1634

The Galileo Affair

Eric Flint
Andrew Dennis

$7.99 U.S.
$11.99 CAN.

ISBN-13: 978-0-7434-9919-4
ISBN-10: 0-7434-9919-0

9 780743 499194

50799

EAN

INFALLIBLE—BUT NOT BULLETPROOF ...

"Who's that?" whispered Gerry, looking at the guy in white, up on what Frank kept thinking of as the stage.

"Dunno," said Frank.

"*Il Papa*," breathed Marius.

"Hold on. Did you say that was the pope?"

"Yes," said Marius, his eyes bright and intent.

"The actual pope? Here?" Frank couldn't believe it. He'd only ever seen one pope, and that was on TV back in the 20th century. This was the actual pope, right here in the church with him! "Cool."

"Yes," said Marius. Something about his tone worried Frank for a reason he couldn't quite put his finger on. But the pope—*the actual pope! Right here!*—was raising his hands like he was a rock star or something, and people were going quiet.

And then Marius drew out his pistol, shoved his way through the row of people in front of him, leveled the pistol at the pope, and pulled the trigger. The gun did not fire.

Silence. Frank felt freezing cold all over, as the sweat started from his skin. Never had he felt so thankful for doing anything as for shaking the primer out of Marius' gun earlier.

"You jackass!" Gerry hollered, charging forward and drawing his own pistol. "You just fucking shot at the *POPE*!"

And then Frank looked up and saw the faces of Ducos and his Roman Committee member, their two guns sliding forward. It all came to him, then. *He suckered us.*

There was no way Frank could get his pistol out in time, he realized.

1634:
The Galileo Affair

Eric Flint
Andrew Dennis

1634: THE GALILEO AFFAIR

Copyright © 2004 by Eric Flint and Andrew Dennis

A Baen Books Original

Baen Publishing Enterprises
P.O. Box 1403
Riverdale, NY 10471
www.baen.com

ISBN: 0-7434-9919-0
ISBN 13: 978-0-7434-9919-4

Cover art by Tom Kidd
Interior maps by Randy Asplund

First paperback printing, August 2005
Third paperback printing, September 2008

Library of Congress Cataloging-in-Publication Number
2003027023

Distributed by Simon & Schuster
1230 Avenue of the Americas
New York, NY 10020

Typeset by Bell Road Press, Sherwood, OR
Production & design by Windhaven® Press, (www.windhaven.com)
Printed in the United States of America.

Dedication

To the memory of Johnny Cash, 1932–2003.

I Fell Into A Burning Ring Of Fire
I Went Down, Down, Down
And The Flames Went Higher

1634:
The Galileo Affair

Prologue: Spring, 1633

That's my last Duchess painted on the wall,
Looking as if she were alive. I call
That piece a wonder, now: Frà Pandolf's hands
Worked busily a day, and there she stands.

Chapter 1

The palace was over-heated, Mazarini thought. That came of Cardinal Richelieu being a man who had more than his share of ailments, despite being only in middle age. Richelieu felt the cold as an old man did. He had his servants build fires if there was even the slightest chill in the air—and early spring in Paris was considerably more than slightly chilly. Fortunately, the cardinal was a polite man. The wait in the anteroom was brief enough that Mazarini was able to fight off drowsiness.

Now Mazarini was in the presence of Richelieu himself, trying to achieve—in spite of the heat—that chilly sharpness a diplomat needed. The cardinal's hard face, now that the pleasantries had been dealt with, indicated that the real negotiation was about to begin.

After only four weeks in Paris, at that; Richelieu must, Mazarini thought, have something in mind. The protocol of his nunciature had been brief. Mazarini had arrived from Rome with a retinue provided by Cardinal Barberini and augmented it from the permanent nunciature in Paris. His American companion, Harry Lefferts, had tried to pretend that he saw the likes of the procession through Paris every day back in Grantville, but Mazarini could see him frankly staring at everything. Pressed afterward, Harry had admitted that the twentieth century had not wanted for spectacle, but that it never came to country towns like Grantville. As it was, Harry had gotten only these few short weeks of mayhem, debauchery and drunkenness in Paris before a message that had missed him narrowly in Rome had called him home to Grantville; he was due to leave in the morning.

As much as he would miss Harry, Mazarini would be relieved to see him go. The flamboyant young American made friends everywhere he went. Unfortunately, the friends were concentrated in two classes of people:

Flamboyant Italian and French young men, who found the exciting and exotic American something of a role model—to the perhaps everlasting ruin of proper attire for proper young men. (Their habits had already included brawling and drunkenness, so those sins could hardly be laid at Harry's feet.)

Shortly after they'd arrived in Rome a few months earlier, Harry had gotten a formal suit done to his own specifications by a tailor who'd done it purely for the chance to take Harry's old rented tux apart to see how to make the style of trousers his customers were demanding. This time around, Harry had reasoned, men's formal wear would be done right. Pockets ranked high in Harry's scheme to anticipate the mistakes of fashion. The gentleman of this future would not be stuck for somewhere to put a wallet, cigarettes, a few items for personal defense and his companion's spare lipstick. Jackets were replaced with tailcoats, as Harry had seen enough performances by someone called Lee Van Cleef to appreciate the practicality of the style for a man who wanted to wear a gun-belt. The swordsmen about town in Rome were glad of it, too.

The city's authorities were not.

The second category of people who made friends with

Harry almost instantaneously were Italian and French young women. Alas. That characteristic had produced even more in the way of excitement than the first.

Mazarini was still a bit astonished that only two duels had resulted. That was probably because of the outcome of the duels themselves. As the challenged party, Harry had been able to choose the weapons. The first duel having been a very informal affair—a tavern brawl which escalated rapidly—he'd naturally chosen pistols, that being the nature of the weapon carried under his coat. Harry had had the mercy and the good sense not to actually kill his opponents—but it had been blindingly obvious to all who witnessed the affair that he could have easily done so instead of inflicting minor flesh wounds.

The second duel, a more formal affair, was worse. Having been accused of cowardice by relying on unfairly superior American firearms, Harry had chosen a different weapon. Another American one, true, but hardly something that could be labeled unfair—a very large knife which he called a "Bowie knife." He had even grandly allowed his opponent to retain his rapier.

The choice had obviated his opponent's greater skill with swordsmanship. Harry had had no intention of trying to match him. He'd simply managed to avoid the first lunge and grappled with his opponent, Bowie knife against main gauche. Thereafter, fighting with knives at close quarters, those qualities which Harry possessed in abundance—great athletic ability and an outlook sanguine enough to be the envy of any Mongol khan—had come to the fore. The end result had been thoroughly fatal and incredibly messy.

Now that he was in the presence of the cardinal, Mazarini suppressed his sigh. Hopefully, Harry Lefferts would be gone from Paris and on his way back to Grantville before the very wealthy and very belligerent Fasciotti brothers—all five of them—discovered that their sister had been dishonored and came to Paris from Rome to seek satisfaction. There would be no

duels, dealing with the Fasciotti. Hiring assassins came
as naturally to them as hiring servants. All the more so
since the sister in question was not complaining about
the episode herself. Awkward, that.

But Richelieu was finally speaking. Mazarini pushed
aside thoughts of his rambunctious American companion. There were many dangers in the world, after all.
Compared to Richelieu, Harry Lefferts was a minor
problem.

"Monsignor," said Richelieu, "You have visited Grantville, perhaps?"

"I have, Your Eminence."

Mazarini responded politely, despite the fact that
the question was moot. It did not do for one *gentiluomo* to admit to another that he had had him spied
on—or, in his response, for the one spied upon to draw
attention to the fact. Mazarini's trip to Grantville had
neither gone unnoticed nor unremarked. The resulting
icy blast of Cardinal Richelieu's displeasure had been
directed straight at Cardinal Barberini, who had in his
turn deposited the whole lot on Mazarini once he'd
arrived in Rome. Richelieu had a long reach; his eyes
were everywhere and there were few within Europe
who could not at least be apprised of his opinions if
not made to suffer for his displeasure. He had latterly
come to have most of the resources of France at his
disposal; in a sense, he *was* France.

"Perhaps," Richelieu went on, "some things passed
between the monsignor and—"

Mazarini interrupted him silently, staring with a
carefully blank expression and placing his hand on his
heart, before casting his eyes down. The gesture of
one who, for ritual reasons, could not speak. If ritual
had an advantage, it was the language of subtlety it
allowed the cognoscenti to converse in.

Richelieu sighed. Ritual could also be a shield for
those who chose to dissemble. He chose not to look

upon the dissimulation. "Monsignor," he said after a little time, "you are aware, perhaps, of the news of the future brought by the Americans?" Richelieu rose and took the two steps that carried him to the window. "I ask in a spirit of genuine enquiry; you need not vouchsafe how much you know or where you have it from."

And such a freight of meaning in that! Mazarini found himself cold despite the heat, his palms sweating. He had never underestimated an opponent in his career to date, but he wondered whether it was possible to do anything *else* with the cardinal who ruled France.

For a wonder, his voice remained under control. "I am aware, yes." He thanked God silently for the calm; it was his best weapon at the card table and in negotiations.

He had already heard enough to deduce what was coming next. More than a few men had emerged, shocked and grinning, from the Palais in the last few weeks. The cardinal was promoting men, young and unknown men, and it was—well, not the talk of all Paris, but certainly noticed.

Richelieu remained at the window, looking out over the garden he had torn down the adjoining buildings to create. He could surely see little, Mazarini reflected. Paris in the spring meant mist and soft, clinging rain as much as fresh air and balmy breezes. The sky was the gray of over-washed linen and the streets a mire, clinging and glutinous. Everywhere was the stink of wet wool.

Richelieu let out a long breath. Not quite—but almost—another sigh. He half-turned, and addressed Mazarini over his shoulder. "It is more difficult, if you will say nothing?"

Mazarini frowned.

Richelieu clasped his hands behind his back and turned further. A long blink, then, both eyes closed for a whole breath before they opened, and he leaned forward a little. Earnestly: "I beg of you, Monsignor, not to take what I said as a suggestion that you might betray a confidence. I fancy we are both"—a little quirk of a smile to underline it—"professionals. Not so?"

Mazarini nodded. Richelieu had used the English word—a word that the seventeenth-century English almost certainly did not have and certainly would not understand the way that up-time Americans did. Mazarini felt his very frame lighten in his chair with the speed of his thoughts. The sheer celerity that came when one matched wits with a master—there was no thrill like it. To gamble all-or-nothing on one's own genius—and with a man who might say so much with the mere choice of a synonym! The mere turn of a clever phrase, a well-parsed statement, these were the common coin of diplomacy. Richelieu was one of a select few in another league altogether.

Richelieu closed his eyes again for another breath. "But I must broach a sensitive subject," he said, and turned back to look out at the dishwater sky.

Richelieu said nothing for some time, and it was Mazarini who broke the silence. He knew it was a trap, a trick he used himself. To break a silence without disadvantage was a delicate business.

"Sensitive?" he asked.

Richelieu, turning, saw Mazarini's raised eyebrow and smiled. "Monsignor, you are the man I crossed wits with at Lyons three years ago, not so? Perhaps I might be candid. *Sub rosa*, and the understanding between us that neither shall bear rancor for what passes here today?"

"Oh, surely." Mazarini permitted himself a broad smile. "Do any of those who were present at Lyon bear rancor?"

Richelieu's face missed not a beat, segueing into a worldly, knowing chuckle. "Ah, yes. Two of my dupes. I am sure that neither bear any rancor, where they are now. I feel sure they have more burning concerns."

Mazarini was impressed by that. Discussing the

execution of two men who had been to all appearances his faithful allies, Richelieu actually twinkled. "Perhaps, Cardinal. But you were mentioning candor?"

Rubbing it in to begin with would not hurt. After all, the cardinal had asked specifically that neither party take offense. Mazarini harked back to what Cardinal Maurice of Savoy had told him about Richelieu: *He must be made to feel that the decision depends on him alone.* And there was little to achieve that better than an initial resistance.

"Candor, yes." Richelieu's eyes grew hooded. "I have something quite outlandish to suggest."

"I am sure, Your Eminence, that this room—" Mazarini waved at a wall at random "—and Servien back there has heard more outlandish propositions these last few weeks. And will again. Does not the delegation from Grantville arrive here in a few weeks?"

Richelieu smiled thinly. "Etienne is behind there," he said, pointing at the wall opposite that at which Mazarini had waved. "He and his clerk take notes. So much more discreet a man than his cousin at the Ministry of War."

Mazarini noted that Richelieu had neither confirmed nor denied what the Holy See's spies claimed to have discovered. "And Your Eminence's proposition?"

"Do you read English?"

"Very well, of late."

"Perhaps I might trouble you—" Richelieu opened a cabinet and took out a thick volume fringed with ribbon bookmarks, "—to read the passage I have marked."

Mazarini frowned at the volume as he took it. It was new, and well made, apparently the work of a Parisian bookbinder. He riffled the pages; they were printed on the smooth and slightly marbled Turk's-paper that French bibliophiles loved so well. He looked inside the front cover to see that the frontispiece was—his eyebrows shot up. "From 1991?" he asked, looking up at the cardinal.

"Just so. I have had printed copies made and more securely bound." A slight sneer. "Whatever else the next three hundred years may bring, improvements in bookbinding were not among them. The books we have from Grantville began to fall apart quite quickly. I needed copies to refer to, and to distribute to . . . various persons. Hand-copying would have engaged every stationer and monk in Paris for weeks and the originals were too fragile to pass around. So I ordered them typeset and the illustrations carefully cut by the best engravers I could find."

"Just so," Mazarini echoed. "And the passage to which Your Eminence wishes to direct my attention?"

"Ah, I do apologize. I began to muse on other matters. Permit me—" Richelieu leaned over to flip a page open by a bookmark. "Here," he said, tapping a bold-face heading.

Mazarini looked. It read: *Mazarin, Cardinal Jules.*

Mazarini focused his eyes on it, confirming that—as with other versions he had seen—they had gotten his birth date wrong. Two days, but still—

He looked up at Richelieu. "I have read this. Or one much like it."

"They are all much alike, that I have seen."

To keep silence now, that was painful. Mazarini could not. "I have spoken with—I have spoken with a number of people—"

And the words dried up. He felt his palms start again with sweat, his pulse hammer in his ears. The abstract—the dry statement of a textbook that spoke of a future world, that spoke of events that would not happen for years to come—was as nothing next to a living, breathing prince of the church directing that he read the future course of his life.

Richelieu took pity on him. "You will have heard, perhaps, that I made a number of promotions rather earlier than"—he took in the cabinet with a languid wave—"these texts say that I would have done?"

"And when last we met you offered then that I might come into—" Again, the sudden drying of the mouth. This time, the words came after only a slight fumble "—your confidence?"

Mazarini wondered that the cardinal did not hear the thunder of his heart. It was like holding the perfect hand at cards, hoping against hope that the betting could be run up to higher and higher levels without—but Richelieu was nodding, slow and liquid, dreamlike, as if under water.

"Confidence," mused the cardinal. "As good a word as any. Knowing what you would do, what you are capable of. I saw some of it at Lyon—I greeted you thinking you came to spy, not to treat, convinced you adhered wholly to my king's enemies. Two hours and you had convinced me of much that turned out to be for the good of everyone involved. And then your theatrical coup at Casale—magnificent!"

"Your Eminence is too kind."

"Ah, Monsignor, but what you will do—it justifies your promise now, if my humble opinion counts for anything. Yes, justifies it amply. Revolution, war, heresy—through all of these to make France the great power of Europe for a hundred years." A sigh, and a deep one. "And for nothing."

"Your Eminence?"

Richelieu smiled in response, small and sad, suddenly wearing every one of his years. "Neither of our other selves was to know. Not Cardinal Richelieu, nor the Cardinal Mazarin who succeeded him so capably. While we made France anew in the image of a beautiful, strong, holy nation, the English simply spread out over the world and . . . stole it."

Mazarini nodded. The governance of the English might be in the hands of fools and outright villains more often than not, but there was no denying the inventive, indefatigable wanderlust they seemed to imbibe with their mothers' milk. Or the roving commission of violent

larceny each Englishman seemed to grant himself as soon
as he could walk. Other nations fought the Algerine or
the Dunkerker to suppress piracy. For the English, it
was to serve the competition a bad turn.

How typical of such, thought Mazarini, to steal
the whole of a future, for there was much in what
Richelieu had said that he had seen in the little of the
future's history that Harry Lefferts had known. Harry
had cheerfully admitted having paid precious little
attention to his studies, but his every act and thought
spoke of the domination of the Anglophone peoples
of the world he had come from.

On the other hand, that hegemony had also created
Grantville. On which, Mazarini reminded himself, he
had felt called to wager so much.

"I see," was all he said.

Richelieu nodded. "I will not find extravagance of
use, here and now, will I? I should keep my hat on,
not so?"

Mazarini smiled. He remembered the theatrics
Richelieu had displayed himself at Lyon, tearing off
his hat and stamping on it. The cardinal as well as
the monsignor could take pleasure in executing a
coup de theatre.

"You wish time to think about this?"

And there it was, finally, laid out as clearly as possible. In another world, another future, another universe,
Richelieu had groomed Mazarini—by then known as
Jules Mazarin—to be his successor. And such a glorious career he had had, under that Francofied name!
Reckoned, in the annals of France, to have been the
equal of Richelieu himself.

There were precious few ministers of state in the
history of the world whose names would be remembered
by any but antiquarians centuries later. Richelieu was
one of them. Mazarin, another.

"If you please, yes." With those words, Mazarini felt
himself grow cool, more ordered.

"There is no urgency," said the cardinal. "For the time being you have obligations as nuncio extraordinary, and doubtless there are many with calls upon your time."

Mazarini nodded. "Monsignor Bischi's office has much work for me, augmenting the regular offices of the nunciature here. And I find my lodgings with le comte de Chavigny most congenial."

"Ah, yes. Young Leon is very much the coming man among my creatures, you know. A promising young fellow, very much in the image of his father. I understand he and young Monsieur Lefferts found much in common?"

Mazarini grinned. "I fear I may not mention much of what they found in the presence of a churchman of Your Eminence's famed piety."

Richelieu chuckled. "There are times when I do feel my age, all—what—forty-eight years of it? I remember when it was thought that I would follow His Majesty's colors rather than take the cloth—oh, the stories I would hear of military debauchery."

"I could tell you more than one such of Harry Lefferts. A man to watch, that." Mazarini smiled at the memories. Now that Harry was leaving, he could afford to do so. Granted, the disemboweling of Agnelli had been perhaps excessive. Then again, Agnelli had been a notorious bully and there had been few, even in Rome, who had mourned his passing. Had he been an outraged husband or father, sentiment would have been different. But Agnelli had simply been a rival for a lady's affections—and one whose own past conduct did not bear close examination.

"As are all the Americans." There was a trace of acerbity in the cardinal's voice. "I shall be meeting some of them in a few weeks, sent by way of an embassy, if my intendants report aright. Apparently they propose to send the wife of their president, Monsieur Stearns. I do look forward to—" Richelieu shook his head. "But you have met the young lady."

"She is charming, of that there is no doubt. Very intelligent and well read, also." Mazarini shrugged. "As a diplomat? Hard to say. She is certainly pleasant to talk with, as well as look upon."

He choked the rest off. Richelieu had almost, he realized, drawn him out into the betrayal of confidence—even by what might be inferred from what he said. None other of the notables he dealt with would cause him to speak so. It was, he felt, unfair to require a diplomat of his comparative youth to deal with beautiful women in the course of his work. What could he say, after, that could not be misconstrued?

Richelieu interrupted his indignant reverie. "While we are on the subject of diplomats, has Sable spoken with you? He has a few things he wishes to discuss about our deployments in northern Italy."

"Sable? Oh, you mean the cousin of—" Mazarin waved at the wall behind which Richelieu's dark-lanternist lurked. It made sense to refer to the senior Servien by his marquisate de Sable when there was room for confusion. Although the near-invisible man in the next room could hardly be confused with the elder Servien in the flesh. The instantly forgettable factotum was one creature. The caustic, bombastic military intendant Mazarini had met at Casale could scarcely be credited to have come from the same family. "Yes, he has sent me a note on the subject. There are doubtless some small issues along the Pinerolo border that we must discuss. Tiresome, but necessary."

"Now, to change the subject. Have you been presented to Her Majesty?" Richelieu returned from the window and perched on the edge of his desk.

"Formally? Naturally, when I arrived. I have not had the pleasure of closer acquaintance, as yet."

"If you will forgive an old prelate's idle curiosity," said Richelieu, stroking a little at his beard, "does the monsignor speak Spanish at all well?"

Mazarini inclined his head in mock modesty. "Your Eminence is perhaps aware that I spent some time in study in Madrid, and learned the language there?"

Richelieu held up a hand. "Of course, of course." He was waxing positively avuncular, and Mazarini felt a sudden twinge of unease. "Her Majesty is a native speaker, and takes great delight in being so addressed."

"Indeed?" Mazarini raised an eyebrow.

"Oh, indeed." Richelieu rose from his desk. "If the monsignor will do me the honor of accompanying me to the Louvre this evening, Her Majesty will be holding an informal levee, where I would be honored to effect a more personal introduction. Her Majesty will be pleased to make your acquaintance, I think. You have something about you of someone she once held very dear. Yes, very dear indeed."

As Richelieu's carriage bore them to the queen's levee, Mazarini had time to ponder his situation. He and Harry Lefferts had set out from Grantville almost half a year before, barely a week after the Americans had fought successfully no fewer than three prongs of attack that had threatened to eradicate them.

Harry had been an officer in the American army that had defeated many times their number at Eisenach, and the next duty he had been given was to accompany Mazarini back to Rome. Mazarini had talked with the President of the United States about Harry before leaving Grantville.

"Monsignor," Mike Stearns had said, weary and rambling, "I've had any number of folks give me lectures about how this place ought to be defended. The longest one was from the guy I'm sending with you. What he thinks isn't my position, frankly. I want to see the new United States prosper, and since King Gustavus is right here it's him I'm talking with. But what I want isn't Fortress America, like Harry thinks we should do. I think it'll be good for him to see why not, eh? And for the people who think there's a military solution to what the United States represents in this time and place, well, I think it'll be good for them to hear Harry talk about what we're capable of."

After that, Stearns' wife Rebecca, the Jewess, had taken over. She had had more to say, and in more detail, and had put the Grantville Constitution in terms Mazarini was more familiar with—passages from Plato and Marcus Aurelius, Machiavelli and Tacitus. It was pleasant to see that at least one of the members of the U.S. government had had a proper education.

It turned out that Harry was, like a lot of Grantville's natives, possessed of some Italian ancestry and knew a few words of the language. He was also nominally a Catholic, although Grantville's priest Father Larry Mazzare could not recall having seen him inside a church more than eight times in as many years. Midnight mass at Christmas—conspicuously filled with Christmas cheer—was about the limit of Harry's observance. And, come to that, his religion.

Mazarini didn't mind that so much. He had only lately even troubled to wear the dress that went with his being, technically at least, a clergyman. No more than a deacon with a couple of lucrative benefices to support him—and his expensive sisters and profligate father, he reflected—as he scrambled at the greasy pole of Europe's power politics.

A revolving greasy pole in a high wind, now that half of the old verities had vanished in the harsh glow of the Ring of Fire that had brought the up-time Americans. Mazarini, gambler, diplomat and showman that he was, had tried to slip a few cards off the bottom of the deck by opening a direct, unofficial channel with Grantville.

He had succeeded in that, certainly. In Grantville he had made friends, left one of his own behind as a contact there, been mightily impressed by the parish priest of the town and dined, with him, with the other pastors there who were all different kinds of Protestant. He had also seen Grantville's civilian population chew up and spit out more than a division of Croat horse, the most reckless and brutal light cavalry that Wallenstein had had under his command.

Mazarini had been impressed by the feat of arms. He had seen two wars at first hand, the first of them—the Valtelline War, to give it a bloodier name than it deserved—as a soldier himself. His captaincy in the papal regiment of the prince of Palestrina had largely been a garrison command, though; his main distinction was in being the only liaison officer sent to Gonsalvo de Cordoba who was not frightened or offended by the fiery Spaniard's rages. By the time of the real bloodletting of the Mantuan War he had been a papal diplomat.

He understood just enough to know how much nerve it took to stand and keep your head in the teeth of a cavalry assault. It had nothing to do with military training or nobility or the peculiar merits of any nation as a nursery of virtue. Just people who did what was needed to do right by the people beside them.

There were so many places in Europe where one found no one but the selfish and the self-glorifying, who wanted nothing better than to be—not even wolves, for wolves hunted in bands, but lone raptors—the better to eat the soft and weak they happened upon. Rare were the places where people felt themselves to be part of something greater and acted as such, individuals who felt the greater good in their bones so deeply that they would not even think to ask the questions that so troubled the philosophers of altruism. Grantville was such a place. Even Mazarini's cynical aide, Father Heinzerling, had taken to behaving more like a decent human being than a wild boar given the power of speech and walking upright.

Mazarini had come away impressed.

He had also come away with a mission. A mission,

what was more, that might well see him humiliated
by abjuration before the Inquisition, if the political
winds did not blow right. Or worse, more imprisoned
than not for the rest of his days, like that poor fool
Campanella.

Father Mazzare, the parish priest of Grantville and
a man who lived up to the vows of his ordination in a
way that verged on sainthood by seventeenth-century
standards, had asked Monsignor Mazarini, priest in
name only, to carry books that showed three hundred
years of the Church coming ever closer to curing the
abuses that Luther nailed to that church door. And
which showed the Church refining and developing its
teaching and tradition and its understanding of Scripture
to the point where wars became impossible to paint as
wars of religion. If the catechism exhorted a man to
reject nothing that was good or holy in the religion of
others, where then for the call to burn heretics?

Either the light at the end of the tunnel of the
Council of Trent or the blackest of heresies. The books
had weighed little in the hands, but in the mind—oh,
in the mind!

Mazarini was no theologian. For him, faith flowed
naturally from all that was good in the world, was part
of who he was and where he was from. But nevertheless he had had to examine himself closely as he picked
his way through the unfamiliar doctrines by lamplight
at inns on the way from Grantville to Rome. Had it
not been for the cheerfully vicious earthiness of the
young American with him—it was easy to think of him
that way, despite there being only a few years between
them—Mazarini felt sure his journey to Rome would
have ended with him in the deepest of melancholy
humors.

That journey had been easy enough. The year's cam-
paigning had settled into the siege of Regensburg, so
there were few enough soldiers about on the route he
led Harry along. The difficulties of the trip had been

those of finding decent inns and good horses. Harry had demonstrated himself a competent rider and, on the one occasion when bandits had accosted them in the Piedmont, an excellent shot. Other than that, no one had troubled with two respectable-looking and well-armed young men with no obvious wealth about their persons.

"We have arrived," announced Richelieu.

Mazarini looked up from his brown study. "Ah."

By the time he alit from the coach and followed Richelieu toward the palace entrance, Mazarini's good spirits were back. Yes, yes, it was all very difficult. Vexing to the soul, trying to the spirit, an endless palpitation of the heart.

It was also supremely exciting.

In person, in casual and intimate discourse, Mazarini found Anne of Austria quite a charming woman. The queen of France was now entering the eighteenth year of her marriage to King Louis XIII—a marriage that had taken place when she and her spouse had been merely fourteen years of age. By all accounts, the marriage was one of name only, and always had been.

Anne of Austria seemed to find Mazarini equally charming. Not surprising, really. In addition to his fluency in her native tongue, Mazarini *was* charming—as one would expect from a man who, despite being a year younger than the queen, was already a top diplomat in the service of the papacy. He was even—or so he had been told—fairly handsome.

So.

On his way back to his domicile after the levee, Mazarini had time to reflect on the full dimensions of Richelieu's offer. That the cardinal would wish to discreetly arrange an affair between a new protégé and Anne of Austria made perfect sense, of course—at least, a protégé intended for the highest honors. The marriage between

Anne and Louis was childless and likely to remain so. In
the absence of an heir, that meant the line of succession
passed to the king's younger brother, the duc d'Orleans,
better known simply as "Monsieur Gaston." And should
Gaston ever ascend to the throne . . .

No one had any doubt at all that the first act of the
new king would be to send Richelieu to the executioner.
Monsieur Gaston was a thoroughly treacherous schemer
who had proved willing to ally with anybody to advance
his designs upon the throne. Rebellious nobles, foreign
enemies, anybody. That he had so far failed—quite
miserably—was due to Richelieu's opposition and the
cardinal's far greater skill in the savage infighting of
French politics.

So.

Chapter 2

"*Bonsoir*, Monsignor." The servant seemed nervous as he took Mazarini's coat.

Mazarini's fatigue-blurred mind was still alert, despite an evening of glitter and repartee that had tired him more than a week's riding. He nodded acknowledgement of the servant's greeting. "Is something wrong?"

"Monsignor?" The question was in an almost affronted tone.

Mazarini had not yet learned the names of all the servants at the *maison* Chavigny—come to that, he had not seen all of them yet—but they were generally a lively lot, less cowed than most. Something was definitely up with this one; his manner went beyond the usual scraping of the servants that so annoyed Harry. "Is Monsieur le Comte at home?"

"*Non*, Monsignor. He is with Monsieur le Vicomte de Turenne."

That would be the younger Tour de l'Auvergne, the elder being largely out of Paris these days, while the younger basked in the sudden favor of the king and Richelieu.

"Monsieur Lefferts has passed the evening in your chambers," the servant finished.

Mazarini was not surprised. Harry was set to depart in the morning, and had decided to take an evening's rest. He needed it. Rome had had its high spots for Harry, but Paris, to any young man with dash and money and a hint of the exotic was a city that opened its . . . arms.

Mazarini smiled slightly at the thought of what he had all but left behind, middle-aged before his time. "I shall retire, then. Have something brought to me in my chambers. I shall take supper before my bed."

"Very good, Monsignor."

Mazarini walked up alone. Now that he thought about it, the house seemed entirely normal. Even with its owner out for the evening, the place was home to dozens of servants. Only in the very small hours was it free from the tick and rustle of people distantly going about life and work. Those sounds—for all that there seemed to be no one around—were still there, muted to their night-time level.

He paused at the door of the apartment that the comte had given to him and Harry for their residence while in the city. "Harry?" he called. The room—the first, a salon—was lit only by the dim glow of red embers. "Harry?" he called again, feeling slightly foolish.

He looked to either side. The corridor was well lit. Lamps, and a chandelier over the stairwell. That was not normal, the risk of fire usually caused all lamps to be doused by this hour. He suddenly realized that standing in the doorway—

Mazarini was on the floor before he heard the snap of a flintlock. A jet of burning powder roared out through the door.

Somewhere in his—*yes! There*—*his pistol!* He tugged at the hilt of the thing through the pocket-cut of his soutanne, at the same time scrabbling across the floor. Out of the door stepped a man—dark-dressed, rough, villainous-looking. Mazarini took in the twist of his mouth where a scar—but he was raising a pistol and Mazarini, cursing, could not get his own free of his soutanne; all he was doing was pulling at his own leg and—

A blast of noise, and scar-face jerked sideways and was crumpling, his face screwed up. Somehow Mazarini could see the detail that his breeches were stained.

Within the room—"*Fuck!*" Harry was definitely alive in there—another shot. Harry's shotgun, by the sound.

Silence, then. Mazarini got to his feet, saw that scar-face was down, unconscious and bleeding in several places. He shook at his pistol, drew it free. He rapped the butt against his palm, then hauled back on the lock. His mouth was dry. He sidled up to the door.

From within, a slight noise. The light was behind him; if he went in, whoever was within would see him first. "Harry?" he called out.

The only answer, two shots. The first, the throaty cough of a pistol. The second, Harry's shotgun. Then a thud. As, perhaps, of a body hitting the floor.

Mazarini swallowed, then thought to check either way along the landing. Movement. "*Arrête-là!*" he called out, spinning to level his pistol. Whoever it was, a shape at the far end of the corridor by the stairwell vanished. He ran, realizing only halfway down the corridor that he had just exposed his back. He got to the head of the stairs, shouted down: "Stop him!"

"Stop who?" came back the answer, and mocking laughter.

The twentieth century had some things worth the Ring of Fire to bring them back. "Motherfucker," Mazarini snarled, and felt better for it. On the wall, there was a display of old swords. Better than nothing. He took one down, felt the weight and ill balance of a weapon meant more for battering armor than the singing phrase of steel. He brought it up to a badly

balanced mockery of a sabreur's guard and edged back
along the corridor, pistol leveled in the other hand, his
back to the wall.

A body flew out of the doorway to his chambers;
the fright made him squeeze the trigger. Somewhere,
something shattered. Whoever it was hit the opposite
wall and landed badly.

"Giulio?" It was Harry's voice. "You there?"

"I'm here, Harry."

Harry Lefferts swaggered out of the doorway, the
bravo's pose only mildly spoiled by the fact that he
was sucking on the knuckles of his right hand. "Three
of 'em, there were," he said, taking the knuckles out
of his mouth. There was a scorch of powder up the
left side of his face. His sawed-off shotgun dangled
almost negligently from his left hand, broken open
and empty.

"Four," said Mazarini. "One ran."

"Two," said Harry, looking down.

Scar-face was gone. The other seemed to be in poor
shape. Mazarini bent to see. "Dead," he said, "or soon
will be. I think his skull, perhaps his neck is broken."
The man had fouled himself where he lay, his eyes
rolled up white.

Harry was looking left and right along the corridor,
his hands reloading the shotgun almost automatically.
"Glad Dan Frost never took this 'un off me. I gave
my other one to Becky."

"Your pistol?"

"I got it. In there." Harry nodded his head back
toward the room. "Stripped down for a little servicing.
When these jokers turned up I was behind the screen,
taking a leak. Lucky I didn't have a lamp on, and the
bastards didn't think to check in the wardrobe, which
was where I hid."

"Monsignor!" It was the servant from the hallway.
"I heard someone shoot—" He stopped, breathless.
"Assassins!"

"Well, that was just as convincing as all hell," drawled Harry Lefferts. A flick of the wrist and his shotgun snapped shut.

The servant's face went into a parody of puzzlement. "Monsignor? What did he say?"

"He wants to know how much you were paid not to warn me."

"But Monsignor, I—" The outraged bluster cut off, as Harry poked the muzzle of his sawed-off into the man's belly.

"Ten livres," he said, simply.

"Fair." Mazarini nodded. "And you did not tell them that Monsieur Lefferts was in?"

"*Non.* I told them he was out. When I heard nothing, I feared the worst for Monsieur Lefferts, and thought that they must have succeeded in killing him quietly."

Harry snorted.

"Now, Harry, let us not be harsh. He thought he could take his ten livres and let these ruffians die at your hand, eh?"

The servant nodded.

"It is probably for the best that I do not know your name, eh?"

Another nod.

"For if I did know it, I might denounce you and you would suffer death on the wheel as an accomplice to murder, yes? But if you leave Paris so I never see you again, you might live a long life."

Nod, nod.

Mazarini took a deep breath. "Go. Now." He did not raise his voice.

The servant ran.

Harry broke open the action on his gun, pulled out the cartridges. "What the hell was that all about?"

Mazarini raised both eyebrows. "But surely you have some idea? Which father or brother or husband—cousin, for that matter—have you outraged most these few weeks past?"

Harry twisted his lip. "Funny, Giulio. Funny. They spoke French, that I do know."

"Which means nothing. Such as they can be hired in any tavern you care to name in this city." He sighed. "I could use a drink," he said, and walked into his chambers.

Shortly thereafter, the real alarm was raised. Servants—frightened-looking ones, who approached nervously, not wanting to get shot—turned up. Harry spoke to them, and they began to remove the two corpses. The one in the corridor had been relatively decorous. The one Harry had shot at close range was missing a face, mostly.

"The fellow who came a-running was just some footman, been here maybe a week."

"Ah. Perhaps he was a little too glib."

"Whatever. He wasn't going to tell us anything anyhow, Giulio. Nor is anyone else. They thought those guys were just regular visitors. For me, that is." Harry paused a moment. "I think your guy was telling the truth, actually. He didn't tell them I was in, did he?"

Mazarini pondered the matter, briefly. Then, shrugged. "He's gone now."

"Well, perhaps it was an outraged husband. Or father. It'd have to be one from Rome, though, on account of I've steered clear of that here."

Mazarini raised an eyebrow.

Harry grinned. "Honest!"

Mazarini felt his head beginning to ring a little, and sat down. Harry sat as well, reached for the drink that a servant had brought. "Never mind. It's got to be something from Rome, yes?"

"Has it?" Mazarini was suddenly not feeling very subtle.

"Sure, I mean here—in Paris, I mean—you're an ambassador. The one group of people who ain't going to kill you are the French."

Mazarini thought about it. True, he was quite sure the assassins had not been sent by Richelieu. Certainly not after the cardinal's veiled offer that very day and the evident rapport between himself and the queen that very evening.

But "the French" numbered in the millions. Had he somehow gotten wind of Richelieu's scheme—or, more likely, simply read one of those cursed American history books—Monsieur Gaston and his confederates had every reason to want Mazarini dead.

Giulio Mazarini, envoy of the Papacy and possibly the future chief minister of France, rubbed his face. Of course, Monsieur Gaston was only one possibility. In the Europe of the year 1633—and never leaving out of the equation, as Americans liked to say, the long arm of the Ottoman Turk—the workings of diplomacy were often hard to distinguish from murder. The American history books had simply—again, to use an American expression—poured gasoline on the flames.

"Motherfuckers," he said again. And, again, felt the better for it.

The next morning, Harry Lefferts departed for Grantville. Once astride his horse—he rode the beast easily and gracefully; it was almost frightening the way Harry had adopted the seventeenth century—the young American looked down at Mazarini.

"You'll be all right without me?"

Mazarini smiled crookedly. "I shall certainly miss the security of your shotgun. Not to mention that barbaric knife of yours. But, yes, Harry, I'll be fine. I *did* somehow take care of myself for thirty years before you showed up, you know."

"Okay, okay. Just checking." Lefferts' face was unusually solemn. "They're all going to be playing for your loyalty, too, Giulio, not just trying to cut your throat. You know it and I know it. Betcha anything the cardinal made you a hell of an offer yesterday."

Not for the first time, Mazarini reflected that there was a keen brain underneath the young American bravo's swagger. Harry had taken to *everything* in this century with panache and gusto—including scheming and maneuver.

The months they had spent together, if nothing else, would allow no dissimulation. Now that Harry was leaving, Mazarini realized with a bit of a start that he had come to cherish the young American's friendship.

"Yes, he did. And, no, I don't know yet how I will respond."

Harry nodded. "Fair enough. I'm glad my loyalties ain't so complicated." He leaned over and extended his hand. "So long, then. It's been a pleasure, Giulio, really has. However we meet again, I promise there'll be no hard feelings on my part."

Mazarini returned the firm handshake. "Mine, neither."

It was all true enough, he thought, watching Harry trot away. Not entirely comforting, of course. Mazarini had also been one of the witnesses at Harry's duel with the brute Agnelli. Whatever fury there had been in Lefferts' bloody actions of the moment, there had been none shortly thereafter.

"There's a man needed killing," Harry had commented casually, almost cheerfully. "Glad to have been of service."

He'd been quite relaxed about it all. Mazarini had no difficulty at all imagining Harry standing over his own corpse. *Sorry, Giulio. No hard feelings, but . . . it had to be done.*

So be it. What would come, would come. Mazarini turned back into the comte's domicile, his mind already turning to the maneuvers of the future. Besides, he still didn't know what decision he would finally make, in the end.

Who was to say? The next time he saw Harry Lefferts, he might be shaking his hand again.

Chapter 3

"Fascinating."

Antonio Barberini looked sharply at Vitelleschi. "I do believe, Father, that that is the first word you have spoken in my presence today."

"My apologies, Your Eminence. I was deep in thought." Vitelleschi gave every sign of still having his faculties at their utmost concentration.

Not surprising, that. The narrow, bladelike man who stood in one of the many elegantly decorated reception-rooms of the Palazzo Barberini in Rome had a potent reputation. Father-General Muzio Vitelleschi, like every General of the Societas Jesu before him back to Father Inigo Lopez de Loyola, was a man to be reckoned with. Part of it was the reputation for ferocious learning. Another part, the famous fourth vow of the Society, of personal loyalty and obedience to the pope. Still another, the Society's iron-hard rule of regular and full reporting that made the man who sat at the center of all its lines of communication arguably the best-informed man in Europe.

Mostly, though, it was the sheer effectiveness of the organization that he headed, an effectiveness that had made the Jesuits the target of every Protestant propagandist in Europe. The Jesuits, they said, were like the night: they always returned.

Vitelleschi was regarding Cardinal Barberini with a cool gaze that few cats could have matched. The Jesuit general was an old man, but not stooped. The high-boned, ascetic face was of a piece with the narrow hungry frame. The calm blue eyes and unwrinkled mien spoke of ice water in the veins. Close-cropped hair, a short beard, both snow-white and fussily trimmed.

"You have some thoughts?"

"I was thinking about Giulio Mazarini. The young monsignor is worthy of watching. I have a man who has marked him, and he is most marvelously disingenuous. But the principal matter has to be the doctrine, no?"

"Ah." Barberini looked at the papers on the table. They were a summary, in essence, of the books that Mazarini had brought with him some months earlier from Grantville. Mazarini had written the summary himself, before he left for Paris. It contained the distilled wisdom and positions of a Roman Catholic Church centuries in the future. The American priest in Grantville, a certain Father Mazzare, had insisted that Mazarini present them to the Holy Father.

Barberini had read the accompanying letter written by Father Mazzare. It had been politely—even deferentially—worded, but neither Barberini nor his uncle Pope Urban VIII had any doubt that the letter and the accompanying documents were, in essence, an ultimatum. A declaration of war, if you would—except that the priest was making a final offer to make peace instead. Provided that peace was made on his terms.

Not that Mazzare would have put it that way. Barberini had the sinking feeling that Mazzare was one of those pestiferous clerics who felt quite firmly that he was simply the organ for a greater truth—in his case, the distilled truth of the Roman Catholic Church to which *he* belonged. He wasn't demanding, however politely, that the Church make peace on *his* terms, but on its own.

Barberini sighed. Another church, in another universe, whose spokesman in this one felt himself to be its voice—and had the documents to back up his claim. And, clearly, not a man easily intimidated. If the matter was not handled properly, Mazzare could become even more explosive than Martin Luther.

"The doctrine. You have read it?"

Vitelleschi stared hard at the cardinal.

"Forgive me, Father-General," said Barberini. "Have you formed an opinion?"

"I have formed—" Vitelleschi paused. "Several opinions. The first is that any hope of another immediate Counter-Reformation is a slim one. The second is that, while I do not know what the reaction of the Protestants of the future might be, the ones of the present day will almost certainly denounce any new doctrine as strongly as the existing."

Vitelleschi lapsed into silence. Barberini waited him out.

When Vitelleschi spoke again, he turned as much away from Barberini as he could without offering his back. He stared into space, his eyes half-closed. "If we are to act on this at all, we must act subtly. An elegant stroke, I think, needs to be found. One blow that sets in motion all that follows. A 'Vatican Council' is not, I think, that blow."

Barberini was inclined to agree. "I know nothing of the council they have in that other time, but now? I doubt we could even hold the Council of Trent again in these times. Not so? After the breviary fiasco?"

Vitelleschi nodded. His Holiness had, a couple of years before, tried to convene a committee to reform the breviary; it was overdue to be done. Months of bickering had resulted in a testy pope ordering the discussions ended with virtually nothing to show and a breviary that was, if anything, worse than before.

"And have you an opinion as to these new doctrines?" Barberini's aesthete manner was as arch as he could make it. He only technically outranked the father-general, otherwise known as the Black Pope for the power he usually chose not to wield.

"When His Holiness has read sufficient, heard sufficient and prayed sufficient to have an opinion, that will be my opinion also." Vitelleschi's eyes seem to close still further. "If His Holiness wishes my advice, I shall give it, of course. I have, as it happens, read the entirety of the books which Mazarini brought back with him, not simply the summary. But I will speak on each point separately, and in public only if His Holiness asks that of me."

"Thank Christ for hierarchy, eh?" Barberini guffawed, briefly.

Vitelleschi smiled. "I believe we need to take one immediate action. Information is our principal need at this time, and I will send to Grantville for a summary of what they have that we have not already seen. That will inform our thinking in more detail. Most important."

Barberini nodded. "It is. And your plan beyond that?"

"It is not a plan as yet. But I believe that Richelieu is suitably warned of what he is up against, as we took pains to send Monsignor Mazarini and his American companion Signor Lefferts to Paris, however briefly either might have remained. And, in the fullness of time, we will take further action if the Church remains beset by France and Spain in concert."

"You believe this United States could be an ally?"

"I believe they may be convinced to be an effective enemy of our enemy. Allies?" Vitelleschi shook his head. "In a hundred years, perhaps. With much reform in both the Church and in the United States. Perhaps."

Barberini stared hard. "Muzio, either you really are addled in your wits or you are playing the deepest game I have ever seen."

Vitelleschi's smile was, again, brief. "I have learned a thing or two from my brethren in the Japans. I commend their reports to your reading."

Barberini cocked his head on one side. "Muzio, you mentioned reform in the United States. What are you planning?"

"No more than the Society ever plans. We open schools and wait. Give us boys of impressionable years, Your Eminence, and we will answer for the actions of the men."

"Including Tilly? Wallenstein?"

Vitelleschi was not smiling, now. "Yes, Your Eminence. Including the Tilly who tried to prevent the sack of Magdeburg. And including the Wallenstein whose administration of his estates is among the most enlightened in Europe. We will answer for them, for good or ill."

Barberini looked away. It was at moments like this that he was reminded of the vast gulf that separated him—and all of the Barberini clan, including his uncle Pope Urban VIII—from the Father-General of the Societas Jesu. All of them were pious men, to be sure. But none of the Barberini, not even the pope himself, had the pure raw *faith* of Muzio Vitelleschi.

It was odd, really. Vitelleschi was much like them, in so many other ways. Immensely sophisticated, learned, cosmopolitan—as astute in the devious and intricate corridors of political power and maneuver as any man in Europe. He even shared the Barberini pleasure in art and science. But, in the end, he was no Renaissance prince of the Church. He was shaped and stamped, molded and formed, in the same manner that had produced the Basque soldier who had founded the Jesuits. There was something ultimately medieval about the man.

Not for the first time, also, Cardinal Barberini was relieved that Inigo Lopez had included that fourth vow of obedience. He shuddered to think what Muzio Vitelleschi would be like as an enemy, instead of—as he certainly was—the pope's most faithful servant.

"Venice, then?" he grunted.

"I think so, yes," replied Vitelleschi softly.

Barberini grimaced sourly. "They're difficult, the Venetians."

"So are the Americans." The Father-General of the Jesuits shrugged. "Where better than Venice, to begin the probe?"

Barberini grunted again. "Mazarini as our go-between? That might be dangerous. The man is leaning in three directions at once—toward us, the French, and the Americans. Who knows where he might wind up, in the end?"

Vitelleschi was back to that unnerving, cool stare. "Who better, then, than Mazarini? Do not forget, Your Eminence, that it remains unclear where *we* might wind up. In the end."

Part I: September, 1633

> She had
> A heart—how shall I say?—too soon made glad,
> Too easily impressed; she liked whate'er
> She looked on, and her looks went everywhere.

Chapter 4

"Trade, Michael, trade."

"I know, Francisco, I know." It was late, and Mike Stearns' office in Grantville was as clean and tidy as the presidential staff could keep it after a day measured in the remorseless rhythm of twenty-minute meetings and a two-hour radio exchange session. That is, not very. It felt . . . in need of laundry.

Opening a window wasn't an option. The autumn night that Don Francisco Nasi was musing on was a filthy one, slapping its rain and wind against the glass. It was the kind of night on which bad novels began. Real life, however, served up nights like this in their season without regard to melodramatic need or—Mike winced at the thought—a President who had a hundred-yard dash through the open to get to his bed. His very empty bed, since his wife, Rebecca, was hundreds of miles away, trapped in the Spanish siege of Amsterdam.

"There is still nothing from the vizier," Francisco sighed. "There will *be* nothing to come."

Mike nodded. Almost a year and a half, from the spring of 1632 onward, of patient and carefully drafted letters, friendly overtures carried to Istanbul by a dozen or more hands, had dropped into a black hole for all the good they seemed to have done. "I'll say this for Richelieu. He may be a damned snake but at least he answers his mail. And accepts ambassadors, even if he does try to——"

Francisco turned and raised an admonitory finger. "Now, we cannot prove that. The English Channel is notoriously thick with pirates."

Mike let out a theatrical groan, and leaned forward to knock his head on his desk. "Francisco," he said, his voice muffled through two inches of paperwork already accumulated for the morrow, "I appreciate you're head of the secret service, but do you have to be quite so cold-blooded? That was my *wife* on that ship."

"Um." Nasi smiled thinly. "Your wife, yes . . . along with Heinrich Schmidt and as tough a selection of soldiers as you could make. Not to mention Gretchen Richter, who causes bowel movements in princes. As I recall the report, the pirates were lucky to survive at all."

His head still lying on the desk, Mike chuckled harshly. Whatever sour thoughts he had toward the world in general, on this sour night, Mike approved deeply of some of the people in it. Tough soldiers and young women who caused princes to squat on oubliettes being right at the top of his list.

Nasi echoed his chuckle. "You would prefer I stormed to Paris and called the cardinal out? Or just offered to meet his *gentiluomo* on his behalf? At dawn, with coffee and pistols?" Francisco twisted his mouth in the wry smile that, with a glitter of his dark eyes, served him as uproarious laughter did other men. "The talk of Europe, it will be—the Jew and the Cardinal! To the death! We would get the attention of the grand vizier's *diwan* then, no error. The sultan, too—he likes a jest, especially if it involves someone getting killed."

Mike sat up. "Yeah, what's the deal there? From your briefings . . ." He suppressed a little laugh. The corps of Jewish merchants who were Grantville's cof-fee lifeline to Istanbul had taken to PowerPoint and overhead projectors in a way that made Mike despair of the soul of early modern capitalism. One thing their reports were *not*, as a rule, was brief. "He's mad as they come, according to you, but he seems to be run-ning Istanbul like an effective and dynamic ruler, for a despot. So what is the problem with the sultan?"

"What is not?" Francisco shrugged. "He is a drunkard, a bully and a raving lunatic. He counts a day wasted in which he does not have someone strangled, or bet-ter yet kill the wretch himself. At the moment he is convinced that purity of Islam will make his empire the equal of Suleiman the Magnificent's, and so wine and coffee are illegal in Istanbul at last news. Any who disagree, die. He reminds me of a phrase I recently heard Harry Lefferts use: 'shoot a fellow for lookin' at me funny.'"

Mike nodded. Francisco's impersonation of Harry's hillbilly tones was good. "Sounds like Harry. One day I'm going to have me a talk with that boy. Assuming he survives Amsterdam and . . . later ports."

"Oh, no—I rather think Harry was warning his men—pack of pirates, rather—off doing that." Francisco smiled. The friendship that had grown up between the quiet Jewish intellectual and the swaggering—but increasingly suave—hillbilly hard-ass was notorious in the world of Grantville's dark-lanternists.

Mike raised an eyebrow. "You surprise me. Still, it's of a piece with the way Harry's—hold on, where were we?"

Francisco held up a hand. "The digression was my fault. Now, where Harry sees the value in restrain-ing his gorier impulses, the sultan revels in them. He genuinely will shoot a man for looking at him—looking at all, that is."

"So he might take another notion tomorrow?"

"No. Insane, but rational, is my assessment. Of course,

I last saw him when he was still a child and under his mother's regency, but—no, leave that aside. Where the sultan's actions may proceed from insane premises, the conclusions and his resolution are remorselessly rational in their deranged context. Mike, have you read Hume's work on this subject? It falls to be published in only a few decades."

"Francisco, I cherish my bone-dumb hillbilly ignorance. Unless it's useful, in which case make sure I get a copy. But for the moment, let's see if I've got this right. We figure he's taken the notion that we're bad news and won't shift unless we make him feel he wants to?"

"Just so. And I think the Hume might be passé in your case, Mike."

Mike harumphed noisily. "Whutaiver," he said, in his best hillbilly drawl. "Don't be telling Frank Jackson about that, willya? The man's looking at me like a dangerous intellectual as it is. Anyway, who put the notion in there, then? His own courtiers, religious leaders, who?"

"Worse. The French."

"Why in the hell—and I ask this in a spirit of pure inquiry—is the sultan taking the word of the French for a single damned thing?" Mike rubbed at eyes grown raw and gritty with a long day's work. "Forgive me, Francisco, if there is something in what you've written that covers this, but . . ."

"I know. We are all at a busy time. What with—" He waved a hand that took in everything from Bohemia to the British Isles, Sweden to Spain. "We are all busy. Now, perhaps some coffee? This discussion may be protracted."

"Sure," said Mike, "a last one for the evening while you tell the story."

Eventually, coffee in hand, Francisco sat on the sofa that was there for the more informal meetings. He looked at it and barked. "Ha!"

"What?" Mike frowned over the rim of his mug.

"Sofa. Kiosk. Divan." He raised his mug in ironic toast. "Kaveh. Coffee. The amount of your language that comes from the Empire—the real Empire, not this cheap imitation Holy Roman thing—."

Mike snorted, nearly having an accident with his coffee.

Francisco continued remorselessly. "All these words in English that started in Turkish. There are probably more, but I have only been here a little less than two years. But I keep hearing little drips of home in a shower of English."

And then he sighed, once, and deeply. "They are all that really survive of the Refuge of the World, as we call it, in your twentieth century's strongest culture. The nation that is there called 'Turkey' was only built, I understand, by sweeping away the rotting shell that it had become. But the glory that was, and still is! Mike, for all that Christian kings of this time talk of dividing the world between them, they are a sorry pack of scoundrels at best. Robber barons, if that. Not all put together could they match the Moghul khan, or the Ming emperor of far Cathay. And even they are as nothing compared to the Sultan of the Two Seas. It is still the strongest empire in the world. Hah! What a thing it is, to know the fate of an empire and mourn the glory it yet has."

Mike nodded, said nothing. For all his own experience of the places Don Nasi talked about, they might as well be on Mars.

Francisco, Don Nasi, man of great affairs in the Confederated Principalities of Europe and the Empire of the House of Osman, sighed again. The weight of four centuries lay heavy on his mind. "Kemal Ataturk and a hundred years of humiliation, Mike. That's what it took, to rescue even a nation from the wreckage of the Empire. You can see it now, if you are told where to look. A people who call novelty heresy, and—but I am rambling. The pith and marrow of the thing, you see, is that France and Germany and England are the edges. The heart of civilization—the very word, *civis*, says it—is the City. And the City—*the* City—is Istanbul that was Constantinople that was Byzantium. Mike, out here beyond the edges of that, we are the barbarians. We are without, and within is civilization with its faction fights and revolts and insanities. Out here we have trinkets to sell, each barbarian coming to set out his stall at the center of civilization. And, as the sultan sees it, the biggest barbarian of all is the padishah of the Franks. After all, half of the empire's European trade is with France, since the empire won't let the Venetians be first in anything."

He grinned, then. "And since Richelieu saw us for a threat when first he clapped eyes on us, every message from the French ambassador has dwelt on our irreligion—no established church, practically atheist!—and dangerous innovations. I need hardly mention the detailed accounts of every sedition and fomentation of unrest practiced by the Committees of Correspondence."

Mike grinned at that. "Trust Richelieu to find a way to make capital out of Gretchen! Wait 'til I tell her! She'll love it."

"Truly, Mike, she will. But it goes this far, and no further. There is to be no ambassador from the CPE or Sweden. There is to be no trading capitulation for us. Any person who enters the empire claiming to be from another time shall suffer death. But we subjects of the empire may go forth and buy whatever we wish and bring it back, and any other trade capitulation may sell whatever it wishes also."

"So provided we can get a sales rep in there, we're fine?"

"Oh, even without a formal representative we can do something. But I think you need to talk more with Messer il Doge of Venice."

Mike chewed on his lip, now thoughtful. The outbreak of war had, in some ways, made his job easier. When there were fewer options, the decisions became clearer and the worry was over what the future would leave open to him when he acted as he was forced to. In some ways, this was easier than fretting over whether he had made the right choice. In all the important ways, infinitely harder. This one was a doozy. Trade within the CPE was all very well, but they needed much more than that; if nothing else, critical raw materials that simply couldn't be found within their own borders.

To the west, England was hostile and most of the Low Countries had recently fallen under the Spanish heel. The rump of the United Provinces had little to offer; aid, rather than trade, was the best the CPE could do there. To the east, Poland and the Russias were hellbent on their precious "second serfdom," shackling half a continent back into medievalism. Given luck, a following wind, and a Peter the Great not written out of history by the changes Grantville had made, they might be worthwhile trading partners someday—but not soon. To the southeast, the Austrian Empire was implacably hostile. Granted, since Wallenstein's recent rebellion, Bohemia had become something of a bright spot. But little Bohemia was scarcely going to do more than dent the CPE's need for foreign trade.

To the southwest, France. With whom they were at war. To the south, Bavaria, likewise. Switzerland was the only adjacent territory that was not hostile, but it wasn't worth much as a trading partner. The status of the Swiss as the world's moneybox remained far in the future, though they would cheerfully take money to let anyone cross their land on the way elsewhere. Fortunately, Gustavus Adolphus held enough of the Rhine as their southwest frontier that there was a clear route to Switzerland.

From where, southward, one might reach the Venetian

Terrafirma, the hinterland of the port that was the home
of the Most Serene Republic of Venice. And, until Switzerland invented the cuckoo clock and no-questions-asked
deposit banking, Venice was the only nonhostile trading
partner in Europe with money to spend. And, through
Venice—if the doge and the Senate and the great houses
of Venice could be persuaded—there was access to the
Adriatic, the Mediterranean and the Levant.

"Who to send, though?" asked Mike of the air
around him.

"Hard. We cannot make the usual consular arrangements there. They don't like Jews in Venice, even if
they tolerate our presence. Oh, they like our money and
our trade well enough, and they are a polite people for
the most part, but we will not get far without a proper
embassy with a Christian in charge of it." Francisco sat
forward, set down his coffee mug. "You have, as I see
it, only two potential ambassadors left who fit the bill
and can be spared from other duties."

"Who?" asked Mike.

Francisco told him.

"Well, I will be damned. You reckon they'll do
it?"

"Yes. There is the matter of their confidence in
their own abilities, but—" He shrugged. "I think they
will overcome those qualms if they are convinced it is
their duty. One of them is a most conscientious cleric,
after all, and the other . . ."

Francisco made a vague gesture, groping for the
words.

Mike laughed. "Ha! The phrase you're looking for
is 'flower child.' Except that he's old enough now to
be willing to grow the flowers himself."

Chapter 5

The Reverend Jones began to cough theatrically.

Father Augustus Heinzerling, SJ, glared at him over the brim of his stout briar pipe. "*Ja?* We are in the open air here, not so?"

Jones looked back at the heavy German priest with an expression of stunned disbelief. "What? Is there such a thing as open air around that—that *substance* you smoke? Dang it, this nation isn't supposed to be using chemical warfare."

"Oh, knock it off, Simon." The third pastor at the table came to Heinzerling's rescue. Father Lawrence Mazzare, parish priest at St. Mary Magdalene's church, Grantville, looked up from the page of the book he was holding open. "Gus, smoke if you want, but get downwind."

"*Auch Sie?*" Heinzerling adopted a wounded tone, but couldn't help his grin. As one of the seventeenth-century clerics who had joined Grantville's cadre of twentieth-century pastors, he had had nearly a year and a half to learn the hard way about the barbaric practice of making the smokers stand outside.

It was, he reflected, one of the odder differences the

"up-timers" showed. The Ring of Fire had brought a town full of twentieth-century English-speaking Americans into seventeenth-century Germany. The exigencies of diplomacy, statecraft and espionage—along with the ambition of Mazarini, one of the pope's more promising young ambassadors—had washed Heinzerling up in Grantville. Settling down with his wife and three children—to the mild consternation of the twentieth-century Catholics in town—he was becoming less and less like the Jesuit that the Society had usually been embarrassed to admit it had. Not so much like a proper Jesuit, perhaps, but he could certainly fake being a decent parochial priest on a good day. With a following wind. It was, he thought, a good life if only one didn't weaken.

And now they were putting the finishing touches on a paper intended for the pope—or, at least, the pope's closest advisers. Somewhat to Heinzerling's surprise—and to Father Mazzare's complete astonishment—the shipment of twentieth-century Catholic texts that Mazzare had asked Mazarini to take to the pope the previous year had borne fruit. In the spring of this year, Harry Lefferts had returned from his long sojourn in Italy and France—bearing with him a polite letter from Cardinal Barberini requesting a further amplification of the texts.

The "paper" that had resulted was more in the way of two massive tomes. One of them dealt with the next fifteen years of the Thirty Years' War, and the other with the history of the Catholic Church to the late 1990s.

Giving the war a name was odd, to Heinzerling. He'd never thought of the troubles in Europe as being one war all taken together. He had bounced around the chaplaincies of two imperial armies and an assortment of other postings out of the sight of people of quality. He had never really seen anything to tell him that the series of unpleasant events and occasional bouts of slaughter were part of some larger whole. Somehow, the war didn't seem to deserve anything so grand as a title when you saw it from the inside. It was just an inevitable part of life's condition that had been with him since, practically, his ordination to the priesthood.

Now, Heinzerling had begun to take a keener interest in peace. He was entering upon his fifth decade of life and his little Karl was nearly ten and clamoring to be a soldier—a soldier, yet, with a company of horse manned for the moment almost entirely by Scots Protestants whose current commander Lennox had had the lights punched out of him only six months before in a barroom brawl. By one Gus Heinzerling, SJ. (Only temporarily punched out, alas. The surly Calvinist had regained his senses and his feet and acquitted himself thereafter better than Heinzerling liked to admit.)

Giving the "paper" practical effect was like being back at school, though. Gus had staggered out of the collegium at Köln with his head crammed full of logic and rhetoric and the rest of the trivium and quadrivium and fit to be a faithful soldier of Christ. And now he was having to go through it all again on this latest project of Father Mazzare's.

They had the garden furniture out behind the rectory in the fresh autumn air. Fortunately, yesterday's rains had been replaced by sunshine. Karl, Aloysius and Matthias were getting the barbecue alight in the intense and scientific manner of small boys allowed to play with fire. Hannelore, to his constant pleasure lately become the Frau Heinzerling, was keeping one eye on the boys and the other on her knitting as she chatted with the Reverend Mary Ellen Jones. The Reverend Simon's wife was a minister in her own right and quite the most bizarre thing or person in Grantville as far as Augustus Heinzerling, SJ, was concerned. He kept watching his own wife for signs of getting ideas in that direction and was ready to put his foot down for the first time since he had married Hanni.

The table was spread, for the moment, with books and papers and scribbled notes. Father Mazzare had received a letter from Cardinal Antonio Barberini the Younger asking—asking, mind—for an appreciation of the three hundred years of history, so far as Grantville had the books to give it, that had led to the doctrines and dogma that was in the bundle of books lately sent to Rome by the kind agency of the good Monsignor Mazarini.

It had been easy enough for Heinzerling; the cardinal gave an order, he jumped to it. For Mazzare, it had been more complicated. The first thing he had pointed out was the hedge of ifs and buts and pleases, not an imperative mood in the whole thing. And that glaring subjunctive in it, inviting a caveat wide enough to ride a squadron of lies through, should Mazzare find it so convenient. Someone was setting a subtler test than Father Mazzare's research and reporting skills. His obedience was on trial as well.

There was also nothing in the letter that demanded secrecy, so Mazzare had made an appointment with Mike Stearns as soon as he could, which turned out to be late in the evening. He had been kept waiting, Heinzerling with him, patient in the presidential offices. Mike had returned from some official business or other with Don Nasi and, of all people, Harry Lefferts. Neither of the priests could figure out why, after Mazzare had explained what he had been asked to do, both Harry and Mike had snorted with laughter.

"Just keep it quiet, okay?" Mike had said, "We don't want anyone getting the idea that it's open season on giving out information to the crowned heads of Europe. And run everything you come up with by Francisco here, he's in charge of this stuff now."

Apart from the outburst of laughter, Harry had kept silent, looking thoughtful as Mazzare had explained what Cardinal Barberini wanted. Later the same evening, the young miner-cum-commando had knocked on the rectory door and spent an hour in conversation with Father Mazzare, a conversation that Heinzerling had only vaguely been aware of as muffled voices from downstairs. Heinzerling knew that type, all right. Decent enough on the straight and narrow, well dressed and polite, what the Italians would call an *galantuomo*. Unleashed or gone bad, nothing but a cold-blooded murderer with a polish of high manners.

The writing-up of three hundred years of theological history was not going to be done overnight, of course. And none of Grantville's Catholic priests—there were five, now, doing pastoral work, two of them in the chapel at what had been a refugee center, one settling in as the high school's Catholic chaplain and Latin master beside the two of them at St. Mary's—had a lot of time to spare. A note went back to the cardinal explaining that the work was in hand amid the pressure of pastoral work and the thing began to take shape.

The pastors of the other churches had pitched in to lend an ecumenical perspective—even the endearingly deranged Reverend Al Green, whose effort to portray three hundred years of post-Reformation rapprochement as the Catholic Church's progress toward the doctrine of justification by faith alone had had to be quietly but firmly edited out. The one exception, of course, had been the Reverend Enoch Wiley, whose blistering denunciation of the papacy as the Antichrist and the Whore of Babylon had smoked its way into the rectory mailbox in response to the invitation. Father Heinzerling, formed in a world in which people tended to take action on the basis of their convictions, had been somewhat dubious about Mazarre's reassurances that no mayhem would follow. His fellow down-timer, the Jesuit Von Spee, had actually admired the letter: "Classical Calvinist imagery, Gus, deftly applied. It's astonishing, really, how well he employs it, given that Father Mazarre has informed me that the man is neither a scholar not trained in rhetoric."

Now there remained only the final edit before any of their dwindling supply of electric typewriter ribbon was committed to the project. And there was another of the many little ironies created by the Ring of Fire. The up-timers considered typewriters "antiques" and made jokes about using them. But down-time artisans would pay a small fortune to get their hands on one—manual typewriters even more than electric—so they could disassemble them and begin designing what would soon become the cutting edge of a new world's literary technology. Indeed, the first seventeenth-century typewriter had just appeared on the market. It was a great, monstrous clumsy thing, which almost needed to be operated by fists instead of fingers. It was also selling like the proverbial hotcakes.

The Reverends Jones had suggested a barbecue, and so the crisp autumn air was being blued with smoke while the ladies maintained Grantville's internal lines of communication and the menfolk finished what Jones kept calling the "First Letter of Mazzare to the Romans."

"Nope," said Mazzare, interrupting Heinzerling's smoker's reverie. "*Unitatis redintegratio* was 1964. We've been admitting you heretics were human for nearly twenty years longer than you thought, Simon, and I suspect even before that."

"Ha!" Jones reached for his beer. "Typical of the Whore of Rome. Denying innocent Protestants the joy of a good propaganda line. You'll be telling me next that all the stuff I got out of Jack Chick comics has to come out, too?"

"Well, if it stays in, we have to explain why the Church in the twentieth century sanctioned the eating of babies at mass—"

Heinzerling broke in. "—when as any fool knows it is only on high days and holy days we do this in these more civilized times, *ja?*"

Mazzare shot him a look that suggested there might

be a lecture later. Damnation, the man was only two years older than he was, there was no need for him to pretend to be some kind of father-figure.

The Reverend Jones was trying not to snork beer out of his nose. When he recovered, he said, "But seriously, though, what do you expect the cardinal will do with all this, beside use it to dither even longer about what to do with all this?"

Heinzerling realized that that was one he could answer. "Perhaps I might assist, *ja*? It is not perhaps the cardinal who wishes it, I think. I have made such reports before."

"Oh?" asked Mazzare.

Both of the up-time clerics looked at him expectantly, and at each other. Behind him, he could all but hear the other Reverend Jones—another cleric, he forced himself to remember—staring at his back. "*Ja*. You do not forget that I am of the *Societas Jesu*? Such reports are the common coin of life in the Society, if one is about its work. All go, eventually, to the father-general."

"And he's asked for this through Cardinal Barberini?" Jones looked thoughtful.

"From what I hear of this particular Cardinal Barberini he is not much given to deep reading." That much he had had from the gossip in Avignon, and confirmed from Mazarini as well. Cardinal Antonio Barberini the Younger was not in the studious, pious mould of his namesake uncle or his elder brother. A butterfly who ended up in the Church for no compelling reason and whose sole mission in life was to beautify his surroundings. Worthy, certainly, but hardly a scholastic heavyweight. "He is more concerned with things of art and beauty, and hang the consequences."

"*Quod non facet Barberi, facerunt Barberini*," quoted Mazzare.

"Uh, whut? This here hillbilly preachuh don't get none of that thar Romish jabber." For all his affected accent, Jones was the only one present not wearing a meshback cap against the bright sun, even if he was the only one with actual hillbilly roots.

Heinzerling could parse the Latin. "'What the Barbarians did not do, the Barberini did,'" he translated. "But what does this mean?"

Mazzare smiled. "I shall add a note to our report. The Pantheon at Rome had its bronzes stripped for a Barberini creation of some sort, I forget what. I do remember the pasquinade, though. I think we need to warn the cardinal that he should not tear down ancient monuments to save a few scudi on the beautification of Rome."

"Well, since we're warning against every other error the Church made, I don't see why not." Jones eyed the pile of manuscript in the middle of the table. "There's a lot there. A good ten inches of history, all stacked up neat."

Heinzerling regarded the pile thoughtfully. He had ended up writing most of it longhand, having the only decent handwriting of the three of them. His hand still ached at the memory of it all. "I was telling about the father-general. Muzio Vitelleschi."

"Oh?" Mazzare looked more alert. "I didn't think you had to do with him, Gus."

"No, ordinarily I do not. The father-general commands the provincial, who commands the heads of houses and collegia, who tell the priests what to do. And reports go back the same way. This is how it is done. But I came here by accident, found myself doing pastoral work, and was ordered to stay. The Society takes the resources it finds to use."

Heinzerling paused a moment. "I speak no secrets, you understand? The Society does God's work as well as it may and with what it finds to hand. It gives the opinion of stealthiness, dishonesty at times. What some would call . . . I am sorry, I do not know the English word. *Scheinheilig?* Holy-seeming, but without the reality?"

"Hypocritical," Jones supplied. "I guess the Jesuits do have a reputation for a certain, uh, moral flexibility?"

"Moral flexibility, no. Moral absolutes, and practical flexibility." Heinzerling nodded. He couldn't think how long it had been since he read Saint Ignatius' Exercises. Or, for that matter, how long since he'd even owned a copy. He felt a pang.

"You were saying, Gus?" Mazzare's tone was gentle.

Heinzerling realized how transparent he had been. "So, the Society does what it may. Here, it has me in place and must needs ignore the fact that I have twice been so close—" he held up thumb and forefinger "—to being declared incorrigible."

The other two priests nodded. Heinzerling was not proud of the way he had been. He was prepared to admit that he had been a sorry excuse for a Jesuit, even if he was about par for a regular priest in the seventeenth century, of any denomination. It was only being able to settle down, acknowledge Hannelore publicly and follow what shreds of his vocation remained to him that had let him be anything other than a brawling, drunken loser. There were very few clerics that weren't, but the Society expected—and usually got—better.

"And so," he went on, "I am instructed direct from the father-general that I must see that Father Mazzare does not stint with his researches, that he is complete and thorough and finds time to do it in a timely manner. Be a good curate, in other words."

Mazzare chuckled. "Actually, you are that. All we have to get you cured of is that filthy thing." He waved at the pipe.

"This is not so bad," Heinzerling said. "It is a less rough smoke than the clay pipe. And lasts longer also. And the Turkish tobacco is much sweeter, not so?"

Heinzerling cringed as his wife spoke from behind him. "No, Herr Mazzare, you tell this fat fool! As soon as I hear from the Doctor Nichols about the canker in the lungs, I am telling him to quit. And telling him and telling him."

"Oh, *leise*," he said over his shoulder. "*Nur ein, ja?* Just a little pleasure?"

Hannelore rolled her eyes to heaven. "Did I think he would listen, when he said he would marry me? Did I? Mary Ellen, tell me it is easier if you are a minister yourself, please? Might I become a nun and make this fool see sense?"

"Hanni," said Mary Ellen, "if there's any of them that aren't so dumb they wouldn't listen to Almighty God Herself, I haven't met him yet."

"Gus, you see what you've provoked?" said the other Reverend Jones. "And I'd give up now, frankly."

Heinzerling looked sharply at Mazzare, who was keeping his face straight. He harumphed. "As I was saying. The father-general writes to me, saying that this report is to be made. And that the order will come from Cardinal Barberini. Of course, it must. How can the father-general of the Society order a lay father like Herr Mazzare? So he asks a cardinal and a prince of the Church, and the pope's nephew, to send the order."

Mazzare nodded. "And so here it is," he said. "Three hundred years. Three hundred years of every book we have left in town, everything the schoolteachers could supply from the French and Spanish history they had at home and, God help us, some stuff we cribbed from historical romances."

"Yup. Just got to get it typed and sent off." The Reverend Jones looked at the pile of notes, and at the beer stein in his hand. "Hmm," he said, "Gus, how are those boys of yours coming along with the fire? I feel a primal urge to burn food coming on."

"I should never have let him read that stuff about pre-Christian religion," said Mary Ellen. "He took to burnt offerings a mite too well."

Chapter 6

The barbecue had done its work and they were munching on ribs and chicken to Mary Ellen Jones' recipe. The boys were sticky all over with barbecue sauce. The adults were being as careful as they could with napkins—which, as always with barbecue, meant just about as sticky. Father Mazzare reflected that on afternoons like this, with a good bellyful of barbecue and a stein of good beer, it was possible to be very content with life.

"Hello the house!" came a call. Mazzare thought he recognized the voice of Mike Stearns, and he got up to greet him.

"Hello yourself!" he called back, heading toward the path around the side of the rectory. "We're in back; come on round."

It was indeed Mike Stearns, and he had brought Francisco Nasi with him. "Resting from your homework, Father?"

"Just about done, as it happens. Have a seat, Mike, Francisco. A few bits left to add, one more read-through and then we can type it up."

"Good, good," Mike said. Mazzare sensed he had something on his mind, and decided to let him come to the point however he saw fit. Nasi was his usual serene self, nodding as greetings went around and deferring to Mike in the making of small talk. The weather continued fair, the Heinzerling boys were looking well, and small wonder, the cooking smelled like it had been good, everyone was well, the pressures of Mike's job were bearable for the moment but, of course, everyone was worried about Rebecca in Amsterdam and the people in the Tower of London.

"In fact," said Mike, after that last topic had been appropriately commiserated on, "that was what I came to talk to you about."

"The situation in England?" Mazzare frowned. He didn't know much more about that than he could have gotten from any newspaper. And if it was a theological problem, it wasn't his field at all. In fact, the nearest thing Grantville had to the Anglican Communion was the Reverends Jones and their congregation, and the history of Methodism didn't start for another century, and that with their divergence from the Church of England. Mazzare idly wondered what Wesley would do when he showed up.

Except he wouldn't, Mazzare knew. There would be no John Wesley in this universe. Wesley hadn't been born until early in the eighteenth century, and Tom Stone had once explained to Mazzare that the so-called butterfly effect would have started scrambling the gene pool in Europe immediately after the Ring of Fire. Within days, apparently, spreading out from Thuringia with incredible speed. By now, Tom had said firmly, it would have swept the entire globe.

Mazzare had found that hard to believe, at first. That the butterfly effect was real, of course, he didn't doubt for a moment. He had only to look around him to see the many ways in which the Ring of Fire had changed Europe in less than three years. But the idea that its effects could be felt *that* quickly, and across such a great distance . . .

Tom had shaken his head. "You're mixing apples and oranges, Father. Sperm cells are a lot more sensitive to the environment than kings and queens—or housewives, for that matter. You'd be amazed how little it takes—"

There had followed a lengthy explanation in far more detail than Mazzare could follow. But, at the end, he'd been convinced that almost anyone who'd been conceived very long after the Ring of Fire in their old universe would never exist in this one. Although he had, smilingly, cautioned Tom not to tell Rebecca Stearns whenever she returned from Amsterdam that her much-prized adopted son "Baby Spinoza" probably wasn't Spinoza at all.

"Not to worry," Tom had replied, grinning. "In the immortal words of Muhammad Ali, 'I'm bold but I'm not crazy.'" Then, much more seriously: "It doesn't matter anyway. Whoever the kid is, genetically, he'll be awfully close to the original. And since his environment's been completely changed, he wouldn't grow up the same even if he does have the identical genome. So who cares? All that matters now is that he's Mike and Rebecca's kid."

It made Mazzare dizzy, sometimes, trying to follow the logic of the causal loops caused by the Ring of Fire. In this universe, "Methodism" would be founded, more than by anyone else, by the only two Methodist ministers in the world: his good friends Simon and Mary Ellen Jones. But when he'd said that to Simon once, his friend had shaken his head. "No, not really. Because we trace where we come from back to John Wesley—so he still does exist in this universe. If you look at it the right way. His soul exists here, even if his chromosomes never will."

Mazzare could hardly argue with that. Whatever other doctrinal disputes he had with Simon Jones, the primacy of the spirit over matter was not one of them.

But he was woolgathering, he suddenly realized,

while Mike had been talking. He was jolted out of the
half-reverie by the last phrase Mike had spoken.

"—like to offer you a job."

Mazzare sat up abruptly. "I've, ah, already got one."
He gestured vaguely at the bulk of St. Mary's over the
fence of the rectory garden. He was uncomfortably
aware of having missed something important. Beer at
lunchtime probably wasn't a good idea, however nice
a day it was, and whatever down-time custom might
have to say on the matter.

"Yes, but this one's important, and for the government," Mike replied. "And I don't think we've got a
better man for the job available, frankly. I want you
to be an ambassador."

"I can't!" Mazzare protested, almost as a reflex.
"Anyway, parish priest's a very important job by itself."
So's ambassador, a treacherous little part of him said.
He grabbed for the first lifeline to hand. "Anyway, I
can't. Separation of Church and State."

"Ah, not so," said Nasi. "We rather ignore your
status as an ordained minister—"

"Priest!" Mazzare barked, wincing as soon he did so.
Just because he was suddenly panicking, there was no
reason to be rude.

"Priest, I thank you for the correction," Nasi continued smoothly, "but we employ you in a secular capacity,
if you follow me?"

Mazzare spotted the flaw immediately. "My parish,
Don Francisco. This is my first responsibility, the cure
of souls or to see it discharged. If you found a curate
for me, another curate rather, while I'm away, that's
the state funding the church right there."

"Again, and with the greatest of respect, not so,
Father." Don Nasi gave every impression of already
having reached this point in the argument and having
passed it some time ago. "Your stipend as an ambassador will be suitably generous to compensate you
for the expenses of the post. Insofar as you choose to

disburse some of it to a curate, that is done by you in your private management of what is, in law, your own household. Not a matter for the State at all."

Mazzare detected the authentic whiff of lawyering. A sort of brimstone reek. He fumed to himself, keeping his face straight the while.

For all of Nasi's smooth legalese, there was still a real problem involved. Since the Reformation, southern Thuringia's Catholic Church had ceased to exist—there were no archdeaconries, no dioceses, no Catholic ecclesiastical administration of any kind. The impact of the Thirty Years' War, especially since Gustav Adolf's decisive victory at Breitenfeld two years earlier, had spread the disorganization into the parts of Franconia that made up the remainder of the territory that Grantville was managing for the Swedish king. The bishops of Wuerzburg and Bamberg were in exile at the Habsburg court, as was the prince-abbot of Fulda. The archbishop of Mainz had fled in the other direction, to Cologne, also outside of the CPE, which removed that link in the religious chain of command.

The normal clear hierarchies simply didn't exist any longer in Thuringia and Franconia. For all practical purposes, there was nobody between Father Larry Mazzare and . . . well, the pope himself. Although Mazzare always insisted that he was simply a parish priest, in fact he'd increasingly been playing the informal role of "the bishop of Thuringia and Franconia."

That was part of the reason, of course, that the Jesuits were so eager to come to Thuringia and set up shop. Protestants in the area tended to view their activities as part of a fiendish Jesuitical plot. But Mazzare knew that most of the explanation was simply that the Jesuits were delighted not to face the usual hassles with a diocesan bishop.

So. It would have to be a curate hired by Mazzare himself while he was off—he stamped down hard on that thought. Granted, it *was* flattering that they thought he was up to . . .

No. Blast it, I'm just a parish priest!

"I can't," he said, trying to be as firm about it as he could. Listening to himself, he thought he was just doing a good job of sounding obdurate.

"Sure you can," replied Mike, relaxed. "In fact, you're perfect for the job."

"I'm not related to you," Mazzare retorted. "That was why you had to send Rita and Rebecca, wasn't it? Put your own good name on the line, and all that?"

"Priests do the same job, you know. Look at what Father Joseph does for Richelieu, or the emperor's confessor, what's his name—"

"I'm not your confessor. You're not even Catholic, Mike." Mazzare had an inkling of where this particular line was going, and didn't much like it.

"I'm not really much of anything, religion-wise," Mike said, raising his hands. Rough hands, Mazzare noted. No strangers to hard work. Hard, unsentimental work. "It's something I rather tend to gloss over, of course, when it comes up. Especially these days, when everyone and his dog in Europe wants to know."

"So you're sending me somewhere Catholic, then? Is that how it is, Mike?" Mazzare realized he sounded peevish, which only made him more peevish. "You want to dissemble yourself as a Catholic?"

Mike never even blinked. "I swear, Father, that thought hadn't occurred to me."

He looked as sincere as Shirley Temple. Mazzare didn't believe it for an instant. Whatever else he was, Mike Stearns was the slickest politician Mazzare knew.

"It *had* occured to me," said Francisco Nasi, suddenly blunt and pugnacious in his manner; from the courtier to the bazaar-haggler in barely a heartbeat. "Father Mazzare, I will not try to pour sugar on this. A mission to Venice, which is indeed Catholic, is vital to our interests—and possibly even our survival. Your presence as leader of that mission represents the best hope we may have of the success of that mission. And, yes, the fact that you are a Catholic priest is part of what fits you so well for the task. For all that nearly everything in Venice turns on money and trade, Father, they need to see a face of Grantville they can trust. Even had we all our pool of potential ambassadors present in Grantville to choose from, most are women, or Jewish."

"Or Jewish women," Mike added, with a brief flash of a grin.

"Just so," said Nasi. "You, Father, are a Catholic priest and, however indirectly"—he gestured at the notes, now weighted down with a brick on the chair where they had been put out of the way—"you have the ear of the pope. Added to this, you are an up-timer and, if you will permit me the compliment, renowned as a man of conscience and integrity among the diplomats of Europe."

"Come again? That last part?" Mazzare shook his head. "Hardly anyone outside this town knows me at all, let alone well enough to give me a character reference."

There was genuine warmth and humor in Nasi's laugh, for all its quietness and brevity. "No, Father Mazzare, many have heard of your reputation. For one thing, you count among your acquaintances one of the rising stars of modern diplomacy, Monsignor Mazarini, and he is, when not keeping secrets, a terrible gossip. Well, not a 'gossip' exactly—nothing that man says is uncalculated. For another thing, surely you cannot think you have escaped the notice of the spies that infest this town?"

"Place is thick with 'em," Mike added. Though he didn't seem terribly aggrieved at the thought.

"Oh, quite," said Nasi, smiling widely. "It is all I can do not to have a guidebook printed so as to be sure that they get everything. Most helpful, in the matter of sending clear messages to our adversaries."

Mazzare gave a little shudder at the kind of mind that would welcome and take advantage of pervasive espionage. For all his affable urbanity, Don Francisco was a deeply devious man. He was, after all, from the city that gave the world the term "Byzantine" in the first place.

"Why would they be interested in me?" he asked, almost afraid of the answer.

"They pay attention to all the churches in this town," Nasi answered. "Also attracting them was the fact that Monsignor Mazarini paid you close attention and in his own person carried your first message to Rome. A message, I might add, that it is widely known was read by either the pope or one of his closest advisers. Hardly the sort of thing that characterizes 'a simple parish priest.'"

Mike snorted. "Hardly. Come on, Larry, cut it out." He gave Mazzare a hard and level gaze. "You know perfectly well that you're in a special position in this world. And, by now, probably the most famous 'simple priest' since a guy named Martin Luther." He pointed a finger at the thick stack of paper on the chair. "Do you really think the pope asks every 'simple parish priest' to send him a tome on theology?"

Mazzare didn't try to meet the gaze. Mike was right, and he knew it. He'd known it since the day he decided to ask Mazarini to take those first books to Rome.

For the first time, he began seriously considering the matter. Where *would* he do more good?

Hesitations came first. "I don't know anything about Venice, especially not in this day and age. And what I know about diplomacy and negotiations you could . . ." Metaphor failed him. "It's not very much. Nothing, come right to it."

Nasi waved those objections aside. "Briefings. Training. Weeks of it. We do not propose to send you on the morrow. Then, when you reach Venice, there will be a staff from the Abrabanel and Nasi holdings in the city to advise you and to handle the details of negotiations. Finally, Father Heinzerling here has some experience as a diplomatic aide."

"Gus?" Mazzare looked sharply at his curate. "Did you have a hand in this, this—?"

Not a muscle moved in Heinzerling's face. "Don Nasi inquired, and I informed him that there would be no difficulty in obtaining the services of a curate or two during any time we spent away. He did not say for how long, where, or on what particular business."

The trouble with Gus, Mazzare thought as he parsed that, was that it was desperately easy to assume that he was plain and straightforward all the time, rather than just most of it. The man could be damnably devious when he put his mind to it, and his loyalty to his parish priest would probably cause him to. The trouble was that his idea of Mazzare's best interests was decidedly seventeenth century. Heinzerling was bound and determined that Larry Mazzare would become—bare minimum—a bishop. In this day and age, that almost required political prominence.

Mazzare sighed. He didn't doubt that Gus' conversation with Francisco had gone considerably beyond the possibility of getting curates while they were away. Nasi seemed to be altogether too well prepared for this meeting for Mazzare's liking.

Nothing for it, then, but to bull ahead. "All right, Gus, who did you sound out for the job?"

"Father Kircher." Again, not a muscle in Heinzerling's face betrayed him. "He is willing, and kind enough to find his own assistant priest if asked to undertake the parochial work here at St. Mary's in addition to his duties at the school."

Mazzare tried not to laugh at his own defeat. *Kircher, no less!*

Athanasius Kircher, SJ. Scientist, scholar, and all

round genius, was willing to cover his parochial work? The Jesuits must be *very* keen to see Mazzare get on. Kircher had made the first serious attempt on Egyptian hieroglyphics, some of the first experiments in rocketry, was a known man in the fields of physics and chemistry. The only reason he hadn't been remembered as a great astronomer was because Galileo and Kepler were his contemporaries and were more dedicated to it than he was.

And this—this genuine *polymath*—was willing to add ten masses, confession, novena and benedictions to his working week? So that Father Lawrence Mazzare could junket to Venice?

"It's a done deal, isn't it?" he said to Mike.

"You can always say no."

"How? With everyone, including at least one leading light among the Jesuits, greasing the rails, all this effort to get me to agree, how can I refuse?" There, that put it in terms his conscience could handle.

Mike had the good grace to look embarrassed. "Look, Father, I'm sorry and all, but I wouldn't be pressing so hard if it wasn't so important."

A sudden wild whim overtook Mazzare. He turned to Jones, who had been watching the conversation in silence, his head following the action like a tennis spectator. "Simon, how about it?"

Jones swallowed, hard, before replying. "Larry, I can't decide for you, you know that. It sounds like there's nothing to get in your way, though, and I think you'd be good with a bit of training. Seriously."

"No, not that. I mean, do you want to come to Venice with me? Call it 'assistant ambassador,' or whatever the appropriate diplomatic title is. Show 'em we're not just Catholics here, and that religion is completely separate from politics?"

"He's starting already," Mike said.

Jones went a little pale. "Me? Why?"

"I'm going to need help."

"You should, Simon, if there's a place for you," said Mary Ellen, over her knitting but not actually looking up. "I can fill in for you while you're gone. And you can bring me back some of that nice Venetian glassware I've always wanted."

Jones, in that moment, looked like Mazzare felt.

Chapter 7

Frank Stone had every nerve, every fragment of concentration on the ball, the wide-open goal, Klaus off his goal-line and with the evening sun in his eyes—

—and so he never saw Aidan pounding in from his left to slide in for the ball in a spray of turf and distinctly seventeenth-century English.

Frank's cry of alarm was part scream, part roar, part a word that would have gotten him a real old-fashioned look from Magda. His new German stepmom had learned about some parts of modern English with surprising speed.

He kept his feet, just barely. The ball went out of play in a low, curving loop, just as the whistle blew for full time. "Damn," said Frank. And, with more feeling, *"Damn!"*

Away on the other side of the eighteen-yard box, Heinrich jogged to a halt. His expression said it all. Had Frank managed to cross the ball, Klaus' sloppy goalkeeping had left the net wide open for the winner to go in: as it was, the game had finished three-all. Freda, back at the other end of the pitch, wasn't much better than Klaus—she got focused on the main attack and a good cross or diagonal through ball could easily leave her off her line and the net wide open for a sneaky striker to score.

Part of the problem, Frank decided, as he heaved air back into his lungs, was that most of the sports-minded Germans seemed to have taken up baseball. That just plain wasn't fair. True, the up-timers had fixed on baseball as a strong reminder of home. On the other hand, they had been dropped back in time into the nation that had produced Beckenbauer and Klinsman and . . .

Frank decided wishing soccer was more popular wasn't going to get him to the showers any quicker. He staggered over to where Aidan was flat on his back in the penalty box, and leaned down to help him up.

Aidan was just about everything Frank wasn't. Frank was an up-time American, raised on a hippie commune dedicated to peace, egalitarianism and really, really good weed. Aidan Southworth was a seventeenth-century Catholic English mercenary, formerly of the Spanish army in Flanders. He'd been taken prisoner at the Wartburg the year before, when the Spanish troops had surrendered after the fortress was bombarded with napalm. Thereafter, he'd elected to stay in Grantville and was now back at school to "get his letters." Aidan had decided to try to make a military career in the armed forces of the CPE, in the Grantville regiments of which literacy was a requirement to advance beyond the rank of private soldier.

Aidan had said he knew no other trade and wanted to learn none for the time being. Soldiering was what he knew and he'd stick with it until he had a little put by. Privately, Frank wondered if Aidan knew what he was letting himself in for. From Aidan's accounts of drinking, fornicating and fighting his way across Europe since going to war alongside his father as a twelve-year-old drummer boy, he was likely to find life in the CPE's increasingly professional armed forces a mite boring.

"Th'art quick, Frank," said Aidan, as he got to his feet, "but not quick enough, eh?"

Aidan's English had been all but incomprehensible when he'd first arrived at school. He'd been from Lancashire, where apparently the English were mostly still Catholic, and had never bothered to learn the more comprehensible speech of the south of England, and simply got by in Spanish and Dutch instead. He'd picked up American English fairly quickly, though.

"Aidan, I'm quick enough not to get cropped by a dirty fouling English bastard like you."

Aidan laughed. "That'd be dirty, fouling, *literate* English bastard, thank ye kindly."

"Cool!" Frank grinned. "You passed, then?"

Aidan grinned back. "That I did. I learned on't this day, and shall have my ticket for it directly."

"Great!" Frank realized his own feelings were a bit mixed on the subject. On the one hand, he'd rather looked forward to a spell in the army—he'd been just that bit too young for the fighting the year before. On the other hand, reforms had just been announced to the effect that the army was going all-volunteer and more professional. Frank Jackson's take on military punctilio—which was largely that it was horse manure that he couldn't be bothered with—was going out of the window. There were already uniforms and drill starting to appear around town, and the U.S. Marine Horse were looking decidedly smart lately.

Frank wasn't sure he wanted any part of that kind of thing. Even if he'd be allowed to join the military at all, for that matter. Frank served as his father's chief assistant and bottlewasher in the pharmaceutical end of his business—with his brothers, Ron and Gerry, being respectively the second and third assistants—and Frank knew that the powers-that-be considered him far more useful in that capacity than as another spear-carrier. He fell into the category of "critical industrial worker." The one time he'd raised the matter with Frank Jackson,

the head of the army had quietly told him he'd be a
lot happier if Frank kept working to save ten sick or
wounded U.S. servicemen than signing up to maybe
kill one French or Spanish soldier.

"Wouldst have a beer with me?" Aidan asked. "In
celebration?"

"Oh, sure. We'll get Gerry as well, and Ron if he's
not busy." That was something neither Frank nor his
two younger brothers had any trouble with. Up-time
and down-time attitudes to drinking had met somewhere in the middle, though probably a bit nearer the
seventeenth-century side of the issue. The down-timers
in Grantville had gotten used to water that was relatively
safe to drink, and the up-timers had gotten used to
beer that was worth drinking for its flavor.

"Uh, I'd better check in with home first, though."
Frank and his brothers Gerry and Ron had come
home the best part of paralytic one night, and their
father had gotten the nearest he ever did to angry.
The sons all thought Tom Stone's attitude was decidedly irrational. Not to mention unfair. *He'd* spent a
lot of his twenties in alternative states of mind, after
all. But now he regarded getting anything more than
a little buzzed as a serious personal failing. Tom had
pulled his usual sneaky parental trick of relying on
his sons' senses of personal honor and responsibility,
and Frank felt he had to check in now when he was
going for a beer.

"Okay," said Aidan, "Telephone after we get out of
the shower, yes?"

The telephone rang and rang. "Come on, Dad,"
Frank muttered.

"No answer?" Frank heard the English accent behind
him, and turned around. Aidan was out of the shower,
and dressed up for the evening. Frank was briefly
thankful that his dad's dyeing business brought a lot
of samples and spare swatches of cloth, so lately the

whole family was very well dressed—except his dad, whose fashion sense had run aground somewhere around 1973.

"No, not yet—" he said, but then his stepmother's voice came on the other end of the line.

"Lothlorien Farbenwerke," she said.

Frank still found his stepmom's telephone manner funny. Magda might have been married to Dad for well over a year and part of an up-time equipped household for a little longer, but for some reason she still retained a slight awe of the telephone. Television she had no trouble with, and the washing machine and vacuum cleaner she regarded as God's fitting apology to womankind for inflicting untidy males on the world, but telephones still left her slightly nervous.

"Magda?" Frank found it best to give her something simple to settle into the conversation with. He knew she would have hesitated while the phone rang, looking to see if someone was around to answer it instead.

"*Ja, hier,*" she said. "Is that you, Faramir?"

Frank winced. Cringed, in fact. The big, big down-side to a hippie upbringing, the thing that completely made up for the freedom other kids didn't get, was the wanton cruelty with which the flower-children had named their own kids. He was, by his paperwork, Faramir Stone. And his brothers—the relationship wasn't quite that clear-cut but his brothers they were—had the names Gwaihir and Elrond to live down. Any one of them would sooner have been called Sue. Every record bar their birth certificates—Dad had had this much decency—recorded them as Frank, Gerry and Ron. Magda, German right the way down, insisted on using the names with which their birth certificates had been *gestempelt.*

On the plus side, there were a lot of folks in Grantville these days with more exotic names, and apart from the few who'd bothered to look Tolkien up they were just three more foreign-sounding names out of hundreds.

Of course, in Thuringia, Frank, Gerry and Ron could be said to sound foreign anyway.

"Yes, Magda, it's me. Frank. I'm calling to check if it's okay if I—and Gerry and Ron if I can find them—go for a dinner and a few beers at the Gardens? Aidan is celebrating finishing summer school."

"Aidan?" Magda was an artist in the kitchen and Dad had high praise for her as a business manager—her own father had taught her to keep books—but she sometimes had trouble matching faces to names before the sixth or seventh meeting.

"Sergeant Southworth." Frank braced himself.

"Ah." There was a freight of meaning in that syllable.

Frank held his breath. The general attitude toward soldiers among the Germans was not good. The professionalization of the U.S. Army—even Frank Jackson's loose attitudes were practically Prussian by local standards—was helping, but few people had shaken off the attitudes of a life during wartime and Magda was no exception. Frank could also see her trying to place Aidan's face among the small army of lifters and shifters that the Lothlorien commune had employed. A lot of summer-school students had supplemented their money by doing a few hours a week casual work at the new dye plant.

"Your father should speak of this," she said at last, "but he is out. With the President, and Doctor Nichols."

Frank could practically smell the snobbery coming out of the telephone, and saw his chance. Magda was still smitten with Dad—and rightly so—but she visibly wanted him to act more like the captain of industry he was well on the way to becoming. Hobnobbing with the President was about the speed she wanted him at. "Well," said Frank, "if Dad's with the President, we don't want to distract him because Gerry and Ron and me are going for a beer at the Gardens with Aidan. Can you tell him when he gets home?"

Silence at the other end of the phone. Then: "Just so. Don't be late, and be respectable, yes?"

"Sure, Magda. And thanks." He put the phone down after saying goodbye with the definite feeling she was no more fooled than anyone had been the last time a couple of Dan Frost's boys had brought all three of them home from where they had "just been tired" on a bench halfway between the Gardens and home. On the other hand, Magda hadn't minded so much. They hadn't been fighting, and as far as she was concerned overdoing it and having to be helped home was something boys did from time to time.

"A'reet?" Aidan was waiting.

"Sure. C'mon, we'll see if we can find Gerry and Ron before we head back to town. I figure we earned them beers."

Aidan grinned. "I've scrip and reason to spend it," he said, and held up a wad of the new funny-looking dollar bills. Frank found them a bit embarrassing, frankly, what with the hand his dad had had in the design.

It was another of those oddities—weirdities, Frank thought of them—that the Ring of Fire had produced in the world, in the Year of Our Lord 1633 in Universe Whichever. With the influx of American technology and the political stability provided by the army of the new U.S., Thuringia had quickly become the strongest economic province in war-ravaged Germany. That meant the U.S. dollar was also the strongest currency in Gustav Adolf's ramshackle Confederated Principalities of Europe.

On the other hand, given that "George Washington" and "Abe Lincoln" meant nothing at all to ninety-nine percent of the population of the CPE, Mike Stearns had decreed that new designs were needed for the various dollar bills. And, since Frank's father Tom was the only manufacturer of a waterproof green ink in the world, he'd more or less been able to finagle his designs onto an unsuspecting universe.

Frank could live with an eight-point buck as the central symbol on the one-dollar bill, hands kneading dough for a five-dollar bill and a loaf of bread for a ten-dollar bill, even if he thought the puns were pretty outrageous. But, even for his dad, putting Johnny Cash on the twenty-dollar bill was going over the edge.

Some people joked that the Thuringen Gardens ought to have been the location of the new Grantville mint. Since the place seemed to have a license to print money, they said, they might as well actually do it there and save on freight.

It was not that there was any shortage of places in Grantville for the hungry—and thirsty—to seek refreshment and unwind. There were places with fancier food, finer drink, and all manner of other selling points.

The Gardens, though, had been there first with the mix of up- and down-time comforts and customs, and had become something of an Official Institution in Grantville. In fact, from what anyone could tell it had become famous all over Germany. Now that central Germany had been politically stabilized—by seventeenth-century standards, anyway—and the armies that had ravaged it driven off, Grantville was not only a boom town but the central tourist attraction for anyone in Europe with the money and leisure time to afford to come there. And each and every one of those visitors sooner or later made a beeline for the Gardens.

The management of the Gardens had cheerfully—and haphazardly—kept expanding the establishment to match the clientele, to the despair of Grantville's more snooty citizens and the sheer outrage of anyone with any sense of proper architectural design. It had become a sprawling giant of a "building," growing up as well as out.

But, like most people, Frank didn't care. If the owners were cavalier about the design of the establishment, they were quite careful to stay within Grantville's building code when it came to what mattered. And, whatever else it was—usually overcrowded, loud, smoky and hot—the Gardens was almost always a good-humored and cheerful place. Even the inevitable and constant disputes over theology and politics always seemed to be friendlier in the Gardens than anywhere else.

Granted, that wasn't perhaps saying much, looked at from one angle. A "moderate dispute" in the seventeenth century would have been classed as a "brawl" in up-time America. But at least, in the Gardens, people settled their disputes with fisticuffs instead of sabers, stones and the gibbet.

Frank pushed open the door and the noise and smoke hit him like a wall. The main bar-and-dining room was colorful and busy. Especially colorful, now that the bright hues that Lothlorien was turning out were making inroads into the brown and tan and goose-turd green of mass-market fabric. It looked like a good night in the Gardens, and it was a pity they hadn't found Gerry and Ron. Frank called over his shoulder: "Get the beers in, Aidan, I'll find us a table."

It was usually as well to get a round from the bar, since the service sometimes got a little slow of a Saturday night. As Frank wandered in, though, he saw that the room wasn't quite as full as it had looked. There were still some tables at the back. People hadn't wanted to get too close to any of the fireplaces, where the fires were still roaring with fresh wood. Later in the evening, when the crowd had throttled back to the die-hards, they would cluster around the softer embers.

"Frank?" Somehow the voice cut through the hub-bub and the tunings of the evening's pickup band. That was all the more impressive because of the mellow and relaxed tone.

Damn. Frank looked around for his dad, panicking slightly before he realized, *No, it's cool, I told Magda.*

He spotted his father's table and headed for it, none

too eagerly. Tom "Stoner" Stone was Grantville's leading ageing hippie, general good guy, pharmacologist, recreational horticulturist and lately owner and CEO of the Lothlorien Farbewerk, the Lothlorien Commune as once was. And, on account of being the aforementioned hippie, almost impossible to generation-gap.

"Dad, hi, what's up, what're you—" Frank dried up. Around the table were Mike Stearns, Balthazar Abrabanel, Doctor James Nichols, Don Francisco Nasi, Frank Jackson, Father Mazzare, the Reverend Jones and—Frank's attempt at calm assurance turned to cold gray slop in his guts—Mister Piazza. Now the secretary of state, but—more to the point—the former principal of Frank's high school.

"Probably the same thing you are, Frank," his dad said. "Did you tell Magda you were coming? Are Gerry and Ron here with you?" There was no note of accusation in his dad's voice, just concern that proper procedure had been followed. He used the same tone of voice to run down the checklist when his sons helped in the lab or the greenhouse, confirming that the sensible things had been done and useful lessons learned.

It would be easier, Frank sometimes thought, if his father was dumber or meaner or a hypocrite or something. What in a lot of hippies—and Frank had met more of the breed than most guys his age—was a lot of New Age hypocritical crap was, in his dad, the genuine article. Tom Stone was reasonable, gentle and good, most of the time, and when he wasn't, he was trying to be. And, unfortunately, he had a fine mind when he felt like using it. He was not impossible to fool, but it wasn't easy.

In short, as a father for sprightly teenage lads, a first-class pain in the ass.

"Sure, Dad. She said you were, uh, with Mister Stearns here. Uh, Mister President, I mean."

Mister President grinned. "You figured the Gardens was safe, then?"

"Um . . ." Frank didn't feel much like talking. Technically he was an adult, now that he was nineteen, but the presence of so many authority figures affected him like so many alarms replete with red lights and sirens. He was not only tongue-tied, he found he was wanting to look down to check he was wearing trousers, and that his zipper was up. He definitely didn't like the way Mister Piazza was grinning. If there was a bright side, he supposed, it was that Miz Mailey—air-raid sirens and maroon flares, here—was in another country. And locked in jail, besides. The Tower of London, no less.

Frank Jackson broke the silence. "Siddown, son. Your dad was saying earlier as how this might concern you, and if you followed proper reporting procedure you've every right to be here. You bring friends?"

"Ah, yes, Mister, I mean General—I, that is, my friend Aidan was celebrating graduating and we figured dinner and a few beers—"

"Excellent, good thinking," beamed Doctor Nichols. "Had the same idea myself every time I passed something, when I took to getting edumacated. Join us, do—is this Aidan friend of yours at the bar?"

"Don't tease the young man, now." That was Father Mazzare, who had always seemed a slightly odd and exotic figure to Frank. "Do, please, join us. As the general says, your father thought it might be good for you and your brothers to come along."

Frank looked around, saw Aidan carefully working his way between tight-packed tables under the weight of four steins of beer. Sigh; leave it to Aidan. Frank caught Aidan's eye to be certain Aidan knew where to head for and sat down. He took a deep breath. "Come along where, Father Mazzare? Dad?" Frank looked from one to the other, trying for an effect of *slightly intrigued* rather than *baffled and terrified*.

"Venice," said Mister President.

"Venice? Cool—but why me? Uh, I mean us? And what about the pharmaceutical work?"

"Mike asked me to go along as the scientific and medical attaché and I agreed," his dad explained. "I could really use your help down there—same with Ron and Gerry—getting a pharmaceutical industry off the ground in Italy. The truth is, that work's gotten pretty routine here. You've already trained enough people to replace you and your brothers."

Nasi nodded. "And a grand tour is a vital part of every young man's education, Señor Stone. I spent some months in Venice myself, at your age. I have a cousin there who is a factor for Messer Mocenigo."

"I wasn't quite so lucky," Doctor Nichols chuckled. "When I was your age, Frank, the educational choice I was given was either a hitch in the Marines or considerable time—never mind how much—in one of those downstate establishments that really don't look too good on a job resumé." The doctor raised his beer stein in ironic toast to Don Francisco's cultured upbringing.

Aidan picked that moment to arrive and set down the beers. "Mister Stone, Doctor Nichols, good e'en to ye. Father Mazzare, good evening." Aidan looked at Frank for introductions.

Ah, thought Frank. Aidan's exhausted everyone he knows by sight. Now for the fun part. "Aidan," he said, taking a beer from in front of his friend. Then he thought a moment, and moved a second one over. This could get—explosive. "I don't believe you know Doctor Abrabanel, Don Nasi, Mister Piazza, General Jackson and—" Frank completed the round of beer-stein gestures "—Mister President Stearns of the United States."

Aidan's face must have been a treat. To his credit, the Englishman didn't spray beer or choke. Whatever he did, though, made Doctors Abrabanel and Nichols suddenly look very professional. Frank's dad grinned, Mike Stearns smiled and Father Mazzare shot Frank a sharp look.

Mister Piazza snorted, briefly, but without cracking

his face. Frank Stone found that oddly satisfying, that all his student pranks hadn't been wasted in keeping the old guy interested in his work back when he'd been a principal.

"So, young feller, I wouldn't wait on your friend to introduce you prop'ly," said Jackson. "And we don't care much about fancy manners anyhow. Pleased to meet you, Aidan, and what are you going to do now you're quittin' school?"

Aidan leapt to his feet. "Sah! Private Southworth, Sah!" he bellowed, and came to quivering attention with a salute that practically echoed off the walls.

"I will get you for this," muttered Frank under his breath, although he doubted Aidan heard him.

"At ease, Private," said Jackson. "Aw, hell, siddown, son. I think you got your own back, there."

Aidan sat down. "Much obliged, General, sir."

"You been a soldier before?" asked Jackson, squinting suddenly in half-recognition.

"Sir, I was a private soldier after I got out of prison for a while, sir. I was a sergeant in Colonel Stanley's Regiment in the Army of Flanders, sir. I took a leave of absence to get my letters again at summer school, sir." Aidan picked up his beer and took a drink. It had been quite a long speech for the usually laconic soldier.

Frank seethed slightly. A moment of surprise was all he'd managed to inflict, damn it. He'd hoped to see Aidan in the grip of that no-trousers feeling, but then a man who had had to take cover from napalm in the line of duty was probably a little harder to faze than most.

"Ah," said Jackson. "Frank said you'd graduated something—you're looking to be a corporal?"

"Sir, yes, sir. As I said, sir, I was a sergeant with the Spani—" Aidan paused a moment, apparently realizing who he was addressing.

Stearns waved Aidan's concern aside. "Don't worry,

son. Lots of folks in this town spent time, uh, else-where. It's where you are now that counts."

"Even some Americans," said Jackson, "weren't on the right side to begin with." He exchanged a look with Stearns that Frank couldn't read. "So, Private Southworth, how have you done with the rest of your training?"

Aidan shifted on his seat. At last, Frank thought, he's having the good grace to be embarrassed. "Sir, I needed but the ticket of having my letters and I shall be fit to be a corporal of horse, sir, and to be an officer some day."

"You go, son," said Doctor Nichols, and the others around the table murmured assent, lifted their glasses or just nodded approvingly.

Mister Piazza beamed particularly widely. "Our adult literacy program," he said. "Most folks hereabouts can read, but a fair few need a refresher or to read some-thing that isn't the Bible. Quite the success, and the best spend of a taxpayer dollar I have seen in some time. Actually, half the battle is teaching folks to read our script."

"Eh?" Frank frowned, trying to pick out the right mental image.

"Fraktur," Mister Piazza said, "Gothic script. If you grew up reading it, you need to learn any different alphabet you want to use all over again. We're doing classes for up-timers to learn the other way around, of course, but Roman script is catching on here in Germany the way it did in our timeline."

"Ah," Frank nodded. He'd known that, actually.

"Venice," his dad said. "We were talking about Venice. Father Mazzare is going to be our ambassador to the Most Serene Republic of Venice."

"What?" said Frank, and realized immediately how that sounded. "I mean, cool, but that's not your scene, is it? Your thing is chemistry, and growing stuff—"

Dad was grinning, as was—no, in fact, all of the

adults were grinning. Adults. *He* was an adult, damn it. Legally, at least. It was just hard to think that way with your high-school principal across the table.

"Oh, such confidence you have in me. I am so stoked." Even being sarcastic, Frank's dad sounded gentle and reasonable. It wasn't *fair.* "Frank, I told you—I am of-fi-cially the medical and scientific attaché." Tom Stone tucked his thumbs in the armholes of his vest, puffed out his chest and sat up straight in mock pride. "The Venetians asked us to send them some medical advisers. Which they certainly need. As you may remember—or maybe not, if you weren't paying attention—Venice just got hit by a terrible plague a couple of years ago."

"Ah." Frank wondered when he would get to either say something meaningful or just get the hell out of there. Beside him, he realized, Aidan might be feigning cool but his spine was creaking with the effort of sitting at attention without looking like he was doing so.

"So," his dad said, "do you want to come? We'll be there maybe a year. I thought we'd all go, Magda and your brothers. The basic processes are working at the factory, now, and Magda's dad can run the business side for the time being. Better than I can, to be truthful."

Frank nodded. "Cool. Uh, that is, that would be just fine, Dad."

"Great." His father grinned brightly. "Maybe you and Aidan want to go find another spot? If you're uncomfortable around authority figures and all? From here on in it's shipbuilding, drains and commercial links, I'm afraid."

Frank and Aidan got while the getting was good.

Chapter 8

The steam crane made things easier, of that there was no doubt.

When the bastard thing was working, that was. Yard Foreman Conrad Ursinus stared at the machine and tried, under his breath, threatening it. The *verdammte* thing was squirting steam in all directions and held a mid-rib in the air like a hooked fish where it was no good to man nor beast.

Threatening it did no good, alas. Conrad took a deep breath and drew on an English curse word or two. Somehow they seemed—filthier? Stronger? More satisfying. Earthier somehow. He certainly felt better for wishing that the stinking thing get fucked. Sideways.

That attended to, he cupped his hands and hollered over the screech of the safety valve. "Was fur shit ist es now? Ist broke, oder was?"

Aloysius the crane-driver leaned out of the cab, his fat Frieslander face sweating red while he wafted steam away from himself. "Das verfuckter packing noch immer. Funf minutes while es kuhlt, dan kann ich es fixen."

That made Conrad chuckle. They had two new

words: *fucken*, straight from English, and *fixen*, which meant to mend something, but sounded exactly like the word they used to use for fucken.

There was probably a scholar somewhere writing about it even now.

Conrad put his fingers in his mouth and whistled for a short break, and heard his gangers along the slip echo the call. There were benches down the side of the slipway, and he went for a sit-down while Aloysius broke out his toolbox.

The boat they were building, having only a contract number and not yet named, was to be a river craft. She could carry light and medium guns at need—everything they built at the U.S. Navy shipyard in Magdeburg had some military capability, even ships being built for civilian customers—but what she would mostly be was a means of hauling cargo along the Rhine and Elbe and whatever canals were built.

One of the very nice things Conrad had discovered about being in the U.S. Navy was that the shipyard had deliberately been planned by the admiral to have more capacity than he needed for his heavy warships. Which meant, especially given how many bottlenecks there were in the production of the ironclads he'd designed, that most of the shipyard was often twiddling its thumbs. "Twiddling thumbs" and "the Devil's work" were pretty much synonyms so far as the admiral was concerned, so he'd eventually started cheerfully accepting the many civilian contracts that had been pressed upon him.

Then, when those contracts proved to be a significant source of income—American up-timers were given to obsessing over "moral issues" that no down-timer could make sense of—the admiral had decided that the civilian work needed to be handled by a separate official concern than the Navy itself. This, to avoid what he called "conflict of interest," something which so far as Conrad could determine was the American equivalent of fussing over the precise status of the body of Christ during communion. So, with the agreement of Mike Stearns, the President of the U.S., Admiral Simpson had created the "U.S. Naval Shipyard Corporation." The USNSC was technically a private corporation and not part of the Navy—even though all the employees and all the facilities did belong to the Navy.

Whatever. The delightful side of it was that, although the admiral himself scrupulously refrained from buying stock in the corporation, he did allow his sailors to do so. So far as Conrad knew, the *only* member of the USNSC who hadn't bought stock in it was the admiral himself.

The Rhine was already a major artery for goods, and the Elbe was bidding fair to join it. Having a paddlesteamer to haul boats and cargo upstream was going to make the new shipping line that had commissioned her very rich indeed. Or spectacularly poor, perhaps—but, either way, the yard would have had their money by then, Conrad's stock options would mature and he'd be into the serious money, maybe even thinking about getting married.

Stern-wheeled, twin-engined and with a ketch rig for fuel-saving, the ship they were currently working on was broad-beamed and shallow-drafted. Her keel was forty meters of rock-elm with an iron keelson on top, and the iron frame of her hull was taking shape from one end to the other. As the frames went on, the carpentry teams bent on the strakes and fixed her lower deck onto the cast-iron cross-beams as the shape of her advanced. At her stern, the carpentry crew making the paddle-box were lighting up for their own break, while one of their apprentices was climbing down to rake the fire over and get some coffee on. Conrad decided he'd wander over in ten minutes or so and take a yard-boss' privilege of glomming a cup.

"Halloooo!" Conrad looked around. Dietrich Schwanhausser, the admiral's mother hen and a prize pain to all sailors while the admiral was out of town, had come through the gate and was walking along the slip to where Conrad was sitting. Well, if Mother Hen wanted to cluck a word or two while the *scheissfressender* crane was being fixed, now was a good time.

"Wie goes it?" Schwanhausser was looking as cheerful as he ever got. Conrad figured he must've counted the frames they'd gotten in so far. He was a *schwein* for only being cheerful with progress and looking like someone hanged his favorite dog if the margin they kept ahead of schedule ever dropped, even if there wasn't any Navy interest in the job at hand. Like everyone in the yards he spoke a mix of German and English—with so many dialects of German, his own different from Dieter's and each of them different again from most of the others (and the Ostfrieslanders communicating largely in grunts and swearwords), they all had to standardize somewhere. Conrad's up-time friend Billy Trumble claimed it was the beginning of a new language altogether. Maybe he was right.

Conrad hawked and spat, his throat good and gummed with coal smoke. "Crane is upgefuckt again. We should save more time to fix him than trying to horse the rib in by hand." And wasn't that a prize *schweinerei* for a job?

"Ah." Schwanhausser nodded and pulled out his pipe. "This is going to be someone else's problem soon, Ensign Ursinus. The admiral has another job for you if you will."

"Eh?"

"*Ja.* Naval attaché." Schwanhausser held up his clipboard and read carefully from the radio office flimsy.

Conrad frowned. "That is a French word, *ja*?"

"Another English word too, it seems. I asked. However fussy the Americans might be when it comes to most forms of robbery and swindling, they are veritable Barbary pirates when it comes to plundering other languages. It means someone with a job helping an ambassador. There is an ambassador to go and you are to go with him to tell the *Fremde* how to make boats. And whatever else he wants."

Schwanhausser handed over the written order. "You go to Venice, Lieutenant Ursinus. The rank is a temporary commission, do not let it swell your head."

Conrad felt his face break out in a big smile. "Fuckin' A," he said.

Truly, the English language had some very useful words in it—and Conrad was bound and determined to see that whatever new language might be emerging contained each and every one of them. He rather approved of linguistic piracy himself.

"Lieutenant Trumble, sir, reporting as ordered."

Lennox was still getting used to the idea of soldiers reporting to him with a salute and the position of attention. His own military experience was as a sergeant in a borderer cavalry company, where things were, if not exactly free-and-easy, at least relatively informal. Watching young Billy come to attention gave him an odd feeling, even after all these months.

"At ease, Lieutenant." That was another thing. When did young officers start looking like children? This one was most famous around town for playing that foolish *game*, and who would credit that? Mister Mackay, now, he was perhaps on the young side to be a captain, but had the cardinal virtue of being able to listen to his sergeants.

That was never going to be a problem for Captain Lennox, USMC, who carried his own Inner Sergeant wherever he went. Young Master Trumble here looked too young to be any kind of officer except an ensign, although the papers that said he was twenty were reliable. Twenty! And that was too old for a proper ensign. Again, the Americans had different ideas, and as they were paying the bills for the Marine Corps Cavalry, they got to write the rules.

Several people had thought the idea of Marine Cavalry was hilarious, and Lennox could see their point. Transporting horses by sea was a chancy business at the best of times, and expecting them to be in condition to fight after any more than the shortest sea passage was ludicrous. King Charles had a Marine Regiment of Foot to send aboard his ships, and that made a certain amount of sense.

The United States had some traditions, though, and one of them was that the troops attached to the President, and the troops who guarded embassies, were Marines. The trouble was that the job of guarding ambassadors in this day and age wasn't an infantry job. Dragoon cavalry were needed, if only so as to be able to keep up with the ambassador's coach, and also to rank properly in precedence with the ambassador himself. Infantry were socially a long way below cavalrymen. Even such salt-of-the-earth sorts as himself.

So the United States Marine Corps had a couple of companies of cavalry, over-officered so they could be sent in penny packets to embassies everywhere under an officer of appropriate rank. The lessons of the earlier diplomatic missions had been well learned.

Not that they'd get Captain Lennox and his horse aboard a ship without dire need. He'd puked every mile across the North Sea to Flanders, and only the prospect of never sailing from Scotland again would get him back to sea.

Lieutenant Trumble was looking at him expectantly. As well he might. Two weeks an officer, and knew nothing yet. May as well start to teach him a thing or two.

"Richt, laddie. D'ye speak Italian?"

"Sir, no sir," said Trumble.

Lennox grinned. "Weel, that's right enough. They'll not be seducing you to Romish ways, then, and ye can't be charming the lassies if ye haven't the language."

"Am I being posted to Italy, sir?"

"The Venetian embassy, laddie. Where I'll be tae

keep an eye on ye, and ye're to report to Lieutenant Taggart. For instruction in ye're officerly duties and sich, d'ye see?"

"Sir, yes sir."

"Dismissed, lad, dismissed."

"Thank you, sir." Trumble saluted again, and left.

Taggart would see to the preparations; they had already picked a solid crew of lads for the embassy guard. It only remained to see if he could spend all those months alongside that sot of a papist Heinzerling without breaking his head for him again.

Part II: February, 1634

Sir, 'twas all one! My favour at her breast,
The dropping of daylight in the West,
The bough of cherries some officious fool
Broke in the orchard for her, the white mule
She rode with round the terrace—all and each
Would draw from her alike the approving speech,
Or blush, at least.

Chapter 9

"Well, here we are, then. Venice." Father Mazzare flopped down on a chaise longue of some sort, producing a small cloud of dust.

"Venice?" The Reverend Jones waved a hand in front of his face. "So that's what that smell is."

It was late afternoon of the day the USE delegation had finally arrived in Venice, after a long and arduous trip from Germany that had taken them up the Rhine by Constance, cross-country through the Graubunden to the Valtelline, and from there down toward Lake Como while being careful to skirt Milanese territory.

Most of the day had then been spent in pageantry, being paraded about and bombarded with pointless speeches entirely free of content. The experience seemed to have caused the Methodist minister to dig deep into reserves of sarcasm that even Mazzare had not suspected he possessed. For some hours now, Jones had taken to calling himself and Heinzerling "cultural attachés."

The Grantville party—Mazzare still had to keep reminding himself that he was now an ambassador representing the newly formed United States of Europe—had been asked to stop for the night at a villa outside La Serenissima while the appropriate reception had been mounted for the embassy. Other states, other nations and cities had all but dispensed with the displays of outright potlatch that greeted a formal ambassador's arrival. But Italy, and especially Venice, was still beggaring itself with Renaissance standards of behavior.

"Renaissance" was being charitable. The standard of organization shown so far by the Venetians had been downright medieval. The overnight stop while the procession had been organized had turned into a three-day jamboree. Three days, it had to be said, of good food, fine wine and general Italian hospitality, but Mazzare couldn't help feeling it was probably symbolic of something to come.

The time had not been entirely wasted, of course. The ambassador would not be so rude as to arrive before his hosts were good and ready to receive him in style, to be sure. But the ambassador's curate and general factotum, the good Father Augustus Heinzerling, SJ, was under no such restriction. Heinzerling had ridden ahead to apply his stout German boot—*ad maiorum Dei gloriam*, of course—to the collective backside of the staff at the lodgings that had been booked for the embassy pending the acquisition of a permanent base. Heinzerling had returned grumbling, with all his prejudices about Venetian housekeeping fully confirmed, but had pronounced himself satisfied. Just.

Francisco Nasi's briefing on the Most Serene Republic of Venice had warned Mazzare of what he was likely to find. Venice positively reeked of a town keeping up appearances. The days when her fleet was the terror of Mediterranean pirates were long gone, her great houses of merchants were losing their ongoing trade war with just about everyone, and cash was tight. The plague that had devastated the city just two years earlier had piled ruin onto decay.

In the streets: gilded barges and processions of

livery; fine dress and sumptuary for public display. Within doors: maintenance budgets had gone by the board, housekeeping was a poor second to ostentation and the fare a sharp contrast with the good living of the countryside.

And so a procession of boldly dressed cavaliers, gilded barges and an escort of stamping, bright-cuirassed soldiers had conveyed them to what Jones had christened the "Roach Hilton" for its mix of gilt and tawdriness. Mazzare couldn't help feeling, with Jones, a certain annoyance at the thoroughly impractical approach these people took to their particular mix of shabbiness and gentility. All the more so since he himself was probably distantly related to them. Nice people, but perhaps not well focused on what was important. They—but he caught himself.

"Better keep a lid on the comments, Simon," said Mazzare.

"The very model of tact, Larry. Tact is my middle name." Jones lasted perhaps two seconds before snorting. "Death in Venice! Ha! How could anyone tell?"

The door opened and Heinzerling strolled in, the very picture of florid, big-boned good health. *"Mein Herren,"* he nodded to the other two clerics.

That clued Mazzare. Heinzerling got more and more German as his thoughts wandered away from the immediate mental effort of thinking about what language he ought to be speaking, especially in English, which was his sixth or seventh language. "Go ahead, Gus," he said.

"Monsignor Mazarini is arrived as nuncio extraordinary." He said it baldly, paused, and then took out his pipe.

"Giulio?" Mazzare was startled. That was unexpected.

"Ja. He came here these few days past. Il Doge has not received him yet. Indeed, he refuses to do so."

Jones turned, frowning, from the window he had

been staring out of. He had been looking off to the east, where the first dark of night was hazed by angry purple bruises of cloud. "Mazarini's supposed to be in Paris. He had a job to do there, last we heard."

"*Genau das.* I have this from an old friend at the Society's house here. His Holiness recalled the monsignor from Paris in the middle of summer, apparently."

"Just after war broke out?" Mazzare raised an eyebrow.

"Yes, but wait a minute." Jones held up a hand. "The recall would have been sent before then, no?"

Mazzare nodded. "That figures. You think—?"

"It's what I'd have done, Larry."

"This I thought also," said Heinzerling. "The monsignor was known in the future history as a cardinal of France, no? So the Vatican seeks to prevent this?"

Jones sucked at his lip, began to pace. "Maybe. But would they? By now, you can be sure the Vatican has gotten its hands on all the histories available, just like Richelieu did. Remember that Mazarini—Mazarin, as he would be by then—sponsored the Peace of Westphalia. And sheltered the Barberini when it all hit the fan after Urban VIII's death. Surely they'd leave him in post to take root?"

Mazzare sat up. "On the other hand, is this place getting to us so soon? Blasted intrigue and double-dealing! Perhaps the pope and his advisers just wanted their best troubleshooter here—especially since he's more familiar with Americans than anyone else they have. Someone good enough to do the job, junior enough to shunt aside if he stalls. Whatever. We're here to do a deal with the Venetians. If Giulio wants to talk, he'll talk. Gus, who else is in town?"

"*Moment, bitte.*" Heinzerling crossed to where a pitcher of wine had been left out, took a goblet and drank. He made a face, perfectly reflected in the polished silver of the cup from where Mazzare sat. "*Ach,* nasty cheap wine. *Essig.* So, the ambassadors. The

Spanish one, the count de Rocca, is a pompous ass. He's
the regular ambassador sent directly from Madrid. But
Cardinal Bedmar is also here for Spain—indirectly, at
least; officially, he's 'special ambassador from the Spanish
Netherlands'—and that is causing trouble, of course.
D'Avaux for France, and he is Richelieu's creature and
bag-man. The representative for the empire is another
nonentity—I've already forgotten the name—since the
empire and Venice are usually so far"—he held up
thumb and forefinger—"from war that any ambassador
is wasting his time here. There is not a Dutchman to
be found for love nor money and the English ambassador does little and says less."

"Dutch are out of it. The English ambassador, though.
Why's he so quiet?"

"He is too busy making money, from what I am
hearing."

"Hmm." Mazzare scratched a chin that, twentieth-
century razors having become largely a memory, was
developing a fine beard. Local fashion was for a properly
trimmed goatee for a reason: it kept the blade away
from all the hard bits to shave. "No surprise that the
Dutch aren't about. Why is Bedmar trouble?"

Jones groaned. "Come on, Larry! Didn't you pay
attention in Causes of the Thirty Years' War, 101?
Bedmar! The Venetian Conspiracy! Osuna's Fleet!"

"Assume I didn't, Simon," Mazzare said patiently.
"And wasn't the Defenestration of Prague the cause
of the Thirty Years' War?"

"Sort of. In the same sense that Archduke Ferdinand's
assassination was the cause of the First World War. It
was just a trigger, that's all—one of many possible ones.
In fact, the other major candidate for the trigger event
happened right here, just a few days before."

"It would be better to say it did not happen, *ja*?"
Heinzerling was now leaning against the buffet table
where the wine-jug was, using his goblet to gesture. "Bedmar had paid a fifth column to open the city to Osuna's

fleet, it was said, and the state inquisitors hanged the
principal conspirators shortly before the fleet sailed—after
breaking their legs, in time-honored Venetian custom.
The conspiracy ended, and Venice remains independent.
There was trouble; I recall it even from the seminary.
But a week later, there was the worse trouble in Prague
and war began in Bohemia instead of in Italy."

"And Bedmar's back? I see the concern that might
raise." Mazzare was pointedly not looking at Heinzerling. A drink or two was fine, but he had promised
Hannelore that he would not let his curate hit the
sauce too hard.

"*Ja*, he is back." Mazzare heard Heinzerling put the
goblet down. "And I hear that he is bribing anything
with hands to hold scudi. I hear only rumors, you
understand."

Mazzare sighed, and looked up at the ceiling a
moment, noting the cracks in the plaster. "It all sounded
so simple when Mike and Francisco set it out for me.
A trade deal, they said. Stand there and look solemn
and sign things, so the Venetians can pretend they're
not dealing with Jews, they said. D'Avaux is your only
problem, they said. Bah!" He swept a hand across an
imaginary chess-board, scattering the pieces of a game
grown tiresome.

"Come on, Larry." Jones' grin looked as forced as
his tone. "If it wasn't hard, they wouldn't need us."

"Well, the women are going to be upset," said
Mazzare.

Heinzerling nodded. "*Ja*. If Hanni saw the filth in
here, she would be *ganz verruckt*."

That set Mazzare to chuckling. The formidable Frau
Heinzerling governed domestic arrangements at the
rectory with an iron will. Preconceptions about early-
modern attitudes to cleanliness were crushed under
her regular blitzkriegs with duster and beeswax. The
place gleamed; not a surface in it couldn't have been
used for surgery.

"Speaking of domestic arrangements," he said, "how are the troops and the various technical missions settling in?"

"*Ganz gut,*" said Heinzerling. "Captain Lennox and his troops are comfortable and probably looking for a drink."

Heinzerling made a face as he mentioned the Scotsman. He and Lennox, in many ways, were two of a kind. One of the more famous brawls in the Thuringen Gardens had transpired when the two of them had debated their competing doctrines of justification one night. The Jesuit had won the debate and—narrowly, he insisted!—lost the ensuing fistfight. Lennox had paid the price in a broken tooth, two broken ribs and the finger he had dislocated on Heinzerling's jaw. Carried back to the rectory, Heinzerling had had a black eye added to his injuries by a furious Hannelore keen to enforce her ambition of getting her man to settle down to parochial respectability. Gus had behaved himself, more or less, ever since.

"And the technical folks?" Mazzare dragged himself back from memories of happier, if harder-working, times.

"Also settled. The Stone boys are suggesting a few drinks with the local Committee, and I mean to go with them."

Mazzare nodded, then frowned. "Is that wise? Should we be seen to have links of any kind with the Committee?"

"He has a point, Gus," said Jones. "If we're talking to the grandees, surely they'll take fright if we're also hobnobbing with revolutionaries and the like?"

Mazzare sat up straighter. "For the moment, let's not take risks. Gus, have the Committee here been in touch yet?"

"Not so far as I know. Frank is a member of the CoC in Grantville, as I'm sure you are aware—all three of the rascals, probably—and he will be looking to make contact." Heinzerling stroked his chin a moment. "In fact, I think it cannot be that the local Committee has been in touch, since it is all staff of the palazzo or the embassy in here so far. They will of course place someone with the servants."

"Right." Mazzare nodded. "What teenage boys do is one thing. You, Gus . . . another. So keep them out of trouble, if you can. And ask Sharon to help."

Jones grinned. "For a man with no children you've got a surprising grasp of teenage psychology, Larry."

Mazzare grinned back. "I have memories of being a teenaged male myself, Simon, before I turned my thoughts to Heaven."

Heinzerling was looking puzzled, so Mazzare took pity on him. "Sharon'll be the key to keeping the Stone boys under control, Gus. Even more than their father and mother. She's the most glamorous woman they know—well, leaving aside Becky Stearns—and close enough to their own age to leave room for fantasies."

Now Heinzerling was frowning. "She is grieving for her dead betrothed, Hans Richter."

Jones smiled. "Yup. Like Larry says: *glamorous*. For Pete's sake, Gus, weren't you *ever* a youngster?"

Heinzerling shook his head. "Americans are all insane. What has 'glamor' to do with anything? Much less fantastical delusions? Fraulein Nichols is a respectable young woman grieving for her betrothed, and those boys are much too young to be entertaining notions of marriage anyway.

"However," he said, shrugging heavily, "I will do as you ask."

After Heinzerling left, Jones cocked an eye at Mazzare. "It might be good for Sharon, too, having to concentrate on keeping those juvenile delinquents out of trouble. Give her something to think about other than . . ." He groped in the air, a bit feebly.

"That's what I was thinking." Mazzare sighed heavily. He was worried about Sharon.

Sharon Nichols had been added to the diplomatic delegation at the very end, just two days before it left Grantville. That had been at her father's urging.

"Anything to get her mind off Hans," he'd told Mazzare. Seeing the question lurking in the priest's mind, James Nichols had chuckled harshly. "Oh, I'm not worried about *that,* Father. My daughter is about as suicidally inclined as a brick. But . . ."

He'd groped in the air too, then, and just as feebly as Jones was doing now. Mazzare understood both gestures. Sharon's romance with Hans Richter had been a storybook one, ended when her fiancé died in true storybook fashion at the Battle of Wismar less than six months earlier. The woman was in her early twenties, to make things worse—that treacherous age when deep grief could insidiously slide into a quasi-romantic melancholy that lasted for years and years. A lifetime, in some cases. The priest had seen it happen, from time to time.

And what a waste that would be! Not just the waste of a life, but the waste of a person whose intelligence and skills—not to mention sheer energy, when Sharon was her normal self—would be an asset to many other people. Including—Mazzare admitted to some selfish motives here—the delegation from the USE to Venice. Sharon's hands-on medical skills would be a valuable addition to Tom Stone's more theoretical knowledge.

He rose from his chair and went over to a window, looking out over the city. "God knows Venice could use her," he murmured.

Loud enough, apparently, for Jones to hear him. The Protestant reverend snorted sarcastically. "And that's another thing the guide books didn't mention! The glamorous pestilence."

Jones wasn't really being fair to Venice, Mazzare thought. Or Italy as a whole, for that matter. Yes,

Venice had lost about a third of its population in the recent plague. But that wasn't an unusual percentage, in this day and age, for a city struck by bubonic plague. Many cities suffered worse. The truth was that medicine and public sanitation were more advanced in Italy in the seventeenth century than probably anywhere else in Europe.

Which . . . wasn't saying much.

Mazzare was a conservatively inclined man, by temperament, and found the constant changes in his life more than a little taxing. In three short years he'd gone from a small town in up-time America where disease didn't include bubonic plague and typhus, through a jury-rigged little "United States" restricted to the southern half of Thuringia, through an equally jury-rigged "Confederated Principalities of Europe," to yet a *fourth* nation—the only-months-old "United States of Europe" which Mike Stearns was busily jury-rigging right now.

And—it needed only this!—one Father Larry Mazzare was the ambassador from that country to Venice. It was almost funny, in a way. He'd been appointed as ambassador from one country—the CPE—but by the time he'd finally been able to take up his post, his country had changed underneath his feet.

Oh, well. He tried to brace his spirit with lines of poetry, which he murmured aloud.

> *"How dull it is to pause, to make an end,*
> *To rust unburnished, not to shine in use!"*

Again, he'd spoke louder than he thought. Reverend Jones frowned. "Sounds like something from the King, although I don't recognize it. Since when did you become an Elvis Presley fan, Larry?"

Mazzare sighed again.

Chapter 10

"Cool." Gerry put the enthusiasm into the word that only someone sixteen could manage.

"Yeah, it'll do," Ron drawled, looking around.

Frank couldn't quite figure out if he was looking at the decor or the help—who clearly thought the Stone brothers' various attempts on the Italian language were funny, but were being polite about it. At least, he hoped that was what they were finding funny. They had also insisted on doing, more or less, everything for him and his brothers when they had lugged their bags up to their rooms, short of—

He let that thought die a natural death. True enough, the help was worth looking at. All four of the servants assigned to them were girls about their own age. If only two of them could properly be called "pretty," all of them could certainly bear the label of "healthy" with great ease.

But if there was one thing that Frank's not-so-great weight of experience with the female of the species had taught him it was that not pushing too hard on the first date—*don't hump her leg*, as his dad had once put it in a jocular mood—did wonders for the success rate in the long run. Things had been decidedly fluid on that front these past two years, though, and he was a free agent for the moment. Part of that was the way in which German attitudes were rubbing off on everyone he knew—including himself, truth be told. Everyone seemed to want to get themselves set up and steady before they got romantic. Which was odd, but then again most of the things everyone had taken for granted as opportunities for dating had gone away. And then the rubbers had run out, and things had gotten decidedly chilly on that front, damn it.

So, he looked around. "It isn't quite how I imagined it."

"Oh?" Ron sounded interested.

"Sure. I looked it all up. You wouldn't believe how many books of photographs of Venice there are. Well, you would now you've seen it, and this town's famous for looking pretty. But all the photos have captions about how such-and-such a palazzo or the Casa-de-that was refurbished in the eighteenth century. So I figured it'd all look more—different—than it did in the pictures, and all."

"Oh," said Ron. Frank's younger brother was trying very hard not to stare at the rump of the chambermaid who was bending down to sort their linen into drawers. Frank sympathized with his struggle. She was the only maid left in the room, since the others had left in a swirl of giggles—and easily the best-looking.

"Whoah!" Gerry called out, "Not that one!" He stepped smartly across the room to where the maid was about to try to lift his bag of tricks. The one that clanked when he moved it.

Frank didn't doubt that someone would take a peek later anyway, but by then the Stone boys would have taken the more outré stuff out of it and hidden it somewhere safer. Gerry was the youngest of the brothers and he'd packed the thing—which meant that "outré" would be outré indeed.

The maid gave Gerry an odd look. Not puzzled so much as . . .

Calculating.

A thought came to Frank, and he decided to take a chance. "Committee?" he asked, making sure to use the English term.

"Yes," the maid hissed softly. "You are the Committee with the Grantville embassy?" Her English was surprisingly good, aside from a heavy accent. But Frank thought the accent was as charming as the rest of her.

"Yup," he said, extending a hand. "All three of us, actually. You learned English for us?"

"No." She took his hand a bit shyly, not shaking it so much as just holding it. "My father make us learn, so we can work with Sir Henry Hider. And then he made us study even harder, when we learned you were coming to Venice."

"Who's Hider?" Frank asked, feeling a sudden twinge of anxiety. Well. Jealousy, to be precise. Did some lousy Brit already have the inside track with the girl?

"Steady on there, podnuh," Gerry said. "Ma'am," he said, sweeping off the silly cavalier hat he'd taken to wearing, "might we have the privilege of your name?"

Frank nodded. The courtly manners thing might be a good idea after all. It had seemed excruciating stuff when a small assortment of Nasis and other gentry had been giving them crash-courses in current manners—Dad's attempts had been hilarious at first until he seemed to just accelerate ahead of everyone—but the effects could be impressive. Frank swept his baseball cap off with the hand that the maid wasn't holding—score one, he realized, she hadn't let go yet. "Lady," he said, in his best shot at the Italian language, "permit me the honor of naming my brothers Gerry and Ron Stone, and I am Frank, very much at your service. And you are?"

The giggles suggested he'd got it wrong, but at least in an amusing way.

"Giovanna Marcoli. My father Antonio is the—what is the word for *capo?*—of the Committee of Correspondence in Venice." The girl straightened proudly. "All of north Italy—even Milan! Even though he is only a metalworker."

She giggled again, and Frank realized her amusement had been at the notion of herself as a *Lady*. Craftsmen were respected enough, in Venice, but very far removed in social terms from the Venetian noble merchant families. The *Case Vecchie,* Frank thought they called themselves—the "Old Houses."

Giggling or not, Giovanna still hadn't relinquished his hand. Frank was in no hurry for her to do so. The hand was of a piece with the girl herself—small, warm, and very well shaped. "Sir Henry is a merchant and a man of some note in Venice," she continued, "if you like I will tell you more of him later?"

"Sure," said Ron. The middle of the three Stone brothers had just turned eighteen, and had a slightly-too-eager tone in his voice. No, make that much-too-eager. He took off his hat, an English foghat he'd gotten somewhere, just to make sure Frank was outdone in the dumbass headgear stakes. "Thanks."

Great, thought Frank, he's going to hump her leg any minute. Actually, he could feel that urge himself. Please, please, please, he thought, let Giovanna not turn out to be attached or something. Short, brunette, dark-eyed, and—and—

Perfect.

Damn. Frank was sure he'd blow it.

As if foretelling his doom, Giovanna finally let go of his hand and frowned. Suddenly, she seemed all business.

"Messer . . . Gerry, it is?" Giovanna asked. "Why must I not touch that bag?"

"This bag?" Gerry said, hoisting it up with a grunt of effort.

"Yes. Is it secret to you or to the Committee?"

"Both, in a manner of speaking." Gerry crossed the room to a table to unpack it.

Frank went over to watch. He'd been kind of curious himself.

"Now," said Gerry, "I expect y'all got a thing or two on sale hereabouts in Venice for the man of action, but I figured on being prepared, one way or another." He looked around to his audience, which was now everyone in the room.

"Y'see," he went on, "I figure never to need any of this stuff. On the other hand, I figure Darryl figured on that, too, and look where he ended up." He paused. "I sure wish I knew what that guy is doing, still locked up in the Tower. I figured he'd have taken it on the lam by now, but maybe he's waiting for—"

"Gerry!" Frank said, pointing. "The bag?"

Gerry visibly wrenched his train of thought back off the track of the mayhem he was missing elsewhere. "What? Oh, sure. The bag. Well, lessee now. We got pistols, six of, modern, for the three of us. Well, not 'modern' modern; I mean state-of-the-art seventeenth-century-style flintlocks. Made by the fellers good old Mister Santee is trainin' up. They're small and look down-time, only they got rifling and they take minie balls. To look at, nothing much, but way better than anything here and they don't say up-time to anyone who sees 'em."

"Messer Gerry?" Giovanna interrupted, "those English words you used? 'Up-time'? 'Down-time'?"

"Oh, sorry," Gerry said. "Up-time is anyone from the twenty-first century. Americans, like us. Down-time means everyone else."

Giovanna nodded. Frank found the effect distracting. Somehow a girl could be a lot sexier buttoned up to the collar than in shorts and a T-shirt. It was all very mysterious. He could see out of the corner of his eye that Ron was not paying a whit of attention to their brother Gerry. It was a mercy his tongue wasn't hanging out.

"Anyway," Gerry was continuing, "we got some explosives and detonators, slowmatch, some corned power for reloads, rope, some tools for bullet-making—oh, and that reminds me, Captain Lennox let me put the ammo crate on the Marines' packhorse, I gotta collect that later."

"Eh?" Frank said. "How much ammo did you bring?" He was surprised that Gerry had brought more than three guns. Still another surprise was that he'd brought enough ammo to show he was expecting to use them seriously, because Gerry wasn't anyone's notion of a good shot. Some plinking and a few sessions with borrowed pistols was all the practice he'd had. Gerry's talents ran more toward pyrotechnic pranks, booby traps and practical jokes. It seemed that Gerry was forgetting that he'd been raised on a hippie commune, not in the hillbilly-hard-ass school that had turned out the likes of Harry Lefferts and Darryl McCarthy. It was kind of sad to watch.

"Just a couple of boxes for the pistols, mostly the special bullets. We can buy powder here, but obviously we won't find any minie balls. I got some sulfa drugs, too. Dad's shop is turning that stuff out at a pretty good clip nowadays, and I figure it'll be a while before we can get set up to do the same down here. Wish it was as easy to make chloramphenicol." He seemed wholly matter-of-fact about it.

Ron beat Frank to it. "Gerry? Are you expecting to fight a war or something?"

That made two mental sighs of relief for Frank. First, that if Ron was spotting it as well, Gerry was clearly off the deep end. And, second, that Ron was finally paying attention to his surroundings and not just drooling down his shirtfront.

"Yeah," said Frank, "hadn't you noticed we have Marines along to do that sort of thing? Like, professional soldiers? Remember? Big, gloomy Scots guys on horses?"

Gerry waved a hand. "Sure, sure. Though Billy's as American as you and me and I'd hardly call Conrad a 'Scot,' much less 'gloomy.' But like I say, better to have and not need, than—"

"Whatever," said Frank, exasperated. "What else'd you bring, Rambo? Nerve gas? Nukes? Punjee sticks?"

"Mock all you want, flower-child." Gerry said it flatly.

Frank could feel the mood turning ugly. All three of them had had to listen to talk like that back up-time, and had gotten a rep for the elaborate revenges they humiliated the offending jocks with. Hearing it from his own brother was . . .

He forced it down. "Cool it, okay, man? Just because I think you're overdoing it, no need to get heavy, all right? Just my opinion, is all."

Gerry took the hint. "Ah," he said. "Mayhem is still on the menu, which is, like a bummer. But the whole destruction trip is just outsville. Because, like, I brought this, in case it turned out this was the bag we were all, like, into, maaan."

He reached into the bag with both hands, grunted a little, and lifted out an oblong steel box with snap-catches holding it shut and wire handles at either end. It was army surplus, and at one time it had been painted olive drab which, along with the rust, still showed through in a few places. Most of it was covered in flowers and peace signs and a really drunken-looking mandala painted on in lurid enamel paint. The lid had *Make love, Not war* scrawled on it in bright orange balloon script.

"Cool," said Ron.

"Heaveeeee," added Frank, giving the voice everything he had before realizing that Giovanna was now looking at all of them funny.

"Yup." Gerry patted the lid of the box gently, grinning from ear to ear. "I brung the Hippie Flower Child Peace and Love Revenge Kit."

Frank nodded, savoring the memory of some truly outstanding pranks. In the years before the Ring of Fire, they'd often enough been confusion to the jocks. "The Lothlorien Hippie Ninja clan is once again ready to wreak havoc in the darkness." He turned to Giovanna. "On no account open that box."

"Please, why?" She looked worried.

"Because, milady," Gerry said, "this box contains everything you need to embarrass and humiliate any-one who annoys you. We are highly trained and highly motivated pranksters, and this box contains the old standards of our repertoire. Guys, it's all in working order, and what with Dad opening his lab I added a few new items."

The new items probably didn't include nitro, or the box would have exploded already. On the other hand, Gerry was inventive, smart, and had a mean streak in him to reckon with. Frank decided it was time to introduce calm and relaxation. "Say," he said, "now we've made out like we're a crew of madmen, where's the Freedom Arches in this town? Any chance of a few beers?"

Giovanna smiled. "No Freedom Arches in Venice! Not with the heel of the Council of Ten on the necks of the populace."

The words were said lightly, though, not with a snarl. Frank had learned enough of Venetian politics to know that the secret police of the Senate's clan-destine governing body were nobody to fool with. On the other hand, they seemed to be more concerned with plots among the nobility than with the doings of Venice's working population. Not surprising, that. The artisans of Venice—especially the workers at the Arsenal—had a rather fearsome reputation themselves, and the Venetian powers-that-be had always been careful not to aggravate them.

Giovanna's smile kept widening and Frank found himself no longer thinking of politics at all. For a wonder, the girl even had straight teeth! Dimples!

He was lost, lost.

"We are free of our duties for the day at sunset—and it is *Carnevale*!" she announced. "We can meet my father and brothers and cousins at one of the taverna. I know which one they will be at, too, because it is right here in the palazzo."

Lost. And didn't care in the least. Even the prospect of meeting Giovanna's father and brothers on their first not-date didn't faze him at all.

"Frank?" said Gerry. "Do you have a problem with that?"

Frank frowned. "Problem?" How could there be any problems on this most sublime of all days?

"Astlay imetay ouyay amecay omehay unkdray, Frank," Ron said in a sing-song voice. "Aren't you going to have to speak with Dad about that?"

"Ah," Frank said. "No biggie. Dad calmed down, and I think you'll notice he didn't mind us staying up on the way down here as long as we were with Father Gus."

"Oh, yeah." Ron nodded. He could see the plan, right enough.

"Guys?" Gerry was looking worried. "If this is going to be anything like—like—" He gave Giovanna a nervous glance. "I mean like a date—"

Now the nervous glance came to Frank. "Okay, dates, I'm not trying to horn in on you but aybemay eshay's otgay riendsfay—I'd like not to bring the priest, okay?"

Giovanna was frowning. "I don't understand some of those words. But if you want me to give you dates, I warn you it is expensive. How much money you have?"

All three Stone brothers stared at her. Frank's heart stopped. The girl he was completely fascinated with—practically the love of his life already—turned out to be a prostitute!

She spread her hands, a bit exasperated. "What you

expect? Dates have to be imported into Venice. From the Levant, I think."

Frank's heart started up again.

"Now, Gerry," said Ron, "leave it to your big brothers to be ahead of this situation. If Frank's thinking what I think he's thinking, I think we're thinking of the same plan." To Giovanna, he added: "Uh, the word 'dates' is just a slang expression. We'll explain it later. It's, uh, complicated. But it doesn't mean those fig things."

Gerry stroked his chin theatrically. "Hmmm. I think I think that I'm thinking what I think you're thinking, Frank, I really think so."

"Then you don't exist," said Frank firmly, "on the best authority, Descartes himself—who's still alive, remember—and so your opinion can and should be discarded. Just try and keep up, okay?"

"We are done here, yes?" asked Giovanna. "When can we go to the taverna?"

Frank hesitated. "Well . . . We won't be unpacking any of the stuff for the pharmaceutical lab today. Dad told me he wanted to make sure we had a safe place to set it up first. But I promised Magda we'd go help them get moved in downstairs and we'll probably run into Father Gus while we're down there. Giovanna, I suspect it's where you're going to get sent next anyway. Our stepmom travels with enough stuff for a medium-sized army and it'll take some doing to get them squared away. Sharon's no piker either, widder's weeds or not."

Giovanna tilted her head on one side. "What is a 'piker' and a 'widder' and why would either of them want weeds? Your father is the *buon Dottore*, yes?"

"Uh, yeah—but he's a chemist, not a doctor."

Giovanna frowned. "We were told that Tomas Stone was a maker of medicine, the Indian Hemp?"

"Well, yes, he makes medicines, and he sets bones and some other simple stuff, but he's not what you'd call a doctor. Sharon Nichols is really the *Dottore* in our delegation—uh, I think that should be *Dottoressa,* actually."

That made her eyebrows shoot up. She rattled off something in Italian that Frank couldn't follow at all.

"What? I mean, please say that again, slower?"

Giovanna tried it in English. "You have such a lot of doctors—even female ones—that your father seems like nothing special?"

"Uh, I guess," said Frank, unsure where this was leading.

"From what we hear, you see, he makes physics and medicines that are better than anything we have ever known. The mist that kills lice—the *diditi,* I think it is called—and the specific against all illnesses, the *clorfeniculo*—"

"Chloramphenicol," Ron said.

"*Sì—chlorafenico,* we hear that your father makes all these."

"He makes some other stuff, too," Frank said. His father would want to be modest, but Frank thought he overdid it. "He makes hash for pain, and some disinfectants and some herbal medicines. He consults for some of the other chemists on the drugs they make. Dad knows a fair bit about making medicines, but it's not what he does for money." He scratched his head a moment. "I guess you could say he's the best . . ." He searched for the word in Italian, but couldn't find it. "—drug-maker in Grantville, but that's practical industrial chemistry. He's one of the two with the theoretical training to understand how it all works, though. Dad's good at research." He grinned. "You won't get what this means, but he made LSD in the sixties."

"No," said Giovanna, looking thoughtful, "I do not know what it means. Do I need to?"

Frank exchanged a look with Gerry and Ron. "On the whole," he said, "I don't think you do. Let's just say it was a hard thing to do, and he did it. Now he makes dye and disinfectant and some other things. Yes, and medicines."

"Anyway," said Gerry, "what were you saying about Dad?"

"Oh," said Giovanna, "only that it is always the way with the natural philosophers that they have a huge amount of baggage. There are many in town, and we have been working in many places that have needed extra chambermaids, and we see a lot."

Frank nodded. "True enough. So let's go see how they're getting on."

Chapter 11

"Tom?" Mazzare put his head around the door. Within was the kind of controlled chaos that Tom Stone either liked or just seemed to generate by his mere presence. The man still clung firmly to his relaxed sixties-era hippie ethics, principles and aesthetics—although he now owned the biggest and most profitable coal-tar dye works in Europe.

Which was to say, the only one. So far, at least. Years of recreational pharmacology on top of a nearly completed masters' degree in the real thing made Tom Stone—also known as Stoner, for reasons that were not hard to deduce—the leading research, industrial and medical chemist in seventeenth-century Europe, if not the world. Not much in the way of spectacular dyeing chemistry was "scheduled by history" to happen until after the Napoleonic period—which meant that Stoner had better than a two-century lead on his competition. In their old timeline, dyes along with soaps had been the first real make-money-hand-over-fist branches of chemistry. So Stoner had a very profitable business ready-made once circumstances—and Magda and her money-minded father—had rubbed his nose in it.

For that matter, the man could probably be making a second fortune in pharmaceuticals, since he was also the principal manufacturer of the new medicines the Americans had introduced into the world. But on that subject, Tom Stone had drawn the line—quite firmly, too, despite the mild squawks of his wife and the loud splutters of protest from his father-in-law.

Medicines, Tom Stone made at cost—and, even there, tried as much as possible to cover his costs through barter rather than money. Given that the electricity he used that was produced by Grantville's huge power plant was essentially free anyway—the power plant produced far more electricity than Grantville could possibly use—he was in effect subsidizing his own pharmaceutical business.

As Tom Stone put it, he was not about to become a bloodsucker on the misery of others. Just about everyone agreed with Stoner's wife and father-in-law that he was a hopelessly impractical man, to be sure. But it was no accident that he was also becoming one of the most popular people in central Europe, especially with the poor German immigrants who were still flooding into Thuringia. If anything, he was even more highly regarded by the rapidly growing population of Magdeburg, the new capital of the United States of Europe rising out of the ruins on the Elbe.

There was even a rumor that one village in Catholic Franconia was petitioning the pope to declare him a saint. Not even a rumor, really—Father Mazzare knew it was true, although he'd seen fit to keep the knowledge to himself. No point in disappointing the villagers prematurely, he felt, with such picayune details as the fact that canonization was reserved for dead people. And had never been extended to someone who was not only not a Catholic but whose religion—such as it was—revolved largely around mandalas and alternative states of mind.

"Tom?" the priest repeated.

Again, Stone didn't hear him. Mazzare wasn't surprised. Frau Stone was somewhere in the background marshalling Frank, Gerry and Ron, a couple of shanghaied soldiers and what looked like a platoon of chambermaids—where had they come from?—into arranging the medical mission's quarters. Although more of a bluestocking than Hanni, Magda conceded the dreadnought-class hausfrau nothing in haus-pride.

Tom stood in the middle of it all holding a small stack of books with the air of a man who would definitely remember where he meant to put them in but a moment. He regarded his wife's drill-mastering of the all-out effort to get order out of chaos with blatant bemusement. He had explained to Mazzare, once, that chaos was not always disorder and dirt not necessarily mess. The natural order of things, per good organic principles, could be persuaded to suck in the gut and make itself useful, but could never be hammered into line.

Magda hewed to a different line, though. The "hash ranch" as the Lothlorien Commune was oft known had looked uncommonly neat and tidy since she moved in.

Finally, Stoner saw Mazzare standing in the doorway. "Hi, Father!" Tom called out, his face a sudden plea for rescue.

Mazzare repressed a smile. "Tom, could I have a word?" He led a relieved Stoner out into the corridor.

Stoner closed the door behind him, leaned on it and sighed, then shook his shaggy head. His hair was graying now, but just as thick and bushy and disheveled as it had always been. "I had me some bizarre domestic arrangements in my time, man, but this just about beats them all. I am o-fish-ully boor-jwah now, henpecked and everything."

"Stoner, that's kind of why I'm here to talk to you."

"Oh?"

"Yeah, it's Hanni." Mazzare chewed his lip a moment. "I, ah, promised her—"

Stoner frowned. "The boys were saying that they might go out for a drink or two with Gus, after he dropped by. I kind of wondered."

Mazzare nodded. It was no wonder Stoner knew. News from Hanni tended to get around fast, and everyone knew Father Heinzerling. It was obvious to anyone with more brains than God gave a rabbit what he suffered from, as well. Even by the standards of a time when drunkenness was the norm, Gus could put it away. And, left to his own devices, he did. It was Mazzare's guess that without Hanni all these years, he would have wrecked himself long since. Not as fast, perhaps, as he would have without Jesuit discipline, but still wrecked. For all his playing of the long-suffering henpecked husband, he actually clung to Hanni like the rock she was.

"Tom," he said, "I promised Hanni I wouldn't let Gus hit the sauce too hard. Now, I persuaded him to persuade the boys to cool it for a few days, since I'm sure they're planning to contact the CoC here in Venice—small as it probably is—but I don't think it makes sense to keep everyone grounded for the duration."

Tom smiled. "Wouldn't work, anyway. Not with my kids. Chips off the old block."

Mazzare managed not to wince. "So, could you ask the boys to keep an eye on Gus? Keep him talking, at least, since that seems to keep him from drinking so much?"

Stoner nodded. "I'll tell them. They're good about that sort of thing. And they like Gus; they consider him a superannuated jock but without the attitude."

Mazzare walked back down to the embassy reception room in a thoughtful frame of mind. On the way, he turned the corner on the staircase and bumped into a small, dark-haired man wearing a pointed yellow hat. Literally bumped into him, since it seemed neither of them was paying much attention to where he was going.

"Please, forgive me," Mazzare said, "Can I help you?" The man was short and slight and looked—yes, Jewish. He was wearing a distinctly lawyerly gown and had a tooled-leather briefcase under his left arm. That would mean he was—

"Signor Luzzatto?"

"Ah, yes," said the little man. "Benjamin Luzzatto, at your service. Might I assume that you are Father Mazzare, of Grantville?"

"Indeed. Were you at the ceremonies earlier today?"

"No, Monsignor. Jews were not permitted to be present at that. I watched from a window. Do I find you settling in here?"

Mazzare frowned. "Should I take it up with the doge? I mean, if you're to be our permanent man here—"

Luzzatto waved a hand. "Oh, please, Monsignor, take no trouble on my account. We must live apart, and are thus subjected to severe overcrowding in the ghetto, but otherwise we suffer only minor disabilities in Venice."

"Really? I thought the restrictions on Jews were severe."

"Perhaps I should restate the matter. Yes—officially— the restrictions are indeed severe. We are required to live in the ghetto; may not pursue many vocations; are required to lend money at unprofitable rates. Oh, indeed, it goes on and on." He shrugged. "In practice? They like to pretend that they have no Jews in La Serenissima, but so long as we are discreet and the pretense is maintained, we are usually left unmolested. In business matters, 'being discreet' simply means finding a Christian partner to be the, ah, what is the expression—?"

"Front man," Mazzare provided, using the English term.

"Yes, precisely." Luzzatto smiled wryly. "Such a devious language, your dialect of English. I have grown quite fond of it. As I was saying, so long as we are discreet the Venetian authorities ignore most of it. For all their pretensions at nobility, you know, the *Case Vecchie* are merchants before they are anything else. To tell the truth, other than the overcrowded conditions of the ghetto—which makes it very bad for us in times of epidemic—the only regulation which causes real aggravation is the requirement"—he gestured at his headgear—"that we must wear yellow hats or veils."

Here, his good humor seemed to slip. "For quite some time now, we have petitioned to have that color changed. It sometimes causes unpleasantness for our women—my own wife was solicited, just yesterday!—since prostitutes are also required by Venetian law to wear yellow veils when practicing their trade on the streets."

"Oh." Mazzare thought on that a moment, and decided to drop it for the time being. "Come, let us go to the reception room. There are some people I should like you to meet."

"That would be the Reverend Jones and Father Heinzerling and Dottores Stone and Nichols, yes?"

"Yes, and some others." They walked back down the stairs. "Are you from Venice originally?"

"No, I was born in Oporto, where my father was a doctor. We left when I was eight years old, for the City, after the great pardon freed him from jail. Then when I was eighteen I came to Italy to study law at Padua. Ever since, I have been a lawyer and a commercial agent here in Venice." Luzzatto smiled. "Much less exotic than your own origins, of course."

"Well, I don't know," said Mazzare. "Until less than three years ago I was nothing more than an ordinary small-town priest. Here we are." He opened the door.

Back in the reception room, some more of the delegation had finished unpacking and had come down to wet their whistles. "Everyone!" Mazzare said loudly. "This is Maestro Benjamin Luzzatto, the man Don Francisco picked to advise us once we arrived."

Luzzatto gave a little half-bow to the people there.

· "I guess it's introductions all round, then," said Mazzare. "We decided that the thing to do was to hand off as much of Grantville's knowledge as we could, to help Venice be as effective a trading partner as possible and to give an earnest of our good faith. We'll be advised by you about that, of course, but for the time being we have a few people with us who're going to be able to help. Doctor Stone, as you call him, is still upstairs getting settled in. No doubt he'll be down later. With him is—ladies first—Sharon Nichols. She's really our doctor here."

Sharon nodded solemnly, as she had done everything for the past months. The statuesque young woman was not wearing "widow's weeds," true—and never had—but she was still grieving deeply.

"Sharon's a doctor of medicine where Tom Stone is a doctor of chemistry." That was something of a fib, designed to augment her status. Sharon wasn't an MD. She wasn't even technically an RN, although she had the equivalent training and experience—even real expertise, when it came to battlefield traumas. But Mazzare had learned early on that nursing when it wasn't done by nuns was regarded as low-rent scutwork in this day and age. Even the nuns only did it as a sort of self-mortification in most places. Besides, given the state of seventeenth-century medical knowledge and practice, a mostly trained twentieth-century nurse was considerably better than a doctor by local standards. A lot better, in Sharon's case. She seemed to have inherited her father James' skill as well as his very dark skin color.

If the Jewish lawyer was surprised to see a Moorish woman in their midst—and he probably wouldn't think of Sharon as anything else—he gave no sign of it. "An honor to meet you, Dottoressa Nichols," said Luzzatto, half-bowing again.

Sharon nodded. "Charmed, Maestro Luzzatto."

Mazzare thought for a moment about how to continue. Then: "As well as the medical side of the health mission we have brought with us, we propose offering some of our learning in the matter of public sanitation. Venice has a unique position in this regard, having the lagoon to drain into, but there is a deal more that can be done. The experts in these matters in Grantville are of the opinion that improved health begins with improved public sanitation, which is why Herr Mauer has come with us. Ernst has spent the last two years as one of the lead contractors in the reconstruction of Magdeburg's sewer system."

Mauer stood up straight from his habitual slouch and made a half-bow of his own. "An honor, Maestro Luzzatto." The greeting was one of the few bits of Italian that Mauer had reliably learned; half of the challenge in his passing anything to the Venetians would be the translation. Mazzare didn't think the translator would be worked too hard, either. Mauer was, at his most voluble, a laconic man. He was, however, a man with a reputation as a civil engineer. A master builder before the Ring of Fire, he had leapt at the opportunities offered by the rebuilding of Magdeburg and grabbed them with both hands. He had not been the only one to do so, but he had been the first to specialize, and had the kind of detailed mind needed to plan and execute a huge sewer system. Over six months he had educated himself in sanitation engineering and the English language, found his metier and laid the foundations of a modest fortune in civil engineering.

"Next," said Mazzare, "it was thought by our principals in Grantville that advances in shipbuilding might usefully be communicated to the shipwrights of Venice's Arsenal. Perhaps some of those advances will prove less than useful, but we anticipate a great volume of trade through Venice. If it can be carried in improved Venetian hulls there is a greater opportunity for the merchants of La Serenissima to profit. Hence we have with us Lieutenant Ursinus from our naval yards at Magdeburg. He has brought plans for a number of different kinds of vessels and has experience in building several types of craft. The young officer standing next to him is Lieutenant William Trumble, part of our Marine escort."

Billy simply nodded. Conrad Ursinus made appropriately polite noises, and Mazzare wondered again how he would go over with the Arsenal. The guildmasters and workers there were said to be notoriously jealous of their skills and prerogatives. Young as he was, Conrad Ursinus was as senior a man as the ferociously busy Magdeburg shipyards could spare, and another trained down-timer.

He was also a man who had grabbed opportunities; in his case, three of them. First, he was an officer in the growing U.S. Navy. Second, he'd parlayed his nearly completed carpenter's apprenticeship into a job as a shipwright and then as a slip foreman, and had the beginnings of credentials as a naval architect. On top of that, he had been part of the first wave of baseball players when the sport had gotten going in Grantville. The heavily plebeian and often-radical German population of Magdeburg had also adopted baseball, with all the ferocious enthusiasm with which they adopted most things American. Conrad was one of the stars of the Magdeburg Yard Dogs, for whom he played first base—and his friend Billy was the star pitcher for the Marine Corps team.

Whether the two of them would succeed in introducing the sport to Venice was another question. Mazzare knew that baseball was a popular sport in up-time

Italy, if a minority interest, but it was as nothing to the Italian national religion of soccer. The Stone boys were enthusiasts for that sport, and Mazzare knew they had plans to introduce it in Italy. They might well succeed, despite Conrad and Billy. Mazzare could remember turning out for a game or two when he'd been in Rome, and the sheer mania that a Lazio crowd was capable of . . .

First, of course, they'd have to figure out *where* to play either game. Venice was not exactly a city with lots of parks and open space—and Mazzare had already firmly explained to all the young men involved that the Piazza San Marco was strictly off-limits. He foresaw enough problems, without having to deal with a doge aggravated by a baseball or a soccer ball breaking one of his windows. Or, worse yet, one of the windows in the Basilica.

He shook his head and went on with the introductions. "Captain Lennox here—"

"Good day to ye," said Lennox. He had a glass in his hand, and was visibly trying not to stand at attention.

"—is head of our embassy guard, which is a function our Marine Corps discharges for reasons of tradition. We also have with us my good friend and colleague the Reverend Simon Jones—"

"Please to meet you," said Jones, raising his glass.

"Who is one of the ministers at Grantville's Methodist church. And this is my curate, Father Augustus Heinzerling. I believe you've already met."

Heinzerling nodded a greeting, and Luzzatto gave another half-bow in return.

"Forgive me," Luzzatto said, "for I may not understand the Christian religion perfectly, but I understood that your Methodist church was Protestant, Reverend Jones?"

"It is, yes," said Jones, clearly anticipating the question. "If you're wondering whether that means Father

Mazzare and I should be enemies, the answer is no, not in the twentieth century. Our churches never settled their differences of doctrine, but outside of a few troubled places and a few small minorities of troublemakers on both sides, Catholic and Protestant never do more than chide each other for their lapses in doctrine. As to our being friends, that is a happy accident of our having shared interests outside our respective religions."

"Indeed," said Mazzare, "a happy accident." He smiled. Jones had learned Italian fairly well in the months they had had before leaving Grantville, but he hadn't quite relaxed into the language. It was bizarre to hear the plain-spoken minister suddenly start talking in that grammatically perfect and excruciatingly pronounced way, in slow and measured sentences, after hearing him in voluble and homey eloquence all these years.

It was a question of practice, of course. Mazzare had grown up with Italian from his parents, refreshed it with a two-year stint in Rome, and was both fluent and colloquial in the language. The twentieth-century version of it, at least. He had had no difficulty with the Venetian dialect once he had attuned his ear to it, but Jones was still having trouble. Indeed, very few people hereabouts could understand his twentieth-century formal Italian, since it was a language hardly anyone in this time actually spoke.

"That is—interesting," said Luzzatto, looking introspective for a moment. Mazzare had an idea that he understood the Jewish lawyer's surprise. Luzzatto had lived most of his life in a place where there were hardly any non-Catholic Christians and non-Christians were formally and punctiliously discriminated against.

Mazzare realized he was being remiss in his duties as host. "Can someone get Maestro Luzzatto a drink? And one for me, as well." He pointed to one of the bottles on the sideboard. "That one—we have some others, too—was sent to you personally from Don Francisco. He asked me to assure you that it was prepared according to the laws of kosher—ah, kashrut."

Heinzerling moved to the sideboard, but Luzzatto intercepted him quickly and smoothly.

"Please," the lawyer said, smiling at the burly Jesuit, "allow me." Luzzatto opened the bottle and poured himself a glass, murmuring something as he did so. Mazzare didn't catch the words but assumed it was a religious blessing. Heinzerling seemed a bit surprised at the notion of a guest serving himself, but made no objection. He simply poured a glass for Mazzare and brought it over.

Mazzare noted with approval that Gus did not take the opportunity to refresh his own glass. But, mostly, he was chiding himself. He'd forgotten that Nasi had explained to him that maintaining kashrut required that the wine not be handled by anyone except observant Jews from the time the grapes were put into the bin to be pressed to the time it was poured into the glass.

He sighed inwardly. This was just one of the many ways in which one Larry Mazzare, small-town American priest, felt inadequate to his new assignment. Grantville's only Jewish family, the Roths, had been Reform Jews and late-twentieth-century variety at that. Dealing with seventeenth-century Jews was another matter altogether. No matter how sophisticated, cosmopolitan and well educated they were, the traditions and customs of Judaism were so deeply ingrained in their attitudes that it was easy to blunder into a minefield without realizing it.

That was even true, in many ways, with nonobservant Jews like Mike Stearn's wife Rebecca and her father, Balthazar Abrabanel. To Mazzare's way of thinking, it was odd. But he was Catholic, not Jewish. He knew that where Christians tended to see theological doctrine as the defining issue of their faith, Jews placed far more emphasis on matters of ritual, tradition and customs. Rebecca had been willing to marry a gentile, and her father had not objected. But Mike had told the priest that, very early on, he had learned to respect and accept the fact that Rebecca kept a kosher house and continued to observe Shabbat and the Jewish holidays. Not as strictly as the rabbis of Amsterdam would require, but to what Rebecca and her father regarded as a reasonable level.

He'd told that to Mazzare one evening in the Thuringen Gardens, as he munched on a ham sandwich. "Only time I ever get to eat pork any more is when I do it on the sly outside the house." But he'd said it cheerfully enough. "What the hell. If Paris was worth a mass to Henry the Fourth, keeping my wife happy is sure as hell worth a few changes in my diet and habits."

Luzzatto came back over to Mazzare's side and held up the glass. "Please pass along my thanks for the wine to my cousin Don Francisco, Monsignor Mazzare." He had a slightly impish half-smile on his face. "The Nasis are quite famous for it, you know."

"Oh?"

"Yes. The Nasis are even famous for it in the City." The words *the City* contained a freight of meaning. As if there was and could be no other city in the word comparable to Istanbul. "Until quite recently they were sole suppliers of wine to Topkapi palace. The business is still substantial, despite Emperor Murad's recent prohibitions."

"I'd think that would be a bit risky."

Luzzatto shrugged. "Simply living in the City has its risks. But it was the great shelter for the Sephardim after the Spanish drove us out of Iberia. Truth be told, the risks are small provided one does not wave the matter under the nose of Murad the Mad. Like most Ottoman emperors, he really does not care much what Jews or Christians do in his capital, as long as they do it quietly."

Mazzare took a sip of his own wine, which had also come from Nasi. Francisco had ordered several barrels sent to the embassy at his own expense. They'd already been here when the mission arrived.

The wine was good; full-bodied and with a sweet undertone that wasn't sickly like so much of the wine they got in Germany. "Delicious," he pronounced. "I must remember to thank Francisco when I send my first message home. Speaking of which—"

He broke off, remembering the need for security. Smoothly, understanding his quandary, Sharon Nichols stepped forward and engaged Luzzatto's attention. Mazzare took the opportunity to move away a few steps and speak softly into Heinzerling's ear. "Gus, how are the radio people doing?"

Heinzerling put his glass down. "I can find out," he said. "I left them untangling wires in the attic."

He spoke as softly as Mazzare. No one really knew if all the capabilities of Americans with radio were still a secret from Europe's princes. But so long as there remained the possibility that the USE's enemies still thought that enormous towers were needed for the devices, they would do their best to keep the knowledge limited. Although Melissa Mailey and her party were imprisoned in the Tower of London, they still had the means to communicate with home. If Charles I—the Earl of Strafford, more likely—ever got wind of the full capability of American radio . . .

He would surely have their quarters in the Tower subjected to a rigorous search—something he had avoided doing so far.

"Please," said Mazzare. "Tell them there's no pressure, I should simply like to know if I can send a message in tonight's transmission window or whether it should wait."

Heinzerling left, padding with that silent gait that went so oddly with his burly physique.

Mazzare moved back to Luzzatto's side. "Speaking of

negotiations, do we yet have a program of discussions with Messer il Doge?"

"Ah." Luzzatto set down his glass and pulled his briefcase from under his arm. "It was for this reason I came to visit." He took out papers and began sorting through them.

"Perhaps we should take a moment to read through . . ." Mazzare broke off, when he saw the amount of paper involved.

"No, Monsignor. These are simply notes, of my own. I find I grow absentminded as I age."

Luzzatto gave a dry little chuckle. Mazzare hoped he was joking. As well as being small and narrow, the lawyer was remarkably baby-faced, giving the impression that he was in his twenties. The life story Nasi had given Mazzare, though, put Luzzatto somewhere nearer to forty.

"Ah," Luzzatto went on. "I am absentminded again. There are some matters for you to attest as plenipotentiary for the United States, the rental of this palazzo and so forth"—he set aside a bundle of documents—"and I shall leave these for you to examine at your leisure. There is no rush before the beginning of Lent, which is some time away yet. Then it will be needful to have your contracts signed."

Mazzare nodded, although he did not relish the thought of reading that pile of legalese in what was rapidly becoming his fourth language after English, German and Latin. Perhaps better to get onto a more immediate subject. "I understand that the diplomacy begins this evening with a reception at the palazzo ducale?"

"This is at once true, and not true, Monsignor. The reception will be to allow the members of the Consiglio to take a look at you and for each to pass some moments, perhaps, in conversation. Nothing can be done or will be done without a vote, and they dislike to act on any vote that does not have a majority of seventy or so."

"Seventy?" Jones had his eyebrows raised. "We have to convince seventy people of everything? I thought it was the doge and a few councillors—ten, wasn't it?"

"Again, Signor Jones, this is at once true and not true. The government of Venice is a complicated thing, and different kinds of decisions require different decision makers. Messer il Doge can decide very little himself; he has influence, not power. Many other decisions require him to act with various other bodies, depending on whether it is to do with the Rialto, the city, the Terraferma, or foreign matters. There are differences for the Empire and for foreign Christian princes. I could not possibly explain all of these conveniently now, signor, although perhaps we might spare a few days at some point?" Luzzatto looked as though he meant it. Mazzare began to speculate, briefly, how much a top-flight commercial attorney in the up-time U.S. would charge to devote his time to a client like this, and that led him to just how deep the Nasi and Abrabanel commitment to the USE actually was. They were spending money like water.

Mazzare wrenched himself back to the present. He was vaguely aware that Jones had made some polite noises about how it sounded a fascinating prospect, but perhaps he might decline to fix a date just now, and Luzzatto was speaking again.

"—and so for diplomatic matters of this character it will be several votes of the Gran Consiglio to test the waters on particular matters and then a final vote to empower il doge to enter into the treaty. They will turn out in full for that, and I should expect to see perhaps a hundred and sixty votes cast. If they believe more than a few will vote against or abstain, they hold off voting. It is safe to do very little without consensus in the most serene Republic of Venice."

Luzzatto was smiling ever so slightly, his eyes twinkling. Mazzare had the distinct feeling that the irony had been intentional and intended to convey a

very real warning of weirdness ahead. It was a warning of another kind, too: that they were in a town
where it paid to be oblique about politics if you were
opening your mouth anywhere near money or power.
That was a kind of town that had been mercifully
rare by the dawn of the twenty-first century, but was
all too common in the seventeenth. Even diplomatic
immunity was no sure guarantee; the Spanish ambassador Bedmar who was supposed to be back in town
had had to get out of Venice one step ahead of a
lynch mob.

Luzzatto was shuffling his notes, apparently prepar-
ing for a more formal presentation. Mazzare decided
to prompt him. "Maestro Luzzatto, what are our
chances of a favorable settlement here in Venice? I
trust Don Francisco sent you a briefing on what we
hope to achieve?"

Luzzatto cleared his throat. "Monsignor Mazzare, I
will say in summary that the chances are good, with
perhaps some reservations. Don Francisco has been
instructing several of us here in Venice, in the ghetto
and the Rialto alike, in rumors and information to
feed to various interested parties. We have, I think,
been successful in making the case for a strong commercial tie with the United States of Europe as it has
now become. Venice has been in a precarious situation
for some years now, and came close to crisis with the
Mantuan war, for there was great risk of losing the
French alliance, such as it is. The designs of both Spain
and France on Venice and the money it represents are
obvious and long standing. Spain is perhaps not so
great a threat as once it was, but France has grown
powerful in recent years. And while the Habsburgs in
Spain and Austria are strong enough to contain them,
the Terrafirma party in Venice have been worried. The
maritime party is also concerned; for all that they pretend to care little for any wealth that comes from the
land and to cleave to the view that Venice will make

all its wealth from the Levant trade, they know that without the landward ties they are less powerful. In this, at least, the two parties see eye to eye."

Murmurs of understanding and assent went around the room. They had all sat through briefings from Nasi.

Luzzatto went on. "I believe that this interest is well recognized to be served by trade with the United States and the commercial opportunities it represents. There is no prejudice about trading with Protestant states, after all. The Dutch and the English have for some years had significant customs concessions here and the merchant houses are grown used to dealing with such. One of the current matters of debate before the Consiglio is the admission of an Englishman to farm the customs on certain goods here, such is the presence of the English in this town. You will doubtless meet this man, Sir Henry Hider, although his interests are in dried fish and cloth and so your commercial aims will not cross with his to any great extent."

Heinzerling came back into the room and padded over to Mazzare. Politely, Luzzatto moved away and began chatting with Sharon, allowing the father and his curate a moment for a quick and private exchange.

"There is good news and bad news," Heinzerling whispered. "The good news is that the radio will soon be functional. Tonight, they say."

Mazzare nodded. Then, braced himself. Gus Heinzerling did not use the expression "bad news" lightly.

"The bad news is that Joe Buckley was just spotted, entering the building next door. With luggage."

It was all Larry Mazzare could do not to groan aloud. As if things weren't complicated enough already!

Chapter 12

One of the great things about the seventeenth century, Joe Buckley reflected, was that you couldn't be left behind. Back up-time, what he had just done would have called for accreditations and passes and all manner of like nonsense and paperwork. If nothing else, airplane tickets.

Here and now, as the coming man in the field of investigative journalism that he was inventing a few hundred years early, Joe had just had to buy a good horse and try to keep up.

There was a downside, of course. A sore ass was only half of it. Name recognition was the other half. Between the Imperial Post and every other one-horse town boasting a printing press, there had been a lot of places on the route that had received his reports from Grantville and Magdeburg. Most of them didn't pay, which was a bind, but copyright and syndication were for the future. Nevertheless, his name was getting well known around Europe, bylined in all manner of odd corners. He'd even seen some pieces he definitely hadn't written but which had his name on them. Which was flattering, even if he never saw so much as a copper groat for it.

Still, he'd hardly put his hand in his pocket from Thuringia through Switzerland to Italy. Even in the rural backwaters where literacy was down around the thirty percent mark, in little towns where lack of practice lost people the letters they'd had, there was generally someone who'd read his stuff out in the tavern. Joe was the only twentieth-century-trained investigative journalist practicing his trade in the here-and-now, so far as he knew—which made him something of an instant superstar.

But—and it was a big but—his every attempt to get something on or about the ambassadorial party to Venice had so far been thwarted. Now, though, he had a top-floor suite of rooms in a building adjoining the palazzo that held the newly arrived embassy of the United States of Europe. The place was something of a dump, even though it had been home to the Swedish ambassador for a while. But there had never been any strong diplomatic presence from Sweden here and, so far as Buckley could tell, most of Venice was a dump anyway.

Joe dropped his bags, and took a moment to reflect on how he had changed. A good eight inches off the waistline, what with a lot more walking and riding and—surprise—a better diet. When the seventeenth century ate well, it generally ate healthily, he'd found. He was also now fairly fluent in three languages and able to get by, just, in two more. Of course, one of the ones he had trouble with was Italian, but he would improve that soon enough.

Behind him, a couple of the palazzo's staff were unpacking his gear and putting it away. He stared out of the window and contemplated the rooftops of Venice. From here he could see—well, no more than two or three streets away, but he was looking east across the city from quite close to the western end. Rooftops, all the way. Under every one, he thought, a story to be told.

And that was the other half of the change in fashion he'd started. He talked to the people who lived just under those roofs, and told the stories of the Rich and Famous from their point of view. Back in the twentieth century, of course, there had been precious little of that. The media was mostly controlled by big corporations, and that meant sucking up to the corporate bosses who owned them. It was the same in the seventeenth century, in a way. Poor people didn't own printing presses here anymore than they had up-time. But there was a big difference in social status. A man who, back up-time, would be a CEO and entitled to some major ass-kissing was, in the seventeenth century, merely "in trade" and thought the less for it.

He turned around and tried his Italian on for size. "Ladies," he said, "what is happening in Venice lately?"

The two maids froze and stared at him. Then, in a moment no choreographer could have bettered, looked at each other and giggled.

Thank you, God, Joe thought. *Another town where everyone ignores the help.*

Claude de Mesmes, comte d'Avaux, considered himself a patient and sensible man. A lawyer like his father before him and his grandfather also.

He had seen little cause for concern in the news from the Germanies at first, but then it had all reached him at third hand in Venice and Rome. True, he had met the king of Sweden and knew him for the brute and the bully he was. But d'Avaux had still been as astonished as anyone at Gustavus Adolphus' rapid success once he intervened in Germany. It had been hard work to extract from the Swede even mild limits on his exactions and depredations. At that, he had broken those promises. D'Avaux had heard of all manner of treasure being carted back to Sweden.

For now, alas, the Germanies were the demesne of the Swede—the Germanies and the assortment of bizarre strangers brought into their midst.

That last was the true source of his trouble. Trouble, mostly, in maintaining the proper and seemly patience of his station. It was difficult, sometimes, in the still watches of the long waits that characterized the diplomat's trade, to remember that in all things there were laws. Laws ordained by God for the natural order. Any scourge of God—like the Hun, or the Swede, or the Turk or doubtless others from the dawn of time to the crack of doom—might temporarily and locally overturn that order. But the sheer force of God's design in the world would soon assert itself, through those who acted as God's instruments in the world of time.

So, d'Avaux reassured himself once again, there was no cause for long-term concern. Cardinal Richelieu had that reassertion of the sublime will well in hand. It was the same argument they had long used with Father Joseph and his *devots*: there were secondary causes in the world through which God worked, and in bringing about the triumph of God's will there was no law save necessity, no matter the distasteful actions required in the short term. Such as, for example, subsidizing the Swede in the past or allying now with Spain. Granted, the *feu-de-dieu* was feeding newer and yet more pernicious heresies into the mélange of European strife. But how often had short-sighted moral and theological imperatives led to the ruin of all?

Best to work subtly. Hence the cardinal's instructions and their urgent tenor:

> *To Venice, Monsieur Le Comte. Nothing within your power must be left undone toward the end of thwarting the work of the ambassador of the United States of Europe. Their entire aim and design at Venice must be set at hazard, in which matter I repose*

*my full confidence in you. There is no scruple
or nicety as regards the Americans you will
find there; there is now hot war between
France and the Swede and his accomplices.
You might spare some small scruple for the
niceties as regards the rulers of the Most
Serene Republic, but there is little injury
in that quarter that sufficient money cannot
repair. Above all, the strategic isolation of
the United States of Europe is vital.*

The comte sat at the window of the French embassy
and brooded on the cavalcade that carried the Americans and their lackeys through town. Naturally, the
Venetians—a frivolous people—had spent their time and
money on a foolish dumb-show. A foolish dumb-show
that d'Avaux had nevertheless ensured, in several days
of furious negotiation, was less ostentatious than the
dumb-show that had greeted his own arrival in Venice
a few weeks earlier.

The Venetians, after all, had learned many of their
habits from the Turk, among whom display and ostentation was all. Reports from Istanbul told always of the
furious fights over ever smaller and smaller slices of
status among the ambassadors.

But enough of past triumphs, and especially such
piffling ones. D'Avaux turned away from the window.

His agent Ducos, awaiting the subtle signal, stepped
forward from where he had been warming himself
beside the fire against the last chill of a Venetian
winter. D'Avaux noted that he had done so by standing on the shadowed side of the chimney-hood where,
between the light of the window, the glow of the fire,
a natural catlike immobility and the Huguenot severity
of his somber suit, Ducos was all but invisible.

D'Avaux found it amusing, from time to time, to
chide Ducos for his religious prejudices. Ducos took
it largely in good part, for d'Avaux was careful never

to press the matter to the point of a serious effort at conversion. There was a use for the hard core of French Protestants whom no edict or religious war would extirpate. There were tasks that had to be undertaken, things that had to be done that the moral flexibility of a theology that denied the value of good behavior could allow where a Catholic, bound to good works for the salvation of his soul, could not in good conscience tread. It would not do to send someone who was not already damned to do such things.

And so Ducos was a heretic servant of His Most Christian Majesty. And a useful one, too. Behind the scenes, in darkened rooms and in places where the likes of Monsieur le Comte d'Avaux could not go, Ducos would go and do and learn things the doing and learning of which were sanctified by the law of necessity and that law alone.

Watching him step forward into the light, d'Avaux was put in mind of some sleek, gray-finned creature of the deep, rising into the sunlit upper waters where men navigated. Woe betide the hapless mariner who found himself in the water when such a one came up from his accustomed darkness.

"Monsieur le Comte." Ducos gave him the little nod of the head that did him the duty served other men by extravagant bows.

"I believe," said d'Avaux, "that we have in place appropriate receptions for the Americans?"

"Yes, Monsieur le Comte. All that could conveniently be laid in advance has been. I have disbursed some three hundred scudi so far."

D'Avaux raised an eyebrow. Not at the sum, which would hire the exclusive services of one of the better class of physicians for a year, but at Ducos' choice of words. "Conveniently?" he repeated. Perhaps he was oversensitive to nuances, but it paid to check. Besides, Ducos was nothing if not precise.

"Conveniently." Ducos nodded.

"I shall leave to your judgment how much I should know, of course."

Ducos paused a moment before replying. "There is another American newly arrived in town," he said at some length.

"Not connected to the embassy?"

"I do not believe so, Monsieur le Comte. A rogue American, I think. He calls himself Buckley. Joe Buckley."

D'Avaux found that intriguing. Joe Buckley was a well-known demagogue and rabble-rouser, for all that his career was a recent one. His vernacular was English but he had a damnable knack of getting translated and passed around Europe by who knew what means. Yet, all the cardinal's spies reported that he was in ill-favor with the Americans themselves, despite being one of their number. "What is that silly term he favors for himself?"

"'Investigative reporter.'" Ducos made a small shrug. "Which is to say, a spy."

"And who to know better than you?" The small witticism was hard for d'Avaux to resist.

"Just so, Monsieur le Comte. Just so. I have a number of schemes, in outline, for dealing with the Americans. I will add this 'Buckley' to the mix. Some depend on contingencies, but under pressure I will be able to—"

D'Avaux held up a hand. "Enough, Ducos. It suffices that, what? He has taken steps against you?"

"Not yet, since he's just arrived. But he will, be sure of it. He will certainly make himself familiar with the staff at the embassy. That will make it more difficult to safely place my own agents there."

D'Avaux waited a moment after Ducos stopped talking. The starveling-looking Huguenot could sometimes be hard to read. He would pause to marshal words, sometimes for remarkably long times. At other times, he would simply stop talking, without verbal punctuation, when in his opinion his master's conscience was sufficiently informed. D'Avaux admired that. Ducos had the casuistry of a Jesuit—but ten times the moral flexibility that had earned d'Avaux himself the ill name of comforter of heretics among the *devots* at home.

The comte brought himself back to the matter at hand. "I had heard this of the Americans," he said, as much to himself as to Ducos. "The cardinal warned me specifically. They have a knack—even the pretended nobility among them—to consort and grow familiar with the lower orders."

Ducos said nothing.

"It may perhaps be," d'Avaux mused aloud, "that will prove their undoing in this time and place. Especially in this place, where nobility is false already—merchants with delusions of grandeur—and thus its appearance may not be diluted. In Venice, the facade is all. Ah, yes. There is much that might be said, in the right ears. Ducos?"

"Yes, Monsieur le Comte?"

"Do I understand that some of your methods include the disbursement of funds among the servant classes?"

"Yes, Monsieur le Comte."

"Then I should like, if it please you, to have reports as to those with whom this Buckley, and all the other Americans, choose to consort. No matter how low their station."

"Yes, Monsieur le Comte. And, Monsieur le Comte?"

"Ducos?"

"Has Monsieur le Comte read the notes I have provided as to the Spanish delegation?"

"Yes, Ducos. I thank you for reminding me. It would appear that Bedmar seeks Spain's advantage in Venice—no surprise there—and by like methods as he used before. He failed before, Ducos. Disastrously, in fact. See that he fails again. Simply because we are allied now, I see no reason to cede any advantage to the Spaniards here."

"Yes, Monsieur le Comte."

"I leave the details, as always, to you, Ducos."

"Yes, Monsieur le Comte."

Chapter 13

Finally, they were finished unpacking. Better yet, Magdalena had charged off to take care of something else. Best of all, Gus Heinzerling had appeared and announced he was done for the night.

All was well in Frank Stone's world. Bases were covered, with his dad and stepmom alike—and the rest of the evening beckoned.

"So," Frank said brightly. "This taverna of yours. How do we get there?"

Giovanna gave him that dimply smile that was doing the weirdest things to his stomach. "The kitchen," was all she said.

The kitchen turned out to be bright, warm, steamy and full of bustle. It wasn't extravagant, there wasn't anything really riotous happening, but there was a definite air of ongoing party about the place.

"Do all these people work here?" Frank asked, as they descended the steps into the room.

"Yes," said Giovanna. "Well, most." She made a beeline toward an open doorway across the large room they'd entered, passing a hearth to her right along the way.

The first big room of several, from what Frank could see. He realized that the "kitchen" should probably be called "the kitchens," in a palace like this one. The rooms were big, and spacious for all their clutter, but they still managed to look full with the number of people who were there.

Not all of them were working, either. The kitchens seemed to combine the attributes of a work place with those of a tavern. Packed into the main room as well as three side rooms that were within his view despite the smoke and steam, Frank could see dozens of people. At least a third of them, although dressed in what he took to be workclothes, were sitting at tables chatting over glasses of wine. In one of the side rooms, out of sight, he could hear what sounded for all the world like a pickup band playing a folk tune.

He followed Giovanna through the doorway, his two younger brothers in tow and Gus bringing up the rear. The room they'd entered was apparently a cellar of some kind, judging from the lack of any hearths or other cooking implements and the casks, jugs, and barrels stacked against two of the walls.

The real function of the room, however, was pretty much "tavern pure and simple." There was a huge table at the center of the room—three tables, rather, fitted together like a T—with at least a dozen people sitting around it on a haphazard collection of stools and chairs.

Using the term "sitting" loosely, that is. Frank immediately recognized one of those people—and Billy Trumble was "sitting" in the manner that a man wrapped around a lot of wine generally "sits." Especially one who was only a year older than Frank himself and almost certainly had less experience with mind-altering substances. His Marine uniform was in such a state of dishevelment that Frank gave silent thanks that Admiral Simpson was several hundred miles away.

"Yo, Frank," slurred Billy. " 'S'up?"

Billy's seat was all the more precarious because the young soldier clearly had a lot on his mind. Or, rather, one single subject upon which he was concentrating as ferociously as a man can concentrate when he's several sheets to the wind. Perched on a stool next to him was a grinning, dark-haired girl perhaps two years older than Giovanna and bearing something of a vague resemblance. A cousin, perhaps, if not a sister.

A moment later, Frank recognized the soldier sitting next to Billy—and with not much more in the way of sober stability. Conrad Ursinus, that was, another of Grantville's star baseball players and one of Billy's close friends. Conrad was wearing a naval uniform that was every bit as disheveled as Billy's. This time, Frank muttered aloud his fervent thanks that Admiral Simpson was across the Alps.

"And they call it a 'security detachment,'" his brother Ron murmured sarcastically. "God help us all."

Now that he listened more carefully, Frank realized that the folk tune being sung in the adjoining room had a definitely Scots air about it. Apparently, Lennox's soldiers had found a better place to ward off the early spring chill than standing at attention outside the embassy.

Heinzerling confirmed his guess. "Lennox will flay them alive, when he finds out," he growled.

"Venizz's great," Billy announced loudly, with the rousing and expansive good cheer of the irretrievably drunk. "Wine, women, song. La dolchy vita!"

Giovanna said something that sounded decidedly arch in rapid-fire Venetian-accented Italian, and the girl sitting next to Billy giggled. She prodded Billy in the chest, and said something in Italian herself. Fortunately, she spoke much more slowly and enunciated clearly, so both Frank and even Billy could understand her.

"Won't you introduce us, Lieutenant?"

Billy tried, and completely failed, to suppress a belch. "'Scuse me and sorry," he said, "but, uh, not in that

order. Or something." He cleared his throat. Then, as
solemnly as a man in his condition could manage:

"Frank, guys, permit me to introduce the lovely, the
charming, Arcangela. Arcangela, this is my good friend
Frank Stone, and his brothers Gerry and Ron. They
may be soccer fags, but otherwise they're great guys.
The beefy old fellow glarin' at me over their shoulder
is Gus Heinzerling." He shifted to English, waving his
wine glass. "Forgive me for not rising, gents, but I am
shit-faced drunk."

Alcohol consumption was making Billy maudlin. In
point of fact, he and Frank were not "good friends."
True, they weren't personal enemies, or anything like
that. As jocks went, Frank had always found Billy
a pretty decent guy—way better than the outright
muscle-Nazis on the football team—and so far as he
knew Billy had no particular animus against him. Still,
they remained on opposite sides of that great high
school divide that both were too fresh from to have
forgotten or forgiven yet. Here, the in crowd, with
their athletes and cheerleaders and class presidents;
there, the polyglot semi-alliance of the outcast nerds
and geeks and hippies.

Far more important at the moment, however, was
that a matter of honor was at stake here. "Soccer fag,
is it?" Frank demanded. His Italian was considerably
better than Billy's, but he stumbled over the second
word. There was undoubtedly an Italian equivalent, but
since he didn't know it he just tried to give the English
word a foreign flavor. "That's a bit rich coming from a
guy who can't even throw a ball in a straight line."

Billy frowned back with grim deliberation, trying to
assemble the glower one eyebrow at a time. It looked
like he was having trouble controlling his face.

"It's true," Frank went on solemnly, speaking now to
Arcangela. "I've seen him. He throws the thing, and it
curves." He mimed a thoroughly banana-shaped pitch.
"Clearly incompetent."

Billy got it at last, and laughed, nearly falling onto the floor. He would have, too, except he got a good grip on Arcangela's arm. She pried it off, but not too quickly and giggling while she did so. Drunk as a skunk or not, Billy didn't seem to have irritated her any. Frank ascribed that to the unfair advantage of the uniform.

But he didn't care, really. Frank's interest was elsewhere—and Giovanna was already passing him a glass of the wine. Then, moving deftly, she poured three more glasses for Frank's brothers and Gus.

Gus nodded his thanks, but Frank noticed that he didn't make any move to drink the stuff. Suddenly cautious—and not simply because he didn't want to make an ass of himself in front of Giovanna—Frank decided to follow his lead.

Gerry was the first to take a mouthful, and his eyes bulged as he got a taste. "Gah! What *is* this stuff?"

"Call it 'grappa,'" Billy slurred. "Great stuff onc't get used to it." He transferred his bleary gaze to Frank. "Say, about pitching and stuff, I been telling the folks about baseball here. I reckon we might be able to get a game on."

That figured. Billy had had a real chance of getting picked up for pro baseball when the Ring of Fire had stopped his career before it started. Rather than just swallow the disappointment, he'd helped organize the first big game after the event. Frank was no great shakes at baseball himself, and didn't really like it much. Soccer was his own passion. But Billy was passionate about baseball and had managed to transfer that passion onto a number of young Germans he'd come into contact with—none more so than his friend and now fellow officer Conrad Ursinus. He'd been on the Marine team in Magdeburg before he was posted away to Venice, and Conrad on the naval yard dog team.

There were five or six other regular teams in Grantville and Magdeburg, and teams were springing up in most of the larger towns in Thuringia and Franconia and anywhere else the Americans had a real presence in the USE. The Germans had taken to the game in a way they hadn't to football or basketball and been slower about with soccer. Talk about organizing real leagues had not gotten far, what with the war and all. But that was just a matter of time, especially after the Committees of Correspondence decided that organizing sports clubs was an excellent way of extending their influence still further.

The whole subject was something of a sore point with Frank and his brothers. They'd done what they could to get soccer adopted as well, but—

And then it hit him. They were in freaking Italy. Italy! For crying out loud, there pretty much wasn't any more promising territory for spreading the word about soccer without going to Brazil or—he was reminded by the sight of Aidan talking to some other soldiers with drunken animation—England. Back up-time, soccer had been Italy's other national religion.

Arcangela broke into Frank's train of thought, all but derailing it. "It is true," she said. "Billy has told us all of this game. But it was not very clear to me."

When he stopped laughing, Frank said: "And now let me tell you about the game they play in Italy in the future."

As he explained, he could see the interest taking hold, people drifting over to listen. He'd been right. Better still, Giovanna seemed as interested as anyone.

One of the Venetian guys—Frank could recall seeing him horsing trunks into the embassy—said, "We need a ball?"

"Sure, about so big." Frank held his hands out to indicate the size of a FIFA standard ball.

"And with just the feet and the head?" the porter asked.

"Yup. Handling it is a foul. What's your name, sorry?"

"Marius," the porter said, rising and holding out a hand. "Marius Pontigrazzi."

Pontigrazzi waved his wine glass in the direction of an intense-looking middle-aged man sitting at the center of the T in the big table. "I work for Giovanna's father, over there."

Frank's enthusiasm came to a screeching halt. *Giovanna's father. Oh, Christ.* Now that he really looked, he could see the family resemblance—just as he could see it in the two younger men sitting on either side of the man.

And her brothers. Oh, Christ.

The father's name was Antonio, he recalled. Antonio Marcoli. Frank couldn't remember the name of Giovanna's brothers, if she'd even told him at all.

Frantically, he tried to figure out where to go from here. Swapping insults with a drunken fellow American and then launching into a fervent speech for the introduction of soccer was probably not, he feared, the best introduction he could have made of himself. He felt like Romeo finally introduced to Juliet's father, and completely blowing it. Might as well pull out the dagger and take the poison now and be done with it.

Alas, Pontigrazzi wasn't going to give him a break, either. The porter was starting to shuffle around. "Just the feet?" he demanded. "Silly!"

"And your head, Marius," Gerry said. He'd gotten a cabbage from somewhere. "Watch," he said, and dropped the vegetable.

Frank winced—*et tu, brother?*—but Gerry caught it neatly on his foot and balanced it there. Fortunately, the one gulp of the grappa didn't seem to have affected Gerry's reflexes—as he went on to prove with a quick flurry of keep-up moves, flicking the cabbage into the air and knocking it up off his left, then his right knee. As it came down again he caught it on his foot, paused a second and chipped it up and over to Ron, who headed it in a shower of cabbage leaves to Frank.

Fortunately, Frank had the presence of mind to chest-trap the cabbage; then, leaned back as it fell to kick it back up. He fluffed that a bit, and had to hop to get his knee under it, but then he was able to get into the rhythm and drunken cheering broke out.

What the hell, he told himself. *Giovanna's dad probably thinks I'm a jerk anyway, so I may as well prove I'm adept at it.*

"Marius?" he called out, and saw Marius nod. Frank flicked it up, wincing a bit as he had to hit the thing a lot harder because it had almost no bounce. He was going to have a bruise in the morning. He got under it as it came back down and nodded it over to the Venetian.

Who chest-trapped it like a pro, and took it on the drop for a shot that would have gone clear to the back of the net, but—

It was a cabbage, after all. It exploded in a shower of healthful greens. The heart shot out at about Mach three and landed in the hearth to a shower of sparks and curses from the cooks.

Then, salvation!

Giovanna's father rose to his feet, bellowing praise, and proceeded to slap Marius on the back. Gerry and Ron went into full-on goal-celebration mode, heaving their doublets up over their faces and waving like loons.

Billy was throwing up now. Whether that was because he had actually laughed himself sick or because he'd just seen his plan to pollute Italy with baseball explode in a shower of cabbage leaves, Frank didn't know. The Italians were all cheering Marius, who was grinning like he'd scored the winner.

Which, in a sense, he had. Definitely, Frank thought, promising territory for three missionaries of the Beautiful Game.

Better yet, Giovanna was hauling her father over and making a proper introduction. Antonio Marcoli still looked far more intense than Frank would ever be comfortable with, but the man was smiling and extending his hand. Best of all, Giovanna's smile was wider than he'd ever seen it and the dimples were on Full Charm Display.

Mentally, Frank put away the vial of poison and the suicide dagger. All was well with the world!

Alas, he should have known.

No sooner did Antonio Marcoli take his hand than he drew Frank close. Then, whispered into his ear.

The whisper even *sounded* conspiratorial.

"Tomorrow. At night. Giovanna will bring you. Full meeting of the Committee. We must conspire to rescue Galileo."

Chapter 14

Slipping away from the embassy the next day to get a boat to Murano was simplicity itself. Ron had suggested holding the meeting with Giovanna's father in the afternoon, so they could with all honesty tell Dad and Magda that they were going to see the sights and would be back by dark.

Giovanna insisted on not letting them row the boat for her. Watching the more-or-less effortless way in which she'd handled the little craft, Frank was inclined to agree it was a good idea that she had. Apart from some kayaking the one time their dad had sent them off to summer camp, none of the Stone boys could have handled the boat the way she did.

Besides, sitting in the stern and observing Giovanna in action was a sheer delight for Frank. The girl might be on the small side—by twentieth-century American standards, if not seventeenth-century Italian ones—but her lush figure was underlain by plenty of muscle. It was all Frank could do not to ogle her outright.

The journey to Murano didn't take much time, and half of that was negotiating the winding little canals and the heavy traffic that Venice always had on its waterways in the daytime. The taverna was on the same model as the one that was in the basement of the embassy: it was in the back of the lower story of a great house. But this one was a dedicated taverna, rather than part of a huge kitchen. It didn't seem to be a public establishment, though. From what Frank could tell, it was more in the way of a private club for the inhabitants of the building.

It was an odd sort of arrangement, to American eyes, even eyes that had grown accustomed to seventeenth-century central Germany. The big building fronting the canal was not a palace for an embassy but a considerably more dilapidated structure. Most of it seemed to be taken up by artisans' shops below and their associated living quarters on the upper floors. The population density was . . . Venetian.

Giovanna's father, Frank had learned, was a metalworker by trade. Which, in Venice, meant something more like a jeweler than a blacksmith. Apparently, he'd traveled to Thuringia not long after the Ring of Fire in order to improve his skills with up-time techniques, leaving his children in the care of his relatives since his own wife had died in the plague. Antonio had returned with a burning enthusiasm for up-time ideology as well as up-time metalworking techniques. In fact, from what Frank could tell, he seemed to be the perfect illustration of the old saw about the zeal of converts. *More Catholic than the pope*—or, in this case, *more American than the Americans.*

The back room was smoky and dark, since at this time of day no direct sunlight was coming through the narrow windows on one wall. Just right for a conspiracy except that it was very large. There was nobody in it other than the Marcolis, Marius, and one other man, standing next to a large table toward the back.

"You know the new guy?" Ron asked Frank quietly.

"No. I wonder if he's part of this or if he just wandered in?"

Giovanna leaned close, and it was all Frank could do not to writhe in pleasure at the feel of her breath on his ear. "It is Michel Ducos, of the Paris Committee. He is attached to the French embassy, but is one of us."

"The Paris Committee?" Frank hadn't been aware there even was a Committee of Correspondence in the French capital. Gretchen Richter must have been busy when she passed through the city as part of Becky Stearns' diplomatic mission!

He wondered how hard a time of it the Committee people were having in Paris. Richelieu's agents were rough, by all accounts. On the other hand, Ducos looked like a mean customer himself, so maybe they were getting on okay if he was any kind of measure of the rest of them. He was a tall, narrow man with a hatchet face—the kind of face that couldn't say *ornery son of a bitch* more plainly if you tattooed it on his forehead. He was on his feet talking to Marcoli senior, a tumbler of something unregarded on the table beside him.

"*Si*," said Giovanna. "Their special embassy came a few weeks before yours, and Michel came with them as one of their servants. He came straight to us, and has given us much information about the comte d'Avaux."

Frank heard the *Michel* and inwardly snarled. *The guy's a fast worker*, he thought, and then told himself to cool it. "Who's this Count Devo, then?"

"The French ambassador, and a very bad man."

"That figures. Works for Richelieu, does he?"

"*Si*. He is infamous for his troublemaking in the Germanies and in Italy, and now he comes to Venice again. Michel tells us he is here to make trouble for you Americans."

Ducos turned his head. "*D'accord*," he said. Frank

realized that while in conversation with Messer Marcoli, Ducos had been keeping track of the conversation on the other side of the room. Ducos went on: "Seigneur le Comte is one of Richelieu's creatures. A man most dangerous to the advance of liberty, Monsieur Stone."

So the guy already knew his name, too. Frank decided to make introductions anyway, and named Gerry and Ron for the Frenchman. Giovanna's father and Marius Pontigrazzi they already knew, and finally he learned the names of Giovanna's brothers: Salvatore and Fabrizio.

There were also Dino and Roberto Marcoli, twin brothers also in their teens, and another older guy in his late thirties or early forties. Frank recognized all three of them. They'd been with Antonio Marcoli in the embassy the day before, although they hadn't really been introduced. The older man turned out to be the father of the twins and one of Antonio's many cousins. He was also Antonio's brother-in-law; or had been, at least, until Giovanna's mother died in the plague.

Frank would have been surprised by that, and a little taken aback, if he hadn't already learned that the general American tendency to avoid cousin marriage was not shared in most of the world. Miz Mailey had once told him the prohibition against it in many U.S. states was a result of a combination of the influence of the eugenics movement in the 1920s and anti-immigrant attitudes. Nowhere outside of North America had it been prohibited and it was actually quite common, even in the twentieth century of the universe they'd come from. He'd found the whole thing rather amusing at the time, given the longstanding wisecracks about inbred West Virginians. In their new world, the former West Virginians were considered maniacal exogamists.

The cousin/brother-in-law was named Massimo Marcoli, and was apparently the intellectual theorist of the group. At least, he had a stack of pamphlets fresh from Germany with him.

"So," said Gerry when introductions had gone around. "When is everyone else getting here?"

"Everyone *is* here," said Marcoli sternly, "now that you have arrived."

Frank's heart sank. Venice's Committee of Correspondence consisted of nine people, seven of whom were all part of the same extended family, one of whom worked for them as a handyman, and the last being a visitor from a Committee in another country altogether. Not to mention that, of the nine, five were teenagers or just barely past it.

And they propose to free Galileo from durance vile? How?

Alarm bells started going off in his mind, This had all the earmarks of a half-baked scheme concocted by enthusiastic amateurs. Well, except Ducos, who seemed to know what he was doing. But he was a foreigner too.

"Okay, then, what's the plan?" asked Gerry.

Frank strained, but couldn't hear a drop of sarcasm. *Damn, he's getting good,* he thought. Either that, or his youngest brother was a nitwit.

Marcoli didn't hear any sarcasm either, and set off in a torrent of enthusiastic Italian. Once they got him to slow down, he explained to them the plan, with contributions from Massimo. Frank's heart plunged lower and lower, into what seemed to be a bottomless abyss.

First, they would circulate propaganda, to ensure that there was popular outrage at Galileo's treatment.

Okay, that's feasible. If we can scrape up the money. And if the authorities don't nab us at it. Not sure how they feel about "circulating propaganda" in Venice, but I rather doubt the First Amendment carries a lot of weight here.

Then, they would travel to Florence, where Galileo was being held under house arrest pending his trial.

Um. Travel takes money—from where? I can just see

Dad's reaction if we ask him for some spare change to mosey on over to Florence. And just how easy is it to travel across Italy these days, anyway? It's not as if the place is a single country in the here and now.

Frank tried to remember the history lessons crammed into them before they left and on the long way here. *Didn't Florence dislike the Venetians? I think so. If I remember right, everybody in Italy dislikes the Venetians.*

Then, they would "fall upon" the inquisitors guarding Galileo.

Frank tried to picture himself "falling upon" an inquisitor. The image that came to mind did not fill him with great confidence. He had a dark suspicion that the average inquisitor in the seventeenth century bore a closer resemblance to American high school jocks than old men rubbing their arthritic hands and cackling with sadistic glee. The one and only time in his life that Frank Stone had ever "fallen upon" a jock—a stupid argument in the high school gym which had gotten out of hand—the affair had gone badly. Very badly indeed. Goddam football players.

Alas, Giovanna was beaming at him. Those dimples . . .

Driven by evolutionary impulses way too powerful to be overridden by mere sanity, Frank squared his shoulders and did his best to look "manly."

And said nothing. Made no protest at all. Such is the folly of natural selection.

Finally, Antonio Marcoli concluded enthusiastically, after freeing Galileo from captivity they would "spirit him away" to freedom in the United States.

Galileo's . . . what, now? Just turned seventy, I think. According to what Dad told me, his health is shaky and on top of that he's losing his eyesight. Frank remembered the rigors of their trek across the Alps to get to Venice. *Great. I can just see us "spiriting him away." In what? A coffin?*

But Marcoli was plowing on, as enthusiastically as ever—and, more to the point, Giovanna was still beaming at him. So, again, Frank kept his mouth shut and just did his best to satisfy the crazed imperatives of evolution by looking as stalwart and masculine as possible. Much like a male peacock spreads his glorious tail feathers in the bright sunshine or a male frog croaks his mightiest in the gloom of night.

Predators be damned.

Marcoli spent the next few minutes explaining how their "great revolutionary exploit" would bring the downtrodden masses of Italy to their feet. It seemed that—according to Marcoli, anyway—every Italian of the exploited and oppressed lower classes spent every waking minute agonizing over the fate of the great Italian genius Galileo. His liberation would be the death knell for medievalism! The tocsin for revolution!

Frank had his doubts. In fact, he was pretty damn sure he now knew what must have been going through the minds of some of John Brown's more level-headed associates when Brown explained his plans for Harper's Ferry.

He's nuts!

But . . .

Apparently, Frank's mimicry of the *male-in-his-prime* had served its purpose. Giovanna left off simply beaming and, in her own enthusiasm, gave him a hug. True, it was a brief hug. No matter. The feel of that nubile warm body against his was enough to paralyze Frank in the critical moment.

Critical . . . because his younger brothers—idiots!— opened the door to madness still further, before Frank could stop them.

"Why do we need the propaganda at all, then?" Gerry asked, running fingers through his hair. "Seems to me we'd be better off keeping quiet until we make our move."

Ron chimed in, after glancing at Giovanna. True, Ron seemed to have reconciled himself to letting Frank have a clear shot. But he was still a teenage boy in the presence of an exceedingly attractive teenage girl. Which is to say, a functional imbecile.

"Yeah, that's what I think too." Ron swelled his chest. "Besides, I'm more of an action sort of guy anyway."

Marcoli leaned over, his intense face more intense than ever. His dark eyes now seemed like coal. Glowing coal. "Because without the propaganda, Galileo's freedom is only the liberty of one old man, messers! The people have clutched his cause to their bosom, to be sure. But the subtleties of the matter must still be explained to them or they will not grasp the full significance of his liberation."

Frank finally saw an opening. *Propaganda. Yeah. Propaganda takes time. Time to stall . . . and stall . . .*

"Good idea!" he said brightly. "I'll start working on something right off. I was thinking a pamphlet— no, maybe a booklet! For that matter—this really is an important and complicated issue—maybe a full-length—"

Alas. Antonio's cousin Massimo smiled and shook his head. "No need, young messer! I have already written it!"

From somewhere on the floor he brought up a satchel, seedy-looking and frayed at the corners. From it he pulled a thick sheaf of paper, closely covered in scrawled writing, cup-rings and other, less identifiable stains. "Everything is explained here, for the people."

"I help to write it," Marius chimed in proudly.

I just bet you did, thought Frank. He'd seen enough of Marius already to realize that the Marcoli family's handyman was, in the venerable old American saying, *not playing with a full deck.* Frank had an awful feeling that the tract Massimo and Marius had written would be of a piece with the rest of the plan.

He had a moment's wild amusement. Maybe he

could send a copy of that screed back to Joachim von Thierbach on an experimental basis. Joachim was the CoC's top propagandist in Germany and a genuine whiz at it. See if a man can really die laughing.

"Maybe you could reduce it to just the essentials," said Ron. "A single, uh, I don't know the Italian. What the Germans call a *Flugblätt*. Means 'flyer' in English."

Massimo and Marius frowned mightily.

"Most people don't have time to read a whole long argument, you see," said Ron. "You're trying to reach the workers and the tradespeople. They spend all day making a living and when they finish they haven't the energy to go through a whole lot. What they might do is read a sheet that convinces them of the main argument."

Massimo and Marius still looked doubtful. So did Antonio. "But we must educate the people fully!" he protested. "They must *understand*."

"Oh, sure, sure," said Ron, hastily. "But full understanding has to come a step at a time. Maybe we can break down your book there into ideas a page at a time, introduce the ideas one at a time, let people work up to it. They'll read a page every few days where they won't sit down with a whole book, right?"

Again, Frank saw an opening. From the look of that thick, closely scrawled manuscript, translating it into comprehensible terms on short leaflets—if it could be done at all; he had his doubts; so much the better—would surely take weeks and weeks. Maybe months.

"Good idea!" he chimed in. "That's the way Joachim von Thierbach always works, you know."

The assembled Marcoli clan studied him with bright eyes.

"*Si?*" asked Giovanna. "That is how the great Thierbach does his . . ." She groped for a moment with the English term. "'Agitprop,' I think they call it."

She looked at her father. "Thierbach is very good, you know. He is the one who writes as 'Spartacus.' I have read some of his tracts you brought back with you. The ones you translated, at least. My German is still not good."

Bless the girl! Frank was still holding on to the hope that the love-of-his-life possessed all of what little common sense God in His Heaven had seen fit to bestow upon the Marcolis. Not much, maybe. But with those dimples and . . . everything else, he was willing to overlook some minor flaws.

Besides, it wasn't as if Frank's own genetic heritage didn't include a fair share of lunacy. *Hypocrisy, get thee behind me. Down with double standards!*

Antonio Marcoli's doubts seemed to be assuaged. In fact, he was positively beaming. "If this is as Spartacus says, then we must do it also!"

"Ab-so-lutely," Ron said firmly. "Joachim's a genius with propaganda, and this is something he found works really well."

That was true enough, actually. Joachim von Thierbach was one of the stars of the Committees of Correspondence, after Gretchen Richter, of course. Other people thought about propaganda as something you just did. Joachim lived it, breathed it, and probably spouted it in his sleep. Of the three Stone brothers, Ron paid the most attention to Joachim's lectures and writing. Frank realized with relief that if Ron could get these guys onto the subject of propaganda and tied up in getting out their message then they wouldn't be thinking about doing anything stupid with the Inquisition. Not any time soon, at least.

Praise be. Frank had mental visions of the Inquisition's goons. Huge, mustachioed guys, he imagined, with those crescent-shaped helmets the Spanish used all the time, prodding people with long, wicked-looking swords into cellars to be tortured. Handing out leaflets and doing a spell in the kitchens at the Freedom Arches was his own idea of revolutionary activity. Taking on huge sword-wielding thugs and their sinister priestly masters was not included.

Ron and Massimo were getting into a serious debate, now. Marius was following the talk back and forth, and looked to be getting a little dizzy. Granted, Marius would probably get a little dizzy trying to follow any extended conversation.

Ducos, on the other hand, was silent and reserved. He'd moved away from the table a little, his face looking more saturnine than ever. Apparently, the Frenchman was a man of action and wasn't entirely satisfied with the new developments. Roberto and Dino were discussing something else at another table, something that involved them making notes on a piece of paper.

And Marcoli himself—Marcoli was now speaking to Frank. "Messer Frank—perhaps your brother Gerry also—this propaganda talk does not need us. May I ask you to help with the technology?" He was awkward in pronouncing the up-time word.

"Uh, sure," said Gerry.

Frank nodded vigorously. He was hardly what you'd call experienced and adept at the art of getting on the good side of the Male Parent of The Intended—even leaving aside the fact that he still didn't really know exactly what he intended—but this was a gimme. In West Virginia, showing off one's mechanical skills to the MPTI was hallowed tradition and custom. Even for someone whose real name was Faramir.

And at least, this time, whatever the MPTI wanted wouldn't involve internal combustion engines. Frank suppressed a wince, remembering that one time . . . Missy Jenkins' father hadn't stopped laughing for three minutes.

"It is for the propaganda. Please, come." Marcoli got up and went over to the back of the room, where a big crate was lying on the floor with three smaller ones stacked next to it. "Our printing press, *si*? But our mechanical skills, they are not great for something like this."

Frank recognized it. One of the things the German Committees were doing—Joachim again—was shipping improved little printing presses out to Committees across Europe. Essentially, they were the seventeenth century's closest equivalent to the mimeograph machines that had been the staple for radical organizations up-time in the years and decades before the advent of copying machines.

"What's the problem?" Frank asked.

Marcoli lifted the lid on the big crate, and pulled out a many-folded piece of paper. "The directions for assembly," he said mournfully, "they are impossible to understand. Even for something in English, it is . . ." He passed the sheet to Frank and threw up his hands.

Frank and Gerry both chuckled. "A law of nature, sir. I've no idea why, but these things are always written by people with no grasp of reality."

"Also, please," Marcoli went on, "what is a 'Philips screwdriver'?"

Frank looked down at the instructions, which were written in English. Sure enough, they had been written by an up-timer. Probably one of the machine-shop guys, who'd assumed that everyone knew what a Philips screwdriver was.

"Gerry, you brought a toolkit, right?"

"Not with me now, but I got one back at the palazzo, sure. We should pass word back to include a Philips with these things?"

"I think we should," said Frank, "although Allen wrenches would be even better, you ask me." Studying the instructions, he shook his head. "Machinists and mechanics are almost as bad as computer geeks, when it comes to assuming that everyone else in the world shares their expertise."

To Giovanna's father, he explained: "Messer Marcoli, a

Philips screwdriver is a special tool. We have one at the embassy. We'll bring it and help set up the press."

Giovanna came up then, standing close to Frank. Very close indeed. "You can make it work properly?"

"Oh, sure," replied Frank, doing his level best to exude *male-in-his-prime*. "No sweat."

Then he had to explain the colloquialism. That segued neatly into an explanation of "piece of cake," which, in turn, segued into "cakewalk" and "milk run."

All was right with the world, again. Better than ever, in fact. Frank was now quite confident that, between the gadgetry and the needs of coherent propaganda, he could postpone any real madness indefinitely. While Antonio Marcoli and his daughter might have been a bit short-changed in the common-sense department—more than a bit, in the father's case—both of them were quite intelligent and were the kind of people who were interested in just about everything. Which meant . . .

Easily distracted. Serenely, Frank foresaw months of distraction, in the most distracting company he had ever met in his life. *Oh, brave new world!*

Chapter 15

Getting back to the embassy, Frank led his brothers up to their apartment. That was an odd notion right there; suddenly they had their own apartment, which was either a gigantic opportunity or put a whole lot more pressure on them to behave. Or, at least, on Frank. Sometimes, being the eldest sucked big-time.

"Okay, guys, time to plan." Gerry was matter-of-fact about it. Frank realized with no little horror that his brother was actually *serious*. *It'd be a lot simpler if he'd just stick to humping the legs of girls he ran into,* he thought. Or worse, maybe he wanted to turn himself into a real hillbilly hard-ass, instead of just the wannabe he was now. Either way, the signs of testosterone poisoning were getting frickin' obvious.

Frank paused to think for a moment. He had to handle this carefully, because there was a real possibility he'd send Gerry off to do the damn thing by himself. Chances were, Ron would go off with him, or at least do something similarly stupid like go handing out leaflets outside the doge's palace.

And leaving aside the need to keep his younger

brothers under control, Frank had to be seen doing *something* or he'd be out of luck real fast with . . .

That though was the real clincher. Cautious enough to keep Gerry and Ron from haring off and getting themselves killed or thrown into a dungeon somewhere—and guess who'd get the blame?—while still daring enough to impress Giovanna.

Worse than that, really. He had to do something daring enough to impress *Antonio* Marcoli. For all her own sprightliness and brains, Giovanna was obviously a girl who was much attached to and impressed by her father. His opinion of Frank would weigh heavily with her.

Damn.

"Yeah, plan," he said, vaguely, distracted by the very clear mental picture he suddenly had of Giovanna.

"We need to find out what the deal is with Galileo's trial," said Ron. "Where he'll be taken, what he's charged with, who his lawyer is, that kind of thing."

That sounded practical enough. "I could see if Father Mazzare knows anything," Frank volunteered.

Gerry looked skeptical. "He's a Catholic priest, remember. Won't he go tell someone if we start asking questions about Galileo?"

"Paranoia, Gerry?" Ron asked. "Been at Dad's stash?"

Gerry didn't answer, but just stood straight up and glared at Ron.

"Well, come on!" Ron snorted. "Father Mazzare, an Inquisition spy?"

"Yeah? You notice why he's called 'Father'?" Gerry demanded.

"Cool it, guys," said Frank. *Testosterone poisoning, for sure.* "Gerry, you're right, but for the wrong reasons. Now, I'm not saying we should go help spring Galileo, and I'm not saying we shouldn't, but Ron's right, first we need info. And if we come right out and say why we want it, we'll be actually grounded for the first time in our lives."

That brought silence. Their dad and the words "harsh disciplinarian" barely belonged on the same continent, let alone in the same sentence. Tom Stone had the sneaky, awful, borderline-abusive practice of being reasonable with teenagers, which was a lot harder to deal with than other kids' parents' ways of dealing with the occasional high spirits. Be that as it may, there was a line across which they had never taken him, a line on the other side of which there was the real possibility of Dad getting old-fashioned. Taking part in a commando raid on an Inquisition prison was definitely on the far side of that line.

"So, what, you're just going to go ask him?" But Gerry had lost some of the snarl from his tone.

"Yeah, why not?" Frank said, shrugging. "I just got to be subtle, but straightforward so's he doesn't suspect anything. How hard can it be?"

"Um, Frank?" said Ron, "You remember what Father Gus told us about playing poker with Father Mazzare?"

Frank remembered. "Yeah, whatever you do, don't do it, not for real money." To hear the Jesuit tell it—and despite appearances, there was plenty of brain to go with the brawn when Gus wasn't pickling it—Father Mazzare could see clear through playing cards, read minds and had ice water in his veins. There was a lot of admiration on Gus' part for Father Mazzare, although how he squared that with Mazzare being a card-shark Frank didn't know.

"Yeah, so be careful, hey?" said Ron.

"Uh, sure," said Frank. "But how's he going to suspect anything? I don't believe we're planning this, and *I'm* involved in it."

That, at least, got a chuckle.

There was a reception room on the second floor of the palazzo, and, the next morning, Frank waited outside it for a good five minutes wondering if they could hear his heart hammering through the big wooden doors. He'd gotten his brothers to agree to leave it to him. Just one of them being curious about the stuff they'd "heard around town" about Galileo was all very well, but all three of them would look suspicious.

Calm, he thought. *Use the force, Frank.*

He went in. He'd checked with the staff, and he knew Father Mazzare was in there. Sure enough, just as Frank came in the priest was sending Gus Heinzerling off somewhere. Mazzare had laid out a whole bunch of stuff on a table by the window, getting the best use he could out of the daylight to go through what looked like the world's supply of paperwork. Frank didn't envy him that one little bit.

"Morning, Frank," said Father Mazzare. "As you see, growing up doesn't stop the homework." The priest indicated the stacks of paper and vellum in front of him. "And this is just to rent a small palazzo. I'm glad we didn't hire a big place."

Mazzare's face twisted up into a wry grin. "How it's going to be when we start putting together trade deals, I dread to think."

"Morning, Father," said Frank, when Mazzare had run down. "Should, I, uh . . ." He looked back at the door.

"Oh, no, no. Sit down, there's coffee in the pot there; good stuff, too. Get yourself a mug."

Frank got himself a coffee and sat down at the table with Father Mazzare. His carefully rehearsed opening gambits were all failing him. "Uh, I . . ." he got out, and then dried up.

"Something troubling you, Frank?" Mazzare asked.

"Well, not as such, no," he said. "Only you seemed to be the best guy to ask about it, and, uh . . ."

"So, not girl trouble, then?"

Frank nearly fell out of his chair. *How did he know?* "No, no, no!" he said hurriedly, thankful for the small mercy that he hadn't had a mouthful of coffee at the time. "It's, uh, it's more of a religion thing, actually." *There, that'd explain the nerves,* he thought.

"Well, don't worry about offending me," said Mazzare. "I've almost certainly heard worse."

"Uh, sure." Frank stopped and thought. He was settling down a bit, and took a sip of his coffee. It was good, just as advertised. Probably the Nasis again, he thought, and then got back on track. "It was just that me and Ron and Gerry were out and about yesterday, and we heard some guys talking about the Galileo thing, you know, with the Inquisition?"

"Hmm. Yes, there would be talk about that, wouldn't there? Where did you hear it?"

"Oh, you know, around." Frank realized that this was heading into dangerous territory. He wondered if that whole silence-of-the-confessional thing would extend to him telling Father Mazzare that he was involved with bunch of lunatic revolutionaries who wanted to stage a raid on the Inquisition, and he was going along because he'd fallen madly in love with the daughter of the head looney even though some part of Frank understood perfectly well that it was probably just youthful infatuation but so what? Look what happened to Romeo and Juliet and they were still talking about it half a millennium later.

Probably not, he decided. Firmly, he fought down the sudden urge to confess everything. If he was grounded, he probably wouldn't see Giovanna again—a thought that was a lot scarier than any number of Inquisition goons.

Mazzare waited, patiently. .

"Just . . . around," Frank said, to fill the silence.

Mazzare gave a sly grin. "And not, in any sense, in any kind of taverna or wine-shop where you might have stopped off for a refreshing glass of wine or two, right?"

Frank felt the whole of Venice give a slight lurch

under him. *How does he do this? Can he really read minds like Gus says?*

The grin was still there. "Oh, all right, seal of the confessional, Frank. It's down to you what you tell your father. Just try to stick to the respectable ones, and know your limits, all right? A little wine for thy stomach's sake is all very well, but it's easy to overdo it if you don't have experience in handling the stuff."

Relief. Mazzare thought he was out drinking on the sly. A small sin to cover a greater one.

Frank grinned back. "Don't worry, Father, we learned our lesson about hangovers and throwing up. It's cool."

"Good. Well, no more lecture, then." Mazzare sighed, reached for the coffee pot and freshened his mug up. "About Galileo, then, what did you want to know?"

"Well, it's the whole deal with the Inquisition, you know?" That about covered it, and it wasn't an outright accusation that Mazzare was an agent of a sinister organization trying to hold back the progress of science.

"Ah, I see. You want to know if we can do anything about it?"

Another lurch. *He can't know—or can he? Who knows what they teach priests how to do in those seminaries. The Catholic Church didn't stick around for two thousand years by being a bunch of dummies. Play it safe.* "Well, it's not so much that, as, well . . ."

"You want to know what I think? Because I'm a priest of the Church that's putting him on trial?" Mazzare's face was taking on a decidedly severe look, now.

"Uh, if it's a problem, or you don't want to talk or anything or if, uh, I should . . ." Frank realized he was gabbling.

Mazzare waved him down. "No, no, relax. I can't say I'm too happy about the whole business, to be honest. Just because I'm on the staff, I don't have to be happy about head office policy, you understand? At least, not on nonreligious subjects, anyway."

Frank felt really uncomfortable about that. Was Mazzare in danger of a visit from the Inquisition as well? He didn't want to think about that. For all that Grantville's priest sometimes intimidated him, Frank genuinely liked the man. He didn't think he knew anybody who didn't. There was nothing ostentatious about Larry Mazzare, but he could have served as a poster model for *Priest, Catholic, small town, finest example thereof.*

Mazzare sighed, deeply. "It was all very amusing when it was three hundred years ago, you know, Frank. Everyone talking about Galileo like he was some plucky pioneer, fighting against the forces of medieval reaction. Of course, when you looked into it, it wasn't that simple. Just like it never really is. And it's even less simple now that we're here, of course."

"How's that?" Frank asked, intrigued in spite of the slightly icky sight of a priest being very definitely human about something. Being brought up the way he had—which was a long, long way away from anything that could even be slightly described as traditional religious beliefs, Christian or otherwise—made ministers and priests seem like slightly awesome figures to Frank Stone. Either ogres—like the televangelists, or the mad-eyed Reverend Green—or uncanny wizards, like Father Mazzare. Watching him in what was unmistakably an irritated mode was unnerving.

"Well, to start with, his trial's late. In the universe we came from, it would have been over by now. He was found guilty and sentenced in June of 1633—almost nine months ago—whereas in this universe his trial hasn't even started yet." Mazzare took another sip of his coffee. "I don't pretend to understand the mathematics of it, but they call it 'the butterfly effect.' You know, a butterfly flaps its wings in South America somewhere, and it affects how tornados form in Kansas."

Frank nodded. He'd watched *Jurassic Park*, too, and at least knew the buzzwords for chaos math.

"Well, it seems that we brought some butterflies of our own. Pretty big ones. Somehow, in whatever complex ways, the Ring of Fire scrambled this 'historic result' just like it's scrambled so many others. Galileo's still in Florence in this timeline. In the old history, he'd been tried and was under house arrest by this date."

"Eh? I thought he'd got burned at the stake?" Frank blurted that out, and regretted it. "Uh, sorry."

Mazzare chuckled. "For astronomy? No, the Church has plenty of astronomers of its own. You're probably mixing him up with Giordano Bruno, Frank, who was burned at the stake. No, you see the real story is that Galileo, to use the cop-show phrase, copped a plea to heresy. And, technically, that was right, he was a heretic."

"What, for saying that the Earth went around the sun?"

"Well, that's technically right, but doesn't tell the whole story. Frank, do you know what heresy is to begin with?"

"Well, uh, it's . . ." He thought about it for a moment. "There's probably a proper definition, isn't there? It's not just disagreeing with the Church, is it?"

"Actually, that's rather close to what the real definition is, if the ugly truth be told. It's like this, and I'm simplifying here, you understand?"

Frank nodded.

"The Church is in the business of guiding people to Jesus, right?"

Nod.

"And, for an assortment of reasons that seem good to us, we have a whole hierarchy set up to decide the best way to go about it, yes?"

Nod. Frank wasn't sure he got it, but this probably wasn't the best time to pick an argument he wouldn't know how to conduct, let alone win.

"And, again, for an assortment of reasons we think are good ones, the Church gets the last word with

Catholics about what we ought to believe. That's supposed to be one of the big differences between us and Protestants, by the way. They're supposed to believe that it's really down to each man with Scripture and his faith to find his best way to God. If the Reverend Jones were here right now, which he's not, he'd be correcting me six ways from Sunday on the subject, but that's about the theoretical size of it. I don't suppose you followed the Rudolstadt Colloquy?"

"The what?" Frank knew where Rudolstadt was, but—no, hold on, now he remembered something. "Wasn't there some kind of big conference there last year?"

"Indeed there was. A big argument between one lot of Lutherans and another lot of Lutherans about what kind of—but I'm getting off the point, here. A good few of the speakers at that conference reckoned that they were the last word on what a Christian ought to believe as well, and don't think for a minute that I'm taking advantage of Simon's absence to make a few cheap cracks at the expense of the competition." Mazzare smiled broadly.

The smile was infectious, and Frank found himself chuckling. "So where you've got one pope, they've got a whole bunch of 'em?"

"Oh, that's good," said Mazzare, "I'll have to remember that the next time I get Simon going on this topic, I really will. And it's sort of accurate, too, although they do deny it. It's why you get lots and lots of little Protestant churches. I mean, there's something to be said for it, they're all Christians at heart and it must be easier knowing you can just head on down the road if you lose an argument."

Frank got the feeling he was getting a look in on an old, old, argument.

Mazzare sighed. "I shouldn't just sit here and slam the competition, should I? I was talking about heresy, and Galileo. Anyway, the formal definition of heresy goes something like this: 'the obstinate denial, after baptism, of some truth which must be believed with divine and catholic faith.' There's a bit in it about obstinate doubt, as well, but I'm not going to subject you to a lecture on formal theology. The thing is, there's a difference between proposing a subject for debate and deliberately expressing denial, you see, and Galileo got himself on the wrong side of that difference."

"But he was right . . ." Frank was wondering where this was leading.

"Yes, well, we knew that by the twentieth century. Actually, we knew it by the eighteenth as it happens, and Church teaching changed."

"I thought dogma couldn't—" Frank grinned. "You're going to explain it to me, aren't you?"

Mazzare's smile was still on his face "I'm carefully not using words like dogma and doctrine and faith and so on, you know. They're actually bits of theological jargon, with subtle shades of meaning. Let's stick with teaching. You know that if you want to be a Catholic, you have to believe the same things that all the other Catholics believe? I think we established that."

Frank nodded. He'd heard some of the things Christians believed, and figured they had some nerve calling his dad a weirdo for what *he* believed in. At least Tom Stone didn't claim to be smoking the body of Christ when he lit up a joint.

"Well," Mazzare continued, "in the time we came from, if you stop believing what all the other Catholics believe, you just stop being a Catholic. That's sad but it happens. In theory, at least. There're are some fairly out-there Catholics in the twentieth century. But I digress. Here and now, if you stop believing what other Catholics believe, it's a crime. Heresy both ways, but different ways of dealing with it."

Mazzare stopped to heave a big sigh. "That's Galileo's problem right there. He disagrees with the Church about what Catholics ought to believe about the shape of the world. Now, the pope told him—back when he was plain old Cardinal Maffeo Barberini, I think, although I could be wrong about that date—"

"What, he *personally* told him?" That sounded odd, to Frank. He'd picked up enough about how the seventeenth century worked to know that who you knew was very, very important indeed.

"Oh, yes. Galileo and the pope are actually old friends. Or they were, at least."

"So how come the pope sicced the Inquisition on him?" This wasn't following the script that Frank was expecting.

"Well, it was more a question of not being able to stop it, or not easily, anyway. I've only gotten this from a book we have back in Grantville, you understand, that was made up of translations of all the papers about Galileo's trial that survived to the twentieth century, plus a book about Galileo's daughter. And, I have to confess, I last read up on the whole thing a while before I went to Grantville because I did a stint as a university chaplain and I got into arguments with scientists about it." Mazzare chuckled. "Actually, I used to really annoy them by pointing out that Galileo got caught by politics, and it was Protestants who suppressed the work of Copernicus and Kepler purely on the strength of it being contrary to Scripture."

"Who and who?" Frank asked.

"Oh, Copernicus was the Catholic priest who first discovered that the Earth orbits the sun, and Kepler was the one who figured out the laws of orbital mechanics. He died only a few years ago, as it happens. But I'm wandering off the point again."

"You say Galileo got caught by politics?"

"Yes. I said before that everyone thinks of it as a plucky scientist battling against the medieval darkness, but it's not that simple. To start with, as I said, Galileo used to be friends with the pope."

Frank heard where Mazzare put the stress on the words, and took his cue. "Used to be?"

Mazzare grinned. "Right up to when Galileo called the pope a simpleton in print."

Frank couldn't think of anything to say.

"Oh, not in so many words," Mazzare added, "but he took every opinion the pope ever expressed on the subjects of science and astronomy and put them into the mouth of a character called Simplicio. Now, at his trial—as I recall—he claimed that was supposed to be Simplicius, a philosopher from classical times. Thing is, he wrote it in Italian, and in Italian, Simplicio means . . ." He pointed to Frank.

"Simpleton. So the pope's really ticked off, huh?"

Mazzare wiggled his hand back and forth. "Hard to know, really. Urban VIII is a very sophisticated man, by all accounts. Not the type to fly into a rage over a minor personal insult—especially since he could, after all, choose to accept Galileo's excuse. Anyway, just to make his own life more interesting, Galileo published his book in Italian, like I say. So he couldn't claim that he was trying to start a learned debate, he'd written for the popular market. Even so, if he could have proven it, he'd have been fine. After all, if nature says one thing and the Church's teaching says another, the Church's teaching has to be wrong and the teaching has to be changed, right?"

"They can do that?" Frank asked.

"We can and we do, Frank. The thing is, a couple of places in the Bible, it talks about the sun going around the Earth. Now, you can read that as a description of what really is going on, or you can read it as the guy who wrote the words down saying what it looked like."

"And the Church is saying that's what it really is, right?" Frank was following the logic, now.

"That's about the size of it. And Galileo couldn't prove otherwise, you see. Part of that was that the astronomer who had the best evidence for the theory he was trying to prove was one of the many people Galileo had annoyed over the years. In fact, he'd denounced the evidence as fraudulent."

"What was it?" Frank was actually getting really interested, now.

"It was a comet, as I recall. Scheiner, who's in Rome right now, or it might have been Grassi, another of the Church's astronomers, I can't remember—"

"The Church has astronomers?"

"Sure. Most of the leading astronomers in this day and age are actually Catholic priests. Did you run into Father Kircher at the high school?"

"*He's* an astronomer?"

"Among other things, yes. He does just about everything; a very bright man. But as I say, there are these two Church astronomers who've got the evidence that goes a long way to prove what Galileo was saying."

"Then why don't they, I mean why didn't they come forward with it? Didn't they want to get accused of heresy too?"

Mazzare laughed. "This is why I said it was more complicated than everyone thinks. They published it, years ago. And Galileo called them both frauds. Galileo thinks comets are optical illusions in the upper atmosphere."

"He thinks what?" That didn't sound like the Galileo he'd heard about.

"Oh, yes. A lot of Galileo's 'science' was off-base. He came up with a wrong explanation for the tides, too. To make things worse, he's a notorious intellectual bully who rarely sees the need for common politeness. Take Scheiner and Grassi: he called one of them a drunk and the other one a plagiarist. Which is why they, between them, reported Galileo to the Inquisition when he published his last book. In which, as I say, he called the pope a simpleton."

Frank mulled over that for a moment. "Can't we send

some astronomy textbooks to Rome, or something? If Galileo can prove it, he gets off, right?"

"Well, again it's not that simple. You know who Galileo works for?"

"I thought he was just, well, a scientist."

"He is, but he has to have a patron to keep him in eating money. There aren't universities with tenure in this day and age, so he gets paid by the Medici family. Now, that means that the Spanish, who as it happens own about half of Italy, are his enemy in order to get at the Medici, who just happen to own one of the bits of Italy that the Spanish want but don't have. Now, I'm simplifying this a whole lot, but basically the pope has a lot of pressure on him to throw Galileo to the wolves to do the Medicis a bad turn. Even so, in our old timeline, the pope stacked the trial as much as he could, and it was his nephew, Cardinal Barberini—"

"Hold on," said Frank, shaking his head with confusion. "I thought you said the pope was Cardinal Barberini?"

"He was, before he became pope. Cardinal Maffeo Barberini, he was then. And his brother's a Cardinal Barberini as well, and both of his nephews are Cardinals Barberini."

"Doesn't that get confusing?"

"Very," said Mazzare, deadpan, and then broke into a chuckle. "We shouldn't laugh, of course. His Holiness had a terrible crisis of conscience over his nepotism later in life, even though it's the way things are done nowadays."

"Right, so one of the Barberini nephews got Galileo a plea bargain?"

"That's right. He admitted that what he'd done gave the appearance of heresy."

"So what did they do to him if they didn't burn him at the stake?"

"Made him promise not to do it again, and sent him home with orders to stay there. He wrote a couple more books after that, and was a lot more careful not to insult anyone." Mazzare sighed again. "It was still a fairly embarrassing business all round, of course, even if the ban on his book never really got enforced outside Italy and was revoked later anyway. I'd like to think that the fact that they're waiting a lot longer to put him on trial than they did in the old history means that someone in Rome is thinking a lot harder about all these issues."

"Isn't there anything we can do? It doesn't seem right, him being in jail. Especially because he's an old man by now. I know that much."

"I don't honestly know what we can do, Frank. I've got a job to do here in Venice, and I wouldn't want to go meddling in a situation I don't fully understand. And no, he's not in jail just now, if they're doing it the same way they did in our history. They've just banned any more sales of his book and ordered him to stay home pending his trial."

"He's *not* in jail?" Again, things Frank had thought about the Inquisition were turning out not to be true. He'd had a firm image of old Galileo shackled with chains in a dungeon somewhere.

"No. I mean, don't get me wrong, the Inquisition's a blight on the Church and does a great deal that is, by any standard, wrong, but they're not complete barbarians. Galileo got very mild, very respectful treatment from them. Apart, that is, from being made to stand trial and having one of his books banned. But he wasn't ever imprisoned or tortured, and he certainly wasn't ever treated with any physical harshness."

"Um." Frank was wondering how he was going to put this over with the guys. And especially with the Committee. He could just see Antonio Marcoli's reaction to him passing on apologies for the Inquisition and then asking for a date with his daughter.

On the bright side, on the other hand, if worse came to worst . . .

Springing him from house arrest might not be so bad. It's gotta beat fighting your way into a dungeon.

Mazzare interrupted the formation of a truly horrible image. Frank Stone, expiring on a pike in the bowels of a castle, his last sight the slime oozing down the damp stone walls . . . a skeleton nearby still sagging from the chains . . .

"Speaking of the job I have to do in Venice, Frank, the day after tomorrow there's a formal reception for us at the Palazzo Ducale. I was going to suggest to your father that you and your brothers come along. Would you be interested in that? I don't want to drag you along for something you don't want to go to, but you might find it interesting, and certainly educational, to see high Venetian society in action. The palazzo is a sight to see, as well, and going to an event like this is about the only way you'll see it, since they don't do public tours yet."

Suddenly Frank was presented with something he understood with perfect clarity. Before his eyes flashed a clear and perfect vision of him escorting Giovanna into a roomful of nobility, of her turning to him and expressing her admiration for how suave and debonair he was, and the rarified circles he moved in, and—

"Can I bring a date?" he blurted out.

Mazzare burst out laughing. "By all means, Frank. When you said you didn't have girl troubles, you weren't kidding, were you? How long have we been in this town? Three days?" He shook his head. "Seriously, Frank, check with your father first. And, I know this is a cliché, but whoever she is, don't do anything I wouldn't approve of, all right?"

Frank nodded, dumbstruck for a moment. He hadn't meant to check with a Catholic priest if it was okay to advance his love life—what had he been thinking of? Still, Father Mazzare seemed to be okay with it.

Mazzare went on: "And keep in mind that you can have worse troubles—a lot worse—than gaining my disapproval. In this day and age they don't just get annoyed about teenage tomfoolery. If she's got brothers or a father, they might actually come and kill you. Or hire it done, if they're rich. In fact, you make sure you check with her father first, all right? I don't want to have to get you on a fast horse out of town."

"Uh. Okay," said Frank. That actually made sense, now he thought about it. "I'll, uh, go find my dad, and, uh, make arrangements. Thanks for the, uh, you know."

"It was my pleasure, Frank." Mazzare smiled.

Frank left before he embarrassed himself any further.

Some hours later, Frank stepped out of the Casa Marcoli into the watery sunlight of a Venetian spring evening and heaved a sigh of relief. Discovering that he was shaking, he leaned against a pillar and tried hard not to throw up.

And then he remembered what he had just done, and whooped for joy. "Yes! He shoots, he scooooores!" he yelled, punching the air and drawing slightly alarmed stares from people in passing boats.

"I gather it went well, then?" Ron called up from the gondola they'd hired to get over. Frank had brought Ron for moral support. He'd not brought Gerry, on account of Gerry being more than likely to try something to spoil his chances. A *kick me* sign on his back would be the least of it, with Gerry.

"Oh, I reckon so," said Frank. He swaggered down the steps to the water.

"You actually got a date, then?" Ron helped Frank into the boat. "I admit, I'm impressed."

Frank grinned. "She said yes! And her daddy said yes, too!" He punched the air again, and drummed his heels on the bottom of the boat in delight.

"You got to bring a chaperone?"

"Nope, Messer Marcoli says he trusts me. Fellow

revolutionist, and all. He also thinks it's a great idea I should take his daughter into a reception full of nobs and such because it strikes a blow against medieval privilege."

Ron laughed aloud as the gondolier poled them into the stream of traffic. "He actually said all that? How big a pack of lies did you tell him anyway?"

"Enough, Elrond," Frank said. "I assured him my intentions were entirely honorable. Um. Which they are, actually, and not just because the assorted Marcoli brothers and cousins have me outnumbered and her father's downright scary. I promised I'd bring her straight home."

"Sure, with maybe a detour on the way?" Ron sniggered.

"Jesus, Ron, you think I want to get killed? Besides, I think this is the real deal. Got to do it right, you know?"

"You said that about Missy. And Gudrun. And—"

"This time it is," Frank said sternly. "And you are, I kid you not, dead meat if you mention any of that to Giovanna, understand?"

"Scout's honor," Ron said, raising his right hand.

"You weren't ever a scout, and that's the Vulcan live-long-and-prosper sign anyway," Frank pointed out.

"Same difference." Ron shrugged. "Besides, enlightened self-interest. I may need your silence about *my* past one day."

"Point." Frank leaned back on the gondola seat. He took a deep, satisfied breath and sighed it out.

In Germany, winter still had its grip on the land. But Venice in March was Venice in spring.

Venice was truly, truly beautiful in the springtime. Even the stink of the canals seemed pleasant.

Chapter 16

There were advantages, Cardinal Bedmar reflected, to being *persona non grata* in Venice. Sourly, he studied the mob packed into the doge's palace. At least he'd been spared *this* unpleasantness since his arrival from the Spanish Netherlands a few weeks earlier. This was the first time he'd been invited to participate in one of the Venetians' beloved gala events, as one of the fish crammed into the barrel.

And why had he been invited at all? he wondered. Probably just because the Venetians enjoyed rubbing his nose in the fact that the ambassador from the infant "United States of Europe" enjoyed more status here than one of the representatives from the ancient and glorious Spanish Empire.

"My feet hurt," the cardinal announced.

"Yes, Your Eminence."

"And my back hurts," he went on.

"Yes, Your Eminence."

"And with all this insincere smiling, Sanchez, my God-damned face hurts."

Sanchez shifted from one foot to the other, a slight wince creasing his face. "Your Eminence bears his suffering well."

"Ruy Sanchez de Casador y Ortiz, did I not know you better I would swear you were being sarcastic." Cardinal Bedmar spoke the words in the low undertone that all diplomats learned for functions like the one they were attending, his face hardly moving from its practiced smile.

"Oh, no," Sanchez drawled, likewise. "For that would be a heretical proposition of disrespect to a prince of the Church, rather than simply suggesting—as one old man to another—that Your Eminence is not the only one who is too old for this."

Sanchez, like the cardinal himself, was two-faced in the service of his country. In theory, a cardinal's *gentiluomo* like Sanchez was simply his master's close-protection man, the last line of defense for a prince of the Church and the bearer of a sword where a cleric ought not to wield one in his own person. In practice, Sanchez ran errands for his master the one-time diplomat.

Sometimes downright odd errands, those were. There had been few enough of them, though, in past years. Bedmar had been in near-retirement on the Council of Flanders, and until the year before Flanders had been quiet. As quiet, at least, as the nearby presence of the pestiferous Protestants in the United Provinces allowed. But all that had changed since the arrival of the Americans in what had come to be known as "the Ring of Fire." Now these bizarre people said to come from the future and their Swedish ally had kicked over the ant-heap in Germany.

On the positive side, most of the Netherlands was back in Spanish hands since the Dutch fleet had been destroyed through treachery and Cardinal-Infante Don Fernando had led a daring seizure of Haarlem. There were new men all over the place, in the Spanish Netherlands, brought by the cardinal-infante. The old warhorse Cardinal Bedmar had been sent back to Venice after fifteen years away. Some genius had decided he was the man to come in and foil whatever plot the Americans were working toward here, despite Bedmar's notoriety in the Serene Republic.

And so, tonight, Bedmar and his trusted assistant Sanchez were in the Sala di Gran Consiglio of the doge's palace, paying more attention to the magnificent Tintoretto paintings on the walls and ceiling than any of the pomp and flummery the Venetians loved so much. Bedmar had spent the evening so far smiling at people whom he had, fifteen years earlier, tried to have killed, ruined, or subordinated to foreign conquest.

That was from the Venetian point of view, of course. From Bedmar's own perspective, it had been a great adventure in the service of his country, widening the empire and taking back some of what the Venetians had leeched from Spain one way or another over the years. Their defiance, captiousness, decadence, whoring and irreligion were a byword across Europe, and there were better uses for the wealth and strategic position of the great city.

But . . . it had ended in humiliation. For some reason these decadent, coin-counting Italians did not want a change of regime at the hands of the greatest power in Europe. The Venetians had caught every one of Bedmar's Venetian partisans. Labeled them "traitors," no less; then, hung them after breaking their legs in the time-honored Venetian tradition. There had been ugly scenes with mobs of Arsenalotti on the day Bedmar had left the Most Serene Republic in a not-very-serene hurry.

A week after that scramble of a day, though, a couple of Imperial ambassadors had been thrown out of a window in the now-famous "defenestration of Prague." Bohemia had risen in revolt under a Protestant king and everyone had forgotten about Italy and what Bedmar had done in Venice—until de Nevers and his claim to Mantua gave everyone another pretext for mayhem in the interest of extending influence in the Italies. That had only just finished when the Americans turned up, but things had now settled down over the border in Mantua. The troops had gone elsewhere, as well, and Italy looked like a relatively safe place for the first time in fifteen years.

Which meant that it wanted nothing but that someone should turn out singly and severally to make trouble. Bedmar wasn't objecting, really. Winter in Flanders was cold and ugly on his old bones; Venice was a good place to be until summer. In the meantime, he would achieve all he could—which was probably nothing. No one trusted him in this town, and never would. He would simply dump a good deal of money in Venice, report failure, and leave with the coming winter chill.

The cardinal thought that old Count Gondomar, back when he was still alive and Spain's ambassador to England, had been righter than he knew when he wrote his famous complaint before the war. He had written of the energy of the newly rising nations, especially the England whose ruin he had conspicuously failed to bring about, and of the waxing commercial power of the Dutch. By contrast, he had said, Spain was buying doubtful loyalties with the better part of every New World treasure fleet.

Bedmar had agreed with him but, alas, the king of Spain had not. Philip IV and his chief minister the Count-Duke of Olivares had opted for a different solution: *war*. If Spain was losing the peace, why, then, the truce was about to expire. Spain was apparently to rediscover her glory at the end of a pike.

The cardinal had been skeptical at the time, and the ensuing fifteen years of what future historians were said to call "the Thirty Years' War" had borne him out. The war had simply continued Spain's slide from the top of the pile, and added a mountain of dead and put half of Europe into near-anarchy to compound everyone's problems.

And here, once again, Bedmar was sent to disburse

another portion of the last treasure fleet on loyalties that were not even strong enough to be called doubtful. The chances were good that all Bedmar would do would be to fund a few petty enemies.

He sighed. Spain would gain nothing here except perhaps a close look at a few more Americans than had been seen outside their new United States to date. And even that was late. The Venetians might be able to run a State Inquisition able to shut down a well-funded fifth column run by a professional spymaster, but they didn't seem to be able to make a convivial drinks reception run on time. At that, Bedmar couldn't fault their sense of priorities.

The majordomo was announcing something. "Did you hear that, Sanchez?" he asked, nudging his gentiluomo.

"Yes, Your Eminence," said Sanchez.

Bedmar turned to glare at him. The Catalan *gentiluomo*'s sense of humor had irritated him for years. Why he put up with the hard-bitten old fool was a mystery to the cardinal. Probably because that same sense of humor amused him also. Most of the time.

Sanchez's mustaches twitched a little. "It is the American ambassador, Your Eminence. He just arrived."

The Sala di Gran Consiglio, the doge's main council chamber, was a working debating-hall without the kind of elevated entrance that permitted guests already arrived to see who was coming in, so they had to wait. In fact, the only raised part of the room was the presiding dais at one end, where the doge was stationed with his retinue of Senators. The middle of the floor was open to allow the new arrivals to parade up to greet the doge. As they passed, Sanchez was all business.

"The priest in front, Your Eminence, is Lawrence Mazzare, the ambassador from the United States of Europe. He speaks for their President—no, he's called the prime minister now—Michael Stearns. The fat priest with him is his curate and factotum, the Jesuit I told

you of, Heinzerling. The other is Mazzare's second in
the embassy, a Protestant cleric by the name of Jones.
Behind them is the alchemist Stone and his wife. The
young Moor is the daughter of the doctor, Nichols;
she was also betrothed to the hero of the battle at
Wismar last autumn. The one named Richter, who
was killed."

Sanchez's voice grew a little distant as he spoke of
the black woman. She was definitely worth looking at,
although Bedmar didn't think she merited quite the
stare that Sanchez, the old goat, was giving her.

Bedmar tried to drag his man back to the matter at hand. "I wonder how Stone will go down," he
murmured, "since everyone is expecting the purest
of rational natural philosophy from these Americans."
Back home, there had been calls for the Inquisition to
deal with alchemists as heretics or, at the very least,
peddlers of superstition. The Inquisition, for the most
part, insisted that fraud was a matter for the secular
courts, although from time to time they proceeded
against the more egregious examples.

"I wonder, too," Sanchez said, his mind still on the
job despite evident distraction, "although I hear stories
that this Stone makes it work."

"Really? And who is this behind, now?" That was
a sight, if anything, even more remarkable than the
prospect of base metal into gold. Well, not anywhere
else in Venice, but here in the Gran Consiglio it was
a bit much.

"These, I think, are Stone's sons. One of them—the
eldest, it would look like—is accompanied by, ah—"

"Quite," Bedmar said. "And such a young and pretty
one, too. I think we might have to be tactful about
that." One of the American boys was accompanied
by a young woman. A Venetian, obviously—and just
as obviously a courtesan, even if she wasn't wearing
the red shoes of her vocation and was pretending to
be otherwise. Nobody else at such an event would be

that young, that good-looking, and that awkward in her bearing and poise. A new courtesan, clearly, unsure of herself in high company. She wasn't even wearing a mask—not even a half-mask. Judging from the stares she was getting, she was completely unknown to the crowd.

That might cause a bit of a scandal. Not her status, but the attempt at disguising it. Several of the younger minor notables of Venice present at the reception were accompanied by courtesans, and no one was taking any real note of it. The Serene Republic was notorious for its moral laxity. On the other hand, all the other courtesans Bedmar could see were wearing the red shoes required by custom. Sin, Venetians tolerated; attempting to rise above one's station was another matter.

"The rest I don't know, Your Eminence," Sanchez was saying. He had moved behind Bedmar now and was murmuring over his shoulder. Around the room, other diplomats were being briefed in like manner. "The stocky soldier is the head of their embassy guard, I think. A Scotsman named Lennox. Until last year he was a cavalryman in the Swede's army."

"Guard?" Bedmar murmured back, as the implications suddenly assembled themselves in his mind. It was vanishingly rare that an ambassador had a formal guard while attending a foreign prince. A small crew of professional soldiers, perhaps, to protect him en route and keep the embassy safe from burglars and such. But a formal liveried guard was either outrageous ostentation or very pointed distrust.

Alas, Spanish intelligence in Venice was at best mediocre since the unfortunate business fifteen years before. It didn't help matters any that the regular ambassador from Madrid was a dim-witted and fussy man, who'd made it quite clear that he resented Bedmar's arrival here as a "special ambassador from the Spanish Netherlands" and had refused to be cooperative beyond the bare minimum required by protocol.

Bedmar would have given a very great deal indeed to get a reliable account of the negotiations that had let that burly Scot soldier into Venice as a formal guard for the American embassy.

Part of it was probably genuine concern, Bedmar conceded, as he contemplated the possibility of protesting to the doge at this unseemly favoritism. After all, the diplomatic mission from the United States to England was immured in the Tower of London, and another was trapped by the cardinal-infante's Spanish army in the siege of Amsterdam. Not to mention that, by now, all Europe had heard the rumors of how Richelieu had attempted to have that embassy ambushed on their way from Paris to The Hague—an embassy led by the very wife of the U.S. President, to boot.

Richelieu hadn't admitted a thing, of course, nor would he ever. But anyone who did not believe that those pirates had attacked Rebecca Abrabanel's ship on French orders was either a purblind idiot or believed that the indefatigable propaganda mills of the Protestant Germanies were lying. Again.

Bedmar watched with interest as the priest Mazzare formally presented his credentials to the doge. It was, as always in Venice, a highly stylized business: the credentials handed over in a fat leather wallet fringed with all manner of tassels and pendant seals. The formal words were spoken aloud, and then a few words of mutual esteem and friendship.

Not many, though. That was either a good sign or a bad one. If they meant to let it all keep for a serious bargaining session upstairs on the morrow, then it was good for the Americans. If the doge was actually treating Mazzare the way he had treated Spain's ambassador extraordinary . . .

Ha! Bedmar had had to hand over his own credentials in private after a four-flight climb up the Scala d'Oro, and the doge had all but cut him, he had been that curt.

But, no, he saw that the doge was smiling. For a wonder, the Consiglio had permitted him that much expression. True, Don Erizzo, the current doge, was rumored to be a ferocious character next to the usual run of Venetian dukes. So perhaps his "advisers" were a bit intimidated by him. Whatever, it looked good for the United States, this week in Venice.

The Spanish cardinal cared little, either way. He was an old and tired man sent here on a mission he considered barely short of insane. What could the count-duke of Olivares have been thinking, to select Bedmar for this mission? One would almost think the boot-faced bastard meant for it to be a failure, and was simply relying on Bedmar to come out of it with as little humiliation as possible.

On the other hand . . .

From long habit, Bedmar considered all the possibilities. As the chief minister of the king of Spain, Olivares had a finger in every pot—which meant he could get his fingers easily burned. There was that interesting circle who had started gathering around the king's younger brother, the cardinal-infante Don Fernando. Most people saw only the martial glory covering the young prince, since his dazzling success in the Netherlands after so many decades of Spanish frustration. In a few short weeks, the cardinal-infante had accomplished what neither the duke of Alva nor Spinola had managed—driven the stubborn Dutchmen to their knees, if not yet to outright surrender.

But the cardinal was starting to wonder. For all his youth—Don Fernando was still in his early twenties— Bedmar was beginning to think he might be playing a very deep game and trying some remarkably complicated steps in the diplomatic gavotte. Bedmar knew that the cardinal-infante had at least two men in his circle—quite close, as well—who were running on very, very long leashes indeed. Bedmar had been asked, by way of several hints so oblique as to make the usual finaglings of protocol look like a barrage of siege artillery, to open up friendly overtures with the Americans on the tenuous authority of Spanish Flanders. Acting on those requests was technically a betrayal of Bedmar's official principal, who was, after all, the king of Spain, not the prince of the Netherlands. On the other hand, his official principal appeared not to care what happened in Venice. Indeed—

"Your Eminence?" Sanchez was nudging him.

It was good that he had. In his reverie, Bedmar had turned his eyes to the marvelous coronation of the virgin that adorned the wall above and behind the doge. Thus he had not noticed that Mazzare had come, in the proper order of protocol, to the extraordinary ambassador from the Spanish Netherlands. Purely out of spite, the Venetians had declined to recall Bedmar's last sojourn as ambassador in Venice and so put him considerably farther from the doyenne—some English coin-counter—than he truly merited. Another point on which his mere presence was helping the Americans, he realized. Any nation that defied Spain and the House of Habsburg was sure of a warm reception from Venice.

The cardinal understood the dynamics of power extremely well. The Venetians had gotten cold comfort from France since the Mantuan War and had been at near war with the Turk these hundred years past. Their best option was the United States of Europe, which was powerful enough to be a worthwhile ally against Spain and the Habsburgs where England—still more distant, always penurious, and of late in turmoil—most certainly was not.

Bedmar stepped forward, noting the carefully blank face of the American priest. "Monsignor," he said, feeling that the man deserved at least that much. Mazzare had risen from parish pastor to, Bedmar estimated, ambassador from the third most powerful nation in Europe to perhaps the fourth or fifth richest. Bedmar extended his hand with its ring of office.

A test, there. Mazzare took it and kissed the ring in the proper manner, betraying the work of a far better tutor in protocol than most parish priests ever ran into.

"Your Eminence does me much honor," Mazzare said, resorting to Veneziano, the local dialect of Italian. That wasn't protocol. The meaning—yes, to meet on neutral ground. Bedmar raised his estimate of the American a notch or two. It had been high enough to begin with, of course. Few were trusted in his position that were not at least confident and competent.

"And how does monsignor find Venice?" Bedmar decided that he would confine himself to the pleasantries. Should Mazzare wish to try a more aggressive approach, he would presumably not do it in front of witnesses.

"Venice is a beautiful city, and I hope to do a great deal of business here."

Oh, so it was that way, was it? At least Bedmar hoped so, although he realized it was perhaps some American quirk that made such a blatant ploy into a mere pleasantry. They were a new folk to him.

"Business?" he asked pleasantly.

"Oh, yes," Mazzare replied, smiling gently with his two aides behind him.

A peculiar arrangement, that. A Catholic ambassador, with a Jesuit and a Protestant as his assistants.

After a moment, Mazzare broke the brief silence. "Many people have expressed an interest in doing business with us, Your Eminence. All save Seigneur le Comte d'Avaux, who gave us his back publicly."

Bedmar had wondered what the murmur had been a few moments before. He had assumed that—no, he had been distracted by the art on the walls and his musings about the situation in Flanders.

Mazzare's words finally registered fully. "Ha!" he barked, amused. Then, cursing himself—getting too damned old!—he got a grip on his momentary lapse and shut his face down while his mind worked. "What was the oily little French toad thinking, to play his hand so publicly and so soon?"

"I had expected some coldness," Mazzare said; wryly now, apparently disarmed by Bedmar's own forthrightness, "with our nations at war. This was more than I thought we might see. The gentleman from England was pleasant, though, and invited us to meet some merchant friends of his. Your own ambassador was courteous, and looked forward to talking with us—"

Bedmar had leapt to a conclusion while Mazzare talked. "Monsignor," he said, interrupting, "disregard that last. My countryman, the permanent ambassador here, Count de Rocca, is a puffed-up fool. He comes directly from Spain and will tell you what he is told to tell you. From me, on the other hand—freshly arrived from the Low Countries, where reality stands in sharp contrast to fantasy—you will get plain speaking. So let me offer my personal hand in friendship, and say that there will be straight dealing between us, as between honorable enemies. We may each of us find nothing to agree on, but it will be fairly haggled for. Like you, I am from a small town. I know what it is to see the women barter in the market-place—" a slight look of bemusement crossed the American's face at that, and Bedmar wondered briefly why "—and perhaps you do, too. Let us be, at least civil; and perhaps reach an understanding as priests, if it can be reached. There will come a time when a larger deal might be done, but let us not force the matter, no?"

Bedmar noted that Mazzare had set his face perfectly for the enlargement and the restriction of what he had said. A professional, then, or at least a gifted amateur.

"Your Eminence, I look forward to it." Mazzare nodded graciously and began to move along.

A moment of mischief filled the cardinal. "By the way," he said, bringing Mazzare back in the very act of turning away, "the young caballero with your party, he moves quickly, no?"

Mazzare's frown of confusion was mild. "Your Eminence?"

"Oh, even in Venice a young man must work a bit to find a courtesan—and such a young and pretty one, too."

The frown deepened. "Your Eminence, I hardly think this is the time or place to cast aspersions—"

"Aspersions, Monsignor? It's quite obvious, despite the woman's improper shoes." Bedmar chuckled, to show he meant no ill-will. "The Venetians may complain about that, you know. They don't mind courtesans here—celebrate them, in fact—but they do insist on the formalities."

Mazzare's face settled into a placid expression. "I thank Your Eminence, for bringing the matter to my attention. You may be assured that it will receive a thorough investigation."

"Shocked, Monsignor? And here I was believing the tales that Grantville was a whole town filled with scantily clad immoral women." Bedmar chuckled. "I am from too rural a town to give much credence to stuffy Venetian notions of proper dress, Monsignor. Lot of hypocrites, they are. But if you have the cure of the boy's soul, Monsignor, you must think on whether fornication between the unmarried is any sin at all or whether, well, boys will be boys, hey?"

It was all Bedmar could do to keep his face straight. Fortunately, he was helped by the arrival of a new party, which distracted Mazzare momentarily. The alchemist was coming along the receiving line in the company of his wife.

"Señor Stone," Bedmar beamed. "A pleasure to make your acquaintance!"

"Thank you, uh . . ." The alchemist looked slightly dazed. Doubtless fumes from some working or other. His wife stood up on tiptoe and whispered into the place where, presumably, an ear was hidden amid shaggy wolf-gray hair. "Your Eminence," Stone finished.

"I have heard that you have divined the secrets of alchemy?"

Another surprised and startled look. "Uh, no. Ah, that is, Your Eminence, alchemy is what they do in this time, and it doesn't work. Chemistry—"

Stone gave the last word a careful and exaggerated pronunciation. As it was a new word, Bedmar surmised that he got asked to repeat it a lot.

"—is what we do in the twentieth century, and it does work. I make dyes, and stains, and paints and medicines, and we may make some other things. Soon. Yes, soon."

He looked uncertainly at his wife, and at Mazzare, as if unsure what he could say and not say.

Bedmar rescued him, or at least pretended to for the sake of a jest he was now thoroughly enjoying. "Dye, eh?" he said. "A coincidence you should mention the color of things. Shoes can be dyed too, of course. It was a matter I raised with the monsignor here, some moments ago. Yes, quite a coincidence."

Mazzare's look in return was pure poison for the moment it took him to get his face under control, a chink in the armor through which Bedmar could see that Mazzare cared for his ambassadorial party. A weakness, perhaps, but one that showed he was a man with whom business could be done. As for the poisonous look, Bedmar thought a man who played the game of princes would do well to be prepared for an occasional unorthodox step in the dance. A mixed metaphor that Sanchez, who had some pretensions to poetry, would wince at.

"Your Eminence," Mazzare said after a long, awkward moment. "It appears we are holding up the receiving line, much though I would like to continue this fascinating conversation. Perhaps later?"

"Yes, perhaps later."

Chapter 17

When the American ambassador had moved on and the lesser lights in their train had passed also, Bedmar turned to Sanchez. "Not bad, for his first time."

"Oh?" Sanchez returned from whatever internal fugue he had been pursuing to save himself from tedium.

"The American priest. There might almost be a diplomat made of him, if he survives this town." Bedmar nodded to himself. The people from the future bore watching, whatever the rest of the hierarchy might say—which was decidedly mixed—if Mazzare was any guide.

"And if he survives your attentions, Your Eminence." Sanchez grinned through his mustaches. "That business over the shoes was a trifle unnecessary, I thought."

"Oh, Sanchez," Bedmar said, "do permit a tired old man his fun."

Sanchez chuckled. "Oh, I will, if he will permit me mine. Did you see the Moorish one?"

Bedmar nodded, although with some reservation. "Looked more like an Ethiope to me."

"You know what I mean. What they all call a Moor here in the Italies that hardly ever see one."

Sanchez's eyes seemed, to Bedmar, to be getting a little dreamy. The man was incorrigible. The old Catalan goat had buried three wives that Bedmar knew about. And while he had been faithful to all of them, so far as the cardinal was aware, he had something of a notorious reputation during those periods he was unmarried. Even now, at his age!

Bedmar reminded himself, on the other hand, that it was that same vigor which made Sanchez such a useful man to have around. Not to mention a comfort, of a certain specific and necessary sort, in the event of dire necessity. Even now, somewhere in his late fifties—no one, including Sanchez, knew the precise year of his birth—only a fool or someone inexperienced in such matters challenged the Catalan lightly. Wives were but a small portion of the people Ruy Sanchez had seen lowered into graves. The chief distinction enjoyed by the wives was that Sanchez had not put them there.

Still, there were times the man annoyed Bedmar. If for no other reason than the many aches and pains from which the cardinal's body now suffered. Sanchez was but a few years younger than he, yet the Catalan still moved with the ease and grace of a man in his thirties.

"Dark meat, Sanchez?" Bedmar asked nastily. "Where did you learn that taste?"

Sanchez gave him a sidelong, blank gaze that would have chilled the cardinal, had he been any other man. Belatedly, Bedmar remembered that the first of the Catalan's wives, won and lost during his youth in New Spain, had been an Indian woman of some sort. He'd also heard that one of the bodies resting in a grave somewhere—Cordoba, he thought, if he remembered the story correctly—was that of a man who had sneered at Sanchez for the fact.

"My apologies," the cardinal murmured. "That was uncalled for."

Sanchez harumphed, clearing the matter aside. Then,

smiled slightly. "Tell me, Your Eminence . . . would it matter if I learned it here tonight?"

Bedmar was still feeling a bit testy. "It would indeed matter, Sanchez, if it turned out you did something foolish to compromise our—" He stopped.

"Ah, Your Eminence has perhaps seen the difficulty with that notion?"

Sanchez trying to be arch was laughable. Bedmar knew for a fact that the man's alleged nobility was an arrant pretense. Sanchez had no less than seven certificates of *limpieza*, not a one of them saying the same thing as the others. A gentleman Sanchez might be reckoned today, but sometimes the Catalan peasant-soldier just shone through.

Bless his iron little heart. Two of those corpses rotting in graves—two, that the cardinal knew of—had tried to kill Bedmar himself.

"No, no." Bedmar waved an admonitory finger. "Am I not a diplomat? A prince of the Church? A man of learning?"

Sanchez snorted. "You are the man I had to get out of this town one step ahead of a mob of angry Arsenalotti. And it was not the step of a man with long legs, I might add." He looked down on his cardinal. Bedmar's short stature next to, well, just about anyone was a running joke between them.

"Hush, you Catalan dullard. Where such as you see only problems, I see only solutions."

Bedmar paused a moment, assessing Sanchez, assessing what little he had yet gleaned of American manners. A foolish scheme, of course—hardly worth calling a scheme at all. But then, there was hardly anything for it but foolish schemes, with the ridiculous mission he had.

A decision. "Yes, Sanchez, pursue your Moor, your Ethiope, your whatever. It may prove helpful."

Sanchez's eyes narrowed. "Prince of the Church or not, Your Eminence, you will not command me to . . ."

Bedmar waited until Sanchez trailed off. "Now, Sanchez, let us not leap to conclusions. We have done much together, you and I, but have I ever asked you to betray the confidence of a lady? Even a Morisco?"

"And how do you know she is not a Christian?" Sanchez was—no, not joking at all. Interesting. The man was usually levity itself, but now he seemed to be on the edge of a frosty pique.

Bedmar sighed. "Be quick, Sanchez. I will tear you away from her soon enough tonight, whatever she may be—and however receptive. My feet still hurt, my back aches, every Venetian here will cut me as if his life depended on it and no one else has any cause to speak with me."

"As you wish, Your Eminence." Sanchez stroked his mustachios and moved off. The cardinal watched him go for a moment.

Irritating, sometimes, truly irritating. How did a man of his years still manage to swagger?

Buckley stamped his feet. It might be spring in Venice, but that didn't mean the warm sunshine of the afternoons stayed on the Piazza San Marco past sundown. It was probably all right if you were moving about, but Joe had picked a shady spot under the Imbroglio to wait for the evening's action.

Well, some of that had been and gone, of course. He hadn't expected to be let in, and had really only tried to insinuate himself for the sheer hell of declaiming, in a loud voice, "Do you know who I am?"

The ducal retainers at the door—bouncers, in any other context—had given him their best sneers and inquired, oh-so-politely, who exactly he was? He had to give them credit for that. He'd told them, in a rather more reasonable tone of voice, and they in their turn had told him that his name wasn't down and he wasn't coming in. Or words to that effect: the bouncer's litany was a little different in seventeenth-century Venice.

As far as he could tell, the last of the diplomatic parties had gone in. He'd only stayed out front to check their various arrivals. Shortly, once the evening's festivities settled in, he'd mosey on around the corner to find what, grand though it might be compared to the ordinary run of doors in this town, must be there to serve the doge's palace as a tradesman's entrance. He'd find the back door in to the story he needed. He just, he figured, had to give it a few minutes.

He spent those few minutes wandering around the piazza, taking in the sights. They were worth taking in, actually. Centuries in the future, in another universe, this was the place the tourists always mobbed when they came to Venice. At least, that's what Joe had read in the travel guide to Venice he'd gotten his hands on—he'd never been any farther outside the United States than a trip to Montreal, himself, back before the Ring of Fire.

He didn't spend much time looking at the famous cathedral, the Basilica di San Marco. Buckley wasn't that taken by any kind of old cathedral, especially not one that was as much of an hodgepodge as the Basilica. His tastes in architecture were pretty much like his tastes in writing—Buckley was a newspaperman, not a pretentious literary author. The one time he'd tried to read a novel by William Faulkner—twenty pages' worth—he'd come away convinced that the entire literary establishment were a bunch of lunatics. Worst prose he'd ever seen.

The Campanile was more to his taste. The ancient lighthouse was the tallest structure in the city, and its clean and simple lines appealed to Buckley. If he got a chance, sometime over the summer, he'd see if he could finagle his way into it. The climb would be strenuous, but Buckley was in decent shape and the view from the top of the lighthouse just had to be spectacular.

Then he ambled around the western half of the

piazza. There wasn't really much to see there, though. If he remembered the guide book correctly, a lot of that area would be changed by Napoleon. The French emperor had even demolished a church somewhere in the pile of buildings to build a dancing hall. In this day and age, however, the buildings were just devoted to Venice's elaborate bureaucracy.

Buckley found bureaucratic edifices even more boring than bureaucrats. So, deciding he'd fiddled away enough time, he headed toward the back of the Palazzo Ducale. There had to be a rear entrance somewhere.

Rounding the corner, he saw it—but that entrance was, if anything, as strongly manned as the front door. Right, nothing else for it. He marched up, and hacking out a sentence as best he could in Veneziano Italian, said: "Joe Buckley, Associated Press," and made to march past.

Unlike twentieth-century bouncers, the bouncers in this day and age had big guys with halberds backing them up. More for show than in any expectation of an armed rush of gatecrashers; but in best guard-style, they crossed their halberds over the door, staring straight ahead the while. Buckley could *feel* the liveried footmen he'd just breezed past smirking behind them.

"There is no entry this way, friend," said one of them.

"Aw, come on," Buckley said. "All I need is to get in and see what's going on. Don't you read newspapers?"

"No, Messer Buckley, I don't," the guy said, still smirking.

Buckley became aware that there was a crowd nearby. Time, he decided, to withdraw with as good a grace as he could. "So," he said, "been a busy night, then?"

That earned him a blank stare.

"You see," he went on, into the silence, "I figure guys like you, you get to see who sneaks in to this place without everyone out front seeing, right? Guys like you could probably tell me more about what's going on at a function like this than I could figure out by going inside, yeah?"

He looked hopefully from one to the other. Usually, by this point, they started bragging about luminaries they'd served at whatever banquet the night before. Or better, dishing the dirt on what lousy table manners they had. That was always a good way in to the real juicy stuff.

Not from these guys, though. One nodded to the other, or some sort of signal passed, and then two guards he hadn't seen stepped up smartly, one to each elbow, and he was frog-marched back to the steps down to the street. He ended up hopping down the steps, trying to keep his balance, his hat and his dignity and managing two out of the three.

He snarled a word that had been old-fashioned in his own time but was futuristic here.

"*Americain, monsieur?*" The voice was somber yet light in tone, the diction oddly stilted somehow.

Buckley looked at the fellow who'd detached himself from the crowd that was, basically, lounging about in the street. Tall and narrow and clad in what looked like dark, dark brown. Buckley pegged him as a high-end servant, as these things went.

"Uh, *Francais?*" he asked, diffidently.

"Ah, *oui,*" and the man launched into a gabble of French that Buckley couldn't follow.

"Uh, *plus lentement, s'il vous plait,*" he said, looking hard at the guy. He had a broad-brimmed hat on, shadowing much of his face, but there were guys with torches moving about and Buckley could get glimpses of what lay under the hat. *So that's what hatchet-faced means,* he thought.

The torrent of French slowed, and the volume went up slightly.

Glad it's not just Americans who do that, Buckley thought. He still wasn't following the guy. He had some kind of broad accent that was giving him serious static.

"You got any Italian?" he asked, in that language.

"Why, certainly, Monsieur Buckley."

"You caught my name, huh?"

"Yes, you announced yourself as well as any major-domo might have done that service for you. Permit me to introduce myself." The Frenchman held out a hand. "Michel Ducos. You are with the embassy from Grantville?"

"Pleased to meet you. As to the other, no, I'm not. Well, not really. I'm from Grantville, though."

"Yes. Tell me, are you *that* Joe Buckley?"

"The one and only," Buckley said, smiling broadly. It was always a pleasure to meet a fan.

"I have read some of your writings, you know." It was said almost shyly. "Are you trying to find news of the diplomatic reception?"

"Yes, I am. Are you with the French embassy?"

"I am, indeed. A humble clerk, which is why I must wait outside with the other servants. The Venetians are most strict about such things."

"I noticed. Their people are a lot less talkative than most, too." Buckley waved up at the doorway, where the bouncers had relaxed back into their formation. He noticed that no one else was trying to gatecrash.

"Ah, that is because they are not ordinary servants on these doors. I think it would take an uncommon sort of fellow to get past such as they." Ducos leaned close. "Agents of the State Inquisition," he whispered.

"No kidding?" Buckley said, raising his eyebrows. That was unusual. Not just rent-a-cops on the door, but the genuine article. Secret police, at that. He suddenly had a burning desire to get inside, and a crushing disappointment that he wouldn't.

Still, he might see what he could do here. "The French embassy, you say? A clerk? Tell me, what exactly does a clerk do in an embassy? And why don't we find somewhere out of the cold night air? My treat."

"That does indeed seem like a most convivial suggestion." Ducos beamed. "I warn you, though, I know very few secrets, and I am duty bound not to divulge what paltry things I do know."

Yes, he could salvage something from this evening after all. A clerk would be bound to know a thing or two he could print. Buckley looked around for the nearest taverna.

Chapter 18

As they left the end of the receiving line the Stones came over to Mazzare.

"Father?" said Tom, "Do we, uh, mingle now?"

It was all Mazzare could do not to break into laughter. Tom Stone was wearing a face that said *Beam me up, Scotty*—which completed the remarkable picture he made in the suit he was wearing. After their marriage, Tom's wife Magda had fallen on the purple velvet drapes at Lothlorien, declaring them too good for mere curtains. How she had gotten a jacket and britches out of them was nobody's business but her own, but the tie-dyed vest and canary-yellow shirt made the whole ensemble truly eye-watering.

And . . .

As nothing next to the Venetians. Nearly two months of the year were *Carnevale* to these people, and conspicuous consumption their national religion. Between the cloth-of-gold and other bright colors, the room looked like a mating dance for birds of paradise. Stoner, if anything, blended in fairly well with the other dowdy birds from northern Europe.

If Tom had been used to being the most garishly

dressed individual in any given room, he was going down in purple-velvet flames tonight. "How are you bearing up?" Mazzare asked.

"Oh, fine," Stone said, frowning the question back at Mazzare.

"Fine too," said Mazzare, suddenly slightly embarrassed. "I thought you'd find this sort of thing, oh, I don't know—" He waved a hand in the air, and was startled when a glass of wine was put into it by a passing servant.

Stone snagged a drink for himself. "Formal?" He shrugged. "Sure. But, you know, folks seem friendly enough. And, frankly, once you've negotiated the hierarchies and pecking orders of a typical commune full of anarchists and individualists, this sort of thing—" He snapped his fingers for it, ducal display and noble hauteur and all.

"I suppose it must come as something of a relief to have rules to follow."

Stoner grinned. "Sure, man. Hippies take vacations from disorder in the army. Two weeks of drill and discipline and orders and we're refreshed and ready for another year of letting it all hang out."

Jones had walked up to catch the tail end of the joke. "Speaking of things hanging out, I just got taken aside by one of the Sestieri's men."

"Who?" Stoner asked.

"Henchman of one of the—well, I guess 'town fathers' does as well as any other way to put it. He wanted a word about the boys. Frank, to be precise."

Almost as one, they all looked down toward the bottom of the room where, spared the ordeal of the receiving line, Stone's three sons were surrounded by a crowd of younger folk and were keeping the waiters busy.

"What about the boys?" Magda asked, suspicion in every syllable.

"Ah, well. That, ah, that is to say—" Jones began

to color slightly, realizing that he was speaking to the boys' stepmother.

Stoner began to look worried, and Mazzare realized his own suspicions were building to match Magda's. The comments that Bedmar had passed were falling into place in Mazzare's mind with a certain lubricious inevitability. He narrowed his eyes. "I think you'd better overcome your embarrassment, Simon."

Jones took a deep breath. He was now a fairly fetching shade of pink. "It's like this. You know we asked the boys to come here with us as much to keep them out of mischief as anything else?"

Nods went around. It had, in point of fact, seemed like a good idea at the time. Mazzare could feel those words in the air, just as damning an indictment as ever they had been.

"And, ah, Frank asked if he could bring a date?"

The penny dropping with Magda was almost audible. "*Schweinerei,*" she murmured.

Stone put a hand on his wife's arm. "Now, Magda, let's not leap to conclusions—"

"I am not leaping to conclusions, Thomas," she hissed. "I am making a reasonable inference from the data as reported to me." She glared at him.

Mazzare winced. That one seemed to be common to all marriages he had seen in action. Hanni gave fair warning that she was about to go nuclear with Gus by quoting theology and Scripture at him. Magda used scientific jargon. In a moment of utter whimsy, he wondered if Stoner had learned any classical philosophy to use in his turn when—

He lost the train of thought to what Jones was saying "—but mostly the Venetians seem to be upset because she's not wearing red shoes."

"Red shoes?" Mazzare said, realizing that for a supposed diplomat he was altogether further behind this conversation than he ought to be. "That means—oh."

Magda's expression was a sight to scare children.

"Tom," said Mazzare hastily, in the faint hope of smoothing this over before the mushroom cloud erupted, "will you have a word with Frank? Not so much about embarrassing us a little—"

"Speak for yourself, Larry," Jones cut in, "but I am more than a little embarrassed."

"Quite. Tom, I think we may have a problem here. We just brought three country boys and turned them loose in a city which is famous for its, ah—"

Magda muttered a very old-fashioned word in German.

"I was going to say courtesans, actually," Mazzare said firmly. Not only had he heard what Magda had called the girl in question, but he'd also heard it used of women who'd been perfectly respectable before, and gone on to be perfectly respectable after they'd played out the bad hand of cards they'd been dealt. Clear moral categorizations were double-edged things, in his view. The world had some very tight corners in it. That was no life for a woman who wanted any self-respect, and he figured the alternative had to be very hard indeed to get her there. The last one he'd spoken to had narrowly escaped burning as a witch.

Then the incongruity hit him. "Hold on," he said. "I thought I recognized that young lady." Maybe two-thirds of the people present were wearing at least half-masks, and most of the people who were masked were wearing full grotesques of one sort or another. The various diplomatic parties were bare-faced, though, as were the doge and his retinue of city dignitaries. So was the girl accompanying Frank, which hardly fit—

"What's the huddle for, guys?" Sharon asked, walking up.

"Hello, Sharon." Mazzare nodded in the direction of the Stone boys. "Do you know anything about Frank's date?"

Sharon grinned widely. "Someone told you?"

"Yes, someone told us," Magda said. She was looking

serene now, Mazzare noticed. Perfectly composed, serene and smooth. Like the flawless concrete curve of a mighty dam.

"Oh." Sharon caught the mood. "I was just talking to the Spanish bishop's guy—more like, he was talking to me—"

"The cardinal's *gentiluomo*," Mazzare murmured.

"Whatever," Sharon said. "I already think of him as Feelthy Sanchez. He's an old lecher."

Magda barked once, a "Ha!" that summarized her current opinion of the male of the species.

Sharon tilted her head to one side a moment, thoughtful. "Well, maybe I'm being unfair. He was kind of twinkly, really. I bet he's pushing sixty."

"Nothing wrong with being mature," Jones said, his face as innocent as all get-out.

"Reverend," Sharon said, "this guy is ripe. Anyway, he was saying Frank had done well to get himself fixed up so quickly."

"Ha!" Magda barked again.

"Oh, Magda honey," Sharon said, suddenly emollient. "It's not so bad. Courtesans are nearly respectable around here. Of course, I didn't realize it was something anyone did part-time."

"Part-time?" Stone looked confused.

"Well, she was working at the embassy this morning," Sharon said it matter-of-factly.

Mazzare suddenly realized why the girl had looked familiar. "One of the chambermaids at the palazzo? That's who Frank brought?"

Mazzare decided the conversation had gone far enough. It also finally occurred to him that perhaps everyone was jumping to conclusions. Venice, he was beginning to realize, was a contagious sort of place. The kind of city where *Think no evil* is a laughable motto and rumors are guaranteed to be as wicked as possible.

"Let's not get into any more detail, everyone. It may

be the girl is just what she seems to be—to anyone except Venetian gossips, at least. Or, well . . . okay, maybe not. If not, we raise the chambermaids' pay so they don't have to, ah—well, you know."

"Quite," Jones said.

"On the other hand," Stone said, "I think I need to have a talk either way with the guys. Like you say, they're young men abroad in a big city for the first time and I think they need to be warned—"

He trailed off, clearly reminiscing. "Heh. I remember the first time I went to San Francisco. The Haight was past its prime, but it was still—" He cleared his throat, seeing the look Magda was giving him. "Well, never mind."

"Did you wear some—" Jones began, but Mazzare waved him down.

"Only you, Simon," he said, "could take that conversation downhill. People, let us mingle. We are supposed to be diplomats. Be nice, listen, give a friendly impression and go easy on the sauce."

"Speaking of which," said Jones, "where's Gus?"

"Unfair, Simon." Mazzare frowned. "Anyway, I left him with the monsignor who's the state theologian here. Gus doesn't usually get to hobnob with the rich and famous, so he's knocking himself out. Anyway, *raus*, the lot of you. Mingle." He made shooing gestures, and as they broke away he saw the first of many coming to pay him their regards.

Mazzare found he didn't even have to think about it. Whatever the other Americans were doing, he was kept busy being affable—easy enough, the company was all witty and polite—to a constant stream of people. He'd done similar duties in the past, and had learned the trick of the thing. Sip only, because otherwise helpful people come along and freshen your drink without you noticing, and before you know it you're paralytic.

He was barely an hour in, on perhaps his fiftieth *how-do-you-do* of the evening, when he realized that perhaps he should have passed that tip on. Especially to Jones, who had no capacity for booze and—but he'd surely been—

With an effort of will, he forced himself to stop worrying.

"Still worrying, Monsignor?" The mask was the traditional Mask of Comedy, worn with a close-fitting hood and a cape and a merely moderately lurid doublet. The voice he recognized, and would have even if it hadn't spoken in English.

"Monsignor," Mazzare said. "I had heard you were in Venice to receive short shrift from Messer il Doge?"

"Indeed. And I must also call you monsignor now, yes?"

Mazzare felt a sudden chill. He had last spoken directly to this man nearly eighteen months before.

Canon Monsignor Giulio Mazarini, Nuncio Extraordinary, was a man who gave Mazzare great hopes and the shivering willies in about equal measure. He was another of the great names of history that Mazzare, and all the other up-time Americans, were having to grow used to sharing a world with. In Mazarini's case, rather earlier than the events for which he was mostly famous, but shortly after his actual rise to prominence.

In the timeline that had been, Mazarini had been a rising star in the Vatican's diplomatic corps. Famous in his twenty-ninth year for rescuing the settlement of the War of the Mantuan Succession that had nearly been blown by Richelieu's creature, Father Joseph. Fortunately for France, the manner of the treaty's near-undoing was completely forgotten in the drama of its rescue. Mazarini had galloped his horse between two armies at Cherasco, waving a blank piece of paper and calling out that peace had been made. His flamboyant *coup de théâtre*, founded in a flagrant lie, had convinced the near-combatants that there was a treaty just long enough for one to be remade in reality.

Later in that timeline, after the time when the

Ring of Fire had split the here and now away from
what would have been, Mazarini had gone on to take
service with Richelieu, and had become a naturalized
Frenchman, changing his name to Jules Mazarin. On
Richelieu's death he had succeeded to the position
of prime minister of France as Cardinal Mazarin, the
architect of the absolute state of Louis XIV. There were
monuments to the man in the Paris Mazzare had briefly
played tourist in, even a Mazarin library.

Grantville had not had a detailed biography of the
man, but the basic facts were there in the better ency-
clopedias. Mazzare was fairly certain that Mazarini's
future career was known, for good or ill, in every
quarter where the knowing was thought worth knowing. Mazzare himself, ordered by the pope to report on
the future, had listed the known details of Mazarini's
career, giving particular prominence to the man's later
support for the Barberini after their patron Urban
VIII—born Maffeo Barberini—died and they began to
lose faction-fight after faction-fight within the Church.
Not that they couldn't have guessed at Mazarini's future
sympathies; he counted at least one Barberini cardinal
among his close friends, by all accounts.

The best bit was his key role in the Peace of Westphalia, the treaty that ended the Thirty Years' War
in 1648. That was important. Mazarini's career, a few
blips apart, was—had been, the normal tenses didn't
seem to work properly—devoted to the making of
peace after peace. The man had been an inveterate
diplomat throughout the life he'd led, and probably
saved a good many lives by his efforts.

Mazzare wondered whether Mazarini had fully
digested any of it. Or if—no, but Harry Lefferts had
come back to Grantville with the news that Mazarini
had gone to Paris. If Richelieu had not used the
knowledge of future history that he undoubtedly had
to make Mazarini an offer, there was no hope at all
for France.

Was there a tactful way to ask?

Mazzare realized that the moment was stretching and that Mazarini's having called attention to his new title was in itself a message. Reminding the American priest that he was a diplomat himself now, that they were both at work in the practice of what was now their mutual trade, and there was no such thing as idle chit-chat for such as they.

"Yes," he said, "although that title is much less official than it was—or will be—back in my day." He grimaced. "Doubtless you too have noticed the trouble that normal tenses have with these circumstances."

Mazarini chuckled. "One's conception of oneself can be a little shaky, as well."

Mazzare had been braced, he had thought, but not for that. One could never be ready for that kind of revelation. He felt his pulse bound and then settle as he decided on a tactical misinterpretation. "Quite," he said, smiling ruefully. "There I was, a simple parish priest in a simple country town, and now here I am an ambassador. Perhaps I could prevail upon our acquaintance to sit down with you for a few pointers from a professional?"

Mazzare realized as he said it that he actually meant that. Whatever Mazarini's final allegiances would turn out to be, he was actually a genuinely nice man. When first they had met, Mazzare had been at the bottom of a long, deep depression brought on by his doubts about his place in this time, and the church that represented God to its people and their world. Mazarini had said and done the right things to make Mazzare feel that there was some hope. It could have been a diplomat's professional patter, of course, but then there had been the raid on Grantville by Wallenstein's cavalry, and the bloody aftermath. Mazarini's response had been too smooth, sustained and practical for anyone to believe that it was entirely or even partly feigned. The man cared, and seemed to have the natural touch of friendship about him.

Mazzare had seen all kinds of faith in his years as a priest, throughout his career in the hierarchy. Some outstanding, in both scales as such things are measured. Most, the workaday belief of those whose faith is part of who they are and their family history. That was the reliable sort, Mazzare felt. A man whose trust in God fell with the dew, that he soaked up in warm spring sunshine and the mists of autumn was a man you could depend on.

The mask in front of Mazzare was nodding. "I would be honored, Monsignor."

"That is good to hear, " Mazzare said. Mike Stearns had told him that listening was better than talking in these sorts of situations, something Mazzare had already known. He allowed himself a silent snort at politicians everywhere, for thinking they had a monopoly on the stratagems by which people could be induced to open their hearts to others. And for thinking that the only reason to use those stratagems was in conflict.

Mazarini had the advantage, since behind the mask his thoughts were inviolate. Of course, with Mazarini, that was something of a moot point. His genial, ever-smiling face was the carefully controlled instrument of a trained negotiator and card-player, as much a mask as the painted thing he wore. He knew it, too, and the apologetic tone sounded sincere. "I should take off the mask, Monsignor, save that I am not here."

Mazzare confined himself to raising an eyebrow.

"Yes. Not here at all. The doge has not invited me and it is strictly forbidden to speak with me."

"Forbidden?"

"Forbidden. Perhaps this should be your first pointer from a professional? If, that is, Don Francisco did not instruct you."

Nasi had, but Mazzare let Mazarini go on, since doubtless he meant to pass on some other information.

"The doge is merely the mouthpiece of the Republic.

Messer Erizzo is, perhaps, more effective than most such. He seems to have the Senate firmly in hand for all that he is no Foscari reborn. But he must still respect the formalities of the thing. My mission, you see, is a matter of etiquette and protocol. His Holiness sees the dignities of cardinals as an issue of the highest importance."

Mazzare nodded understanding. There was a joke about it, he had heard, that the three bees of the Barberini coat of arms had once been horseflies, a joke prompted by the numbers of Barberini and Barberini placemen that were now in Rome, taking their share of the Church's revenue. There were no less than three cardinals Barberini, and the pope himself was another; he was yet to have the famous repentance of his nepotism. Between the current situation and that repentance in the old timeline was a near war over a failure to show the proper respect and to employ the correct etiquette in dealing with one of the Barberini cardinals. Part of that etiquette was the new title of "Eminence" for all cardinals, and their rank in protocol as princes. Both were Barberini innovations under Urban VIII, and part of Mazzare's briefing had been about Venice's refusal to acknowledge either.

"Venice," said Mazarini, "is—as it always has been— unwilling to knock its head on the floor at Rome's bidding. This is a city that has laughed off Interdicts in its time. On the other hand, Venice wants Rome's support in the matter of Cyprus. Let the pope declare in favor of Venice, the doge has said, and the pope may have his cardinals addressed however he pleases. That may affect you, incidentally."

"How does that affect me?" Mazzare asked.

"Because, Monsignor, Cyprus is part of the mercantile party's holdings at sea. The sway of the island represents a powerful symbol for the merchants. With Cyprus in Venetian hands, and the doge of The Most Serene Republic able to number 'King of Cyprus' among his titles, the merchant party can maintain their claim that the Terrafirma is of less importance than the seagoing trade."

"And so we deduce that those merchants are strong enough in Venice to procure that the doge defies the pope's own nuncio extraordinary?"

"Just so," said Mazarini. "*Quod erat demonstrandum.*"

"Ah," Mazzare smiled. "You have picked up some of our scientific jargon as well—"

He stopped. He had been about to turn the talk to the scientific mission Tom Stone was leading, as a way to turn the conversation away from potentially dangerous topics with some mild and harmless bragging, but he could feel the grin even through the mask.

"Monsignor," Mazarini said, his tone deeply and comically reproachful, "the scientific jargon is ours, not yours. I spent some hours in that wonderful library at Grantville. I found a number of interesting biographies in there and I see that two of the most famous natural philosophers of the twentieth century were born in this one."

Mazzare realized, watching those eyes twinkle through the eyeholes of the mask, that he must have let his bafflement show.

"Newton, the Englishman, and our very own Galileo Galilei," Mazarini said.

Mazzare laughed, rueful. "Of course. And Germany's Leibniz is from this time as well, and many give some of Newton's credit to him. And Father Descartes, as well."

"Just so. But please, Monsignor, let me not keep you, for I suspect that Messer il Doge will want to speak with you, as *tête-à-tête* as may be permitted him, before this function is over. I should be gone by then. Monsignor, if I may, I shall visit with you at the embassy before long."

"That would be a genuine pleasure," Mazzare said, meaning it.

"Seeya," Mazarini said, and vanished into the plum-aged crowd.

It was a second or two before Mazzare realized that the parting word had been spoken in a West Virginia accent, and a fair imitation of Harry Lefferts at that.

He kept the surprise off his face, he hoped. He took a quiet moment, then, standing alone in the crowd and listening to the faint strains of the musicians at the other side of the room playing something with a lot of strings in it; Mazzare was ill-equipped to recognize it. He tried to focus on the memory exercises to match names to faces in their proper pairings. Then the flow started up again, no important business to be done but introductions being made and pleasantries offered and returned in their turn. It was perhaps another fifteen minutes before the flow of introductions dried up again.

Jones, who had been at his elbow throughout, took advantage of the lull. "What was all that about?"

Mazzare chose to misinterpret the question. "I believe the last fellow was a factor for the Foscari."

"Larry." The tone was reproach enough.

"Didn't you recognize him? Don't say it, though, he's not supposed to be here."

"Oh. Someone we met back when?" Jones was looking around, apparently trying to see if Mazarini was still present.

"Back when, yes," said Mazzare, resisting his own urge to rubberneck. "Gus mentioned that he was in town earlier."

"Sure. Not a popular man, in Venice. Got some nerve, showing his face in here. Or not, as it happens."

"Got some nerve, period," Mazzare agreed.

"What's he doing it for, anyway? If someone recognizes him, he's in big trouble. Blows whatever chance he's got of getting on the doge's good side." Jones had finally stopped looking around, and took a sip of his wine. Which was a full glass, and not appreciably lowered by the sip, Mazzare noted with a mixture of silent relief and self-admonition for not having confidence in his old friend.

"His chances were slim and none anyway," Mazzare said. "But if there's one thing that man is down in the history books as liking, it's a touch of the theatrical."

Jones simply chuckled, and then: "Eyes front, Monsignor."

The doge was approaching, much in the manner of a ship under full sail in his robes—although, to American eyes, there was something faintly comical about the ducal cap. It resembled nothing so much as a smurf's hat.

The doge was flanked and trailed, as everywhere, by a small retinue of Venetian nobility. Not so much an honor guard as a prisoner's escort, the Venetian constitution being what it was.

There was a famous piece of architecture in Venice—Mazzare had read about it once in a travel guide—which tradition said was a gallows to hang misbehaving doges from. The office was a strange one, so hemmed about with checks and balances and separations of power that Venice appeared to be governed in spite of the doge, not because of him. In practice, the position carried a lot of influence that made up for the near total lack of power, an influence that the Venetians thought worth having and foreign diplomats had to cultivate. And, Mazzare thought, recalling their first formal meeting earlier that day, had to cultivate after climbing four flights of the Scala D'Oro to get to his receiving room.

It was a classic Venetian trick, that. Classical, including the sense of bygone, greater days. The times when the Venetians were genuinely a power in the Mediterranean rather than just a major player among several were long past. Every year, still, the doge symbolically married the sea. But the joke about him being cuckolded by the Turk was almost a century old by now.

"Monsignor," the doge said.

"Your Grace," Mazzare replied, making the formal bow. Not being Venetian, he had no right to address him as plain old Messer il Doge, without salutation. And in these years of declining power and waning influence, of shortened profits and rising costs, the Venetians clung to every little artifice of power and petty trick of haughtiness they could. Method acting in reverse, you might call it. They acted like haughty patricians granting audience to unlettered barbarians, in the hope—fond hope, really—that their audience would come to believe in the reality of it.

Especially, Mazzare thought, after that four-story stair climb.

"It will, we are sure, be a pleasure to receive your formal embassy. The Gran Consiglio meets in three days' time. Doubtless one of our secretaries will deliver your invitation tomorrow. We look forward to increase in trade and friendship with all who would truly be our friends."

Mazzare resisted an impulse to add warm praise for sunlight, motherhood and apple pie, or whatever dessert the Venetians favored. Doge Erizzo, it seemed, spouted meaningless hot air like a hairdryer, at least in public. The meeting earlier had consisted largely of a similar speech. Mazzare looked past the doge at the halo of attendants around; he could put names to some of the faces, but not all, and they seemed to be arrayed to give truth to the polite fiction that the doge was first among these equals.

Francisco Nasi had told him not to trouble himself about what stood behind the doge, though. He was to deal with the doge as if he were really the Renaissance prince he assumed the styles and airs of, and further to assume that every senator he met was one of the Ten. Every single one, bar a few misfits, reported to at least one of them.

Mazzare satisfied himself that he could not in fact

pick out any obvious members of Venice's shadowy ruling council—no tattoos on foreheads, alas—and reflected on Nasi's advice. The Ten were the real government of Venice, when they could agree. Certainly there was not one item of Senate business that that anonymous, unrecorded body would not have carved up in detail before the Senate met to vote on it, with the result that every vote of the Senate was nearly unanimous. There would always be three or four dissenting votes, of course. Venice, as everywhere, had its leavening of misfits and the occasional downright lunatic among its governing classes. The Ten was one of the many compromises and anomalies by which the Most Serene Republic of Venice actually worked. It was an oligarchy, true enough, but one which allowed for democratic decision-making among the oligarchs themselves.

The doge might even be one of the Ten himself. Since the Ten was not officially part of the Venetian constitution, there was room for more than a modicum of doubt about who was saying what in its councils.

But, as Nasi had said, from the outside at least, the doge was a prince. Sometimes, it paid to focus on the illusion and ignore the reality. Nasi had then proceeded, with malice aforethought, to use words and phrases like *interface* and *interaction metaphor*. Mazzare was sure that Nasi made those things up just to enliven dull briefings, after having been mightily amused by twentieth-century management-speak as recorded in the few MBA texts Grantville had had. The man's sense of humor was oblique and bizarre. Both Jones and Mazzare had laughed about his account of the ducal promises that governed the doge's role in Venice's government. The one about his being obliged to buy five ducks for every adult male patrician in the city as a New Year's present had especially entertained them.

At the time, Mazzare and Jones had assumed the story was one of Nasi's embroideries—until they'd arrived in Venice and discovered that it was actually true.

The pleasantries concluded, with no mention of ducks for good or ill, the doge moved away.

"We're not in Kansas any more," Jones murmured.

Mazzare smiled, and looked around. That left only— but no, the entire French party were visibly and pointedly giving Mazzare their backs.

The rest of the soiree passed quietly.

For Mazzare, at least.

Frank thought it would probably take surgery to get rid of the cringe he was feeling.

Tom Stone had a truly awful way of reaming out his sons. Perfectly reasonable, calm and polite, his soft-spoken admonition littered with hippie ethic and the wisdom of the nineteen-sixties. That was why Giovanna looked thoroughly bewildered. As well she might. She'd been born and brought up in seventeenth-century Venice, and on the wrong side of the tracks at that. So the sight and sound of a twentieth-century hippie deploying his thoroughly weird parenting skills in a lecture on the rights of women, sexual politics and Respect For Cultures Not Our Own was completely outside her experience.

Frank didn't feel that it helped any that his father, hippie that he was, still referred to women as "chicks" despite being nearly three centuries away from the sixties.

Chapter 19

"I embarrassed you?" Giovanna asked, her tone an odd combination of cool challenge and nervous anxiety. She was now sitting next to him in the gondola taking them back to her father's establishment—she'd not tried to work a boat herself, this night, not wearing those fancy clothes—and regarding him with narrowed eyes.

"No, Giovanna," he said. "I'm not embarrassed by *you*. It's just . . . It's just that, well, I'm told it's not a big deal in Venice—prostitution, I mean, uh, courtesanship rather—but it is a big deal where we came from. And, uh, it's a different kind of big deal depending on who's talking about it."

He could sense he was babbling but saw no alternative but to babble further. Babble he did, thus, with all the fervor that a drunk with a hangover seizes upon the hair of the dog. "What I mean is that some Americans will denounce you for consorting with harlots and others—like my dad—will denounce you—well, my dad doesn't really denounce anybody, it's a lot worse than that—for being a sexist pig and exploiting women." *Keep babbling, keep babbling, maybe there's a bottom to this pit.* "And, uh, we didn't know the customs, and it took us by surprise. And we're supposed to be part of a diplomatic mission."

Giovanna's eyes weren't narrow now. They were slits. It suddenly dawned on Frank . . .

Giovanna put it into words. "You think I am a whore?" Her tone of voice was decidedly dangerous, and Frank could feel panic rising. He hunted frantically for reverse gear.

"No, no!" he said, louder than he'd meant. "That's not what I meant! I never thought so, please—not once!—it's the filthy minds of those aristocrats, that's what really caused the trouble!"

Bingo. Even a babbler, now and then, babbles his way clear of disaster. Giovanna's eyes were still slits, but her hostile gaze shifted from Frank to scan the surroundings. By great good luck—*oh thank you whatever gods may be*—the gondola was passing a stretch of Venice where the mansions of the *Case Vecchie* were concentrated. The mansions, like the merchant nobility themselves, had the feel of tawdriness under the glitter.

"They are *pigs*," Giovanna hissed. "Just like them—to flaunt their whores by making them wear red shoes!"

A light at the end of the tunnel. Frank could only hope it wasn't a freight train coming. "Yes, yes—that's pretty much what my dad was talking about." *In his own screwy way,* but Frank saw no reason to dwell on *that* subject. "I had no idea it would cause any problem, honest! I just wanted to take you to a party where we might have some fun, and, and—"

Go on, say it, said a little voice in the back of his mind; but he couldn't, not yet. "I'm sorry," he managed at last. "I thought you'd like to be taken somewhere fancy like that. I should have thought about what kind of mess it might drop you in."

Giovanna was visibly softening now. Very rapidly, in fact. She even put her hand on his. It was like she'd touched him with a live wire.

"It is not your fault, Frank."

"I guess. I just screwed up tonight. It was me embarrassed you. I'm sorry." He wondered if he should try puppy-dog eyes, and then thought better of it. The dating tactics that had worked in up-time America—okay, occasionally worked, Frank was really no Lothario—were completely out of place here. Hippie upbringing or not, Frank was no fool. The Marcolis might be revolutionaries, but they were still seventeenth-century revolutionaries. Their radicalism, he was quite sure, only went so far—and probably not that far at all on some subjects. One of which undoubtedly included what they would regard as matters of family honor. With a capital H. In red ink, with a border of daggers and skulls-and-crossbones. The fact that Antonio Marcoli had magnanimously waived the necessity of a chaperone didn't mean that he would have casual up-time attitudes about sex. "Freedom" was one thing; "free love" another.

And besides . . . Frank wasn't really just interested in getting laid. Not that he *wasn't* interested in that, of course. For an instant, he had to fight down a ferocious surge of hormones that threatened to addle his wits completely at the worst possible time. But sex was only part of it. He didn't understand why, exactly—maybe he had a taste for the exotic—but something about Giovanna excited him far more than any American girl he'd ever had the hots for.

Giovanna sniffed, putting her nose in the air. It was a very pretty nose. For the first time, ironically, it dawned on Frank that it was also what people usually called an "aristocratic nose." A lot like Sophia Loren's, in fact. Odd that he hadn't noticed that before—since he'd certainly noticed the resemblance to Sophia Loren's figure. Um. Well, maybe his dad was right. A little bit. Maybe Frank did suffer from a touch of callow adolescence. What his dad called "infantile boob fixation."

Giovanna sniffed again. The sound, this time, had the flavor of doom about it. A very aristocratic sound, as it happens. "You should not apologize, Frank! I will not have it!" Then, more softly—oh, very softly indeed—and with suddenly warm and open eyes: "I am not embarrassed to prick the pretensions of the parasites who grind the blood and flesh of the Italian nation under their filthy heels."

Frank almost choked. The tone was of a piece with the moonlight on the water of the lagoon, with the soft strains of distant music that reached them from a myriad of *Carnevale* parties. The words? Straight from *Revolution 101*. Or *Introduction to Storming the Bastille*. No, wait, that was the French revolution. What had the Italians called theirs? The *risorgimento*, he thought. It was led by some guy in the future named . . .

The only thing Frank could remember was that the name rhymed with Pavarotti. Of course, that was no help, since half the names in Italian rhymed with Pavarotti.

Verdi? No, that was the opera guy.

Whatever. It didn't matter, because that had all happened in another universe. In the here and now, it looked like the name was going to be "Marcoli." At least, that seemed to be the ambition of Giovanna's father. Frank had a horrible feeling he had no choice but to get with Messer Marcoli's program completely, if he wanted to get anywhere with Giovanna.

"Well," he said, trying to be as gruff and manly about it as he could, "if it's all right with you. I should have checked first, though. Wasn't respectful to just drop you in all that with no warning." *Yeah, make out you planned it all along, that's right. Dumbass.* At times, Frank wondered if there was any way to get rid of that treacherous little voice in the back of his mind. Stand it against a wall and shoot it, maybe.

But he couldn't dwell on the political risks involved, not with Giovanna looking at him like that. She had a smile on her face again. A shy one, to his surprise—though not so shy that those glorious dimples weren't showing.

A moment of truth dawned on Frank. That moment of truth, he dimly understood, that eventually comes to young males who aren't hopelessly self-absorbed—which, of course, excluded most of the beastly critters—that girls have minds of their own. And that they, too, have treacherous inner voices that they'd often like to send to the chopping block. They, too, plan and plot and scheme and—most of all—wonder what they look like to the young man they're fascinated with.

Hot damn! The little voice was back online, and finally saying something he wanted to hear. *She's actually interested in me! REALLY interested! No fooling!*

He gave himself a little mental shake. The plain truth of it was that he was now almost certain that she was The One. The last thing he could afford was to lapse into teenage folly. *Be cool, Frank. Maintain!*

But she was talking again—and, Frank guessed, had made her own decision that The Right Thing To Do Now Was Stay Cool. "As to the diplomacy, Frank, I think you are fretting unnecessarily. Who cares what the stinking *Case Vecchie* think? My father will have his own opinion."

Oh, swell. Antonio Marcoli's reaction, when he heard about the evening, was exactly what Frank was worried about.

That he *would* hear about it from Giovanna, Frank didn't doubt for a moment. What separated Giovanna's father from a comic opera figure was that the man was genuinely charismatic. Even Frank had felt the pull of Antonio Marcoli's magnetically intense personality. And that charisma was something he exuded as a father, not simply as the leader of a political group. Giovanna and her brothers—the cousins, too—were closely attached to him and obviously trusted him and confided in him. It simply wouldn't occur to Giovanna *not* to tell her father.

Frank cringed, right there on the gondola seat. Another vivid image had just flashed through his mind.

If earlier fantasies about Giovanna had caused certain organs to swell, this image caused them to shrivel right up. The Marcolis, lined up in order of seniority, each with a knife in his hand, waiting their turn to carve a large and painful piece out of Frank's hide. Or—

The organs in question raced for cover, gibbering with terror. Frank almost clutched himself. Fortunately, a further image brought surcease from pain: Antonio Marcoli, passing out pistols to his clan, so that the lot of them could riddle Frank's poor mutilated body with bullet holes for good measure . . .

To his astonishment, Giovanna burst into laughter. He gaped at her.

"Oh, Frank! The expression on your face—it's priceless!" She covered her mouth with a hand, trying to stifle the laughter.

"I don't see what's so funny," he growled.

"Why do you think—" She had to break off, overcome by giggles. By the time she recovered, Frank saw that the gondola was about to moor.

I'm dead. The organs in question seemed to have vanished entirely, now. Not that it mattered, of course, since Frank Stone would never have any use for them. Not in the short span of life left to him.

As the gondola drew up, Giovanna came lithely to her feet and extended a hand. "Come. My father will react differently than I think you expect."

Seeing no option—what the hell, at least he'd go down holding her hand—Frank started to follow her. Over her shoulder, Giovanna smiled and said: "But do not forget to pay the gondolier. That is something to really worry about."

With a start, Frank realized that he had completely forgotten that small matter. Hastily, he handed over some coins without even trying to figure out if they came to the right amount. From the look on the gondolier's face, though, he'd overpaid him considerably.

Frank didn't stop to get change. He had other things

on his mind; and, besides, at least the gondolier would mourn his passage.

Once he stepped ashore, though, he felt himself relax a little. The gondolier had let them off at a pier rather than enter the narrow canals of the island. Murano was a small island just to the north of Venice's main islands, where Venice's glassblowing industry had been concentrated since the thirteenth century. But since Murano had a somewhat unsavory reputation, most gondoliers refused to enter it directly.

That meant they had a bit of a walk to get to the Marcoli building. Blessedly.

Even more blessedly, because Giovanna tucked her hand into his elbow. She was almost snuggling him. She'd never done that before.

"If you don't mind, I'd like to use your arm," she said sweetly. "The footing is not good here. And it's very dark."

The excuse was transparent. The footing was no worse than anywhere in Venice, and Frank had seen her earlier, practically dancing across it with light and sure feet. True, that had been in daylight, and it was now well after sundown. But there was a full moon out, and visibility really wasn't that bad.

Not that Frank was about to object, of course. He felt quite light-headed. In the moonlight, Giovanna seemed more beautiful than ever.

"Oh, yeah. Sure. Of course. Be my pleasure."

So, they made their way. Slowly. Giovanna didn't seem to be in any more of a hurry than Frank.

Alas, it couldn't have been more than a few minutes before they were in among the alleys and courts inside the block that held the Marcoli building. It seemed like mere seconds. A dim and still-sentient corner of Frank's mind—insofar as Frank could be said to have a "mind" left at all, between his fretting over Papa's Fury, the Venetian moonlight on Giovanna, and she on his arm—was trying to shrill a little alarm at him. This neighborhood at night really did have the appearance of a rough one. A downright nasty one, in fact. Distant sounds of arguments in tenements high above the street, the wail of a cat on a roof somewhere, dark and lurking shadows in narrow alleys—

One of those shadows moved, and Frank tasted the cold coppery flavor of fear. All other thoughts fled from his mind, as adrenaline worked its magic.

Another movement.

They were brought up short by two grimy customers stepping out from a doorway in front of them. Grimy customers with knives that were far and away the best-kept things about them. Shiny, bright, and obviously *sharp* knives.

A low, deep growl came from somewhere behind. "Hand over the purse and strip off the good clothes."

Frank looked around. Surrounded. Two in front, two behind. A mugging. Just *great*. The perfect end to a disastrous evening.

He sighed. No way to deal with this heroically; they wouldn't stop at kicking his ass, not with those knives.

Besides, he was Tom Stone's son. Frank's dad considered "macho" a synonym for "moron." He was known to say that he hadn't trusted the theory of evolution since he'd seen his first John Wayne movie. His first and only.

So, as he reached into his pocket, Frank summoned up the spirit of his hippie father to guide him through this momentary unpleasantness.

"Okay, guys, you got us. Everybody just relax. Take the money with no argument, but we keep the clothes, all right?"

"Frank—" Giovanna's hand was clutching his arm tightly.

"No, it's okay. It's only money. Money can be replaced. And these guys look like they need it more than us, anyway." That was true, at least. Scruffy wasn't even close to being the word for the way these guys looked. You'd have to add scrawny, unshaven, mean and ugly to get anywhere close. If you looked upon it as aggressive panhandling, which was pretty much the way his father would, it was almost compassionate to give them some eating money.

Not that Frank looked at it that way. He really didn't see eye-to-eye with his father on this subject. Granted, Frank wasn't any too fond of *machismo* himself. In fact, he'd been known to express pretty much the same skepticism concerning evolution as his dad, except that Frank's preferred example was the average high school jock. Still, Frank was just naturally more combative than Tom Stone, even if he usually tried to figure out a way to get even instead of getting mad.

On the other hand, as long as all that was involved was money . . . Well, the truth was that Frank didn't care about money much more than his dad. So piss on it.

But then the guy who seemed to be the head thug spoke again, and all of Frank's reasoning fled in an instant. Genetics and upbringing can lead a boy to pacifism, but they can't make him drink.

"Not just the money," the guy said. "The clothes too." His eyes moved to Giovanna, roaming up and down like a visual tongue. "And we'll want your whore for a while. Maybe we'll give her back."

Frank discovered that an old hackneyed expression was actually true. A red mist appear in front of his eyes. The fury was so intense that he couldn't make himself do anything. Like in a bad dream—

And then Giovanna ended the moment. Her intake of breath was quick, and sharp. The scream that came back out was high, piercing and incredibly loud.

The sound broke Frank's paralysis—at the same time that it held the thug in front of him momentarily frozen.

There was no thought at all involved. Just the immediate lightning reaction of a nineteen-year-old in very good health who was also—false modesty aside—one hell of a good soccer player. Frank's kick to the crotch didn't double up the goon. It lifted him about a foot off the ground; and, when he landed, he was curled up like a spider caught in a flame.

Unfortunately, muggers have good reflexes too. Vaguely, Frank realized that shutters and doors along the alley were beginning to bang open, letting light into the alleyway. But his attention was on the thug next to the one he'd kicked, who was already swinging his knife.

Frank managed to avoid the first stab by just backing away. Giovanna's hand yanking on his arm helped a lot too. Frantically, he grabbed Giovanna and pushed her into a doorway, which was the best he could do to get her out of danger. When he turned back, the same thug was coming in for another stab.

Frank had no training at all in the martial arts. Luckily for him, some things are just automatic reflex—and blocking an awkward looping stab with a forearm is one of them. The thug's snarling face was now less than a foot away from Frank's own.

Again, soccer substituted for kung-fu, and Frank had one hell of a head-butt. The goon staggered back, dazed, blood pouring down his face. Frank was pretty sure he'd broken his nose.

He backed up again, protecting Giovanna in the doorway as best he could, his eyes ranging, looking for the two other muggers. Giovanna's lungs were as impressive as her bust. Coming from just inches behind, her second scream almost blew out his eardrums.

But it was all over. Those opening doorways were open, now, and people were spilling out of them. Among those people—right in the fore—were Marcolis. Marcoli males. Many Marcoli males.

And they were looking even meaner and angrier

than they had in Frank's nightmare reverie. Oh, lots meaner and lots angrier.

The muggers hesitated, and that was their undoing. None of them got more than a few steps before they were brought down.

Shortly thereafter, Giovanna hugging him tightly—boy, did that feel great—Frank was able to observe an interesting tableau.

Antonio Marcoli was at the center of it, standing in front of four would-be muggers held by what seemed like eight pair of none-too-gentle hands apiece. Well. In the case of the one Frank had kicked, "held up" was probably a more accurate description than "held." The guy was still curled into a ball. Even with Antonio's cousin holding him by the hair, his head wasn't more than waist-high.

You couldn't actually say that Marcoli was swaggering or strutting. But that was only because "swaggering" and "strutting" were words that had a slightly comical connotation to them, and there was nothing at all comical—oh, no, no, no, no, no—about Antonio Marcoli's body language.

Frank found himself titling the tableau like a picture. *Street-life, with lynch-mob.* A moment of murmured reassurance that his daughter was unharmed, and then Marcoli had taken charge. By then, all the Marcolis had plenty of neighbors and friends to lend them a hand. Not that they probably needed it. Truth to tell, the Marcolis looked right at home in a dark alley. Natural denizens.

And Messer Marcoli suddenly wasn't the screwball radical he'd been in daylight, either. The guy looked about as comic opera as a rattlesnake. He had a thin smile on his face, which contained no humor at all.

Marcoli bestowed the razor smile on the man Frank had kicked. "I guess we won't need to cut his balls off." He swiveled his head and bestowed the smile on Frank himself. For an instant, there actually seemed to be some warmth in it.

But the instant passed. Marcoli's head swiveled back to regard the captured muggers. "I warned you," he said softly. "And now—you assault even my own daughter."

Frank could only see the faces of two of the muggers. Well, three—but it was obvious now that he had broken that man's nose. His face was still covered with blood.

They looked very scared already. The moment Marcoli said the last sentence, Frank discovered that another hackneyed old expression was true. Men actually *could* turn as white as a sheet.

They must not have recognized Giovanna, Frank realized, wearing that borrowed finery. Apparently, they really had thought she was—

"They called me a whore, Papa!" Giovanna hissed. "Hissed" as in locomotive. Very healthy lungs.

Marcoli nodded judiciously. "Yes, outrageous. But we must not allow personal animosity to enter the business. This is a matter of revolutionary justice, not family vengeance."

That didn't seem to cheer up the muggers any. Frank suddenly had a very bad feeling about the situation.

"Uh, Messer Marcoli," he said, half-protesting. "If it had just been the money, you know, I would have given it to them. I mean, it's only money."

Again, that judicious nod. "Yes, I understand. Very generous, your spirit—and it is true that money is not something we should worship. But that is not the point."

He gestured, his hand sweeping the surroundings. "See where these carrion lurk? They prey on their own kind. Too cowardly to rob the nobility. We will put a stop to that, by making this more dangerous still. I gave them one warning, and they paid no heed. Let us see if they will pay attention this time."

He didn't pause at all, so far as Frank could see. "Beat them to a pulp. Slit their noses. Then cut off one ear each. We will nail them up in prominent places."

The Marcolis and their confederates set to it immediately, and with a will. The one Frank had kicked and the one he'd head-butted got no bonus points for their existing injuries either.

But Frank didn't watch it, after the shock of the first few seconds of violence held him immobile. He blew out his breath and turned away. Giovanna was still hugging him and now he finally returned the embrace. With a will.

Frank didn't really know what to think. He'd heard of stuff like this happening in Magdeburg. That raw boom town had nothing much in the way of a police force, outside of the few areas where Swedish or U.S. soldiers patrolled, and the crime rate had initially rocketed. Until the Committees of Correspondence had established their own rough-and-ready street law. "Rough-and-ready" was the right expression, too. Frank knew that some criminals had wound up in the Elbe river.

He'd even approved of it himself, when he'd heard about it. But somehow "street justice" was harder to take in person than at a distance. He found himself wishing—for the first time in his scapegrace life, ha!—that Dan Frost were here. Grantville's one-time police chief had been a pain in the ass often enough, sure. But nobody had ever worried about being beaten in a cell, much less the *ley de fuega,* when Dan Frost took them into custody. There was a lot to be said for professional law enforcement, when you got right down to it, at least when it was done fair and square.

By then, though, Frank discovered that he was nuzzling Giovanna's hair. Which was every bit as luxuriant and healthy as her lungs and . . . well, everything else. So he found it easy enough to forget about the rest.

At least, until he realized that Antonio Marcoli had

left off supervising the mayhem and was standing at his elbow.

Frank froze. Okay, so he wasn't doing anything with Giovanna you could really call "feeling her up," but . . .

On the other hand, she *was* practically feeling him up—boy, those little hands felt great—and he suddenly remembered that The One's papa standing at his elbow was the very same guy who'd just calmly given orders on the subject of broken bones, slit noses, sliced-off ears . . . judicious decisions that castration wasn't probably necessary even though it was a charming idea and maybe another time . . .

I'm dead.

But all Marcoli did was slap him on the shoulder. Then, pried him loose from Giovanna and pulled him close for a very Italian embrace of his own. And then, back at arm's length, one hand on each of Frank's shoulders.

"Splendid man!" Marcoli pronounced. "You are a credit to our cause—and to your own nation, of course."

Back into the embrace. Back out again, at arm's length, hands on shoulders. Frank couldn't help being reminded of any number of mob movies he'd seen. It was kind of eerie. The father of his girlfriend—well, he had hopes, anyway; and things were sure looking good—was a cross between John Brown and the Godfather.

Eek.

"Frank," said Marcoli, "your generosity speaks well of you personally. But—trust me!—fine feelings are wasted on such as them. Criminals in the end are but lackeys for the exploiters. Because of their poor origins, we allow them one warning. More would be a waste of our time and effort—both things of which the revolution is in short supply."

He was dead serious, too. There wasn't a dishonest

bone or a poseur's fingernail anywhere on Antonio Marcoli's body. Goofy or not, Frank realized, this man was no parlor pink. Words he used like *exploiters* and *lackeys* and *The Revolution*—you could practically hear the capital letters—came trippingly from his tongue. He might be an impractical man given to harebrained schemes, but a faker he wasn't.

Oh, well. For Giovanna . . .

Frank did make a note to himself that, if there was ever a next time—not that he wanted there to be—he'd try to pick a Love Of His Life with a different kind of father. Maybe a bookkeeper whose idea of adventure was reading a novel. A Jane Austen freak. No westerns or thrillers. Short. Scrawny. A ninety-seven-pound weakling. Nearsighted—no, practically blind . . .

"Come, Frank," said Marcoli, putting one arm around Frank and the other around his daughter. He guided them back down the alley toward his door, away from the final grisly moments of the street justice he'd dispensed. "You must stay the night with us. You should not carry that away as your memory of Venetian hospitality, eh? We can send a note to the embassy by a gondolier, so they won't worry."

Frank hoped like hell Marcoli meant the mugging, and not what had been done to the muggers. The guy might seem like a rather endearing, barmy coot when it came to his enthusiastic plans. But when it came to action, he had all the old Venetian charm of a mob capo.

On the other hand . . . there was the prospect of spending the rest of the evening with Giovanna. Not the night, of course. The one thing Frank Stone was not about to contemplate—in Antonio Marcoli's own house!—was trying to sneak into his daughter's bedroom.

"See?" Antonio demanded. "It is too cold to return, this late at night. Already you are shivering."

Chapter 20

Joe Buckley drained the last of his glass, and thought about pouring another. He thought better of it. He'd matched the Frenchman Ducos drink for drink in the earlier part of the evening, and the hangover was already starting to nibble at the frontal lobes of his brain. He looked over his notes and decided they were legible, although how they'd look in the cold hard light of morning was anyone's guess. His last ballpoint had died months ago. Thankfully, the modern-style fountain pen had proven a massive hit with Germany's stationers and while they weren't cheap they were very good indeed. In fact, the only ones being made yet were the kind of finely crafted high-end items he'd always liked back up-time. Good notepaper was the problem, since the Turkish stuff fine enough for handwriting tended to be expensive, and the newsprint of the time turned into a blotched rag if you wrote on it with anything harder than a feather pen.

The embassy's reception room was quiet, the silence marred only by the crackling in the grate and Captain Lennox's heroic snoring. Jones and Mazzare were looking bone-weary and ragged. Everyone else seemed to have gone straight to bed. If they'd had a debrief, they hadn't done it anywhere journalistic ears might catch a word or two. Buckley was bone-weary himself, and wanted nothing so much as to drag himself across the way into his own building and his own bed. But he was still on that fine line between drunken bravado and sober enough to know better, which was why he was aching to start asking questions but keeping quiet anyway. Besides, with no deadline to meet, he told himself, he could leave the polite request for an interview for the morning, when everyone would be better rested and feeling more accommodating. There was that to be said for biweekly publication and filing stories by horse-borne mail; you could take a few hours off now and then. He had the Ring of Fire to thank for never having had the tyranny of a daily news hole to fill, and this week's was already nicely plugged with a damned good story about d'Avaux.

Tom Stone came in as Buckley mused on the ruckus that was going to cause. The old hippy-turned-industrialist—and wasn't that a switch!—picked an armchair by Jones and plopped into it.

"Man, am I beat!"

"Tell me about it," said Jones. "My feet are killing me." He had kicked off his shoes and had both much-darned socks on public display on a handy hassock.

Mazzare sat up straighter. "How's Frank?"

Stone grinned. "Mortified, Father. You'd be pleased."

Mazzare chuckled. "Somehow, Tom, I doubt you play the stern father very well."

"Honesty and sweet reason, gentlemen, has always been my watchword in raising those boys."

"Ouch," said Jones. "That's just *cruel*, with teenagers. Makes me glad my own father believed in sparing not the rod. Or the belt, in his case."

"Man, I don't even like jokes about that."

"Sorry, Tom," Jones said, sounding like he meant it.

Buckley, almost automatically, wondered what lay behind that exchange. He knew altogether too little about any of the three leading figures in the United States delegation. Mazzare's background he had from the State Department press-pack on him, at least as far as his clerical career went. Chaplaincy for the USAF posted in England, a spell at the Vatican, work in the office of the archbishop of Baltimore before coming to pastoral work in Grantville. From Chicago originally. Other than that, *nada*.

Jones . . . Buckley had only what Rita Stearns had told him. No—Rita Simpson; he'd gotten the information from her after her marriage to Tom Simpson. He and Rita were friends from college, which was why Joe had been in Grantville on the day of the Ring of Fire.

All he knew about Jones was that he was a Grantville local boy, settled as the town's Methodist minister alongside his wife, who was from out of state. There had been that business back in 1631 when he'd somehow come by a sudden surge in church funds. The story had dried up in one cold lead after another and Buckley had reluctantly dropped it, but not without putting acres of bad blood between the two of them, however polite Jones might be to his face.

Stoner—what about him? *There* was a story waiting to be written. Probably an easy one to get, too, with the man's hippie openness. The problem was finding a time when Stoner was free and available. For a supposed counter-cultural slacker he worked long hard hours. Hippie, commune founder, chemist—like the reason for that wasn't obvious—and growing hash for the government.

Joe had tried to work that angle precisely once, when word got out. There was always good copy to be had from the War on Drugs. But then he'd had a visit from Doctors Nichols and Abrabanel after he'd published the first piece. Nichols had offered—no, insisted on—an interview in which he and Doctor Abrabanel had explained, in excruciating detail, all of the medical uses of cannabis, opium, cocaine and just about every narc—Buckley stopped himself. He'd used the word narcotic precisely once in relation to the drugs under discussion, which had prompted a long, technical and utterly patronizing digression from Doctor Abrabanel about how precisely none of these medicines were in fact narcotics at all, but euphoriants, analgesics, anti-whatevers and whocaresiates.

Whatever. The DEA came in for some trenchant comments from Doctor Nichols, before he'd gotten back to the topic at hand, which was how banning any one of the formerly illegal drugs would condemn hundreds, thousands, to unnecessary pain and hardship.

It had been a thoroughly dispiriting interview. Especially since, for a doctor, Nichols was a thoroughly menacing individual when he put his mind to it. Doctor Abrabanel, on the other hand, had been a lot more urbane and Buckley had turned his "suggestions" on how to make a face-saving retraction and change of line into, though he did say so himself, damn good copy. But the memory was still tender.

Mazzare was speaking again as Buckley's mind wandered. "Does he understand what the problem was?"

"Sure," said Stone, "although I think Frank figures we're being a bunch of old squares about it."

"What did he do?" Buckley asked. He decided it wouldn't be honest just to sit there and listen in, and besides it sounded like a story. If one of Stone's kids had gone along to the first major diplomatic function of the USE embassy to Venice and screwed up—maybe an article on the scandal of nepotism—the viper in the bosom of liberty—

"Not *him*," Stone said. "He's just having his first real crush. That's the teenage version of trying to get laid with panache and style." The old hippie was grinning. He clearly didn't think that whatever the offense had been was that great, although Mazzare and Jones were both frowning pastoral disapproval.

Buckley didn't ask the obvious question, but Stoner answered it anyway. "His date turned out to be a girl from an artisan family, dressed up in finery. No sweat—except the Venetian upper crust assumed she must have been a whore—since no lower-class girl could have afforded those clothes—and they were a bit miffed that she wasn't wearing the customary red shoes. Go figure."

"Oh." Buckley saw the story vanish before it even formed. Who wanted to hear about horny teenage boys and the fixes they got themselves into thinking with their dicks? Any villager in Germany could tell you *that* story. By the baker's dozen.

But maybe there was a different angle. A political angle. "Was she one of the chambermaids here?"

Stoner nodded.

Buckley smiled thinly. "Bet you dollars for donuts she was inserted into your staff by the local Committee of Correspondence, then. I know there's one here in Venice, although I haven't been able to find out much about them."

"Mister Buckley," Mazzare said sternly, "I'd really appreciate it if you'd be a little careful there. We are trying to avoid obvious links with the Committee. I realize asking that of you is probably a waste of my time. Still, I am asking." He sighed. "How many of our staff do you think belong to the Committee?"

Buckley shrugged. "Hard to say. For women, membership in the Committees of Correspondence tends to be elastic in areas outside of the United States itself. At a guess, I'd say Frank's new girlfriend is the only actual member of the Venice Committee—but if you looked closely, you'd find that lots of the other chambermaids are friends and relatives of hers. Think of them as Committee, once removed. Most of your staff, of course, are Francisco Nasi's people."

Jones groaned. "Our security's perfect, then, and

we're totally compromised anyway. Wait'll I see Luz-zatto again."

The Jewish commercial agent was back in the ghetto for the night. Venetian law might be elastic on the restrictions on its Jewry, but Luzzatto liked to observe the proprieties. Doing so practically defined the man, in Joe's limited experience with him. Buckley real-ized that Jones had a point about Luzzatto's handling of the set-up of the embassy. His own sources said that Luzzatto had regarded the Committee as a good voucher for the reliability of prospective staff. If he hadn't, he'd have had trouble getting any help at all for the embassy. The plague a couple of years before had sorely depleted Venice and everyone from the doge on down was having trouble keeping servants. Being picky about who one hired was a recipe for a very short queue of applicants.

Still, it sounded like Mazzare didn't want to frighten the notables, and there was every chance that the Committee connection would be spotted. Whatever the history books might say about Venice being in the first years of its decadent period, the Council of Ten's agents were still justly feared.

"The girl probably wasn't a prostitute," he said, in an attempt to change the subject. "She could have borrowed the clothes, easily enough, assuming she's connected to the local Committee. The CoCs almost always have a presence in the needle trades. It's easy enough to get your hands on finery for an evening, if you know a seamstress working on something. Just hope you don't run into the real owner or that she doesn't recognize her own outfit on someone else."

"If you wind up doing a story on them, Joe, let me have a copy. Although I did get a briefing and I should have—" Mazzare let out another deep sigh. "What's done is done. I suppose we should look at what we're paying our staff, make sure the girls don't have to sell themselves."

Buckley bit down on what he'd been about to offer, that the embassy was in fact paying very generously—even by the standards of Venice, a town where plague had made pretty much every job market a seller's market. He was, he told himself, a reporter, not a researcher for the embassy.

"I gave the boys a lecture about exploitation, just to be on the safe side," Stoner said, looking considerably more serious now. "Maybe we should say something to the soldiers?"

The two pastors digested that in silence.

"Doubt it'd do any good," Jones said at length.

"True," Mazzare agreed gloomily. "Although I suppose they'll be discreet about it. Maybe we should say something to them about security?"

More silence.

Buckley thought the gloom was misplaced. First, there was something downright comical about two ministers fretting about security lapses on the part of the soldiery when they had a Scotsman named Lennox in charge of that very matter. Buckley knew for a fact—he'd gotten two different accounts, both agreeing on all the major points and both wickedly amusing—that Lennox had thoroughly reamed out Billy Trumble and Conrad Ursinus for their behavior the night the embassy had finally arrived in Venice. Since then, the two young officers looked to have ramrods up their ass.

Secondly, and more important, Mazzare and Jones underestimated—by about an order of magnitude, Buckley thought—the difference that up-time social habits made in the attitude of their hired help. Just being treated like a regular working stiff was a major step up from the condescension of the served to their servants that was the norm in the seventeenth century. Half of Buckley's journalistic success depended on that simple fact, which infected even the journalists of the time. They went for interviews with the Great Men and their hangers-on and wrangled for admission to the councils and conferences at which great matters were discussed and decided. Buckley just asked the waiters and footmen what they'd seen and heard, and so got in on things that others were excluded from. He had to be careful sometimes to cover up sources, but it worked every time.

He'd gotten the idea while doing a story on Admiral Simpson. The man's household staff had fallen over themselves to dish on the man and his wife. To Buckley's surprise, it had all been praise. But getting that experience stood him in good stead in Venice. The French embassy, in particular, leaked like a sieve.

Which reminded him of what he'd actually written. "I'm for my bed," he said, gathering up his papers and nodding to the other three.

They bid him good night, and he left with all the dignity of a half-drunk journalist getting the hell out before anyone asked him what he was actually going to file for this week's story.

After Buckley's departure the two pastors and the hippie lapsed into companionable silence for several minutes. Lennox's snores took on the breathy, whistling tone of a man well away in the land of Nod.

"You think pinching that Scot warthog's nostrils would help?" Jones finally grumbled.

"Oh, I don't know," said Stone, "I find the noise kind of restful. Almost as good as a ticking clock."

Mazzare chuckled at the banter. Jones's acid wit and Stone's casual, good-natured humor had eased a lot of the frustration of their journey to Venice. Switzerland in winter had been no joke, even for the hard-bitten cavalrymen of their Marine guard. "What we could do with, I think," he said, "is pinching Buckley's mouth."

"You think he's up to no good?" Stone asked.

"Depend on it," Jones said, still glaring at Lennox. "Man's a damned nuisance. He's bound to be up to something that'll bite us all on the ass."

Jones' run-in with Buckley had been a fairly quiet business, for all the newsman's efforts at scandal-mongering after the Ecumenical Relief Committee had gotten its mysterious boost in funding over the winter of 1631. Away from prying ears in the garage at Mazzare's rectory, Jones had waxed positively sulfurous, using a great deal of what he called "agricultural metaphor" to describe the journalist and the inquiries he'd been making.

"Has anyone heard what he's been up to?" Mazzare asked. "I asked Gus to look into it, but he hasn't gotten back to me. Fortunately, Joe can't use the radio to file anything—although I'm sure he knows we have one. But Joe's plenty ingenious, so he'll figure out some other way to get his stories across the Alps."

"Set Gus and his sneaky Jesuit tricks onto him," recommended Jones. "Of course, knowing Gus, he'd probably start by laming every horse in Venice."

Mazzare laughed out loud at that. Whatever the reputation of the Society of Jesus for subtlety of approach and cunning casuistry, Father Augustus Heinzerling, SJ, was one of the most direct and straightforward men anyone knew. Gus was about as devious as a charging boar.

"We can't just shut him up, can we?" Stone asked, sounding a little worried.

"No, Tom, we can't." Mazzare said. "I just think we should all be very, very careful about what we say when Joe is around."

"And then some," Jones grunted. "Man's a muckraker. Emphasis on muck."

"Should we give him press releases to distract him, then?" Stone asked.

"Tell him Elvis was spotted rowing a gondola, be about his speed," Jones snarled.

Mazzare snorted. "Leave off, Simon. Two years—more than that, now—is a bit much to be bearing a grudge, even for you. But yes, Tom, I think giving him a prepared statement or two to use would be a good idea. If we can plant ideas in his mind we may influence what investigations he actually goes off on. In fact, if he thinks he's going to get the straight goods from us without having to work for it, he'll go off and annoy someone else."

Jones grinned, and snapped his fingers. "That," he said, "for the Jesuits."

The next morning, as he returned to the embassy in a gondola in bright sunlight, Frank was in a much more sanguine mood. All was well with the world.

It must have still showed when he reached the embassy. His brothers took one look at him and simultaneously shook their heads.

"Boy, do you look like the cat's meow," Gerry commented.

"Something exciting happen?" asked Ron.

Frank was grinning from ear to ear. "Sure did. Giovanna kissed me. Twice. Once before she went to bed—right in front of her dad! Okay, it was more like a peck on the cheek, but still. And this morning, she kissed me again when I left—and that was a real one, since her dad wasn't watching." The grin was in serious danger of dislocating his jaw.

"That's *it*?" Gerry demanded. "Nothing else? Then what caused that bruise on your forehead? That's one hell of a hickey."

"You have a dirty mind." Frank thought about it. "Well. There was a spot of trouble with some goofs outside her house. No big deal. Did I tell you she kissed me?"

Part III: March, 1634

She thanked men,—good! but thanked
Somehow—I know not how—as if she ranked
My gift of a nine-hundred-years-old name
With anybody's gift.

Chapter 21

Francisco Nasi looked out of the window at the winter snowscape, savoring the cool air of the window alcove after stifling in the heat of the offices. Growing up in Istanbul, he had come to relish, cherish even, the cool of northern Europe. When, that is, it was not raining. The first year in Grantville had been marvelous, while the air conditioning still worked. Most of it had broken down since, one way or another. Still, the summers had been tolerable.

The winters were still marvelous, though, even here in Magdeburg. Nasi missed the hills around Grantville, but there had been no way to keep that town as the capital of the now greatly expanded United States of Europe. Henceforth, Grantville would be the capital of a province, not a nation. The small United States restricted to Thuringia had not lasted even two years. It had given way—given birth, more accurately—to a much larger nation that encompassed perhaps half of the Germanies. A nation great enough, in fact, to add "of Europe" to its title without causing the slightest snicker anywhere. Many scowls, of course, and more than a few curses; but no snickers.

Magdeburg was the capital of that new nation. And, since Mike Stearns had been appointed as its prime minister by the USE's Emperor Gustav II Adolf, he'd transferred himself and his staff to the city on the Elbe.

It was a brand new city, in everything but its name. Tilly's army had destroyed the old Magdeburg less than three years earlier, massacring most of the population. The people living here now—pouring in every day—were as new to Magdeburg as were the buildings they moved into and labored in. Between becoming the capital of the USE and the industry rising up in and around the city, Magdeburg was now a boom town, with all the completely uncharming characteristics thereof.

Still, Nasi liked the place, at least in the winter. The raw, flamboyantly industrial ugliness of the city was disguised by snow; it even seemed to improve the flatness of the landscape. Nasi had always had to travel to see snow, in his youth. To have it right outside his door could make him forget his dignity. He'd even been known to throw snowballs.

He smirked slightly about that. Rising before dawn— no great feat at this latitude—he had walked to work past a small gang of schoolboys earning pocket money by shoveling entrances clear. Out of the corner of his eye, he had seen one of them bend to prepare a snowball practically behind him, and had turned and let the junior-league bushwhacker have it between the eyes with the snowball he'd had in his pocket. He'd gotten pelted, of course, but it had been worth it for the look on the little rascal's face.

And now he was going to savor another expression. He'd had time to read the morning paper before Mike Stearns came to the office, and Mike was now at his desk taking a moment to look at the day's news. He should be reaching the offending piece about . . .

Now.

"Why, that son of a bitch," Mike murmured. Then, louder: "What an asshole."

Nasi permitted himself a small moment of self-congratulation. He was coming to anticipate the prime minister perfectly—his reaction to some things at least—and certainly his reading speed.

"Francisco?"

"Yes, Michael?" Nasi had also learned some of the American habits of informality. That mode of address, used back in Topkapi, would have earned him a bowstring around the neck and a place of his own at the bottom of the Sea of Marmara.

"Did we send Joe Buckley to Venice?" Mike's tone could have been used to etch steel.

Nasi turned away from the window and smiled. "No, we did not."

Mike rested his elbows on his desk and his head in his hands. "Francisco, are our spy networks up to finding someone in France—a village idiot, maybe, in a remote province—who will actually believe that?"

Nasi pantomimed giving the matter heavy consideration, cupping his chin in his hand and frowning, brow furrowed and eyes narrowed. "No, Prime Minister. Perhaps, did God lend us the service of his every djinn and angel—to use your heathen terms—we might scour Europe and find one such unworldly trusting fool. But certainly not in France."

Mike didn't look up. He just groaned, deeply and theatrically. "What does this do to our own operations in Venice?"

"Surprisingly little, as it happens." Nasi had checked that first thing. The story—more like an editorial—that Buckley had filed on d'Avaux's intrigues in the Venetian state had come as no great surprise. Only a few details differed in Buckley's account from the reports Nasi had gotten himself. Francisco suspected that was due to the journalist making mistakes rather than to any defects in the organization his cousin was running in the Most Serene Republic. Unlike Buckley's, those reports came with sources attributed and with reliability assessments.

"Little?" Stearns was looking up and frowning. "Surely they're about to have the mother of all mole-hunts right about now?"

"Oh, surely they will. The French embassy there has an efficient and effective man in charge of—things." Nasi didn't want to put it more specifically than that. A man handling espionage and counterespionage could have surprisingly wide duties. Especially if his name was Michel Ducos.

"He probably already knew that Buckley was speaking to the servants at the embassy, Michael. It is a standard enough ploy, even if few people do it as effectively as Joe Buckley. The only surprise will have been the publication of the material. As far as we can tell the French were assuming that Buckley was one of our spies—one of the reports they filed even suggested that he wasn't the real Buckley but an impostor."

Stearns chuckled. "Makes a change for them, doesn't it? Decades of journalists who either printed the press release, relied on rumor and hearsay or just flat-out lied. Suddenly they've got a for-real investigative journalist out after them. Ha! Do that French viper some good."

"D'Avaux or Richelieu?"

Mike snorted. "Pair of 'em. Had far too much freedom of action, you ask me. Bit of publicity beyond pamphleteering and state-approved sermons, just what they're short of." He grinned.

Nasi snagged a tablet and a pencil to make a note. "We will encourage—oh." Nasi looked at that grin.

The grin got wider. "Time to stir this particular pot, I think. Get the propaganda guys on it. The line is that we deny all knowledge of Buckley, and while we deeply regret any inconvenience caused, we can't intervene and the appropriate remedy would appear to be a slander action—no, strike that, let's just have some standard ringing declaration for freedom of speech and the press, rule of law, contrast with the despotism of other and by definition lesser nations, France and her tyrannical Hapsburg allies, iron heel of Charles Stuart, et cetera, et cetera."

"But we keep our distance from Buckley?"

"Oh, sure. Maybe warn our folks in Venice to do something if it looks like he's going to get killed. Say, how likely is that?"

"In Venice? Should the Venetian authorities decide he should die, he will die. Quickly, overnight, with no one to see how the thing is done."

Nasi remembered a scene he had witnessed as a boy, visiting Venice. Corpses, hanging with their legs broken, twisting in the light sea air over the Piazza San Marco. They had been hung there overnight, with no witnesses to the deadly and secret work of the Council of Ten. The same day, a mob of Arsenalotti at the Spanish embassy chasing Bedmar out of town. A little later, all of Europe catching light, and the sparks seeming to flare up at home. The mad sultan Mustapha enthroned and deposed three months later, the world gone mad.

He brought himself back to the present, away from the pull of memories of a former home. "So unlike the civilized manner in which these things are done in the City," he said. "The pasha who offends the sultan is ordered to report for execution, and report he does. If he does not, the executioner goes to him, and—" He drew a finger across his throat. "All done out in the open. Honest. Healthy."

Mike nodded solemnly. "Oh, couldn't agree more. Can't be having executions in the dark and on the quiet, oh no. Publicity, that's the ticket."

Neither of them held their faces straight for more than a second or two, breaking out in matching broad smiles. Nasi treasured moments like this, when Mike was not feeling the load so much. The world that

Nasi had grown up in had far more idle nobles and underworked functionaries, a wealth of sinecures for hangers-on to occupy and work at in dilettante fashion. It might make for a great deal of waste, but it also made for plenty of leisure time among the governing classes. The sultan, to pick the most obvious example, generally had all his state business over with by lunchtime—and him no early riser, at that—on any given day. It left him with his afternoons to fill with a regular schedule of the arts, literature, science and drinking. Mostly drinking, as it happened.

Mike, meanwhile, was running one of the biggest political units in Europe, by most measures, with a staff that in the empire would be thought barely sufficient to run a small provincial town. Even here in Europe, where they made do with less government—and in Nasi's humble opinion it showed—the running of the United States of Europe was a lean business.

The result was a set of chronically overworked politicians and civil servants. That last was being remedied, slowly, as *Amtmänner* and their like took retraining in the new style of government and began to take on federal responsibilities in their areas. It was half jury-rigging and hodgepodge, but it did the job and rationalization could wait for the war to end. As could, apparently, any hope of anyone taking a vacation, which was why Nasi tried to make a moment or two, now and then, for the slightly oblique gallows humor he liked and that Mike was getting a taste for.

But Mike was back to scanning the news again. "This one, Francisco," he said, stabbing a finger down a few columns over from the Buckley piece. "Franconia's still not settled down?"

Nasi heaved a weary sigh. That one escaped him, truly it did. Getting any intelligence on the situation in Franconia—and a dozen other places like it—was like trying to read fog, even if he had thought he had a hope of ever understanding the underlying business.

It seemed that when they lacked Jews to pick on, Christians would name some of their own "heretic" or "witch" and vent their spleen on them instead.

"No, Mike," he said, "although now they have a regiment or two to worry about and hopefully that will settle them down. Instead of fantastical *Hexerei*, they can worry about real—and unruly—soldiers and how they will feed them."

The policy was a simple one. It was a while yet before the monstrous size of the army could be made more manageable; simply demobilizing tens of thousands of men at a time was a recipe for disaster. So they were being used as a crude police force, sent to sit on an area that was becoming unruly for reasons unconnected with the government, such as witch-panic, and giving the populace concrete concerns to deal with to take their minds off burning their neighbors.

"Still. Two near-lynchings this week and another riot. We know what that's about, yet?"

Nasi shook his head. "No. I expect the reports shortly. The last time it was the rumor of Jesuits."

Mike grunted. "Figures. Why they can't be like every other place and not give a damn if there's no one breathing down their neck—" He waved a hand, as if to clear away the stink of bigotry. "Part of it's just the way folks who are a gnat's ass away from poverty behave, I suppose, when they get to thinking about it."

Nasi waited. Silence. He raised an eyebrow. "Usually there is more to this particular Stearns rant," he mused.

"I know, I know. This—" Mike stopped, chewing on his lower lip. "Francisco," he said at length, "I am getting sick of this crap." The last word was punctuated with a slam of his big hand, palm down, on the desk.

"It could be worse."

"Sure, it could be worse. They could be sitting there in sullen resentment and boiling up like a frigging abscess. God, I wish they'd march on the capital and

burn this place to the ground, it'd make more sense.
It ain't gonna happen, though. What burns my ass is
that instead of folks actually getting on and making
something out of it, or saying they're mad as hell and
not gonna take it any more, we get this penny-ante crap
whenever there's a hitch. Never because they're pissed
at me—although God knows there's plenty are—but
over religion or the number of Jews in the town or
because some idiot thought he saw a witch or—" He
ran out of wind.

Nasi waited.

"This business in Franconia. Not a damned thing to
do with witches or Jesuits. It's really happening because
the rural places—you look, Francisco, and you find all
these riots are in backwater little towns—are losing out
to the bigger towns that are getting the factories and
industries. Nothing I can do about it, either, except
try and sit on 'em to keep the peace. But do they get
pissed at me? No, they don't, they mob up and pick
a neighbor to lynch."

"There are troubles in the cities, too. There is a
new pamphlet, by someone you may recognize, from
the style."

There had been a particularly nasty one, entitled
Pestis Pontifica, Pestis Judaica. It had started with
unpleasant suggestions about Rebecca Stearns and
Cardinal Richelieu. Tracing the thing to the printing
press was a tall order; in Germany every town, many
of them not even big enough to afford so much as a
one-fourth share in a horse—and a second-rate horse
at that—regarded having its own press as a must-have
status symbol.

Dan Frost had taken some persuading to help with
the search. Grantville's former chief of police was now
in private practice as a police consultant, but he was
just as much of a stickler as ever. He'd only agreed on
Nasi's promise to leave the printer alone and follow the
trail back to the source of the money that had paid for

the typesetting and printing. Whatever the pamphleteer was saying, Frost had argued, he was free to say it. Tracking down and suppressing dissenters was against the Constitution.

Dealing with restrictions like that had been Nasi's biggest learning experience as an official of the United States government. He had had a good theoretical understanding of the science of government. It had been, of course, a favored subject of learned writers these two thousand years past. A grasp of the theory and an understanding that came from growing up in a system were, however, completely different things. There was what the Americans called a "learning curve." The system of government Nasi had grown up in might have its rules, laws and established custom, but anything in it could simply be decreed out of the way if it proved inconvenient to a sufficiently powerful official. If the sultan ordered a thing done, the choice was obedience or rebellion. That set the usual political limits, of course. But the system included, required on occasion, that the sultan or one of his pashas should make a *firman* to cover some unusual situation. Such an order was just that: an order.

The American tradition was very different. The laws covered far more, to begin with. The room for an official to maneuver in was stiflingly small, or so it seemed at first. In practice, the constraints forced one to move in different ways, and exercise other political faculties. In many ways, actually, Nasi had more freedom of action as head of the United States' intelligence service than any Ottoman pasha below the grand vizier had ever had. The ability to make special rules for special cases was gone, though. The Rule of Law, they called it, although when he looked that up it turned out that the technical definition was slightly different from the practical one, which was that everyone had to be treated by the same rules. Bending them was as bad as breaking them and no one wanted to set a precedent that would be hard to live with.

Dan Frost had a particularly hard line on the issue of the unknown pamphleteer. The objections he had raised to the treatment of Freddie Congden had been, in essence, that there was no precedent for what they were doing and he didn't want to set one. They'd made an end-run around the policeman's logic by pointing to his own precedent. He'd bent a few rules in his own time. It had been a logical misadventure that Dan hadn't spotted, and one which Nasi still felt a little guilty about not pointing out at the time.

Still there had been a good solid gain from that operation, and since it was kept very nearly entirely secret, it had not set any kind of precedent. A considerable amount of misinformation had been fed to an assortment of rival powers and great chunks of perfectly accurate scientific and technical knowledge had been spoon-fed them as well. That was knowledge that would do little short-term good and might tie up their better intellects in blue-sky projects. It was also knowledge that they would never have taken, Nasi remained convinced, if they had been freely offered it. The operation had turned a modest profit, too, funding a few of the more outlandishly secret projects Nasi had running.

Mention of that particular pamphlet had put Mike into a brown study to match Nasi's own. "Pamphlets," he said at length, musing on the *Pestis*. The improbable sexual geometry of his wife and Cardinal Richelieu had been funny, to Mike, in a way Nasi would never have found it. Had it stopped there, it would have been another blowhard political diatribe to laugh off, like the ones that featured woodcuts of Americans eating babies, or "Use of nonnes to triall hell's-armes upon," with engravings of habited sisters being napalmed by leering Americans under the direction of Satan. This one, though, had included lengthy quotations from the *Protocols of the Elders of Zion*, which the author alleged the witches from the future had brought back in league with Jews of the present time.

That had made Mike go quiet for the longest time Nasi had ever seen. The so-called *Protocols* must have come from an up-timer, since the text was quoted literally and it had not been created until the nineteenth century. In fact, the final version quoted in the *Pestis* pamphlet was forged by the Okhrana, the Tsarist secret police, in the 1890s. There was no way to make enquiries as to who had had the thing and brought it back to the seventeenth century. Freddy Congden had certainly denied it, hadn't even heard of it, he claimed. Nasi wasn't sure, but he thought he could believe Congden. He hadn't the imagination to lie convincingly.

After a while, Mike spoke again. "*Pestis* guy is back? That one?"

"The same. The latest is more temperate, alleging, among the wilder material about Jews and Catholic treachery, only that the mission to Venice is in truth a mission to Rome, to sell the whole of the United States of Europe to the pope."

"How's it being distributed this time?" Mike sounded genuinely curious. The first *Pestis* pamphlet had enjoyed a day or two of uninterrupted sales, mostly from street vendors who, when questioned, had invariably been given bundles of them to sell by a man they'd met in a tavern. A stranger to them, German or so they thought, of varying descriptions. From the times of appearance of the pamphlets across Germany, there were perhaps four or five different people distributing it.

After the Committees of Correspondence had gotten a look at the thing, sales had dried up quickly. A good threat of a beating backed up with an occasional demonstration—with the promise of broken bones to follow—would discourage even the most avaricious vendor. Of course, the actions of the Committees were thoroughly illegal. But not even Dan Frost had made any serious effort to put a stop to it. Tactically speaking, the author of the pamphlet had made a serious error by including the obscene material about Mike Stearns' wife Rebecca.

Anti-Semitic prejudices or not, a big percentage of the USE's population regarded Rebecca as something in the way of their commoners' princess-of-choice. Even those who didn't tended to get surly when she was attacked personally. In Magdeburg's province, the percentage was well-nigh astronomical. Mike Stearns didn't expect to win a nationwide election running against Wilhelm Wettin, whenever the first regular election was called. But neither he nor Wilhelm nor anyone else doubted for an instant that Rebecca would sweep the senatorial election in Magdeburg province—even if she ran in absentee from Amsterdam. Maybe *especially* if she ran while still in Amsterdam. Hopefully, of course, the siege would be over before the election, but . . . who knew? The election wasn't even scheduled yet, much less the end of the war.

Still, the Committees weren't everywhere and the *Pestis* pamphlet had kept turning up from time to time in the smaller towns and the villages. Apparently at random, although Dan Frost reckoned that to be an artifact of the reporting. He thought there was probably an underlying pattern to it that they'd see if they only had reports from everywhere that got the things.

"This time?" Nasi said. "This time, they are trying not to draw the attention of the Committees. The pamphlet contains no slanderous attack on Becky—ha! the cretins!—and they simply leave stacks of the things in tavern privies, under the tables and so forth. Left anonymously in places where they will be found and picked up. They're no longer even trying to use open vendors."

"I'm surprised the Committees aren't hoovering the things up," Mike said.

"When they find them, they are. Usually when the tavern owners bring it to their attention—and quickly, lest suspicion fall on them. Heh. The Committees of Correspondence—especially here in Magdeburg—are, ah, territorial about propaganda."

Mike chuckled. He, too, knew many of the firebrands involved with the Committees. They had no such troubles as the anonymous pamphleteer in getting their message across. They didn't even have to threaten anyone to get vendors to distribute their propaganda in the open. Well, not in Magdeburg, at least, or in Thuringia. It was hard to know what practices they might be following in the smaller towns in such provinces as Pomerania or Mecklenburg.

"What they did not notice," Nasi went on, "is that the author is the same as the author of *Pestis*. I, however, am certain of it. The style, the word-choices. As good as a fingerprint. Dan Frost's suggestion of examining the letters in their small details allows me to say the two pamphlets come from the same press. We have, though, yet to find that press."

"You're assuming it's in Germany?"

"Yes, I am assuming that. I have to. Loose as our borders are, from the point of view of smugglers printed matter is bulky and hard to transport unseen. Did a foreigner wish to circulate this material among us, he would do better to buy a press within our borders and produce it here."

"Figures," Mike agreed.

"We are trying to trace the type, and the paper. Dan's experience of the police techniques of the future gives us methods that the perpetrators do not, I think, know of. The problem is that there are thousands of presses and hundreds of papermakers in the Germanies. Until we stumble upon something from that particular press which we can trace, we are stymied. The paper is even worse. No two batches are alike, whereas in the twentieth century there was quality control and everything was milled to the same grade. Now? The papermaker probably isn't using the same mix of rags any more. Although we do know something about the shape of his roller."

Mike sat silent for a while. "You think this guy's a threat," he said finally.

Nasi decided he had to approach this carefully. "Mike, no. This fellow, by himself, whoever he is, is not a threat. His pamphlets appear too infrequently and too widely scattered for me to think there is a big organization with him. It's just . . ."

Stearns was ahead of him. "You want to know who's funding this stuff. It's the money that bothers you."

Nasi nodded.

"You're sure it's not just internal, then?" Mike was talking slowly and carefully. Nasi understood his concern. However ebullient Mike had been with Dan Frost over the Congden business, he had himself had misgivings about it. Sometimes, he'd said privately, what looks like a crime is in fact the exercise of a right.

"No, Mike." It was as well to lay the whole thing before him. Nasi had seen Mike's response to faits accompli and it was not pretty. Not that Herr Prime Minister Stearns wasn't above doing it himself, but he regarded it as a tactic for use on opponents, not on one's own side. "I'm sure of nothing at the moment. It takes no great stretch of the imagination to find that there is a group—a small group, I would guess, or they would be more overt—who have done badly, but not too badly, out of the last three years."

"Why not too badly?" Mike asked, and then: "No, forget that. Printers have to be paid. Papermakers, too."

"Just so. Such a group would be smart enough to evade ruin, but not so smart as to see what is taking shape, in these United States of Europe."

Mike flashed a grin, leaned back and stretched. "A mess, Francisco. An unholy, godawful, don't-know-my-ass-from-my-elbow mess."

"Quite." Nasi stepped away from the window to pace a little. "The problem is that such a mess is a novelty to much of our population. The spoliation of armies and the ravages of plague, these things they could take for granted. They have been facts of life for so many for so long."

"Too many, too long," Mike growled.

"But they have had a taste of better, now. This economy is in a boom, if I understood the theoreticians I have read correctly. People are learning—forgive my borrowing a rather foolish metaphor, coined so far as I can determine by someone who had never so much as gotten his feet wet—that a rising tide does not lift all the boats. Something which the first author of that metaphor missed, Mike, but that many people here and now do not, is that the rising tide has surges and eddies that smash boats and drown people."

"Francisco, I know all this, please—"

Nasi gave a slight bow of apology. He knew he had a slight tendency to lecture. "Forgive me. The point I seek to make, Mike, is that it is not those swimming for the wharf or outright drowned that need concern us. Our malcontents are those still in their boats, watching the harbor water come in through sprung planks. They have time enough from bailing to blame you for the light damage to their boat."

"And I am to blame," Mike said, "and don't think I don't know it. Thing is, I don't think it's an inescapable law of nature, like a lot of folks back up-time did. It's the casualties you take to win a battle. Ask Gustavus Adolphus some time. It's not pretty, but it beats losing."

"Nothing, save a battle lost, is half so melancholy as a battle won." Nasi liked that quote.

"You get that from Eddie Cantrell?" Mike asked. The young naval officer, for the time being in Danish captivity, was fond of quoting Wellington.

"Originally, yes. But I first heard it said in what I suspect was its original spirit by Colonel Wood."

"Ah." Mike nodded, suddenly more solemn than angry. Colonel Jesse "Der Adler" Wood had won—helped win; Eddie Cantrell had been maimed and then captured in the same action—the battle of Wismar late in the year before. In that battle, the colonel had lost his star pilot, Hans Richter. Jesse had become a grimmer man, since then.

Nasi let the silence gather a moment. Hans' death had been a dreadful personal loss to many in and around Grantville. Still keenly felt, for all that his death had been the standard around which the new United States had rallied.

"You know," Mike said, "all that—" He gestured to take in the last few months, the mass demonstrations and the flood of volunteers to the new brigades. "—is probably scaring the daylights out of our pamphleteer. Out of a lot of them, actually, but especially this *Pestis* guy."

Nasi answered that with a grin. "Probably. For it speaks to him of yet more success for the Jewish conspiracy to ruin the honest and spill the blood of Christians."

Mike chuckled. "So we could believe *Pestis* guy is a native-born asshole. But you suspect—?" Mike raised an eyebrow.

"Mike, I find myself asking who benefits by incitement and sedition."

"Free speech," Mike corrected him.

"Free speech, fine," Nasi allowed, "but directed at provoking criminal activity. And who has a proven record of working with *agents provocateurs* . . . ?"

"A French term," Mike said. "Richelieu? You think he's funding this?"

"I have no proof. But the telling factor, for me, is how unlikely it is that someone might suffer misfortune enough to provoke this much hatred without becoming bankrupt. Without, even, losing that level of funds required to get several thousand *Flugblätter* printed and bound. That suggests to me that a better hypothesis is that the disaffected party is getting its funding from somewhere else."

"Stipulated. It still isn't a crime, is it?"

"No. But it may be something that criminals are doing. If they will take money from foreign powers—I do not assume, entirely, that it is France—to print leaflets, they might well take it to do other things."

Mike chewed his lip. "What does Dan think?" Dan Frost had gone from being head of Grantville's tiny police department to being a consultant to a good many town constabularies throughout the United States. Social advances were not just limited to the making of tools, they covered developments in technique as well, as Dan was proving. Like a lot of small-town cops, he had had little time away from the job for formal training and had substituted a slew of subscriptions to professional journals. He was putting the articles to good use, now, reselling copies of them around the USE and, everyone hoped, raising the usually pitiful level of European law enforcement in this day and age. That library of technique had also proved helpful to Nasi, when he had detection problems that conventional seventeenth-century counterespionage was ill equipped to handle.

"Dan agrees that the behavior is suspicious, and merits investigation. If only to rule out the possibility of sabotage or some other, actively criminal, subversion."

Mike nodded, slowly "Fine. Francisco, trust Dan's instincts on this one. I mean no disrespect, but your instincts in these things come from a culture that—no, that's not right, and I'm sorry. You know what you grew up with, and what the United States is all about, and how it's different."

Nasi grinned broadly. It was rare that Mike dropped into such lazy habits of thought, and the effect was amusing, not offensive. Still, that was no reason not to have a little fun.

"True," he said, deadpan. "The sultan would have set his torturers to work, found out who was responsible, and devised some suitably humorous way to put him to death. Run through his own press, most likely, before an appreciative audience of pashas and beys."

Mike gave him an old-fashioned look.

"No, Mike, seriously, I take no offense. I do try to take account of how my upbringing and training and the standards of this brave new world may differ. It was for this reason I consulted with Dan, you know. A good spymaster checks his assumptions."

"Sorry, Francisco. I'm teaching granny to suck eggs again."

Nasi dismissed the apology with a wave. "In truth, the operational details need not detain us. The substance of the report I sought to make this morning was the report from Venice and that this pamphleteer is back at work, both of which you needed to know."

Mike raised his coffee cup. "Cheers, then," he said, and took a gulp. "Damn fine coffee your cousin is getting for us."

Nasi sniffed. "Which you Americans then proceed to ruin. I was served a cup yesterday that I could actually see the bottom of." He sniffed again. "I shall not repeat my opinion of the barbaric pollutants used."

"Be off," Mike said, waving his coffee cup toward the door, "and take your coffee snobbery with you. Some of us like to have a cup of coffee and not take three days to get the use of our taste buds back.

"Anyway," Mike went on in a more sober tone, "I need time to compose myself for my first meeting. Wilhelm's coming in to tell me what he's viewing with alarm this week."

"Exasperating?" Nasi asked, knowing what the answer was. As Wilhelm Wettin—formerly Duke Wilhelm von Saxe-Weimar—grew into his role as the leader of the newly founded Crown Loyalist opposition party, he was giving Mike more and more trouble.

Mike sighed. "Very. The man's got more sense than to be anything other than totally straight with me, all the time, even in private, and it's getting wearing. I was thinking at first that he'd' have no experience of this kind of politics, but if he's learning on the job he hides it well."

"And what is he viewing with alarm this week?"

"I don't know yet," Mike said. "He's got the media part down pat, I have to say. I get a long list of grievances, condemnations, views-with-alarm, occasionally—very occasionally!—some point of commendation. And it all appears in the same day's papers. I could do with a press office that good, really I could."

"Do you want to know in advance—" Nasi began.

Mike stopped him. "No, Francisco. In fact: *hell, no*. Did you read about Watergate?"

"Yes, Mike," Nasi said, recalling his own reaction: that Richard Nixon would have fit right in at the Sublime Porte. "No, what I meant was to suggest that you ask the Crown Loyalists to set the agenda for the meetings. The day before, perhaps, so that you can be ready with the facts at hand to answer questions?"

Mike smiled. "Nice try. That works in Congress, for Prime Minister's Questions, but Wilhelm's too good an operator to give me any advance warning for one of these little chats. Wide-ranging discussion, he'll say. Loyal opposition, not the foreign delegation at a summit, he'll say. And more like it, and he'll look like he means it all. No, he suckered me into having these briefing sessions for the leaders of the opposition parties, and now he's got them he's not going to let me take the teeth out of them for him. So, no agenda." Mike sighed.

"Well, I might hazard a guess as to what is on the agenda you do not have for this morning might be."

"Venice, what else?" Mike said, with more than the merest hint of a groan in his voice. "As it has been these six weeks past. Viewing with alarm the possibility of any extension of the mission in the direction of Rome. Drawing to my attention that our enemies are all among the Catholic powers, our friends among the Protestant ones. Except for England and Denmark, of course, but Wilhelm claims that doesn't count since Charles Stuart is a notorious papist sympathizer and Christian IV an equally notorious drunkard."

Mike sighed again. "I am resolutely not using the phrase 'religious bigot' either here or in public. So far, he hasn't used the words 'Catholic Menace,' either. So I guess we're even—or, at least, still being reasonably civil."

"He needs at least a goodly chunk of the Catholic vote if he hopes to win a nationwide election," Nasi pointed out. Then, shook his head. "But I leave that to you."

"Along with Wilhelm," Mike said, gloomily.

Chapter 22

It was good for Michel Ducos that he was quiet and impassive. The comte d'Avaux could feel a rage boiling in the quiet depths of the man's heart, a rage that would take no more than a word, a gesture, an expression out of place to make good on its threat that he would abandon the pretense of calm reason that he was maintaining. There was something not sane at the core of Ducos' soul, the comte had long known. Of course, the same could be said of any heretic, he supposed; but of Ducos, more than most. He reminded d'Avaux of one of the watchdogs the comte owned on his estate back in France.

It was a dangerous beast, improperly handled. On the other hand, also the best watchdog on the estate—and d'Avaux knew himself for a superb handler, of either dogs or men.

Ducos had delivered the news-sheet without comment beyond a grave, "Seigneur le Comte should read this."

So he had, and having gotten no more than a third of the way down the page he had put the piece of refuse down. Bad enough that this Buckley had outwitted a staff of professional spymasters to penetrate to their more secret counsels, although such was more or less to be expected. There was this much to take comfort in: the encyphered dispatches that only d'Avaux, Ducos and their cypher clerk had seen appeared not to have been relayed to the wretched American.

But to publish! That was the larger half of d'Avaux's upset. There were customs in such matters, hallowed by time so as to be all but law. By his actions, Buckley had put the American delegation in flagrant mockery of that law. D'Avaux wondered, with unwonted grim humor, whether this meant that the Swede's creatures wanted matters in Venice played out *à l'outrance*? They had certainly spared no pains to provoke such. For what purported to be a communiqué of news the thing had the brutal tone of an incendiary pamphlet.

The Americans had almost certainly acquired that habit in the Germanies. Or, rather, added it like a gloss onto the boorish customs they had brought with them. The Germanies sprouted presses like mushrooms, waxing in the fecal darkness of their Protestant benightedness. The product of those presses was no more wholesome than what they grew in.

But that brought the metaphor of mushrooms to an abrupt halt, since d'Avaux was partial to the delicacies. So, he forced himself back to the matter at hand.

To write, in what purported to be news, in the tone of a demagogue exhorting the mob, was—exactly what he might have done, or at least ordered done, had he thought of it first. The realization drained the unaccustomed rage away, unexpressed now save as mild annoyance.

"Ducos, how did he come by this?"

A brief smile was Ducos' first answer. Then: "Monsieur Buckley fancies himself as a spy. An amateur, only."

D'Avaux cocked an eyebrow.

Ducos nodded. "He fancies himself quite the master of espionage, seigneur. He speaks with servants."

D'Avaux felt his own face twitch into a smile. It was, of course, impossible to keep many secrets from one's servants. Ducos was as good an example as any, and better than most, but below Ducos' exalted level as factotum, the footmen and valets could not help but overhear a great deal. The astute spymaster would cultivate such sorts and their gossip, and it was seldom needful to disburse more than nominal bribes to procure an essential appreciation of one's opponent's counsels and habits of thought. The trick was to sort the wheat from the chaff in the information thus gathered, the genuine intelligence from the idle talk of the lower orders. It did not do to be vexed by this, of course, since those same lower orders were constitutionally incapable of genuine, higher loyalty.

All that mattered was that the most central secrets be kept. And, when he thought further on the matter, d'Avaux realized that not only had Buckley not penetrated any of those, he had no hope of doing so. He pursed his lips, and set to thinking hard; a calm consideration was called for.

He tapped his finger on the offending newspaper where it lay on his desk. Once, twice, thrice. "He has, of course, insulted us."

"Yes, seigneur."

"Ascribed to us base motives. Suggested that all we have said to the doge of our mission is a sham. That we seek to continue the war on neutral ground."

"Yes, seigneur." Ducos impassively awaited instructions.

"Is there a statement yet from the Americans?"

"Not as yet, seigneur."

"I thought not. I shall compose a letter to the doge. Naturally, we are upset at this callous libel, which we regard as *damnum iniuria atrox*, calling for satisfaction. Naturally, His Most Christian Majesty Louis XIII of France is likewise insulted, and would esteem it a great favor were the Americans proceeded against,

or at least expelled from the Most Serene Republic."
D'Avaux drew pen and paper toward himself and
contemplated the feather of his quill as he flicked it
back and forth.

"It is my assessment, seigneur—"

D'Avaux waved him quiet. "No, I know, Ducos.
The Venetians have had gold waved under their noses.
They would insult God Himself to get it. But they
will respect the forms and take the counsel of their
fear of our doing them harm at Istanbul. They will at
least reprimand the American priest, and repairing the
damage will set him back somewhat."

Ducos nodded.

D'Avaux decided to check before dismissing Ducos.
"Is there anything further?" he asked.

"Yes, Seigneur le Comte." Ducos produced another
paper. "Word is sent us from Istanbul, as it happens. The
grand seignor of the Turks is to send an emissary."

"This came from our own embassy there?"

"Yes, seigneur. Our courier believes he got the message here a full day before the official message from
the Sublime Porte, which will be for the doge first in
any event."

"Good," d'Avaux said. "We are, I believe, much in
favor with the Grand Turk lately."

"Seigneur?"

"Well, I suppose there's no reason you shouldn't
know," the comte said, putting down his pen for a
moment and using his best tone of condescension.
Ducos responded well to that; the Huguenot underling
treasured the little tidbits d'Avaux handfed him as much
as did the savage watchdog on his estate.

"His Eminence has spared no pains in his efforts
to confine the Swede in northern Europe. Cardinal
Richelieu has had profuse warnings carried to the grand
vizier, to the sultan and to the priests of the Maho-
metans. The Turks much dislike novelty and disorder,
you know, and are easily persuaded by news of the

Committees of Correspondence that the Swede's new United States is a wholesale fomenter of revolt."

"Which is true," Ducos said, in a rare excursion into commentary.

"Naturally," d'Avaux agreed. "The truth was all it needed. And by representing the League of Ostend as a matter of distracting the Spaniards from the Mediterranean where they compete with the Turk's Algerines, we ingratiate ourselves further with the Turk. It is simple work to advance ourselves in this matter by the most traditional of means, while the rest of Europe is more pressingly engaged elsewhere and trade outside the Mediterranean is disrupted."

"And so the emissary?"

D'Avaux permitted himself another smile; this session was proving quite pleasant after its inauspicious beginning. "The emissary has been sent—you may depend upon it, Ducos—to satisfy the Grand Turk's curiosity about these peculiar Americans and to warn Venice to have no truck with them, on pain of the sultan's displeasure."

"What does the seigneur want done?"

D'Avaux paused, while he composed his thoughts. Ducos was a good servant in this, especially. He stood always ready to do his superior's bidding. "I believe," d'Avaux said at length, "we should see that the Turk's undoubted prejudices are validated in full."

Ducos remained silent and attentive, while the germ of an idea sprouted in d'Avaux's mind. "See that Buckley's attention is diverted toward the Turk. Let us see how they react to perceived insult."

"Yes, Seigneur le Comte."

D'Avaux fixed his man with a steady gaze. "The Turk's response, of course, will most likely be sanguinary."

"Yes, Seigneur le Comte," Ducos said, and withdrew.

When the room was silent and d'Avaux was sure he was alone, he permitted himself a small chuckle, and then a brief prayer of thanks. Sometimes, the secondary causes through which God worked were truly remarkable. The Turk, indeed! How pleasant to use such a tool, atop another like the Huguenot heretic.

It was, of course, a given that the Mahometan religion was of the devil. They were also notorious funders of Protestant arms in the Germanies. The current Grand Turk had a reputation as more of a monster than most. A prodigious brute of uncommon size and strength, he was by repute taking the Turkish state all the firmer in his grip by the simple expedient of terrorizing all who opposed him. Executions by the thousand were reported in some years. Of course, lacking the Law and the Order that it brought with it, such brutal measures were all that would answer the Turk's purposes.

And having to resort to such in his own home land, who would doubt that his emissaries would do otherwise to someone who offended them in Venice?

Did d'Avaux care to wager, he felt, he could do worse than to hazard a small sum that Ducos would not need to act on his instructions at all.

"Well, that didn't go quite as I expected," Sharon said.

Magda's only response was to stump along toward the gondolas tied up at a pier, muttering a litany of some kind in German. Sharon was catching, perhaps, one word in three. She understood those because they were swear words. It was a wonder that the paintwork on the palazzi they were walking past didn't blister. Even the Marines who had been sent along because they were carrying cash were probably learning some words, and Sharon was mildly worried because their officer was Billy Trumble, who seemed like such a sweet kid under the uniform.

"I wonder what we were doing wrong?" Sharon tried, when the pyroclastic flow had subsided.

"Going to the place of business of an ill-mannered

arschloch, that is what we were doing wrong!" Magda snapped. And then: "Oh, please forgive me, Sharon. I should go back and give that, that—" She shuddered. "I should give to him a piece of my mind, that is what I should do."

Sharon tried a smile on for size. "You already did that, honey."

She was rewarded with an answering grin. "Oh, *nein*. I gave him a talking-to, quite mild for me. I should go back and insult him properly, I think."

Sharon pantomimed horror. "But, Magda, we'd get arrested. He all but died of fright right there on the spot."

That was almost true, she thought. They'd gone into Casa Falier to keep an appointment with one of their senior agents. Maestro Luzzatto had given them a list of brokers who dealt in the goods on their "shopping list," and they had decided that the simplest way to go about it was to visit one of them and ask him. Luzzatto had cheerfully admitted he was not a specialist in the kind of trading they were doing, but would hunt up some friends and acquaintances who could help more directly when they had scouted the lay of the land. After all, most of the stuff on their list he'd never even heard of.

At Tom Stone's request, his wife and Sharon had taken on one of the secondary tasks of the USE mission to Venice, which was to try to fulfill as much of the wish list of chemicals, raw materials and useful items that had been thrown together by the combined efforts of Grantville's and Magdeburg's corps of technologists. A lot of the stuff—certainly the material in the smaller quantities—was needed for research into things that probably weren't going to pay off for years to come. Others were vital strategic supplies. Zinc, for example, which was already being imported from Asia but which few Europeans outside of Grantville recognized as a distinct element.

Magda actually chuckled. "I think we need to make a better plan, Sharon."

"I think we may well, at that. It seems they want us to buy wholesale."

"If we do not want to buy retail, 'with the other peasants,'" Magda muttered.

"Did he really say that?"

"*Ja,* he did! He muttered it, but I heard him. Filthy manners, that swine."

There was a rumble from the Marines behind them.

"Ma'am?" asked Lieutenant Trumble, "you want we should go back and maybe have a stronger word with the man?"

"Oh, no, Billy," said Sharon hastily. "That won't be necessary. He just doesn't get any more of our business, is all. Bad service, and we tell everyone who wants to hear. Simple." She smiled at him as brightly as she could, having visions of the repercussions of three of the USE's uniformed finest turning up to terrorize a respected Venetian merchant house. Billy Trumble would be for diplomacy what a bull would be for a china shop.

Magda sighed. "We go back to the embassy, then, and plan afresh."

"Well, maybe." Sharon was seized by a sudden wild impulse. "How about we go do a little personal shopping instead? We've got money of our own, after all—and three big strong boys here to carry our purchases. That's a rare opportunity, let me tell you."

"Shopping?" Magda looked intrigued.

"Yeah, shopping. We call it retail therapy. Just the thing after a disappointing experience. One of the finer inventions of the twentieth century."

Magda smiled her agreement. "Shopping!" she said.

Sharon looked back at the Marines. Billy was the only up-timer of the three, and his face was a picture.

❊ ❊ ❊

The embassy was quickly settling into a routine of drinks before dinner, which was just getting going when Sharon and Magda got back. The down-time Marines had been introduced to the pleasure of accompanying ladies in a serious retail frenzy; thereby proving, to Sharon's satisfaction, that blank-faced stoical response was hardwired into the male genetic code. Born three hundred years before the invention of the mall, they had developed the stance and the face without even having to think about it. Sharon had been amused, despite herself. And besides, shopping was just plain fun.

They'd gotten back, squared accounts from their own funds, and changed for dinner.

"Any success, ladies?" Father Mazzare asked.

"Not yet, no," Sharon said. "Explored a blind alley this morning, and took the rest of the day just exploring. We're going to get hold of Maestro Luzzatto as soon as we can and work up a real plan of action."

She and Magda hadn't just been shopping, actually. They'd crossed and recrossed the Rialto district as they'd picked up souvenirs, clothes and assorted pretties, and watched deals go down left, right and center. Venice was a town that, however tight margins currently were, lived and died by dealing. When the weather was good, Venetians came out and did it in the street, strolling across the piazza and in taprooms and tavernas everywhere. Wander into the right part of town and you heard everything being bought and sold. They'd even taken a look at the Palazzo Ducale, and walked through the Imbroglio, which had given its name to the kind of insanely complicated political and commercial deals that were put together there.

Eavesdropping had been fruitful. Sharon and Magda had gotten some idea of the kind of trading they wanted to do here, and they were already revising their plan of attack.

Tom was over by the fire, sprawled sideways across an armchair and perusing his notes. Given the volume of requests that had poured in as soon as the embassy arrived in Venice, Stoner had decided to postpone setting up his own laboratory in favor of purely educational work. He was about to start his lectures with a series on the practical problems of scaling lab processes to industrial ones, right here in Venice. He would be going to the university in Padua later, to do the more academic stuff on scientific method and real chemistry. He was absorbed in his material, so much so that he wasn't paying any attention to the room around him.

"I should go reassure my husband," Magda said. "He seems nervous."

"I think you're right," Sharon agreed. "And Magda?"

"*Ja?*"

"I think we maybe ought to turn out for Tom's lectures, don't you?"

"Well, naturally . . ." Magda said, frowning at the implied suggestion that she hadn't been going to support her man.

"No, that's not what I meant. I mean we should go with our trading hats on. Not every chemist is as unworldly as your Stoner." She smiled to take any possible sting out of the words. To hear Magda tell it, as well as being the most frustrating thing about Stoner, his impracticality was one of the things she loved most about him. "And maybe there's a slice of that action to be had."

Magda, grasping what Sharon was driving at immediately, grinned back. And it was not a friendly grin, either. Sharon realized that there was something deeply predatory about her friend, something that had been aroused to a terrible hunger by the scent of deals in the water.

She suspected that the next few weeks were going

to be very interesting indeed. As Magda crossed the room to mop Tom's fevered brow, Sharon began looking around for Luzzatto to make an appointment.

Chapter 23

Singing. Some damned idiot was singing, somewhere in the street below. He'd been at it for some time, too, long enough to wake Buckley up. Joe rolled over and grabbed his watch. No need for the backlight function, it was already full day.

That helped wake him up as well. The fact that he'd gotten a suite of rooms with a nice, big, east-facing window that gave him a view of the Isola di Sant'Elena and its cathedral, and beyond that the Lido and the sea, was all very well. But the sun came up right in the window and the first thing it did in the morning was heat the room up to somewhere near boiling point. The bull's-eye panes in the window didn't help; they focused the sunlight onto the far wall in a strange and eye-watering pattern of rippled light.

Just after midday, he saw from his watch. He could probably have figured that by the position of the sunlight on the wall. Joe lived in a permanent paranoia of his watch breaking. He'd had the good fortune to have a self-winding model, nothing fancy, but it was one of the few timepieces from the old universe that was still working. He'd only been half-joking with himself when he'd thought to mark the position of the sun on the wallpaper at every hour. A couple of times he'd had scares that his watch was about to wind down. He wound it anyway, for the reassurance of having the time right.

He rolled out of bed, and stood swaying for a moment before rooting around for the chamberpot. He hadn't gotten into bed before about four o'clock that morning. He'd stayed light on the sauce, but that didn't mean he felt particularly human this morning. Afternoon, rather.

This was a town that liked to party, and party good and hard at that. Would it be too much, he wondered, to do a tourist guide piece? Venice could certainly use the income, and there were plenty of people in Europe with money who might want to come down here for a week or two.

He coughed, good and hard. Those tavernas could be damned smoky. The prevalence of tobacco in seventeenth-century Europe had come as a surprise to Joe, as it had to most of the up-timers. But where many up-timers had been relieved that their addiction could still be fueled, Joe had quit smoking as soon as the cigarettes ran out. Unlike some others, he'd not been able to bring himself to try what passed for pipe tobacco in this day and age. The stuff was so wretched that just sitting in a tavern was as good as going through a whole pack in an evening.

Buckley opened the window and spat out of it, watching the phlegm drop four floors to the canal. Then he sent the contents of the chamberpot after it, flinging it out so it didn't land on the footpath that ran along the edge of the water. He wasn't supposed to do that, but everybody did anyway.

He was right at the other end of downtown Venice from the embassy, now, up under the roof of a mostly empty tenement block. The rent wasn't bad, as no Venetian really wanted to live this high up if he could afford to be lower down. Besides, after the plague tenants were thin on the ground. The landlord had been almost ecstatic to find a renter.

For his own part, Joe liked it well enough. Someone who'd had the room before him—could have been any time in the last couple of centuries, from the rickety feel of the place—had liked to have plenty of light in the mornings, so they'd enlarged the windows. That kept the rent low, as well, because Joe was quite sure the rooms would be very cold in the winter. But he didn't care; he liked the light himself and planned to be gone by midsummer anyway.

The only real downside to the place was that his guidebook stopped working hereabouts. The map in the back had been drawn in the twentieth century and according to the street plan he was living in what would be, from the nineteenth century onward, a park. Finding the embassy was tough, too—where that stood would be Venice's railway station in three hundred years' time.

Buckley opened the package of laundry that he had picked up yesterday afternoon. That was an odd business. The modern clothes generally came back ruined, other than jeans, but the contemporary stuff usually got through fine. He guessed that was due to the local folks knowing how to deal with what they were used to, and not having a clue with care labels. That said, he'd never had a clue either. He'd gotten used to shapeless pullovers and faded colors in college.

Another change for the better in the seventeenth century: he was dressed better now. Natural curiosity had led him to go find out how they did it before the invention of the Laundromat. It turned out that they took the clothes apart to launder them, and then put them back together, an effort that made him appreciate all the more the pleasant sensation of pulling on clean clothes. Not that he did that as often as he used to.

Wearing a shirt once and tossing it in the hamper was a luxury he couldn't afford any more.

What to do with the day, he wondered? He got his little stove going and began to brew breakfast. He'd gotten hold of one of Grantville's supply of primus stoves early on in his travels. He'd read a quote from Casanova's memoirs—a local boy, that one—some years before the Ring of Fire, and been mightily impressed by the old seducer's habit of carrying with him a bag packed with a stove and breakfast fixings wherever he went so he could "break his fast like a gentleman."

Living out of a suitcase in upper-floor garrets, Buckley appreciated it more for the ability to get hot coffee down him first thing in the morning without having to lay a fire he wasn't going to need to keep warm.

Still, as the coffee perked, he had a day to fill and no clear plan for what to do with it. And that idiot was still singing by the canal-side. He wished he'd spat on the caterwauling fool. Or worse. Something about love and the springtime, a folksong of some sort.

That put Buckley in mind of Frank Stone, and he grinned. What a perfect illustration of teenage maleness that was! Off at all hours hanging out with the Marcolis, a family of complete loons, because he was besotted with Giovanna. Okay, sure, the girl herself was gorgeous, but still. And hauling his brothers along with him every time! The three of them were fixtures at the Casa Marcoli these days, helping to spread the word of the coming new world order to the largely indifferent population of Venice.

Although . . .

Now that Joe actually thought about it, there was something a little odd about that picture. The two younger Stone boys weren't even Frank's brothers. They were really step-brothers. And Giovanna was the only Marcoli daughter, so what the hell were they getting out of it? Hanging out with an obvious crank while their brother tried to get into the pants of the crank's daughter?

Odd. Was something else going on out there? Something more exciting than just sitting around and jabbering about politics?

Joe decided he'd find out. If nothing else, he supposed, it would be a way to spend the day. Besides, it was probably time he took a look at the Committee of Correspondence in Venice, even if he was pretty sure it was mostly a joke. He checked his watch again. There was plenty of time to get there for the daily public meeting they tried to get a decent turnout for—and failed miserably, from what Joe had heard.

And the idiot was *still* singing. He'd reached the end of the song and started again! The way it echoed up from the canal and the buildings opposite made it doubly, trebly annoying. Buckley found himself wishing for some traffic noise, a sound he hadn't heard in nearly three years. Definitely, he decided, time to get out of the house. Even if he got nothing from the Venetian committee, he could mooch about Murano and play tourist.

A boat over to Murano was easily had, and getting out from among the filthy canals of downtown Venice and into the seabreeze and the salt air of the lagoon did Buckley a world of good.

Murano, even in midafternoon with the sunlight across it, looked like a seedy and disreputable pile. Sure, it had its nice neighborhoods, and the glassblowers had always been one of the better-off classes of Venetians. Not dirt-poor, anyway. But like almost everything in Venice, Murano was looking down-at-the-heels. The smoke from the kilns gave it a positively brooding air.

He got off the boat at the right pier for the neighborhood he wanted. Looking around, his imagination immediately painted a set of tracks along the water's edge with a big sign, saying: *You are now entering The Wrong Side.* All of the clues were there. Peeling stucco, even more than usual for Venice. Great patches of plaster missing, the brickwork grinning through from underneath like the teeth of bleached skulls. The laundry strung across the streets—alleyways, in any other town—was gray and patched. More rats than in the neighborhoods that could afford catchers. And, above all, a hunched, wary surliness about the inhabitants, such of them as there were.

He was almost immediately accosted by a grimy little kid. *Urchin, to the life*, he thought. Sighing, he dug in his pocket for a coin before realizing that the kid was holding out a piece of paper. He took it. It was as grimy as the kid was, the print slightly smeared.

He looked back down at the kid. The look of pathetic gratitude and the thick sheaf of handbills still in his hand spoke volumes. Buckley looked around. So did the litter of discarded . . .

He checked the paper in his hand again. *Ha! Yes!* Committee of Correspondence flyers scattered along the path and floating dejectedly in the water.

"No one interested, kid?" Buckley returned his hand into his pocket for that coin. For some time now he'd been keeping a hefty handful of small change in his pocket for just this sort of occasion. Besides, the poor little brat looked like he could use a meal.

"No, messer," the kid said. "Messer Marcoli, he is a good man, he gives me soup and money to give out the papers, but no one wants them." The tone was mournful and the big, brown, hang-dog eyes positively heartbreaking.

"Something for you, then, kid," Buckley said, handing over the coin.

The eyes started to glisten, the lower lip started to tremble. "Aw, hell, here's another. Take a break, on me."

"No, messer. Messer Marcoli wants to tell everyone about the new world coming, and I want people to come and hear him, so I stay."

"How old are you?" Buckley asked, beginning to

see his story taking shape and glad he'd followed this whim. "And what's your name?"

"Eight years, I think, and my name is Benito." Benito sniffed, and added a streak of snot to the grime on his already filthy shirtsleeve.

"Does your mama know you're working for Messer Marcoli? Your papa?"

"Messer, I'm an orphan. Messer Marcoli, he feeds some of us and we help him with his papers, *si*?"

"How many orphans? I mean, kids like you, helping Messer Marcoli?"

"Maybe ten, fifteen. It's not always the same kids. The messer, he is good to us, yes?" Then, suddenly, suspicion was written all over the little face. "What you want to know about Messer Marcoli for, anyhow?" The kid put the sheaf of flyers behind his back, and it was all Buckley could do to keep his face straight.

"It ain't just agents of the authorities who ask questions, kid," he said. He could understand the concern, though. Venice's secret police apparatus might not bother the likes of little Benito. The Council of Ten had bigger fish to fry. But the mercenary soldiers who served the city as its police force were, from the point of view of kids like him, nothing but a goon squad.

"What are you, then?" The insecure little boy had vanished, replaced with a street-smart, hard-boiled little gangster.

"I'm a reporter, Benito. I find out things and write them in a newspaper, like the papers you've got there only bigger, and we sell them. So people can read about things and know what's going on."

"Can't read," Benito said, defiant. Another sniff, another stripe of snot. "Messer Massimo, he's always at us to learn it."

"It's a good thing, Benito. A very good thing."

Another sniff, this time contemptuous. "What's the use of it, eh?"

Hoo-boy. No sense in trying to explain the value of

learning for its own sake, or tell him about the wonderful world of books. *Cut to the chase, Buckley.* "I get paid money because I can read and write."

Head on one side. "For your newspaper?"

"Catch on fast, don't you? Back in the USE, people pay a few pfennigs for every paper they buy. Those pfennigs mount up, and I get enough money to come all the way to Venice looking for new stories to put in the paper." No sense trying to explain syndication, and freelance fees, and staff writers and stringers just yet.

"Stories? You want to ask old Tomaso, when he's sober. He got all kinds of stories about how he's gonna get rich one day." The kid snickered. "And about the real big fish he nearly caught one time. People buy him drinks to get him to tell that one."

Buckley smiled in spite of himself. "Not that kind of story, Benito. True stories, real stories. About people like you, if you'll tell it to me."

"Me?" Benito's eyes were wide. His mouth was open wider still.

"Sure, kid. I mean, not now, you're a busy man, got a lot to do and all. But maybe we could talk after the Committee meeting?"

"You're going to that?"

"Sure I am. That's the story I'm after today, Benito. How the Committee in Venice is getting on."

"Will I be in your story?" Benito asked, now clearly intrigued by the sight of his approaching fifteen minutes of fame.

"Figure you'll get a mention, sure." Buckley made a mental note to focus on Benito and his friends. A thought occurred to him. "Say, that Messer Massimo you mentioned, is he with the Committee?"

Nod. "He's Messer Marcoli's cousin."

"And he's teaching you kids to read?"

"Some of the guys are trying it, a bit. He gives them cakes if they stay for lessons." Sniff. "Me, I never.

Figured it was dumb, a guy like me learning to read. Don't wanna be a priest or nothin'. Anyway," he waved the sheaf of flyers, "I gotta job."

Buckley offered up a silent prayer of thanks to whatever the patron saint of journalists was. This one was going to be real, real easy to write. "Say, Benito, before I let you get back to work, you want to know how to do the thing with the flyers? I had to sell papers myself before they let me write in 'em."

That was a little white lie. Joe had distributed flyers for a nightclub a couple of times for a few extra dollars. But it was better to give the kid the idea he was on a career path, here. Do wonders for his self-confidence, with any luck. "Here, gimme a few."

He read one over, and then demonstrated the technique for Benito. Smile, accost, smile, patter, smile and hand over the flyer. There was a rhythm to it, even.

"See?" he said to Benito, after he'd unloaded a dozen or so. "You have to smile and have a little chat with them. They're more likely to take something from you. Lots of confidence, lots of good cheer. They're more likely to buy something from you, too. Go on, kid, give it a try."

A couple of diffident tries and then Benito got the hang of it, getting maybe half the people he approached to take a flyer. Some still tossed the things aside when they'd read them.

"Thank you, Messer . . ." A frown. "I don't know your name."

"Buckley. Joe Buckley."

"Thank you, Messer Buckley. See you at the Committee!"

Buckley grinned. Before he left Benito, he got directions from the kid, but took his time about going there. He had a couple of hours to kill and the Murano glassworks were, if not fascinating, then at least relatively interesting. Until it dawned on him that the bizarre and brightly colored glassware on sale was exactly the kind of thing his mother had liked to annoy his dad by buying. Joe spent a long time after he realized that, staring into the lagoon, homesick as all hell.

Evening was drawing near when he entered the neighborhood where the Marcolis—he had trouble thinking of them as the Venetian "Committee of Correspondence," accustomed as he was to the political machine that operated in Magdeburg—held their meetings in a taverna. As he turned down the street where it was, he noticed something brownish nailed to a wall. He looked closer. It was a severed human ear, just starting to turn maggotty. Choking his lunch back down, Joe walked on hurriedly, sticking to the middle of the street and trying not to make eye contact. *Talk about your rough neighborhoods!*

He knew he was in the right place as soon as he turned a corner and saw some young guys kicking a soccer ball up and down, although with what level of skill he didn't know. That would be the influence of the Stone boys, he thought. Stone had been a "soccer dad," back up-time. The Venetian precursor of the sport wasn't anything Joe wanted to see up close, though. He was sure it would be best described as a gang fight with a ball in there somewhere.

There was a signboard, a rather nicely lettered one, proclaiming a meeting of the Committee of Correspondence somewhere around to the rear of the big building. Buckley wound his way to the back and went in. Inside, once through a short corridor, was a standard type of Venetian taverna. It was more in the way of a big room attached to the kitchens that was primarily used by family and residents rather than being a public establishment as such, although they had it set up at the moment to serve drink at a temporary counter under the windows along the western wall. Despite being open, the one row of windows didn't really allow that much air into the place. Between the poor circulation and the direct sunlight coming through the windows, the place was on the hot and stuffy side.

And this was still March. Buckley didn't want to think how hot the place would get in midsummer. He got himself a jug of wine and sat down to wait for the show to start.

"Hi, Mr. Buckley, doing a story on us?" It was Ron Stone, coming over from somewhere in back.

"Hi, Ron, yeah, I thought I might."

Ron grinned. "Do we get copy approval?"

Buckley grinned back. "What, you're here five minutes and you're head flack already?"

Ron laughed aloud. "Sort of assistant to the head flack, which is Massimo over there." He pointed to a slightly rounded-looking fellow having an animated discussion with a shock-headed older guy. "That's Messer Marcoli he's talking to," Ron went on. "You want an interview, just ask. We can use all the publicity we can get, I figure."

"Happy to oblige. A lot of my readers are Committee types, or at least sympathetic. They'll want to know what's going on. Say, what's the deal with Massimo teaching little kids to read?"

"Yeah, he's a nice guy about that sort of thing. He covers it all up with a lot of guff about advancing national consciousness, raising the awareness of the Italian masses and all, but I think he's basically in it for the goodness. Get a square meal into the little scamps and hope some of the three Rs takes root."

"He having a lot of success?"

"Some. A lot of the kids, the boys especially, think they'll turn into fags if they can read."

"I noticed." Buckley gave Ron a wry grin. "I met one of your Baker Street Irregulars on the way here. Name of Benito. Nice kid, under the dirt. I might have given him a clinching argument about learning to read. Told him I made money writing."

"I can't say I know all their names. But I'll mention

him to Massimo, see if we can't follow up on that for you."

"Thanks," Buckley said, and then he saw Ducos. He stood up and called out, "Michel!"

Ducos looked around, face blank, and then he saw Buckley and smiled back. "Joe!" He came over. "You know, Monsieur Buckley, you nearly got me into terrible trouble at the embassy, publishing what you did."

"Eh? What's that?" Marcoli rose and came over, a suspicious note in his voice. "How in trouble, Michel? And who is this?"

"Monsieur Marcoli, permit me to name Monsieur Buckley to you, American journalist. Monsieur Buckley, if Monsieur Stone has not already had the honor, this is Monsieur Marcoli, who is the leader of this Committee of Correspondence."

"You know each other?" said Marcoli, and then, "Jesu! *That* Buckley? Are you?"

Buckley nodded and Marcoli favored him with an enthusiastic embrace and a flurry of protestations of how honored he was to have *Buckley* there.

"But what is this talk of trouble?" Marcoli asked at length.

"Monsieur Ducos was kind enough to give me some information for my story about d'Avaux," Buckley said.

Marcoli beamed. "Michel? That was you? You kept that quiet!" And he was off again, this time embracing and congratulating Ducos. Phrases like *blow against the oppressor,* and *struck the serpent with the sword of truth* drifted out like flecks of foam from a torrent.

And with that, they were all friends. Marcoli promised Joe a full interview, perhaps the very next day but not today, since they had a private business meeting right after the public meeting.

Buckley saw Gerry Stone with oil up to his elbows emerging from the back room, where apparently he was chief of maintenance on the Committee's printing press. Frank wandered in too, but hardly seemed to notice Joe's presence beyond a murmured: "Oh, hi, Mr. Buckley."

Come to that, the lad hardly seemed to notice his own presence, when Marcoli's daughter was in his line of sight. Which was . . . almost always. Buckley snickered to himself. *Teenagers.* It was pretty clear that Giovanna herself was very happy with the situation.

Not that anything was "going on," Joe was certain. Frank Stone and Giovanna Marcoli moved around each other like a double star. Constant glances back and forth did for the force of gravity—pretty damn ferocious force, judging by the frequency of the doe-eyed looks they gave each other—but Buckley noted that they almost always maintained a certain distance. The double handful of Marcoli sons and cousins were watching the couple all the time, from what Joe could tell. Not with any hostility, no—in fact, it was obvious they all approved of Frank. But there'd be no hanky-panky here, either, fervent revolutionists or not. Lurking somewhere under the approval was the hint that if their sister might cry—or ought to, even if she didn't—one Frank Stone might bleed.

But that was the only positive note. The meeting started as advertised. A few of the urchins drifted in—Benito among them, Buckley noted. But other than them and the members of Marcoli's extended family, Ducos, the Stones and Buckley himself, the meeting had the traditional audience for such events: three old men and a dog. One of the old men remained fast asleep throughout Marcoli's hour-long speech. So did the dog.

There wasn't even anyone Buckley could peg as the Obvious Cop, who might at least have explained the execrable turnout. Which was a shame, in a way, because while Antonio Marcoli was not rowing with both his oars in the water, he was a damn fine speaker. Buckley got most of it down, and figured he could let the guy revise and extend it later to fill in what he'd missed.

And that was it. A chorus of good-byes and good nights, and almost the entire inner corps—Messers Marcoli and Massimo, Giovanna, three of the boys, Ducos and the Stones—departed. They were going to deal with "routine administrative business," according to Ron Stone.

Fair enough, Buckley thought. He stayed in the main room of the taverna for one last drink before quitting for the evening and returning to his rooms to sit down and write up his notes.

He was halfway down his glass of wine when he realized something didn't make sense. *Routine administrative business?*

That didn't require three USE visitors or their visiting rep from the Paris Committee. *My journo-sense is tingling,* Buckley thought.

One advantage of narrow alleys and no street lighting was that it was comparatively easy to sneak around the back unseen and crouch under a shuttered window.

He listened to what was being discussed. Something about Galileo, was all he caught at first. Then, as his ears adjusted after maybe a minute, he silently reached for tablet and pen.

Dynamite. That patron saint is getting candles for a year. And if I can't find out which saint it is, the way my luck's running tonight, I might as well give up.

Chapter 24

Maestro Luzzatto's office wasn't what Sharon Nichols thought of when she heard the words *Expensive Commercial Lawyer*. It was more what she thought of when she heard the words *broom closet*. Actually, given the amount of paper and vellum stuffed into every available nook and cranny and piled atop the desk—albeit in neat, fussy piles—it was still more what the words *filing cabinet* brought to mind. The office was absolutely tiny, and part of a building shared with about thirty other lawyers. Some of the less well-established ones were crammed two and even three at a time in rooms about this size. With her and Magda and the man Luzzatto had brought them here to meet, the place was stuffed wall to wall with bodies and legal impedimenta.

She would have ascribed it all to ghetto crowding, but she knew this was pretty much what real law offices always looked like, even back in the century she'd come from. She'd dated a law student in college for a few months—whose father had been a lawyer before him—and he'd told her that all law offices had a population-and-paper density that shamed Calcutta.

The aim of the game was to pack as many fee-earners as possible into as little rented space as possible. The elegant, book-lined rooms they showed people on TV shows were modeled on the conference rooms reserved for client meetings. The actual working space, he'd told her, usually looked like an explosion in a paper mill followed by a commando raid by the coffee-ring gnomes.

Still, she was sure this level of crowding was extreme. That was, of course, the ghetto effect. The word still gave Sharon a touch of conceptual whiplash, not least because this neighborhood was the original "Ghetto" for which all the others would be named in the centuries to follow. Plus, this was the place where the Jews lived, rather than the black folks. Not that Sharon had any real personal experience herself with the black ghettos of the old United States. She only knew the ghettos of up-time America from stories her father occasionally told, and the few months she'd spent working for him in his clinic.

The Jewish ghetto in Venice wasn't really a poor neighborhood, either, even if the severe crowding could make it look that way at times. The inhabitants might live packed in like sardines, but they did pretty well—although they suffered disproportionately from fires and disease. Venice might not like their company much, but Jews could do business just as well as Christians on the islands of the lagoon; and when it came to making a deal, they made the same deals as everyone else. They even had the advantage—if you were prepared to go looking for a bright side to the seventeenth century's equivalent of Jim Crow laws—of sumptuary regulations which forbade them the extravagant finery of the Venetian upper crust. Maintaining that facade could be extremely expensive, so the Jews probably weren't doing quite as badly as the rest of Venice out of the current lean time.

"Not doing as badly" was a relative term, of course.

The ghetto was as down-at-the-heels as most of Venice, and the plague had probably hit it worse than it had the rest of the city. Having met them on the way in and walked them up to his office, Luzzatto had remarked that the place felt empty these days. Hard as it was to imagine, before the plague it had apparently been much more crowded.

Luzzatto sent an office-boy running for coffee and began with introductions. "Signora Nichols, Signora Stone, may I present to you Messer Giuseppe Cavriani, who is the agent in La Serenissima for the Cavriani family." That provoked a round of *charmed-to-meet-yous* and a rather lengthy one, as Cavriani insisted on rising and bowing. Sharon wondered how he managed it without knocking something over.

Coffee came, presented on quite a nice tray—although the tray itself had to be balanced between two stacks of parchment briefs tied up in bundles with actual by-God red tape. While Luzzatto was fussing over the tiny cups and the Turkish-style coffee pot, Sharon took a good long look at Cavriani.

She knew the name—the family name, at least—even if she'd never met the man. That had been part of the briefing which Ed Piazza had given them, before they left on this mission to Venice. Today, Piazza was the appointed governor of the province of the USE known either as "Thuringia" or "East Virginia." (That depended on who you talked to. No official decision had been made yet regarding the eventual name of the province which had once been a semi-independent nation under Grantville's leadership. In fact, the official government stationery of the province still read "United States.") But before that he'd been the secretary of state of the original small U.S.; and, during that time, he'd been approached by one of the representatives of the Cavriani clan. Ed hadn't gone into the details, for reasons he had declined to give—which, to Sharon, meant diplomatic skullduggery and maneuver. She'd asked her father about it, and he'd told her he was pretty sure the Cavrianis were also agents of the Neapolitan radicals as well as legitimate continental businessmen.

Although he hadn't explained his reasons, Ed Piazza had asked all of them to report to him if they ran across any Cavrianis in Venice. And . . .

Now they had.

Sharon was a bit intrigued to see that a Cavriani in the flesh didn't look at all like the combination of bomb-throwing anarchist and suave Genevan man-of-affairs she would have imagined. If anything, he looked like a younger, shorter version of Father Mazzare. Less gray at the temples, a little fuller in the face, he had the same aquiline profile and deepset eyes. He smiled rather more readily, though, and had an animation that contrasted with Mazzare's habitual cool demeanor.

Luzzatto explained that he wanted them to consult with Messer Cavriani, because although he wasn't *Case Vecchie* or even a retainer of one, he did have a lot of connections throughout Europe by way of his extended family, which was based in Geneva. After Luzzatto had finished explaining all the things the Cavrianis did, what Sharon gathered was that they were professional middlemen. Luzzatto did not say anything about whatever their political proclivities might be.

Well . . .

Sharon decided she'd go along with Luzzatto's inclinations. He was probably right, she reflected, that using a middleman like Cavriani gave them better prospects than trying to deal directly with the trading houses themselves.

"So, please," said Cavriani after Luzzatto's prologue was done, "tell me what you are trying to achieve on the Rialto. Maestro Luzzatto has given me sight of your list of desiderata, and I have heard a great deal from my cousin at Geneva about how you Americans work."

"Nothing bad, I hope," said Sharon.

"Oh, no, no, no—quite the contrary. Dear Leopold attended your Rudolstadt Colloquy, you know, and heard the argument there."

Leopold Cavriani. Yes, that was the name Ed Piazza had mentioned, Sharon could now remember. She relaxed a bit. If this Cavriani wasn't trying to hide his connection with the other one, he was presumably not up to anything worse than middling-level skullduggery. Of course, in Venice—all of Italy, so far as she could tell—middling-level skullduggery probably put you somewhere on the third or fourth level of Dante's *Inferno.*

"He was much impressed," Cavriani continued with what seemed to be real enthusiasm, "by the contrast between the manner in which these things are traditionally done in the Germanies and the way in which you Americans approach business. He also had high praise indeed for your Maestro Piazza. A very able and forthright man, according to Leopold."

Sharon nodded, but decided to say nothing. In point of fact, she thought Ed Piazza was a very able and forthright man herself. She also liked him personally. On the other hand, he'd spent most of his adult life as a high school principal. High school had not agreed well with Sharon Nichols. She'd been one of those bright-but-easily-bored kids who had been habitually labeled an "underachiever" in high school and hadn't really come into her own until she reached college. She'd admit it was probably childish, but even after several years of college and almost three years of the seventeenth century, she was still nursing something of a grudge. In her opinion, high school principals were probably assigned somewhere to the fifth or sixth level of the Inferno.

"Now, let us to business!" Cavriani said brightly. "Just how were you proposing to get some of this? Half of it I never heard of, to be honest. And I hear you got short shrift from the Casa Falier a couple of days ago. Yes?"

"We certainly did, and the fellow was very rude!" snapped Magda. "I should like it if we do not use their services at all for this business."

Cavriani rocked a hand back and forth in doubt. "I think maybe you got Messer Petro Falier on a bad day." He snickered. "Not that he has many good days, you understand. He's a sharp customer, that one, although as you say, lacks in the manners department. You aren't the first he's been that way with, and the story surprised no one when it got around that you'd had bruises off him. And, Signora Stone, may I add that all the Rialto heard what you called him to his face, and two-thirds of it agrees with you. But, as I say, he's good and his House is good, too. So, if we need Casa Falier for anything, we try to delay it until we've got you, ah, raised in the profile a little, yes?"

He'd tried out an English phrase on them. "I think you mean, 'until we've raised our profile a little,'" said Sharon. She'd heard some of that about the Rialto. Occasional boulders of English in the stream of Veneziano Italian. She'd decided it was because there were a lot of English merchants in town, handling this end of the Levant trade, and that she was probably missing other imported words from other languages that she didn't recognize. On the other hand, that phrase was straight out of the twentieth century. Had the tendency of visiting Nasis and Abrabanels to pick up MBA-babble started to spread to other communities than the Jewish one? Sharon hoped not.

"Ah, I thank you," said Cavriani. "When we are visibly making deals in this town, there will almost certainly be a brief fashion to be seen trading with your good selves. Brief, but if we work quickly we will be able to do much in that short time to establish ourselves. And if, in that time, such business as you take to Casa Falier is expressly reserved for factors other than Messer Petro Falier, the prestige he will lose . . ." Cavriani's face was the very picture of *schadenfreude*. "And, of course, just to rub it in, his fellow factors will ask him for advice on the deals they are doing for you, so we will even get the benefit of his experience."

"Will he not simply lead them astray?" Magda asked.

Cavriani's grin turned wry. "Petro? I think not. The man's a notorious pedant. And besides, what price his good name as a trader, for everyone acknowledges that he knows his business, if he publicly gets it wrong?"

"Ah, I see," said Magda, nodding in satisfaction.

Sharon almost giggled. Magda, concurring in a plot to visit humiliation on the pompous, abrasive Messer Petro Falier, looked like she was going native in Venice real fast. "Thanks for that pointer, Messer Cavriani. Now, to our own business, we've spent the time since we arrived going about and getting a feel for the place, and we've revised our ideas about the kind of deals we want to put together. You see, we've got some money that might well amount to down payments on everything on our list, but hearing the traders talk we thought we might be a little more ambitious and perhaps use it as seed money. Also, we've been cultivating the people to whom Signora Stone's husband has been talking, some of the businessmen he's been advising on chemical industry—"

"Ah, the good doctor! Yes, he has been making a stir. For a long time before he came, as well. New dyes, new medicine, some of it coming through Venice, and getting richer by the day, so we hear."

Magda preened. "Also, he has spoken with many artisans and master dyers and apothecaries here in Venice, and we have begun to make deals for the new processes they will be trying."

"We think a lot of them will be ordering things from our list as well," added Sharon.

"Ah. Then perhaps we will want to organize a *collegamento* and send a ship to some of the places—"

began Luzzatto. But Cavriani cut him off in a sing-song voice:

"*Oh, you who follow in little boats . . .*"

Luzzatto gave him a half-glare. Cavriani waved him down. "Please, please, no offense! I am here to consult, maestro, so let me consult."

Luzzatto held up a hand. "Fine. But—please—keep the crazy schemes to a minimum."

Cavriani harumphed. "He's going to tell you what they call me," he said to Sharon.

"'Crazy Giuseppe.'"

Cavriani harumphed again, and louder. "Yes, yes. But you'll notice they don't call me 'bankrupt Giuseppe.' Or even 'poor Giuseppe.'"

"Granted," Luzzatto admitted. "But I hear the Christian God has a special providence for the incurably mad."

"Luck is where you go looking for her. And if I choose to go looking for her in places where no one else is looking, who is the crazy one, eh?"

Luzzatto rolled his eyes. "Was I mad myself, to invite him?" To Sharon and Magda: "Ladies, I will allow that Messer Cavriani is very good. But I will advise you to leave him to risk only his own money on the more insane ventures. Yes, he does well, but he's not always so lucky, and it's only the big wins he brings home that keep him ahead."

"Risk, that's the thing." Cavriani turned visibly more serious. "But if the ladies wish to be safe and secure, I can do those kinds of deals as well. To tell the truth, they're the deals we make the money on, to risk on the crazy ventures. And I do come out ahead more often than I come out behind, or I wouldn't still be in business. I wouldn't be the first Cavriani to get put behind a desk somewhere and left in charge of ordering the wherewithal for more capable Cavrianis."

Sharon found herself smiling at the byplay. "Gentlemen, assume that we are prepared to run perhaps a few risks. What do you propose?"

"Ah, now that's proper talk!" Cavriani actually rubbed his hands. Sharon was beginning to realize that beneath the unprepossessing exterior lurked the soul of a ham actor. "First, do I understand that you have the radio between here in Venice and the Baltic?"

Sharon and Magda looked at each other. That was *supposed* to be a secret. It was Sharon's turn to roll her eyes. Magda just looked pained.

Cavriani went on: "Please, please! It's all in confidence here. I assure you that the Cavrianis have ways of knowing things that are beyond the grasp of the miserable Spanish and French heretics. Not to mention the pitiful Venetians, who are long past their prime." He gave Luzzatto the kind of raised-eyebrow look that Sharon had only seen before in the movies. Bad movies. "The Jews are another story; they will naturally know also. They are an especially clever people. Why else would they have attached themselves to you so readily? So there's no danger there of idle words slipping."

Now he sighed, histrionically. "A pity they are all condemned to everlasting torment, of course. It grieves me to think of my good friend Benjamin Luzzatto, his flesh torn for eternity by hot pincers in the hands of demons— But!" Again, that histrionic sigh, coupled with outstretched hands. "What can you do? These are a stubborn folk as well as a clever one, and insist on denying the Savior."

Throughout, Luzzatto had simply smiled serenely. Sharon had the feeling this was an old game between the two of them. She also had the feeling that Cavriani wasn't lying at all when he referred to Benjamin as "his good friend." For reasons she couldn't begin to explain, she was starting to like Cavriani. Whether that was because of the ham acting or despite it, she wasn't sure.

For the moment, though, she decided there was

no point in trying to deny the existence of the radio. She'd tell Father Mazzare about it afterward, of course. But whatever damage was done—if any—was already done.

Sharon nodded. "Yes, we have a radio here. We can reach as far as Grantville, most evenings. Sometimes as far as Magdeburg. Through relays, as far as Luebeck and Wismar with no more than a day's delay."

"And Hamburg?" Cavriani asked. He was all business now. "Hamburg is, ah, very important."

Sharon thought about it. They got only condensed news reports, down here, of the progress of the war. But with spring coming, nobody had any doubt at all that the League of Ostend was going to try to finally capture Luebeck and Amsterdam. Nor that, if they failed, Gustav Adolf's counterattack would roll over a good chunk of northwestern Germany, in the middle of which—right smack in the middle—sat the still-neutral city of Hamburg.

She shrugged. "Impossible to say, at the moment. But even using couriers, I'd think no more than a few days' delay. Why? What are you thinking of, messer Cavriani?" She had a feeling she knew what was coming.

"Well, if we had advance news of cargoes, ahead of anyone else . . ." Cavriani grinned, looking more sharklike by the second. "You might find that you could make some very good trades in futures."

"And get yourself hanged!" Luzzatto snapped. "Some of those cargoes will be underwritten with state bonds. Insider trading"—again, an English term—"is illegal where state bonds are concerned. And the penalty is death."

"But the ladies have diplomatic immunity—" Cavriani began.

"You don't!" Luzzatto said forcefully. "More to the point, *I* don't—and I won't even be able to get away from it the way you might, with enough money. A Jew on the run in Italy is as good as a dead man."

"Who'll know?" Cavriani said, brightly. "Besides, we can just make discreet enquiries and make sure we don't play a trade on anything with state bonds riding on it."

Luzzatto seemed to relax. Apparently, Cavriani's willingness to avoid anything that involved state bonds—whatever those were, exactly—was enough to mollify the agent. Sharon had been in Venice long enough to understand how the city worked, that way. Crossing the Council of Ten was a desperate business. Whereas simply crossing commercial rivals, while it had its own dangers, was more or less taken for granted.

Sharon was impressed with Cavriani already. As far as she could tell, no one so far had thought of that as a way of making money out of radio. No need to tell Cavriani that, through relays, they had radio all the way to the embassy in London—overlooking the main commercial port, at that—and in Amsterdam as well.

"Would this enhance our working capital?" Magda asked. "Maybe we could use this to generate quick cash flow?" From the tone of her voice, Magda was starting to get into the excitement of the scheme. She smelled money in the air. And for all that Magda was happily married to a hippie, she'd been brought up the daughter of a hardnosed German merchant.

"Oh, certainly," said Cavriani, leaning forward. "Now, Signora Stone, here's what we do to begin with."

Sharon demoted herself to note taker for what followed. It seemed Magda had found a kindred spirit in Cavriani. About halfway through, just as the German hausfrau and the Venetian wheeler-dealer were concocting a scheme that would, if Sharon followed it right, involve them selling futures to themselves in a cargo they'd never actually need or want and which would never come within five hundred miles of Venice, she stole a look at Luzzatto who had become almost invisible in his own office.

His shrug and upturned eyes spoke volumes. But so did the sly smile on his face.

Sharon wondered about that. Mostly, though, she wondered at herself. Unlike Magda, Sharon had been brought up in the household of a doctor. To be sure, her father had always provided well for his family. But he could have provided even better if he'd been willing to forego his ghetto practice for more lucrative work. He hadn't, because money had never been the principal motive in the life of James Nichols.

Nor was it in the life of his daughter. So why, now, did she too feel that growing, almost feral, excitement?

The answer came to her on the very heels of the question. She rose quietly from her chair and moved as far off as she could in the tiny room, staring blankly at a wall. At first, just to fight down the spike of sheer pain. There were times, even after all these months, when she wondered if the hole ripped in her soul by Hans' death would ever heal.

Maybe not. But, if it did . . .

Quiet fury came to flush aside the anguish. If it did, Sharon knew, it would be a fine clean anger that managed the trick. Only if she struck her own blows at the world that had led her beloved to fly his plane into an enemy warship, would she find surcease from sorrow and acceptance of his passing. She understood that now.

She smiled at the wall. She would do it in her own way, of course. Hans had been flamboyantly heroic, which Sharon would never be. Had no desire to be, really. Still, there were many ways to strike a blow at that cold, callous aristocracy that ruled all of Europe and most of the world beyond.

One of them was money. A predatorial, ruthless willingness to use every advantage to cut the bastards where they lived.

Oh, yes, money was where they lived—their pretensions about "blood" notwithstanding. A bankrupt nobleman was just another beggar, after all. Sharon thought the aristocracy of Europe and their factors and financiers—as many of them as she could manage, anyway—would look splendid lined up alongside the roadway. All of them with signs around their neck.

Will act haughty and superior for food.

The image made her laugh aloud. Smiling, she returned to her seat and took up her notepad and pen.

"So let's get rich," she murmured. "Stinking, filthy rich."

When they returned to the embassy, the doorman handed Sharon a note. It was written on fine paper and sealed with wax. The only thing written on the outside was her name, in handwriting she recognized immediately.

"Another one, signora," the doorman said with a small, half-apologetic smile. This has gotten to be something of a joke between them.

"What's this, now?" Sharon snorted. "The twelfth? Thirteenth? I'll say this for the man. Whatever else he is, he's a stubborn bastard."

Magda came up to look at the note over her shoulder. "Feelthy Sanchez again! What is wrong with that man? By now, even an old lecher should understand the situation."

Sharon shook her head. She'd never opened and read any of them after the first two. Not that what Sanchez had written had been anything other than respectful. Simply polite requests to allow him the privilege of accompanying her to some public event or other. Perhaps the opera? Whatever the signora desired.

She started to hand the note back to the doorman to be disposed of as all the others. But, then, a new thought brought on by the day's work came to her and she drew it back. On impulse, she broke the seal and read the note.

As she expected, it was another request to accompany her to a public event. She was a bit surprised, though, to see that Sanchez had added a few self-deprecating lines allowing as how he could only hope she might deign to read what he'd written. It was rather droll, actually.

So. Witty Sanchez as well as Feelthy Sanchez. Hmm . . .

"You can't seriously be considering to agree!" Magda hissed.

Sharon tapped the note against her chin. "Well . . . maybe. You know, Magda, it occurs to me that we should have paid more attention to Ed Piazza's briefings. One thing I do remember, though, is that he stressed that any contacts we could make with the Spanish Netherlands would be exceedingly valuable. And if what I've picked up here and there is accurate, there seem to be some doubts—fuzziness, anyway—as to exactly who holds Sanchez and his paymaster Bedmar's leash. The king of Spain—or his younger brother the cardinal-infante?"

She reopened the note and studied it. "Be interesting to find out, don't you think?"

Magda still looked dubious. *Very* dubious.

Sharon couldn't help grinning. She and Magda had gotten to be pretty close friends, all these months they'd spent together as the only two women on the mission since leaving the U.S. late the previous autumn. But, now and then, she was reminded of their very different life experience. Magda had no experience with the freewheeling American custom of dating.

Sharon did. Quite a bit. She'd be the first to agree she was hardly what you'd call a beauty queen. But her features were attractive enough and she had the kind of full-bodied figure that plenty of men were drawn to.

Um. Drooled over, some of them.

She patted Magda reassuringly on the shoulder.

"Relax, girl. I've got no intention of sleeping with the old goat. But how hard can it be fending him off, at his age? Especially if he's got a sense of humor? Someday I'll tell you about a basketball player I went out with once. Him, I had to threaten with a kitchen knife."

Again, she felt that spike of anguish. Briefer this time, fortunately, and not so painful. She hadn't had to fend off Hans Richter, for all that he'd made his interest in her crystal clear. In that, as in everything, he'd been transparent and . . . sweet, was the only word.

She pinched her eyes, for a moment. When she took the fingers away, her vision was a bit blurry.

"Still," said Magda. "I think you should get advice from someone. Perhaps . . ."

She glanced up the staircase which led to the ambassador's suite. Then, simultaneously, she and Sharon burst into laughter.

"Oh, right!" choked Sharon. "I can see it already. 'Father Mazzare, please guide me through the proper maneuvers involved in keeping an old Spanish lecher out of my pants while I try to finagle information out of him.' Yup. I bet he'd be a fountain of wisdom on the subject."

Magda shook her head, still chuckling. "Still. You should ask *someone*."

The answer, also, came to them simultaneously.

"Cavriani!"

"The very man!"

Chapter 25

"It's like negotiating with a committee, Larry," said Jones as they mounted the stairs to the reception room of the embassy, which they used as their main center of operations.

"In a sense, we are," Mazzare said. Then, thinking about it: "No, we are negotiating with a committee of the Council of Venice. The Grand Council is Doge Erizzo's compromise between all the factions he has to please."

They reached the top of the stairs, where one of the maids was waiting to take their coats. Mazzare was never quite able to keep them straight, except for Frank Stone's would-be enamorata Giovanna—impossible to forget her, and not simply because she was the prettiest!—although he thought this one was Maria.

"That's what I meant, Larry," said Jones. "Thank you, Maria."

Mazzare handed over his own coat, thanking the maid as he did so. Then he turned to Jones. "I know. It's frustrating, thoroughly frustrating, having to listen to twenty senators say more or less the same thing in seventeen or so subtly different ways."

"Well, except for—" Jones said, reaching for the doorknob.

"Yes, Simon," Mazzare said as Jones opened the door, "and I think we can lay that before the principal offender, ah—right now."

"Buckley!" Jones called out, seeing the young journalist across the room sharing a bottle of wine with the civil engineer Ernst Mauer. "You idiot!"

"What?" Buckley looked around in surprise.

Jones strode across the room, playing the agreed-upon role of Bad Preacher to the hilt. Mazzare ambled after him, taking his time so that the Good Preacher could go in after the preparatory barrage. He stopped halfway to collect a glass of wine from—he guessed—Raffaela.

Jones was in full pulpit fire-and-brimstone form and giving it his Methodist best. Buckley was, to his credit, not flinching, but getting a word in edgewise was proving beyond him. Mazzare decided to let him roast a few minutes longer as Jones enumerated his various defects of character, intelligence and consideration for his fellow-man.

The rest of the room was gawking. Ernst was edging discreetly out of the splash-zone and Sharon, who seemed to be dressed up to go somewhere for the evening, had gone from open mouthed amazement to badly concealed amusement.

He decided it was time, and sauntered over. "Joe," he said, "Why?"

"Reverend," he said, "I have a right—"

Mazzare held up a hand. "I know. Back in the USE, freedom of the press is written into the Constitution. Here, there are—differences. You can have all the rights you want, but—"

"The silly bastard—" Jones began.

Mazzare stopped Jones with a look, as much to control his laughter at the sight of Buckley flinching when Jones swore as anything else. It still shocked people when it came from a pastor.

"Reverend Jones is annoyed, Joe, because we both just got chewed on, politely, by the doge of Venice for permitting one of our servants to slander another ambassador."

"Servant?" Buckley grew a little flushed. "I'm not—" Then, he dried up, apparently having started after all this time to think about how things looked.

Mazzare smiled while Jones glared. "Joe, almost no one believes that. The French embassy is seething right now. Because, as far as they're concerned, we just pissed"—another cringe from Buckley—"all over every canon of diplomatic protocol."

Buckley was now visibly bewildered.

Jones' voice was fit to pronounce curses in. "Sure, we're all polite. You idiot. We're all good friends with the greatest of respect for one another. We're all reasonable men, diplomatic-like. And one thing we do *not* do, idiot, is carry on our private fights on the territory of our generous, benevolent and above all neutral host. This includes, dumbass, publishing—across a third of Europe, yet, and how a pissant muckraker like you got syndicated beats me—a full indictment of what one of our fellow-diplomats is doing."

"It's also dangerous for you, Joe." Mazzare gestured at one of the windows. "That's not Magdeburg out there, much less Grantville."

"Safety's not something I lose sleep over," Buckley said breezily. "Father, look, I'm sorry if I've caused you a problem, but—"

Mazzare frowned, realizing what was coming next. "Joe, I think you should think hard about that. 'Just doing my job,' when you get down to it, is only a hair away from 'just following orders.'"

"Now hold on, Father! My job is to get important information to the people who matter, which is all of them."

"And the hell with the consequences?"

Buckley wasn't going to back down. "Well, not all

of them. It's just that most of them are worse than shutting up."

"Point," Mazzare admitted. He notched his estimation of the journalist up a point or two. Joe had been caught in the Ring of Fire when he turned out for Rita Stearns' wedding. He'd been a friend of Rita and Sharon's at college, a graduate student in journalism, and he'd found himself in at the birth of modern journalism. The first newspapers of a recognizably modern type had been in print for perhaps twenty years, with pamphlets and broadsides before that. Nowadays, the Imperial Post service carried news dispatches around Europe to feed hungry presses.

Like everything else, news reporting had developed an arsenal of tricks and techniques over three and a half centuries, and Buckley was equipped with a beginner's arsenal of them. So when he'd discovered that there was work for him in this time, he'd gone at it with enthusiasm. Dedication, even.

Mazzare had read some of his stuff. Buckley would never have won a Pulitzer Prize. On the other hand, by seventeenth-century standards he was polished, crisp, informative, original and readable. Whether he was popular for his originality or whether the twentieth-century style would catch on remained to be seen, of course.

"Look," Joe said, "I moved out of the building next door a while ago." He hesitated just an instant, then: "I did that precisely to put some distance between you and me, so nobody would think we were connected politically. I live all the way across Venice now."

That was a fib, Mazzare thought. He was quite sure that Joe had moved simply because he discovered he couldn't afford the rent in this rather ritzy part of Venice. Buckley's argument was silly anyway, since the reporter spent perhaps half his nights taking advantage of the hospitality at the USE embassy. Not that Mazzare begrudged him the free food and drink. He had his own memories of life on a tight budget.

Mazzare wondered how Buckley had managed to stay so fundamentally naive after almost three years of the seventeenth century, and especially after all the digging he seemed to have done in Venice. Beneath the patina of a tough street-wise news reporter was a young man who still really thought it was all something of an exciting game.

"Joe," he said gently, hoping Buckley wouldn't take it as condescension, "the fact that you don't live nearby anymore means exactly nothing to the people you need to worry about. These are people who routinely scheme and maneuver on a continental scale. Please—be careful. Try to be at least a *little* discreet. Powerful people in these times can have you killed or jailed, and they will get away with it. Or you'll find yourself having to fight a duel, or getting sued or something."

Buckley's grin was pure *joie de vivre*. "But, Father," he said, "I'm young and popular. That makes me invulnerable!" After a moment, he went on, "Seriously, though, I do watch my back. The thing is, there's a lot of journalists out there, and the powerful tend to ignore us. They think that they're taking the long view that a lot of yapping nuisances—"

"Good phrase, that," Mazzare put in, in a sudden spirit of pure mischief.

Buckley snorted his amusement, acknowledging the hit, and went on. "They think that sooner or later everything blows over. But it doesn't, of course. Woodward and Bernstein are a long ways off yet, but there's already a lot of light being shone on the doings of the muckity-mucks."

"Some of it's less than honest, though," Mazzare said. "I know they've already invented the press release. What's that piece of slang? 'Tear off and print'?"

Buckley smiled ruefully. "I know, I know. Laziness wins nine times out of ten. But the principle is there."

"Still. Be careful."

"I will, Father, don't worry. Both ways before stepping into the, uh, canal."

Mazzare chuckled. Anyone who fell into one of Venice's canals had more pressing problems, even assuming he could swim, than being run over by an oncoming boat. There was all manner of ordure and filth in them; the ebb and flow of the lagoon as the Adriatic's gentle, almost nonexistent tides washed back and forth cleaned them a little, but there was still the unmistakable whiff of eau de sewer down close to the water.

"Anyway," Buckley said, draining his glass, "I should get going. It's a long way home for me these days." He rose and left hurriedly.

Jones came back over, now with a drink in his hand. "He's really a pretty nice guy, underneath that damn Woodward and Bernstein act," he admitted. "Not that I'll say it to his face."

"Yes. Although lacking a little in forethought."

"Who wasn't, at his age?" There was rather more charity in Jones' tone than Mazzare had been expecting. "Think I registered my displeasure strongly enough?"

Mazzare laughed outright. "I think he's as chastened as we've any right to expect."

"Whatever." Jones handed over a slip of paper adorned with the seal of the Most Serene Republic. "While you were having your little heart to heart, this came."

It was a note from the doge, inviting Mazzare to a reception at the Ducal Palace for the Turkish delegation which had arrived in the city recently.

Oh, wonderful. Just what we needed. The Ottomans added to the mix!

Mazzare decided he needed some expert and informed advice. He turned, to pick out Benjamin across the room, where the lawyer was going over some kind of paperwork with Magda and Sharon.

"Benjamin? Can you spare a moment? No, better, we'll come over."

As Mazzare and Jones went over to the table they were using, Mazzare asked, "Where's Tom, by the way?"

"Gone to Padua for the week, lecturing," Jones said. "It's just up the river, about twenty miles. A day's boat ride, or a little less, and a bit less back."

The arrived at the table. The paperwork spread across it did indeed look excruciatingly commercial. "So while Tom's away you're handling the chemicals-buying business," Mazzare said to Benjamin and the ladies.

"Sure are," Sharon said. "The going got tough, so the tough went shopping."

"We do well, I think," Magda said, evidently satisfied with how it all seemed to be stacking up, although unlike Sharon she seemed to be settled in for the long haul with the mound of contracts and balance sheets. "Much now awaits my husband's signature."

"Oh, yes," said Benjamin. "We have a number of advantages. Being in—ah, more rapid than usual contact has let us buy some excellent futures in the Baltic trade."

Mazzare sighed. That was a euphemism for "radio contact," of course. Yet another problem! Sharon had told him of the disturbing ease with which the Cavrianis had penetrated the security surrounding the USE's use of radio, which Mazzare had passed along to Nasi in Magdeburg. They could only hope that the Cavrianis would keep it to themselves and that the League of Ostend hadn't figured it out as well.

"Trade is still going on?" Jones asked. "Surely the war—?"

"Nope," Sharon said. "Remember: we're in the seventeenth century, not the twentieth. Wars are the business of princes, got nothing to do with merchants except being another factor in the equation. Trade carries on right through. Prices are way up, is all, and we get killer margins on anything we know got out of the Baltic safely. *Killer* margins. You wouldn't believe it."

"Oh," said Jones. "But don't we just buy stuff from the Baltic direct? Why are we getting it through Venice?"

"Oh, we are not," Magda said. "But while we are here with the radio to get information, we can make good trades, which means more money to buy the things we need and which we must get through Venice."

Something besides Ottoman politics began to nag at the back of Mazzare's mind. *Trading—?*

"Hold on," he said. "Isn't that a bit unfair? Insider trading, or some such?"

Sharon flashed a rare smile; she was usually a solemn woman, these days. This smile, though, was purely predatory. "It's not illegal *here*, Father."

"Except for trades in state bonds," Benjamin put in firmly.

"Sure, sure," said Sharon, "but we didn't buy any of those, and besides, in this town they respect you for sharp deals and stacking the deck."

Mazzare decided he had enough other things to worry about. "Well, if Benjamin says it's legal, and no one's going to be sore at us over it, fine. Just don't get anyone else annoyed at us, please. Mr. Buckley—"

"We heard," Sharon said, smiling.

Jones looked downright smug. The strip he'd torn off Buckley had been country-wide.

After Mazzare showed him the note from the doge, Benjamin nodded. "I will make enquiries. Although I think you might do better to inquire of Don Francisco. Any intelligence from the City will reach him directly, and he has the advantage of knowing most of the principals personally."

Mazzare chided himself, briefly, for the relief he felt at dumping the problem of the Turks in someone else's lap. He'd still have to act here on the ground, after all. He nodded agreement to Benjamin. "You're right about that last, Benjamin. The radio's going to be busy tonight, I fear."

He took the invitation back from Benjamin. "Now," he said, "about this reception. Magda?"

"Yes, Monsignor?" she said.

"Will your husband be back from Padua by the day after tomorrow?"

"No, Monsignor, unless we send for him."

"Invite didn't mention him, Larry," Jones pointed out.

"You're right, Simon, of course. They knew he was out of town for the moment. Wouldn't want to embarrass us, or inconvenience the professors at Padua." Mazzare tapped the invitation onto his palm once, twice, three times. "Can't be helped," he said. "Sharon, can I prevail on you to come back to your attaché role tomorrow morning, and get with Gus to organize our turnout?"

"Sure."

Sharon's elaborate costume finally registered on him. "Sharon? Are you going out, tonight?"

"To the opera," she said cheerfully, rising to her feet. "With Feelthy Sanchez. In fact, he should be here any moment. Ta-ta."

Waving a casual hand, she breezed through the door. Mazzare stared after her for perhaps half a minute.

"Oh," he said.

Chapter 26

Castel Gandolfo, Mazarini decided, would be a beautiful place when it was finished. The villa was perfectly sited, the gardens perfectly laid out, and the prospects magnificent. The gardens themselves were fit to walk in, and His Holiness was wont to do so when he was at his new summer retreat.

Mazarini was not a man to be awed by authority, but there was nevertheless something nerve-wracking about being invited to go for a walk in the pontiff's own *rus in urbe*, particularly in such august company. Not, he reflected, that there was much *urbe* around for this to be *rus* in—Castel Gandolfo was well away from the stern and stony majesty of Rome. He quelled the thought. His Holiness Pope Urban VIII had confined himself to inconsequentialities thus far in the day, but there was certain to be a shift in the conversation at any moment. It was perhaps ordinary for the pope to summon his nephew the cardinal Barberini into his presence. Not an everyday occurrence to bring the father-general of the Society of Jesus into his counsel, but certainly nothing to remark upon. What was unusual was to invite a junior legate to his summer retreat to discuss business, without at any time mentioning what that business might be. France? Grantville? Venice? Mazarini admonished himself. *Patience, or your nerve will betray you.*

"Young man," Urban said, rising from a minute inspection of something green that was growing by the path. "How much do you know of the keeping of gardens?"

"Almost nothing, Your Holiness," Mazarini said, his mental thread snapping.

"Then I shall explain something I have learned in gardens, Monsignor. Look here—" Urban pointed into the foliage. "There is an insect, if you look closely."

Mazarini bent low. Sure enough, there was something like a grasshopper, big and ugly, though. A cicada, perhaps? "I see him, Your Holiness."

"Some years ago, I essayed a short monograph on the subject of natural philosophy. Part of a small debate I had with a man more famous in that field."

"Ah, I understand, Your Holiness. I had the pleasure of reading that same monograph. Most interesting, and insightful, if I may say so." Mazarini couldn't see where this was leading, and uttered the compliment to cover his confusion. Surely the business with Galileo, however it shook out, was a matter for the Holy Office and, insofar as the pope took part, a matter of political wrangling between His Holiness and the Spanish party? Galileo's patronage made him a target for Spain, and his writing made him a target for accusations of heresy. Mazarini's own concerns were all with the troubles in northern Europe, how did this connect?

"I misdoubt you do, Monsignor," Urban chided him gently. He was nobody's idea of a young man, well into his sixties, but with the wiry frame of an old man who was active. The cares of office had used him reasonably well, but he still gave the impression of greater age than his sixty-six years would account for. Add to that the white soutane of his office and there was a real force to his admonishment. For a moment, Mazarini felt himself back at school. "You wonder, perhaps, why I have digressed on the subject of Galileo Galilei?"

Mazarini nodded. "Yes, Your Holiness," he said, remembering his manners enough to speak. The first meeting between himself and the pontiff, the day before, had been one of excruciatingly correct etiquette and protocol, and therefore easy. To be informal with the head of the church was hard. How far to go, what to leave out of the full panoply of formal address?

"Please, be at ease. I approach this matter in a roundabout way because I wish to have you in my confidence. I wrote, when Galileo was first coming to trouble the counsels of the Church, of the understanding of a cicada, the ability of a naturalist to understand it, and the ability of a cicada itself to understand its world. You understand how we are as insects in our understanding before God, yes?"

"His folly is as the wisdom of the wisest men, Your Holiness," Mazarini quoted, almost certain he had mangled the Scripture.

"Yes, yes, most apropos, my young monsignor," Urban beamed widely. "And I in my turn, learned myself and surrounded by the learned all eager to advise me as best they may, am as nothing before the wisdom of God, would you agree?"

"Your Holiness is most modest." Mazarini was unsure where this was leading at all. Could it be that the pope was going to ask *him* what to do about a question of dogma?

"Not modest at all, Mazarini. Or should I say Mazarin?" Urban's tone was quiet, now, and in Mazarini's ears the soft breeze and the singing of birds became as thunderous gales and wild screeching.

He stood, straight and barely able to control his shaking. How much of this was genuine intelligence from Paris, and how much from reading of future history? Was he here to be accused of disloyalty, in person, by the pope? He looked across to Vitelleschi, the emaciated and closed-faced head of the Jesuits, and saw no clue. Cardinal Barberini's face was serene and pudgy as ever, and no more than mildly intrigued. "Your Holiness," he said when he felt certain of his voice, "I am aware of the future that might have been, and indeed His Eminence the cardinal-protector of France has—"

Urban waved it aside. His smile remained absent, his eyes a little narrowed like a schoolmaster about to chastise. "I know, Monsignor. I know. The important point for me is the welfare of the Church, not the jostles and stratagems of those seeking authority within it. I pray God that the results of such are guided by the Holy Spirit, but I know enough of my own poor dealings to be cynical about these things. No, I am not concerned that you might take yourself to the party of France in the fullness of time. I also saw in those histories, if it is permissible to call them that, that you retained your loyalty to the Barberini throughout, and sheltered my people at some political cost to yourself after my own play was done."

Mazarini relaxed. Either this was a side issue leading to something else, or there was nothing he could do to escape what was about to pass.

Urban went on. "I have a greater concern than that other Urban did, do I not?"

Mazarini decided to forego subtlety and nuance. "Which greater concern does Your Holiness refer to?" There were, after all, several possibilities.

"In particular, the United States of Europe, Monsignor. A terrible problem, and if this priest from our future has the right of it, a great and terrible opportunity. For both good and ill, depending on the choices I must make."

Mazarini remained silent, waiting for the pope to go on. Vitelleschi moved closer. The man they called the Black Pope had walked a few paces behind, listening intently. In a garden glorious with noonday sun, he created for himself a metaphorical shadow to remain in, behind the scenes. Mazarini tried to imagine what went on behind that blade-thin face, and failed utterly.

"If I might interject, Your Holiness?" Vitelleschi asked. When Urban nodded he went on: "There is a simple point about these United States that many, if not all, have missed outside these counsels, Monsignor. And that is the complete abandonment of *cuius regio, eius religio.*"

Mazarini murmured assent. That was, if anything, the most radical element of what the up-timers had brought. The principle that the ruler decided the religion of his people had been a given in the politics of Europe since shortly after Luther, and was yet another means for princes and prelates to justify their armed robberies under color of just war.

"This principle of freedom of religion, Monsignor," Vitelleschi continued, "bids us reconsider our attitudes to the recatholicization of the Germanies. The Swede can no longer expel the Society, for we have freedom of our own religion there. The Swede can no longer mandate to his people that they shall not hear us, nor be converted. This much the Society shall do of its own initiative. We will win converts for Christ. His Holiness has had other possibilities drawn to his attention as well."

"Indeed," Urban said, "and I am grateful to my brother in Christ for his summation and for the most wise counsel he has offered me. For your own part, Monsignor Mazarini, would you regard this Padre Mazzare as trustworthy? Reliable? A worthy priest?"

"Ah, to what end, Your Holiness?"

Urban's expression turned wintry, a sharp contrast to the sunlight. "To the end of all our service to God, Monsignor. I seek an assessment of the character of the man."

"I beg forgiveness of Your Holiness. I thought to

shape my answer to Your Holiness' political needs."
Mazarini thought furiously. The pope could not possibly
be neglecting his duties as monarch of the Church, or
could he? Mazarini dismissed that thought from his
mind. There was really nothing for it but to simply
tell the truth as he saw it.

"Perhaps if I recount for Your Holiness all of my
direct experiences of him? I think this will give you
the same material on which I form my assessment of
the man Mazzare. I think very highly of him, as it
happens."

"Then tell me all, Monsignor," Urban said, smiling
a little again. "Tell me all."

Mazarini told the whole story, beginning from his
first news of Grantville, brought in with the intelligence
reports to Avignon. He had written to Grantville's parish
priest, seeking a way in to what looked like being the
new politics of the Germanies. Why he had foreseen
that, he did not know. It had just seemed so obvious
at the time. He had sent the letter with Heinzerling,
at the time his assistant and aide de camp, and the
opening of communications in that way, coupled with
Mazarini's attempts to lever himself into a peacemaker's
role, had attracted the ire of Richelieu. Mazarini had
had to cool his heels in Rome until the autumn of
1632, when he had traveled, quietly and without fuss,
to Grantville to meet Father Mazzare.

He had not gone without foreknowledge. Forbidden
to pass any message to Mazzare or anyone in Grantville, Mazarini had sent Heinzerling with no message
at all, but required to report back. Vitelleschi nodded a quiet appreciation for a neat piece of casuistry
as Mazarini recounted that. Mazarini had eventually
gone to Grantville lacking anything better to do. He
had seen Grantville at both its best and worst: hard-
pressed and in fear of its life, fighting desperately for
survival, and also triumphant, haggling the terms of a
new ascendancy.

Just so had he seen Grantville's parish priest. At once the harried and overworked small-town pastor, nervous over events which he did not control. And then, after the battle, concerned to see that the right thing was done by a woman who had died, by all accounts, the most obnoxious of his parishioners.

"A true shepherd, then?" Urban remarked, when Mazarini came to a halt in his tale. There was an intrigued expression on the pope's face, an expression that spoke of a renewal of interest.

"Yes, Your Holiness," said Mazarini, suddenly deflating. He realized that as they had walked he had grown animated, had poured much of his own agitation over the business of Grantville into his words.

"Perhaps indecisive," said Vitelleschi, from where he walked behind Mazarini and the Pope.

Mazarini realized that even in his customary terseness, Vitelleschi was saying more than the usually garrulous Barberini, and it was all Mazarini could do not to grin when he realized that Cardinal Antonio Barberini the Younger was somewhat overawed by his uncle's presence, and was being seen and not heard, like a good boy.

"How say you, Monsignor?" asked Urban, after mulling this over for a moment. "Is the priest from the future indecisive?"

"Any appearance to that effect," Mazarini said, realizing that he had at last relaxed in the presence of these two great men and recovered his facility for smoothness, "derives, if I may make so bold with the father-general, from Padre Mazzare's habit of taking as much time as he can to think before acting. I have seen him, in the thick of difficulty and danger, act with decision and dispatch. If the father-general and Your Holiness will recall, he passed only a few hours in thought—perhaps as little as an hour, although I cannot say when the thought first came in to his mind—before deciding to send those first books to Your Holiness through my humble self. I think if there is pressure of time, or great passion working on the man, he will act decisively."

A few more paces, now in silence.

"If Your Holiness . . ." Mazarini trailed off, letting the silence be his request for permission.

The pope nodded his consent.

"If Your Holiness will vouchsafe his intent for Padre Mazzare, perhaps I might make my humble opinion better tailored to the fit of Your Holiness' ideas?"

"Will he make a worthy advocate before an Inquisition?" The question was put with disarming simplicity.

"Your Holiness?" Again, the pope had caught him off guard.

"I am minded to direct that he plead Galileo's case. After all, if it can be proven that Nature gives the lie to our interpretation of Scripture, we must change our interpretation. There is Scripture, Nature, and the theology of men. The creation of men cannot be allowed to gainsay the creation of God, after all, and such revisions to the Church's teaching have happened before and will doubtless happen again. And if this new learning that Grantville brings will spare the Church the embarrassment of causing to be abjured what later is proven true, then—" Urban waved a hand, a hand that sketched all manner of pleasing possibilities in the air.

Barberini spoke for the first time. "Scheiner and Grassi may yet complain."

Vitelleschi answered him. "Scheiner and Grassi are priests of the Society. They will obey." In such tones a man might declare that the sun would rise in the east.

Mazarini had thought about Mazzare as the others spoke, and remembered hearing the American priest speak at Irene Flannery's funeral. A final homily for a woman who had hated everyone, and yet he had spoke eloquently and perfectly for the time.

"Your Holiness," he said, "It is a duty which I believe that Padre Mazzare will discharge well, given time to prepare."

"That he shall have. It will be some time before Galileo stands his formal trial. Time enough for Father Mazzare to come to Rome."

"By your leave, then, Your Holiness," Mazarini said, "I shall depart as soon as may be for Venice. Padre Mazzare is there now, and I can give him warning of your summons."

"Go with God's blessing, Monsignor."

Chapter 27

Cardinal Antonio Barberini watched Mazarini's retreating back for a while. The man had made his excuses—travel to organize, packing to supervise—and set off as if his boots were afire. It was a mark of the man that under the soutane were a cavalier's breeches and boots, a holdover from his younger days. Days, Barberini reflected with a wry smile, when Mazarini had been his own age. Antonio was still shy of his twenty-sixth birthday, and owed his rapid rise in the church entirely to family influence.

Behind him, his uncle was speaking to Vitelleschi. "Muzio, reassure me that this will achieve more than I sacrifice."

"Your Holiness." Vitelleschi acknowledged the command, and paused. At length. "I have repeated several times in advising Your Holiness that it is the doctrine that must be our grounding. I confess alarm at the prospect of further reforms so soon after the Council of Trent, but we cannot ignore what seems so clearly to be messages from our future brethren in Christ."

"And the truth of those messages?" Cardinal Barberini was more of a skeptic about this than either of the two older men. He would cheerfully admit he was no natural philosopher—was not any kind of philosopher or theologian, come to it—but he did make a point of patronizing those who were advancing the arts, letters and sciences. Leave aside the essential implausibility of the story—"Ring of Fire," indeed!—and it resolved to this: that the Americans had more and better devices and engines and weapons than anyone else.

One could either believe that a secret coterie of geniuses had gotten ahead of the rest of the world in artifice and invention, and sprung like a *deus ex machina* onto the stage of the Germanies with their marvels fully formed, or that they had been hurled back in time three hundred years from an age when such things were commonplace. Perhaps the older generation, unused to seeing what modern natural philosophy could do, might see something miraculous and wonderful in the American engines and weapons. But Antonio Barberini had seen demonstrations of all manner of newly discovered principles and the only feeling they stirred was envy that elsewhere there were better—scientists, to use the new word—than he had been able to attract to his own salon. Yet.

By itself, that was no problem. After all, the watch-word of natural philosophy was what worked. Galileo had seen to that, with his trials and experiments. What matter the outlandish story the inventor told, if his invention actually worked? Who cared that he was changing fashion throughout Rome, or was the creator of a string of scandals?

Yet the older generation were looking at the wonders Grantville had released as a token of the truth of their claim to be from the future. And when something that necessarily did not admit of proof—such as religious doctrine, or political theory—was being expounded, the speaker's truthfulness in one sphere was often taken as a measure of his honesty in another.

Both of the older men were looking at him now.

"Your Holiness, Father-General, it may be that the Americans can prove Galileo's claims. I for one would welcome it, frankly. The discussions at the Inquisition grow tiresome, and privately the astronomers are saying that Galileo's claims are helpful, even if he cannot prove them. But that logically says nothing about the truth of their other claims."

"It does furnish me with a good excuse, though, Antonio." His Holiness Urban VIII had developed a twinkle that was literally as well as figuratively avuncular.

Barberini seethed inside. These two had concocted something between them, decided on something, and were now mocking him! Or as much mockery as the constitutionally humorless Vitelleschi was capable. "Does the pope require an excuse in matters of faith?" he asked, knowing they probably had an answer already.

"Certainly," Urban said. "If the pope was not visibly commanded by God to reverse himself, what price infallibility?"

"Which is no more than a tradition!" Barberini snapped, regretting it immediately. "Your Holiness, I most humbly apologize for my tone."

"And so you should," Urban said. "But as to infallibility being a tradition, yes, it is. And a most valuable tradition it is, for without it there is no last authority on the Church's teaching and thus no certainty."

"And so we need an excuse to proceed from what is certainly wrong to what is probably right?" Barberini smiled to show he jested.

"Indeed."

"And there is more," Vitelleschi said. "We will have some chance to see the American priest in a sore trial of his wit and learning. A man may lie well and convincingly at his leisure. Under pressure even the most glib will err."

Understanding dawned on Barberini then. "The Galileo affair is not the real trial?"

"Not the real trial," Vitelleschi said.

"Then what is? Your Holiness?"

"That I do not know. I pray for guidance, Antonio. Your elder brother believes there is much to be gained by proceeding down this path, word-for-word and as fast as possible. He is more of an enthusiast than you for the new learning in every sphere of life. San Onofrio, my brother and your uncle, believes that we should place this material from Grantville in some musty corner of his library at the Lateran. Then, admit of its existence to only a few of our more trusted theologians and let the ideas out slowly and with great caution, if at all, and beginning only when we have seen the new politics established for perhaps a century, so as to be certain this has in some sense God's blessing upon it."

Barberini could barely keep himself from laughing aloud at that last. "He thinks that God has ordained a trial by combat in the Germanies?"

"Not really." Urban's smile was a little wistful. "He and I are less than an hour apart in age, but very different in some ways. He has always been the more studious of us, and I think he fears these things for which there is not ancient authority. May God bless him, he has not been well of late, and some of the things he has to say on these subjects are not entirely lucid."

"He grows unwell?" Barberini crossed himself, offered a silent prayer for his other uncle.

"Not so bad that he cannot get about. He grows . . . testy." Urban sighed. "I would that I could grow so testy as well. I prayed God to spare me this, such turmoil. And yet I see no way out of engaging with this new learning. This—*basta!*"

Both Barberini and Vitelleschi moved closer to the pope, whose face was now drawn and lined. "Are you unwell, uncle?" Barberini asked.

Vitelleschi's mask had cracked, for a moment, and was then back in place. "Shall I have a physician attend Your Holiness?"

"No, no," Urban said. "I am well enough, in body. It is in the spirit I ache, in the spirit. At once an opportunity and a challenge. I am reminded of that English saint, Thomas à Becket."

Neither of the other two priests spoke. Barberini, for his own part, could not place the Saint Thomas that his uncle was referring to.

Urban went on. "He was commanded by his king to overlook some matter of the church's interest, and refused. I misdoubt that that king's penitence after the fact made the swords of his knights hurt any the less."

"I can assure Your Holiness that there is no sign of any current plot—" Vitelleschi began, almost hotly. Whatever the efficiencies of the Holy Office in Rome, the Society of Jesus had its own fearsomely effective apparatus of informers and spies, and had indeed been first on the trail of the last, albeit comical, plot to murder the pope.

Urban waved him aside. "No, no, I do not doubt you or your eyes, Muzio. I know for a fact that there will be such a plot, however."

"Your Holiness has decided—?" Vitelleschi's voice had a note of doubt in it.

"Not in any formal sense, no." The pope's face had turned brooding. "But in my heart I see that there is a way to step ahead of the errors and missteps of the next centuries. I pray every hour for the courage to take that way. For, more importantly, the wisdom to see the path that leads on that way."

"Ah," said Vitelleschi, and fell silent.

"I do not understand," said Barberini after a moment trying to follow. "What way?"

Urban smiled. "My dear, dearly beloved nephew, have you *read* those papers that the American priest sent?"

"Some of them, yes, but . . ."

"But you are no theologian, or at least no more than

you need to be a priest on those occasions when you discharge that small part of your office?"

Barberini felt himself blush. Holiness and piety were no great part of his character and in the august presence of his uncle there was no way to hide that fact. He said nothing.

"Ah, Antonio," Urban said, "even if there is no truth in the picture that the American priest paints for us of that future, there is a terrible plausibility and such a great weight of learning. In itself, this speaks to its truth, does it not? How well might one man fabricate such a thing, with all its inconsistencies and blank spots? A liar would try harder to dress up the rough parts, plaster over the cracks."

"You believe the Americans' accounts of future history?"

"With caution," Vitelleschi murmured.

Urban nodded. "In some regards they may be being selective with the information they release, the father-general tells us. It is what he would do in their place, for in the father-general's eyes the only word that should be passed freely is the Gospel, is that not so, Muzio?"

Vitelleschi nodded.

"But there have been too many unplanned releases, I think. The book that caused such trouble in England, for example, and the Congden Library, which may be under control in Grantville now—" Urban paused to let Vitelleschi speak.

"The change in the information coming out of Congden argues for it. It is no longer the original printed books, but manuscript copy. Who knows what is added by the copyist?"

Urban chuckled. "Muzio, I take counsel of your caution. But it remains"—he grew serious again—"that I have either an opportunity or a sure route to disaster and it lies in a Protestant nation."

"You seek to ally the Church with the Swede?" It

was the only Protestant nation Urban could mean, and Barberini could hardly refrain from blurting out his amazement.

"Ah, there is the beauty of it, Nephew," said Urban. "There is no establishment of religion in the United States of Europe. I cannot be their ally, can I? If nothing else, meeting the priest whom their prime minister trusts enough to appoint as an ambassador will give me some clue, some hint about how to harness their strength to the betterment of the Church."

"And what is that?" Barberini asked.

"I do not know, Antonio," said Urban, and turned away to look at his new-growing garden. "I do not know."

The pope spent some time studying a moving insect. "I only know that I had never imagined it would come to this, in the long decades of my life. That, in my old age, God would place me before that same choice he gave Becket. What thoughts move through His unknowable mind, that He would choose two such worldly men for such a test?"

When he had been silent for a quarter hour or more, both Barberini and Vitelleschi left, in different directions.

Chapter 28

Ducos coughed discreetly at the door. D'Avaux
nodded, once, permitting the man entry. At least
Ducos remembered that Seigneur le Comte deserved
a modicum of dignity and took pains to respect it.
D'Avaux, feeling guilt at indulging a passion so strong
as hatred, darted his glance across the desk to the pile
of papers on the corner. All of the reports on Buckley,
and by him. He forced calm upon his troubled soul. To
grow irrational through the righteous anger of wounded
honor would simply not do.

"Seigneur le Comte," Ducos said, after the silence
had grown uncomfortable, and bowed.

D'Avaux collected himself. Yes, he had grown distracted and omitted the proper protocol. Permissible
between familiars, but with even so exalted a servant
as Ducos—not unpardonable, but nevertheless *noblesse
oblige* required otherwise. "Ducos, if it please you, do
you have something to report?"

"Several matters, master," Ducos said. His face hardly
moved as he spoke, but there seemed to be a faint
smile in every syllable his voice spoke. The smile of a
cat sauntering away from a mousehole licking his chops.

D'Avaux pulled his desk lamp closer—the hour was late, midnight close at hand—and turned to face his man. A crook of the eyebrow invited him to proceed.

"As to the American Buckley, I have arranged matters. Seigneur le Comte's proposal that the Turks be involved or implicated proved impractical, and I have therefore suborned a member of the Holy Office's retinue to the deed."

D'Avaux felt a thrill of shock. "Ducos, I gave orders for no such . . ." He trailed off. "No," he said when he had collected himself again, "first give me the remainder of your report."

"Yes, seigneur. The Turk delegation declines to speak of Buckley. They are well disciplined and bring all their own slaves, so it is very difficult to make any progress with them. Had they a long-established presence in Venice there would be known avenues of approach, but this mission is ad hoc and improvisation has availed nothing in the time I have had. The short time since they arrive also means that Buckley has had no time to give plausible offense. I can do nothing to place any Turk even near the scene of the deed, or Buckley plausibly in the company of any Turk."

D'Avaux leaned back in his chair and steepled his fingers. "Pray continue, Ducos. How did you proceed from there to the Holy Office?" This was beginning to sound intriguing, particularly as Ducos had had to improvise, a practice foreign to his nature. To both their natures, if it came to it. The unexpected was not an experience d'Avaux relished.

"Seigneur." Ducos made a little bow before going on. "I proceeded with ordinary matters after my rebuff early in the day with the Turks. I had news, perhaps some small moments earlier than the seigneur did, of the latest developments in the business of the astronomer Galileo, when I paid a visit to my contacts with the Holy Office."

D'Avaux began to wonder where this was going.

The business with Galileo was a slightly vexing one, to be certain. Few people of education regarded the matter as anything too serious; perhaps the interpretation of Scripture required to be looked at afresh, as the Lyncaeans suggested, or perhaps the astronomers were chasing proverbial moonbeams as well as the real thing. D'Avaux considered himself a man of parts, but there seemed to be a new advance in natural philosophy every year—this Galileo responsible for a fair fraction himself—and just keeping up with his own country's advances in the mathematics was hard enough. Although . . .

D'Avaux had heard, he now remembered, that this affair with Galileo was apparently something of a notoriety in the history books brought by the Americans through the Ring of Fire. Those wretched, miserable history books that had caused so much unexpectedness in d'Avaux's well-ordered life. Cardinal Richelieu could say what he wanted. In private, the comte was quite certain the Ring of Fire was of diabolic origin.

He blinked once, twice, suddenly aware he was wandering away from the point. "He is to be tried, yes?"

"He is to be tried. This will come as something of a relief to the Holy Office, I understand, which will be pleased to stop paying bounties on copies of Galileo's book." There was a hairline smile on Ducos' face. "There are some enterprising souls in Venice who, when they heard there was a bounty on each copy, began printing cheap and shoddy copies and turning them in by the box-full."

D'Avaux frowned back. "I should think such a mockery was hardly a laughing matter, Ducos." To a pious man like d'Avaux, the situation was all the more aggravating in that the Venetian authorities were obviously complicit in the matter. Tacitly, at least. Such a clandestine printing press was quite illegal in Venice, and the Council of Ten's agents were perfectly capable of closing it down had they chosen to do so. Just another instance in which the Venetians were subtly thumbing their noses at the Church and its institutions.

Ducos' face straightened immediately. "Seigneur, my apologies. I simply have regard for an audacious scheme, while at once condemning the motivation for it."

D'Avaux felt his own face cracking. "And the fact that the Holy Office is made the butt of this joke is of no account, eh?"

Ducos nodded acknowledgement. There were subjects troubling even for his icy demeanor—the Holy Office had hardly been needed for his Huguenot coreligionists in France. It was only understandable that Ducos should find jokes at the expense of organs of Mother Church to be entertaining. But it would not do to let him laugh out loud without reminding him he was, when all was said and done, a heretic.

"Seigneur," was all he said. Though his face seemed tighter than ever.

"And how will Galileo's trial assist?" d'Avaux asked, after granting Ducos a moment to compose himself.

"It had been said that the pope would surely instruct the Holy Office that there was to be no revision of scriptural interpretation, seigneur. It was further said that there was no prospect of Galileo's book remaining lawful to possess anywhere in Italy, and there had been some suggestion that Galileo might be prevailed upon to flee to the Swede's territories. To that end, he had been kept under close watch while his ill health prevented him from traveling to Rome."

"And you have reason to doubt this?" D'Avaux was intrigued.

"Until today, seigneur, no. However, there is a factor that is the talk of the lower ranks of the Holy Office here, and that is Mazarini."

"The legate?"

"The same. He has been to and from Venice and Rome repeatedly while the Americans have been here, and it is now emerging that the American priest, Mazzare, has been in communication with Rome. He is commanded to Rome to speak at the trial of Galileo, seigneur."

"I confess I cannot see why." D'Avaux spent a moment turning it over in his mind. "What is the pope thinking? The American is neither inquisitor nor natural philosopher, and he has no name as a doctor of theology."

"It is thought that all these Americans have a great command of natural philosophy, seigneur. It is reported to me—with what accuracy I cannot at present judge—that Mazarini impressed this upon either the Holy Office or the pope himself. For this reason they seek this American priest as *amicus curiae* or some such." Ducos made a small, dismissing wave of the hand. "I confess I know little of the proper procedure in such matters, and this may be entirely normal."

"It is not, as it happens," d'Avaux said, musingly. "It is not at all. I cannot see that even the See of Rome will lightly prevail upon a priest's vows of obedience to call him away from a secular mission imposed by his prince—even if, in this case, the prince involved calls himself a 'prime minister.' There must be more to it."

However, this troubling issue was not a matter to be discussed with a heretic like Ducos, d'Avaux reminded himself. He crooked a finger to invite Ducos to continue. "But we digress. You were explaining why the Holy Office will kill Buckley."

"Seigneur. Buckley has publicized the scheme with the Galileo books. Every town with a printing press can print copies of the book for a sum less than the bounty offered, and so—"

"A profit margin, yes. And I see the humor in it, Ducos." There was a trace of frost in his voice. "Up to a point."

"The seigneur is most kind. I understand that there was an argument some weeks ago whether a bounty was to be paid on copies that had been bound with the ink still wet. Many pages were apparently blurred and unreadable. The concluding argument was that if the Inquisition wished to announce that the book was now acceptable in the booksellers of Venice, the pious citizens would cease buying up the copies and turning them in. Since there is as yet no firm order banning the book, the Inquisition is in a tricky position carrying out its orders to suppress the thing."

D'Avaux was impressed. Even for Ducos, that had been deadpan. "Do go on."

"Yes, seigneur. Buckley has published a further piece roundly denouncing the folly of the scheme and encouraging others to use the printing press to break the Inquisition. He has even coined a phrase: 'Information wants to be at liberty.' It is beginning to be passed as a slogan, seigneur."

"'Information wants to be at liberty.'" D'Avaux turned the idea over and over in his mind. "What a remarkable proposition. Is he some manner of pagan, then, believing that mere thoughts and words have their own animating spirit that might express such a desire?"

"Most droll, seigneur. It is nevertheless a slogan that people may act upon. The Holy Office is most concerned." Ducos reported it flatly, in the tones of one remarking that the weather continued fair, rather than the tones of one suggesting that the feared Inquisition was growing vexed with someone.

"And yet it is not heresy, which surely makes it not the concern of the Holy Office?" D'Avaux found the argument of the *avocatus diaboli* surprisingly easy to formulate. "Is it not the case that absent palpable heresy, there is value in freedom of speech? Many advance this argument."

"None among the Holy Office, seigneur. And Buckley advances the argument in support of suspected heresy. They grow concerned and turn to stratagems to silence Buckley."

"And you have provided them with one?"

"Indeed, seigneur. And in the same stroke I believe we will also prevent any closer contact forming between the Swede and Rome."

"Between the arch-Protestant of northern Europe and His Holiness? Surely there was no great danger of that?"

"There is according to the Inquisition, seigneur. They fear that His Holiness will undertake to co-opt the Catholic presence in the United States of Europe to press further reforms in the Church. There is talk of correspondence already passing between Rome and Magdeburg."

"Ah, so those rumors have reached Venice, have they?"

"Seigneur?" Ducos inclined his head a little. It was rare that d'Avaux's factotum was caught by surprise.

"A briefing at the highest level . . ." No sense in naming His Eminence. "I am given to understand that Mazarini made a number of trips to Grantville shortly after its appearance, and proceeded from his last trip there straight to Rome. It is also reported that the priest was moved to send a great deal of material to the Vatican, although we have been unable to discover precisely what. It centers on what the Americans claim is the future development of the Church, that much we do know. Doubtless the Holy Office is suitably concerned, since many of them in Italy are creatures of Spain, or at least under their direction."

Ducos nodded. "They certainly wish Buckley to be silent, for the moment."

D'Avaux smiled. "Well, if it assists in saving the Church from American heresy at the very highest level, I see no good reason why they should not be suitably obliged. See to it, Ducos."

"As the Seigneur le Comte directs." Ducos acknowledged the order with a bow. "There is further intelligence," he went on. "I am informed that the Venetian

Committee of Correspondence, such as it is, has some notion of taking further action over Galileo."

"Further than printing copies of his book? How significant could they be, here in Venice?"

"The seigneur is most perspicacious. Indeed, they are said to be a rather pathetic grouping. Not much more than one malcontent and his family. My assessment is that even with the aid of the youths with the American party they will proceed no further than making tedious speeches to each other in draughty rooms. But my informer tells me they are at least talking about a scheme to rescue Galileo from his impending trial."

"Are they, now?" d'Avaux mused. "You say some American youths are involved with them? Is there not then an opportunity to further divide the Vatican from the Americans?"

"As I observed to the seigneur, there is perhaps little prospect of these particular radicals taking any effective action. They are regarded as something of a joke by virtually every organ of the Venetian state and by the Holy Office."

"And yet more unlikely groups have delivered themselves of great coups in the past, have they not?" D'Avaux stroked his beard, thinking furiously. "Are we certain that there are Americans with them?"

"Yes, seigneur. The three sons of Doctor Stone. They have attended several meetings." Ducos was firm on this point.

"Perhaps they might be impressed with the desire to proceed further?" D'Avaux could hardly hope for a result like that, although Ducos' resourcefulness had surprised him before. "Perhaps a new member with some spirit and drive, a spark of, dare I say, competence?"

"If the seigneur gives leave, I might serve as such an agent provocateur, yes." The idea seemed to amuse the cold factotum, as much as anything did. "I regret I have no operative in Venice who would pass as a genuine adherent, not on such short notice."

"So be it, then. Except I think that perhaps we might press them to go further than simply attempting to spirit Galileo away. The first objection to any such accusation would be that the Americans had sent an advocate to the trial and would hardly cheat themselves of victory. I feel sure that so radical and dangerous a group must be plotting some greater outrage against a prince of the church. Perhaps—perish the very thought—another plot against His Holiness' life?"

"Perhaps, Seigneur le Comte. But again, I would suggest that such a plot might not be considered very credible, even compared with the last such. These are not hardened revolutionists, seigneur, but a small group of wild-eyed artisans and rebellious youths. Competence is not easily to be found among them."

"True," reflected d'Avaux. Indeed, the last publicized plot on the pope's life had been a farce, an attempt to do him to death with image magic, sticking pins in a doll dressed as the pope. "Nevertheless, if we add a soupçon of competence to their armory?"

"I still hold out no great hope of success, seigneur." Ducos sounded almost disappointed.

"That will not be necessary, Ducos. Simply a spirited effort will do. All I ask is that they appear to have intended a prominent outrage. For our purposes, a near thing will be better since it will achieve all of our aims without bloodshed."

"Yes, Seigneur le Comte. With your permission, I shall be about it. You understand, this will almost certainly require me to absent myself from Venice?"

D'Avaux nodded and waved him away. He steeled himself to do without his factotum for a few weeks. In some ways, that would be a relief. Having Ducos around was more than a bit like having a mad dog on a leash. Taxing to the spirit.

D'Avaux's spirit would have been considerably more taxed had he seen the smile on Ducos' face after his factotum left the comte's chamber. All of Ducos' careful planning had finally come to fruition. Every piece of his scheme, finally in its place.

The smile of a man, finally slipping the leash.

Part IV: April, 1634

—and if she let

Herself be lessoned so, nor plainly set
Her wits to yours, forsooth, and made excuse,
—E'en then would be some stooping, and I choose
Never to stoop.

Chapter 29

Stoner began to realize, as he stared at the forbidding stack of documents in front of him, the truth of two essential propositions.

First, that there was a very real value in the rejection of materialism, which was that it saved you a lot of work.

The second was that a cheerful willingness to be helpful was going to get taken cheerful advantage of sooner or later.

Magda and Sharon and Benjamin Luzzatto had come in grinning from ear to ear. Well, Sharon was grinning from ear to ear, Magda was smiling demurely and Benjamin was wearing his professional po-face with a hint of cheer. It didn't matter. Sharon was grinning enough for seven or eight people, let alone three.

"We have been shopping," Magda said brightly.

"Exactly," Sharon added, "when the going gets tough, the tough go—"

"—shopping," Stoner capped the quotation, just as he went weak at the knees because Benjamin had produced what looked like about thirty kilos of paper and actual by-God parchment, done up in no-messing-around

by-God red tape. He dropped the package on the table
with an expensive-sounding thud.

Benjamin then cracked a smile himself. "We have
been very busy, but we need some signatures and seals
to make it proper and legal."

Stoner looked from the paperwork to the short, bright-
eyed Jewish lawyer and commercial agent. And back
again. And back to Benjamin. At least Benjamin wasn't
grinning his head off, although Stoner suspected that
was because he took money seriously and not because
he wanted to help Stoner mourn his final passage into
the world of bread-headdity. Nevertheless, the sight
of a lawyer, smiling—even a short, runty, friendly one
like Benjamin—would normally have sent Stoner diving
through the window into the canal. Had Benjamin been
grinning as widely and sharkily as Sharon was doing,
he doubted whether he'd have bothered to open the
window first.

"So, what is all this?" he asked, gesturing weakly.

"Money," said Magda, uttering the code-word that
told him to more or less leave it to her. "And com-
modities for all of the industries at home, and some
other deals to make it all work."

"All this just to buy stuff?" he asked, fishing for a
full explanation of some kind. He supposed short words
and a diagram were too much to hope for . . .

"Ah," said Benjamin. "I have here—" He reached
inside his kaftan. Benjamin sometimes found it convenient to get by in Venice by dressing as a Turk rather
than wearing the distinguishing marks of his Jewish faith,
and the Venetian authorities seemed willing to tolerate
the minor subterfuge as long as he didn't overdo it.
Stoner didn't understand the social complexities involved
in the little dance, but he always found that garment
a bit amusing. The garb of a hippie back up-time had
originally been the garb of a rich Muslim.

What wasn't so amusing was what Benjamin was
pulling out. Stoner felt his heart sink as Benjamin

produced one of Grantville's precious stock of laptops. Powerpoint slides and spreadsheets had been treated as the direct Word of God by every seventeenth-century businessman who had arrived in Grantville. The Sephardim, though, had been particularly enthusiastic; the Viennese scion of the Abrabanel clan, Don Moses, was widely known as a slideshow bore of truly terrifying proportions. Stoner held up his hands. "Benjamin, can I just have the edited highlights?"

Benjamin looked perplexed. "Signor Stone, all of it is important. And the Signora Stone, she has made some most excellent trades in your behalf. There is, first the share in the Mocenigo fleet to—"

Sharon put a hand on Benjamin's shoulder and the birdy little lawyer ran down to a halt. Stoner realized, with the first spark of joy he had felt since the three of them had walked in, that she was genuinely, freely grinning, not just keeping her end up for company.

"Stoner," she said, "it breaks down nice and simple. We sold shares in all the potential mines that our exploratory crews have been finding. We sold metals futures in the mines that are ready to start producing this year. King Gustav's copper concessionaires have been coming through us for the Mediterranean market because we agreed to work—what was it, Benjamin?"

"Del Credere," said Benjamin.

"Del Credere, and maybe I'll explain that later. But we got a few good copper contracts and beat the price up here, which made our friend in Bohemia sweat a bit. He sent a couple of angry messages saying that we were messing up the market deliberately. I understand a number of folks back in Magdeburg told him not to be such a baby. Anyway, that's as may be. Once we started shifting the copper here, and the mining shares in all manner of other things, we had some seed capital and took up a number of margin loans to get into the serious action—"

Stoner sank down to sit cross-legged on the floorboards,

feeling rather the way he did after a good deep toke: a little dizzy with hypoxia before the real rush hit.

"I surrender," he said in a weak voice. Then, more firmly: "How much of the stuff on the list could you get? You've been at this for nearly two months, but we haven't had anything delivered yet—"

He looked up, from face to face. He couldn't quite read the expressions. "What?"

Silence. First Sharon, then Magda, and finally Benjamin picked a chair and sat down. Looking harder, Stoner saw that Benjamin was looking faintly pleased with himself, but was waiting for his clients to talk. Magda looked like she had gotten the cream, and was now smiling as widely as a properly-brought-up guildmaster's daughter could. Sharon was back to grinning like a maniac.

"What?" Stoner asked again. The grin was proving infectious, although he didn't know why.

"Well, you know that the biggest item on the list was the hundredweight of lac?" Sharon asked.

"That wasn't one of mine," Stoner said, "but, like, I'll take your word for it."

"Well, we went for that one first and found a place downtown that had some."

Magda sniffed. "That man was *no gentleman.*" She uttered the phrase with the same tone and spin and venom some people used for the phrase *baby-eating satanist.*

Sharon snorted. "The jerk told Benjamin that if his clients wanted a hundred pounds of anything but spice we could buy retail like the other peasants."

"Ha!" Magda said. "Sharon does the poltroon too much justice. He used coarse language as well."

Sharon looked hard at Magda.

Magda looked back, perfectly calmly. "Well, I know what that word meant in Latin, and from the tone of voice he used I presumed he meant it in Venetian."

"Oh," said Sharon, evidently surprised.

Stoner wasn't; sufficiently riled, Magda could take the hide off a wild boar with her language, much of it from the classics at that.

"Anyway," Sharon went on, "I said to Benjamin that we should buy in bulk and from source if we could."

Benjamin nodded. "The signoras were mostly insistent that we not deal through that house for anything. Naturally, I was proactive on my clients' behalf."

Stoner wondered if his wince had shown. Laptops and PowerPoint weren't the only things that the Istanbul Sephardim—and, apparently their Spanish and Italian cousins—had taken to. Godawful MBA-speak was catching among them like the clap in a whorehouse. Stoner recalled discussing that with Sharon's dad, Doctor Nichols. The good doctor's theory was that the Abrabanels had gone over Grantville's limited stock of legal and financial textbooks looking for any tricks they had missed. Whatever else they had found in the course of those studies, they had been particularly taken by the management jargon. The fact that they seemed to have an eye for the most anus-clenching excesses was, Doctor Nichols reckoned, their big joke at the expense of the twentieth century that most of the up-timers hadn't gotten yet.

Stoner saw that there was a question expected of him at this point. "So, what did you do?"

Sharon put an arm around Benjamin, who looked briefly alarmed and then appeared to force himself to relax. "Benjamin was magnificent," she said. "We spent a couple of days over in the ghetto picking up local information and making contacts, getting notes of introduction, that kind of thing. And then we went shopping. You see, Stoner, this is one of those towns where they don't make much of anything except the glass, which I'll tell you about, but they do make deals. You should take a walk through the Rialto sometime, it's wall-to-wall deals."

"I, uh, heard."

"Yeah, and part of it was all of those shares you got."

"What? What shares?"

Magda sighed, and she and Sharon looked at each other. Magda looked hard at Stoner. "You recall that you have been giving lectures and seminars on alchemy and physic—?"

Stoner leapt to his feet. "Now hold on—you charged admission?" He realized as the words escaped that he had raised his voice. He took a deep breath. "Guys, I'm sorry and all for shouting, but I wouldn't have agreed to that."

Magda was first to get over the shock of Stoner looking angry. "No, Tom, *schatz*, we did no such thing!" Stoner could see that she was a little upset that he might have thought so.

"That's right," said Sharon. "It's just that when all those guys were asking to hire you on as a consultant, Magda was getting you stock deals instead of just the flat fees they were offering."

"Eh? They have those here and now?" Stoner had hardly been up to speed with capitalism as she was spoke in the twentieth century, let alone the seventeenth.

"Oh, indeed, Signor Stone," said Benjamin, drawing breath for what promised to be a serious lecture. "You see, we have had partnerships and anonymous societies and joint-stock companies for many, many years now and there are—"

Stoner laughed. "Benjamin, please! Have mercy, man. Even if you explain it in short words I'm not going to grok it, okay?"

Benjamin frowned the uncomprehending frown of someone whose learning of the English language had missed the word "grok" entirely. But he did shut up.

"So, what now?" Stoner asked into the ensuing silence. "You got me a bunch of stocks. So. I just wait for my 401(k) to mature?"

Only Sharon got that, of course. "What we did was

a hair less formal there, Stoner. We got everyone we had stock in to pool their buying through us, and that got us some excellent deals. They're all acting like our subsidiaries now, one big corporate group rather than a lot of little businesses that just feed their margins to middlemen. With which, I might add, this town is infested."

Benjamin didn't even twitch.

Stoner mentally vibed some respect for Benjamin; the poor guy had spent weeks in the company of two of the hardest chicks in Venice right now, and he still seemed to have it all together.

Speaking of which, Stoner realized, he'd better take some positive action before his old lady lost all respect for him. "So, all I gotta do is sign?" Stoner levered himself to his feet and reached across the table for a pen. "Is there a downside?" he asked, poised to sign the first paper. He grinned, trying to disarm his pretense at shrewdness.

"Um, well—" Sharon looked at Benjamin, "do I have this right, Benjamin, that if we lose everything—"

"This would be difficult, Signora Nichols. Very difficult, as we have interests in four fleets and nearly thirty ships."

"Yes, but—" said Stoner, realizing that Sharon probably needed this, since she was in as clear a case of done-deal euphoria as Stoner had ever seen.

"Don't worry," said Sharon, "it's hardly likely to happen. Thirty ships, all in different parts of the world sailing at different times. They can't *all* sink at once. Anyway, even if it all drops in the pot, we've got so many people in this town tied up in our deals that they'd never . . ." Sharon trailed off.

"What?" By now, Stoner was fairly sure that he had punctured the balloon a bit, but he still wanted to know what the downside really was. "What do we do if we lose everything?"

"Get imprisoned for debt."

"Oh. Is that all?" Stoner immediately began to sign and seal where Benjamin had penciled for him to do so.

As he did, he mentally counted off, and was up to twenty-eight before Sharon spoke up.

"You don't mind?" she asked, apparently surprised.

"Nope," Stoner said, pressing his Deadhead signet ring into soft wax.

"Nope?"

"Nope." Stoner was gratified that Magda hadn't been suckered. "How long do you think I've been in business, Miss Boojwah Nichols? You think the old hippie gets confused and scared around bread?"

"Uh—" was all Sharon could manage.

Stoner found this helpful, when Magda made him turn out to do business that she needed his face or signature at. Everyone expected Magda to be ruthless. When he did it, though, the shock somehow made it more effective. He finished the last indenture, and straightened up to look straight at Sharon. "Pain," he said.

"Pain?" Sharon was the only one of the three to say anything, but the looks Stoner was getting from the other two clearly implied the question.

"Pain," Stoner repeated, as the text of a little sermon he hadn't given in a long, long time.

"You see," he said, straightening the pile of documents and shoving it across the table to Benjamin, "all of this stuff is about pain and when and how we can inflict it. It's the big problem we all have—uh, we all had, I should say, back up-time with the bread-heads and money and all that junk. Every one of those contracts was just a charter for pain and sadism."

He let that one linger a moment.

"Run that by me again?" Sharon said, wearing a grin that had definite undertones of *I'll keep him talking, someone call the guys in the white coats.*

"It's simple, Sharon. Guys like Benjamin here write

a whole bunch of stuff down about what the deal is, and we call it a contract, which is just a deal written down on paper or whatever. But because of this insubstantial substance we call law—ha! and they called me an impractical flower-child who believed in mystical nonsense—the deal becomes stupid serious and metaphysical instead of just a simple matter of trust and friendship."

Sharon frowned. "Well, you've got to make busting a deal more painful than keeping to it, or—"

"Or what?" Stoner demanded. "Outbreaks of gratuitous promise-breaking and other asshole behavior everywhere? Sharon, if I bought that depravity of mankind propaganda I never would have started in a commune in the first place, much less stuck with it. It's just pain-worship, that's all it is; totem and taboo; superstitious dancing before golden idols. I've had nothing but contempt for most of this stuff since, oh, before you were born, and so it doesn't surprise me that debtor's prison is a lot nearer the surface here in the down-time. It's the same deal, it's just in the shop window instead of out back for the special customers."

Stoner looked around the room again. Benjamin's face had gone very professional indeed. Magda was used to his foibles, and was giving him a look that promised a pleasant rebuttal later. Sharon's grin was now just relaxed. She obviously still thought he was nuts, but wasn't looking over her shoulder for the guys in the white coats.

"So, let's recap some, hey, guys? Stoner said. "We've got, what, all the feedstocks that the guys back at Grantville wanted?"

"Yes. The people who wanted zinc will be pleased in particular," said Magda. "We will have two hundred tons of Japanese zinc within a year of midsummer's day."

"Oh." He wasn't too thrilled to hear that. Zinc was handy stuff, all right, but Stoner wondered about the market for galvanized buckets in a time that still had as many coopers as it did. Of course, the stuff could be used for making brass and batteries too, but—he bit down, hard. It was nearly a year and a half before that zinc arrived, and a lot could happen in that time.

"What else?" he asked, in lieu of the rant he could feel building. "Or, perhaps you should say what we didn't get?"

"Well, thorium," said Sharon. "We're probably going to have trouble with the borax, too. The Turks seem to be the only ones who've got it, and they're not being real friendly so far."

"Right," said Stoner, "that's not actually much of a downside, is it?" Apart, he thought, from all that goddammed zinc.

"We have done well, I think," said Magda. "The telephone people are particularly pleased that we were able to source good English graphite, they thought there was not any. Sharon saw it in a pencil from Naples, and asked around about where it came from, and it seems that we should have been asking for wad from England. We have ordered much of that. We also have much lac coming from India, which will come soon. There was a difference between what they said that they needed and what was the smallest lot we could buy. So we have sent a trade fleet with English fustians—"

"What?"

"Cloth," Magda explained, "made with wool and cotton, and woven in the north of England. The return trip will bring batiks and spices and some other things we can sell on for profit."

"Some of the phone stuff," Sharon interjected, "we got right here in Venice. All of the insulators are being made in Murano, just across the lagoon. They're doing them to quality standards to train apprentices, they said, rather than working to the tolerances that the people at Prague said would do." She smiled. "I sent a wireless message to Tanner and Ellie telling them about the tolerances we'd gotten on the samples, and they sent back asking how we'd mechanized so quickly."

Stoner nodded. He'd been surprised himself a few times by that sort of thing, since he'd assumed that craftsmen around Thuringia from whom he'd ordered glasswork for the dye factory could do quality or volume but not both, and been pleasantly surprised. Of course, if you watched how fast a competent journeyman could work and then sat down and did the math, it wasn't so surprising. And if they had to turn out a big batch of something quickly, they reorganized the workshop to throw man-hours at the project until it was done.

"Tell him about the aqua vitae, Sharon," Magda said.

"Oh, yeah, that's a good one. There's a fair bit of wine gets rejected when it's imported here, and some of the local product is pretty poor too. There are a fair few good old-fashioned 'shiners as well. When I drew a Liebig condenser for them, there were a few guys slapping foreheads, and a couple of the glassware shops did a roaring trade in the things for a couple of weeks. They use copper pipes and leather fittings, but they work. Now they're making alcohol a lot cheaper and purer than anywhere else, and with about 7eleventy-seven businesses back in the USE fighting over the supplies of good alcohol there's a good market. We did middleman trade on that for a while, and got a cut out of nearly a whole year's production even before the factories we took shares in turned a profit. Anyway, we got paper for most of those payments and cash for some of them, which was good, since we fed that back into the mill on the Rialto. Some of the alcohol factories have managed to do mail-order deals back to the USE and cut out the middlewomen, but that's okay, we'll make it up elsewhere. For now we've got cash flow."

"And what are we doing with that cash flow?"

"Servicing the term loans," said Magda promptly,

with the air of a woman who regarded memoranda and ledgers as management tools for lesser minds. "With the term loans we underwrote the stock issues. The ghetto already has SEC rules and—"

"What?" Stoner began to feel he was really, really overusing that word.

"Ah," said Benjamin, sitting forward in his chair. "Perhaps I can explain this one best. There was a brief description of your Securities and Exchange Commission and your stock exchanges in several of the management and business textbooks in Grantville, and Admiral Simpson was kind enough to furnish some excellent seminars in the matter. We already had most of the things they variously described, and combining them into more organized and consistent markets impressed many of us as a good idea, if it could be made practical. So we circulated the ideas we found most helpful."

"How?" asked Stoner, pleased at a chance to vary his vocabulary a little, "and who to?"

"Well, first we passed it—ah, I should mention that Don Francisco Nasi wrote a most incisive monograph on the matter, which we had printed. It was circulated here in Venice first, since the Rialto is such an important market among those to which we had easy access in these troubled times. It also went to Genoa, and by some less direct routes, I hear, to Antwerp and Amsterdam and Paris. It has also gone to the City and some other places further east. Everywhere I have mentioned has done some of the things in Don Francisco's monograph and now a few of them are doing more. On some subjects, Don Francisco can be very . . . persuasive, when he is minded to."

"Persuasive?" Stoner chuckled. He had gone in to see Mike Stearns about maybe writing some stuff up to go to the doctors in Venice and Padua and Florence and so on, and maybe make himself available to do seminars and classes for visiting alchemists who wanted to raise their game. If he had time, he'd thought, he might volunteer to train some folks up to teach basic chemistry of some kind. Pay forward a little, he'd thought.

When he came out, he'd agreed—he wasn't quite sure how, but he was certain he *had* agreed—to learn Italian, decamp his family to Venice for a year, give lectures until his throat was dry and his feet hurt to, as it turned out, chemists and doctors and alchemists and natural philosophers and heaven only knew what else from all over Europe who wanted to hear the new learning from Grantville but thought Venice was a much less chancy prospect for a working vacation than Germany in wartime. They had heard some alarming stories about Croats, it seemed.

Not that Stoner was complaining after the event, of course, what with Venice being a nice town and some of the professors being great guys. But Benjamin was still talking.

"—and so the underwriting and market-making rules proved to be good innovations, and the most widely practiced. Here and at the Antwerp Bourse they have been making daily quotes in this way for nearly six months now. It remains only to persuade the Wisselbank at Antwerp to issue proper banknotes instead of just deposit certificates, although with the manner of their recent move they can hardly be blamed for feeling inclined to conservatism."

"Eh? What about our greenbacks?" Stoner frowned. He actually liked those notes, not least because making the fast green ink was a good, solid government contract and they'd actually gone with his joke of putting Johnny Cash on the twenty-dollar bill. Hopefully that'd make people take the stuff less seriously, although he'd had long and bitter experience of how that kind of dream usually turned out.

"Keep up, Stoner," said Sharon. "We don't spend those outside the USE, we buy them. Because of the exchange rate it's cheaper to borrow Wissel notes. They're as good as bullion and everyone knows that. They absolutely do not issue notes for silver they don't have, and their letters of credit are watertight. We spend greenbacks where they will buy the most."

"Then what's the problem?" Stoner had an awful feeling that he was going to get an answer.

Benjamin saw his chance. "This is about a marvelous concept you had up-time called the money supply. You see, deposit certificates and bills for title to specie are well known in these times. Since Sweden uses those foolish copper plates for money, they must perforce use notes or spend more in carting their money around than it is worth. Now, if we can persuade the Wisselbank to go over to a fidu—"

Stoner straightened up. Time, he felt, to put into practice a little of that business management stuff he'd read about and mostly laughed at. Decisive, that was the key.

"I think I've heard enough," he said. "Benjamin, have we broken any laws?"

"No, signor," said Benjamin, plainly taken aback.

"Good. Sharon, is all the stuff we're doing going to, you know, help people get medicines and stuff?"

"Yes, Stoner."

He nodded and resolved that he would discuss the assorted warlike uses of zinc with her later.

He turned to Magda. "Magda, I think I've signed everything. Would you come for a walk with me?"

Magda grinned and practically skipped to his side as he stepped around the table toward the door.

Once outside it, he dropped from the straight-backed, square-shouldered, chin-lifted pose he'd struck. "Man, that is so, so, not where I'm at," he sighed in relief.

Magda nuzzled up to him. "But, Tom, *mein schatz*, see how it is you can be a tough and purposeful man of affairs?"

. "Sure," he drawled, "I just don't want to make a habit of it, okay?"

"Just from time to time," she said, squeezing him a little harder.

"All right. Except I think tonight we should rent a boat and get some wine and go out on the lagoon in the spring moonlight, and maybe smoke a little. You know, stars, moonlight, rippling water. Because otherwise I'm going to get a haircut and start acting serious and probably get a regular job. Or something."

"I think I should prefer the something," she said.

Chapter 30

Buckley put down his pen. There, finally done. A complete write-up on the current activities—plight might be a better word—of the Committee of Correspondence in Venice. Tiny numbers, worthless budget, reliance on street kids, the lot. Combined, however, with a wild plan to liberate Galileo from the clutches of the Inquisition.

Damn, damn, damn, damn. It might be the greatest story of the year, maybe the decade—like being able to scoop John Brown's raid on Harper's Ferry—and Joe wasn't sure if he could print it. No, scratch that. He could print it, all right. But the consequences . . .

He thought back ruefully to a conversation he'd had with Father Mazzare only a couple of weeks before. *Worse than the consequences of keeping quiet,* indeed.

He'd heard a lot from eavesdropping, and filled in the rest from conversations with Michel Ducos. The French sympathizer of the Committee was generally taciturn, but put a few drinks in him and he sometimes became downright loquacious. Joe had met Michel's type before. The kind of guy who, a few sheets to the wind, just couldn't help bragging about things.

360

Somehow they'd gotten news of Galileo being moved to Rome. Somehow they'd gotten hold of weapons, too. What kind and from where Joe hadn't been able to find out, except that he was sure that at least some of them had been provided by the Stone boys.

And that was an explosive element to the story, right there in itself. Even if the Stone boys hadn't provided weapons, the fact that they were knee-deep in the plot would be enough to connect it inseparably with the United States of Europe. Only the week before, Buckley himself had done a piece on the copies of Galileo's book that were flooding out of a press somewhere, and he figured he could guess the source now.

Knee-deep? Joe smiled to himself. Say better: *up to their elbows in it.* He remembered Gerry, smeared up to the elbows with oil and ink, the very image of a hillbilly jackleg mechanic. He must be running one of the Committee's presses into an early trip to the great scrapyard in the sky. How they were getting them out and to the Inquisition was anyone's guess. On the whole, given Joe's record in finding out things he'd rather not have known, he wasn't sure he wanted to make any efforts in that direction.

Buckley himself had spoken out in his article in favor of Galileo, of scientific freedom, of freedom of speech. And here he was with an opportunity to make damned sure the man stayed in the toils of the Inquisition and do himself a good turn into the bargain. On the one hand, the scoop of the year, maybe the decade. On the other, Galileo—*Gali-freaking-leo!*—in a damp cell somewhere. That was a nice clear image in Buckley's mind. Galileo's fierce, bearded visage, unbowed and defiant, glaring out through the bars of some dank cell.

It was all horsepuckey, of course. Buckley knew about the house arrest and the soft treatment the old guy was getting. No slouches in the PR department themselves, the church, they weren't going to give the man at the cutting edge of seventeenth-century science any treatment anyone could describe as medieval. In truth, there was something more than a little comical about the idea of the Marcolis and the Stones busting him out of a luxury apartment in Rome.

Buckley sighed deeply, looking at the tablet full of notes from which he'd compiled the story. Many of those notes he'd scribbled from hiding under that window. He'd managed to divert any suspicion by spending quite a bit of time in the open with members of the Committee on Murano and elsewhere. Interviews with Marcoli and Massimo, the lot, all of it purporting to be—which was truthful enough, in itself—material for an article on the Committee's overt work.

Well . . . Joe decided he'd send that part of the story in the mail to Magdeburg. He'd send it in the morning, after a good night's sleep. And when he'd done that, he'd think about the rescue story. Maybe he'd send it, too. Maybe he wouldn't. He was too tired to think clearly right now.

He got up from his desk and went to bed.

The shock brought him awake. He blinked to clear sleep out of his eyes and then focused them. Floorboards. He was lying on the floor. *How did I get out of bed?* Then someone grabbed the back of his nightshirt and hauled on it.

"What?" he yelled, and scrambled to get his legs under him. *Pistol under the pillow,* he thought. He made a dive for it, got a hand on the bed, and then pain exploded through the back of his head and he went out again.

Drowning! Buckley came to from a delirium vision of suffocating under water, to find himself soaked and cold. Something was over his face, clinging and wet, over his whole face; he couldn't see. He couldn't get his breath through it, not properly. He tried to rip it away, but his hands were tied to something, down by his lap. *Only a nightmare, I can wake up at any time.*

"Good, you are awake," someone said. Murmured, rather, into his ear.

"Who?" It sounded blurred even to Buckley, as he gasped it out through what he could now identify as wet cloth.

"You don't know me?" There was a trace of sly amusement in the voice. "Ah, but no one really knows me any more."

The cloth was whipped away. There was no one there. Looking down, Joe saw that he'd been tied to a chair, wrists and ankles both.

Then the click of boot heels on floorboards, and a figure stepped between Buckley and his desk lamp. Even in silhouette, there was no mistaking that file-thin build.

"Michel?" Buckley asked. His guts sank as he realized what this was about. "Marcoli sent you, right? Look, I wasn't going to publish, all right? I got the notes right there on the desk, you can read the piece I was gonna file. It was just about the Committee, I swear to God. I wasn't gonna say anything about the rest of it. I want Galileo busted out as much as you guys—"

A slap across the mouth silenced him. Bare-handed, but a hand that somehow seemed clawlike, bony and callused. *Callous*, Buckley thought. Not a flicker had crossed Ducos' face. Suddenly he was Ducos, not pleasant, friendly-if-a-bit-reserved good-old-Michel. The slap hadn't hurt much, more insult than injury, but there was a huge, brimming reservoir of hatred behind the dam that was Ducos' face. And Buckley realized he was starting to see cracks in the concrete. Ducos' eyes, and Buckley could see them now as his eyes adjusted to the light, were boring into Buckley. Intense. Mad.

"Fool," said Ducos, in English. "I have read your scribblings, *reporter*."

"Then you know—"

"Everything. Marcoli doesn't, of course." A small smile twisted that narrow blade of a face. "Another dupe. A shame. He may be the one honest man in this city. Such a shame, that he should be an imbecile also." Ducos shook his head, slowly and theatrically.

Buckley remained silent. *Don't provoke him.* He wished he knew more about hostage situations than he'd been able to gather from the movies. *Sure as hell nobody's dialing 911 right now,* he thought. He put his head down, to avoid catching Ducos' eye.

"You made my own spy most upset, Monsieur Buckley. He wanted to know, did I not trust him to maintain a watch on the building for him? Did I think he was too stupid to keep a proper watch? I had to pay him extra because of you. Pfui. No matter."

Ducos began to pace. "No, that is not the problem I must solve tonight, Monsieur Buckley." He pointed to Joe's article on the table. "No, the problem is that you know nothing about the plot to kill the pope. There is not a word in there about the matter."

He sounded deeply aggrieved, but Joe could sense that it was a pose. Underneath the sorrowful tone was just that hint of maniacal humor.

"What am I to do?" Ducos mused, pacing back and forth. Again, he pointed to the table. "That article must be found, of course. Crucial evidence, pointing the finger in the proper direction. But nothing about the pope!"

Buckley's head spun, and not just with uninterrupted sleep and lingering concussion. "The pope? What are you—"

Ducos was behind him, and slapped him across the head. "Silence!" The Frenchman hissed the word. There was no trace of the earlier humor now. "Of course you know nothing! Imbecile. Seigneur le Comte only gave me the orders last night."

Buckley fought down the question. The last two he'd

asked had earned him blows. He stared at a knothole in the floorboard between his feet, and concentrated very hard on not being there.

Another little chuckle. "Ah, the manner in which I have played my would-be master! D'Avaux, the fool, has never—not once!—considered the risks of taking a Huguenot so closely into his confidence. Smug, noble fool!" The voice changed, became a baritone snarl. "As if Saint Bartholomew's Day could have been forgotten. Or La Rochelle. Or the Languedoc."

So Ducos really was a traitor to France after all, Buckley realized. He was working for the count in name only. And he had reason to be pissed about his country, if he was a Huguenot. The Saint Bartholomew's Day massacre of the Huguenots, although it was now over six decades in the past, was still a byword among Protestants for Catholic tyranny and butchery. La Rochelle had seen Protestants similarly slaughtered, starved and penned under siege to die of disease. Buckley hadn't heard much about the suppression of the Huguenots in the Languedoc, but that was probably only because the savagery had had to compete with barbarisms in the Germanies. La Rochelle and Languedoc were recent, too, within the last five years. The wounds were still fresh.

"Liars, the Catholics, all of them," Ducos continued. "Did they think I would not read their stolen histories? Did they think I would not learn about the revocation of the Edict of Nantes?"

Joe's brain was still a little muzzy from the effects of the blows. He tried to remember what he could about the Edict of Nantes. Not much. It had been decreed by an earlier French king—Henry the Something-or-other, and given some rights to the Protestants. But what . . .

Oh, hell. He remembered now. He'd read about it. Fifty years or so in the future—the future of another universe—King Louis XIV would declare it null and void.

"Look, Michel," he said urgently, "that's still a long ways off. By then all kinds of things will be different. Just calm down and we can talk—"

Ducos raised his hand and Joe choked off the rest. The Frenchman was obviously in no mood to discuss the matter. And, for the first time, as Ducos raised his hand—his left hand, this time—Joe spotted the hilt of the dagger in the sleeve. *Oh, shit.*

"Ah, France!" Ducos sighed the name of his country, pacing in circles around Buckley, lost in some reflection of his own. "At least the cretin d'Avaux seeks the advantage of France, even while he mires her in the Roman heresy. He knows I am a patriot also, which is why he trusts me in what I do."

Another long silence. Three, four, five more circuits around the room. Buckley stole a glance out of the corner of his eye, and realized with a chill that Ducos was toying with the handle of the knife in his sleeve. Then, he pulled it out. A short, thin, and very wicked-looking blade.

"Saint Bartholomew's Day." Ducos sighed the words, almost in the same tone as he had spoken the name of France. "It has not been forgotten, Monsieur Buckley." A long pause. "And certainly not forgiven. Finally, after long years of biding my time, I have my chance to strike all France's enemies with a single blow."

The chuckle was becoming more like a cackle, now, as it returned. Ducos squatted in front of Buckley, and grabbed his chin roughly to lift it up. "Several blows, rather, the one riding on top of another." Back to a soft chuckle. Buckley was horrified to see that Ducos' face hardly moved at all as he laughed. "You American heretics—and you will receive one of those blows—even have a name for it. 'Piggyback.' Seigneur le Comte wanted me to mount a piggyback operation on top of Marcoli's ridiculous scheme to liberate Galileo. Make it seem as if the imbecile intended to assassinate the pope as well."

Ducos rocked back on his heels, his mouth open in a rictus than might have served someone else for a grin. "*Petits cochons!*" he whooped. "All climbing on each others' backs. I clear the way for Marcoli and his children's crusade to go to Rome. I have evidence planted in the Marcoli house after they leave, saying they meant to kill the Antichrist of Rome. So much for d'Avaux's scheme. That, of course, clears the way to lay my own plans. You see, d'Avaux wants Marcoli to fail to kill the pope. Not even to try, in fact—simply to have looked as if he intended to try. Whereas I want him to *succeed.*" Ducos hissed the last word.

Another long silence. "The cardinal is right about that, of course. The English stole the world. Better, though, that it be stolen by foreign Protestants, I think, than French heretics."

Joe was desperately trying to follow the way Michel's mind seemed to skitter from one subject to another. He was quite sure by now that Ducos was not really sane. "You work for Richelieu?" he asked, not really knowing why but simply hoping to divert the maniac. He tensed himself for a blow.

Which never came. "But of course, Monsieur Buckley. Why else would I send back a dispatch describing the foolish, insane, desperate venture that Seigneur le Comte has instructed me to carry out? Seigneur le Comte will be most lucky if he is merely broken and ruined. A traitor's death would suit him better, I think." A pause, and then another soft little chuckle. "Administered by the arch-traitor and heretic himself. Savor the irony, Monsieur Buckley. Savor it."

Ducos stood. "It is perfect, perfect in every detail. Your American abomination, this 'religious freedom' exposed as a cover for bloodshed and duplicity. The Roman Antichrist sent back to the Pit, to be chained by Christ for a thousand years. And the Beast's henchmen on earth, they all suspect France. All the further from Rome goes France. Ah, perfect."

Ducos stopped behind Buckley and laid a hand gently on either of the American's shoulders. Joe could see the edge of the blade protruding next to his cheek. The thing looked razor sharp.

"And there is more, oh, yes," Ducos said, purring. "Monsieur Gaston has his man here in Paris, too. And he has agreed to assist with the plot to discredit d'Avaux. And such a simple matter to show that he, too, compassed the death of the pope. Yes, all of it is perfect—except that one unfortunate detail. There is no mention of the plot to kill the pope in your writings."

Ducos began stroking Buckley's wet hair with his left hand, and in that moment Buckley realized he was going to die. He began to shudder, and felt warmth on his thighs as he lost bladder control.

"You tremble, Monsieur Buckley. You urinate from terror. Just so will France tremble and soil herself, as she is first-born into the Millennium. Just so. As Richelieu and Gaston squabble over the bleeding body of the Antichrist, the new world will come. Yes, the new world. Born of little pigs, climbing on each other's backs. *Petits cochons.*"

He kept stroking Joe's hair. It felt like a vulture's caress. "And both these little pigs blaming the American pigs. I care not who wins, for by then there will be the reign of Christ. And France, reborn. The new Jerusalem, and I shall be the one to lay the first stone of that heavenly city. Mortared with the blood of the Antichrist, Monsieur Buckley, and of the little pigs who pollute France with their heresy."

Another soft little chuckle. "I meant to have an Inquisition guard come to murder you, Monsieur Buckley. What better sport than to set your Americans, and that Jew who is your spymaster, on the heels of the Inquisition? But I must now hurry, for you learned of Marcoli's plan. Alas, the real plan, not the one I require. So I am afraid—my apologies—that

I must do my best to question you in the style of the Inquisition."

Torture! Buckley moaned, and began to shake again. The chair he was tied to had a short leg, and it drummed on the floorboards. "I'll talk!" he said, suddenly and oddly embarrassed that his voice was squeaking. "I'll talk!"

"Why? How? I don't mean to ask you any questions." Stroke, stroke. That hand on the top of his head, as Ducos murmured to him softly, almost intimately. Buckley cringed at every touch. Stroke. "I have read all your notes, Monsieur. I know all you know. And I shall send off your writing for you. In this way your death will not go unnoticed. Though for the moment, of course, it surely will. This building is empty, but for ourselves."

Buckley swallowed. He was dead, as dead as if he'd already stopped breathing. What to do? He was still shuddering; his testicles seemed to be burrowing into his belly. The piss on his thighs was cooling, making him shudder all the more.

Hurt him, said a still, quiet voice in his mind. He remembered a line of poetry he'd always liked a lot. From Bob Dylan—no, it was Dylan Thomas.

> *Do not go gentle into that good night,*
> *Rage, rage against the dying of the light.*

The hand holding the blade was next to his cheek. Joe snapped his head around like a snake or a snapping turtle and bit the hand. Hard.

Ducos roared with rage and pain. Buckley ignored everything except sinking his teeth into that hated hand. Ducos tried to pull the hand away but it was impossible. Then he grabbed Joe by the hair and lifted him, chair and all, and slammed his head against the edge of the table. The skinny madman's strength was incredible.

Joe was dazed by the impact. Finally, his jaws loosened enough and Michel ripped his hand away. Buckley saw the knife fall to the floor.

Get the knife! Get the knife!

The chair was off-balance anyway. He managed to tip it over and fall next to the knife. There came then the greatest sensation of triumph Joe had ever felt in his life. He managed to clamp the hilt of the knife in his teeth. *Try cutting me now, you son of a bitch!*

He never felt the slender cord sliding around his neck. Never felt it at all, even when the garrote tightened in the madman's grip. The knife was everything.

Chapter 31

Cardinal Antonio Barberini the Younger—that last an important distinction with his Uncle Antonio in the room—felt mildly out of his depth, and completely out of place. The most he could find to think of himself in this company was that he knew more of art than all of them put together. And that, alas, most of the people in the chamber would be fascinating company if they weren't all concentrating so hard on the business at hand.

Could there be anything in world so tedious as this affair with the miserable creature Galileo Galilei? Not for the first time, Antonio found himself wishing that the nasty old man would simply have the good grace to drop dead. He was seventy years old, after all. It was not as if Antonio were asking for a miracle.

Alas, the terms *good grace* and *Galileo Galilei of Pisa* were not to be found in the same sentence. Restraining yet another sigh, the young cardinal's eyes moved across the chamber. The sight brought him no relief. It was a very well populated chamber.

There were his brother Francesco and his Uncle Antonio—for whom he was named—and Cardinal

Zacchia. All were theological authorities and Inquisitors and well suited to the business of these interminable weekly meetings.

Fra Vincenzo da Maculano and the Jesuit Inchofer were also well suited to the task. An engineer and a classicist, each well learned in his field. Both of them were also experienced in Inquisition business. But the lead in that matter, among the members of the Commission of Inquiry who were not cardinals, was taken by Sinceri; who, during the rest of the week, was a prosecutor of the Holy Office.

Barberini half-listened to Sinceri's droning, dry-as-dust exposition of the laws of the Church pertaining to heresy. Picking his way, with difficulty, through Sinceri's salvos of *hold-and-defends* and *teaching contrary to magisterium*, and what-not else. Privately, Antonio thought that the Inquisition would be better feared for its tedium than its tortures. He prayed, silently, that his other uncle—Maffeo, now Pope Urban VIII—would unilaterally settle the issue with regard to the ranting Pisan so that Antonio would not have to take any decision in what was becoming a wholly vexed matter.

From the sound of the thing, Galileo had tried to weasel out of the charge. That was a joke, if one cared to laugh. After decades of sneering at everyone who dared to contradict him, of publishing viperous sallies against his opponents, he had finally stumbled against the one tribunal that could call him to account. Years of being the biggest bully in Italian natural philosophy had come to a halt when the bigger bullies of the Inquisition summoned him to Rome.

They had been gentle with him, though. They had told him to rest and get well before traveling, seen to it that he had an escort and a litter to ride in, bid him choose his own lodgings and requested, not ordered, that he not make public appearances while awaiting his trial. When they examined him—Antonio read between the lines, here, not having been present as Sinceri and da Maculano had been—Galileo had tried to pretend that the whole point of his book had been to refute the Copernican hypothesis, not to hold, defend or teach it. Had he not written Simplicius in as a character? Aristotle's great interpreter, who gave the philosopher's view and gave it ably and well? Surely, Galileo had asked, the Holy Office could see that he had defended Aristotle against Pythagoras?

The truth was, no one could see any such thing, which was why Inchofer had had to read the whole of the damned turgid book and write a review of it. Antonio felt sure that Inchofer had been more bothered by the tone of the text than anything it might say about the motion of the heavenly spheres. What was the phrase? *He slights as mental dwarfs all who are not Copernican or Pythagorean.* As well he might, in some cases, since the mental dwarfdom of some of his opponents was not wholly beyond doubt.

Which thought led Antonio, somewhat unfairly, across the room to the other three members of the Inquisi—not the Inquisition, Antonio reminded himself, never to call it that—the Commission of Inquiry.

Scheiner, whose presence was inexplicable since he was the prime complainant. Or, at least, had provoked all the complaints about Galileo—so rumor had it, with some evidence on its side—out of nothing more than desire for vengeance. Perhaps that was one of Uncle Maffeo's little jokes: to make the man who least wanted to be impartial, swear before God that he would judge without partiality. Scheiner would do it, too, out of his fourth vow as a Jesuit if nothing else. But it would take monstrous prejudice in Galileo's favor to acquit him.

Grassi was also an agitator against Galileo, and he again had had good personal reason. Over the years, Galileo had called him about seven sorts of idiot. Including, at one point, for advancing evidence in favor of the Copernican hypothesis that Galileo didn't agree with—which was some measure of the defendant in this trial. Grassi's presence was, if it was to be explained at all, part of the same game that had put his fellow Jesuit on the trial panel. Even if he, too, was scrupulously fair, the only question was Galileo's penalty.

Finally, Cardinal Gaspar Borja y Velasco. Probably not even the direct intervention of God Himself would cause him to vote in Galileo's favor. Too many of the people around the pope, people who opposed the Spanish party in Rome, were Galileo partisans as well. The Spanish Inquisitor would not be in the least partial to Galileo, even if he had come before the Inquisition looking more Catholic than the pope.

The fact that His Holiness Urban VIII had violated every canon of Inquisition procedure with this Commission of Inquiry had almost certainly caused the Spaniards to smell a rat. Six of the regular Inquisition cardinals had been asked to step aside, and been replaced with a third Barberini—Antonio himself, whom nobody including Antonio thought was in the least bit qualified to judge such a matter—and five assorted lawyers, theologians and scientists. And yet His Holiness had not explicitly said that he wished to see an acquittal. The message seemed to be that the committee was to deal as gently with Galileo as it could. It would all be much easier if Uncle Maffeo and Father-General Vitelleschi would let anyone else see the papers that had come from Grantville. Then perhaps the game they were playing might be more obvious to the less exalted members of the hierarchy.

Putting Grassi, Scheiner and Borja on the Commission seemed to be a sop to the anti-Galilean opinion and, perhaps, to the Spanish. Even together, and even assuming Scheiner and Grassi went against their vows, they would not change the outcome. Unanimity was not required, from what Sinceri had said in an earlier meeting. The lawyer seemed to be enjoying his chance to be a judge and was now holding forth, from the one word in three Barberini was catching, on whether the evidence permitted a conviction as it stood or whether all they could find was vehement suspicion calling for a public abjuration.

Barberini half-turned in his chair to see what Inchofer would say to that, and was not disappointed.

"He holds it, it is certain," Inchofer said. "He did his best to respect the formalities, but the man is so full of conceit that he put every contrary case—"

Cardinal Francesco Barberini waved him down. "So long as there is room to say that he did not mean heresy, the details don't matter."

Scheiner cleared his throat noisily, and spoke for the first time in one of these meetings. "If Your Eminence will permit, heresy was the last thing Galileo would have *meant*—but it was still the first thing he wrote in this book."

Antonio sat up straight. There seemed to be some life in these tedious meetings after all. "Father Scheiner, do you say we should absolve him of heresy?"

"No, Your Eminence," Scheiner said, half turning to address Antonio. "And with Your Eminence's permission, I shall explain."

Barberini nodded. Indeed, everyone in the room sat up straighter to hear Scheiner's contribution. Having their complete attention, Scheiner went on. "What one must always remember of Galileo is that he is capable of great personal malice."

"He is an ignoramus, and arrogant!" Grassi snapped.

"Just so," agreed Scheiner, "and a plagiarist, and bereft of manners. Above all else, a monstrous conceit afflicts him, far above that which must motivate any natural philosopher."

Grassi barked a laugh in agreement. Of those in the room who had had encounters with the Pisan, his had been the most bruising.

Scheiner went on again, glaring. "The fact that he is often—not always!—right is no great soother of our hurts." He paused, and laughed briefly. "And that hurt led me, until these last few weeks, to think him a damned heretic. Which he is! Not a page of his book passes without he arrogates to himself matters of scriptural exegesis."

Sinceri nodded. "The very pith and marrow of the grave crime of heresy," he said, in his best graveside manner.

Scheiner harumphed. "But he meant to win an argument, and perhaps guide and persuade those for whom deciding what is and is not heresy is their duty under God."

"You, too, are Copernican now, Scheiner?" Borja demanded, from his seat beside Scheiner. Grassi just glowered.

Scheiner took a deep breath and folded his hands. "As God is my witness, and may He forgive me, but I despise that man and I pray that he may be wrong in every particular and iota of his work. It may be that he is wrong about the Copernican hypothesis. But then again, he may not be."

Scheiner raised his eyes to heaven. "I would give all I have and all I ever will have to see Galileo Galilei humbled for all the wrongs he has done me. I am a natural philosopher and an astronomer, Grassi, and unlike you I have seen my own work stolen by this fraud, not just reviled as yours was. But in this"—he picked up Galileo's book—"he says much that is true. Did you but compare him with Kepler and the Tycho you championed yourself, Grassi, and with this new learning—"

"Basta!" Grassi got to his feet, shaking a finger at Scheiner. "I can read Kircher's letters from Grantville as well as you can!"

There was a silent moment. Antonio Barberini tore his eyes away from the two Jesuits. Borja was rigid, his small mouth pursed tight as a cat's ass. The regular inquisitor-cardinals were leaning forward, impassive but watching and listening carefully. The other priests were looking decidedly uncomfortable. They were used to the gentle tones of theology or the sedate protocols of cardinals. To see the kind of mayhem that natural philosophers regarded as convivial debate practiced in front of princes of the church was embarrassing them. For himself, it was all Barberini could do not to burst out laughing.

But Grassi was continuing. "There is that in the Congden Library, yes? That was a child's library, full of books for the instruction of children, yes? And they teach the Copernican hypothesis to children in the future! To children! And, I might add, I was right about that wretched comet and Galileo was not. Optical illusion, indeed."

Grassi sat down, evidently much satisfied to have said that last.

"Then where are we in disagreement?" asked Scheiner, spreading his hands in as disarming a manner as he seemed capable of.

"That you want to excuse him his heresy, and excuse him being a bad scientist!" Grassi snapped back. "With these I will never agree."

"Bad?" Scheiner asked, suddenly wearing the face of a man three steps ahead of the argument. "Because he was once wrong and you were once right?"

Grassi snorted. "Because he holds an opinion he cannot prove at a time when such opinion is heresy."

"Then," said Scheiner, "can we perhaps declare his hypothesis true and contrary to Scripture?"

Barberini nearly lost control of his face.

To his credit, Grassi laughed aloud. "Such a contagious heretic, this Galileo! He corrupts his very inquisitors!"

A rumble of chuckles went around the room. Barberini noted that even Borja twitched a corner of his mouth.

"Just so," said Scheiner. "I think the worst we can

lay before him is that he has made a thoroughly misguided attempt to convince the Church of a genuine error. And if it be no error, we can add that he is wrong to his tactlessness, indiscretion, plagiarism and arrogance."

Grassi struck a pose of astonishment straight out of the commedia dell'arte. "You—after all we did to bring him here? You find that he—that damned winetaster—acted out of the best of motives?"

Scheiner slumped down heavily in his seat, like a puppet with cut strings. "But it is still heresy," he sighed.

Neither of the two astronomers said anything further in that meeting. Antonio Barberini was again finding it hard to concentrate. Soon enough, he gave up the effort entirely and went back to the contemplation of matters in which he *was* an expert.

He was on the verge of deciding to throw his patronage in support of Artemisia Gentileschi. Very generous patronage, to boot. Female or not, the woman was one of the most superb painters of the day. Antonio considered her variant on the famous theme of Judith slaying Holofernes—both her variants, in fact—of being the best ever. Yet neither one of those paintings, magnificent as they were, compared in his opinion to either her youthful *Susanna and the Elders* or the recent *Self-Portrait as the Allegory of Painting*. True, her latest variant on the theme of Cleopatra was perhaps a bit prosaic—but only in comparison to the magnificent version she had painted some ten years earlier.

In truth, Antonio's remaining hesitation was entirely political, not artistic. Despite her sex, Artemisia Gentileschi now enjoyed the patronage—miserly, to be sure—of no less a figure than King Philip of Spain. King Charles of England too, it was said, as well as the duke of Modena.

But those last two were irrelevant, in political terms.

It was Philip who mattered, all the more so now that Gentileschi had moved from Rome to Naples. The Spanish were already aggravated with the Barberini clan. If Cardinal Antonio Barberini, nephew of Pope Urban VIII, were to steal Gentileschi away—perhaps he could even persuade her to move back to Rome . . .

Antonio cast a considering eye on his uncle Maffeo. The pope, as he had throughout these proceedings, was sitting silently and simply listening. His face, utterly impassive to anyone who did not know him well.

For a moment, their eyes met. Then the pope looked away.

But Antonio *did* know his uncle. Maffeo Barberini, he thought, was on the verge of some great and momentous decision. And Antonio thought he could guess which way he would decide. Underneath it all, the man now known as Urban VIII was something of a gambler.

Why else, Antonio thought wryly, would he have taken the risk of elevating so many of his clan to positions of such prominence in the church? That had risks and well as gains. Looked at the right way, it was almost Antonio's duty to gamble himself.

The least he could do! It was not, after all, as if Antonio would be gambling the same great stakes that sat on the table before his uncle the pope.

So. This session on the Galileo affair seemed to be coming to an end. Thankfully. Antonio was careful not to be the first to rise. Only the third. By the time he came fully erect, he had made his decision.

Yes. He would send an emissary to Naples on the morrow. No point in dallying. Great matters were coming to a head; it was his simple duty to do the same with smaller ones.

Besides, there was this. The Spanish would be furious. But the Americans would be pleased. The reason for that was somewhat mystifying to Antonio. Such odd notions those creatures had regarding the position of women. Still, he'd paid careful attention to the political reports and didn't doubt the reaction at all. Artemisia Gentileschi was the most prominent female artist in all of Europe, of the few there were at all. Were Cardinal Antonio Barberini to advance his public and munificent patronage to the woman . . . stealing her right away from the king of Spain . . .

Once again his eyes met those of his uncle.

Yes. Antonio was sure of it, now. The Americans even had an expression for the thing, he suddenly recalled. *Knows which way the wind blows.*

Chapter 32

"He's in here, Father." Billy Trumble stood at the door of the suite of rooms Buckley had occupied, leaning against the doorpost in the nerveless way that had come to mean "death room" to Mazzare over the years.

Mazzare studied the young Marine officer for a moment. Very young, he was, just out of his teens. Billy's complexion definitely looked a little green under the surface.

"Perhaps you should stand your guard outside, Billy? Fresh air might do you good."

"Uh, Father, I can't. Lieutenant Taggart told me to take guard here."

Taggart must have been standing somewhere in the room beyond. Mazzare heard his voice drift through the open door. "There's no need for that now, Lieutenant Trumble. I think the father is right. Go outside and get some air."

"Uh, thank you, sir." Billy gave Mazzare a flashing glance of thanks and started marching away. A very military-looking stride it was. The boy's back was ramrod-straight. Mazzare knew the posture was simply young Trumble's way of maintaining himself under the circumstances.

The priest sighed, wishing now he had brought Gus along. The big Jesuit somehow seemed to anchor the world around him to solid, physical verities. The presence of the earthy German would do Billy good that Father Mazzare wasn't entirely equipped to deliver. Silently, he wished the lad well—hardly a lad, now, he reminded himself, a commissioned officer as he was—and went through the doorway.

Inside was the gloomy, smoky half-dark of a candelabra-lit room. Buckley had picked one of the smaller, more cluttered suites higher up in the house, apparently for the view. Or possibly for the profusion of overstuffed and riotously carven furniture it held. In the far corner, by the long drapes that hid the night sky outside, stood Lieutenant Taggart, looking down at something that was hidden from Mazzare by a chaise-longue. Mazzare stopped and waited to be noticed.

Taggart was only a moment before seeing him. "Father," he said. "There's been a murder."

"Is it . . . ?"

"Aye. Mister Buckley." Taggart nodded, downward to what was on the floor by him. "Mistress Nichols has the laying out of him."

Sharon stood up, then. Mazzare hadn't spotted her, kneeling next to the corpse behind the chaise-longue. "Hello, Father."

"Good evening, Sharon." Mazzare nodded to her. The candlelight revealed nothing of her complexion or how steady she was, but she had the hooded eyes and upward tilted face that were the universal signal of the young lady retaining her composure under stress. Professionalism in every line of her poise, Mazzare thought. Her father's influence. He could guess that in a good light the blood would be visibly drained from her face, but that there would not be a tremor in evidence. "How, ah—how did Joe die?"

"I think, um, that is—" She took a deep breath. "I think you should take a look, Father. There's no easy way to describe this."

"Forgive me, I shouldn't stand here like a spare part." Mazzare began to walk over. This seemed all wrong. He had lost count of the deathbeds and sickrooms he had attended. The places where people came in their time to the ends of their lives. Somehow it was easy to give comfort, to be the calming presence, in places like that. Violent death was harsher. Bad enough when it happened in the street, or was carried into the emergency room. To find it like this, in an almost domestic context—Mazzare had never tried to wear what he thought of as his professional face in such a situation. This was something the police did. For the first time in years, he felt himself resist the first step forward. The prayer for strength was almost wordless. *Our Father, who art in heaven*—and then mute appeal.

Forward he went, feeling his face set into the serenity of his office. Around the chaise, to see the scene that Sharon had found. There was scarcely more to see than Buckley's form, face-down on the floor, dark and shiny stain around him. A dark and shiny puddle, as the candlelight flickered and reflected in it. Red.

"This is how we found him, more or less." Sharon's voice was cool as could be.

Mazzare did not look at her. Felt, somehow, that even so slight a touch as his gaze would cause her composure to collapse. His own didn't feel too strong. Strange, after seeing so many battle-corpses. The context made so much difference.

"Have you determined a cause of death?" He realized as he said it that it was pure cop-show. The urge to giggle was fortunately faint.

"Someone really wanted to make sure." Sharon's voice was flat now, as if the familiar routines of second-rate scriptwriters made the thing seem somehow homey. "I think he died of strangulation, this cord around his neck here. But then they bashed in his skull at the back here and cut him across the belly. They . . . did a lot of other things, too. There are multiple traumas." She put a sleeve across her face and breathed in, deeply.

Mazzare wished she hadn't. The smell was overpowering. He closed his eyes, tried to breathe shallowly through his mouth, to ignore the smell of the corpse and the final stinking indignity of Buckley's death. "How do you know?"

"That he was dead first?"

"Yes."

"If they'd cut him before they killed him, there'd be more blood. He's draining, not bleeding."

Mazzare opened his eyes, looked up a moment. The words. He concentrated a moment, to bring them to mind. Somehow, he didn't want to speak the Latin over this one. It had to be the up-time version. "Eternal rest grant unto him, O Lord, and let perpetual light shine upon him. May he rest in peace."

"Amen," said Sharon.

"Aye. Amen," added Taggart.

Mazzare nodded, once. Taggart was stoutly Presbyterian, and made no secret of his dislike of popery. But, a good man to the core, he would not begrudge the dead the right words by the lights of whoever chanced to speak them. "Thank you, Lieutenant. Thank you, Sharon. I think we should see that Mr. Buckley is attended to, yes? Lieutenant, can you have one of your men find someone—"

Before Mazzare could say anything further, Sharon interrupted. "Uh, Father. I'd rather we didn't do anything. Not until Ruy—Ruy Sanchez, I mean—gets here." She glanced at Taggart. "I asked the lieutenant to send for him."

Ruy Sanchez? Mazzare drew a blank for a moment. Then he placed the name. The factotum—to use a polite term—for Cardinal Bedmar, the special ambassador from the Spanish Netherlands. The old Catalan soldier—to use another euphemism—whom Sharon had been spending so much time with these past few weeks. Mazzare was still completely mystified by the relationship.

"Ah. Why Sanchez?"

Judging from the expression on her face, Sharon herself was a bit mystified by her relationship with Sanchez. For just that moment there, she seemed like a confused little girl. Quite unlike her normal self. As a rule, Sharon Nichols exuded a level of poise and composure far beyond what you'd expect from a woman in her early-mid twenties.

It was all Mazzare could do, for an instant, not to bark a laugh—insane laugh, under the circumstances. The nickname of *Die Fürstin* which the German population of Magdeburg had bestowed upon Sharon—the word meant "princess"—had been more of a tribute to her martyred fiancé, Hans Richter, than anything else. But . . .

The name had stuck, as such things sometimes do. Stuck, and then begun to spread, as other people observed the young woman's stately manner in public. The fact that Sharon was black—and very dark-complected at that—simply added to the glamorous myth. Black people were not unknown in the Europe of the 1630s. They were even somewhat common, now, in some of the major ports like Amsterdam. But they were still exotic, and the continent of Africa itself was almost completely unknown.

The damned human race was quirky, as Father Mazzare had long recognized. God had some purpose there, he was quite sure, though he didn't pretend to know what it was. People had their prejudices; but they also had their love of legendry. So, a woman from an unknown continent and a mysterious future, daughter of a doctor whose medical wizardry was now a legend in itself across half of Europe, betrothed of Germany's great martial champion Hans Richter, had taken on the aspect of royalty. Something similar, if not identical, had happened to Rebecca Abrabanel.

Even worldly wise and often-cynical Venice was susceptible. Mazzare had observed any number of times that, at the public gatherings the Venetian elite was so fond of, the *Case Vecchie* clustered around Sharon more than any other member of the delegation. Nor were all of them—even most of them—young men with obvious motives. She was even more popular with the daughters and matrons of the upper crust. They tended to mob her a little, in a genteel sort of way. In much the same manner, Mazzare suspected, that Princess Diana had been mobbed in the years before her death by American socialites at charity functions. Even though she too, in her last years, had not technically been a princess at all.

Sharon looked back down at Buckley's corpse. "I'm not exactly sure myself, Father. I did it on the spur of the moment, without really thinking. Ruy, well . . . he doesn't talk much about it, but I'm quite sure he has more experience with—ah—this kind of thing than anyone else I know. And . . ."

She shook her head. "There's something wrong here, Father."

Mazzare choked audibly—half a suppressed, hysterical laugh; half a protest at a naked, bestial universe.

Sharon smiled grimly. "I guess that sounds idiotic, doesn't it? Yeah, gee, no kidding, there's something wrong about a murder. Especially one this brutal. But that's not what I meant. There's something wrong about the *murder.*"

Coming around the corner, the first thing Frank Stone and his brothers spotted was Billy Trumble. The young Marine was leaning against the wall next to the entrance in front of Joe Buckley's building. Even from a distance, he looked . . .

"He's practically green," hissed Ron. "It must be true. Shit!"

Gerry was scowling in the exaggerated manner that only teenagers can manage. " 'Shit,' is right. Joe was a good guy."

Frank didn't really share his youngest brother's attitude toward Buckley. *Hadn't* shared, he reminded himself bleakly. Frank had always found the reporter a bit two-faced. Not a bad guy, no, but way too self-absorbed for Frank to like him all that much. Still, he'd hardly wanted anything like this to happen to him.

"Let's go see what Billy can tell us," he said. He began marching over, his brothers trailing in his wake.

When they came up, Billy gave them a weak little nod. "Hey, guys. You heard about Joe, huh? Yeah, it's true." He paused for a moment, clearly controlling his gorge. "Jesus, you oughta see him! No—don't."

Billy glanced at the door. "Don't go up there, guys. Just take my word for it. Lieutenant Taggart probably wouldn't let you in, anyway."

Frank swallowed. So did Ron and Gerry.

"Bad?" asked Gerry, half-whispering the words.

Billy wiped his face with the back of his uniform sleeve. "You wouldn't believe it. They tortured him first. Then . . . oh . . ."

He turned away and doubled up. Vomit splattered the side of the building and the garbage-strewn ground in front of it.

"Jesus," hissed Ron. He looked like he might puke himself.

Frank thought he probably looked about the same. His stomach sure didn't feel good. He was definitely feeling light-headed. Not even so much at the horror of what had happened to Buckley, but at the greater horror of what might happen in the future. To Giovanna.

But he managed to control himself. More than anything, Frank needed to figure out what to do. *Now.*

He waited impatiently—some part of his mind feeling guilty at the impatience—until Billy was done. As soon as Billy drew in a deep breath and managed to half-lift himself, hands now placed firmly on his knees, Frank stepped up and patted him on the back.

"You okay?"

Billy nodded.

"Look, Billy, I'm sorry but I've gotta know. You say they *tortured* him? I mean, Joe wasn't just murdered?"

Billy shook his head. When he spoke, his voice was thin but firm. "No. Christ, Frank, there are pieces of him spread around. His fingers—belly—" He broke off, giving his head a shake so violent it was more like a dumb beast trying to rid itself of a swarm of insects. "Just take my word for it, will you?"

Frank nodded and gave Billy another pat on the shoulder. "Okay, man, no sweat. I just . . . needed to be sure." He glanced at his brothers meaningfully. "I guess we'd better . . . uh, be off, now."

Billy finally managed to raise himself erect. He took another deep breath and then gave Frank something that might in really bad light have been able to pass for a smile.

"Probably a good idea." Billy glanced unhappily at the doorway. "I need to get back up there anyway." He took an uncertain step toward it.

But Frank and his brothers were already around the corner before Billy made it to the door. As soon as they were out of sight, they started running.

When Ruy Sanchez came through the door after a young officer nodded him past, the first thing he saw was Sharon Nichols. The sight of the woman, as it had for weeks now, arrested him for a moment. Had Sanchez known that Mazzare had, not long before, been puzzling over the matter of Sharon's relationship with him, the Catalan would have been mightily amused. Since he himself was only—finally!—beginning to sort it out.

It was not so much that the woman herself was confusing, though there were many times that Sanchez found her so. It was more a matter, he'd finally realized, that Ruy Sanchez de Casador y Ortiz—as he'd called himself for several decades now; to his amazement, with complete success—had managed, not for the first time in his life, to place himself in a quandary.

Sharon still hadn't noticed him, standing in the doorway. Neither had the priest standing beside her. So, Sanchez took the moment to examine her.

Then, very softly, sighed. Two weeks earlier, after as serious and determined a campaign of seduction as Ruy Sanchez had ever launched—and he was quite good at it—he'd come to accept the fact that he'd met his match. Not for the first time, to be sure; but it was still a rare enough experience to cause him to sulk for several days. The cardinal had been quite sarcastic about it, too. Not that Bedmar knew any of the details, of course, because Ruy Sanchez never discussed his amatory affairs with anyone. But he and the cardinal had been together now for many years, and the old bastard was hard to fool.

That left only two options: abandon the campaign with a gracious salute to the victor; or . . .

Sanchez had spent a week mulling over the "or." And, by the end, decided he much preferred it to the alternative.

As he'd feared he would, alas. Whatever else he was, the Catalan was no fool. His pretense at nobility had gone unchallenged, true enough, but that was mostly a result of his connection with the cardinal and the fact that few men who knew Sanchez would challenge him lightly. Few, indeed, would challenge him at all; even now, as he approached his sixtieth year of life. In his own way, he was somewhat famous in the insular world of hidalgo Spain and its territories. Well known, at least; and if not esteemed, he was certainly given wary respect.

None of which, he well knew, would make—to use the American expression he'd picked up from

Sharon—a "spit's worth of difference" to her. He might as well advance an offer of marriage to a Spanish infanta. Granted, Sharon Nichols would be gracious in her refusal, where an infanta—or her father, more likely—would have Sanchez clapped into a dungeon. Refuse him she would, nonetheless—if anything, even more decisively than a Spanish princess. The Catalan had only a dim sense of the way in which Americans gauged these things, because they viewed the world so differently than other people he'd known. But he understood enough—thought he did, at least—to know that he would be considered an utterly unsuitable spouse for such as Sharon Nichols. By she herself, leaving aside her father or anyone else.

It was all . . . very confusing, and left Sanchez feeling uncertain of himself and what he should do. There was nothing in the world that Ruy Sanchez de Casador y Ortiz *detested* more than being confused and uncertain.

That detestation made him clear his throat more noisily than he meant to. Sharon and the American priest looked over, startled.

"You sent for me, dona?" Stubbornly, as a sop to himself, Sanchez used the Catalan term instead of the Spanish *señora* or the Italian *signora*. He knew it was silly, but not even Ruy Sanchez could bring himself to call Sharon Nichols by the girlish diminutives. Not in any language. Unmarried or not, she was simply impossible to address other than with the fullest respect.

"Thank you for coming, Ruy," said Sharon. She gestured at the corpse whose feet were the only thing Sanchez could see from where he stood. "You were told what happened?"

He nodded. "The soldier who brought your summons informed me."

"It was hardly a 'summons,' Ruy," Sharon murmured, smiling. It was a little smile, and a sad one. He wondered about that sadness. Most of it, to be sure, was due to the death in the room. But some, perhaps . . .

Old habit swept his hat from his head in a gallant flourish. "From you, dona, any request sent to Ruy Sanchez is considered a summons. I would no more think to disobey than—"

Sharon barked a little laugh. "Oh, Ruy—give it a rest!" She shook her head, smiling more widely. "I will say you can always cheer me up. Even here, even now. But, still, put a cork in the testosterone, would you? Just for a few minutes—I know it's a lot to ask."

Sanchez smiled back. He understood the term "testosterone" now. Sharon had explained it to him. Twice. The second time, laughing, after he'd strutted for minutes when she explained it the first time. Ha! The truth! Confirmed even by Americans, with their dazzling science!

She motioned him over. "Come here, please. I want you to look at this. I think—no, I'd rather hear what you think, before I say anything."

It took Sanchez no more than three minutes to draw his conclusions. It was not difficult. Certainly it was not upsetting. Sanchez had seen far worse, as a young man, in the course of the endless border wars in New Spain with the savage indigenes of the mountains and deserts. Not all of which barbarisms, by any means, had been the work of the indigenes themselves. By the time he was twenty, he'd understood that savagery was the common property of mankind. The same skin, whatever its color.

He might have despaired then, had he not discovered in the arms of his first wife that other properties were shared and common also. Those he chose to treasure. For the rest, there was always his sword.

He rose. "This is fakery. The man fought. Not well, I think, but fight he did. Those teeth broke; they were not broken. The rest—"

He made a contemptuous gesture. "All done after he died. The garrote is what killed him. Not a good death—what is?—but better than most. It would have been quick, at least, as deeply as that cord is driven into his neck."

The priest was frowning. "All . . . *that?* But—why?"

Sanchez shrugged. "Much of it, I think, was done from sheer fury. The murderer probably did not expect his victim to strike back, and flew into a rage when he did." He pointed to the intestines spilling onto the floor. "Why else inflict such a wound? No torturer would, for a surety. And most of this was done to make it seem that the man was tortured."

The priest was still frowning. Whether that was because he was puzzled or simply because a frown was his way of maintaining composure in the midst of barbarity, Sanchez could not determine.

"I still don't understand *why.*"

Neither did Sanchez—and the matter was beginning to intrigue him. Given Buckley's past activities, of course, there were a multitude of possible suspects. One of them being . . . well, Sanchez himself.

He decided it would be best to depart now, before that thought occured to the Americans also. Besides, Cardinal Bedmar needed to learn of this matter at once. So, with a flourish, he made his farewells and came as close to scampering out the door as Ruy Sanchez de Casador y Ortiz ever came to scampering.

Which was not very close at all. After he was gone, Sharon Nichols shook her head and said: "I swear, that man will swagger into his own grave." But she was smiling when she said it. The first genuine smile on her face since she'd entered that horrible room.

Chapter 33

The funeral that took place the next day was wholly lacking in Venetian pomp, but drew a ceremonial all of its own. The arrangements had been simple enough; Gus had dealt with it. It had turned out to be easy to persuade the nearest church to let them hold the service, and a grave was to be had for ready money. Given the state of the corpse, no one even proposed employing the services of a mortician. The Marines, sharing Gus' own grim attitude, had taken care of wrapping the body. The casket, of course, was closed.

Mazzare had not even the beginnings of a notion what religion Buckley had had, if any, and Sharon hadn't known either despite their being at college together. So it was a requiem mass, by default, since there would have been complications at the very least had Jones, as the only Protestant minister in town, done the service in his own native liturgy.

He had expected a quiet affair, with just the staff and the ambassadorial party turning out.

Not a bit of it. Mazzare had stepped out of the sacristy, accompanied by a small squadron of Venetian altar boys, to see a church packed wall to wall. In the front pews, the embassy party minus the corporal's guard they'd left behind. Behind them, Mazzare recognized several Venetian dignitaries. None of them of the first rank, and the highest of them would need to puff himself out to make the second rank, but nothing happened by accident in this town. Someone—likely several someones, some number between one and Ten—was sending a message of support.

Mazzare was not really surprised. Outside, he'd been told by Gus, a small mob from the Arsenal had gathered for the funeral also. Joe Buckley's articles had been passed around the Arsenal too, in special editions printed by the Venetian Committee of Correspondence. For whatever reason—always hard to know with that mysterious body—the Council of Ten had chosen to turn a blind eye both to Buckley's activities as well as the propaganda work of the city's small and oft-derided Committee.

Heinzerling himself thought it was because the Council of Ten saw Buckley and his popularity in the Arsenal as an asset to Venice. True, the Venetian elite itself had often been the target of Buckley's muckraking. Buckley had had the touch, however unpolished he might have been, and the Venetian masses had especially enjoyed one article he'd written on the Council of Ten, which he or some wit of an editor had entitled "A Conspiracy of Harlots."

But Venice had not survived for so many centuries in Europe—a republic among monarchies for a thousand years—because its upper crust was given to fits of pique. The real danger they faced was not rebellion on the part of the city's masses, it was foreign intervention. More than once, Venice's powers had used the Arsenalotti to drive out an alien presence which, for one reason or another, the Council of Ten had not wanted to confront directly.

Mazzare wondered if such a maneuver was being undertaken again. And who would be the target?

The Spanish? Maybe . . .

But, if so, Sanchez seemed determined to be the joker in the deck. He'd turned out for the funeral also, and in full hidalgo formal attire. A message from his master, or just here because of Sharon?

Following the service, Buckley went by boat from the church to his grave, accompanied by a fleet of, not mourners exactly, but people who wanted to be seen to be mourners. It seemed a little unreal to Mazzare as he spoke the words and watched the crowd gather. He had visions of political funerals in South Africa and Northern Ireland, and stumbled over the words of committal as visions of riot crossed his mind.

But the funeral was wholly lacking in drama as well. The gravediggers stepped forward on cue as the mourners began to file out of the graveyard. Mazzare took off his stole, and looked to the gray sky that threatened rain but had not yet delivered.

"Larry?" Jones interrupted the reverie that Mazzare always fell into after funerals. "There's a message from Benjamin."

The Jewish lawyer had remained at the embassy to mind the store. "What does he say?" Mazzare asked.

"The State Inquisition is declining to investigate."

Mazzare frowned. He had, naturally, reported the matter to the appropriate authorities as a murder. "Why?" he asked.

"They think it's the Spanish or the French, and they can't arrest any of the diplomats."

"What?" Sanchez had heard.

Jones colored. "Señor Sanchez," he said, "I'm only repeating what was told to me."

Sanchez blew through his mustaches. "Did they have the courage to make this accusation to my face, I should be much tempted to take advantage of my diplomat status." He smiled in a way that was all the more unnerving coming from a man of almost sixty.

Mazzare decided to try conciliation. "Now, señor,

I feel sure the accusation was not meant for you personally—"

Sanchez threw back his head and laughed. "Your Excellency forgets that I was here for the conspiracy. Took part in it, in fact. The Venetians would believe anything of me."

A cold wind was idly toying with the clothes of the few mourners who yet remained in the graveyard, but that was not all that made Mazzare shiver. The sheer Latin ferality of the man, when he chose to show it, was quite intimidating. In that moment Mazzare realized he himself could well believe anything of the stocky Spaniard, whom Sharon had once described to him as "Don Quixote on steroids." It was easy to see him smiling in badly feigned innocence while a windmill was blown to smithereens by stealthily planted charges. Tilting he would regard as pointlessly ineffective.

"Behave, Ruy," Sharon said.

"Forgive me, Dona Sharon." Then, turning back to Mazzare: "And forgive my manner, Excellency. The plain fact of the matter is that our nations are in arms against one another. But neither I nor His Eminence the cardinal would resort to such as this. If nothing else, I am pricked by the suggestion that we should do something so foolish. The man Buckley was an annoyance to us, as I understand he was to you—"

Sharon had the good grace to look a little embarrassed at having apparently released a little diplomatic communiqué of her own. Mazzare decided he would do no more than issue a word to the wise—later.

"—but there are other means to deal with annoyances of his kind."

"Quite," Mazzare said. He'd heard rumors of prosecutions for libel and slander, challenges to duels and so forth. It had been only a matter of time before something had descended on Buckley; it was just that the murderer got to him first.

"Please accept my assurance and my word," Sanchez

continued, speaking very formally now, "Your Excellency, that to my knowledge this matter was not conceived of at the embassy of His Most Catholic Majesty."

"Thank you, Sanchez," Mazzare said.

Sanchez bid them all good day, and left immediately. That made sense. If the Venetians were casting aspersions of that character, his master the cardinal Bedmar and the Spanish embassy in general needed to know so as to start protesting immediately. Loudly and in strong terms; Mazzare wondered how Bedmar kept a straight face. The old cardinal was one of the sharpest operators in Venice, for all he played the role of feeble old man in over his head.

And, at that, he might well have to keep a straight face through all those protests. Sanchez was himself a competent operator, and had not gone so far as to pledge his word absolutely for the clean hands of the whole Spanish presence in Venice. There were, in effect, two missions from His Most Catholic Majesty in town right now, and no firm guarantee that the left hand knew what the right was doing. Mazzare had met Bedmar several times, and the other Spaniards likewise. Never in the same place, and always on neutral ground. The regular mission—the one from Madrid—was polite, reserved and distant, saying nothing and giving away less. Bedmar, on the other hand, seemed to be hinting at a second agenda, a possibility that there was more to discuss than just how little personal rancor there was arising from the fact that their mutual nations were at war. There was, however, nothing of substance in that as yet. It was, at best, frustrating.

Jones interrupted this rather gloomy train of thought. "Penny for 'em," he said.

Mazzare looked around and saw that he and Jones were the last to leave, apart from the gravediggers, who were settled into a steady rhythm as they buried poor Buckley in Venice's soggy silt.

"Poor value for money," he grunted.

"Stuck for ideas?" Jones said. "Me too."

They began to walk away from the grave, toward the gate, threading through the ornate monuments under which the Venetians buried their dead. "The Venetians say it's the French or the Spaniards," Mazzare said, "and Sanchez denies it. The Spanish part."

"You believe him?" Jones asked, pulling his coat tighter about him against the chill breeze of early spring.

"I'd like to."

"Larry, don't get all gloomy on me again. Last time I turned out for one of your funerals, you went all serious on me. Did everything but start another Reformation."

Mazzare, suddenly reminded of old Mrs. Flannery's funeral, bit off the smart answer he'd been assembling practically from the moment Jones had opened his mouth. Irene Flannery, retired schoolteacher, dragon and stalwart of St. Mary's back in Grantville, had died in a cavalry raid on the town, too stubborn to leave her home for the safety of the downtown buildings where Grantville's heavily armed population had ambushed and defeated a horde of Wallenstein's raiders.

It had been four days before she'd been brought in for burial, and that sodden, rain-lashed graveside attended by not a single genuine mourner had been the place where Mazzare had suddenly decided to stand up under the weight of his vocation. To finally heed what God had been telling him for over a year since the Ring of Fire.

He sighed. "No, Simon, it's not that. It's just that poor Joe's been murdered and I don't know what more we can do."

"Find out who did it," Jones said, simply, as they came to the graveyard gate.

Mazzare said nothing. He hoped Jones's irrepressible sense of humor wasn't taking a turn for the morbid.

"I'm being serious, Larry," Jones said. "Even if we

can't take it to a trial and the hanging someone richly deserves, we need to know who's out to get us."

"Everyone." Mazzare gave a single bark of laughter. "We're not paranoid, Simon, everyone really is out to get us."

Jones chuckled. "We could at least try to identify which of them is prepared to murder us in our beds."

"True."

"Of course, this isn't a cliché yet," Jones added.

"What?" Mazzare looked askance. Jones was being even more oblique than usual.

"Oh, you know. Father Whazzisname investigates." Jones held out his hands in the shape of a frame, to see how Mazzare would look on screen, or possibly in something by Chesterton.

"Knock it off, Simon." Mazzare waved to call for a boat back to the embassy. They were busy a few moments getting in and negotiating with the gondolier.

"Seriously, Larry," Jones continued as the boat pulled away, "we need to look into this."

"Finding the time will be a trick. And how do we do it anyway? I can just see me going to Count d'Avaux and asking him where he was on the night in question."

Jones looked at him sharply. "Why'd you think it's the French?"

Mazzare gave back his best Poirot impersonation. "I zuzpect evreewahn, and I zuzpect nowhan." Then he shrugged. "No, the count was just the first example to spring to mind. Although if I had to draw up a short list of suspects, most of the names on it are French ones."

"Figures. Anyway, since you seem to be in the right frame of mind, who are our suspects?"

Mazzare counted on his fingers. "First, all the countries we're at war with. France, Spain, England, in that order."

"You think Sanchez was lying?"

"No, it's that he almost certainly doesn't know everything. There are really two Spains, these days. He's with the one we might be able to do business with some day."

"Flanders," Jones said.

"Quite. Except it's a lot bigger than Flanders, nowadays. Bedmar's definitely on that side, I think, if he's on any side bar his own. We can probably rule him out."

"England too, on that basis."

"True," Mazzare said. "Fielding's as smooth and two-faced a limey as ever I met."

"Prejudice, Larry?" Jones clucked his tongue slyly.

"No, I lived there, remember. I'm not suggesting he's smooth and two-faced *because* he's a limey—and they found that term funny, by the way. No, as I was saying, he's as smooth and two-faced as they come, but if he's a schemer then he's a schemer who's doing nicely, I hear, out of us being in Venice. And even if he wasn't, Hider would be sitting on him, and Hider right here has a lot more clout than Charles Stuart at the other end of Europe. So, you're right, not the English. The Danes? We've had hardly a peep out of them here, and I doubt they care what happens all the way over this side of Europe. No, they've got more parochial concerns."

"The Austrians?" Jones suggested. "Come to that, Wallenstein? Yeah, sure, he's supposed to be an ally now, but with that man . . ."

"Doubt either. Wallenstein's hardly on the radar. What are we doing in Venice to annoy him that even comes close to matching his need to rely on us where he lives? Undercutting his interest in the copper market? Sure, he sent off a nasty letter or two, but that's piddly stuff. As for the Austrians, the Empire's pretty much resigned to us cocking a snook at them."

"Really?" Jones raised his eyebrows.

"I'm sure of it. All the bloviating they've been doing has been pretty much for form's sake. They've had to put up with the Venetians for so long they don't seem to care any more, and we're not likely to do them any harm here that we're not doing bigger and better closer to home. Besides, the Spanish Habsburgs regard this as their theater, not for their cousins to dabble in."

"Stipulated. For the moment. That leaves us with France and Spain proper, then, and—who else?"

"Everyone Buckley annoyed," Mazzare said, with a sigh.

"That's me on the list of suspects, then," Jones said. "You too, actually."

"Right. But the first people he annoyed were the French and the last were, at a guess, the Turks."

"Turks?"

"That was going to be his next piece, as far as Benjamin could tell, and I found some notes to that effect in his room. He'd been making himself a nuisance around Bey Koprulu's staff. I understand he'd been told his presence wasn't wanted and would be, ah, reduced if it was detected again."

Jones nodded. "Should have remembered the reports. I do recall reading that a couple of days ago."

They rode the rest of the way in silence, watching the sights and sounds of Venice slide by. It was, Mazzare thought, living proof that there was such a thing as too beautiful. The palazzi were carefully constructed to be light and airy in their facades, of properly balanced proportion and perfectly tasteful adornment. Even the lack of maintenance was part of the charm. Still and all, he couldn't help feeling that a little more austerity would improve the place no end, or at least let some of the poorer neighborhoods front onto the canal.

As they turned onto the narrow canal that led to the embassy, a maneuver that always put Mazzare in mind of sailing into a cave-mouth, they saw an unfamiliar boat tied up in front, slightly ornate despite Venice's ferocious sumptuary laws that insisted on the same kind of gondola for everyone.

"Visitor, then," Jones said as they disembarked and paid the gondolier. He nodded at the new boat. "Someone important, from the looks."

"Wonder who?" Mazzare mused.

Mazarini met them inside the door, chatting with Sharon Nichols. He must have been practically standing sentry. "Your Excellency," he said, in very solemn tone of voice, "I have a letter for you here. It's from the Holy Father."

Mazzare took the proffered note. It was a very fancy looking thing. He could only stare at the missive, for some moments, while his mind raced over the possible contents. He had a sense that the blood had drained from his face.

What was most likely, he thought, was that the pope had decided to firmly and decisively reject Mazzare's views on the Church's proper theological and historical perspective and future course. If so, Larry Mazzare would finally find himself in that place he had most wanted to avoid since the Ring of Fire. The place where Martin Luther had once stood—almost half a millennium back, in the world Mazzare had come from, but not much more than a century in this one.

Or was it, perhaps, the place where Thomas à Becket had once stood, when he made his decision?

But there was no point in delaying. Very pale, but composed, Mazzare broke the seal and opened the letter.

It took him some time to read it. The Latin was even more flowery than usual. Mostly, though, it took him some time because the contents were the last thing he had expected. In fact, they didn't even qualify as "last." He had never once imagined he might receive such a letter—neither in his dreams nor his nightmares. He had to read it three times over before he finally absorbed it.

"I am summoned to Rome," he said harshly. "I must appear before the Inquisition."

On the landing above, where he'd been eavesdropping, Gerry Stone pulled his head back and tip-toed away as fast as he could.

"Michel was right," he muttered to himself. "Every which way from Sunday. The bastards are pulling out all the stops."

Seeing the shock on the face of Simon Jones—Sharon's too—Mazzare belatedly realized that he'd perhaps chosen his words poorly. Simon was such a close friend that the priest sometimes forgot that the Protestant minister would automatically place a different twist on certain things.

He cawed a little laugh. "Oh, for Pete's sake. Simon, to 'appear before the Inquisition'—which is slang to begin with; the correct term these days is 'Holy Office' or 'Commission of Inquiry'—just means about the same thing as 'to appear in court.' In case you'd never noticed, *lots* of people have to appear in court. The defendant is only one of them. There is also the prosecutor, the witnesses—"

"They want you to be a witness, then?" Jones' sigh of relief might have knocked down walls. The thatch walls of the lazy first little piggie, anyway. Maybe even the second.

Mazzare looked back down at the letter. "No, as a matter of fact. They want me to appear as the attorney—well, that's not the right term exactly—for the defense. I'm to defend Galileo before the Holy Office."

It was all Mazzare could do not to crumple the letter in his fist. Not in anger, but in a sudden and almost uncontrollable surge of triumph.

Simon Jones might be a Protestant, and thus unfamiliar with the intricate workings of the Roman Catholic

Church. Not to mention something of a hillbilly naïf. But the Methodist minister had a very good brain, and it didn't take him more than a few seconds to realize the truth.

"Lord in Heaven," he murmured. "It's cracking, isn't it? Cracking wide open."

With some effort, Mazzare took the time to fold the letter back up in a neat manner. Then, handed it back to Mazarini. "How soon?" he asked.

"Immediately, Monsignor." Mazarini smiled. It was a thin smile, but a cheerful one nonetheless. "Not even a man of my modest station is used simply as a courier."

Mazzare nodded. "No, of course not. You're to be my escort and—ah—"

Mazarini raised a stiff hand. The smile was on the verge of cracking open itself. "Please! I assure you, Father, that no one—certainly not Giulio Mazarini!—has ever once contemplated such crude terms as 'jailer' and 'watchdog.' The Holy Father has great trust in you."

The diplomat cocked his head a bit sideways, narrowing his eyes. "Um. Actually, I think that last bit may even be true. And what a rare wonder that would be, in this odd business we practice."

Mazarini now gestured to the door. "I have made all the arrangements, Father. A boat to take us to the mainland. Thereafter, an excellent carriage. We can leave as soon as you are ready."

"I'll just need a half hour to pack some things." Mazzare turned to Jones. "This is something I have to do, Simon. *Must.* But . . . can you come with me? I'd find your company a help and a comfort."

Simon didn't hesitate for more than a second. "Yes, of course. But who'll hold the fort for us while we're gone? Stoner's back up in Padua."

"I'll send word for him to get right back," said Sharon firmly. "In the meantime, I imagine I can handle whatever needs to be. It can't be that hard, right?

Basically, I just pass the buck until Stoner gets back, and then he passes the buck until you do. Stoner's a world-class buck-passer and I'm no slouch either, if I say so myself." She gave Mazzare a dazzling smile.

Neither statement was actually true at all. Sharon was almost compulsive about doing her duty and, in his own inimitable way, Stoner was even more so. Still . . .

Mazzare had other things on his mind, and the fact was that he had a great deal of confidence in Sharon Nichols. Even, for that matter, in Tom Stone. Besides, he understood enough already just in the short time he'd had to think about it to realize that the pope's decision to appoint Mazzare to defend Galileo was going to transform Europe's politics. Whatever real diplomacy would be practiced in Italy for the next period would be practiced in Rome, not Venice.

"All right, Sharon. Thanks." He started to turn away to attend to his packing, when a last thought arrested him. "Oh. And—ah—explain it to Mike Stearns as best you can when—"

He managed not to glance at Mazarini. "—whenever you can send off a letter."

Sharon's smile was really quite dazzling. And Mazzare noted with approval that she didn't even glance up the stairs toward the radio room. "Yeah, sure, Father. Consider it done. I'll start writing the letter as soon as you and the monsignor are gone."

"We don't have any *choice*, Frank," insisted Ron. "You heard what Gerry said. I mean, we're talking about the *Inquisition* here. They're not even respecting Father Mazzare's diplomatic immunity any more. You think they won't cut our throats—or your girlfriend's—without blinking an eye? Okay, sure, Antonio's a little too sure of himself, maybe. But, you ask me, he's an island of sanity in this crazy place."

Frank ran fingers through his hair, glancing at their youngest brother. For once, the sixteen-year-old wasn't looking in the least bit cocksure. Gerry looked just plain scared.

Frank didn't blame him. He was scared himself. Joe Buckley tortured and murdered—the authorities making it clear they were going to look the other way—and Father Mazzare now hauled off to an Inquisition dungeon in Rome. Michel Ducos hiding out from his own French embassy at the Marcolis—they'd tried to kill him, he said. Given how crazy everything had suddenly gotten, Frank had no trouble believing it either. Michel certainly had a nasty-looking defensive wound on his hand

Worst of all, in some ways, was that their dad wasn't available to talk to. He and Magda were in Padua. As much as Tom Stone could often drive his sons nuts, at bottom they trusted him more than most kids did their parents. Even his good judgment.

The thought of his father in Padua did the trick. Frank knew that Antonio Marcoli was planning to travel through Padua on the way to Rome. Frank could at least get Giovanna out of the murder hole that Venice had turned into and maybe keep her safe. And he could ask his dad what he thought about Marcoli's plan when they reached Padua. Frank had always thought the plan was pretty nutty, but . . .

All of Italy looked to be a madhouse. So maybe it wasn't so crazy after all.

"All right," he said, "we'll do it. As soon as that bastard Mazarini's gone with the father."

Gerry had drifted over to the window in their rooms as Frank had ruminated. Suddenly, he stiffened. "They're leaving now. And—damn it, look!—they're hauling away Reverend Jones, too."

The look on his face combined indignation and fear. "I thought they couldn't do that? I mean, he's not a Catholic to begin with."

Ron shrugged. "I'd say they can pretty much do whatever they want to. What's Mike Stearns gonna do?

Send an army across the Alps at the same time we're fighting everybody else in Europe? Not hardly."

Fifteen minutes later, they slipped out of the back door of the embassy and headed for Murano.

The radio at the embassy wasn't capable of reaching across the Alps during the daytime, so Sharon would have to wait until the evening window to send a message to Magdeburg bringing Francisco Nasi and the prime minister up to date on the most recent developments. In the meantime, she decided she *would* write a letter.

In the end, after dillying for a bit, Sharon decided to make it a brief note. That would be enough to bring Sanchez to the embassy, and she found herself unable to write anything more extensive. She needed to be looking him straight in the face when she said what she had to say.

Whatever that might be. She still wasn't really sure. She needed to *look* at him.

Chapter 34

Sanchez arrived the next morning. After he was ushered into the salon in the embassy where Sharon had decided she would meet him alone, she took some time to study him. Sanchez underwent the scrutiny patiently. He simply stood before her where she sat on a chaise, saying nothing. Patience? she wondered. Or was it simply fatalism?

Abruptly, she spoke. "Did you have anything to do with it, Ruy?"

Sanchez began to stiffen. Suddenly angry, Sharon slapped her hands on her thighs. "Stop it, Ruy! This is *me*. I don't care about your damned hidalgo honor and your solemn vows and your so-called oaths." It was all she could do not to grit her teeth. "I've never seen where any of that precious crap—and that's what it is, crap—has kept any of you from butchering anyone you felt like. Or committing every other crime in the book."

She lifted her head. "So tell it to *me*, this time. Just straight up. Did you kill Joe Buckley? And if you didn't, do you have any idea who did?"

Sanchez blew through his mustaches. Then, his

broad shoulders moved in a chuckle. "Such a difficult woman! In this, as in everything."

He shook his head. "No, Dona Sharon, I did not do it. Nor did Bedmar. The cardinal would have used only me for such a deed. I cannot vow that it was not done by the regular Spanish embassy, the one representing Madrid directly. We have, in truth, little to do with them. But . . , I do not think so."

She believed him. She wasn't sure why, exactly, but she did. It came as a great relief.

Greater than she'd expected, in fact. She found herself starting to wonder about that, but Sanchez continued to speak.

"Your second question, of course, is much more difficult to answer. Do I have *any* idea who killed him? Oh, certainly—many ideas. But that is all they are, simply ideas. Do you wish me to expound upon them?"

She shook her head. "Not at the moment, no. Later, yes. In fact, that's the reason I asked you here. Well, one of them. I want to ask you to help me try to find out who murdered Joe. You're the only person I know in Venice who'd have any idea where to even start."

Sanchez cut right past that. "Yes, certainly. And the other reason? Or reasons?"

She studied him again for a moment. Then, looked away and studied the Venetian sky beyond a window. "Me. You and me." Impatiently, she flicked her hand. "I'm not saying this well. What I mean is, that I think we need to define our relationship. Finally."

She smiled at the sky. "I really do *not* want to be fending you off while you and I play Sherlock Holmes and Doctor Watson—your Sherlock to my Watson, I'm quite sure. I wouldn't mind so much—well, I would, but at least it wouldn't be hard—if you did your groping with your hands instead of your brains. But, you don't."

Which was true. In all the many occasions they'd spent time together, Ruy had not laid a finger on her

except for an occasional polite offer of a hand to help
her out of a gondola or to cross a difficult patch of
ground. He had been courtesy incarnate—while never
ceasing his endless flirtation. At times when she'd not
been immersed in her quiet melancholy, she'd found
it quite amusing. Even, yes, quite flattering. Even, yes,
sometimes—not often—quite attractive.

The first time she'd met the man she'd thought of
him as *Feelthy Sanchez*. That image had faded away,
as the weeks went by in his company. Ruy Sanchez
had the sex drive of a goat, true enough, even at his
advanced age. But there was nothing filthy about it.
Lust, yes; leering, no. Just the honest if not particularly couth drive of a man with more than his share
of testosterone.

And . . . so what? The same had been true of Hans
Richter, after all, even if the outer shell had been as
different as could be imagined. Hans, a sweet and shy
young German boy; Ruy, a self-confident and swaggering old Catalan hidalgo. But Hans, too, had flooded
her with that same raw desire. And if you wanted
testosterone—Sharon issued a soft, sad little laugh—all
you had to do was get in a motor vehicle with Hans
at the wheel. Or—a stab of pain, here—fly with him
in his beloved airplane. He'd sometimes driven Colonel Wood a little nuts. Sharon could remember one
occasion when Jesse had ranted at him: *Why don't
you try—just once, Hans!—thinking with your brain
instead of your balls?*

She looked back at Sanchez and discovered an odd
expression on his face. It took her a moment to place
it. Then, when she did, she couldn't help but laugh a
second time. Softly, again, but not sadly.

They'd been speaking in English, as Ruy always
preferred. He said that was to improve his command
of the language. Sharon knew that for a little lie.
Sanchez, an old seducer, would take any advantage he
could get. Better to fumble a bit with the intended

seducee's language—perhaps she'd find the accent charming—than to place oneself in the dreaded position of an instructor.

It was the word *relationship* that had confused him, she realized. How delightful. She'd have to remember that. Confusing Ruy Sanchez was an accomplishment. Not like climbing Everest, maybe, but perhaps up there with climbing the Matterhorn.

He understood the word itself, of course. But Europeans of this day and age—the Spanish, for a certainty—simply did not think of people in terms of their "relationship." The word was at once too broad and too individual. They thought in terms of *specific* relationships. Class, status, age, whatever. Behind that American concept lay centuries of technical and industrial advance and the social looseness that came with it. A world where custom and tradition had lost its firm grip needed that individual substitute. In the world of Ruy Sanchez, it fit about as well as a square peg in a round hole.

A glimmer of understanding came to her, then. Just a glimmer.

"What do you *want* from me, Ruy?" Sharon looked down at herself. Once again, she slapped her thighs. "Besides this, I mean? Or is there anything else?"

Even covered by the rich material of her gown, the sound was distinctly meaty. Not surprising—the thighs strained at the fabric just as the breasts did. No one would ever mistake Sharon Nichols for a *Vogue* model. Still, it was the sound of firm flesh, not flab.

She looked back up at Sanchez, challenging him with her dark eyes. "What do you *want*? Or is it impossible for you to even think that straightforwardly? Do you always need to fit yourself—and me—into categories? Like 'conquest'?"

She looked over at a settee nearby. "I swear, I'm almost—not quite—ready to march over there and spread my legs just so you can get it out of your system." She brought her gaze back to him. "We've got a term for that, by the way. Americans, I mean. It's called a 'mercy fuck.' But it's usually something bestowed on boys."

To her surprise, he did not bridle at all under the implied insult. True, he stroked his mustachios; but, with Ruy Sanchez, that was a given. As well ask a rooster not to crow at dawn; or a tomcat not to prowl at night.

When he took the fingers away, there was a smile there. A sad one, she thought.

"Do not ask, Dona Sharon. The answer is . . . impossible." His square shoulders seemed to get squarer still. "I shall no longer attempt my—ah—courtesies. Although—" His eyes flicked to the settee. "—should you reconsider at any point . . ."

The humor, Sharon realized, was simply a cover for sadness. Why?

The realization came to her almost like the proverbial thunderclap. It was all she could do not to clap her hand over her mouth in shock and surprise.

He wants to PROPOSE? He's old enough to be my father! That was quite literally true—Ruy Sanchez and James Nichols were almost exactly the same age. *An old goat is one thing, but . . .*

Another realization came to her, then. Not like a bolt from the blue, but welling up from underneath. There had always been something about Ruy Sanchez that had struck an odd chord with her. She'd called it "twinkly," she remembered. For the first time, she understood what it was.

Ruy Sanchez reminded Sharon of her father. The two men were so different in so many ways that she'd never thought of it before. But now . . .

She rose and went to stand by the window. Yes. Two men born and raised in a society's underbelly who had clawed their way out of it. Yet, beneath the smoothly polished exterior, always retained something of that primal origin. Including the sheer testosterone ferocity that served some men in such places as their shield and sword.

That was not often in evidence, with her father, but it was there. Always there, somewhere, beneath the doctor's surface. Sharon remembered, once—she'd been twelve at the time and her mother was still alive—coming out of a movie theater with her parents in a rough part of Chicago. Two young men had moved toward them. Their purpose? Impossible to know, but there had been that sense of aggressiveness about their movements.

Their purpose would never be known because her father had gone through an instantaneous transformation. Dr. Jekyll to Mr. Hyde—or was it the other way around? Sharon could never remember. One instant, a courteous and sophisticated professional man in early middle age; the next—

Sharon could remember being far more frightened by her father than the two young men, even though none of his—anger? pose? who could tell?—was aimed at her. *You got some kinda problem, motherfuckers?* James Nichols was not a big man. But, in that moment, his entire upper body had seemed to swell, his face jutting forward, the muscles in his neck like stretched cables. If he'd had hackles, they would have been raised. The beast below, filling the man.

The two young men had lost whatever purpose they'd had, immediately. They hadn't run away. Not quite. But Sharon was sure they'd set a new Olympic record for the fifty-yard walk, if there was such an event.

She looked back at Sanchez. He was still just studying her, silently, through hooded eyes.

Yes. Oh, yes. *But there is that one great difference, isn't there?*

Sharon's eyes went back to the window, moving across the seascape of Venice below. For all the surface glitter of the city and its undoubted beauty, it was ultimately tawdry. Even foul, in this time and place. It was a world with many wonders, to be sure. But it was still the world that had destroyed Hans Richter. A world she loathed, hated and despised, when all was said and done.

Yes, that difference. James Nichols had come into a world which, however uncaring it might often be about its underbelly—and a big, foul underbelly it was, too—allowed individuals from it to claw their way out. Even sanctioned it; even praised the act of clawing. James Nichols was known to publicly joke about his "close encounter with that downstate institute of learning I don't think I'll get into the details about"—and the joke invariably elicited laughs from the men who heard it. Men of a different background and a different color, but it mattered not at all. Always, beneath the laughter, there was that genuine respect. Even admiration.

There would be no such respect and admiration for Ruy Sanchez. Not in this world. The trajectory of his life mattered not at all. The origin was enough. He was tolerated for his skills, and accepted because he had the good grace to cover his origins with the requisite lies. But there would always be certain limits, certain boundaries—and, always, the silence of a man who really couldn't even understand the source of his own bitterness.

How odd it seemed to Sharon—shocking, even—that he should extend those limits to her. Would see her as a suitable object of his lust—his world would accept a seducer, and enjoyed its salacious gossip about nobility—but . . . nothing further. Such a gulf there was between them. The difference in age was the least of it.

The gulf itself drove the decision. In this, too, Sharon Nichols would use anger as her tool.

She turned to face him, squarely, her hands pressed to her thighs. "Ruy Sanchez de Casador y Ortiz—or whatever your real name is, and how about telling me some time? I'd actually like to know—and . . . that's a run-on sentence. Sorry. Weakness of mine."

She took a deep breath. "There is only one human being in this universe who will ever decide whether you belong in my bed. In whatever capacity. One-night stand—never mind; I'll explain that some other time, I'm sure you can figure out—ha! you!—the gist of it, anyway—or lawfully wedded husband. That person is *me*. Understand that in the marrow of your bones, or get out of my sight and don't come back. *Comprende?*"

Sharon was discovering that there was a real pleasure to be derived from startling Ruy Sanchez. It was fascinating. She'd never been at all interested in climbing mountains, but now she could understand at least some of the thrill involved.

The Matterhorn, all of it, beneath her feet. Ruy Sanchez, all of him, completely taken aback.

"Ah . . ."

"What is so hard to understand?" She gestured angrily at the window. "You think I give a damn what *those* people think? You'll see hell freeze over first, Ruy Sanchez. Freeze up like an Alaskan glacier. Siberia, with the Devil buried ten miles down."

Sanchez chuckled. "I was actually not concerned about them, Dona—"

"And cut the stupid *Donna* business! My name's Sharon, not Donna. Plain and simple Sharon. Been that since I was a toddler. Except for that jerk Falasha Jones when I was ten who thought it was funny to call me 'Cherie' until I pounded the crap out of her."

"Um. Yes. Somehow I do not find that difficult to believe. But what I was trying to say—ah, Sharon—is that it was your own people who concerned me. I would not give offense."

It took her a moment to understand what he was talking about. That just made her angrier. "To hell with that. If Mike Stearns doesn't like—whatever I do—I will explain to him that the difference between 'prime minister' and 'prime rib' doesn't mean squat to a nurse. As for my father . . ."

She couldn't help but wince a little. "Oh, sure, he'd have a fit if I decided—which I probably won't, Ruy, I'll give you fair warning—but so what? Won't be the first time. He had a fit about Hans, too, at first. Had an even worse fit over Leroy Hancock, although I'll admit my dad turned out to be right about that one. What a sleaze bucket he turned to be."

She tried, for a moment, to picture Ruy Sanchez with her father in a room somewhere. Discussing it like gentlemen. The image caused a burst of laughter. "Do me one favor, though. In the event—not likely—that you wind up meeting James Nichols, do try to maintain, will you? I don't even want to think about a room filled waist high with testosterone, between you and my dad putting on the act."

Sanchez suddenly bowed. It was a purely formal gesture.

"Very well, then. I shall respect your wishes, Do—ah, Sharon. Yes. I wish to formally request—what is that American expression?—'your hand in marriage,' I believe."

When he rose, he looked very dignified. Ruy did "dignified" extremely well, too. Sharon had noticed that before. It was one of the things she liked about the man.

One of many, in truth, now that she thought about it. Granted, there were other things she found quite unlikable. However, that had also been true of Hans Richter. The span of centuries could be bridged, but it could not be waved away.

And, so what? Sharon had made no attempt to change Hans, after all, beyond a few habits. She'd always thought it was stupid anyway to accept a man only to immediately try to turn him into something he wasn't. On a practical level, why bother? Find someone else, dummy, if it bothers you that much. On a deeper level, because something about the idea offended Sharon Nichols' concept of basic human dignity.

That concept also included honesty, she reminded herself. "Ruy, understand that the answer will probably be 'no.' There are many—ah—problems—"

"I understand." He gave the mustachios a little flick of the finger. Not a stroke, just a gesture to highlight their color. The mustachios were thick and rich, to be sure. They were also more gray than black. "My age."

Sharon shook her head. "That's the least of it. Well, maybe not the least, but—"

She broke off, startled. It actually *wasn't* that important to her, she suddenly understood. Not trivial, certainly, but not vital either. Why should it be, really, other than the certainty—if she made *that* decision—that she would be a widow at an early age. "Old goat," Ruy Sanchez might be, but he was a very, very vigorous goat. The many decades of his life were apparent in the lines of his face. Few of them showed in that stocky, broad-shouldered body, so obviously still muscular even under the rich costume of a hidalgo.

For just an instant, and for the first time since she'd met him, Sharon had an image of Ruy in her bed. Naked, as she herself; coupling. The image vanished almost as soon as it came. But, as she considered the residue, she realized that it was not . . . unpleasing. Certainly not repellent. In some ways, quite the opposite. She'd more than once, laughing, accused Hans Richter of being a goat, after all. To which he'd replied with a grin and an eager nod. The simple fact was—Sharon had to be honest with herself—she reacted with animal heat to that kind of rambunctious male, provided it was a man she cared for. Hans had kept her well exercised in bed, and she didn't doubt for a moment that Ruy would do the same. Nor—*don't lie to yourself, girl*—that she'd enjoy it immensely.

And, again, Sharon was startled. She'd just crossed

a boundary here, she knew. Or made a transition, it might be better to say. Since the morning of October 7, 1633, when she'd seen the column of smoke rising from the Baltic and known that Hans was dead, this was the first time she'd even thought of sex, as anything other than an abstraction.

Only six months? She probed, to find the guilt, and was surprised to find . . . well, some. But not really very much.

You slut. Then she shook her head. It had just been a *thought,* after all. It wasn't as if she had any plans to act on it. Not soon, certainly.

"No, Ruy, that's not the most of it. Let's start with the fact—awkward little detail, here—that you are the agent of a foreign power with which my country is at war. Eh?"

Sanchez smiled. "That is indeed . . . ah, awkward, as you say. Still—" He waved his hand theatrically. "Here my age comes to advantage! Wars come and go, alliances change—overnight, often enough. We are a wicked, wicked race, much given to depravity and duplicity." He pressed his right hand on his chest and gave her a look of utmost sincerity and ardor. "All except in matters of the heart."

Sharon burst into laughter. John Barrymore couldn't have done that better! Sir Laurence Olivier would have knelt at the feet of his master. Lesser actors would have fled in despair. Many, committed suicide.

She shook her head weakly. "You do make me laugh, God knows you do. All right, Ruy, we'll let that sit on the side for the time being. Do keep in mind, though, that my own loyalties are rock solid. Don't doubt that for a moment."

He examined her with none of his earlier drollery. "Yes, I know that, Sharon," he said quietly. "I have understood that from the beginning. Well, very soon, at least. But—I am serious now, for the moment—my age does have certain advantages. That your loyalties are rock solid, I do not doubt. The fact remains—how to say it?—that 'rock solid' simply describes the substance of the thing. It says nothing about the form."

Her puzzlement must have shown. Ruy stroked his mustache, as if to concentrate his thoughts. "Let me put it this way. The same end can often be achieved by an alternate means. So it may be—I have my loyalties also, you understand—that both loyalties can find a different place to meet than on a field of battle."

He placed his hand over his heart again. The gesture, this time, was solemn rather than theatrical. "More I cannot say, at the moment, because of those same loyalties."

"Oh." Sharon looked away. She thought . . .

Maybe. Could this be another glimpse of that possibility that both Francisco Nasi in his briefings and Father Mazzare in his—usually frustrated—musings had talked about? A distance between Spain itself and its supposed province in the Netherlands? The king here—but the prince there? If so . . .

She lapsed into a bit of theatricality herself. "Well. In that case, it might almost be considered my duty to receive your courtship, wouldn't it? Very depraved and duplicitous of me, of course."

Ruy smiled. "To be sure. A new Mata Hari."

Sharon wondered where he'd heard about Mata Hari. Not for long, though. If there was any principality in Europe that *hadn't* stolen or finagled or just bought in the open market copies of Grantville's prized history books, she didn't know where it was. Maybe a clan chief somewhere in the west of Ireland.

She grimaced. "That woman got shot. Or hanged, I can't remember which."

"Please!" Ruy drew himself erect, exuding outrage and indignation. Again, Barrymore couldn't have done it better. "That was done by the French!" He scowled. Olivier would have swooned at the sight of that tight-set jaw, the quivering mustachios, the frown like

Jove's. "The *French.* Just like them. Shoot a woman! Yes, it was a firing squad. The ungallant bastards. No Spaniard—well, perhaps the Spaniards—but certainly no Catalan—"

"Oh, give it a rest!" Sharon shook her head, laughing. "You'd shoot a woman in a heartbeat, Ruy, if you thought it was your duty."

"Well. Duty, yes. Simply because it was ordered, no."

There was a finality to that last sentence that Sharon didn't find herself doubting at all. Whatever else he was, she'd understood for some time now, Sanchez was not dishonorable. If anything, she suspected, he would hold himself to a tighter standard than most men would.

I can live with that, she decided abruptly. "All right, Ruy. Still, the answer will probably—almost certainly, to be honest—wind up being a 'no.' But . . . if you're willing to risk the most-likely waste of your time and effort . . ."

Barrymore and Olivier, both, would have collapsed then. Struck down by the sudden realization of their hopeless amateurism.

Sanchez had taken off his plumed hat when he'd first entered the room, and placed it on the back of an armchair. Now, he snatched the hat up, swept it across in a flourish, and gave a bow that no courtier in Madrid could possibly have bettered.

"Dona Sharon! A minute wasted in your company is time better spent than a millennium in paradise! I, Ruy Sanchez de Casador y Ortiz, swear it is true!"

When she stopped laughing—she had to sit down, for a moment there—Sharon rose and slung her purse over her shoulder. It was very big purse—more like a traveling bag, since she always carried an emergency medical kit in it—which a smaller and less broad-shouldered woman would have found fatiguing to carry

for very long. For Sharon, it was almost an inseparable
part of her. She even took it to the opera.

She ushered Sanchez out the door. "Come on, Ruy.
The *main* reason I asked you to come here—I, Sharon
Nichols, swear it is true—is to ask for your help in
finding Joe Buckley's murderer. Remember?"

She cocked an eyebrow at him.

"Certainly! And notice that I did not give it a moment's
thought. So sure may you always be of me."

As they moved down the corridor, she couldn't keep
the laughter from bubbling up. "Like I said—Don
Quixote on steroids."

"Indeed. Whatever 'steroids' are. If they are something like 'testosterone,' it is certainly true. And . . ."

His voice trailed off for a moment. When he looked
at her, sideways, the brown eyes were soft, a bit sad,
and . . .

"You are indeed my Dulcinea, Sharon Nichols.
Believe it true."

*Jesus H. Christ. The guy is actually in love with
me.*

That he'd read Cervantes, didn't surprise her. That
he'd embraced the book . . .

Didn't surprise her either.

The answer is still probably NO, she told herself
firmly. *Tomorrow, next year, whenever.*

But she couldn't deny the warmth the knowledge
brought to her heart. Nor that it was the first real
warmth that had come into it since a column of smoke
rose over the sea. She wondered if she were being
unfaithful to Hans? Just the warmth, alone?

No, she decided. Hans Richter had been many things,
including rash and reckless and often unthoughtful.
Petty and spiteful, never once.

In the foyer below, they encountered Benjamin
Luzzatto and Ernst Mauer. Billy Trumble was standing
guard at the entrance, along with two other Marines.

"Oh, good, you're both here. Hold down the fort for the day, would you? I won't be back until sometime this evening." Sharon gave Billy a somewhat imperious look. "Lieutenant Trumble, would you be so good as to accompany us?"

"Uh, sure, ma'am. Whatever you say. The father left you in charge until Mr. Stone gets back." Billy's eyes flicked back and forth from Sharon to Sanchez. The youngster was obviously both surprised and more than a little dismayed. "Ah, going out on a date?"

"*Today?* Of course not!" No duchess could have said it more frostily. *The very idea!* Then, seeing Billy suitably abashed, Sharon relented.

"No, not a date. Although—" Struck by an impulse, Sharon took Ruy's hand in hers. "I may as well take the occasion to let everyone know that Señor Sanchez has just formally proposed to me."

That brought a delightful round of eyes-wide-as-saucers. It was all Sharon could do not to giggle.

"Of course, I told him there was no question of my accepting his offer, though I was deeply honored. Not for the moment, certainly. But I would think about it. Perhaps, in the future . . ."

She let that trail away. "However, today we are about another matter—which is why I'd appreciate your assistance, Lieutenant. I've asked Señor Sanchez to help us find and apprehend the murderer of Joe Buckley, and he has agreed to do so."

She'd relinquished Ruy's hand by then. The hand went straight to the mustachios, stroking them fiercely.

"The villain may as well cut his throat and be done with it," Sanchez growled.

There was always that about Ruy Sanchez de Casador y Ortiz, in the end, whatever else might be said of him. He could make a statement like that—and not one person who heard it so much as cracked a smile.

Billy just about snapped to attention. He swept open the door to the embassy. "After you, Mr. Sanchez."

Chapter 35

Once they got out of the embassy, Sharon felt decisiveness leaving her. Pouring out, rather, like water through a ruptured dam.

She looked around, uncertainly. "I really don't have any idea where to start." She gave Ruy a look of appeal.

Sanchez rose smoothly to the occasion. "The last activities of Buckley, I think. I know he was attempting to interview the Turks. Ha! Speak of folly."

Billy Trumble straightened. His hand slid to the pistol holstered to his waist. As an officer assigned to an embassy guard, he was entitled to one of the precious up-time automatics. Sharon knew little of guns, beyond how to fire them—her father had insisted she learn that much—but the thing was certainly wicked-looking.

"You want to start with the Turks, then?" the young lieutenant asked gruffly. As gruffly, at least, as an twenty-year-old could manage.

Sharon saw Ruy disguise a little smile with another stroke of his mustachios. He was amused by the young American's bold front, obviously. But, just as obviously, was not prepared to deride him for it. No doubt Ruy had many memories of bold fronts himself, as a youth.

"No, there is no point," the Catalan responded. "I do not really suspect the Turks."

"Why not?" Sharon asked.

Ruy shrugged. "They are certainly callous enough. But, first, that was not a callous killing, it was a savage murder done by a man in a rage. I am quite sure of that; and I suspect the murderer was not entirely sane as well. Hard to explain some of those wounds otherwise. The Turks would have simply sent an assassin—they have very good ones—who would have strangled him and been done with it. Or slid a stiletto between his ribs. Why torture him? Still further—why *fake* the torture? The Ottomans have no motive to do such. Not that I can see."

His eyes ranged the canal for a moment, as if he sought inspiration in its filthy waters. "Secondly, they have simply not been here long enough. Even a man as heedless as Buckley could not have infuriated them so quickly. No, whoever it was, it was someone who had known Buckley for some time."

Billy's expression underwent a peculiar shift. From bold front to . . . startled?

Sanchez didn't miss it either. "Yes, Lieutenant?"

Billy rubbed his face. "Well . . . I can't see any reason why they would . . . they seemed to like him, in fact. But, well, he'd been spending a lot of time, there just before the end, hanging out with the Committee of Correspondence." The lieutenant pointed toward the north. "Over there on Murano. You know, at the building where the Marcolis live."

"You have been there?" Sanchez asked.

Billy gave Sharon a nervous glance. As an officer in the Marine guard, he'd presumably been subject to Mazzare's instructions to keep a diplomatic distance from the Committee in Venice. "Well . . ."

Sharon smiled sweetly. "Your secret is safe with us,

Lieutenant. Ruy could care less, and me—well, I'm just the temporary buck-passer. Temps are always forgetting to pass things along, you know."

"Uh, thanks. Yeah, well, I did go out there. Twice. Once with my buddy Conrad and once alone. Conrad couldn't come along the second time because, well—"

Sharon smiled more sweetly still. "Yes, Lieutenant. I know about his girlfriend. The whole embassy knows. I remember Father Mazzare muttering just the other day that if one of our Navy officers manages to get the daughter of an Arsenal guildmaster pregnant, he'd strip his hide off. More precisely, he'd have Gus Heinzerling strip his hide off."

Billy grimaced. Then, shook his head. "Not much chance of that! You wouldn't believe the way they watch their girls around here."

"Come on, it's not *that* bad." Sharon gestured toward the embassy building. "After all, none of the chambermaids have chaperones watching over—oh."

It was Billy's turn to smile. "Yeah. Oh. Sure, they let them work out of the house. But the minute there's a whiff of anything . . . You *have* noticed, maybe, that Giovanna Marcoli hasn't worked here for weeks. Soon as Old Man Marcoli got wind of Frank—*zip*—out she came. He hasn't let her out of sight since, let freedom ring be damned. She's under his eye or that of her brothers and cousins every minute."

Sharon frowned. "I'd gotten the impression that the Marcolis approved of Frank. They certainly haven't ordered him to stay away from Giovanna, I know that much."

"Approval's got nothing to do with it, ma'am. They *do* approve of Frank. I think if he asked her to marry him—and he just might, too, he's that bowled over—they'd agree in a heartbeat. But there won't be any hanky-panky going on before then, if you know what I mean." He glanced toward the Arsenal. "It's the same with Conrad's girl. He's actually gotten pretty damn popular over there, even with the guildmasters. I think they admire his cussing ability, if nothing else. It is pretty impressive."

That was interesting. Sharon hadn't paid any attention to the embassy's progress in the Venetian shipyards, since the first days after their arrival. Between her heavy nursing duties—more like half-faking a doctor's consultations—combined with Magda's round-the-clock commercial ventures, she'd been too preoccupied with her own affairs. The last she'd heard, Conrad had been encountering sullen resistance in the Arsenal to his new-fangled American notions.

She suddenly remembered the heavy turn-out from the Arsenalotti at Buckley's funeral. "What's the sentiment over there, these days? About Joe's murder, I mean?"

"They're really pissed, ma'am—uh, pardon the language. But, I mean, they really *are*. Conrad told me just last night that if they ever figure out who did it, the bastard'll be lucky to get out of town alive. There are thousands of those Arsenalotti and they're tough as nails. They've run people out of Venice on a rail before, you know."

Belatedly, he realized who was present. He bobbed his head nervously toward Sanchez. "Uh, meaning no offense, Don Ruy."

The Catalan grinned cheerfully. "None taken, I assure you. And you are indeed quite right. I have personal experience with those fellows from the Arsenal. Most forthright, they are, in moments of displeasure. I was reminded at the time of the running of the bulls in Pamplona. Except the bulls were more civilized. And considerably less insensate."

"They do that already, Ruy?" Sharon asked, her curiosity momentarily piqued. "Running the bulls at Pamplona, I mean. I thought—I don't know." She issued a little laugh of embarrassment. "I thought maybe Ernest Hemingway invented that."

"Oh, no. La Fiesta de San Fermin dates back two centuries already. He was the saint who was gored by the bulls, you know. He was probably drunk at the time. He often was, they say. The manner in which this made him a martyr of the Church escapes me at the moment. Saint Ernest, I believe, is the one who was martyred by a great fish of some sort."

He said the last with a perfectly straight face. Sharon didn't dare ask if Ruy had any idea who Ernest Hemingway was, or if he'd ever read *The Old Man and the Sea*. With Ruy, you never knew. He was just as capable of inventing a story on the spot, and improvising it to incredible lengths without missing a beat.

Sanchez was now looking toward the Arsenal. "Hmm. Interesting," he murmured. "And such a pleasure *that* would be . . ."

He turned back to her, smiling. "But let us not jump to hasty conclusions. To be sure, it probably *was* the French. Ungallant bastards. Shoot a woman! Still, other possibilities cannot be overlooked. Perhaps a triton or some other fantastical creature took offense at Buckley." He waved at the canal. "These waters are said to be full of them."

Sharon snorted. "Your prejudices are showing, Ruy."

He shrugged. "Perhaps. For the moment, I think we should begin on Murano. Most likely the Committee had nothing to do with the affair. They are said to be most ineffective. Still, it is a beginning."

Padua was a nice-looking town, at least in silhouette. As the boats pulled up at the river-dock below the town, Frank couldn't see much more than that, what with the midafternoon sun begin to set behind it.

"We stay here tonight," Antonio Marcoli said. "I know an inn."

"A lot of work to do getting unloaded first," Frank remarked.

"Oh, sure," said Marcoli. "We got plenty of big strong boys with us, though." He grinned. His own hands were no strangers to hard work, it had to be said.

It was still going to be hard work. Frank and Messer Marcoli were in the third boat of three. Rather than get faster, oared boats, Marcoli had hired three smallish sailing boats. Big dinghies, Frank supposed they were. There were twelve of them on the mission, and any of the three boats would have held them all comfortably with any reasonable amount of baggage. For some reason, though, trying to fit all seven Marcolis and the word "reasonable" into the same plan was something that just couldn't be made to happen.

First of all, Massimo had to be forcibly dissuaded from bringing the printing press. Yes, it was portable. Yes, it disassembled into easy-to-carry sections. Yes, you could have the thing up and running from its box in under two hours—once you had a Philips screwdriver and were familiar enough with the thing to do without the instructions. On the other hand, "easy to carry" meant two strong men on each of three boxes, and if it got dropped it'd probably be ruined.

What had clinched it was the simple argument from time and speed. Four hours a day just setting the thing up and taking it down, not counting the time spent actually printing. Time spent buying paper en route. Time spent composing propaganda en route. Time in which Galileo was being held in Rome awaiting trial, and a date would be set any day now.

Massimo had given in. The idea of instant, reactive propaganda . . . Frank hadn't dared ask, but he suspected that Massimo had been thinking of passing out progress bulletins on the rescue as it went along. Frank privately thanked whatever deities, watchful spirits, guardian angels and even Great Cthulhu that they didn't have TV or radio in Italy yet. Massimo would have been trying to lug a transmitter along to do a play-by-play.

Of course, Massimo had only given in for small values of "given in." Then the negotiations had begun as to how many crates of preprinted propaganda they would take along for distribution en route . . .

So now they were approaching Padua slowly, when they could have been here by lunchtime. They were doing it in three boats—eating still further into their store of funds—where they could have used one. And before they got to dinner and a bed for the night, apparently with a friend of Marcoli's wife's sister's husband, they had about a ton of revolutionary propaganda to haul out of the boats and up to wherever they were staying. They wouldn't even start on trying to hire a couple of wagons until the next day. Coaches were out of the question, of course. They had too much baggage for anything that was likely to move.

Bright side, Frank, bright side. Spending the night meant they'd have time to track down their father. In fact, as soon as the boat docked—he'd already arranged it—Gerry would make himself scarce and set off to find him. None of the Stone boys knew exactly where their father and Magda were staying, here in Padua, but they knew it was somewhere in or right next to the university where he gave his lectures.

Once they were on the mainland and into the carriage Mazarini had obtained for them, Mazzare decided they'd reached a point where their travels would be uninterrupted for a time. They'd be on the road for approximately two weeks, stopping only at night for food and lodgings. The carriage rode much too roughly for Mazzare to even think of writing notes. So roughly, in fact, that the trip itself would be tiring. Too tiring, he suspected, to allow him to make notes during their overnight stops, either.

He'd just have to make do with days of extended conversation. Hopefully, he'd be able to remember what was said and systematize it in writing once they reached Rome.

He turned to Jones, sitting next to him on the plush seat of the carriage. "Simon, can I ask you please to put aside the things you've heard about the Inquisition?"

The Reverend Jones nodded, although Mazzare was a bit amused to see the wary look on his face.

"The truth is this, Simon: Galileo got in trouble, more than anything, for annoying some well-connected scientists within the Church. The fact that he was usually ahead of what he could prove from his data didn't help. Made it look like he was contradicting the Church's interpretation of the Bible out of heresy. So what happened in the universe we came from is that they sentenced him to life in jail and commuted it to house arrest after he, ah, copped a plea. The Inquisition held a trial, but that was all. Galileo went voluntarily and cooperated rather than upset the Church."

Mazarini straightened up from his comfortable traveler's slouch on the seat bank across from them and sat erect, his hands planted on his knees. "It is different now."

"How?" asked Jones.

"There was no Inquisition. His Holiness called a Commission of Inquiry. Half of its membership are Inquisition cardinals. They have a report from a number of astronomers who say that there are errors of fact in Galileo's work and that he holds, defends and teaches something considered heresy at present." He glanced at Mazzare. "The exact words are significant, you understand."

Mazzare turned that one over in his mind a little. *At present*. "Do we know who the astronomers were?"

Mazarini grinned. "One of them was Scheiner."

Mazzare raised an eyebrow. Scheiner was one of Galileo's most bitter enemies. "And he used that form of words?"

"Yes. I guess it this way, that he is still angry with

Galileo, but has begun to read Grantville's astronomy."

"Hold on," said Jones. "If they're prepared to accept that the earth moves on Grantville's say-so, why are they bothering to give Galileo grief? Am I missing something?"

"Politics, Simon," said Mazzare. "The church isn't just the pope, and he can't just order the whole church to follow his lead. There has to be some negotiation, you see, or it's the Church of England all over again."

Mazarini nodded. "There is this, too—the father-general of the Jesuits is involved this time. If anyone can put words in the mouths of kings it is him."

"So it's a show trial in a good cause, then?" said Jones, beginning to catch on. "*Tennessee v. Scopes*, and this time the monkey wins?"

Mazzare looked at Mazarini, quite intently. "That's my guess, Simon, yes." The last word had an upward tilt to it, which made it seem more like a question than a statement. A question addressed at Mazarini.

The Vatican diplomat smiled serenely. "My guess also. But, who can really know?"

It was all Mazzare could do not to glare at him. Mazarini turned his hands over and spread them wide, still smiling. "I am simply telling you the truth, Monsignor. I really do not think the pope himself knows yet what he intends to do." Mazarini turned his head and looked out at the passing Italian countryside. "The father-general . . . perhaps."

"Be careful, Magda," Stoner cautioned. He extended a hand to help her into the boat.

His wife gave him a glance that was just short of sarcastic. Magda was some twenty years younger than Tom Stone, more athletic, more coordinated, in better physical condition—and considerably more practical about most everything. Stoner's awkward perch on the side of the boat made his helping hand a dubious proposition. He was more likely to fall off himself and drag her into the river with him than anything else.

However, Magda was a dutiful German wife, at least for public consumption. Besides, she was also a better swimmer than Stoner. So she took her husband's hand—the fingertips only, in case she had to let go—smiled, and hopped nimbly into the rivercraft. Nimbly enough, in fact, that even the slender vessel—designed for speed, not cargo-handling—barely rocked under the impact.

The vessel's captain and crew were also attuned to speed. The instant the captain saw that the woman was securely seated and that her idiot husband was no longer actively attempting to capsize the boat, he gave the order to push away from the pier. Within seconds, the oars were in the water and the boat was making good speed toward Venice. They'd be there by nightfall.

The captain was pleased. That meant a good bonus. The young soldier who'd come up the river with them to fetch the man and his wife had promised as much. And while this was the first time the captain himself had ever done business with the people from the Swede's embassy, they had a good reputation with the boatmen on the river to Padua. The man was some sort of savant, who made this trip regularly. And, by all accounts, paid well, paid promptly—and never tried to skimp on the bonus.

Thankfully, he hadn't drowned yet. Given his clumsiness in a boat, the captain supposed that was just a matter of time. Still, he'd make sure the man stayed in the boat long enough to pay the bonus for this trip.

Looking around at the riverbanks, the captain noticed some sort of stir at the commercial docks now some distance behind. Other people, it seemed, had difficulty staying out of the water.

The passengers had craned their necks around and

were observing the same little ruckus. Idle curiosity, nothing more. It was really too far away to see much.

"What is happening back there?" the woman asked. Her Italian was not bad, though the captain found the heavy Veneziano accent a bit amusing. Heavier than a native's, it was.

"Nothing significant, signora," he replied casually. "I think someone fell into the river and others are trying to fish him out."

"Oh, the poor fellow. I do hope they manage to rescue him."

But her concern was more perfunctory than anything else. She didn't spend more than a moment observing the distant commotion before turning back and facing forward. Her husband and the young soldier escorting them did the same, a few seconds later.

The captain didn't share even her minimal concern. He'd been a successful boatman for almost thirty years now. He'd never even bothered to learn how to swim. What sort of boatman can't manage to stay in a boat? Let the incompetent ones drown. They had no business plying the trade in the first place.

Chapter 36

As soon as they'd left Venice, Michel Ducos had pulled a tarp over himself and the bag he'd brought, and promptly gone to sleep. In truth, Frank thought Ducos looked exhausted. The wound he'd suffered on his hand seemed to be bothering him a lot, too.

Ducos had snored all the way up the Brenta, provoking giggles from Giovanna every time he turned over and grunted. That would have been interesting if they'd been pulled over by whatever passed for cops hereabouts, although Messer Marcoli had said Frank should relax, they were running ahead of even the news of their departure, let alone any pursuit.

Michel woke up in good time to help the boatmen tie up, and while Messer Marcoli paid the last quarter of their passage—his credit wasn't good for much in Venice, apparently—Frank decided to let the Venetians organize the unloading. He and his brothers would take advantage of the moment to see Gerry off quietly to go find their father.

That was no problem, as Frank had expected. Gerry was good at making himself scarce without being seen, and the Marcolis weren't paying the slightest bit of attention anyway. Frank had known they wouldn't. After all these weeks in close proximity to the family, he'd come to know them quite well. As much as he liked them—and he did, all of them, even if Giovanna was the only one he *really* cared about—he'd long since realized that if this new universe had had a television industry, the Marcoli family would have made the ideal subject for a situation comedy series.

The Marcoli Bunch, maybe. No, that was too sedate. *The Seven Screwballs.* No, that wasn't fair to Giovanna— which wasn't just natural prejudice on Frank's part. Even Ron would admit that when God had been passing around common sense to the Marcolis, he'd given all of it to the one and only female in the pack. *Giovanna and the Six Loose Cannons on the Deck.*

Alas, no. The problem with that title was that it implied that Giovanna was in some sense the captain of the crew.

Alas, no. The Marcoli males, revolutionary firebrands or not, were every bit as mired in some customs as any Italian. *Listen to what the girl says? Nonsense! Practical matters are for men.*

Besides, the title omitted the biggest goof in the bunch—Marius, the handyman. Whatever the Marcolis didn't mismanage, the hired help would invariably make good the lack.

Oh, well. Frank went back to his favorite pastime, which was watching Giovanna. She was something to watch, too, scampering around with her usual energy and giving constant advice to her father and uncle and their assorted sons—to which, of course, they paid no attention whatsoever.

It went well enough until they started to haul out one of the big boxes with the propaganda in it. The boatmen had been about to simply toss them up onto the wharf one by one, two men to a box, but Massimo would have none of it. He had a better idea. He insisted that the whole operation would be smoother and easier if they rigged up a tripod of spars on the wharf and swung a block and tackle off it. They could sway up the boxes onto the wharf without any effort, that way.

Thus spake Archimedes. And so he and Messer Marcoli fell to work, using materials from the boats that were lying around as well as such things as are wont to be found on wharves, even small river wharves like Padua's.

Frank stood to one side with Ron while Massimo and Messer Marcoli fiddled with their jury-rigged crane. Michel had wandered off somewhere. Giovanna had finally given up trying to inject reason into madness, and had found a seat on a barrel. The barrel was close to Frank, but just far enough away so as not to incite the territorial instincts of her family watchdogs. Had the matter not concerned Frank himself, he would have been mightily amused. No matter how enthusiastically preoccupied the Marcoli males got with one of their projects, they never got so preoccupied as not to notice where Giovanna was in relation to Frank. It was downright weird—as if they possessed some kind of automatic daughter navigation radar.

They were never nasty about it, he had to admit. By their own light, he supposed, they could even be considered tolerant. They did not object to Giovanna sitting next to Frank at the dinner table, and never made any attempt to look under the table to see if their daughter and her enamorata were playing footsie. (Which, they invariably were. By now, Frank's ankles were almost callused.) Nor did they object if she and Frank held hands whenever there was the slightest excuse for them to do so—such as helping Giovanna negotiate a street she had been walking since she was two years old. They didn't even object when Giovanna kissed Frank every time he left—although, after enough time had passed, comments would be made. Jocular ones, initially, rising steadily in serious timber thereafter. Frank and Giovanna had learned exactly how long they could maintain the kiss before Antonio would rise huffily to his feet.

They even made earthy jokes about the matter in Frank's presence—so long as Giovanna wasn't around to hear them. On one occasion, they'd been repairing the printing press and had had to fit a new drive shaft into its appointed slot. It proved difficult to get it in, as was often the case when mating a brand-new part to a used one. The Marcolis had lightened the burden with fifteen minutes' worth of ribaldry on the subject of how much more difficult it would be to mate two brand-new parts together—especially in the dark. Grinning at Frank the whole time. Frank's ears were red by the end of it.

They were, in truth, nice people. But they had their customs, and that was that. They weren't prudes about sex, they just set certain limits. By now, Frank was quite sure that if he proposed to Giovanna her family would agree instantly. Enthusiastically, in fact.

And . . . he was almost there. In truth, he would have done so already except that the prospect of having the Marcolis as his in-laws was just that little too daunting to accept yet. Especially when they were on the eve—no, not even that, anymore—of undertaking what was probably one of the screwiest stunts Frank had ever heard of. *The Marcolis Go to Rome.*

A little flurry of shouts broke Frank out of his reverie. The Marcolis were in the middle of hollering orders and advice at each other. Six opinions, not one of which matched. Naturally.

Frank reflected that in the time Giovanna's father and his cousin Massimo had spent lashing spars together and rigging the thing up, the boatmen, who were standing in the bottoms of their craft, grinning at this display of lubberly ingenuity, could have heaved up all twenty boxes and been on their way. They were both born engineers, that way. Perhaps the two finest examples in the world of the perils of being an autodidact.

Naturally, the boatmen had stopped work to watch the fun. Frank was suitably embarrassed on Messer Marcoli's behalf, although Antonio himself didn't seem to notice the grins, nudges, and sly chuckles he was getting from the peanut gallery down on the water. Giovanna just watched with cool disinterest. Frank was getting good at reading her expressions, and this one said *Papa will grow bored of this game soon, don't worry*.

That was the other thing that made Frank still hesitate. On most subjects, Giovanna was a levelheaded girl. Well, as levelheaded as a girl just turned eighteen ever gets, anyway. But that was still more levelheaded than Frank himself, half the time, he'd cheerfully admit. The problem was that Giovanna's good-humored sanity seemed to come to an abrupt halt when it reached that border which she and her beloved father both called *The Revolution*.

It wasn't the ideology that bothered Frank. Except for an occasional curlicue or excess here and there—he didn't think demanding that the church melt down all its gold—the artwork, too?—and distribute it to the poor was really such a great idea—Frank shared most of it himself. Hardly surprising, of course, since the core of the ideology came from the American up-timers in the first place. It was just that . . .

Did they *have* to be so impractical about everything connected to politics? Look at Mike Stearns, for Pete's sake. He was probably even more radical than the Marcolis, in lots of ways. But that never stopped him from being as canny and slick as you could ask for. Alas, in the Marcoli lexicon, the word *tactics* seemed to be a synonym for *unthinkable*.

"Done!" Marcoli shouted, dumping Frank back into the here-and-now. Marcoli and Massimo had spent some minutes pulling on things and, in the finest tradition of pioneer engineers since the dawn of time, kicking at the spars and lashings to make sure they were secure. Massimo sat on the back leg of the tripod to weigh it down. At a word from Messer Marcoli, one of the boatmen put the hook of the lower block under the sling of a stack of boxes.

"Marius!" Marcoli called, beckoning his handyman to come help pull.

Frank and Ron looked at each other, amused. They'd noticed before that whatever Marcoli's pretensions to liberty and equality, he invariably stuck Marius rather than one of his own sons or Massimo's with the worst of the grunt work. Not that Marius wasn't eminently suited to the lifting and moving of heavy objects. That was just about all he *could* be relied on for. And at that you had to watch him carefully. It wasn't just that the poor guy was on the dimwitted side. He also tended to be watching a completely different channel to most everyone else, most of the time.

And, of course, he was strong as an ox.

Antonio Marcoli shouted "Pull!"

Marius pulled. The boxes shot into the air.

Now, Massimo had paid attention to his Archimedes. He'd figured out where to sit so as to balance the boxes exactly. What he hadn't counted on was having the leg of the crane he was sitting on, left loose as it was, suddenly jerk under him like a spooked mustang. He also hadn't counted on this happening without sufficient warning. He really, really, hadn't counted on losing his balance.

His weight came off the spar, the spar shot into the air, and, in a neat demonstration of angular momentum, inertia, and slapstick comedy, Massimo was turned end-for-end in the air and landed head-first on the cobbles. Meanwhile, the boxes swung on the end of the tackle and plunged into the water between boat and wharf. Marius, ordered to pull on the rope, kept trying to do so—instead of just being sensible and letting go. All that he accomplished was being slammed into his boss' back. Marius fell, still holding the rope, and sent Antonio Marcoli flying into the water.

There was a thud down below, and then a splash. Frank ran over. "What happened?" he called down into the boats,

"The messer hit the boat and then fell in!" came the reply. They were fending their boats away from the wharf, peering into the water.

Frank looked. No sign of Messer Marcoli. *There!* Bubbles were rising. He looked again. Perhaps three feet to the water. He sat on the wharf, pulled off his boots, and let himself down into the river.

And was brought up short with a jar. It was only three feet deep! Frank felt around in the brown and turbid water and—*there!* He grabbed a handful of clothes and heaved. Marcoli came up, flailing and gasping, wild-eyed and obviously stunned. He coughed once, twice, and then began to retch. Frank tried to turn him over, put himself under, and then stood up with an arm under Marcoli, letting him throw up what looked like a gallon and a half of the Brenta's finest mud.

And then a groan. Frank tried to help Marcoli to a standing position, and was rewarded with a choked-off half-scream.

"My leg!" Marcoli screeched. He drew in a ragged breath between gritted teeth. "Broken, I think."

Frank looked up. The rest of the Marcolis were still standing on the wharf. Frank realized that he'd moved faster than all of them. A fact that was not, he was pleased to see, lost on a radiantly smiling Giovanna.

He shoots, he scores!

That was habit, though, more than anything else. Whatever else Frank had to worry about in the world, gaining Giovanna's approval was no longer one of them. He knew damn good and well that if he proposed to her she'd say "yes" before he even finished the sentence. She'd told him so. Three times already.

Still, it was hard not to crow with glee. *Saved by*

the bell! He was sorry Messer Marcoli had gotten hurt, of course, and hoped the injury wouldn't be too serious.

Just serious enough to scuttle this whole crazy expedition. That's all Frank asked for. By nightfall, Gerry would have found their dad. Whatever his quirks, Tom Stone just had a naturally calming influence on the people around him. Between him and the leader of the pack being laid up with a busted leg . . .

What could go wrong?

By the time they finally got Antonio Marcoli into a bed at the inn they'd be staying at that night, Gerry was back.

"Dad's gone. He and Magda both. Got called back to Venice." The youngest of the three Stone brothers looked miserable. "I can't believe it. We must have passed them on the river, going the other way. Nobody even noticed."

Frank sighed and ran fingers through his air. "All right. Bad luck, that's all. Look at it this way. Every project gets its fair share of bad luck. So we just got ours. From here on . . ."

He couldn't finish the sentence. It was too asinine, under any circumstances, much less these.

Combine *The Marcoli Bunch* with "project" and you just automatically raised bad luck by an order of magnitude. By now, Frank was pretty sure that was a law of nature.

"That may be the stupidest thing I've ever heard anyone say," mused Ron.

"I know," said Frank glumly. "Best I could come up with."

Chapter 37

Sharon had never been across to Murano, before. Within five minutes of arriving on the northern island, she hoped she never would again. Even by Venetian standards, Murano was run-down.

To make things worse, it soon became apparent that Billy Trumble didn't really know his way around the island. He'd set off confidently enough, once they'd disembarked. But after guiding them through part of the island's maze of alleyways—as often as not, just spaces between artisan shops, kilns and dwellings—he more or less drifted to a halt. Then, took off his cap and started scratching his head.

"Lost?" Sharon asked.

"Not exactly, ma'am." Billy pointed to his right with the cap. "I know it's off that way—not even too far from here. The problem is that I don't know how to get there."

Sharon immediately provided the logical solution. "Let's ask somebody."

Billy and Ruy immediately bestowed upon her the inevitable frown.

Sharon sniffed. "I guess some things remain constant,

442

one universe to another. I'd still like to know the evolutionary logic of males being hard-wired never to ask
for directions."

Billy smiled crookedly. "I don't think it's really that,
ma'am. Just, you know, a guy thing."

Sharon snorted. "Yeah, that's my father said when
I asked him. He claims it's too deeply rooted in our
culture to do about anything it. He might be right. Why
else would it have taken that doofus Ulysses ten years
to get home? If he'd just asked for directions . . ."

Fortunately, the directions stumbled upon them.
An urchin came around the corner, paying the usual
urchin attention to his surroundings, and just barely
kept from bumping into Sanchez. A bit apprehensive,
the boy backed up a couple of steps.

"Hey, I know this kid," exclaimed Billy. He looked
more closely, stooping a bit. "Name ends with an 'o.'"

Sharon rolled her eyes. "Billy, in Italy that's not
exactly a big help."

The urchin came to the rescue. To Sharon's sur-
prise, he understood English. "Benito," he pronounced.
He craned his neck up at Billy. "You are one of the
American soldiers, yes? I remember you."

"Yeah, that's me. We're looking for the Marcolis. I
can't remember how to get there."

The urchin looked woebegone. "They left. All gone.
Yesterday."

Sharon felt herself stiffen. "Gone? Where?"

Benito shrugged. "I'm not sure. I think they went
to Rome. I heard them talking about it, anyway."

Sharon and Ruy and Billy exchanged meaningful
glances. Meaningless glances, it might be better to
say. The kind of looks people give each other who are
utterly bewildered.

"*Rome?*" Billy almost choked. "Why the hell would
they go to Rome? That's—that's—" He groped in the air.
"That's hundreds of miles away. It'd take them weeks,
unless they could afford the best carriage."

Benito shrugged again. "I don't know. I think maybe they're going to see an old friend of theirs. A relative, maybe. Some old man who's sick or maybe in some kind of trouble. It didn't make much sense to me."

It was Sharon's turn to choke a little. "Oh, Christ . . ." A feeling of dread was coming over her. The only old man in Rome she could think of who was in any kind of trouble was . . .

"What was the old man's name?" she demanded.

"I told you, I can't remember." The urchin gave Billy a sly look. "Oh, wait. I remember now. The name ends with an 'o.'"

"Never mind that," said Ruy quietly. "When you say 'they all went,' boy, who are you talking about? Exactly."

Benito frowned. "All of them. Everybody in the Committee." He started counting off his fingers. "All the Marcolis—Massimo and his kids too. The girl, of course." A fleeting grin passed across the urchin's face that was at least a decade too leering to fit a boy whom Sharon estimated was not more than eight years old. "No way they'd leave Giovanna behind. Besides—he's no fool, Antonio Marcoli, whatever people say—that way he could be sure Frank and his brothers would come, too."

Sharon heard herself groan. Benito tugged at his fingers, remembering his count. "Oh. Yeah. Two more. Marius the handyman. He always goes anywhere Antonio does. And Michel. He went with them too."

The name "Michel" had an odd flavor, in Benito's mouth. The way a kid determined to seem sophisticated will fumble at foreign words.

"Michel?" Ruy's face was suddenly blank; all the underlying amusement that had been there a moment before vanished. "Michel who? What is his last name? And don't tell me you don't remember, boy. Or what letter the name ends in. *The name.*"

Sanchez could be genuinely intimidating, Sharon

reflected. She'd tell him to stop bullying the kid, except . . . well, she was a bit too intimidated.

So was the urchin. Whatever smart remark Benito might have been contemplating died on his lips, as she stared up at Ruy's face. The mustachios didn't look like a flamboyant affectation now. They looked like they fit that face perfectly. The face of a conquistadore, contemplating a field of battle.

"Oh, I know it," Benito protested. "It's Ducos. Michel Ducos." He pointed to the main islands to the south. "He's a French compatriot. He tells Antonio what's happening in the French embassy."

Ruy straightened. *"Ducos."* The word came out like a snarl.

"You know him?" Billy asked.

"Yes, I know him," Sanchez said softly. The Catalan looked at Sharon. "This is no longer a joke. Not of any kind."

Sharon had guessed that much just from the expression on Ruy's face. "Who is he?" she asked.

"D'Avaux's agent. Spy, assassin, whatever the comte requires."

"He's a compatriot!" Benito protested.

"He is nothing of the sort," Sanchez pronounced. "If he spent time with your Marcolis, he was acting as a spy. No. More likely as a provocateur." A thought seemed to come to him. "Tell me, young Benito. When the American reporter Buckley came here, did he speak with Ducos often?"

"Oh, sure. He and Michel were good buddies. Once or twice they even came together."

Ruy nodded. "Yes, it makes sense. All of it, now."

"What's happening, Ruy?" Sharon asked quietly.

"Ducos is your murderer. I am almost certain of it. He would have been stirring up some sort of trouble. Ingratiated himself with Buckley as well as the Marcolis—and then used the mutual friendships to reinforce each other." Sighing, he took off his plumed hat and ran fingers through stiff, gray hair. "It is an old trick. Only amateurs would be taken in by it, of course. Use one connection to provide the authenticity for another. Then, back again. Buckley and the Marcolis each vouch for Ducos, and it never occurs to any of them that the principal reason they do so is because the other vouched for him in the first place. Idiots."

He gave Billy Trumble a hard look. "Did you meet this Ducos, the times you came here?"

Billy shook his head. "No." He hesitated. "I do remember somebody mentioning the name 'Michel' once or twice, but . . . I didn't think anything of it."

"No, of course not." Ruy put the hat back on his head. "Ducos would have made certain not to appear at the Marcolis if anyone other than the Stone boys were there from your embassy. Too much risk someone might know who he really was—or start asking questions."

Sharon was trying to follow the logic and making hard going with it. "I still don't understand, Ruy. The Marcolis and the Stone boys, okay. But why would Joe be taken in? He *was* a pretty damn good investigative reporter, you know. There's no way he wouldn't have found out Michel worked for the French embassy."

But, by the time she'd finished, she already knew the answer. "Oh. Of course. Ducos wouldn't have even tried to deny it, would he?"

Ruy smiled grimly. "No, Sharon. He would have boasted of it. And then provided Buckley with so much good information—what's your American expression? the 'inside dope,' I believe—that Buckley would have been dazzled by the opportunity. You recall that article he wrote on d'Avaux's machinations, the one that caused all the trouble? He got the information from Ducos. Never thinking once that a man who gives silver intends to get gold in return."

"Bait," Billy muttered. "You're right. Joe was a good enough guy, but he was . . . oh, I don't know. Cocksure of himself."

Sharon went back to something Sanchez had said earlier. "Why do you think Ducos is the murderer, though? With this good a setup, I'd think he wouldn't want to upset anything."

Ruy's little frown made Sharon realize that he hadn't understood the colloquial term "setup." The Catalan's English had gotten so good that she tended to forget he didn't necessarily know all the slang and idiom. She began to explain but Ruy stilled her with a raised hand.

"I understand the gist of your question. The answer? Two-fold. First, Ducos would have had no interest in simply spying on the Committee. Why should he? This is Venice, not Paris. His interest in them would have been simply that of tools to accomplish some other purpose. By all accounts, this Marcoli fellow is given to rashness, yes?"

The last question was aimed at Billy, accompanied by the kind of up-tilted eyebrow that translates as *Don't bullshit me, buddy.*

Billy took a deep breath and let it out. "Oh, yeah. I liked the guy, mind you—almost impossible not to. But, yeah, he wasn't exactly playing with a full deck. Well. That's not quite right. Marcoli's not actually nuts—and he's certainly not stupid. It's just . . ."

Sharon sighed. "I get the picture. I have a cousin like that. Did, anyway, back when and where. She was bright as a tack, and you couldn't really say she wasn't sane." A little chuckle emerged. "I played cards with her, now and then. Not often, because she drove me nuts. She always assumed every card coming up was either an ace or a face card. Just because that's what she wanted."

"Yup. That fits Marcoli to a T." Billy looked to the south. "I guess we'd better get back, ma'am. There's only just a few more hours left of daylight. If Stoner's kids have gone with him . . ."

Sharon could imagine the hell to be paid herself,

with no trouble. But she still wished she knew more. She was now pretty sure that Marcoli had decided to try some kind of rescue attempt for Galileo. But that was just a guess on her part. And any assumption that the Stone boys were part of whatever scheme Marcoli had cooked up—assuming there was really one at all—would be sheer speculation at this point.

Nobody really *knew* anything. From an street urchin's simple statement that the Stone boys had left with the Marcolis, there was only so far you could leap.

Uncertainly, she looked in the direction Billy had indicated earlier was where the Marcoli house was to be found. Ruy put her thoughts into words.

"Yes, I agree. Since we are here, we may as well see if there is any information to be found there. Marcoli or one of his confederates may have left something behind." He tugged at his mustache, smiling a bit derisively. "Judging from their reputation, perhaps a broadside boasting of their not-yet-accomplishment."

The Catalan looked down at Benito. "Take us there," he commanded.

With Benito's sure feet guiding the way, they arrived at the building where the Marcolis lived within just a few minutes. The building was old as well as big, one of those edifices that gets added on to decade after decade, century after century, in a city as ancient as Venice. Much of the front consisted of workhouses, to Sharon's surprise, which were humming busily at their trades. Glassmaking, judging from what little she could see.

"The Marcolis live in the back part," Benito explained. "This way."

He led them down the side of the building, through a passageway almost too narrow to be called an alley. Then, made two quick turns to thread his way through a little labyrinth of outbuildings. They found themselves in front of a large door.

The door was ajar. "That's funny," Benito said, frowning. "I know they closed it when they left. Locked it, too." The boy looked a little guilty, then. Despite the seriousness of the moment, Sharon had to suppress a chuckle. She had no doubt the little scamp had tried to get himself in. Maybe not to steal, just . . . an opportunity too rare for a respectable street urchin to pass up.

Ruy, though, didn't seem to be suppressing any kind of humor. "The door has been forced." He stepped up and pushed it open. "Dona—ah, Sharon. Please remain outside." A moment later, moving quickly and silently, the Catalan was through the door.

Sharon and Billy looked at each other.

"Like hell," said Sharon. "If there's trouble, he's not facing it alone."

Billy nodded and went in, Sharon on his heels.

Once inside, they found themselves in something of a vestibule. A narrow staircase led up on the left. At the end of a short corridor, on the right, a door stood open. Sanchez himself was nowhere in sight.

Sharon decided he couldn't have gone up the stairs that quickly. "That way," she hissed, pointing to the door.

Billy nodded again and hurried toward it, Sharon crowding him as closely as she could.

So closely, in fact, that when Billy came to an abrupt halt as soon as he passed through the door, Sharon collided with him.

"Goddamit," she heard Billy mutter. Sharon was surprised at the anger in his voice. She hadn't bumped into him *that* hard. But then, looking over the lieutenant's shoulder, she realized that the curse had been directed elsewhere.

Oh, damn.

They had entered a very big room, lit only by windows along one wall. Despite the narrowness of the windows, the lighting was rather good this time of day, with the afternoon sun shining through. It was the sort of central kitchen-and-taverna that the USE embassy itself contained. Sanchez was standing near a small table toward the center of the room, staring at six men crowded around a much larger table at the back. The men were staring back at him. Most of them were seated. Judging from their postures, Ruy had caught them completely by surprise. They seemed to be doing something with documents spread out on the table.

All of them, alas, were armed. Sharon thought so, at least. She couldn't see any guns in evidence, but two of them were bearing swords and all of them had knives of one sort or another scabbarded to their waists.

Ruy swiveled his head and looked at her. Then, his lips quirking, brought his gaze back to the strangers. "Why am I not surprised?" she heard him murmur. "I predict it will be a stormy courtship."

Suddenly—the Catalan could move very quickly when he wanted to—Sanchez plucked off his hat and sent it sailing toward a row of coat-pegs on the far wall. The hat landed atop one of the pegs and perched there neatly. Despite everything, Sharon almost burst into laughter. Only Ruy would make sure of that detail!

"Lieutenant Trumble," Sanchez said loudly, "I will rely upon you to keep Dona Sharon safe. These are Ducos' men. I recognize three of them."

The word *Ducos* seemed to break the paralysis of the strangers. One of them shouted something which Sharon didn't understand, although she thought it was French. An instant later, working together, all the men still seated had upended the big table and tossed it aside. And all of them were drawing out weapons.

Three swords, damnation! One of the men seated had been armed with one also. Sharon hadn't spotted it beneath the table. The others simply had daggers. Big, nasty, sharp-looking daggers.

Sanchez planted a boot on the small table next to him and sent it flying against the same wall his hat was resting upon. For all the smooth ease of the motion, the table shattered when it hit the wall. One of the legs landed five feet away. There was now a clear fighting space in the center of the room. Ruy's hands went to his waist. The rapier and main gauche came out easily, hissing their steely way.

For just that instant, as the Catalan's back and shoulders swelled in the act of drawing his blades, Ruy Sanchez reminded Sharon of nothing so much as a cobra flaring its hood. She'd long understood that the man was deadly, beneath the veneer of wit and drollery. The veneer was gone now. Not a trace of it left. Ruy Sanchez was once again in a familiar place—and he was almost sixty years of age. He'd survived that place before. He intended to survive it again.

His opponents sensed that feral confidence themselves. Their initial lunge toward the center of the room, fueled by the bravado brought by greater numbers, stumbled to a sudden halt. The rapier and main gauche had been almost like lightning bolts, flashing in the rays of late-afternoon sun pouring through the windows.

To their misfortune, they'd paused too late. The cobra struck. How a man as stocky and relatively short as Sanchez—he was perhaps an inch shorter than Sharon herself—could manage that sort of lunge was beyond her. Manage it he did, though—and it was a perfect fencer's lunge. Poised, balanced, no awkwardness at all.

The intended target screeched and tried to deflect the blade with his own sword. But Sanchez had not aimed for the easily protected chest and belly. The rapier flashed beneath the parry and sank into the man's upper thigh, just below the hip joint. A quick vicious twist of the wrist and the blade was back out again.

The man groaned and stumbled back, collapsing. He dropped his sword, both hands clutching at his leg. The blood was already spurting out as if through a hose.

Sharon felt numb. She was a nurse and, at that, better versed than most in human anatomy. The man's femoral artery had been sliced right through. He'd bleed to death in a few minutes; lose consciousness much sooner than that. She was pretty sure Ruy had hit the femoral triangle straight on—Scarpa's triangle, as it was sometimes called. He'd probably severed the great femoral nerve at the same time.

The blow was deadly; as deadly, to an expert, as more obvious cuts to the throat or heart. And, seeing the grim look of satisfaction on Ruy's face, she had no doubt at all that the Catalan had known exactly what he was doing.

Sanchez smiled mirthlessly. "My name is Ruy Sanchez de Casador y Ortiz," he growled at the five still-standing French agents. "Prepare to die."

This time, Sharon couldn't stop the laugh from bursting out. A semi-hysterical laugh, to be sure. But still—

Where in the hell had Ruy Sanchez gotten his hands on a copy of *The Princess Bride*?

"Jesus," she heard Billy mutter. "He's not kidding."

The eruption of violence had paralyzed Billy Trumble for a moment. Soldier or not, Marine officer or not, he was actually a complete stranger to this kind of sudden mayhem. But while Billy had caught the same reference—he'd seen the movie—he understood something immediately which Sharon didn't.

Sanchez *hadn't* read the book. He'd probably never even heard of it. The character of Inigo Montoya was just an author's comic twist on an ancient and very real model.

Meet Ruy Sanchez. The original.
And he ain't being funny at all.

"Oh, Jesus," he repeated, clawing at the flap of his holster. One of the French thugs screamed something,

threw his knife at Sanchez and then stooped to retrieve
the fallen sword. The Catalan took a quick step to the
left and swept the main gauche across, batting the
thrown knife harmlessly into a far corner. Billy knew
that he'd taken that little step, despite the risk, to make
sure he didn't deflect the knife toward Sharon.

*Goddam knight of the round table, too! Sixty years
he's spent stewing in that crazy macho stuff.*

He had the flap open finally. Thank God. Out of the
corner of his eye, he saw a sudden burst of swordplay.
Just a quick clash of blades before Sanchez and his
opponents backed away. This was no idiot Gene Kelly
or Errol Flynn movie where swordsmen pranced and
danced all over the place smiling gaily and matching
sword strokes for minutes on end. This was a deadly
serious business where one good stroke or cut left a
man dead or dying in a split-second. It was like watching angry rattlesnakes in a cage.

The pistol was coming out. Billy reached over with
his left hand to work the slide and jack a round into
the chamber. It was an old .45-caliber automatic, the
Colt army model, with a heavy slide. He fumbled at it.
He felt light-headed, the way he never did in a baseball
game no matter how tight the situation. *I'm not used
to this!* some part of him wailed silently.

The slide banged down. The weapon discharged and
recoiled out of his hand.

It shouldn't have happened, but a worn sear—or
one a gunsmith had stoned to a knife-edge—could
slip. *I should've checked the goddam thing when I
had time!*

The bullet ricocheted harmlessly from the floor and
off into a corner. The pistol itself skidded across the
floor. Right toward the Frenchmen.

How Sanchez knew what had happened Billy would
never understand. The Catalan must have had eyes
in the back of his head. He stamped a boot, lunged
once—twice—skipped aside . . . caught the sliding pistol

with the toe of a boot and send it neatly sliding back across the floor.

Okay, it wasn't done perfectly—the pistol was heading toward the far corner instead of the one where Billy and Sharon were standing. Still. Any sarcastic thoughts Billy had ever had about Ruy Sanchez and his flamboyant ways died a sudden death. *Jesus, that crazy old man is good.*

But the horror wasn't over. Sharon pushed past him and practically tackled the pistol.

"Sharon—it's *armed!*" Billy shrieked. The hammer was back, anyway, and the recoil might've been enough to cycle the weapon completely, jacking another round into the chamber. If so, that thing was as deadly as a rattlesnake itself. Some part of Billy's mind made a solemn vow—piss on the admiral and his goddam rules—that he'd never use anything but a revolver in the future.

Sharon hit the floor on her belly and scooped up the pistol. Billy held his breath . . .

Thank God, again. Apparently she knew enough about firearms to realize that the pistol was armed. She had the butt in both hands and was coming up to her knees. Billy started to step toward her, reaching out his hand.

But Sharon didn't even glance at him. "Ruy, look out!" she screamed, leveling the gun.

Billy twisted his head. Another one of Ducos' agents was down. Somehow Sanchez had slashed the man's throat. Damn near cut his head off, in fact. He was obviously deader than a mackerel.

Sanchez had picked up a wound himself along the way. Billy could see a red stain spreading across the doublet on the left side above the waist. It couldn't be too bad a one, he guessed, since the Catalan was still in fine fighting form. The wound didn't seem to be bleeding that much. Nothing like that horrible gushing spray of blood that had happened after Sanchez stabbed the first man in the leg.

The wound on Sanchez wasn't why Sharon had screamed, though. Billy felt himself grow more light-headed still. He wondered if he had any blood at all left in his brain.

One of Ducos' agents had a pistol. Where the hell that had come from, Billy had no idea. The Frenchman had backed up a few steps so he could get a clear shot at Sanchez. Unfortunately—even if Sharon was a good enough shot in the first place—Sanchez was between her and his opponents.

The pistol was some kind of smallish wheel-lock, not the big cavalry variety. An assassin's weapon, and probably no more accurate than—

Billy felt his head clear instantly, as well-trained reflexes took over. There was a small table just next to the door, not more than a step away. Atop sat a bowl of fruit. Those small Italian apples that Billy didn't like because they were too sour.

Right now, he could care less about their taste. They were also very hard—and, if not quite a big as a baseball, close enough.

The apple came into his hand as easily and comfortably as the pistol had not. A quick pitcher's stride—Billy had never dawdled on the mound—and the apple went flying.

Billy could hit the plate, three times out of four, from the sixty-foot range of a pitcher's mound. At considerably less than half the range, the apple hit the man right between the eyes.

His coach had clocked his fastball once at ninety-seven miles per hour. Billy was pretty sure he'd just broken that.

The apple splattered. It was just soft enough that the man didn't die. But he was hurled against the wall, the pistol flying out of his hand.

The pistol hit the same wall Billy was near. Wheel-locks were even touchier than old automatic pistols once they were cocked. The weapon discharged. The bullet hit the bowl of fruit and sent the apples flying everywhere.

I . . . do . . . not . . . fucking . . . believe . . . this . . . shit.

Frantically, Sharon tried to get a bead on someone. But it was impossible. The way Ruy was dancing back and forth, she'd be as likely to shoot him as one of his opponents. Even at this range, Sharon had no confidence at all in her marksmanship. She'd only gone to the firing range at Grantville—then, later, at Wismar—when her father or Hans had absolutely insisted. She didn't like guns and felt no affinity for the things whatsoever. Especially a great big heavy monster like this one, whatever the hell it was.

There was another of those sudden, terrifying clashes between Ruy and his opponents. Like watching men turn into sharks for an instant. It was all too quick for Sharon to follow clearly. When it was over, though, another of Ducos' agents was stumbling back against the far wall, his sword spilling to the floor. Blood spurted through the hands clutching his throat. That was pure reflex, though. As soon as the man smashed against the wall his eyes rolled up and he slumped to the floor.

There were only two French agents left standing, now. But to her horror, Sharon saw that Ruy had been injured again himself. She hadn't seen it happen, but one of Ducos' men must have stabbed Ruy in the leg. Not the fatal kind of strike Ruy had landed at the beginning of the fracas, no; just a cut to the meat of the thigh. As wounds went, from a purely medical perspective, nothing much to worry about. Sharon was a lot more concerned about the wound that had now spread blood across the left side of the Catalan's doublet.

However, what was dangerous in a hospital was not the same thing as what was dangerous in a fight. Ruy was limping, now, pretty badly. And he'd lost a lot of blood, and—Sanchez or no Sanchez—he was a man in his late fifties. He couldn't possibly last much longer.

The two surviving Frenchmen sensed it. They started moving in for the kill. Slowly and carefully, to be sure.

Sharon glanced to her left. Billy was scrabbling on the floor for apples. No help there.

She took a very deep breath. She'd never smoked, was a big woman—and had a pair of lungs to match the rest of her chest.

"GODAMMIT RUY SANCHEZ GET THE HELL OUT OF THE WAY! LISTEN TO YOUR WOMAN!"

Sanchez instantly flung himself aside, coming to rest on his rump plastered against the wall right below his hat. He gave Sharon a grin that, for all the strain in his face, seemed genuinely cheerful.

"A request from my intended is like a command from God," he pronounced.

Sharon snorted. Took another breath and drew a bead. The two agents were staring at her now.

She decided marksmanship was pointless. She really had no idea what she was doing. On the other hand, she understood why they called these damn things "automatics."

"It was frickin' amazing," Billy would tell his friend Conrad later. "Truly awesome. She emptied the whole clip. Musta set some kinda time record, too. Sounded like it was on full auto."

A shake of the head, another quaff of beer. "A Colt .45 M-1911A1, to boot. Sure, it's an old warhorse—none of the fancy few modern ones we've got for plebes like you and me, Conrad old buddy—but it's still got enough firepower to shred a bull."

Another shake of the head, another quaff. "Point-blank range. Couldna been more than twenty feet. Frickin' amazing. She never hit the one guy at all and only managed to hit the other once. I grant you, in the chest, perfect center mass shot. Killed him deader'n a doornail. But. Still."

Billy wondered if he'd ever hear again. It felt like at least one of his eardrums had burst. Paralyzed, for sure. He'd never actually heard what a .45 sounded like fired in a closed room—thick walls, too—and wearing no ear protectors. It didn't help at all that he'd been positioned alongside the firearm instead of behind the shooter.

The one Frenchman still left standing seemed even more dazed than Billy was. Slowly, the man spread his arms wide and stared down at his body. He seemed a little amazed to see no blood.

Billy was downright astonished. How could she *possibly* have missed—at that range?

Sharon lurched to her feet and tried to do with the pistol itself what she'd failed to do with its ammunition. Hollering something that was probably obscene as all hell—Billy couldn't make out a word of it—she hurled the pistol at the Frenchman.

Alas. She was no more accurate than before. Ducos' agent didn't even have to duck. He just watched the pistol sail by at least two feet from his head.

When he brought his head back, though, there was a smile on his face. A damn cold one. Sharon was disarmed and while Sanchez was struggling to get back on his feet the old man was obviously having a hard time of it now. Leaving aside the wound to the body, his left leg was just about literally soaked in blood.

On the other hand, Billy had finally gotten his apple.

"Hey, shithead," he said. The Frenchman looked his way. Billy beaned him.

A little high. Out of the strike zone. The apple had struck the man on the slope of his forehead instead of right between the eyes. Most of the impact had been deflected with the apple.

Still, that had been one hell of a fastball. Somewhere between ninety-five and a hundred miles an hour, at a guess. The apple itself was now just a fruit stain across the far wall. Ducos' agent was reeling, barely able to stand. And he'd dropped his sword.

Billy started to reach down for another apple but changed his mind. "I never liked that damn designated-hitter rule anyway," he muttered.

He stalked over and picked up the leg of the table Sanchez had shattered. Then, proceeded to start beating the Frenchman into a pulp.

Sharon stopped him, unfortunately, before he could really get into a good rhythm.

"Hey, don't kill him! We want him to talk." He could just barely make out the words through the ringing in his ears.

Billy took a deep breath. She was probably right.

"Okay. But. Still. This is why pitchers never bat too well, y'know. Nobody lets us get enough practice."

Chapter 38

After Mike Stearns had finished reading the latest report from Venice, he raised his eyes—his head still lowered—and looked at Francisco Nasi.

"Did you expect this? Any idea at all?"

Nasi chuckled. "Would you believe me if I claimed that I did?"

Mike smiled and slid the file onto the desk. "I'd call you five ways a liar. I sure as hell didn't. Never in my wildest dreams. Larry Mazzare summoned by the pope to Rome to defend Galileo. Lord in Heaven, you want to talk about an *opening.*"

He rose from his chair and went over to the window he favored at moments like this. Francisco suspected that looking out the window helped Mike take his mind off his wife, his sister, and his friends who were trapped in cities far away, and about whom the prime minister could do very little, just then. But what Mike found to look at out there, in the still-ugly raw newness that was the city of Magdeburg being reborn, Francisco had never been able to determine. Most likely the Elbe rather than the city itself. Nasi knew that Mike Stearns found looking at moving water something of an emotional comfort and an aid to concentration. That might be part of the reason he had insisted on having the new building which housed the USE's executive branch built along the riverbank.

A small part, though, if any. The main reason was that the building fronted along Hans Richter Square and was named—also at Mike's insistence—the *Richterhof*. If there was any trick of propaganda and public relations that Mike Stearns would shy away from, Nasi had never encountered it. Magdeburg was the political capital of the new United States of Europe as well as—so far, at least—its major industrial center. Over time, the two aspects of the city would most likely reinforce each other. There was no way to tell, as yet, and wouldn't be for many years. But Nasi thought that Mike's estimate that Magdeburg would eventually come to provide the same center of gravity for Germany that London and Paris provided for England and France was probably correct.

If so, Mike Stearns would take the time and effort now to stamp the city in his own political mold as best he could. Using the memory of Hans Richter as the stamp, every chance he got. *Richterhof*, *Richterplatz*, *Richterstrasse*—there were at least three of those in the city—Richter Park; for all Francisco knew, a Richter lamppost somewhere and no doubt a profusion of Richter Alleys.

Stearns was utterly shameless. Francisco glanced at a nearby wall of Mike's office, which was covered with enlarged portraits. A few of them were photographs; most were paintings. Mike agreed fully with Mary Simpson that drawing artists to Magdeburg was yet another way to ensure that Germany's most radical city also became its most important. As Paris goes, so goes France; the same for London—and if Stearns had any say in the matter, the same would be true of Magdeburg as well.

Most of the portraits were what you'd expect in the office of the new nation's prime minister:

A large portrait of the emperor, Gustavus Adolphus.

A not quite so large—perhaps by half an inch—portrait of Mike Stearns and Gustavus Adolphus and Axel Oxenstierna solemnly discussing political affairs. The emperor seated, his two principal advisers standing. Francisco was particularly taken by those poses: Oxenstierna with his hand atop a globe of the world—well, that was reasonable enough—and Mike Stearns with a sword belted to his waist and one leg turned out in the finest courtier style. Given that Mike Stearns did not own a sword, had no idea how to use one, and had never been seen by man nor beast in any stance that was not either relaxed or what you'd expect of an ex-pugilist . . .

Those type of portraits.

Ah, Magdeburg. Nasi loved the city, despite its multitude of flaws. It was the only city in the world other than great Istanbul that he found truly exciting.

His favorite portraits, however, were two others. One, by far the largest, covered almost the entire wall in the back—where visitors would first enter the room. The enormous painting had been only recently completed by the young Dutch artist Pieter Codde, a student of Franz Hals who had managed to escape Amsterdam just before the siege closed in. The painting was entitled *Allegory of the Rebirth of Magdeburg*, and it was all Francisco could do not to burst into laughter every time he entered the prime minister's office and looked at the thing.

His amusement was caused not so much by the image of Michael Stearns standing just beside Gustavus Adolphus—but carefully portrayed as barely more than half the emperor's size. Not even by the truly ludicrous spectacle of Mike Stearns as the loyal spear-carrier, wearing a Roman centurion's armor, no less!

Nor was it caused—well, perhaps a bit—by the inevitable mob of cherubs lifting the soul of slaughtered Magdeburg to Heaven, accompanied by the inescapable angels blowing upon their horns.

No, it was the centerpiece that Francisco could never look at without having to suppress the urge to riotous laughter. The babe, of course, was to be expected. Magdeburg reborn, looking much like any babe. But the young mother so tenderly cradling the infant . . . the obvious symbolism, the allegory to the birth of Christ . . .

He must have choked. Mike glanced at him. "What's so funny?"

Francisco shook his head. "Oh, nothing. I was just thinking of the mother in that grotesque new painting of yours." He hooked a thumb over his shoulder, not daring to actually look. They *did* have serious business to conduct, this day.

Mike glanced at the huge painting, and smiled. "I have to admit I get a kick out of it myself. I will say that Pieter did one hell of good job, having to work from memory the way he did, with the model still back in Amsterdam." He went back to staring out the window, the smile still on his face. "Spitting image of my wife. Who is, ah, no longer a virgin and has never been a Christian at any time."

He hooked his own thumb over his shoulder. "But don't lie, Francisco. I know you think that other one is even funnier."

Nasi examined the portrait to which the thumb was pointed. It was not a portrait, as such, but one of the few photographs hanging up on the walls. A classic example of that peculiar sub-genre of the visual arts known as *Politics, American, Crass Beyond Belief.*

"Indeed. Michael Stearns. Cheerfully eating the first Hans Richter Victory Sandwich produced by the Freedom Arches in Magdeburg. What are the ingredients, again?"

"Baltic rye bread, ham and cheese, with, of course, the essential splash of French dressing. It's not bad, actually."

The prime minister turned away from the window.

"All right, Francisco, enough of the drollery. I know you could bring down the house with your comedy routines. Well, anywhere except in Istanbul."

Nasi winced. "Risky business, that. Murad the Mad is prone to assuming that all jokes are at his expense."

Stearns pointed to the file. "I also know that you're just stalling because this is one of the few subjects you don't feel particularly knowledgeable about. I understand that. I don't expert a Sephardic Jew from Istanbul to be the world's expert on the inner workings of the Roman Catholic Church. Still, what's your best estimate?"

"The truth? I think we are sensing a tremor beneath our feet. The first sign of a coming political earthquake."

Mike stared down at the file, his hands now planted on the desk. "That's what I think, too. Jesus, Joseph and Mary."

Nasi shook his head. "The man will not take sides, you understand."

"Don't be silly, Francisco. He *has* been taking a side, whether he liked it or not—which, by all reports, he didn't much." Stearns rapped the file with a finger. "Simply the act of declaring neutrality is taking a side, when you're already on one."

"Not what I meant. Sorry. I only intended to say that I think there is no chance—no chance at all—that the pope will do or say anything overtly which could in any way be construed—formally, you understand—as an alliance of any kind with the United States of Europe."

Mike gave Nasi a very placid look. Francisco braced himself. That sleepy expression invariably signaled the coming sarcasm.

"At a rough guess, Francisco, I could get the same assessment from two out of three urchins in the streets of Magdeburg. Nineteen out of twenty, in the streets of Rome. Maffeo Barberini who was, Urban VIII who is, has been accused of a lot of things in his sixty-some-odd years. Deviousness, manipulation, cynicism—not to mention a truly breathtaking devotion to nepotism—but never once, that I can recall, being a moron. Try again."

Nasi sighed. "Michael, this is *not* a subject—"

"Try again."

"Tyrant!"

"Try again."

Nasi puffed out his cheeks. "You'd do better to ask von Spee. He's back in town, you know."

"Good idea. I will. Try again. And I'll make it easy for you, since you brought up von Spee. Who is still, I remind you, a Jesuit."

Stearns gave Nasi a little encouraging jiggle of the chin, the way a mother encourages her toddler to say *mama*. "Don't try to start with a pope maybe undergoing a real and profound crisis of conscience. Start with what you know. Would Urban even consider this if he didn't think he had Vitelleschi in his corner? And I'm not talking about that famous fourth vow of obedience. I'm talking about the father-general of the Jesuits—the Black Pope, they sometimes call him—being *really* in his corner."

Francisco felt the ground stabilize beneath his feet. "No," he said firmly. "Not a chance."

"What I think, too." Stearns stared at the file on the desk. Then, suddenly, slammed his open palm down upon it. Stearns had big hands. The loud noise almost startled Nasi out of his chair.

"Hot damn!" Mike exclaimed. "Hot diggedy-damn. Chew on *that*, Richelieu. And you can downright choke on it, you stinking emperor of Austria. And you, puke-face elector of Bavaria, you can take your so-called Catholic League and stick it where the sun don't shine. Y'all just lost your fig leaf. 'Bout to, anyway. If that wasn't enough—you morons!—you just lost the help of what is probably still the most effective political organization in Europe. Maybe the whole world, the way the Japanese seem to be squawking. Sure as hell the most experienced."

Suddenly energetic, Mike slid himself into his chair. "Okay. First. You're right. Get von Spee in here, ASAP. Second, get in touch with Spartacus and tell him I'll want a private meeting. Private as in *private*. If I have to, I'll use regular soldiers and goddamit firing squads to put a stop to any and all anti-Jesuit riots from now on. But I'd really prefer it if the Committees handled the problem informally."

"Ah, I believe what you're alluding to is actually illegal, Michael, not 'informal.'"

"Sure is," Mike said cheerfully. "And be assured that I will so inform Spartacus in no uncertain terms. If I catch the Committees doing anything illegal like pounding the crap out of stinking bigot lynch mobs, I will have them charged and prosecuted to the full extent and rigor of the laws."

"Amazing, really," mused Nasi.

"What?"

"I do not believe I have ever heard a sentence that long which had almost the entirety of its emphasis upon a single word in it. 'Catch.' The rest was practically a murmur."

Mike just grinned. "Third. Get in touch with Morris in Prague and have him feel out Wallenstein. Shouldn't be a problem, I don't think. Wallenstein's always been partial to the Jesuits. He'll probably be tickled pink." The prime minister paused for a moment. "I don't suppose there's any way we could get him to think we're trying to make amends for the ruckus over the copper business, is there?"

Nasi enjoyed the opportunity to bestow a placid look upon his boss.

"Right," Stearns snorted. "Grow up, Mike. 'Wallenstein' and 'moron' don't belong in the same sentence either. So it goes. Fourth. Start sending out feelers—quietly, you understand; I don't need my stubborn Lutheran emperor hollering at me—suggesting that any Jesuit educational project will be more than welcome to set up shop in the USE. Um. Well, hold off on that until we've had a chance to consult with von Spee. We gotta be slick, here. We really can't afford to show our hand openly. Gustav Adolf hollers really, really good, if I say so myself as shouldn't."

Nasi nodded. Mike Stearns was capable of hollering superbly well himself, though he rarely chose to. But Gustav Adolf was in a league of his own. "We should be able to manage well enough, I think. Freedom of religion *is* the law in the USE after all—"

"—until Wilhelm wins the election," Mike interjected sourly.

"—and in any event, alas, the emperor is preoccupied on the war front. He's not likely to pay much attention to the complex minutiae of educational affairs. Which—you'd be amazed—can get incredibly complex and minute. And don't exaggerate, Michael. Wilhelm and his Crown Loyalists advocate the restoration of established churches in those provinces whose legislatures elect to do so, but he's always been very careful to stipulate that no minority faiths—even non-Christian ones—will be penalized in any way. He even insisted on writing that in as a formal part of his party's program."

Mike didn't look noticeably mollified. "Yeah, swell. So members of nonestablished churches get taxed to support the established ones, and then have to pay for their own out of their own pockets." He blew out a breath. "Oh, well. I admit it beats pogroms and inquisitions and *auto-da-fé*. We do what we can, one step at a time. Mostly, by taking ten steps forward and nine steps back."

"Which is still a step ahead," Nasi replied. "That's a quote, by way, from a speech I recently heard. Given by a man who, I regret to say, I have come to conclude is the most brazen politician in Europe."

He swiveled in his chair and gazed back upon the *Allegory of the Rebirth of Magdeburg.* "It's astonishing, really. I can—just barely—understand how a superb artist could visualize you in that preposterous Roman armor. But how did he manage the expression on your face?"

Mike glanced at his portrait. "That suggestion of stalwart dim-wittedness? The hint of adulation for the emperor? The mouth that looks like butter wouldn't melt in it?"

Nasi nodded.

"I gave Pieter firm instructions, what do you think? Paid him a good bonus, too. Worth every penny. Gustavus Adolphus thinks very highly of that painting, did I mention that?"

"As I recall, you boasted about it for ten minutes straight."

"Don't be sarcastic, Francisco. It's very unbecoming. Okay, back to business. Fifth—"

Chapter 39

Sharon almost stumbled when she came into the salon of the embassy which, by dint of feverish work throughout the night, had been turned into an impromptu operating room. Fortunately, she caught herself in time to turn the stumble into what she hoped would pass for a dignified pause.

"Jesus, Stoner," she hissed, "you didn't say anything about a *mob*." She forced herself to scan the room slowly, instead of doing what she felt like doing, which would have resembled a small girl frantically looking everywhere at once, trying to find a bolt hole.

"It's hardly a 'mob,'" Tom Stone murmured. "Okay, yeah, it's a lot of people. But—trust me on this one— they're about as hoity-toity as it comes. No rabble here."

He glanced into one corner of the huge salon, where, atop one of the many heavy tables that had been positioned around three sides of the room to serve as an jury-rigged observers' gallery, Lieutenant Ursinus and two men from the Arsenal were standing. "Well, leaving Conrad and his people aside—but I think both of those guys are guildmasters anyway."

Stoner scanned the room also. The gaze, in his case, was genuinely serene—perhaps even smug—rather than Sharon's desperate attempt to fake it. "You've got just about every doctor in Venice worth calling by the name in this room. They're all good ones, too, I know them. They even scrupulously followed my instructions about being freshly bathed and wearing clean clothes, so far as I can tell. The rest of the people—the ones I made stand in the back because I'm not sure about how closely they followed my sanitation instructions—are political bigshots of one kind or another. According to Taggart, they include one of the doge's aides and at least four senators. He thinks one of them might be on the Council of Ten. Hard to know, of course. There's even a cardinal of the Church—Bedmar, the Spanish guy. I sent somebody to invite him, too, seeing as how it's his main man going under the knife. I didn't think he'd show up, actually."

Sharon's eyes went to the great bank of windows along one wall. The windows faced almost directly to the east, which was the reason she'd picked this salon for her operating room. She had agonized over that decision. Given the nature of Ruy's wound, she'd wanted to operate as soon as possible. Waiting twelve hours was a terrible risk—an unconscionable one, had she still been in the world she'd come from. But that world had electric lighting and this one didn't. Sharon had finally decided that the risk of trying abdominal surgery by lamplight was worse than the risk of waiting till sunrise—and would have been, even if she were an experienced surgeon instead of a nurse trying to pass herself off as one.

"It's not even six o'clock in the morning," she protested.

Stoner smiled. "Yeah, but the light's pretty terrific, you gotta admit. The sun's been up for almost an hour, shining right in now, and—" He bestowed a lingering and very approving look upon the eclectic collection of lighting aids that surrounded the operating table. "Billy did one hell of a job. And he was right about those tailor's globes. Filled with water, they make a lot of difference. Especially with the mirrors."

"That's not what I meant," Sharon hissed again. "How the hell did you get all these people here this early? Especially when you just got back yesterday yourself?"

By way of an answer, Stoner simply gave her an ironic little cock of the eyebrow. Sharon understood it, of course. She'd known the answer before she even finished the question. A world which, outside of Grantville and parts of Magdeburg, still had only oil lamps and candles to illuminate the night was a world where *early to bed, early to rise* was taken for granted. Even for political bigshots.

"I'm nervous enough already, damn you, Tom. The last thing I need is to try to pull this stunt off in front of a crowd."

Stoner started to say something—one of his usual variations on *be cool*, Sharon was sure—but then hesitated for a moment. Good thing for him, too. If he had said it, Sharon thought she'd just haul off and belt him one. He might be a pacifist, but she wasn't.

What he did say surprised her. The tone more than the words themselves. It was the first time Sharon could ever remember hearing Tom Stone say anything harshly.

"That's crap, Sharon. You want to know the truth? You're one of those people who does better under pressure than they do any other time. That's partly why I did this. Everybody—except you—knows that about you. Your dad makes jokes about it. 'Best way to make sure Sharon aces a test is to give her no warning.'" He pointed a finger at the operating table. "So just shut up and Sharon, will you? There's a man dying over there. What do you care who's watching? Fuck 'em."

The vulgarity jolted her as much as the tone. Unusually,

for a hippie—at least, the two-generations-later brand of hippie that Sharon was familiar with from college—Tom Stone very rarely used foul language.

The jolt made her think about what he'd actually said. Was that true, she wondered?

It might be, actually. She'd always ascribed her tendency to goof off in school until the last minute to plain and simple laziness. But maybe that was her own unconscious way of maximizing her strengths when the time came. Sharon had never once turned in a paper until the very last minute, and for her the words "study" and "cram" were pretty much synonyms. Still, she'd graduated from WVU *magna cum laude*. Would have made *summa* if that bum Leroy Hancock hadn't blown two whole semesters out of the water, jacking her around with his lies and promises.

"You're treacherous, Stoner," she murmured. But she was smiling by the end of the sentence, and taking her first step toward the table. "Come on, then. At least I managed to get two hours' sleep, which is more than I usually did before a final exam."

She gave him a sidelong glance. "I *do* hope that you didn't forget to anesthetize the patient. Being so preoccupied like you were with plotting and scheming."

"Oh, he's under all right. I'll keep dripping ether onto the gauze on his face to keep him under, and just have to hope I gauge it properly. I can tell you all you need to know about the chemical structure of ether and how to make it. But how much of it to use . . ."

Stoner glanced at the crowd. "I did tell all of them—really clear—that if anyone so much as looked like they were going to strike a match, we'd wrestle 'em down and slap *them* onto the OR table. Do an immediate brainectomy to remove what is obviously a malignant foreign body."

Sharon chuckled and put a hand on his shoulder. Like she herself, Stoner was wearing a scrub gown.

She'd brought several with her from Grantville, on the off chance that she might be called upon to do ... well, exactly what she was going to do. She could tell from the warmth and feel of the fabric that Stoner's gown, like her own, had just recently been sterilized in the steam cleaner that had been one of the first innovations the embassy had made in their little palace.

"Relax, Tom. I'm a lot more likely to kill him than you are, much less a casual smoker. Remind me to compliment Billy, by the way. He's done a fantastic job here."

They were only halfway to the operating table, since Sharon was moving slowly to help compose herself. Billy Trumble was lying on a cot not far away with an IV in his arm. One of the older Marines was lying on a cot next to him. Only two donors, which Sharon wasn't happy about at all. Unfortunately, they knew the blood types of only two of the Scot soldiers who made up most of the embassy guard. Lennox was the other one, and he had A-positive which was no use at all since they didn't know Ruy Sanchez's blood type either.

"It's that silly guilt-trip business," Tom murmured. "Billy's feeling bad because he thinks he screwed up yesterday. Dropping the gun the way he did."

Sharon's lips quirked. "I thought he did great, myself. Hey, look, two of us in that madhouse were amateurs. The pro's the only one who got hurt."

"Well, yeah. But Billy probably figures if he hadn't screwed up the pro wouldn't have been scratched." He gave his head a little shake. "As it is, I had to stop him from donating too many units. Especially with him also running around organizing so much stuff. I wish we'd had somebody besides him and Dalziel still here with type O-negative."

Stoner's lips tightened on that last sentence. Sharon knew that Tom had his own worries. His son Gerry had the universal donor's blood type also. But Gerry had vanished, along with Frank and Ron, nobody knew where. The documents they'd found at the Marcoli house after the deadly brawl had referred to crazy schemes to liberate Galileo and murder the pope. True, those documents had obviously been planted by Ducos' agents. But there had also been notes from Joe Buckley—no doubt about it; Joe's handwriting had been distinctive—which seemed to at least confirm the part about liberating Galileo. Lennox and most of his men were out scouring the city, trying to find out what the truth was.

Sharon shook her head. They'd reached the table now, and there was no time to think about anything other than the work ahead of her. The OR table itself was something Sharon had had designed weeks earlier, blessedly, in case of an emergency. It was a well-made local product, heavily shellacked and polished, and now covered with sterilized absorbent fabric. It wasn't quite as good as an up-time OR gurney—and certainly a lot harder to move around, between the weight of the wood and the lack of wheels—but it would do fine.

She looked down at the patient lying on the OR table. She'd wondered if it would bother her, having to operate on someone she knew. To her relief, she discovered that it didn't. The man on the table bore a vague resemblance to a man named Ruy Sanchez, what she could see of the face above the gauze over the nose and mouth that Stoner would use to keep administering the anesthetic. But that was all it was. Just a resemblance. The animation was gone. The skin was pale, the cheeks were flushed. That was fever and blood loss.

The key, though, was the eyes. The patient's eyes were closed now, but Sharon had seen the dullness come into them in the hours after the fight. Not even Don Quixote on steroids could shrug off these kinds of injuries. The cut to the leg, maybe; that had been a simple flesh wound which Sharon had treated and sewn up quickly hours earlier. But certainly not the other trauma.

That one was a killer. The type of abdominal wound which, at any time prior to the late nineteenth century, would have been accepted as well-nigh certain death. A slow and tortured death, to boot. Sharon knew full well that the reason Stoner had been able to pack the huge salon with observers was because they all wanted to see if the exotic American *Dottoressa* could do what had always been considered impossible.

She took a slow, deep breath. A man named Ruy Sanchez with dull eyes simply did not exist in the world, she told herself firmly.

Could not exist. A contradiction in terms. All that lay here was a patient. A body. If she did her job, a human being might return into that body. But, for now, it was just a body. One of many. She'd studied and handled bodies for years now. The father who had sired her and raised her and given her his own talent and love for medicine had done the same for decades before that.

She felt calm, now. She'd gained that emotional detachment which, however inhuman it might be from one angle, was utterly necessary for what lay ahead of her.

Stoner had already moved to his part of the OR table and was checking the patient's vital signs.

"The last urine sample we got wasn't too bad," he said. "That was a little over an hour ago. Low volume, but I don't think there's any danger of immediate kidney failure. His pulse right now is . . . pretty good, I'd say. Weak and rapid, of course, but I don't think he's missing any beats."

"What's the systolic pressure?"

"That's the good news. A hundred and ten."

Sharon hummed a little note of satisfaction. She needed a minimum of ninety to risk an operation like this, and had wanted a hundred. A hundred and ten was higher than she'd dreamed of.

For an instant, a treacherous little thought tried to

worm its way forward. *How could I do otherwise? A wish from my intended is like a command from—*

She squashed that, right quick. "Please introduce me to my colleagues," she said, more loudly than she'd meant to. "And I think we should begin speaking in Italian"—that last sentence said in the language—"except in such instances where I might encounter an emergency."

In which case, all bets are off and I'll probably start hollering at them incoherently. But she saw no reason to add that. The two Venetian doctors standing at the table in their own scrub gowns looked to be even more nervous than she'd been.

Tom nodded. "To your left, Dottoressa Nichols, is Dottor Fermelli. He has agreed to serve as your first assist and scrub."

He used the English word *scrub*, not the Italian translation of it. The full term in English would have been "scrub nurse," but that last word needed to be avoided. In the parlance of the seventeenth century, "nurses" were purely scut-work menials with about as much skill and training—and social status—as a janitor. That was the reason, of course, that the embassy had from the beginning introduced Sharon as a *Dottoressa.* And since the Italian word for *scrub* was every bit as prosaic as the English term, Tom had apparently decided to fall back on the ancient trick—perfected by French chefs—of making something sound glamorous by using a foreign term for it.

Fermelli nodded politely. Sharon returned the nod and took the opportunity to gauge the man as best she could. He'd be the key assistant. The second Venetian doctor would be the circulating nurse. Which meant, under the circumstances, nothing much more than a gofer. That doctor was standing next to the small table that held the instruments and absorbents. She'd be curious to see what title Stoner had decided to bestow upon him in order to avoid the dreaded "nurse" label. *Circulator,* probably.

But it was Fermelli she'd be counting on, in case of trouble. And, perhaps more to the point, it would be Fermelli who'd have to be able to help her with the really grisly parts of the operation. Sharon could well remember her very first experience in an operating room. The operation she was about to do wasn't that much different. It had been an abdominal hysterectomy. She'd almost lost it when they pulled the woman's guts out and plopped them on her chest. To this day, she couldn't eat sausage links.

And she'd just been an observer. Fermelli was the guy who would have to hold the patient's guts once Sharon hauled them out so that she could examine them.

Because of the surgical mask Fermelli was wearing, Sharon couldn't see most of his face. But the calm and steady look in his eyes reassured her. She'd told Stoner to make sure he found someone who had real hands-on surgical experience. Most seventeenth-century doctors—in Germany at least; she wasn't sure about Italian practice—were really more in the way of medical theorists. Advisers and consultants, potion-prescribers and the like, not what Sharon thought of as a "surgeon." The word itself was ancient, her father had once told her, deriving from the Greek *kheirourgia* and passing through the Old French *serurgien* before entering the English language. But, despite its majestic lineage, it had entered English through the cellar, not the front door. Until fairly recently in the universe she'd come from—not much more than a century, she thought—the distinction between doctor and surgeon had been entirely in favor of the doctor. The "surgeon" was the lowlife who sawed off legs, using booze for an anesthetic—and, like as not, did so while half-drunk himself.

Satisfied, Sharon looked at the other Venetian doctor. "And this is Dottor d'Amati," Stoner completed the introductions. "He has agreed to serve as the gofer."

D'Amati's chest swelled and he beamed at her. It was all Sharon could do not to burst into laughter. She

should have known! Leave it to Tom Stone to call a
gofer a gofer. There were times Sharon really liked
that old hippie. She had no doubt at all that by the
time Stoner finished with his lectures in Venice and
Padua, Italian medical practitioners would have *gofer*
firmly planted in their prestigious lexicon. He'd probably even manage, somehow, to get them clawing for
the honor of being called a nurse. Which, as far as
Sharon was concerned—she really looked at the world
from a nurse's perspective, not a doctor's—would be
just dandy.

She felt good. Really good. She'd been almost petri-
fied in the hours leading up to this, knowing that for
the first time in her life she'd have to be the one in
charge of a critical operation. Now . . .

Flesh and blood. She could almost feel James Nichols' big, capable hands settling over her shoulders, as
if from half a continent away his spirit was calming
her and guiding her.

The sensation was powerful enough that by the time
Sharon finished sterilizing with alcohol the area where
she'd be operating—she'd have preferred iodine but
they hadn't been able to turn up enough in the short
time they'd had—she decided she would explain what
she was doing while she worked. She'd seen her father
do that, before students. He'd told her afterward that
he found it a steadying influence on himself.

"I'm going to begin with what we call an exploratory
laparotomy." She gave Dottors Fermelli and d'Amati
a smile, hoping they could detect it under her own
mask. "That's just a fancy phrase that means I'm going
to cut the patient open and go exploring to see what's
happening in there."

They seemed to be smiling back. Judging from his
eyes, Fermelli's smile was even cheerful.

Splendid. She made sure of her grip on the scalpel.
"The initial incision needs to be made in one firm
stroke. It must be firm enough to cut through the skin

and part of the initial subcutaneous layer. That's just another fancy word for 'fat.' Judging from appearance, I don't think we'll find a very thick layer of that with this patient. For a man of his age, he appears—make that any age, actually—to have a very low percentage of body fat."

She slid the scalpel in. "I'll open him from an inch or so below the breast bone to about four inches above the pubic bone. Like—"

It was a good cut. Really good.

"So."

Cardinal Bedmar was not the only spectator who looked away, at that point. But he suspected he was the only one who did so for spiritual reasons.

Like—

So.

The cardinal from Spain understood many things now which had been murky to him before.

Some, which had been murky for a short time, he understood very well. Ruy Sanchez's obsession with the woman had become a mystery to Bedmar, as the weeks had gone by since the doge's levee. The cardinal had assumed, at first, that the Catalan's fascination was nothing more complicated than a taste for exotic flesh.

And indeed, so it might have been, at the beginning. In the costumes they favored for their wealthy women, as in so many things, the Venetians enjoyed thumbing their noses at the Spain that controlled half of Italy. Where the Spanish style that still dominated much of the continent encased the female form in rigid, stiff—above all, high-necked—apparel, the Venetians preferred to see their women. Decadent and lascivious, in this as in all things.

And, see them they did. The first time Bedmar had ever attended a Venetian levee, as a man in his mid-thirties born and raised in Spain, he had thought himself somewhere at sea—with surging half-bare breasts making up the waves. He'd been quite shocked at the time, though he'd diplomatically kept it from showing.

He had not been shocked, of course, when he saw the Nichols woman so attired at the levee in February. By then, the man of thirty-five was a man of sixty-two, the marquis had become a cardinal, and Bedmar was as well traveled, cosmopolitan and sophisticated as any man in Europe. Yet even he had been arrested, for a moment, by the sight of such a magnificent and well-displayed bosom. All the more so when the flesh was as darkly colored as undiluted coffee.

But he had misgauged the Catalan, he now realized. Seeing the same woman wearing garments that, though they could not hide the female form did nothing to display it either, had laid bare the truth.

All his life—and Bedmar had known him since he was a young man—Ruy Sanchez had never been able to resist a challenge. In that, he was much akin to the hero of the Cervantes story that he so adored. The flesh was not the challenge, of course. For a man like Sanchez, flesh was no longer a challenge at all. The challenge came from meeting the first woman in the Catalan's life who intimidated him.

And how delightful a thought that was! Ruy Sanchez, abashed.

A woman so young, yet who moved like a queen, serenely and calmly—even more so in the garments she wore today than she had in the costumes she favored for the levees and operas—and could slice a man open while she described the deed itself. Calmly, serenely; not a tremor in her voice.

It was all the cardinal could do not to laugh aloud. Don Quixote, indeed, facing the largest windmill he had ever seen. No wonder Ruy had seemed so perplexed; yet, at the same time, so exultant. To such a windmill, such a man would devote the rest of his life. If he could only figure out what sort of lance would do the trick. The one between his legs that had served him so well in the past was hardly up to this exploit. Not on its own, certainly.

Bedmar's eyes drifted to the windows. The light was blinding for a moment, as if the rising sun were challenging the cardinal.

Which, indeed, it was. Bedmar sighed softly, all thought of laughter gone. The sun was made by God, as He had made all things. And now, after a long lifetime devoted to matters of the flesh—politics and intrigue, if not the cruder forms—He who had created Alphonso de la Cueva, marquis de Bedmar, was reminding him none too gently that He could and did make much greater things than a marquis and a cardinal.

The sound of many gags being suppressed simultaneously drew Bedmar's attention back to the center of the room.

One of those things was the man lying on the table. Not for many years now had Bedmar fooled himself which was the greater, the master or the servant. Did the rest of mankind fulfill their appointed roles on Earth with as much unflinching courage, honor and loyalty as that Catalan once-peasant, Satan's domains would be far more sparsely populated.

Granted, Purgatory would be full.

Another—and Bedmar suspected a greater still—

There came another and louder simultaneous gag; in two cases, not suppressed. Idly, Bedmar wondered which of these disturbingly efficient Americans had thought to provide those useful sacks he had wondered about, positioned conveniently here and there.

His own stomach, however, had never been given to queasiness. He leaned forward, to see what was happening better.

Yes. As he'd thought. The woman was handing the intestines to her assistant. As much of them, at least, as she could pry out of the body. Bedmar wondered, for a moment, if he might someday be able to prevail upon her to allow one of those magnificent Flemish painters—he was partial to Van Dyck himself—to do a portrait of her in the act.

Probably not. There would also be the problem of keeping the painter to the work, of course. Some of them were delicate fellows.

A pity, really. It would make such a splendid allegory. The world had many queens—and far more kings—who could disembowel men at a distance using the instrument of their armies. How many did it have who could disembowel a man with her own hands in order to save his life?

The sun shone in the cardinal's eyes, asking him God's question. Bedmar, no fool, did not fail to note that it was a rising sun.

"—can see only one nick on the intestines themselves. I'll sew that up later. That's worrisome, because any cut in the intestinal tract is almost sure to result in peritonitis. But I was a lot more worried that I'd find one of the loops completely severed. That would have been a real nightmare, given what we've got available. This cut is small enough that I'm pretty sure we can contain the infection with the sulfa powder I'll be using as well as the chloramphenicol we gave the patient a few hours ago."

Sharon was almost done running the intestines now. "I'd be a lot happier, of course, if we didn't have such a small supply of the chloram. Uh, that's a nickname we made up for chloramphenicol. But at least we're in pretty good shape with the sulfa drugs."

She then took a couple of minutes to double-check herself and make sure she hadn't overlooked anything. "I don't need to check the liver or the bladder, given the location of the wound. I will need to check the stomach but I'll do that later. Right now, the spleen's in the way."

She pulled her head back. "How are the vital signs looking, Stoner?"

"Holding up. I don't think he'll make the marathon, though. Not next month's, anyway."

Sharon chuckled, making no attempt any longer to maintain her earlier reserve. By now they were well into the operation and her team was shaping up as a good one. Fermelli was splendid. D'Amati was still catching up, but doing better than she'd expected. A little relaxed banter was just part of the process.

That was the way her father ran operating teams, anyway. Sharon knew that some other surgeons didn't. There was one surgeon back in Chicago whom James Nichols always privately called "the pencil sharpener." The reference was not to his bookkeeping fussiness— though the man had that in full measure also—but to a portion of the surgeon's anatomy.

Graveside humor, granted. But what else do you expect to hear on the edge of a grave? Of course, if the patients could *hear* the jokes, they'd probably die right then and there. Of terminal indignation, if nothing else.

For the first time since she'd begun the operation, that treacherous little voice crept back.

Ruy Sanchez wouldn't. He'd probably kill himself from making the surgeons laugh too hard. His English was even getting the right idiom.

Never has a man been felt up so well by his woman! I, Ruy Sanchez de Casador y Ortiz, swear it is— SQUASH.

Once she was sure the damn thought was flat as a bug, Sharon straightened and took a deep breath.

"Okay. The main damage was to the spleen and I'm going to remove it entirely. We call that a splenectomy. The 'ectomy' part of it is just a fancy way of saying 'yank it out.' And why am I telling you that, anyway? I'm sure your Latin is way better than mine."

Her assistants chuckled; then again, and more loudly, when Fermelli added: "Actually, it's Greek. We Latins are more inclined to putting things in. Unfortunately, the common term for that does not adapt well to medical terminology."

Sharon bent over, smiling, back to the work. "There's going to be a lot of blood coming out here. From the looks of it, the capsule that surrounds the spleen tampanaded the bleeding. That's good—I was hoping for it—because it means the capsule would have acted as a temporary pressure dressing and slowed the bleeding. That's really important with spleen injuries, since the spleen is the most vascular organ in the body and is normally perfused by something like three hundred and fifty liters of blood a day."

It was an odd little speech. The sentence structure was Italian but so many of the words were English. Sharon knew Fermelli and d'Amati would barely be able to follow her here. So why had she spoken at all?

Was she losing her nerve? Stalling?

The self-doubt made her hesitate until she realized the truth. She was just immensely relieved, and the relief was as much personal as professional. She'd agonized over her decision to wait until daylight. Wondering if Ruy Sanchez would bleed to death internally because of her own fears.

Well, he hadn't. The man's spleen was as tough as the rest of him.

To be sure! The spleen of Catalonia is famous! Ask the wretched Castilians if you don't believe—

"Oh, shut up, Ruy," she murmured, still smiling.

After she perforated the capsule, she reflected that shutting up Ruy Sanchez was easier said than done. Even when the man was under full anesthesia.

"Would you wipe off my face, please, Dottor d'Amati? And we'll need to use plenty of that sterilized gauze to soak up as much blood as we can. Despite appearances, most of it went into the abdominal cavity, not onto me. Loose blood like that is a culture medium for infection."

She waited until she could see well again. "Thank you, Dottor. Okay, I'll start the cut here because—"

Bedmar had been perhaps the only man in the room not to gasp. Where all others seemed to think a desperate emergency had arisen, because they focused on the frightening gout of blood, the cardinal had been watching the woman's face before it struck. That small, expectant smile.

He could not see the smile itself, to be sure, because of the mask the woman was wearing. But he did not need to. Something in the calm dark eyes, the set of the jaw, the poise of the body, made it obvious. If anything, it was accentuated by the mask.

It was quite amazing, really. Bedmar was reminded of Diego Velasquez's *The Adoration of the Magi.* Not the wise and solemn face of the black king but the serene face of the Virgin. It was said that Velasquez had used his wife, Juana, as the model. The cardinal could well believe it, now. The serenity in that Virgin's face was not the usual ethereal business. Just a young woman's calm acceptance of God's miraculous handiwork. Whatever the Child's conception, after all, pain and labor had still been needed to bring Him forth.

Quietly, without fuss, the cardinal left the chamber. He would return on the morrow, to see after Sanchez's welfare. That the Catalan would survive this day, Bedmar had no doubt at all. Not any longer.

And he had other matters to consider. Much greater issues that were still murky to him, but less so after this day's instructions. That hidden but so obvious smile, like the blazing sun, had been another challenge from his God.

A warning, it would be better to say. Sixty-two years of life God had now granted Alphonso de la Cueva, once the marquis and now the cardinal Bedmar. God, he suspected, was beginning to lose patience with him.

As well He might. A life of stature, wealth, comfort

and considerable ease. Also a life slowly ebbing away in frustration and self-pity as Bedmar watched his once-glorious nation fade in its colors and become frayed in its fabric. A frustration which, over time, had become its own seductive melancholy.

Vanity, all it was. In the end, just vanity. Whose only distinction from pride was perhaps its sheer stupidity. But the cardinal was fairly certain that God would not accept a plea of stupidity as an excuse for one of the seven mortal sins.

Especially given that Alphonso de la Cueva was very far from stupid.

So, it was finally time to *think*. The cardinal believed in a personal God. He also believed in personal damnation.

Far better, he thought, to while away a limited number of millennia in the company of such as Ruy Sanchez. Even in Purgatory, the disrespectful Catalan was bound to make jokes.

Good ones, too.

It was over, finally.

"Two hours and nine minutes," Stoner announced. "I am genuinely impressed."

"Vital signs?"

"They're all okay. I'm not going to say 'good,' of course. But if he doesn't catch pneumonia or something down the road, this tough bird should live about as long as he would have."

Sharon winced a little.

"Oh, come *on,* Sharon," Stoner scolded gently. "Under these conditions, not even your dad would have tried to repair the spleen. Besides, I doubt if Ruy Sanchez was destined to die of old age anyway. Him? Be serious."

"Is something wrong, Dottoressa?" asked Fermelli.

Sharon shook her head. "Not . . . really, Dottor. I considered at one point attempting to repair the spleen rather than remove it. The problem with having the spleen removed is that it helps protect the body against infection."

She looked down at the patient. For some reason, he was starting to look like Ruy Sanchez again. Odd, really, since nothing in his appearance had changed except he had a large new scar to add to an already impressive collection.

"So, Ruy—ah, Señor Sanchez—will be more susceptible to such things as pneumonia from now on. He'll just have to be more careful, that's all."

Ha. Weren't you the one making speeches on this subject not so long ago?

Ruy Sanchez, careful and cautious. Walk with a cane, beware of inclement weather, wear warm clothes—who cares what they look like?—eat the right foods, avoid ruffians. At all costs, stay away from risky women. Which is you, judging from the record, right at the top of the list. Maybe the only one on the list.

Hell, frozen over.

She took refuge in trusty jargon. "That can be done using what we call the omentum—that's part of the lining of the abdomen—as a patch over the site. But it's tricky. If it goes wrong—which it very likely would working as I am now—I'd have had to go back in and remove the spleen anyway. With a much weakened patient and probably much worse infection. I decided it simply wasn't worth the risk."

The crowd was gathering around now, as Stoner and three burly Marines picked up the operating table—no wheeled gurneys here—and began hefting Sanchez out of the room. They were gathering to congratulate her, Sharon understood.

Do more than that, really, judging from the faces she could see. That was applause gathering there, applause and admiration. For the first time, she got a glimpse of what Stoner had been angling for when he invited that damned mob to come in.

She couldn't resist. Just couldn't. It was only a little fib, anyway.

"My father would have undoubtedly attempted the repair," she announced loudly, after removing her mask. Then, with a demure, well-nigh virginal smile: "But a young woman should know her limitations."

Stoner heard her, on the way out the door. He winced a lot more than she had.

"T'st too heavy then, sair?" asked one of the Marines. "We ken git anot'er man—"

"No, no. I can handle it. I just worry about Sharon sometimes. Bad vibes. The way she can be so nasty and sarcastic, I mean."

Chapter 40

Blinking in the sunlight, Frank Stone turned to look at where the shouting was coming from. Although it was well into the spring, the sun was still low in the sky at midmorning. Some of that blinking was fatigue, too. He'd gotten very little sleep in the day and half since Antonio Marcoli and Massimo's accident. Frank and his brothers had been as quiet as they could, sitting nervously in the next room as the doctor who'd been called out for Messer Marcoli and his cousin Massimo had done his work on the injured men.

They'd had no choice. The problem was that every medic in this town would know the name Stone, and be sure to ask after them. Their dad had been the star lecturer at the university here for weeks now. The Marcolis had expected only to pass the one night and be out of town with the dawn; and here they were, still debating the difference between asses and elbows.

The noise was Salvatore and Dino chest-to-chest screaming at each other. They were both soccer-mad, and with more than just the zeal of recent converts. They had the zeal of Marcolis. They'd been playing a little one-on-one up and down the street outside the inn, where they were all waiting for Roberto, Marius and Fabrizio to get back with the wagons they were going to be using for the next stage of the expedition.

And . . . now they were about to start brawling in the street. Frank took a moment to bring down a silent curse on the entire Marcoli clan, with the sole exception of Giovanna. Then, hurried toward them.

"Guys! Guys! Knock it off, okay? We've got enough problems already."

Both began a blustering explanation of how it was the other guy, and then trailed off, looking past Frank.

Frank looked round. It was Michel.

"Frank is right," Michel said. Somehow, he had chill pouring off him like an open freezer. When he wanted to be, Michel could be a damn scary customer. Dino and Salvatore nodded meekly and scurried off.

Frank turned away, sighing. "Thanks, Michel."

His face must have been a picture. "I, too, worry," said Ducos. "We are about a desperate and dangerous business, and such as this is cause for great worry."

Frank nodded gloomily. "If I didn't know we were being chased, I'd give up now."

Michel clapped him on the shoulder. "Courage, *mon brave*. We can surely not have been missed until late yesterday, and no pursuit will be properly on its way until today. If we are vigilant, we will see any assassins on our trail before we are struck."

"Assassins?" Frank's stomach churned. "You think so?"

"It comes as naturally to Venetians as hiring a gondolier, especially to their Council of Ten. The Spanish as well." The narrow face creased with something you might call a smile if you were inclined to be charitable. "And so, to be perfectly honest, my own French." Michel held up his heavily bandaged right hand in the way of rueful proof.

Frank had a vivid mental image of some Venetian

senator at a big desk somewhere, barking orders to kill someone into one phone and for an anchovy pizza into another. The image wasn't improved by Michel's next words.

"The creature that did for Monsieur Buckley is almost certain to be the closest one on our heels."

Frank shivered. Having poor Joe murdered back in Venice was bad enough. The thought that the murderer or murderers would be chasing after them across all Italy . . .

"Do we, uh, do we need to change our travel plans then?" he asked uncertainly. "I mean, we're taking the main road to Rome, after all."

Michel rubbed his chin with his uninjured left hand, pondering briefly. "There is reason in what you suggest. In fact . . ."

Another ponder, before the hand came away from the chin and clenched into a decisive fist. "Yes! We should change our route! There will certainly be ample opportunity for the assassins of the Inquisition and of the Council of Ten to lie in wait for us on the road to Florence. We should take a less obvious route. Well thought out, Monsieur Stone! Perhaps the route by way of Ravenna?"

"You know the way?"

Ducos shook his head. "Not as such, no. I had to deal with maps and the like when I worked for the embassy, but I have no clear memory of the roads as they are in Italy."

"Maybe Messer Marcoli will know?"

"Better yet, he almost certainly has a map," Michel said. "Let us consult with him."

Antonio Marcoli looked better than he had the night before, that was for sure. He was sitting up in bed in his room in the inn, being tended to by his daughter. Frank had his usual moment every time he caught sight of Giovanna—warmth; tenderness; okay, yeah, sheer lust too—seeing his girl play the ministering angel for her poor hurt daddy.

Damn, I love her. If only—

He shook the hopeless thought away, and looked around. Massimo was lying in another bed, still out cold. He seemed to be breathing normally, though. In fact, he was more than breathing normally, he was snoring. At least the Paduan doctor who'd attended Massimo also the night before hadn't done any actual harm. Frank had been worried about that, from all the stories he'd heard of the standards of seventeenth-century medicine. But, according to Giovanna, the doctor had never even mentioned using leeches.

"How's Massimo?" Frank asked.

"He rests," Giovanna said. "He was awake a little while ago, while you were outside. He had some bread and some water, and went back to sleep."

"Uh, okay," Frank said, although he was troubled a little. *Weren't you supposed to keep concussion victims awake?* But he didn't really have a clue. Sharon Nichols would know, but she was left behind in Venice. He hoped she was okay, but then the embassy had guards and that old Spanish guy she was seeing a lot of lately—for reasons that Frank couldn't begin to fathom—seemed to be able to handle himself.

Maybe they should send Massimo back to the embassy? He decided to see what Messer Marcoli thought.

"Maybe we could ask the embassy for asylum or something, for Massimo? I mean, he's not going anywhere like that. They could get medical help, proper up-time medical help that is. I mean, they wouldn't want to help with the Galileo business, but they'd keep Massimo safe while he gets better."

Marcoli digested that for a moment. Then, mournfully: "It is not just Massimo who will be going no further."

Frank nodded. And then realized what that meant.

"We're not going back to Venice, are we?" he asked, incredulous.

Venice . . . with its assassins and murderers and inquisitors and who knew what-all else. Not to mention having to face the wrath of Magda without having pulled off the rescue first. Getting reamed out and then assassinated was bad enough; getting reamed out and then assassinated after having failed was just about the most awful prospect he could imagine. He dwelt a moment on the memory of one of Magda's more impressive ass-chewings, multiplied it about tenfold, and realized he was less scared of the assassins than he was of his stepmom, right at the moment. It was all he could do not to smile at the thought of standing in the street and shouting out who he was so that the assassins would get to him first.

Marcoli interrupted his flight of whimsy. "No, of course not!" he said, sounding quite indignant. "Galileo must still be rescued! You must go on without Massimo and me." He sighed deeply. "The doctor, he said that there was a risk I might lose the leg without the hygiene your father taught, and I should stay here and keep clean."

That nearly set Frank off again. His dad had included lectures on aseptic technique, that he did remember. There had been a strong smell of grappa—the stuff was a pretty good antiseptic, even if drinking it took the lining out of your stomach—while the doctor had been working. And it seemed they were taking no chances with how far you had to go with it, either. As well as setting and splinting the bone, the doctor had insisted that Marcoli be washed all over and put to bed in freshly laundered linen. The bed bath, Frank decided, probably wouldn't do any harm and would help keep his temperature down. Dad's teaching hadn't been even close to comprehensive, but basic sick care had been a must, living as they did on a commune with no health insurance.

Frank was no judge, but he didn't think Antonio Marcoli had suffered a very serious break. Just bad enough to keep him off his feet for a while, following any kind of intelligent medical regimen.

Frank realized it was turning into a long, uncomfortable silence. "What do we do, then?"

Another long silence.

Marcoli took a deep breath, and looked Frank firmly in the eye.

Uh-oh.

"Messer Stone," he said, giving the name a portentous roll to it. "You must lead the rescue of Galileo."

Somber, it was. The tone of a man reading a death sentence, Frank thought. How *did* they execute people in Italy nowadays, anyway?

Was there *any* limit to folly?

But all he could manage was:

"Uh. Me?"

"What is it, Lieutenant Trumble?" Sharon asked, doing her level best to keep irritation and exasperation out of voice. Since the operation the day before, Ruy's condition seemed to be stabilized for the moment. But she was still gnawed with deep fear—somewhere in the corner of her brain the words *peritonitis! peritonitis! peritonitis!* wouldn't stop gibbering at her—and in no mood to be called to the embassy's front entrance to settle some kind of squabble with—

Oh.

She cleared her throat. "Good morning, Your Eminence."

Just beyond the door, Cardinal Bedmar gave Billy Trumble a triumphant little glance. "And good morning to you as well, Signora Nichols. I have come to inquire about my servant, Ruy Sanchez. I have been given to understand that you intend to keep him here at your embassy."

Been given to understand, Sharon thought sourly. That was spook-speak for *my spies tell me.*

On the other hand, she could understand why the special ambassador from the Spanish Netherlands would be concerned at discovering that his top spy was now residing under the roof of a foreign nation's embassy. All the more so when that nation was at war with his own—and, by the latest reports, the war was heating up rapidly.

"Yes, he is here." A sudden impulse swept over her. Probably undiplomatic as all hell, but . . .

Oh, she just *couldn't* resist.

"Indeed," she said firmly. "After an extended and relentless campaign—a veritable Champion of Lust, that man—Ruy Sanchez de Casador y Ortiz has finally succeeding in worming his way into my bed."

She pressed the back of her wrist again her forehead; the gesture was as flamboyantly histrionic as anything Ruy himself might have done. "I fear I was taken completely off-guard. The flatteries, the flowers—certainly the plying with wine—all that I expected. But I had not foreseen that the man would stoop so low as to take a sword in the guts. That duplicitous stratagem succeeded where all others had failed. I fear my reputation is now ruined."

Sharon was immensely proud of herself. She'd kept a straight face all the way through.

The old cardinal smiled thinly. "Yes, indeed. The man is amazingly stubborn and persistent. He's driven me to the edge of madness with it, at times."

But the smile didn't extend to the eyes. Sharon suddenly realized that Bedmar was a very worried man.

"Signora . . . please." The Spanish ambassador swallowed. "Ruy and I go back many years together. I would know how he is. Please."

Sharon found herself swallowing a lump. However the relationship between Bedmar and Sánchez had gotten started, and whatever its formal nature, she understood in that moment something she should have

understood simply from knowing Ruy himself. Ruy Sanchez, ruthless as he might be, was no Michel Ducos.
And Bedmar was no Seigneur le Comte d'Avaux, who
would treat his most trusted agent and bodyguard as
a mere lackey.

"My apologies, Your Eminence," she murmured. Then,
stood aside and motioned with her hand. "Please, come
in. I'll take you to him immediately. He's awake now.
Was, at least, when I left him two minutes ago."

As they moved through the salon leading to the great
central staircase, the cardinal gave Sharon a sidelong
look. "Did you really put him in your own bed?"

"Yes. It's a good bed—one of the best in the
embassy—and I can easily manage in one of the Stone
boys' rooms. He is absent at the moment." She decided
not to mention that the Stone kids seemed to have
all decamped on some hare-brained scheme. Bedmar
probably already knew, but . . .

She hurried past the problem. "I'll be spending most
of my time in that room anyway, except when I'm
actually sleeping. It's big and I'm used to it, so . . . it
just seemed like the best place to put him."

She saw no reason to mention the confusing swirl of
emotions that had been involved in the decision also.
Listen to your woman! she'd screamed at the man, less
than two days before, in what could quite literally be
called the heat of action.

Had she meant it? She still didn't know herself.
Looking back, she could see that it had been, tactically, exactly the right thing to say to get Ruy out of
her line of fire. *And that's* still *the party line,* she told
herself firmly.

But . . .

She hadn't been thinking tactically at all, at the
moment she said it. They had just been words, boiling
up out of a cauldron of fear and fury. *In vino veritas,*
the old saying went. In wine there is truth. Could the
same be said of adrenaline?

She didn't know; wasn't even prepared to think about it now. What she *did* know was that Ruy Sanchez could quite possibly be dead very soon. That bed was, perhaps, the last bed he would ever sleep in. So had come the decision, as of its own volition, just like the words she'd screamed.

If that was to be Ruy Sanchez's last bed, then it would be hers. Even if it had never been put to its accustomed use between man and woman. He would still die in it.

And, on the plus side, it might help keep the pestiferous man alive. Most doctors and all nurses understood that a cheerful patient—especially a sanguine one—had a better chance of surviving serious illness than one who was morose and gloomy. Finding himself in Sharon's own bed when he came out of anesthesia had certainly seemed to pick up Sanchez's spirits.

Old goat.

The first victory! Then had come the inevitable stroking of the mustachios. *Now I must only persuade the slippery woman to get back into her own bed. An interesting twist* . . .

Bedmar seemed to understand at least some of what was involved. As they moved up the stairs, he gave her another sidelong glance. "It seems important to tell you that Ruy Sanchez has spoken of you many times." The cardinal's old lips thinned. "Sometimes to the point of sheer tedium. For me, if not him. But he has—never once—told me anything of what, ah, you might call his amatory success."

Bedmar shook his head. "He is something of peculiar man, you know. Where others would lie in order to boast before their fellows, he would—ha!" He gave Sharon an almost gleeful cock of the head. "Do you know that—just five days ago—I had to drag him away from a levee lest he challenge one of these Venetian merchants to a duel? The man had offended him by making sly innuendos complimenting Sanchez on his success in bedding you."

Sharon's eyed widened. "You have *got* to be kidding. Ruy was going to fight a guy"—she grimaced, now having seen what a Ruy Sanchez fight looked like—"because he assumed that Ruy had seduced me? Which, in point of fact, is exactly what Ruy has been trying to do these past many weeks."

"Oh, indeed." Bedmar barked a laugh. "And they make jokes about we Castilians and our touchy honor! I sometimes think a proper Catalan would take offense at the movement of the heavenly bodies, did the mood take him. Challenge the moon to a duel. Rise before dawn to meet it sword in hand. And then accuse the moon of cowardice and dishonor when it refused to appear on the chosen ground."

Sharon shook her head. "You may well be right. I don't know. Ruy is the only Catalan I've ever met, so far as I know."

They'd reached the door to her bedroom. Sharon opened it and ushered the cardinal in.

Ruy was lying in the bed, glaring at the window.

"You malingering bastard," growled the cardinal. "And who gave you permission in the first place to go pick a fight on behalf of these heretics? Who are also, I might remind you, our king's mortal enemies. For the moment."

"Never mind that," Sanchez growled. "Spanish kings change enemies as often as they change clothes, and you know it as well as I do."

He pointed an accusing finger at the window. "Something's going out there! What is it? I can't hear well enough because the window is closed."

Now he glared at Sharon. "And I can't get up and look for myself because *she* told me not to move."

Bedmar's eyes widened. "And you obeyed her?" He turned and gave Sharon a very courtly bow. "My deepest congratulations, signora. You have succeeded where princes of state and church alike have failed often enough. Ignominiously, at times."

Ruy slapped a hand on the bedcovers. "Damnation! What is happening?"

"Oh, hold your horses," Sharon snorted, moving toward the window. As she drew near, she realized that Ruy was right. There *was* some kind of commotion going on out there.

She hurried a little, the last few paces, to throw open the window. Then, leaned over to look out.

"Oh, my."

"What is it, signora?" The cardinal had come to stand behind her. Then: "Interesting."

He took his head out of the window and looked back at Sanchez. "It will be a bit more difficult to escape this time, I fear. With you in that absurd condition!"

Sanchez winced. "The Arsenalotti? Again?"

But Sharon had been listening more closely. And she was probably the only one of the three in the room who could have really followed the—ah, debate—going on below. Most of the exchange between Billy Trumble and his two Marines and the mob gathering outside the embassy was taking place between Billy and his friend Conrad Ursinus. Who, naval officer of the USE or not, seemed to be the leader of the mob.

Well . . . not exactly. Leader, perhaps, but also one who was trying to convince his followers to follow him.

It was her turn to wince. Ursinus really *did* have an impressive command of the cruder forms of invective. Billy Trumble was no slouch either, come to it.

"Just stay put, Sanchez," she commanded. "The gist of what's happening is that Billy is assuring the crowd that you Spaniards were not complicit in the foul and dastardly and—oh lots of other words—murder of Joe Buckley. Indeed, he is casting some aspersions on the crowd itself—he really shouldn't use language like that—for their, ah, stupidity is the mildest term he's used so far, in even thinking so."

She pursed her lips for a moment, whistling a little. "Um. That was a particularly unnecessary flourish, I think. Now he's pointing out to the crowd—mostly in what we'd call four letter terms—that even sorry imbecilic—ah, that last expression refers to incestuous persons—should have enough sense to understand who was really to blame. The more so since the Venetian residents on Murano who came to our aid immediately thereafter will vouch—I'm really cleaning this up a lot, you understand; maybe in another universe I should look into getting a job as a UN translator—that we found evidence planted by Ducos' agents as well, of course, as having two of the agents themselves now in the custody of the Venetians—although God knows what's happened to them since—and—"

She broke off, recoiling from the window as if suddenly splashed by a wave. "Oh, Lord! Now Conrad's getting into the act—his language *really* stinks—I wonder if he and Billy set this up ahead of time?—and the gist of what he's saying, leaving aside about five hundred *I-told-you-sos*, is that they ought to be heading for the French embassy."

The crowd started chanting something. The name "d'Avaux" figured prominently in the chants. Within seconds, the sound of the chants grew dimmer in the distance.

Sharon closed the window. "And that's that. I do hope, for his sake, that the comte has a fast horse."

"Sweet it is," murmured Bedmar. He took three little prancing steps. "I could die now, happily. That stinking Frenchman, on the run!"

Ruy shared none of his glee. Again, he slapped the bedcovers. "Curse you, woman! I want to *watch*."

"You don't *move,* Sanchez," she hissed. "You don't even *think* about it."

Bedmar, grinning, plunked himself on the bed next to Ruy. "So, Ruy, tell me. How were you so foolish as to let"—he pointed a finger at Sharon—"that Gorgon, that Medusa, that black demoness from the Pit, inveigle you into her bed?"

"She tricked me," Ruy insisted. "It was most foully done. Lured me into an ambush, the witch."

Chapter 41

"Yes, Frank, you." Marcoli said. In just such tones might he have ordered Frank to form up a party of men and Take That Hill.

Frank stole a glance at Giovanna. She was gazing at him, eyes shining. Frank knew in that moment that whatever they did to convicted felons in Italy in the seventeenth century, he had no choice but to face it with a smile. *Her eyes!*

He couldn't see a way out, unless . . . "What about Michel?"

"*Non*, Frank," Ducos said firmly. "I am really little more than a clerk. Oh, for certain, I am from the back alleys of Paris and I own myself a fair hand in any desperate business. But I have not the temperament to be a leader—whereas you do, Frank."

"Me?" Frank found that particularly mystifying. He'd been brought up a hippie, not an army brat. At least he *thought* army brats grew up knowing about this chain-of-command stuff. Kids on a commune sure didn't.

On the other hand . . .

Well, yes, he supposed it might be true that he was often the guy who seemed to get things organized. That wasn't just true with his brothers, either, something which could be explained by the fact that he was the oldest. He'd been the one who got the soccer league organized and off the ground, too.

Um. And now that Frank thought about it, if he hadn't been along on this expedition they'd probably still be in the outskirts of Venice. Frank had been the one who'd constantly finagled the Marcolis to settle on a course of action—*any* course of action—and just do it. Antonio Marcoli was a natural leader in terms of charisma and decisiveness, to be sure. The problem was that his enthusiasm for just about everything led him to change his mind about four times an hour—each new change of plan being advanced just as enthusiastically and decisively as the preceding ones. Following the man was a bit like following a child leading the way in an amusement park. He wanted to take all the rides at once.

Still, there just *had* to be a better way out of this. "Messer Marcoli, I'm only nineteen years old—well, okay, almost twenty. Still, by your standards—even, some ways, the standards of my own folk—I'm not a grown man yet."

"Nonsense!" Michel exclaimed. "Age has nothing to do with leadership. Consider Alexander the Great. And you have already devised a plan to avoid our assassins!"

Frank stumbled over the analogy with Alexander. "Huh? I did? What are you talking about?"

"The route through Ravenna!" Michel clapped him on the back. The kind of hearty, manly reassurance that raised the hackles of every hippie-trained instinct Frank had. He really didn't like Ducos, he finally decided.

"Hold on, Michel!" Frank protested. "*You* decided on Ravenna."

"Ah, but I would not have thought to go another way than the main road to begin with! Truly I would not, Frank. I have some small command of the geography of this country, but I lack the supple mind, the decisiveness. You supplied these lacks. I can assist with the details in some small way, but . . ." Michel trailed off with a very expressive, and very Gallic shrug.

"I don't even know where Ravenna is—"

"Have no fear, Frank!" Marcoli said. "I came prepared. I have a map!"

Great, Frank thought. *A seventeenth-century map, I'll bet.* He wondered whether they should have thought to bust out one of the up-time maps that he knew the embassy had. Too late now, of course. One foot back in Venice and they'd be lucky to get as much as ten yards off the boat before they were jumped by assassins. Did they dress all in black, with masks, he wondered? Or was that just ninjas?

Maybe they had ninjas in Venice. There'd be a hell of a market for their services, he thought sourly. Maybe there were adverts in the *Ninja Times of Japan.* "Come to Venice for the most lucrative working holiday of your life!"

At that point Frank realized he was on the verge of decidedly unmanly hysterics—which was definitely not the thing to do with *that* look in Giovanna's eyes. Dark brown or not, the eyes seemed as bright as anything he'd ever seen. "Okay," he muttered.

"So you will lead! Okay! Splendid! And your plan for Ravenna is a good one, for it lets you avoid Florentine lands, where we might have had trouble." Marcoli positively beamed. Like a lot of folks down-time, he'd picked up the word *okay* very quickly. No wonder, it was a useful word.

Frank had a whole lot more useful words assembled to go, too, right on the tip of his tongue. Words and terms he had to firmly suppress, like *out of your mind* and *you gotta be kidding.*

There was just no way, not with that look on Giovanna's face. Her expression was an odd combination of adoration, serenity and smugness. Frank understood that he'd crossed some kind of invisible line here. Giovanna's beloved father had just more or less officially declared him a Certified Adult Male, Prime Cut. Eminently suitable for his daughter in all respects. That magic moment—simultaneously treasured and dreaded in varying proportions by all involved parties—when the Prospective Father-in-Law solemnly avers and avows that The Young Fellow Is Okay With Him.

It was a bit like being branded. As Frank recalled from various movies he'd seen, the calf always bellowed in protest. As much, he suspected, due to its fear of the future—*yup, young fella, you're now certified Grade-A meat on the hoof*—as the pain of the moment.

He felt like bellowing himself. *How in the hell did I ever wind up in this fix?* It was as if fate and destiny had guided him as surely—and with as much malice aforethought—as ranchers herded their cattle into the slaughtering pens.

Firmly, he shook his head. Giovanna was at the center of this, after all, as least so far as he was concerned. And she was hardly the equivalent of a slaughtering pen.

Frank took a long slow breath, his eyes closed, doing his best to think everything through. Everything that mattered to *him,* leaving aside what he thought about the Galileo affair. Getting married at an early age didn't hold the same fears for Frank that it might for most nineteen-year-olds. Rather the opposite, in fact. Most kids hadn't been raised on a hippie commune. Yes, there were advantages; and, all things considered, Tom Stone was probably about as good a dad as you could ask for. But Frank also understood the limits of the "free and easy life." Truth be told, there was something deeply attractive to him about the kind of traditional marriage that he was looking at here. "Traditional," as in seventeenth century.

He opened his eyes and looked at Giovanna. She

met his gaze happily, confidently, serenely. The girl was almost two years younger than Frank. But she had made her decision and had no problem with it at all. That she wanted Frank as much as he wanted her, he knew for sure by now. *Till death do us part* and all that, too. Whatever her ideological notions, Giovanna was really no modern girl. That was part of the attraction, Frank knew. He had no idea where his own mother had wandered off to, after she left the commune. Neither did Ron; neither did Gerry. Whereas none of Giovanna Marcoli's kids would ever wonder about what had happened to her. She'd either be there, or she'd be in a grave.

Say whatever else you would about the Marcolis, not one of them was faithless.

Okay, done, he said to himself. It was time to decide, and the decision was really easy to make. Even if it did lock him into the goofiest set of in-laws anybody could hope to have. And even if it did commit him to lead what was probably the screwiest political caper anybody had ever come up with.

See if you think that on the rack, lover boy, came a little Voice of Treason.

But Frank chose to ignore the voice. Much as Alexander the Great, he fancied for a moment, chose to ignore the odds at Issus.

Yup. He died young too, snickered the Voice. *Thirty-three. You'll beat that by a country mile. Here lies Frank Stone. 1984 to 1634. The only Great Hero on record dumb enough to kill himself off three hundred and fifty years before he was even born.*

Dino put his head around the door at that moment. "The carts, they are here."

"I guess we better get loaded up, then," Frank said firmly.

He turned back to Antonio. "Messer Marcoli, I want to marry your daughter."

He heard Giovanna clap her hands, once, but kept his eyes on the father.

"Of course," Marcoli said immediately. "I can think of no man I should rather have for a son-in-law." He gave his daughter a quick, sly glance. "Nor do I foresee any problems in convincing the child to respect her father's wishes."

Frank risked a glance himself. Giovanna's smile was the widest he'd ever seen on any human being. Anatomically speaking, it was a little scary.

But he brought his eyes back to Marcoli at once. The hard part was still to come. "We can't get married today. It's just not possible."

Marcoli frowned. "Well, of course not. Posting the banns alone would require—" He broke off suddenly, glancing back and forth between Frank and Giovanna. "Ah."

The frown deepened. For a moment, threatening to become Jovian. Then, to Frank's relief, began to fade away.

"To be sure," Marcoli murmured. "You will want your intended to accompany you to Rome."

"Yes, sir. Ah . . ." How to say it? "It will be dangerous for you here, sir. You and Massimo both. What with the assassins coming after us."

Marcoli waved his hand. "Yes, yes, I understand. A desperate business. Massimo and I will shortly be on the run, I have no doubt at all. Our chances? Not good. No, not good. I agree. Giovanna would be safer with you."

He swiveled his head and gave his daughter an intense scrutiny. "Intense," as in Marcoli-intense.

Then, seemingly satisfied, Marcoli looked back at Frank. "I give my permission. I will trust you not to take advantage of the situation until you can find the time and place for a wedding. I would not see my daughter dishonored."

"My word on it, sir."

Massimo had awakened, apparently, somewhere in the middle of all this. Frank heard him issue a derisive snort.

"You are mad, cousin. Look at them! As well command water not to run downhill."

Marcoli glared at his cousin. Massimo was now levering himself upright on his bed. "Still," he said, "I agree with the decision itself. We must be decisive at all times—here above all others. Better to risk—"

Massimo gave Marcoli a glare of his own. "—something which has been *known* to happen in this family—my own sister! Giovanna's mother! two days before the wedding! don't try to pretend!—"

Antonio Marcoli flushed and looked away. His eyes carefully avoided his daughter's.

"—*without* any noticeable catastrophe, I would point out." Massimo cleared his throat. "Better that than to fail in saving our great Italian savant. The young man here—fine young man, yes, I fully agree—will do far better if he can concentrate on the task without worrying about what might have happened to his betrothed."

Massimo was now sitting fully upright and, concussion or no concussion, was gesticulating with his usual intellectual's enthusiasm. "Besides—I am the theoretician here, don't forget—I suspect we need to modify our program on this matter in any event."

He came to an abrupt halt, eyeing Frank and then Giovanna. "After these two impressionable youngsters have departed, however."

"Leaving right now," Frank announced. He extended his hand. "Giovanna?"

She skipped to her feet. "Coming!"

"You're sure?" Tom Stone demanded. "I mean, like, positive? They didn't just, you know, maybe go off on a long picnic or something?"

Lennox was shaking his head before Tom had finished the sentence.

"Goan," said Lennox, in a tone lugubrious even for him. "I found yon papist drunkard bemoanin't the lack ae 'em."

Sharon felt a chill run down her spine. This was too much. Buckley dead, Ruy fighting for his life, and now Lennox had brought Heinzerling in to report that all three of the Stone boys had definitely vanished. And, more to the point, that they had discovered several people who'd seen them leaving the city in the company of the Marcolis.

That had been the last, lingering hope—that, maybe, the bizarre "evidence" of a plot against the pope's life which they'd found in the Marcoli house had been entirely faked by Ducos' agents.

Sharon didn't have any doubt at all that the so-called evidence about a plot to kill the pope was fraudulent. No matter how scrambled his brains might be by hormones, she knew Frank Stone well enough to know that he'd never have agreed to something like that. But the other business . . . about rescuing Galileo . . .

It was all she could do not to groan out loud. When she'd passed on the information to Ruy just an hour ago, he'd immediately confirmed her own private assessment.

"Oh, yes," the Catalan had said confidently. "It all makes sense, Sharon. The business about assassinating the pope is nonsense, of course. But a rescue of Galileo? That would be exactly the sort of idiot scheme that a man like Marcoli would develop—and which would seem attractive enough to naive boys. Very romantic. It also explains Ducos' involvement—as well as his murder of Buckley. He would plant evidence trying to implicate them in a much worse design, in order to embarrass your embassy still further, increase the Venetians' ties to the French, and drive a wedge between Paris and the Vatican. But, then, he had to murder Buckley to keep Buckley—the one man everyone would believe, in this matter—from being able to deny it."

Lennox had had the first report from one of his sergeants, the Catholic one named Southworth, that there had definitely been something afoot in Venice among the Committee crowd. The urchin Benito was not the only one, apparently, before whom the Marcolis had carelessly prattled. Lennox had gone looking for Heinzerling then, to ask him if there was anything he was mindful of. When he found Heinzerling, he had practically taken the Jesuit by the scruff of the neck to make his report.

"Gus?" Stoner asked.

"*Ja*," Heinzerling said, his voice croakier even than usual. "It is that we had drinks—Ron Stone and Fabrizio Marcoli and myself—in the Casino dei Tre Radi, several days ago, and there were more drinks at another Casino whose name I forget. It is Carnivale, *ja*?"

Stoner nodded. "Go on."

"There was discussion of the Galileo book, which has been recalled recently by the Inquisition." Heinzerling stopped and rubbed his forehead. "It is there that I began to debate with Monsignor—I cannot remember his name—but he is now the state theologian at Venice."

"He was at the casino, consorting with Committee members?" Sharon was a bit intrigued. The monsignor in question was a notorious firebrand who had spoken out for Galileo. The thought of him squaring off with Heinzerling's drunken eloquence was—entertaining, she realized, but not relevant. And the issue of what a senior theologian was doing in a casino knocking down drinks with the likes of Ron Stone and Fabrizio Marcoli could also abide. "Never mind that," she said before Heinzerling could respond, "when did you realize the boys were missing?"

Heinzerling bit his lower lip and sighed deeply. The glum expression made his muttonchop whiskers bristle, reinforcing the impression he gave of being a prize boar in a clerical outfit. "Well. Not until today, for a certainty—but I should have seen it coming then. The problem is that I was preoccupied. The monsignor and I came to words over the proposition of whether *summa fideei* should be expressed through—"

Sharon held up a hand. Gus' capability for theological excursion was vast, creative and best stopped before it started if there was any urgent secular business at hand. "*What* should you 'have seen coming'?"

"Galileo." Gus's tone managed to grow a notch gloomier. He looked to Sharon like he was on the verge of tears. "They would rescue him, I am now sure of it."

Stoner's voice was soft, although he sounded like he was on the verge of shouting. "Rescue," he said. "Rescue." And then a long pause. "The Inquisition have got him, then?"

Heinzerling gave a little groan, by way of running up to coherent speech. "The Inquisition have had him since last year," he said. "He was ordered not to travel or to print further copies of his latest book, which is about the motion of the Earth. The news is that he is recovered the illness by which the Inquisition excused him travel to Rome, and is now going there under guard. Some stories say he is in irons. I do not believe that myself but—"

He was interrupted by the door banging open. "Where are they gone?" shouted Magda as she swept in. She was flushed and looked—dangerous. She was a young woman, slender and usually dignified, grave even, in her manner. Spitting fury was not a state Sharon had ever seen her in. Even Magda's anger at the boor Falier had been moderate in comparison.

There was this to be said for Hanni's tendency to haul off and belt her husband upside the head—she could cool off fairly quickly when she had vented her rage and never quite seemed to be unhappy for long. Sharon began to wish one or another of the Stones would cut loose properly at Gus—

And Magda did. She paused hardly a moment before letting rip. Fully five minutes of sustained invective in two languages—no, three, it sounded like there had been some Latin in there.

"And you!" she said, rounding on Lennox. "You will send men! All your men if you have to! You will get them back!"

Lennox joined Heinzerling in the group cringe that looked set to take in every man in the room. "Aye. I'll do that, right enough. I'll take yon papist, wit' y'r permission?"

It was unclear exactly who was being asked for permission. Sharon glanced at Stoner. He seemed in too much of a daze to think clearly.

Sharon decided her temporary ambassador status was still operating. "Yes, certainly. Will you leave some of the guard?"

"Aye. Lieutenant Taggart will hae command of't. Young Trumble I'll take wit me—'e can be the second, for his education. No tellin' what mischief the lad would get into if left behind. Sergeant Southworth and four lads will come wi' me too. Sergeant Dalziel will have the running of the guard here, since he's the senior man."

"Why Southworth?" Sharon asked. The young English sergeant seemed to be something of an outsider among the mostly Scots troops, an infantryman who had joined the Marines and been assigned to the wholly anomalous Marine Cavalry Troop.

"He's a friend o' Frank Stone, to start wit'. 'At may coom in handy. Beyond that, Aidan's a guid lad, right enough, f'r a sassenach, an' wi' the lads short-handed I want an old hand here and Dalziel's that. Besides, if yon drunkard"—he nodded toward Heinzerling—"takes to his cups, Southworth has the heathen talk o' these parts better than any other man w'hae."

Sharon nodded. For all Lennox talked a bigoted line, he was actually a lot less prejudiced than most men she knew.

Lennox snapped a salute. "Richt. C'mon Father Heinzerling, ye sot of a Jesuit. Ye're to come and lead us tae Rome or wherever."

"Wait a minute," Sharon said. She had a sudden nightmare vision of Lennox and Heinzerling blundering about northern Italy with no real clue where they were going. "Start by going to Maestro Luzzatto. He won't be any use himself, but he can put you in touch with Giuseppe Cavriani. Tell Cavriani that I—Magda and I, rather—insist that he serve you as a guide."

Stoner stared at her. "Why would he agree to do that? He's got a business to run."

Magda snorted. Sharon just grinned. "Stoner, you really need to pay more attention to all those papers you sign. You *are* Cavriani's business, these days. Well, in the real world, me and Magda are. It's just disguised by this idiot business—and where's Gloria Steinem when you really want her?—of not accepting women as signatories on commercial deals. The point is, you are now one of the richest men in Italy."

"I am?"

"Yup. And she and I"—Sharon pointed a finger at Magda—"are two of the richest women. She because she's your wife, and me because I don't do anything in business without getting a cut. My father's a bit oblivious to these things, but my momma didn't raise no fools."

Stoner looked back and forth between them. "You are?"

"Are what? Rich, or a fool? Yes to the first, no to the second. But to get back to the point, Crazy Giuseppe is by now easily the most successful Cavriani on record. The one thing he will *not* want to do is tick off his meal ticket. If we tell him to go, he'll go. Knowing Giuseppe, he'll even go cheerfully. They don't call him Crazy for nothing."

"T'will lose us time," Lennox objected. "Be a full day afore we c'n nab yon swindler and muscle him along."

Sharon managed not to sneer. Barely. "Big deal. You lose a day at the beginning—instead of losing two weeks getting lost. And what's a day? You're tracking the *Marcolis,* Captain. By all accounts, their progress across Italy will look like Buster Keaton building a sailboat."

That got a round of laughs. Anyone who lived in Grantville for any length of time became a Buster Keaton aficionado. For some reason, Keaton's brand of silent slapstick comedy struck a chord with down-timers that Charlie Chaplin rarely did.

"True enough," Lennox grunted. He gave Heinzerling a glance. "Let's be off, then."

The two big men went out, grimly silent.

"Uh," said Stoner, "shouldn't they be going with more men?"

"I'm sure Captain Lennox knows best how to organize a chase," said Sharon.

"He had better," said Magda. "He had better."

For his sake, Sharon hoped he did.

Part V: May, 1634

Oh, sir, she smiled, no doubt,
Whene'er I passed her; but who passed without
Much the same smile? This grew; I gave
    commands;
Then all smiles stopped together. There she stands
As if alive. Will't please you to rise? We'll meet
The company below, then.

Chapter 42

It was, of course, too hot. Lennox had grown up near Dunbar and spent the last few years rattling around northern Germany. This, by all accounts a balmy spring day for Venice, was what he would think of as a scorching summer day. Venice was still just visible as he looked back, blued in the distance and hazy with the miles.

The horses were sweating already, although part of that was the nervousness of crossing on the flotilla of boats they'd hired in a hurry to take them to the mainland. They'd brought two remounts for everyone except the commercial agent, Giuseppe Cavriani, who'd joined them at the last minute. Cavriani seemed to know what he was doing around a horse, though, even with Lennox not inclined—between the heat and the shudders of his stomach after so short a boat trip on the virtually flat lagoon—to be in the least charitable.

And charitable he'd have to be to describe that fat papist Heinzerling as any kind of horseman. Oh, he was a fine enough fellow, for a damned Jesuit, but putting him on a horse was a cruelty to man and beast alike. Not just for the weight of the man—there were such

things as big horses—but for the way he sat the poor
creature. They could put a lad behind the horse with
a shovel, pile the results in a sack across the saddle,
and there'd be a definite improvement in the overall
grace of the whole picture.

For all that, the Jesuit could stay in the saddle
and ride well enough to cover ground. They'd have
to keep to roads, though. The thought of Heinzerling
going neck-or-nothing across the Borders of Lennox's
youth was almost as good as a Buster Keaton movie
for laughs.

Lennox kept his gaze carefully away from the hustle
and shift of his fellows getting their gear triced up and
themselves mounted, until an expectant silence told him
that his sergeant was satisfied with the state of things.
That was the hardest thing to do, something that came
easy to the likes of Mister MacKay, who'd been born
to his gentleman's station and was used to being done
for. The Inner Sergeant kept telling Lennox to turn
about and fuss over the detachment he'd brought. He
resisted it, though, and turned to his men.

Good turnout, he thought, looking over them.
Heinzerling and Cavriani were beside him, discussing
something about their route in an undertone. Both of
them spoke in Italian, Cavriani's first language despite
being born in Geneva, and one of the huge number
Heinzerling spoke. Lennox didn't have a notion what
they were on about, so he addressed his men.

"Lads," he said, "We've tae catch the Doctor Stone's
boys before they get in any mair trouble. So we've not to
add to yon trouble our ain selves. Beggin' your presence,
Sergeant Southworth, we're Protestants in a nation o'
Catholics and soldiers o' the United States Marines abroad
on duty. So we've to give no bad account o' ourselves."
He dropped to a growl. "T'at means keep ye're thievin'
honds tae yersels and ye're britches buttoned."

Not that that much needed saying, he thought.
He'd picked good lads against that eventuality. Ritson,

a sassenach but a solid, older man. Chosen man, in the regiment that was but didn't have his letters well enough for the new armed forces, he'd do if Southworth ever didn't. MacNeish, a teuchter but a solid man for all that, and Faul and Milton, both Scots. Southworth was a new lad, on the young side for a sergeant. He'd been a corporal until recently—the new American word for a chosen man still sounded odd to Lennox—but he had his letters and seemed to want to prove himself as the only papist noncom in the largely Protestant Marine Cavalry.

Good troopers—Marines, rather. Lennox still found himself occasionally using the old term. Well, to business. He turned to the priest and the facilitator, as Cavriani chose to call himself. "Have you gentlemen decided on our route?"

Cavriani nodded. "Captain, if you can lay us a course due southwest?"

"Aye, right enough I can." Lennox pulled from his pocket one of the new compasses that were being made in Grantville. They weren't much like the Silva ones that had been brought back—those had all gone with the engineers surveying for new roads, canals and mines—but they were a good deal better than the kind of instrument Lennox was used to seeing officers getting lost with.

"I've no good map, mind." The best one, which fit in his sabretache, had been traced from one that showed all of Italy on one small sheet. The major roads of the old Roman Empire were on it, and not much more. The other one, in a roll he'd tied across his saddle, had been drawn a few years before, and they had bought it in Venice just after they had arrived there. Lennox had realized, looking at it, that he had been badly spoiled by the kinds of maps Grantville had had; even the kind of maps they were making now in the USE. From the point of view of a cavalryman, down-time maps . . . sucked.

"We will be able to manage, I think," said Cavriani. "Southwest from here, cross the Adige as soon as we may and continue until we reach the road south to Ferrara. We should be there by tonight. Perhaps thirty, forty miles?"

"We'll be ahead of them?" Lennox liked the sound of a mere thirty or forty miles before sundown. With this small a party and with remounts, that should not be difficult.

"Assuming that they proceed to Rome, and I have every belief that they are going there, yes. I also have information that Marcoli chartered boats to Padua." Cavriani was beginning to sound less like a commercial agent and more like a soldier with every word, Lennox noticed. He supposed it was like riding a horse; you never really forgot how. He'd be interested to find out what the man's history had been. He hadn't always been a facilitator, of that Lennox was well-nigh certain.

"Padua?" Lennox frowned. From memory that was off to the west of Venice, and Rome was almost due south.

Cavriani nodded. "From Padua, the road south takes you through Ferrara, Bologna, Firenze, and thence on to Rome. Very simple, very easy, and the most direct route. Coming to Chioggia and going across country to Ferrara, I think we will cut the corner and arrive there first. They will have passed much of the first day traveling to Padua, stayed there the night, and set out for Ferrara on the morrow. Despite having started three days before us, they'll be moving much more slowly. My reports tell me that they are hauling a volume of baggage which borders on the insane. We should expect them either late tomorrow or early the next day."

"You're sure they'll do that?" Lennox had to check, although doing so was ringing all manner of internal alarms. His Inner Sergeant was reacting to Cavriani as an officer, not simply as a civilian and a foreigner to boot. That said, he recognized the tendency and the man had a plan that made sense by Lennox's map. The other route, by way of Ravenna and Rimini, was farther off the straight line, and required that they take back roads that would be hard to find their way on. The embassy was fairly certain that none of the good maps were missing, and none of them showed the small routes either.

Cavriani nodded. "Ferrara it is," said Lennox. He took a sight with the compass. "To yon village first. Lead on, if you would."

Cavriani touched the brim of his cavalier hat in salute, wheeled his mount and moved off at trot.

Lennox turned in his saddle. "Marines! Walk-march! Trot!"

And they were off.

"*Merde.*"

Frank had a rough idea what that word was French for, and the feeling with which Michel said it removed all doubt. "We're lost, aren't we?"

They were sitting on the driving seat of the first of the two wagons. Giovanna, Gerry and Dino were perched on their gear in the wagon-bed behind them, and the others were in the second wagon. They'd managed to stay somewhere near southwest for most of the morning, while the sun gave them some kind of clue which way they were headed. But then they'd taken a wrong turning somewhere. The sun was coming down in front of them, which definitely wasn't right.

It didn't help that the transport they had was pulled by what had to be the two oldest horses in Italy. Frank had seen, and dealt with, more horses in the three years since the Ring of Fire than he'd had to do with in the whole of his life before. He was never going to call himself any kind of equestrian expert, but this pair of nags were candidates for the glue-factory any day now. As a result, neither of them were in any great hurry to be off anywhere.

"You think we could get more horses? Or just different ones?" Frank wondered aloud, as he watched the bony ass in front of him plod along. They'd tried inspiring the beasts with the buggy whips that came with the carts. The only response had been a flick of an ear and a look over the shoulder with a round, white-edged and rheumy eye that said, in clear Equine, *You must be joking.* They hadn't tried again. "I think this one's older than I am."

Michel snorted. "Messer Frank, I think this horse is older than *I* am. I did not like to say at Padua, as Messer Marcoli had gone to such trouble, but . . ." Michel gave one of those wonderfully expressive French shrugs. The one that said, *In a perfect world, monsieur, it would be otherwise. But what can you do?*

Frank opened up the map, trying to get some notion of where they were again. He was no more successful than he had been the last time he'd tried. That had been—he looked at his watch—five minutes ago. The damned thing had been hand-drawn on something that felt like leather—too thick to be parchment or vellum, he thought, or maybe it was just expensive, hard-wearing stuff. Whoever had drawn it had been a whiz with curlicues and fancy writing. He'd been a world's expert on spouting whales and dreadful serpents in the sea. Frank doubted there was a better man anywhere for intricate little details in the corners or stylized representations of the Four Winds. He had, however, had no truck with fancified modern notions of a map actually representing anything on the ground. If nothing else, Frank knew for a fact that Italy wasn't that shape. The famous boot looked more like a fat slug crawling its way toward Africa.

What the hell were they going to do? This would be a good one for the Committee propaganda mill, he thought. *Heroic rescue party dies of old age trying to find first major town on their route.* Or, better still: *Bold rescue party gets halfway there, horses boldly die of old age, film at eleven.* What to do?

There was a rustle of skirts. Giovanna leaned over the back of the driving bench between Frank and Michel. "Should we ask for directions?"

Both Frank and Michel looked at her. "Eh?" Frank said.

"One of these fellows"—she waved to the side of the road—"might know where we are. And the way to Ravenna."

"What, you mean just ask?" Frank demanded. The little voice in the back of his mind muttered, *Stereotype warning! You are acting like a stereotype male! Warning! Warning!*

There were times when having been raised by Tom Stone was a real pain in the butt. On the other hand . . .

Well, actually, it *did* make sense. "Sure," said Frank. "Stop the cart, Michel."

Ducos' expression was as sour as you could ask for. But he was hoist on his own petard, since he'd insisted himself that Frank was the leader of the party. So, however grudgingly, he did as he was told.

Frank got down, trusting to Salvatore on the cart behind to stop in time. Or, more accurately, trusting the horse. Near as Frank could tell, the horses were both better drivers than anyone on the carts.

They'd been ambling slowly into a village that consisted of a small cluster of houses and a church. There was a orchard of some kind next to the road. Frank was pretty sure it was an olive grove, although he wouldn't swear to it. They had that dusky grayish-green color to them, anyway, which he associated with olive trees.

By the gate to the orchard was a stone bench. The little old guy who sat on it, taking his ease in the late afternoon sunshine, was straight from central casting. *Peasant, wizened, Italian, one of.* Frank suspected that he'd probably not get much sense out of the guy. But, nothing ventured, nothing gained.

"Excuse me, how do we get to Ravenna?"

"Eh?" The oldster cupped a hand behind one ear. Frank's heart sank. *Great, he's deaf.*

He repeated himself. "Excuse me, how do we get to Ravenna?"

The response was a torrent of . . . gibberish. Well, nearly gibberish.

Recollection shyly raised its hand at the back of class. Of course! Italy was full of dialects, and Frank only knew Veneziano. His heart sank. If he could barely talk to the locals this close to Venice, what was it going to be like when they got further away?

Still, Frank managed to pick out a few bits. "*Babble babble*, the priest, *garble garble*, reads books, *babble babble*, foreign parts."

The machine-gun speed hadn't helped. "More slowly, please?"

The old guy raised the volume as well as slowing down. "Talk to the priest," he said, then a few words Frank didn't recognize at all, finishing with "Foreign parts." The oldster added a hefty wad of phlegm onto the ground beside him to show his opinion of the said foreign parts.

"You say the priest?" Frank tried, slowly and loudly.

"*Si*, the priest." The old guy lifted a gnarled stick— also straight out of central casting—and pointed down the road toward the church.

Frank turned back. "I think he means we should ask at the church. I'm not sure that's a good idea?" He made it a question.

Michel shrugged. The man had a vast collection of shrugs, each subtly different. Frank wondered if the French had a school somewhere where they taught shrugging. If so, Ducos had graduated *summa cum laude*.

This one said *Maybe, maybe not. I think maybe we should chance it.*

"Okay," Frank said. After all, why not? The chances of their pursuers coming here any time soon were slim.

If they didn't know where they were themselves, how were assassins going to track them down?

The priest, when they finally found his house behind the church, turned out to be a little, cheerful, bouncy fellow, who at least had enough Veneziano to get by in and actually spoke formal Italian, which knocked down the communications barrier. And yes, he knew the way to Ravenna, and gave them directions. And indeed, there was a coaching inn only a little way further on, the establishment of his brother-in-law's uncle, who could sell them fine new horses, excellent beasts. They could be in Ravenna in two days with no unseemly haste. Perhaps they could be so good as to do humble Father Rizzi the honor of remaining for a little refreshment? He should so, so like to hear news of the wider world, what they had heard of the war in the Germanies and these strange people who had come, it was said, from the future.

Frank almost had a heart attack at that last bit, until he realized that the priest was just talking in general terms. Father Rizzi clearly understood that Frank was a foreigner of some kind, but in rural Italy—as anywhere in rural Europe and even in most cities—the concept of "foreigner" was blessedly all-inclusive. If you weren't from here—*here* being the immediate locality—you were a foreigner.

Oh, no, they couldn't possibly impose . . .

But he insisted! Positively insisted! He would not hear of a suggestion that he be inhospitable!

By the time it was all done, they had agreed to stay a little while, to have a light repast of cold chicken and ham and cheese and good, fresh bread, to sample some of the local wine and generally shoot the breeze with the good father and bring the news of the world to his sleepy hamlet.

Frank was nervous, at first, but eventually he realized the priest had no suspicions whatsoever. He was the kind of cheerful soul who simply found suspicion even more foreign territory than the nations whose news he wanted to hear. He even put them up for the night when it got late, and had his housekeeper see to their breakfast in the morning. And refused all offer of payment from their limited stocks of coin, for he had received, he said, quite enough recompense in the news they'd brought of the wider world. The villagers laughed at him for reading books and being interested in foreign places, and so it was a double joy to be brought such a wealth! He hefted the thick stack of broadsheets with Buckley's articles on them.

Setting off down the road to Ravenna, via Father Rizzi's brother-in-law's uncle's inn and used horse dealership, Frank felt kind of guilty about the whole thing. The priest had been kind and generous, feeding and sheltering them out of all proportion to what they'd given him in return. And here they were on their way to strike a blow at the church he represented.

Mostly, though, Frank was just frustrated. Really, really, really frustrated. He'd spent most of the evening wondering if he dared asked the priest to marry Giovanna and him on the spot. But . . .

It just wouldn't have worked. Las Vegas–style quickie weddings were a universe away. Leaving aside all the lengthy procedures that Frank knew a Catholic marriage required, even in his old universe, Father Rizzi would have insisted on proof of parental permission—for Giovanna, certainly, if not for Frank. To be sure, Giovanna's brothers could have vouched for the legitimacy of the whole enterprise, and there was enough a family resemblance for their sibling status to be accepted. But the priest would still have wanted a full explanation for the reason the father himself couldn't be present.

And what was there to say? *He broke his leg in Padua playing engineer and we had to leave him behind and keep going so we can rescue Galileo before the assassins catch up with us . . .*

Probably wouldn't play in Peoria. Much less here.

Frank sighed. Giovanna's hand slid alongside his ribs and caressed him. She leaned over from where she was sitting behind him and whispered in his ear. "Maybe when we get to Ferrara. If not, Rome." She punctuated the whispers with a lingering kiss to his ear that was not even remotely chaste.

Frank sighed. The new horse was a lot better, sure, but what he really wanted was a jet airliner. Rescuing Galileo—or dying in the attempt—ranked a long way second to his principal preoccupation.

On the positive side, he didn't notice any of the tedium of their slow progress through the country roads of Romagna. Neither that day, nor the next. So marvelous were the erotic fantasies that flooded his brain. Which was light-headed, anyway, because most of his blood supply seemed to be permanently concentrated in more netherly regions.

Somewhere, that nasty little voice of treason was muttering uncouth phrases about thinking with other organs than brains, but Frank paid no attention at all. Giovanna's hand was now resting more or less permanently on his ribs. Caressing, and caressing, and caressing. Compared to that promise of joy and delight, what was Reason?

Nothing more than the pathetic Persian hordes gathered at Issus. Frank sneered at it like a veritable Alexander.

Chapter 43

"Can we hae missed 'em?" Lennox was an old campaigner, used to the hurry-up-and-wait pace of a cavalryman's life, but for some reason a single day spent in Ferrara was grating on his nerves. They had spent most of it just outside town, by the north road that led back to Padua.

Heinzerling grunted a "maybe."

They'd gotten in late the night before. Naturally, the weather had picked last night to drop an unseasonal rain on them, so they had all the extra trouble of caring for horses that were muddy as well as tired. They'd mounted a watch on the road over the night, and didn't really have enough men to make it an easy watch, so everyone had been tired all day. He'd had Lieutenant Trumble stand the lads down by twos for a nap in the shade of some trees by the road, and that had helped, and there was a roadside inn just outside the town which had been only too glad to take USE silver thalers for food and wine. No sense in wasting their hard-tack, or eating it for that matter, when there was real food to be had. Not that Lennox was overjoyed to be eating the stuff they called food hereabouts. The sausage was all right, he grudgingly allowed, but the rest of it wasn't a patch on what they got back in Grantville. Or even Magdeburg.

It was an improvement on what they got in Venice, though. He'd remarked as much to Cavriani, who'd laughed and told him that Venetians were renowned as the worst cooks in Italy. That made sense. He'd been surprised to discover, when the innkeeper brought dishes out to where the Marines had taken their station, that the stuff called pasta was a lot better if it wasn't served up as near sludge, stuck together in a gluey mass that was a sore trial to a man missing as many teeth as Lennox did. It still wasn't a patch on—

He squashed the homesickness hard, and looked to the sun. Then, remembering, took out his watch. "Four of the afternoon clock," he remarked. The shadows were already starting to lengthen.

Virtually no one had passed their position during the day. He'd ordered the weapons kept out of sight and the horses picketed off the road a short way. It wasn't the way he'd ordinarily have done things, since looking well-armed and alert was a sure way to prevent attacks. On the other hand, they were within sight of a grand big town and he didn't want to have to explain anything to the town guards, or watch, or whatever they had. Best not to provoke any complaints.

Cavriani was pacing across the road, back and forth. Lennox wandered over to join him.

"Could they have taken another route?"

"Hmm?" Cavriani seemed distracted by something.

"Could they have taken another route"

"Ah?" A pause, it looked like for thought, and then, "Not without going far, far out of their way. And taking back roads, at that. I doubt that Messer Marcoli has traveled much outside Venice other than his trip to Grantville, you see. He must rely on whatever map he could afford, which will not be much. He will see the old Roman road through Bologna—"

"Which we're on, aye?" Lennox asked.

Cavriani smiled. "I beg your pardon, Captain. Roman road built by ancient Romans, rather than the road to Rome, which this most assuredly is."

"Aye?" Lennox nodded for the man to continue, intrigued in spite of himself. He'd heard some things about the pagan Romans of old, largely from hearing better-learned men than himself talk. If nothing else, a lot of the officers he'd served under got their drill and tactics out of Julius Caesar, or claimed to.

But Cavriani was carrying on, and Lennox chided himself for getting distracted. Old, and tired, and mithered with this sod of a job. "You see," Cavriani was saying, "on most maps the other route to Rome is shown as departing from this one along the Via Emilia, and that runs through Bologna. I feel sure they will have trouble even finding the route through Ravenna, let along knowing it is there. It is not so important a town as it once was, a backwater you might say, and many maps do not even show it. Especially the cheap ones."

Lennox nodded. Had he not been thinking about the worthlessness of most maps only the day before?

"Aye, weel," he said with a sigh. "Happen they passed us in the night, or hae yet tae get on the road. Or they're coming after us e'en now." He stretched the back he'd made ache by standing up most of the day. "We'll stand our watch here until last light, and have sentry-go on the road from yon inn tonight. We'll wait out tomorrow as well, and then make good speed with rested horses for this Bologna at first light the day after. If we've missed them, we've remounts and we're good Borderers all. If yourself and the big yin there"—he jerked a thumb at Heinzerling—"canna keep up, we'll see ye's in Bologna."

"Oh, I can keep up," Cavriani said, with a smile. "And Father Augustus might surprise you."

Lennox grinned. "Oh, aye, that'd be a surprise, all right."

❊   ❊   ❊

By the following morning, Lennox had changed his
mind about waiting the day. "We hae missed 'em," he
pronounced.

"Probably," agreed Heinzerling, stamping his feet
against the dawn chill. He was looking down the road
back to Padua, although the chances of anyone coming
down it at this early hour were nil.

Lennox grunted. Well, at least Heinzerling could
see something that was as plain as the nose on
his face. "We'll make a fast ride to this Fee-rensey
place, then, since Messer Cavriani says that's where
the road goes after the nearest place to cross yon
mountains." He nodded over to where the tops of
the Appennines were shining in the dawn light over
the mist.

"You mean Firenze?" Heinzerling grinned. He pronounced it exactly as Cavriani did. The Jesuit spoke
several of the Italian dialects, from being chaplain to
an assortment of mercenaries over the years.

"However they say it, mon," Lennox snapped back,
but without real anger. He had good English and German and enough of the Gaelic to swear at the few
highlanders he'd commanded over the years. A bit
of Swedish too, lately. Heinzerling liked to flaunt his
learning, one of his more annoying habits. The fat fool
still knew as little proper theology—just as Lennox had
learned at kirk!—as any other papist. One step from
heathens, the lot of them.

He stamped his own feet again. He'd heard Italian
summers could be scorching. For him, this was about
the only time of day with a civilized temperature and
it was only spring. Aye, weel . . .

"Get Messer Cavriani up, will you? I'll see the lads
are getting ready for the road. We'll either pass the
boys on the way or be waiting for them there. We
happen might have Messer Cavriani's people hire a
few local lads there to help watch, eh?"

"Turning spymaster, Herr Kapitan Lennox?" Heinzerling grinned through two days' worth of stubble.

Would it kill him to bloody well shave? "Hiring local scouts, ye daft gobshite," Lennox retorted. *Spymaster, indeed.* It was not as though he had any low opinion of the good Don Francisco, mind. It just wasn't honest work for a soldier. "An' no' another word, ye bugger, o' spyin' or the like. And while we're aboot changes o' career, do ye think to make a cavalryman? For today's ride'll see that fat German arse broken."

Heinzerling's sneer was magnificent; Lennox had to allow him that. It was just possible to admit a sneaking regard for the drunken tub of guts. He might sit a horse like a side of fat bacon, but at least he stayed on the thing and, more or less, kept up. He seemed to be able to look after his beast as well, although he'd passed the word for the troopers to keep an eye on him. Any horse bearing Heinzerling's weight was bound to see more wear and tear than a mere Romish priest could remedy. Lennox himself was no small man, but at least he wasn't carrying a half-hundredweight of butter with it.

The sniff that followed the sneer was another masterwork. "We shall see, *Herr Kapitan*, which arse is broken, this day. I have the better padding, I think you will agree. Am I not the fat papist?"

Och, the bugger's a smart one. Took ma ain line off me and turned it around. And there was a sting in it, too. Lennox wasn't the young man who could once have ridden days and nights on end and not noticed it, and truth be told he was considerably bonier about the behind than Heinzerling. "Aye, ye've y'ain cushion, right enough. It'll be threadbare by dusk, mind. Now run and get Messer Cavriani up and about."

"You called?" Cavriani stood in the inn doorway, a buff-coat wrapped tightly about him. "Curse these cold mornings."

The worst of it, the man was not joking. Lennox sighed. "The day'll warm up. And I was just saying we'll ride on for—" he paused to get the sound of the placename right "—Firenze straight away. Mind, we'll stop as little as we can, press the pace good and hard."

Cavriani groaned. "Christ, have mercy!" he exclaimed. "My ass is already about broken."

Lennox and Heinzerling looked at each other.

"What?" said Cavriani.

Florence seemed like a neat and pretty enough town, although Lennox would be the first to admit he was no great admirer of architecture and buildings and what-not.

The ride had been just as bloody painful as advertised, for the horses as well as his own backside. They'd pressed hard for the best part of two and a half days to get to Florence, and gotten away without any serious problems. That the embassy had enough funds to see them right for two remounts apiece had been their salvation, of course, even if it did make them look like a gaggle of tinker horse-copers.

Heinzerling, rot him, had coped admirably. Lennox supposed, all other things being equal, that the fat priest wasn't such a bad fellow, if he could endure a ride like that without complaint. He had to be hurting just as badly as Lennox was.

Cavriani was a sight to inspire pity. Suffering though Lennox was for not having been in a saddle for weeks before this wild goose chase, Cavriani had last sat a horse years before. And he was by no means the youngest man in their party, either. The lads—none of whom seemed to be feeling a damned thing, God rot their callow souls—had ribbed him with a good nature and seen to him without orders. They all, no doubt, remembered their own first days in the saddle.

They'd left Lieutenant Trumble in charge of keeping a watch on the road while the horses were cared for and rested at a livery on the edge of town that had been positively ecstatic to see so much business in one fell swoop. Cavriani had ambled about—conspicuously bow-legged; Lennox would have to see about getting the man some goose-grease for his sores—asking after the Marcoli party.

There had been no sign, yet. So Lennox and Heinzerling had rented a couple of nags—nothing much to look at, just not half-blown from nearly three days' hard ride across mountains—to take a look in town. Walking would have been agony, and a carriage was no way to see a town. They weren't expecting to see anything, it was just that Lennox liked to get a feel for a new place as quickly as he could. They'd wait here for a few days, he thought, keeping a watch, and if Messer Cavriani could—

Heinzerling reached over and tugged his sleeve. "Herr Kapitan? If I might disturb your rest?"

Lennox realized that he had, in fact, been nodding a little in the saddle as they rode along a cobbled streets and into a large, open square. "Aye?" he said, daring Heinzerling to comment further.

"Father Mazzare." He pointed.

Lennox stared. "Aye, so it is." The American priest was standing on the other side of the square with, it looked like, the Reverend Jones, studying the front of some building or other. A Romish church, from the looks of it. Even the outside of the thing looked idolatrous. "I'd thought myself he'd be nearer Rome by now. We should report."

"*Ja,*" agreed Heinzerling, and they rode across the square.

Mazzare and Jones both did double takes when they turned at the sound of approaching hooves and saw Lennox and Heinzerling. It turned out that they'd reached Florence two days before, and were proposing to depart in the morning.

"You nearly missed us here," the priest-turned-ambassador said. "I'd finished writing up my notes from the things we discussed in the coach, and we were just sightseeing before getting a good night's sleep and moving on. You must have just missed us at Ferrara, if I'm keeping any track of the time we've spent on the road."

"Seems like," said Lennox. "And you didn't pass anyone you recognized on the road?"

"Should we have?" Mazzare frowned.

"Aye, weel," said Lennox, sighing deeply. "It's like this, y'see . . ."

The report took a few minutes. The Reverend Jones simply let his face drop open. As well he might.

Father Mazzare's face grew progressively blanker as Lennox progressed with his report.

"Well," he said, when Lennox had finished.

"Aye," Lennox responded. "It's a muckle great stew of a thing, right enough."

"And Ducos is with them," Heinzerling added.

"Aye," Lennox added. "We were wondering about that, as it happens. Yon Marcoli fellow's none of your great schemers, it seems, and the French want to see him succeed and embarrass us all."

"That'd work," Jones said. "What were the boys thinking?"

Mazzare's face was growing eerily still. "I can guess what Frank was thinking," he said, in a voice with almost no tone to it at all.

Lennox saw that Heinzerling was growing even redder in the face than he normally was, and shifting from foot to foot.

"Father Mazzare," the big German said, "*Vielleicht* we can be charitable toward the boys, *ja*? They think to do good, by their lights, *ja*?"

"Good?" Mazzare's tone was still mild. Lennox realized, with more than a little discomfort, that Mazzare was one of those dangerous men who got more controlled and calm the angrier they became. The man was positively icy, now. Lennox realized that he really,

really did not want to be the Stone boys when Mazzare next saw them. Come to that, he didn't want to be himself if he didn't stop the Stone boys before they did whatever it was they were planning.

"Yeah, steady there, Larry," Jones said. "You said yourself lots of folks have some, ah, slightly wild ideas about what's going on with the Inquisition and Galileo and all."

Mazzare took a deep breath, murmured something quietly to himself—probably a prayer, Lennox realized—and: "Okay. Getting angry isn't going to help. Captain Lennox, you say you've not passed them on the road?"

"Aye, Your Excellency," Lennox said. Out of reflex, he was calling on all his reserves of sergeantliness.

"And you're certain they headed for Padua first?"

"Aye, Your Excellency."

"Such was the news Messer Cavriani got for us from the watermen, Father." said Heinzerling, "The Marcolis were poor at keeping secrets, it seems."

"Except from us, apparently," Mazzare snapped. "Sorry, Gus, it wasn't your fault. Will they have met Tom at Padua? Maybe he got them to turn back, and you've chased down here for nothing."

"*Schade,* no," said Heinzerling. "Herr Doktor Stone returned from Padua without meeting his sons. He is very worried, *mein' ich.*"

"As well he might be, Gus. Not that I'm telling you anything on that score. Lord knows I did some dumb things as a teenager, but this has to beat all." Mazzare heaved another deep sigh, pondered for a moment and then seemed to reach a decision. "Let's assume they're definitely on the way to Rome. Captain Lennox, continue your attempts to find and stop the boys on the road, but please try and make sure you're in Rome before they can possibly arrive. Don't let trying to catch them keep you out on the road while they're up to mischief in Rome. I'll be staying at the palazzo Barberini, apparently; get

word to me there. I'll let you know where Galileo's being
held and when and where the trial's to be, and you can
mount a discreet watch. Stop them quietly but firmly,
please. Gus, Captain Lennox, I don't know much about
the Marcolis, but Tom's boys are three good kids at heart
with all their lives in front of them. Try and keep them
out of trouble, eh?"

Lennox and Heinzerling murmured their assent.

"And another thing," Mazzare went on, "make your-
selves scarce in town until say noon tomorrow. We're
traveling with Monsignor Mazarini, and I'd prefer not
to have him know anything he might feel duty-bound
to report."

As Gus and Captain Lennox rode away, Jones said
"Larry, I'm not sure this is the best way to handle
this."

"Why not, Simon?" Mazzare wasn't sure himself,
but it was the first improvisation that had occurred
to him. Trying to explain about American traditions
of teenage independence, about youthful high spirits
and the sheer improbability of them doing any harm
would cut no ice at a trial for what was, by anyone's
standards, a plot to commit a major felony.

"Well, if we explain and all . . . oh." Jones dried up
as his thought processes caught up. "Yeah, I see what
you mean. 'Cardinal, we need extra guards. The three
sons of a friend of ours—one of our delegation, in
fact—are plotting to spring the star attraction at this
summer's biggest show-trial out of the pokey.'" He
snorted. "Go down real well."

Mazzare nodded. "Thinking aloud, here, Simon,
we're dealing with a propaganda event. If things really
are starting to crack open on this, if it's really like we
hope it is, then we can't let anything throw grit in
the gears. Although I'd throw it all up in a heartbeat
if I could keep those boys from doing something that
they'll regret for the rest of their lives."

Mazzare realized, as he said it, that needn't be a very long time at all. While he wasn't familiar with any of the local penal codes, he was pretty certain what the penalty would be for trying to organize a prison-break. This was an era where people could get executed for petty theft.

"Come on, Larry," said Jones, after a long silence. "I think I'm done sightseeing."

Chapter 44

"Well, Rome's better found than Venice was, I suppose." Jones was looking around the apartment that they had been given in the Palazzo Barberini for their stay. "Not as roomy, but it's clean, at least."

"You know, Simon, for a married man you can be a real old woman at times." Mazzare chuckled.

Jones blew a loud raspberry and sat down while a small platoon of servants scurried to sort out their baggage.

Mazzare looked around, feeling uncomfortable sitting down where someone else was working. The Barberinis' general program of beautification of their surroundings had its upside, and staying in their palazzo was part of it. Many years before by his own time—the three-and-three-quarter-century-wide fault line notwithstanding—a much younger Father Lawrence Mazzare had come to Rome for the first time and checked off the tourist sights methodically.

The Palazzo Barberini, by then a museum, was one of the ones he'd gone back to. The place was wall to wall with art and treasures and just plain beautiful things. It was a little sparser now than his own memory of it, but then the place had had over three hundred years to fill up by the time he'd last seen it.

"Simon?"

"Yes, Larry?" Jones had lain back in his chair and draped a handkerchief over his face. The trip down from Venice had been wearing, for all it had been taken in the most comfortably sprung coach they had been able to find. Jones, slightly the older of the two, had a far less ascetic disposition than Mazzare and gave vent to his discomforts and took the load off whenever he could.

"Point of grammar. If I remember having been in this very room, but won't have been here for another three hundred and—let me think—fifty-one years, is that deja vu all over again?"

"It is this business about Sharon Nichols and the man Sanchez that concerns me perhaps the most, Michael." Nasi leaned back in his chair across from the prime minister's desk and somewhat cattercorner to it. "Mostly, perhaps, because we can do nothing anyway about this Galileo affair, except hope that the Stone boys refrain from sheer madness or that Lennox catches them before they don't. Whereas . . ." The sentence drifted to a halt as if it had simply run out of gas.

Mike Stearns laced his fingers together and leaned forward on the desk. "Explain."

Unusually, the Sephardic banker needed time to organize his thoughts. He'd spoken somewhat impulsively, which was quite unlike him. Since Rebecca was trapped in Amsterdam and Ed Piazza had had to relinquish his duties as secretary of state in order to administer Thuringia as the new governor appointed by Gustav Adolf, Francisco had come to assume many of Rebecca and Ed Piazza's roles for Mike as well as being the head of the USE's intelligence service. There were some ways in which he was very diffident about the business. Rebecca's tasks as national security adviser he felt confident to handle, but he could hardly serve Mike as the same sort of personal confidante. And this was . . .

Perhaps a touchy matter. On this, unlike most subjects, Americans could be quite unpredictable.

"Well, to begin with, Michael, as a spy myself—'spook,' to use that phrase you so enjoy—I am naturally given to suspicion. I am uncomfortable with the fact that a known agent of the Spanish empire with whom we are at war has now been residing for some days in our embassy in Venice." That was the easy part. He cleared his throat. "Yes, I understand the seriousness of his medical condition—Tom Stone explained in reply to one of my queries; at far greater length, I might add, than he normally explains anything; which itself disturbs me a bit because he too seems to have become something of a partisan of this peculiar Spanish fellow—"

"You're prattling, Francisco," Mike said mildly. "Not like you at all. And he's not really 'Spanish' anyway, he's Catalan." There seemed to be a trace of humor there. "Weren't you the one who gave me a briefing not two months ago on the significance of the distinction?"

Francisco smiled, acknowledging the hit. "Well, yes. Still . . ."

"Oh, just spit it out, will you? I won't bite, I promise." The prime minister unlaced his fingers and leaned back in his own chair. "What you're really wondering is why—let's be precise, here—the bed he's been recuperating in belongs to Sharon Nichols."

Nasi must have looked a little startled. Mike smiled thinly. "I *do* occasionally read the entire reports, not simply your summaries. I made it a point to do so, in this case. If for no other reason, because James Nichols is one of my closest friends."

For some obscure reason, Francisco felt compelled to play devil's advocate for a moment. "You will have noted then that there is no evidence—unless she sneaks about at night, which doesn't seem to match her profile—"

Mike scowled, as he usually did when Nasi lapsed into jargon.

"Well, you know what I mean."

"'Course I do!" Mike snorted. "So why don't you just come out and say it? Sharon Nichols and 'sneak around at night' is pure bullshit. Bull-shit. A nice, clear term that beats all that psychobabble six ways from Sunday." Mike levered himself back upright. "We're talking about a woman here who told her father straight to his face that she was going to spend the night with Hans Richter. Then did it. In his house. The way he tells the story, even instructed him to have breakfast ready the next morning—although I'm sure James made that last bit up himself. I could tell. He doesn't hardly ever brag about anything except his daughter."

Mike was back to leaning on the desk, using laced fingers to support the weight. "So she's not screwing Sanchez. To use another excellent nonbabble term. Even if that were possible, anyway—which, if I interpreted Stoner's technical details correctly, it probably isn't. Not recuperating from that wound, not this quickly. Not even if this Sanchez guy was a man in his twenties."

Nasi relaxed. He'd never be as comfortable as so many—though certainly not all—Americans were, in the casual way they discussed sex. His own culture was very far from prudish, but had a more circumspect way of dealing with the matter. Still, it was at least obvious that he had not inadvertently stumbled into what Americans liked to call a "mine field."

"I am still concerned, Michael." He forced himself to be honest. "Mainly, I will admit, simply because I am puzzled. Being puzzled tends to make me very suspicious."

Mike smiled crookedly. "There are times I think you are the only fully functional paranoid I know. 'Francisco

Nasi' and 'puzzled' is a contradiction in terms; so, on the rare occasions it happens, you immediately suspect the universe of having foul designs."

Nasi chuckled. "Something like that."

Mike rose from his chair and moved to a nearby window. "I think what we're seeing here is just deja vu all over again," he mused. "Do you know much about grief, Francisco? Personally, I mean."

Nasi was having a hard time following Mike's thoughts, but knew from experience that they were headed somewhere. Eventually, even somewhere coherent. "Ah . . . no. Not really. My parents are both still alive and healthy, as are my brothers and sisters. At last report, anyway. A cousin, three years ago, who died in childbirth. But I cannot say I was personally close to her."

When Stearns spoke again, his tone was a bit harsh. "I have quite a bit of experience with it. More than I wish I did, although I think it's probably been good for me in the long run. Emphasis on 'long.'"

"Yes. Your father."

"I wasn't thinking about him at the moment, actually." Mike turned his head toward Nasi. Not looking at him, just showing a three-quarter profile. "Did you ever wonder why I went to Los Angeles? And then left?"

That had all happened long before Nasi had met Mike Stearns. Long before the Ring of Fire, in fact. "Ah. No."

Stearns nodded. "Her name was Kathleen Michael. We used to joke about the coincidence. Kathleen insisted we should name our first kid Michael Michael-Stearns, if he was a boy. Claimed it was her simple feminist duty."

The smile that came to his face was one that Francisco had never seen before. Impossible to analyze; even to describe.

"I met her in Clarksburg, while she was out here visiting distant relatives. This led to that—I even wrote letters, and was that a miracle—and eventually I moved out there. I couldn't in good conscience ask her to move here, seeing as how she had a real career under way and I had the mines, at best. Lawyer, no less, and was that another miracle. Except I could never figure out which way it went—a miracle that I fell in love with a lawyer, or that she'd fall in love with me?"

He was silent for a time, that peculiar smile never leaving his face. "It was the best two years of my life, until I met Becky. She never minded at all that I mostly scraped up work on the docks. Even came to my prize fights, until I finally had the good sense to quit, although she was after me the whole time to give it up. But she always made it a point, at those damn lawyer cocktail parties I hated, to brag to her colleagues about my latest victory. That was Kathleen's way of saying 'this is my man; if you don't like it, tough.' She was the most junior lawyer in the firm, too." There was another long silence. "God, I loved that woman."

Francisco cleared his throat. "You were never married?"

The smile shaded into something more familiar; that wry little twist that Francisco had come to know so well. Mike Stearns had a very fine sense of irony; perhaps the best Nasi had ever encountered.

"This was LA, Francisco, not a small town in West Virginia. Nobody worried too much about such things. The only reason we eventually decided to get married was because Kathleen was starting to get worried about my folks' opinion."

The smile faded away. "She was on her way up to Fresno to tell her own family about our decision when it happened. One of those sudden thick fogs that come into the San Joaquin valley. Kathleen always drove too fast, and she had a bad habit of tailgating. It was a twenty-car pileup and hers was the third car in it. Sandwiched by trucks, front and back."

He took a long, long breath. "The only comfort I ever had was that at least it was quick. She probably never really even knew what was happening."

Another long, long breath. When he spoke again, the voice was almost a sheer rasp. "You have no idea what it does to a human heart to be suddenly ripped in half, Francisco. You really don't, until and unless it happens to you."

For the first time since he'd risen from the chair, Mike looked at Nasi directly. "Grief is weird, Francisco. It's like a drug, really, after an operation. You need it desperately to handle the pain, but it can become its own addiction. You've got to get rid of it, eventually. And that's the dangerous time. I think that's the reason so many societies prescribe a fixed and formal period of mourning. Probably a good idea, to tell you the truth. Because you can wind up doing the screwiest things to start draining it off."

To Nasi's genuine amazement, there came a cheerful little laugh. "And that's why I left Los Angeles. Not because of Kathleen's death—that had happened almost a year earlier. It was because my screwy way of dealing with it was a woman named Linda Thompson. Linda LaLane, to use her stage name. Who, to this day, I think may have been the screwiest woman in the entire LA basin, which pretty much defines 'screwy' to begin with. Three months of that and I was finally ready to come home. Everybody thinks I came back because of my dad's accident—and I saw no reason to correct the assumption, since I figured the less said about Linda LaLane the better—but the truth is that I'd made the decision a week earlier anyway. I'd already given notice to the landlord and was half-packed when I got the news about my father."

Moving easily, now, he slid himself back into his chair. Laced his fingers together, leaned forward on his desk, and gazed upon Francisco serenely. "Does any of that make sense?"

Francisco nodded. "You fear that this Sanchez is Sharon Nichols'—ah—Linda Thompson.'"

Mike grimaced. "Fer chrissake, Francisco, how can anybody be that dumb? Sharon's . . . what, now? Twenty-four? Pretty close to what I was, at the time. Except she spent her what they call 'formative years' doing sensible and socially useful stuff right down the line—I leave aside some business with a jackass named Leroy that James is occasionally known to still grumble about; but that only lasted a year anyway before she booted the bum out the door; quite literally, the way James brags about it—whereas I spent those years trying to become the best head-basher in my weight division. You see what I mean?"

Nasi was by now completely baffled. "Ah. No. I don't."

Mike rolled his eyes. "It's so frickin' obvious. I didn't say that *every* relationship a person finds to handle their grief is screwy. I just said mine was. Sharon Nichols is not me. At a rough guess—when I was that age, anyway—the woman's got more good sense in her big toe that I had all put together."

He unlaced his hands and tapped the folder that contained all the files on the Galileo affair. "Look at the *age*, Francisco. That's the key to it. I picked a woman who had to use a fake driver's license in order to be a go-go dancer in a place that served liquor. Sanchez is pushing sixty."

"Seeking maturity, you mean. Wisdom."

Again, Mike rolled his eyes. "How can a man as smart as you be this dumb about some things?"

He issued a majestically sarcastic snort. "*Wisdom?* Francisco—you *have* read the reports, right?—we're talking about a Catalan swordsman who's spent most of his adult life in the service of Spain's most notorious diplomatic intriguer. If that's your definition of mature wisdom, I shudder to think what you'd call 'youthful folly.' I leave aside the fact that the reason the man is lying in Sharon's bed in the first place is because at the age of fifty-whatever he thought getting into a sword fight outnumbered six-to-one was a perfectly reasonable proposition. And I thought Linda was crazy!"

Francisco stared him. Eventually, he realized his mind was a complete blank.

"My mind is a complete blank." He stared out the window. "I'm not sure that's ever happened before."

"Do you some good, masterspy. All right, then, listen to the old wise man. The oldest and wisest one you've got, anyway, when it comes to stuff like this. Which, all false modesty aside, I am damn good at."

That was certainly true. Francisco had understood for some time that a large part of Mike Stearns' superb political skill was that the man had an uncanny knack for understanding the human mind. Even more, the human heart.

"It's the challenge that matters, Francisco. It's got nothing to do with wisdom or maturity. Grief will roll over those like an APC over an anthill. I challenged my grief by picking a woman, who, on the best day of her life, couldn't have reached up high enough to shine Kathleen Michael's shoes. Sharon . . ."

His fingers idly stroked the folder. "Oh, I think something very different is happening down there in Venice. I think she stumbled, quite by accident, across a man who—as different as he might be—is something of a match for Hans Richter. And had enough sense to recognize it, despite the lines on his face. Even despite her own grief."

That wry smile came back. "He won't live all that long, of course. But, deep in her heart, I don't think Sharon really thought Hans would either. She just didn't ultimately care. Well, not that exactly. She cared, certainly. It's just that she's the sort of person who will always choose quality over quantity, whatever the cost."

Finally, it all came into focus. If Nasi did not have

Mike's intuitive grasp of these things, he had made good the lack—to an extent, at least—by his extensive study of literature. That of the west, as well as his own culture.

"Ah." He leaned back in his chair, steepling his fingers. "How odd. She is indeed a very sensible and levelheaded young woman. Who would have thought, beneath that deceptive surface, lurked the soul of Achilles?"

Stearns was looking very smug. "Besides you, I mean," Francisco added sourly.

"Oh, I imagine her father won't be that surprised. He'll have a fit, of course. I think James does that mostly so he can brag later about how she told him to take a hike if he didn't like it."

Nasi still had some lingering doubts. Hesitations, at least. "It remains a very delicate situation, Michael. Politically, I mean. Dangerous, too. I grant you, the Achilles of the world, whatever their other flaws, are not given to treason. Still—the man is, by all accounts, as good an intriguer as he is a swordsman—"

Mike hauled out his wallet and extracted from it a twenty-dollar bill. He took a moment to admire the portrait. "God, there are times I really like that old hippie." Then, slapped the bill down on the table.

"My money's on Sharon, Francisco. I'll give you ten-to-one odds. No, make that twenty. Put up or shut up. Match it with a dollar."

Francisco eyed the bill. The cost was not the issue, of course. Nasi was wealthier than Mike Stearns by at least two orders of magnitude. He could have reversed the odds and still paid his losses out of what amounted to pocket change.

He had, exactly once, taken Mike Stearns up on a bet. The memory still festered.

"Pass."

"Thought so." Mike scooped up the bill and returned it to his wallet. "Now. What's happening in Bohemia?"

❊   ❊   ❊

When Sharon came into Ruy's room, she saw that he was reading Herman Melville's *Moby Dick*. The copy belonged to Conrad Ursinus, who'd purchased it simply because he thought that a USE naval officer should probably be familiar with a classic American sea story.

Conrad hadn't made it through more than the first thirty pages. He'd been more than willing to lend it to Sanchez. Who, for his part—to Sharon's certain knowledge—was now rereading it for the third time in as many weeks.

Sharon hadn't really been that surprised to discover that Sanchez was a voracious reader. But she did find that his tastes could be . . . eccentric.

"What is so fascinating about that novel, anyway?" she demanded. "I barely managed to get through it in college—and wouldn't have, if I hadn't had a test coming."

Sanchez didn't look up from his reading. "Americans. Ha! The most—what is that word you used the other day? referring to me?—'schizophrenic,' I believe. Yes, the most cross-headed people in existence. What other nation could produce such a book and then misunderstand it completely?"

When he finished the paragraph, he lowered the book and gave Sharon a sly little smile. "The most magnificent hero in all of literature, matched only by those of Cervantes and Homer."

Thus spake Sanchez.

Sharon shook her head. "How any man in his right mind could think Captain Ahab—"

"Ahab? Who spoke of that pathetic creature? Ahab is simply the literary foil. A mere device." Ruy closed the book—carefully keeping his place with a finger—and held up the cover for Sharon to see.

"Did the author need to be more obvious? Look at the title, woman! It's the whale, the whale."

On some other day, Sharon might have laughed. On this one, her purpose was too solemn. She had spent three days bringing herself to this point.

"What is the traditional period of mourning in Catalonia?" she asked abruptly. "For a widow, I mean."

Sanchez studied her for a moment. "It varies, from place to place. Most often—my village as well—it is a year and a day."

Sharon nodded. "October 8, then. Ask me your question again on that day. I will probably not have the answer, Ruy. But at least I will be able to think about it. Really think about it. I just can't, right now. I've tried, but . . . I don't trust any of the responses I get. They seem to veer all over place, from one hour to the next."

Which, they certainly did. Right now, looking at the man, the response was veering toward sheer passion. Ruy Sanchez could look very, very good, lying in a bed. Especially these days, when his wound had healed well enough to allow him to sit erect. She couldn't imagine, any longer, how she had ever thought of him as *Feelthy Sanchez*. All she usually saw now were the broad shoulders, eyes younger than springtime in a well-lined face—she'd come to know every line, too—and, perhaps most of all, that seemingly endless and antic wit.

Other days, true, it was all Sharon could do not to throw him out of it. But, even then, the cause was never disgust or anger. Just that Ruy could be the most *exasperating* man she'd ever known.

What bothered her most of all was not even the wild swings in her mood. It was that she had not failed to notice that the swings were beginning to develop a pattern. An hour, perhaps, wishing that Sanchez was out of the bed. Two hours—more like three, lately—wishing she were in it with him.

She didn't trust any of it. Regarded it all with deep suspicion. Simultaneously faithless to Hans and unfair to Ruy. Not to mention, stupid for her.

"I need structure," she said. "Rules. Or I think I'll go crazy."

"No danger of that," Ruy said firmly. "*Do* something crazy, yes; go crazy, no." The Catalan stroked his mustache. "Trust me on this matter, young maiden. I am an expert on the distinction."

"I am not a maiden. Haven't been, since I was seventeen."

Sanchez gave the ceiling a long-suffering look. "Leave it to me to fall in love with an imbecile. What else could she be, to confuse Ruy Sanchez de Casador y Ortiz with a callow stripling?"

The look became a glare. "Not even that! Even as a callow stripling, Ruy Sanchez understood the proper place of the hymen in God's scheme of things. It was obvious. Higher than the feet, lower than the woman."

When he brought his eyes down—damn the man!— they were twinkling again. "Sharon Nichols, as a crone of eighty, with a veritable horde of children and grand-children gathered about, you will still think like a maiden. And, thus, will be one." He hefted the thick novel. "If you took the time to *study* this book, you would understand. What is Moby Dick, but the best man of the day?"

Fortunately, the mood swing had brought Sharon abruptly to her own center. She advanced upon Sanchez, smiling serenely.

"It occurs to me that a man of your advanced age needs to be inspected regularly for the first signs of colon cancer." She described for him, in some detail, the traditional medical procedure to do so.

Ruy's eyes were wide, his cheeks flushed. "You wouldn't!"

An instant later, the cheeks were pale. "You would!"

To her surprise, Sharon heard a little laugh coming from behind her. Turning, she saw that Cardinal Bedmar was sitting in a chair in the corner. She was not surprised to see him, since he came to visit Ruy quite often. But she was still somewhat chagrined that she hadn't thought to check when she came in the door. She'd been that preoccupied.

Perhaps it was the residue of the mood swing, but she decided that she was well centered enough to handle that problem also.

"And how long must I wait for you to ask me your question, Your Eminence? I gave Ruy a date. Give me yours."

Bedmar frowned. "I do not—"

"Cut it out. How long will you continue to mourn the passing glory of Spain?"

The cardinal looked away. After a moment, he murmured: "I thought . . . with the ambassador gone—even Signor Stone, now, I understand . . ."

"Yeah, that's right. Tom Stone—boy, can he be a doofus—finally realized he made a lot better father than a diplomat. So, six days ago, he and Magda packed up and headed for Rome to see what's happening with their kids. That leaves me in charge. So give me a date, Your Eminence."

She cocked her head a little. "How old are you, by the way? Older than Ruy, I know. Are you aware that the risk of colon cancer increases dramatically after the age of fifty? Annual inspections are strongly recommended. When did you have your last one? Let me rephrase that. When did you have your first one?" She waited maybe three seconds. "Right. Never. No sweat."

Sharon glanced at the corner where she kept medical supplies in a chest. "I even have a few latex gloves in there, handy as could be. Each one of which, these days, is worth its weight in gold—and worth a hell of a lot more than a so-called diplomat who goofs off on the job."

Bedmar's eyes were even wider than Ruy's had been. "I'm a cardinal of the Church!"

"And before that a marquis. I know. Ask me if I care. Better yet, let me tell you what do I care about. I am a nurse, Your Eminence. I am not a soldier, I am not a diplomat. Soldiers destroy people when diplomats tell them to. Nurses are the ones who try to put together what they can afterward. I'd like to get about my job, which, judging from all reports from the war front, is going to be a monster. But I can't even start—not really—until the war ends. And even then it won't do much good if the war doesn't produce a good peace. Which is what you're supposed to be doing. Instead of sawing away at the violins, playing a sorrowful tune. Badly. You're not a musician."

From the bed, Sanchez spoke.

"Do it, Alphonso. Do it now. We have talked about it enough."

It was the only time Sharon had ever heard Ruy use the cardinal's first name. She looked over and saw that Sanchez was closing the book. Firmly, without leaving a finger behind. "How did I put it, just yesterday?" he mused. "'How many barrels of oil will thy melancholy bring thee in Nantucket market?'"

The cardinal sniffed. "Don't give yourself literary airs in front of me, you wretched Catalan peasant. I am no maiden and never thought like one. You didn't say 'Nantucket,' wherever that is. You said 'Amsterdam.'"

"Ah. So I did." Sanchez grinned. "Always practical, my slogan!" He eyed Sharon uncertainly. "Well. Perhaps not in my choice of women."

But the uncertainty was feigned. Not even Ruy Sanchez was that good an actor.

"October 8," Sharon told him softly. Then, bringing her eyes back to the cardinal, she spoke not softly at all. "You, I will expect to see downstairs within the hour."

※   ※   ※

The following day, when Nasi slid a new file in front of Mike Stearns, he murmured: "Came in on the radio last night. Good thing I didn't take your bet."

Mike scanned the file quickly. "Boil it down for me, Francisco. Your best shot."

"Well, he won't spy for us. Certainly not regarding military affairs."

"Don't want a spy," Mike grunted. "Got plenty of those already. And I leave the soldiering to Gustav Adolf and Lennart Torstensson and John Chandler Simpson, who've forgotten more about it than I'll ever learn. It's their job to win the war. My job, to win the peace."

He cocked an eye at Nasi. Then, seeing the great smile spreading, nodded his head and went back to studying the report.

"What I think, too. How soon can Bedmar get back to the Netherlands?"

"Not immediately. He'll need to find a plausible excuse to leave Venice. Then there's the travel time itself. That's a bit tricky, between his age and the risks of passing through France."

"France, baloney. Let's smuggle him right through our own territory. Who's the best we've got for that, with Harry Lefferts not available?"

Nasi paused, estimating. "Probably Klaus Grünwald, for something like this."

Decisively, Mike closed the file and slid it toward Nasi. "Set it up, Francisco. Let's get him back right next to the cardinal-infante's ear as fast as we can."

Francisco didn't pick up the file immediately. "Did you see the personal note from Sharon? At the end."

Mike hadn't spotted the note. He pulled back the file and reopened it. Within seconds, had found the note. Not many seconds later, closed the file again.

"Sure. Anything to please such a charming young lady. Tell him he's got to leave Sanchez behind.

Invent some kind of plausible reason if he squawks. Sweeten the pot, somehow, if you think he needs an incentive."

Nasi picked up the file, smiling. "Oh, I doubt that. I suspect the young lady has already given the cardinal an incentive to agree."

Chapter 45

"Damn, it's cold." That was about the fourteenth time in—Frank checked—an hour that Gerry had said that.

"Can you change the record, Gerry?" he asked, at last exasperated.

"Are we nearly there yet?"

Ron snickered, and Frank found himself smiling. Truth be told, it wasn't that bad. Chilly, up here in these mountains even in springtime, but nothing compared to a Thuringian winter. During the day, out in the sun on top of the coaches they now had, it was quite pleasant. Of course, all of the Marcolis were inside the coaches, complaining bitterly at the weather. They'd dressed for spring, after all.

Coaches. Frank decided that Michel was on average, a blessing. Mixed, sure. Creepy as all hell, and sometimes exasperatingly French, but useful. He knew the drill for negotiating with innkeepers and livery stables for changes of horses. And he'd stolen all that money from the embassy where he'd worked. That had bothered Frank at first, but then he'd decided, what the hell, we're at war with 'em. If they got caught, a larceny charge wasn't even going to register on the grisly-execution-o-meter. Besides, it was Michel going to the chair for that one. Or whatever they used.

Other than that, Michel seemed to be spending a lot of time on the driver's seat of the second coach, talking to Marius, and both Frank and his brothers wondered what was up with that. Neither of them was what you'd call an astounding conversationalist. Half of Michel's utterances seemed to trail off into that damned shrug that was really getting on Frank's nerves these days; and Marius, while he could string sentences together at great length, was, well, not gifted, put it that way. Not to mention the fact that he managed the rare feat of being the maddest Marcoli, even if only a Marcoli by dint of working for the head of the house. Plus, Frank wasn't too keen on the way he was looking at Giovanna these days.

There was another sore subject. Giovanna had made it perfectly plain she now regarded the whole thing as a done deal. There was, she had hinted, a whole new world she wanted to explore with Frank. But she still had two brothers and two cousins and that damned handyman watching her like a gaggle of slightly goofy hawks. Frank wondered why it was that this was such a glaring exception to the general rule of Marcoli behavior. In every other freaking way they were easily distracted, apt to wander off the point, goofy as all get-out. But they never missed a beat when it came to protecting the sacred sisterly virginity. Whether the sister herself wanted it protected or not.

Your future in-laws, pal, said the Voice of Treason, earning itself another very short stand in front of the heavily scarred wall Frank kept sending it to.

"Are we nearly there yet?" Gerry asked.

"Gnnnh," Frank commented. "Gerry, that was funny once, okay? We are making maybe four miles an hour, tops, my ass aches, I think my leg's gone numb, this breeze is making my ears hurt, and I've been staring at one horse's ass after another for weeks. Just recently, we have joined the ranks of the high rollers, and I get to look at two horses' asses. This is not an improvement. If you start with the are-we-nearly-there-yet joke, I will by God kill you."

"Chill, man. I'm just saying, okay?" Gerry sounded genuinely alarmed.

"It's okay, Gerry," said Frank. "I guess I'm a little tired."

"I know what you mean. If we had a car, we'd have done this in a day." Gerry nodded sagely.

"Sure, and if we had some ham, we could have ham and eggs, if we had eggs." Frank regretted being so testy immediately. "Ah, skip it. Yes, it's taking a long time. On the other hand, it's taking them a long time to get to Rome, too, and one thing we know about down-time proceedings and bureaucracy and like that there, it takes a while to get anything done. We'll get there in time. And remember, slow for us is slow for anyone chasing us as well."

"Michel thinks we could go faster," Gerry offered.

"Yeah, well, Michel's the only one of us who's driven a coach before, all right? I'm going as fast as I dare on these mountain roads."

In three hundred years time, Frank supposed, these same roads—maybe even this well-found Roman road—would be a treat for the drivers of the high-performance cars that Italy was famous for. Hairpins, switchbacks and all manner of other delights for the connoisseur of skilled driving in a powerful car with good road-handling. Of course, in that time, such civilities as blacktop and crash barriers would be added. More than once Frank had held his breath and not dared look, convinced he had at least one wheel out over empty air. Most of the time, like now, he didn't go much faster than a walk.

"I'm just saying—*whoah!*" Gerry's exclamation had come as they rounded a bend on the shoulder of a hill.

"Yeah," said Frank, "I agree. And yes, relative to where we've been up until now, we're nearly there yet."

The view had opened out in front of them. There was still plenty of mountain road to go, of course, but it looked like they were definitely going down from here. Stretched out in front of them was the rolling countryside of Lazio, and somewhere in the blue haze of the distance was Rome.

"What do you reckon that is, fifty miles?"

"Not a clue, sorry," Frank said, and then hazarded a guess. "Maybe a couple of days more?"

"Cool. So we are nearly there. Hey, what say we let our hair down at our next stop? Party a bit before we press on for the last run to Rome?"

"I dunno." Frank chewed on the idea. It certainly sounded good, but he thought maybe it wouldn't be the responsible thing to do. "We'll probably stop earlyish anyway, and if we leave late because we partied—and I say late here bearing in mind how damn' hard it is to get Fabrizio out of bed when he hasn't had *anything* to drink the night before—we might give whoever's on our back trail time to catch up."

"Aw, c'mon Frank, there's no one on our back trail. Changing routes the way we did threw 'em off."

Frank snorted. "Yeah, who but a madman would decide to come the long way 'round to get to a daring rescue? I keep being afraid we'll arrive a week after the frickin' nick of time."

"Uh, Frank?" Gerry said, "Before you said not to worry, we'd be on time?"

Frank waved the objection away. "Consistency, who needs it? But . . . yeah, I think we're probably all right, too. And you know, I could do with unwinding a bit myself. But I think we should have someone stay sober, keep a watch or something. I don't want to get ambushed because we're all three sheets to the wind, okay?"

"Hey, bring 'em on, I prefer a straight fight to all this sneakin' around."

"Gerry?" said Frank.

"Yes?"

"That has *got* to be the worst Han Solo impersonation I've ever heard."

"Glad you liked it," Gerry said, climbing down from the moving coach. "I'll pass the word about the party."

There, it was done. Another Leadership Decision. Frank felt they deserved capitals, even though he had the horrible feeling that he was largely being led himself—by events, and by the need to try and keep everyone pointed in the same direction. It was a . . . he strained for a word foul enough for it. He'd not slept properly since they started, his back hurt, and he was grinding his teeth a lot. The constant jaw-clenching as he bit down on what he really wanted to say, what with having to be The Leader, was taking its toll on his teeth. Once more, he took a deep breath of invigorating mountain air, and forced himself to relax.

They found an inn about two hours later. As these things went, it wasn't bad. A farmhouse, a large villa type of thing; with a big room where, apparently, the locals would come in for a drink or three, and rooms for travelers. They were on a main road, so they got plenty of business.

Michel returned after a few moments haggling with the owner. "No change of horses here, Monsieur Frank." Shrug. "We must continue with tired horses. A pity, for we might go faster now we are to descend from these mountains." Another shrug.

Frank just nodded. Damn, he was weary. He looked around for his usual pick-me-up, a sight of Giovanna, and saw her in animated discussion with Gerry and Ron. More clenching of the teeth. He wasn't even going to think about hauling off at his brothers about it.

And then the party got going. Say that for the Marcolis, they knew how to cut loose. Michel's purse got raided again—more Gallic moping, another shrug, and he retired to a corner with Marius for the evening—and the good wine got brought out, and a few of the locals got friendly, and dinner got going and, well, a good time was had by all. Except for Frank.

No one seemed to be talking to him much. Oh, sure, have another, Frank. You okay, Frank, from his brothers. Giovanna was dancing with her brothers and cousins over in one corner, where a couple of local guys had gotten musical instruments—lutey things, and a couple of flutey things—and were playing something fairly lively. And everyone was getting drunk. Three or four glasses of wine into the evening, Frank realized that if he didn't stay sober, no one would.

Damn. He started to just sip, and stopped letting anyone top up his glass. Gerry and Ron were reeling around the room making sure everyone had refills and freshen-ups. Indeed, they were making sure everyone, mine host and his family included, got good and lathered. They seemed to have the message about Frank, though, and left him alone in his corner.

Was this what they called The Loneliness of Command? Frank didn't know. If it wasn't for the prospect of certain death awaiting them on their return—even more, the fact that it would take longer to get back now than to go on—he'd give it up in a heartbeat. It wasn't like he could talk to anyone either. *Hey, guys, I'm getting bored with this game, now. Let's go back, right? Guys?* The resulting scene, as it played before Frank's mind's eye, began with a slap across the face from Giovanna, and that was the most painful part of all.

He watched the others get progressively drunker and drunker. Sure enough, the grappa had come out, and the fiery rotgut was wreaking its usual havoc. He looked at his watch. *Guess I should get some sleep while they're all still up and watchful,* he thought. He watched Fabrizio and Dino trying and failing to play keep-it-up with a jury-rigged soccer ball in the middle of the room to the massive amusement of the rest of the company there assembled.

He got up and, quietly and without being noticed by the others, made his way to bed. Away from the roaring hearth and the bodies in the inn's main room, the place was cold. Mine host clearly didn't believe in spending too much on fuel for the bedrooms, since everyone would be in blankets anyway. That was fine by Frank. He was still warm from downstairs and he simply kicked off his boots and crawled under the blankets fully dressed. He'd done that right through the mountains. He was getting more than a little ripe, to his own way of thinking, but he was too tired to care. He was almost too tired to notice.

What he wasn't too tired to notice was that there was only the one bed in this room. So that was what it had come to, eh? They really, really didn't want anything to do with him. He pulled the blankets up around his ears and tried to sleep. Not that that was any easy task with the near-riot still going on downstairs.

What had he been thinking? The condition they were getting in, they'd be lucky to get out of bed tomorrow, let alone go anywhere. They'd lost a day as surely as if he'd ordered them not to move. For all his bluster to Gerry, Frank was worried that they'd not arrive in Rome in time to find out where Galileo was being held, case the place, and arrange to get him out.

For that matter, they needed to get down to some serious planning of their route away from Rome; trying to flee back the way they had come was going to be impossible. The map he had showed a road heading northward away from Rome up toward Florence and Pisa, and maybe they could head that way. Or maybe go straight south and hope to get a ship somewhere at . ...

But how would they afford passage on a ship? Frank wasn't even sure how much it would cost, and they'd spent better than half what Michel said he'd stolen along with all the money the Marcolis had started with . . .

He was awakened—damn, how long had he been asleep?—by the creaking of the door. He muttered and rolled over, pretending to still be asleep, but he wanted to see the door. There was no light in the corridor outside, so all he had were dim chinks of moonlight to see by. A dark figure, sidling around the door . . .

Was it just imagination that filled in a dark hood, a mask?

Slowly, Frank slid his hand up to where he had his pistol under the—

Oh, hell! Every night of this journey he'd put a pistol under the pillow, loaded and wanting only to be cocked. Where was the damned thing? By his bed? In his bag? Where? Surely the assassin could hear his heart pounding, knew he wasn't asleep—

Another stealthy step, the door pushed softly closed behind, a quiet rustle. Frank began to think desperately. Shout the alarm and then make a break? Throw a blanket and then shout? What? Would anyone wake up? Was he the last one left alive, everyone else murdered in a drunken stupor? He resolved to throw his blanket over the assassin, scream a warning and get the hell out into the corridor. Keep moving, make as much noise as possible, see what could be done with speed and surprise. He tensed himself to spring. One more step, you son of a bitch, just one more step . . .

"Frank?" the voice was a soft whisper.

A soft, *feminine*, whisper. One he recognized perfectly because it had been whispering in his ear for weeks now.

"Giovanna?" he breathed.

"Yes. You are awake?"

"Uh, yeah?" He began to tremble. "Jesus, Giovanna, you scared the life out of me!" He clapped a hand over his mouth, realizing he'd spoken aloud. "Oops," he murmured.

She giggled. "I hope I didn't scare all the life out of you," she whispered. "So tragic, a widow before I even marry." She took two more steps, quickly now, and with one motion flipped up the blankets and squirmed under.

Fireworks and cheering started going off in Frank's head. And, he realized, other parts of his anatomy.

And then, hard on their heels, that vision of the queue of Marcolis, lining up with knives and murder in their hearts . . .

"Giovanna, you can't be here, if your brothers—"

"They're all drunk asleep, Frank. A volcano couldn't wake them up. It's cool." She said the last two words in English. Another phrase that was definitely catching on in these parts. Although not in the parts of Frank that were currently getting his urgent attention, where things were growing very warm indeed.

"How, I mean, uh—"

Whatever the linkage was between Frank's brain and his mouth, it stopped working just then. Come right to it, his brain was shut down completely.

And his mouth for that matter, as Giovanna found it and comprehensively shut him up in the best way known to man. She'd kissed him before, but never like *this*. The fact that the girl was figuring out how to do it as she went along just made it all the more exciting.

Time passed. Something was happening to Frank's sense of time. It was either seconds, or hours. He breathed in, deeply, savoring the scent of her. God, they were both good and ripe. To his surprise, he found it good. That sneaking little voice came again. *If you're caught, Romeo . . .*

"How?" he asked.

"Gerry and Ron, they helped. We plotted, them and me. Them and I? Whatever. They made sure everyone got good and drunk. Except you. I drank almost nothing, too, I just pretended." Her voice now sounded just that little bit cross. "But forget them. Thank them in the morning. Tonight, you concentrate on *me*. How can you do a proper job of taking my virginity—you fiend!"—a little giggle there—"if you're worrying about anything else? And I warn you!" She lifted herself up on an elbow, grinning like an imp, and wagged a finger under his nose. "I want it taken lots of times!"

"Uh, I don't think you can do that."

"Yes, you can! If you only concentrate!"

Frank didn't really feel like arguing the point. To put it mildly. As erect as he was now, who knew what was possible?

The problem was that same ferocious erection—they'd all been sleeping in their clothes and seventeenth-century styles didn't go in for handy zippers and whatnot—he was fumbling with the fasteners like an idiot—

"How do I, uh—

"Like this." Her nimble fingers worked quickly. "Here."

Suddenly, gloriously, he was free. A veritable statue of liberty. Giovanna's hand moved from the fasteners to close around him.

"Oh," she said softly, wonderingly. "I never thought it would be so big. Even though I thought about it a lot."

Then, choking down a laugh of pure glee: "Oh! Ten times at least!"

Part VI: June, 1634

Nay, we'll go
Together down, sir. Notice Neptune, though,
Taming a sea-horse, thought a rarity,
Which Claus of Innsbruck cast in bronze for me!

Chapter 46

Frank wondered what the hell he was doing calling himself a leader any more. Michel had made the plans that got them into Rome. Michel had done the scouting when they'd laid up in the grotty tenement house that—yes—Michel had found. Michel had sketched out their route into the church where the trial was being held; their way back out again. Michel had found the coaches and the trustworthy drivers who'd get them down to the boat on the Tiber which would take them and Galileo to freedom. Just like he'd found a reliable captain and crew. The coach drivers and boat crew were all members of Rome's Committee of Correspondence, he explained. That had come as a surprise to the Marcoli youngsters as much as it had to Frank and his brothers. None of them had even known there *was* a Committee in Rome.

Sure, the others had contributed, too. They'd all done a turn casing the Villa Medici, where Galileo was being held. That hadn't gone anywhere, though. All of them agreed that there was no way they could fight their way in past a small horde of Medici retainers, find out which room the old guy was being held in, and get him out.

So, they'd have to spring Galileo from the trial itself. They couldn't even be sure of their moment to do it, but they reckoned it would go best if they waited until the last minute. After all, then would be the best moment. Right after he'd been convicted and they could wring the maximum amount of propaganda out of the forces of reaction. There was no sense not giving them enough rope to hang themselves with, Ron had said—an image that Frank felt he might have chosen a little more carefully.

Still, Michel had planned most of this. He'd really been the one running the show since they'd finally arrived in Rome. Frank was finding his dislike for the man growing all the time, but he was too honest with himself not to admit that Ducos seemed a veritable wizard at this sort of thing, all of his modest protestations notwithstanding.

And, truth be told, the closer they got to the actual deed, the more Frank felt as if he'd entered some kind of weird virtual universe where he didn't trust his own judgment. Too many things just . . . didn't make sense to him, even though he could never figure out exactly why they didn't.

Take the location of the trial itself. The whole thing was freaky, to Frank. The Inquisition held its trials in an ordinary church, it turned out, not a dungeon. A church that happened to have some extra side rooms, but a church nonetheless. Made sense, Frank supposed, when you tried to look at the thing with the sort of bizarre logic that put a man on trial for saying the Earth went around the sun, but Frank still couldn't get his head around it.

The days of leaving church buildings locked were a long way in the future, so everyone had taken a turn over the last couple of days to go in, kneel down, and case the place. That, at least, was easy to do. It wasn't like there weren't whole bunches of other people in there at the same time. It had come as a surprise to

Frank to discover that the church was used as something of a social center when it wasn't being used as a house of worship. People met there, and talked, and sat around to shoot the breeze. Frank had actually never set foot inside a church before, which was maybe a little freaky when he thought about it, but it was true. The only idea he'd had about how you ought to behave in a church came from television: hushed tones; respectful whispers; slow-moving priests with hands folded before them, coming to offer wise counsel to troubled souls.

Come right to it, that was mostly where he'd gotten his impression of Father Mazzare from, since he barely knew the man.

And there was something else for Frank to worry about. Despite the best efforts of Michel Ducos, they'd been unable to learn anything about where Mazzare was being held or when his trial was scheduled.

Well, they could only do so much. If Father Mazzare wound up in a second trial in that church, he was going to have to rely on the USE's diplomatic efforts to get him out, or be a martyr or something. That left Frank more than a bit dry-mouthed, but there was just no way they'd be able to pull off a second rescue, even if they managed the first one.

The plan had been to get to the church at the crack of dawn and take their places down front. Fabrizio was the biggest problem there, although the other Marcolis had warned him the night before that he was getting a bucket of water if he wasn't up smartly just before dawn. Perhaps more to the point, Ducos—in that utterly chilling manner he sometimes had about him—had predicted that the bucket of water would be followed by immersion in the Tiber. An immersion, he gave the distinct impression, that would be permanent.

But . . . it worked, as so many things Ducos did worked. Fabrizio got up with the rest of them.

And now they were on a wide, cobbled street looking across at a church that, later in the morning, was going to be the scene of the Venetian Committee of Correspondence's greatest triumph.

Or greatest disaster, a quiet little voice told him.

He looked around. For, he realized, probably the fifth time in as many minutes. Everyone was here. Well, everyone who was coming. Thankfully, that didn't include Giovanna. Frank had put his foot right down with Giovanna, to keep her back with the coaches. Frank never thought he'd say it, but Gretchen Richter was a prize pain in the ass on that score, just for the example she set. After all, if Gretchen could take part in all manner of daring adventures—fighting off pirates, even—why couldn't Giovanna? The fact that Gretchen was a big and frankly scary Amazon who'd been around soldiers and fighting since she was a kid and Giovanna was, well, none of the above.

It had been a long and ferocious argument. Truth to tell, Frank was pretty sure that there was only one reason he'd won the argument at all. Ever since— his thoughts got really misty and warm here, for a moment—*that night,* Giovanna's behavior had changed subtly. She was reacting to him as a husband, now, not a boyfriend; and Italy, after all, was the country that had given the world the term *paterfamilias.* Okay, it was cheating, but Frank was willing to cheat if it'd keep Giovanna alive.

Still, he was pretty sure he'd be hearing about it for a long, long, long time if they got out of this alive. That too, he suspected darkly, was part of the tradition.

Ron and Gerry were along, Marius, Michel, Dino and Fabrizio. Michel had also insisted on bringing one of the members of the Roman Committee into the church with them. He'd even insisted that the man had to be given one of the six flintlock pistols, which left Dino and Fabrizio unarmed. Local liaison, he explained, in case something went wrong and they had to use a different escape route. Frank didn't even know the guy's name.

Salvatore was back with Giovanna at the coaches and Roberto was going to be watching the route back, ready to spring a couple of the surprises from the Revenge Kit that they'd brought with them. Michel had approved of those, and Roberto turned out to have a knack for the gadgetry. So, Gerry had spent days eagerly lecturing the Marcoli youngster on the subjects of pyrotechnics and related mayhem. At least it had kept Frank's often rambunctious youngest brother out of his hair for a good long while.

"Nervous, Frank?" Ron asked. He was doing his best to look nonchalant on the street corner in the first light of dawn. The church was open, all right, there were guards there ambling about and, off to one side, having a quiet smoke. That was a worry in itself.

"Sure, who wouldn't be? I think we wait until we see someone else go in. I want to know if those guys are searching folks at the door."

"Sure." Ron yawned widely. "These early mornings don't agree with me."

Frank laughed. "Yeah, and this is early-early, too. Electric lighting can't come too soon for me, these predawn starts are a killer." The street was starting to get light, though, and Rome was already fairly busy. Not a patch on Venice, packed as it was into a much smaller space, or Magdeburg with its industrial bustle, but there was still plenty going on.

Michel was standing nearby, silent and impassive. Naturally, he'd found a shadow to stand in, and had gone from his usual Gallic morosity to something harder and colder, something that gave Frank more than a bit of a chill. Marius stood next to him; the two had somehow grown quite close over the last few weeks. Talk about an Odd Couple.

"When's the trial start, Michel?" Gerry asked.

"As soon as all is ready, Monsieur Gerry," Michel

said. "Everyone must wait on the convenience of these prelates." Another shrug, this one conveying Michel's disdain for the prelates in question.

"Someone's going in," Ron said.

Frank looked. It was hard to see whether the figures going in were old women or priests. The light wasn't good. It seemed fairly clear, though, that the guards weren't searching anyone on the way in. That was damned odd. A courthouse up-time would have cops and probably rent-a-cops around it as a matter of routine, surely? They did on TV, anyway.

Oh, well. A lot of things about the seventeenth century didn't make much sense to Frank. He took a deep breath. "Okay," he said. "Dino, since neither of you have guns, take Fabrizio and see if you get searched on the way in. I figure you can come back out if there's a search and let us know."

"And if there is?" Michel asked.

"Then we've got a real problem," Frank said. "Probably have to figure out a different plan altogether. Maybe wait till Galileo's been moved somewhere else."

Oh, please let there be a search, came the Voice of Treason. Frank squashed it as best he could. Which was not too well at all.

"Maybe we could find some other way in where they're not searching," Gerry said, "Get the weapons in that way."

"Whatever," said Frank. "Get going, Dino. Fabrizio. If you don't come out in ten minutes, we'll follow you in."

And so it was done.

There was no search. Ten minutes later, they all went in.

The church was all but empty.

Outside of the church of San Matteo where Galileo's trial would be starting soon, the crowd was seething but quiet.

Lennox looked around to Heinzerling, who was holding him up on a stone balustrade. "I can see naught," he said. "Leave me doon, Heinzerling."

"Can we go in?" Heinzerling was already going beetred in only the mild morning sunshine of a Roman summer.

"Nae the noo. Yon Swiss laddies hae the place ringed." He nodded to himself. "Just as I would do't. The maist fowk'll aye be in an' set, and the place needs closed while the quality arrive."

"The quality, you say?" Heinzerling's voice had taken on a slow, thoughtful character.

Lennox pulled his canteen from his belt and took a drink. By all that was holy, if he'd known he was going to be this thirsty he'd have had another drink the night before. "Ye've a notion how we're to get in, have ye not?" he said, as matter-of-fact as he could be.

"*V'leicht,*" murmured Heinzerling, his eyes growing a little far-away as if he was unfocusing them to see the inside of his own mind a little more clearly. Lennox sympathized; his own head was throbbing gently, and the heat and smell of this abominable city of papists was not helping.

He waited a moment. For all he cursed the big German for a fattened, drunken papist gobshite, he was a frighteningly smart man when he sobered up. What was coming might not be perfect, but—

"*Ja!*" said Heinzerling, beaming suddenly and snapping his fingers. "We shall need two good horses, the rest of the Marines and for you and Billy Trumble your dress uniforms with all speed. Und Lennox?"

"Aye?"

"Can you sneer?"

"Sneer?"

"*Ja,* like *ein Adel*—like a nobleman?"

Realization crept up on Lennox. "Oh, aye," he said, "I can do that wee thing right enow." He grinned.

Heinzerling grinned back. The pair of them threw

their weight against the crowd to get back to the hostelry where the Marines were sleeping off the exhaustion of the last hard-driving stretch of their journey.

"Simon," said Mazzare, "I'm scared."

Jones snorted. "No kidding, Larry. The pope has ordered you to talk the greatest scientist who ever lived—most famous, anyway—out of the clutches of the Inquisition. This is called a 'pressure situation.'"

The priest chuckled, feeling the tension lighten a bit. Today was the day of Galileo's trial, and Mazzare had prepared as well as he felt he could. Still, and it was a heavy burden he had borne these past weeks past since he received the pope's summons, and there was not a lot that all the science that Grantville had to offer would help. Mazzare knew full well that, when all was said and done, the issue was really theological and political. Both of which were frequently the same thing in this town.

Mazzare sighed, heavily. He had retired early the night before after one last consultation with Galileo, who was now fluttering between terror and ill temper. Now that was most of the problem—but no. This was Mazzare's own burden to bear. He and the Reverend Jones, who was along as his clerk and moral support for the trial, had been given an anteroom in a palazzo next door to the church of San Matteo. Ostensibly it was for use as a workroom, but all the use Mazzare had been able to find for the cool marble floor dotted with elegant furniture was as a space to pace in. On an escritoire by the window there was a bundle of paper, his notes for the day. Every turn he took at that side of the room showed him those notes, and each time he felt his gut sink a little.

"What's eating you now, Larry?" Jones asked after a while.

Mazzare looked at the Methodist minister, where he sprawled on an antique of the future that looked too gracile for his weight. He realized he had known the wise-cracking Methodist for the best part of twelve years, and neither of them could much fool the other any more. They were too alike, for all their differences. Jones was just as full of stage fright as Mazzare was, but he was carefully wearing his professional face in these slow hours before the proceedings began. Jones would doubtless insist that that was for Mazzare's benefit, but it was as much for Jones' own peace of mind. Seeing Jones trying so hard to pretend he wasn't nervous gave Mazzare a sudden sense of warmth. It was all he could do not to fall to his knees and loudly thank God for the blessing of friendship. Al Green, Grantville's Baptist minister, would have done just that. But a pastor had to stay in his own character.

Mazzare stopped his pacing squarely in the bright golden patch of light from the big window that lit the room. He took a deep breath. "It's my client, Simon."

"Galileo? What's wrong with him? Apart from being an ornery old coot without a good word for anyone?"

"He's guilty, Simon." There, far easier to deal with now it was out in the open. There was that much truth in the old sixties saying.

"Guilty." Jones repeated the word flatly. "Go on, then, Larry, tell me about it?"

Mazzare walked over to where the window stood open and leaned against the plasterwork of the jamb. Outside, and some way below, there was the murmur of a crowd. Hushed, like the ordinary street noise of Rome never was, but noisy as thousands of people all together must always be.

"He's charged with heresy, Simon."

Jones frowned. "Well, yes. That's why we're here, isn't it?"

"Yes and no. When he was tried in our history, it happened a year earlier than this. And there was the

Bellarmino memorandum, which they hung the plea on that they got him to cop. But that isn't in the papers for this trial, so they can't find him guilty of violating a direct order."

"That's to the good, isn't it?" Jones looked at the stack of trial papers, most of which he could barely read. "I mean, we don't have to answer that charge?"

"We don't. It means, though, that the Holy Office—and forget this stuff about Committees of Inquiry, it's the Inquisition—that, as I say, the Holy Office are only charging him with what they can convict him on."

"Yes, but it's still only vehement suspicion of heresy, isn't it?"

"That's the charge. The trouble is, the only defense for Galileo is to admit the actual charge of heresy."

Jones was silent a moment, working though the implications. "Oh," he said after a while.

"You see? He got off the main charge last time and they caught him on vehement suspicion of holding and defending Copernican opinions he couldn't prove."

"But we *can* prove them, surely?"

"It won't do any good, Simon. Didn't you pay any attention to the make-up of the court?"

Jones sat up straight and laughed, although there was little humor in it. "Sure I did. Especially the bit of the list that went Barberini, Barberini, Barberini."

"That didn't amount to a message?" Mazzare straightened up from the window-jamb and sat on the window-sill, which was at just the right height and sun-warmed. The sun on his back made him realize how tired he really was.

"Sure. The pope stacked the court with his brother and two of his nephews. He wants Galileo let off."

"Or convicted."

"Eh?" Jones stared hard at Mazzare with narrowed eyes. "That's not what you've been saying. What made you change your mind?"

Mazzare shrugged. "Perhaps simply being in Rome.

It's an ancient city, Simon, and the Catholic Church is almost as ancient. The pope, in the end, will do whatever he does because he believes it is for the good of the Church." Mazzare felt strangely light and calm as he spoke. "I find myself much less prepared to state that I am certain what he will decide. His Holiness does not necessarily agree with you—or me—what the interest of the Church might be. And if he decides otherwise, he has made certain that he has a tribunal which will accommodate him."

"Now hold on—" Jones rose out of his chair and wagged a finger at Mazzare. "Don't you be getting all paranoid on me, Larry. The issue is as straightforward as it gets."

"It certainly is not!" Mazzare grew sharp, then, and stood up from his warm perch on the windowsill. "Simon, we aren't preaching to small-town congregations any more. With the best will in the world, Grantville is a rural town full of plain people who don't truck with subtleties."

Jones made a sour face. "Peasants, you mean—"

"Knock it off, Simon, you know what I mean. Pollyanna it up all you want, old friend, but there won't be any straw-man arguments in that church this morning. Every single person in that tribunal is at least as good a theologian as either of us, and most of them are better. And any of them can tell you the difference. Since you're pretending not to know better, and bless you for trying to cheer me up with it, the difference is between assuming that all that is, is by the will of God, and assuming that all is according to God's ineffable plan for the universe."

Jones held up his hands. "Pax."

"Thank you, Simon, graciously done." Mazzare smiled, resuming his pacing with his head bowed and hands clasped behind him. "The prosecution will certainly advance an argument in favour of the law of necessity that is straight out of scholasticism."

"Which I'm too rusty on to know if that's right or not, but go on."

Mazzare waved Jones's objection aside for the mere bagatelle it was. "You can look it up later. The important thing is that among the schools of philosophy His Holiness Urban VIII clove to was—" He smiled encouragingly at Jones.

"Scholasticism." Jones finished the sentence in a weak voice. "And His Holiness is also a temporal ruler who will see an immediate increase in temporal power if he steps on Galileo and publicly thwarts the USE, as represented by you, and especially me, the Protestant."

"Just so."

"Oh, damn," said Jones, with feeling. "I hadn't thought of that. We've been suckered! Set up!"

Mazzare chuckled harshly. "Don't get all paranoid on me, Simon. I didn't say that's what His Holiness *would* do. Just that it was indeed a very possible option."

Jones cocked his head. "What's your best estimate?"

The American priest shrugged. "My guess is that Pope Urban VIII hasn't really quite made up his own mind yet. He wants to wait and see how the trial shapes up. Which means . . . I'm on the spot, Simon. I think he *is* leaning in our direction, actually. But I don't think 'the fix is in.' I think he wants to see if I can do the fixing."

"Ah." Jones thought about it for moment. "Pressure situation, then, like I said. But don't forget our trusty motto, Larry. When the going gets tough, the tough go theologizing."

That brought a genuine laugh from Mazzare. "The ending of that, as I recall—the last time you recited it, anyway—was 'the tough change the oil filter.'"

"There's a difference?"

One of the palazzo's servants ushered in Monsignor Mazarini.

"It is time, Father," he said. Mazarini's voice, as usual, was calm and soft-spoken; intimate, even, without being presumptuous. The voice of a master diplomat, despite still being short of his thirty-second year of life.

Mazzare stared at the young man who, in another universe, would become France's great minister of state in the fullness of time, in that era when France was the center of the Western world. A universe in which Galileo had been convicted.

A universe where the Ring of Fire had never happened.

It all fell into place for the American priest, in that moment. Larry Mazzare had wondered himself, for three years, what God's purpose had been when he ripped Grantville out of its own time to send it to another.

Many others had as well, of course, and come to their own conclusions. Gustavus Adolphus thought it was a warning to the world's princes. So, in a different way, did Cardinal Richelieu.

But they were princes themselves. Mazzare was not. He was simply a small-town priest; ultimately, a very humble man.

Yes, that was the key. Humility, nothing more.

The Ring of Fire had not been a warning at all. Just the Lord's subtle reminder that, in the end, it was not for mortals to presume to know His purpose.

"Good," said Mazzare. "I am ready."

He gave Mazarini a comforting little pat on the shoulder, on his way through the door. The man needed reassurance, he thought. In his own way, Mazarini too was a humble man—perhaps the only such, among Europe's great diplomats. Mazzare had great hopes for him.

Chapter 47

Lennox felt a prize fool. It was a lot easier to wear a couple of pounds of gold braid, a buffed cuirass and a cavalier hat in front of a rank of smartly turned-out troops than—no, he reminded himself again, Marines. It was important to remember the difference, because that was mainly why he and his men were being thoroughly gawked at.

And no wonder. President—now Prime Minister—Stearns had been caught with his pants down once due to a lack of fancy uniforms. Mike Stearns rarely made the same mistake twice. He'd certainly seen to it that this one wouldn't be repeated, even exceeding Admiral Simpson's budget request.

The new USMC Cavalry dress uniform was therefore very flashy and high-class, even by seventeenth-century standards. No utilitarian BDUs here. The crowd lining the street was suitably impressed. Even the Swiss guards were craning their necks for a good look as he rode past. Was this the normal condition of life for the quality? No matter, he was on parade no matter how foolish he felt.

Perhaps best of all, the uniforms were *new*. That

meant, down here in Italy, that probably no one would recognize them. It would be more than a bit awkward to explain what troops from the USE were doing in Rome at all, much less prancing toward the church of San Matteo where Galileo was being tried.

They'd decided to pass themselves off as Polish, if anyone asked. Heinzerling spoke enough Polish to fake the matter, from that side; and, from the other, the commonwealth of Poland and Lithuania was not only a distant country but one whose political structure was confusing enough to the Poles and Lithuanians themselves to make well-nigh any uniform plausible.

Lieutenant Trumble, decked out almost as fancy as Lennox, rode to his left; to his right, Heinzerling; and to Heinzerling's right, Sergeant Southworth. MacNish, Ritson, Faul and Milton rode behind as an honor guard, in their rather plainer dress blues.

The touch of outright farce came from Heinzerling, who had changed out of his clerical black shirt and jeans and was now sitting ramrod straight in the saddle of a mule, tricked out in sauterne and sash, bands and biretta. Lennox decided he looked like an·overweight, sweaty·chess-piece.

The mule was the final touch. Heinzerling needed a big horse, a strong and sensible beast that would carry his weight and decidedly rough-and-ready horsemanship both. As it was, it looked like having the Jesuit carry the mule under one arm would probably be more comfortable for the both of them. It was all Lennox could do not to snigger. The picture was truly absurd, but it did seem priestly humble, in its own extravagant way. All it lacked was a hairshirt for the mule.

Sergeant Southworth at least looked the part, riding next to Heinzerling as being the only Marine who could possibly pass for Catholic if pressed. Although, as far as Lennox could see, that appeared to consist entirely in being as drunk and debauched as any other Marine and vanishing to a different chapel on Sundays.

As for passing for nobility, that was even easier:

Flout the livery laws;
Surround yourself with armed retainers;
Sneer.

Lennox grinned to himself. That last was easy. He had but to remember that he was a Scotsman.

Scotsman or not, noble or not, he still had to wait in line. His own patience wasn't a problem. Lennox had suffered a career's worth of—and this was a phrase he loved the Americans for—hurry up and wait. The horses weren't too bad either. They'd used their own mounts, which they'd been careful with on the way down from Venice and kept as well as they could in the stables they'd found. They were better fed beasts than most hereabout, and plenty of grain had been bought for them since their arrival in Rome.

They were well trained, too, to the parade and to battle, and so they could stand a good while in this street. A beast that had been taught to trust its rider in the heat of battle would not spook at the smell and the noise and the tension of the crowd. His own mount barely snorted as a scuffle broke out somewhere off to his right. Either a cutpurse had worked or someone had jostled too roughly.

Ahead of them in line, as well as behind, there were riders who were not so lucky or sensible in their choice of horses. Several of the retainers and not a few of their masters were only barely keeping their mounts in check.

Lennox shaded his eyes with a gauntleted hand—kid leather, the like of which he'd never have afforded himself—and looked up to the sun. It was getting well up; perhaps nearly eight of the morning clock by a reckoning he'd gotten thoroughly used to. Unfortunately, he'd had to leave his watch behind. Yes, it gave the

time splendidly; it would just as splendidly give him
away to any observer. No officers in this day and age
except those of the USE had watches like that. Certainly
not the Poles and Lithuanians.

The line of noble parties moved forward a place.
Then, after a little while, moved forward another.
Lennox simply let his brain bake under the sun, not
thinking, allowing his horse to amble forward to make
up the gap. The crowd remained quiet, but restive,
although they seemed to be straining less against the
Swiss halberdiers than they had been. Looking closely
into the colonnades and the mouths of alleyways, he
could see gawkers who had grown bored slipping away
to be about other business of the day.

Lennox nodded to himself. That would be about
right. If they couldn't get in to see the show, there
was still the daily bread to earn. A few moments later,
another half-gallon of sweat under his cuirass, he had
another and less pleasant thought.

That meant only the real hooligans were left . . .

There was a click. Quite a loud one.

Marius was standing next to Frank in the nave of
the church they'd selected as their spot. He grunted;
then spoke a word that caused everyone nearby to turn
around and glare. Fortunately, all of them were members
of the Committee. But, revolutionary firebrands
or not, they still disapproved to a man of that kind of
language in church.

Frank looked too. Marius grinned weakly back. He
had both hands inside his tabard and his eyes were
watering. "Sorry," he said, through gritted and grinning
teeth. "I got my pistol-flint in my hand."

"What?" Frank looked around, trying not to appear
frantic. The cleared area around the sanctuary of the
church of San Matteo was busy with clerks and servants,
shuffling papers and making ready. There were pews
waiting for nobles and a path was kept open between

the sanctuary and the pulpit. Everywhere else, it was breathing-room only for the crowd in the nave and the transepts and more were still coming in. At the doors, the Swiss Guard were growling at the pressed crowd to keep them back from the building. The Committee had gotten in early, and they had all been standing for several hours.

And in all this, Marius, the idiot, had started playing with his pistol. Well, it was of a piece with everything else about him.

"I said," Marius repeated with the deliberation of a man in richly deserved pain, "I got my flint in my hand. She went off in my hand, and I got my hand in the way of the flint." He took a deep breath. "My hand is trapped."

Frank groaned, softly.

Gerry leaned forward and tugged Frank's shoulder. "What's the putz done now?" he hissed in English.

"Trapped his hand in his flintlock," Frank hissed.

"Typical," Gerry grunted. He leaned back again. A short moment and a little whispering later, Frank heard a soft groan ripple right along the row behind. Marius Pontigrazzi was becoming a legend in his own lifetime, truly he was.

Another loud click. Frank tensed up. Not content with playing with the lock of his pistol and—surely he didn't deserve the luck—only getting his hand trapped, he had now cocked it to get his hand out.

"Marius?" Frank said, very carefully and slowly.

"*Si?*"

"I want you to freeze perfectly still with your pistol just as you are." Frank kept his tone of voice perfectly level, which really took some doing.

"Why?" asked Marius, turning his head and frowning back.

Frank's voice stayed low, but he couldn't keep the threatening note out of the monotone he spoke in. "Because if you don't, I'll fucking shoot you myself. I can't believe you'd be dumb enough to mess with your pistol in an Inquisition courtroom."

To his surprise, Frank saw that the Marcoli youngsters were now glaring at *him*. Why—?

Oh. It was all he could do not to scream with sheer frustration. Revolutionary firebrands, one minute; prim and proper old ladies the next. Frank's Italian was getting very, very fluent, including the profanity.

In church, remember.

He moved his lips closer to Marius' ear and whispered. "Don't. Move. I. Will. Fix. The. Gun." He found himself wishing that Ducos were standing nearby. Frank didn't like the man, but Michel would be the best one to handle Marius. Unfortunately, Ducos was standing some fifteen feet away. Far enough that he wasn't even aware of what was happening.

Marius started to scowl, in that oxlike manner the man had when he decided to be stubborn about something. But then Gerry leaned forward. He was wearing a long coat despite the heat the day promised; from under it came the sound of a lock clicking back. Fortunately, as distinctive as it was, the sound was not loud enough to be heard beyond a few feet in the soft murmur of the crowd.

"Like my big brother said," he hissed into Marius' other ear, "hands out away from the fucking piece. Do as he says."

The Committee boys knew better than to glare at Gerry for his language. The youngest of the three Stone brothers was easily the most pugnacious. He'd just glare back at them. Besides, by this point they were all as desperate as Frank to get the situation under control. And, whatever his language, Gerry had done that.

Frank realized that they were speaking loudly enough that the people in the row in front were trying to lean away from them. Not because they'd heard the specifics of the dispute, but simply because they understood some sort of dispute was happening. Shuffling was

out of the question, but they were trying it anyway.
Frank knew that the solid block of Committee guys
were in danger of starting their own Mexican wave.
Worse, once the guys at the edge started shoving back,
Marius might get jostled, or worse, someone might
take offense and—

"Marius!" he hissed. Marius jerked his hands out of
his tabard in a way that made Frank age about fifty
years in an instant. A second or two passed in which
Frank listened for the sound of priming and . . .

The pistol didn't fire. Frank let out a long, loud
breath. From the row behind there was the soft click
of a lock being uncocked that told him that Gerry
had relaxed too.

Marius, meanwhile, had raised his hands about level
to his armpits. "Don't shoot, okay?" His face was white.
Frank looked up and saw a deep, painful-looking gouge
where the flint had struck. It was bleeding. Serve the
idiot right.

"Just hold still," he whispered. Frank reached into
Marius' tabard and discovered that, just to add to
the list of Dumb Stuff Marius Did Today, he had his
pistol stuffed down the front of his britches. It was
all he could do not to snarl: *You know, I ought to
just pull the trigger so's you don't breed and pass on
your stupidity.*

But he restrained himself. His dad's influence, there.
One of the few things that would get Tom Stone really
pissed was hearing people make fun of dimwits, even
if he didn't like the dimwits himself.

Frank found the priming pan and, by feel, flipped it
open. A tap, a shake, and he spilled the powder out.
It would dribble down Marius' legs inside the tabard,
but Frank couldn't think of any alternative. He didn't
dare bring the pistol out into the open.

That done, he reached his other hand in so that,
two-handed, he could uncock the thing safely.

Good enough. He didn't even consider repriming the

pistol. Given Marius, it would be best to just leave it disarmed. When the breakout happened, Marius could wave it around and bellow. Nothing else, he'd add to the confusion.

Leaving the pistol behind, Frank pulled his hands out of the tabard. "Don't do that again, Marius. Understand me?"

Some part of Frank's brain was astonished at his own tone of voice. The words he'd spoken, however softly, had been sheer menace. Sounded like something young Corleone would have said in *The Godfather.* Either one of them, father or son. Soft, calm, guaranteeing instant and sure oblivion.

Marius lowered his hands. He was visibly trembling, and his eyes were wide and bright with the starting of tears. As the man could do, he'd shifted in a split-second from a somewhat surly and none-too-bright adult to a bewildered, childish simpleton. Frank was glad now that he'd left those words unspoken. In this as in so many things, his sometimes goofy dad was still smarter than most people—not to mention a lot nicer.

Frank sniffed, and then looked down. Marius was standing in a puddle. A puddle that was already steaming slightly, in a church that was warming up rapidly with the sunshine and the press of bodies. Luckily, like most big cities of the time, Rome tended to smell a bit like a cesspool anyway. Frank didn't think anybody would notice unless they actually looked—which was none too likely, in this jam-packed mob.

He sighed softly. It was going to be a fuc—a long wait. Frank glanced guiltily at the nearest image of Jesus and silently apologized to him for even thinking about thinking a swearword in church.

It was still going to be a fucking long wait.

"I still dinnae believe that worked," Lennox muttered.

Heinzerling turned back around to him, and grinned. He was aiming for disarming, but the nearest the fat priest could manage was mischievous. "This city is so hierarchical, Captain. What they expect to see, they see."

Lennox grunted. Like all soldiers, he was a practical man, and he wasn't about to argue with success. Besides, he was too busy trying not to gawk. Accustomed as he was to the dour Calvinist chapels of home, and their equivalent in Germany, the interior of the Inquisition's church of San Matteo was a mild shock.

Not the gilt and art and ostentation, in itself. Lennox had seen plenty of that in his travels, and had gotten used to the idea that rich men decorated their homes and places of business in that manner, even if he disapproved on general principles. Seeing it all in a place of worship, however—he'd seldom had cause to step inside a Catholic church before—brought back the fiery sermons he'd heard over and over since his youth.

Idolatry. Whore of Rome. Gilded harlot. Babylon reborn.

Too, now that he thought about it, the last Catholic church Lennox had set foot in had been St. Mary's in Grantville, a church of stark and elegant simplicity inside. Almost Calvinist, compared to this confection of gilt and plaster and stone and just about every artifice or decoration imaginable.

He shook his head to clear it of the gleams of gilt and marble, and craned his neck to peer down the nave. He'd tried to keep an eye out to both sides when he had walked up to the seats reserved for the nobility, but either he'd looked left when he should have looked right or the Stone boys were hiding. "Can ye see 'em?"

"*Nein,*" Heinzerling murmured back. He too was craning his neck, one boot on the pew behind him. Lennox fought down the urge to tell him to get his foot off the seat.

"I see them now," Heinzerling hissed. "In the nave, on the left."

Lennox looked. Now they were pointed out, they were obvious, even though they all had their heads down. Frank was the most visible of the three, and seemed to be preoccupied with someone standing next to him. The other two brothers had to be there, though; the rascals were practically inseparable—something of which, under most circumstances, Lennox highly approved.

Sure enough, he caught sight of Gerry in the next row back. He, too, was staring hard at the man next to Frank.

Frank Stone picked that moment to look up, and his eyes caught Lennox's.

"I think he recognizes you," Heinzerling said. Indeed, Frank's expression was practically a beacon of despair.

"Likely so. And if no' me, ye're ain mug's yin he'll ken right enough," Lennox muttered back, not taking his glare away from Frank for a second.

"Gerry?" Frank said, when he realized who it was that was staring at him. "It's Lennox."

"He caught up? Where, man?"

"Up front, in the seats." Frank didn't dare point. He retained the fond, slight hope that they hadn't been spotted. Even though Lennox was staring right at him. And, um, glaring. Really glaring. Like Clint Eastwood glaring at a criminal in a Dirty Harry movie.

"I see him now. We still with the plan?"

"Plan? Uh, maybe we should . . ." Frank couldn't think of anything to say. His mind was drawing a complete blank.

"Should what?" Gerry asked, his voice getting a little warmer. "Give up?"

"Well, we—" Frank tried again.

"Don't say it, man. Just don't, all right?"

"Say what? All I was thinking is we're busted, you know, and—"

"You reckon?" Frank's heart sank. He could tell from his tone of voice that Gerry wasn't worried at all. With Gerry, that was a bad sign. A very very bad sign. When he was in that state of mind, Gerry could drive off a cliff and insist he wasn't in trouble until he hit the ground.

"What do you mean, busted?" Gerry snorted.

Frank groaned, softly. "They're right there, man. I see Lennox, and Father Gus, and I bet they got the Marines somewhere nearby. We're busted, I tell you. Totally busted."

"Relax, will you? They can't do anything. They can't just waltz over here and haul us away, because they can't tell anyone who we are or why we're here ourselves. We're talking major diplomatic incident here, man. They've got to pretend they don't know us. We won that one as soon as we got here before them, Frank. We carry on just as we planned."

"Sure, but do they know that?"

"I reckon Gus is smart enough to figure it out."

Gerry spoke with the tone of an empiricist whose evidence is in. Frank, though, was uncomfortably aware of the number of times he'd seen Father Gus get an idea stuck in his head and stick with it past all reason. And Lennox was right there with him. The bare-knuckle "theological debate" the two of them had once gotten into at the Thuringen Gardens was a thing of legend in Grantville.

But . . . Frank couldn't think of anything else to do either, except play it by ear. This supposedly well-planned scheme was about to get very unpredictable. Lyrics by Antonio Marcoli; music by Michel Ducos. What else could you expect?

"I pissed myself," Marius whined. "My legs are getting cold."

That wasn't helping Frank's nerves any, either.

❊ ❊ ❊

"If ye've any suggestions, Augustus, ye ken richt weel this is the time for 'em," Lennox murmured to Heinzerling.

The Inquisition's public hearing—an innovation in itself—was being held in San Matteo because that was the Inquisition's "home" church. The ruse Heinzerling had devised had gotten Lennox and himself inside the church; had even gotten them some of the prized seats—but not, unfortunately, the squad of cavalrymen. Those had had to remain outside, with Lieutenant Trumble in command.

They'd gotten seats with the quality at the very head of the nave, close to the pulpit. The sanctuary was behind them, and the Stone boys and their Venetian cohorts had picked a spot to stand right at the front of the common peoples' part of the nave. A small knot of them, right by the aisle. No doubt they had meant to have an escape route clear, but the aisle was also filling up.

"I should have more ideas, *mein' ich*, if I knew what these *knaben* were planning, *ja*?" Heinzerling tried to match Lennox's fixed stare at the Stone boys with a constant scan around the place.

"Och, I ken that right enough."

"*Ja*?"

"All we've to do is dream up the stupidest thing the bampots could possibly do, and there is their plan."

The note of humor in Lennox's voice was genuine. Heinzerling realized he, too, had a sneaking regard for the Stone boys. At their age he'd been a prize little prig, and would never have dreamed of doing something so glorious, adventurous and utterly *verrückt*. It had taken him *years* to learn how to be so daft.

"Perhaps it is so easy as to go over there and insist they leave with us before the business begins?" Heinzerling couldn't think of anything else to do. Besides, simplicity was usually the right solution to a problem anyway. "In fact, we shall, yes? Stop them before they start. They will not know that we dare not try and force them for fear of diplomatic embarrassment."

"Oh, dare we not? I'll hae th'idjits oot o' here by the baw-heers and never mind their eyes watr'in nor any diplomacy, Augustus. Ye've confession an' absolution and like Romish stuff, so it strikes me we'd do better to think on forgiveness and no let frae any man, eh?" Lennox's face was turned away from Heinzerling's, but the brawler's grin was loud and clear in his voice.

"Speak so to our boys, and I think they will believe you." Heinzerling looked down at where the Stone boys, all three, and their Venetian friends had their eyes fixed on Lennox. He could see the effect Lennox's grim smile was having on them. "Shall we not go, then?" he proposed. "Before the trial begins, and while they are still nervous."

"Aye. Wi' me, then," said Lennox, rising from his seat.

At that moment a chime rang and the entire congregation rose.

"Hold," Heinzerling whispered. "It begins."

"Och, bully, we dithered too long. Maybe we should—"

Heinzerling hissed for quiet. Sitting side on to the main axis of the nave, they had to crane to look in either direction. Stealing a glance over his shoulder, Heinzerling saw Cardinal Barberini—the youngest of the three, the one his former master Monsignor Mazarini had worked for—walking down the sanctuary, accompanied by a small flotilla of deacons and altar boys. Barberini was clearly about to make some kind of speech. Behind him came another eight men in the vestments of Inquisitors. Only four of them besides Barberini himself were cardinals, which was unusual in itself.

Barberini stood at the sanctuary rail and cleared his throat.

Probably a standard speech, Heinzerling thought. As the cardinal began to address the congregation, he turned to watch the boys carefully for any signs of movement. Now that he was in a standing position he could see more of the row behind them.

There, suddenly, he saw a man whose description he recognized. All traces of humor vanished.

"Ducos. *Scheisse!*"

Chapter 48

Cardinal Antonio Barberini had the rare experience of proceeding into a church without knowing exactly what would take place, and knowing he would not. Scheiner was to make the principal speech against Galileo, Grassi having finally agreed that perhaps he was a little too involved, a little too likely to attach undue personal vehemence. And, on the other side, the American priest Mazzare had been ordered to speak on Galileo's behalf.

The church was packed. The day was growing warm, and all Rome seemed to have turned out to see Galileo tried. Or, rather, not tried, but inquired into. The Inquisition had done so much of its business behind closed doors, for so long, that a public hearing raised a great deal of curiosity. Much of it morbid, the cardinal suspected.

Barberini's presence, and the presence of the other inquisitors—it would be as well to put the name to them that everyone else would, even though they were not, lawfully, of the Holy Office—brought the assembled congregation to silence.

"Brethren in Christ—" he began, and realized that off to his right, the silence was not complete.

The cardinal had little of either German or English, but he recognized the one word, a German obscenity. And then something he couldn't follow.

Another voice, in English this time, or so he thought. He glared, trying to place the grossly improper interruption. He could feel his face purpling as his ire and outrage increased—

There! He saw them. A nobleman of some kind and his attendant priest. They fell silent, staring back at him in silent apology, murmurs spreading out from them.

What to do? Any response would carry the whole proceeding into farce, he decided. Today was not a day to stand on dignity at the price of solemnity. He kept silence for a beat or two, and carried on.

"Brethren in Christ, today's proceedings are novel, an innovation before you all. What falls to be decided today is the terms of advice to be given to His Holiness the Pope by the Holy Office and the other learned fathers you see behind me. Let us pray that the Holy Spirit is upon us all—"

He said a simple blessing. The amen that followed it was a quiet thing, but from a thousand or more throats almost thunderously loud.

A few more preliminary remarks, upon the great weight of theological questions, the mortal peril to men's souls of error, and then Galileo was brought in. Another murmur. This was the man about whom the Holy Office had ordered sermons preached. The man whose ideas they had all been told were dangerous. What would they think to see him given an open hearing?

He told the congregation that Scheiner would deliver the first address and sat down.

Mazzare nodded to Scheiner as the man rose in response to hearing his name. A small area in the transept had been screened off for them to remain in, to take notes toward the addresses they must give if they so chose. Scheiner went to the pulpit to begin the process of damning Galileo, who even now was being seated in the sanctuary, a chair having been brought in for the old man. Mazzare could just see where Galileo sat, facing the congregation, slumped in the chair, head bowed and hands in his lap.

It was hard to square the meek, frightened old man with the fiery disputant who had delivered so many kicks to the backside of Europe's scientific establishment over the last thirty years. And, being honest, more than a few to the crotch. Galileo had often been wrong, too, especially when he delved into astronomical matters, a field in which he really accomplished nothing as a theoretician; his great contribution there was his invention of the telescope and his observational data. He'd been wrong about the nature of comets, when he opposed Tycho Brahe; wrong again when he opposed Kepler on the cause of the tides. Ironically, the popular image of the man as a great astronomer that would emerge over the centuries was due almost entirely to his trial.

Galileo's real contribution to science had been in the field of mechanics, not astronomy. But no matter where Galileo's interests took him, one thing had remained constant through the years: his arrogance, and his abusive conduct toward any who opposed him. Galileo had rarely hesitated to pile personal insult onto scholarly sarcasm. Nor was he given to any great scruples when it came to grabbing credit for himself or denying it to others. He paid no attention to his great contemporary Johannes Kepler, the first two of whose famous three laws of planetary motion had been published as far back as 1609, and the third law ten years later. Newton's three laws would derive from Kepler, not from Galileo.

Galileo had fumbled the defense of the Copernican theory, too. Because he refused to pay attention to what Kepler was doing, Galileo had been unable to solve the apparent contradictions of the Copernican theory—and it was that, as much as anything, that had ultimately led to his trial for heresy. The fact would become obscured in the historical record because of the glamour surrounding Galileo's "martyrdom," but the simple truth was that in the early seventeenth century Ptolemaic theory predicted the movements of the heavenly bodies better than Copernican theory did—with the exception of Kepler, who finally discovered that the planetary orbits were ellipses rather than circles.

Anyone who knew Galileo Galilei, and Mazarre had spoken to several of them, knew that he was abrasive and obnoxiously self-righteous if he was not impressed with the need to be mannerly. His months under the orders of the Inquisition had agreed with him to that extent, at least. The reports that he was by nature a bully had been made false at last, in the way most such reports were made false: the man had encountered a bigger bully.

Out in the main body of the church, Scheiner had ascended to the pulpit and was beginning his oration. In traditional style, in Latin. How much of it the congregation was following was anyone's guess, but the important part of the audience was all fluent in the language. Latin in this day and age was the primary language of science as well as religion.

And there was another of the historical ironies of Galileo's trial, Mazzare thought wryly. The world would come to remember it as a clash between science and religion, the latter embodied in the Catholic Church. Which, to a degree, it certainly was. But the world would forget that most of the great scientists of the day were also Catholic clerics, including Copernicus himself—and that the early track record of the Protestants on the subject of science was considerably more dismal than the Catholics. It was Protestant theologians who first denounced the Copernican theory for being contrary to Scripture. Both Luther and Melanchthon had inveighed against Copernicus, where Popes Leo X and Paul III had provided him with support.

Mazzare had scripted his own speech, and was confident enough in the language to be taking notes. Not at the moment, though, as Scheiner was beginning with a rehearsal of the facts of the matter that, Galileo had agreed, was pretty much accurate.

"Stage fright, Larry?" The Reverend Jones put a hand on his shoulder.

"Yes, Simon," Mazzare murmured, one ear on the dry, German-accented Latin coming from the pulpit. "It'd be easier if what I'd had from Galileo wasn't just a lot of wheedling about being misunderstood."

"Sure. How did the stuff on the space program go down with him? I meant to ask, but you know how it is." Jones waved his hand in a small motion that took in the church, the congregation they could see through the fretwork screen, the inquisitors sitting across the sanctuary like a jury of vestmented vultures.

Mazzare chuckled humorlessly. "Galileo, bless him, whimpered and insisted that it had to all be fraud, because obviously Copernicanism was contrary to Scripture, and hadn't I read his defense of it?"

"Seriously?"

"He thinks I'm an inquisitor, Simon."

"No kidding?" Jones blew out a long, silent whistle, as much sigh as anything. "I suppose two years of the Inquisition could make a man paranoid, at that."

"I reckon it could. I've tried to convince him, of course, but I've only really had a couple of chances to talk to him. I could've pushed it, I think, or at least Francesco Barberini was hinting that way, but at the end of the day this isn't about what the fellow thinks, it's about what he wrote."

"A masterful summation, if I may say so." Mazzare and Jones turned at the new voice.

"Your Holiness," said Mazzare, rising to his feet.

"I did not—" He stopped, and began to rephrase his response in Latin.

"Please, in English if you prefer," said the pope. He had entered alone, although behind him in the aisle that led back to the sacristy there was a small cloud of priests and deacons. "But, yes, it is about what he wrote. Please, try not to fear. The worst I propose to sanction is a reprimand to Galileo, and an order that—but no mind to the details. You need not fear that you will fail your client to the extent of his losing his life or liberty. That is an error you have already convinced me away from."

"Your Holiness . . ." Mazzare stopped. What to say? He stole a glance at Jones, whose mouth was hanging open. "Your Holiness, why? If you propose no more than to reprimand Galileo for his ill manners, why do we have this—" He waved over his shoulder, where Scheiner was still droning, not having come to the part of his speech where oratorical flourish would serve.

"You think it a cheat?" If Mazzare did not know better, he would swear that the poker face of His Holiness Urban VIII, Vicar of Christ and head of the Roman Catholic Church, concealed a broad grin.

Somehow that was comforting. "Perhaps I would not use *that* word," said Mazzare, feeling the tension drain out of him. "But perhaps this has more of the character of the *commedia* than the congregation think?"

"A dumb-show?" Now the pope was definitely grinning. "Not without purpose, though."

"Does His Holiness care to make that purpose known?"

"Ah, perhaps later. For now, my blessing, my son." Urban raised his hand, and spoke the Latin words of benediction.

Mazzare crossed himself in response, and his ultimate superior—realizing that he genuinely thought of him that way was a great comfort—left the room. He saw, out of the corner of his eye, that Jones had his

arm partly raised. Had he been about to forget and
cross himself as well? Somehow Mazzare found the
idea hilarious.

"I think your nerves just went away," muttered
Jones, with an expression that said his were still out
in force.

Mazzare just grinned.

"Come on, Larry, you know more than you're letting on." Jones's face was a study. *Preacher, growing
tetchy.*

"I know exactly what you do. I may reach different
conclusions from it than you do, but I'm reasoning from
the same premises." Mazzare hummed softly beneath
his breath. Listening to himself, he realized it was the
theme from, of all things, *The Magnificent Seven.* What
that had to do with orbital mechanics or theology—or
the price of fish, for that matter—he had no idea.

"Is this going to go on much longer?" Gerry hissed
in Frank's ear.

Frank tried telepathy. *Shutupshutupshutupshutup.
We'rerightdownfrontyoumoron. Shutupshutupshutup.*

It didn't work. "Only we need to do something or
get off the pot, you know?"

Frank half turned and whispered out of the corner
of his mouth. "Let's just wait, okay? We already agreed
we can't make our break until the end of the trial,
when there's a crowd leaving anyway. We get in there,
drag him back, and use the cover of the crowd to get
out. If they can't shoot and they can't shut the doors,
we got a much better chance."

"Yeah, but I don't understand a word and he could
be reading out a death sentence for all I know." Frank
caught the undertone in Gerry's voice that said he was
right on the edge.

Of course, there was an undertone from Marius that
said he was well and truly over that edge, but it wasn't
a voice undertone. More of a warm, ripe, smell. He

hadn't just had one bodily accident—now he was farting
loudly every thirty seconds or so as well. Frank could see
where Gerry's patience might be wearing a little thin.
The smell of gunpowder spilt down the inside of Marius'
tabard wasn't helping matters any. If anyone caught on
to *that*, they were really in the soup. In a way, it was a
mercy he'd wet himself; it kept the smell of gunpowder
faint and disguised, which Frank thought only someone
standing right next to Marius could detect.

Frank considered that for a few seconds, and had
a moment of utter horror. *How have I gotten myself
into a situation where I'm glad I'm standing in a
puddle of piss?*

"Frank," Gerry hissed again, and then: "Knock it
off, Ron!"

At least one other person back there was thinking
straight, Frank realized with relief. From the sound of
things, Ron had elbowed his brother in the ribs. He
couldn't follow the hissing whispers behind him, but
from the sound of things it was pretty intense and
Ron was getting the upper hand in the game of Shut
Gerry Up Right Now.

And then the priest who was droning on came to
a halt. There was a little polite applause, mostly from
the old guys who were sitting up by the altar, and
everything went silent.

The short fat young guy who'd kicked things off got
up again. Before he spoke, he glared to his right where
Lennox and Heinzerling were sitting. Then he paused
and began to speak in the unmistakable manner of a
man announcing the next act. And Frank realized he
recognized two names in all that Latin:

One, the name of the town he had grown up in,
and the other . . .

Surely not! Here?

Heinzerling wondered what to do now. There was
a definite French agent with the Stone boys, and the

big Jesuit needed no reminding that the phrase *agent provocateur* was seldom translated from its original language whenever it was used. Heinzerling's own parish priest was about to speak at the trial that that agent had come to, probably with the American boys as his unwitting dupes. What had seemed to be nothing worse than adolescent idiot enthusiasm now had a far more sinister flavor. Whatever the role of Ducos, the fact remained that everything was happening in the presence of Grantville's Catholic priest; an accredited ambassador of the United States of Europe; a commissioned officer of the same nation—and any outrage would be committed by three of its citizens.

Right in the home church of the Roman Inquisition, just to make it all perfect.

After chewing on the situation, Heinzerling decided it was comforting. From the absolute bottom of the Pit, after all, the only way is up.

Mazzare found his nerves returning as he mounted the steps to the pulpit. The congregation was enormous; he had never seen St. Mary's so packed, other than on Christmas Eve at midnight mass. He took a moment to arrange his notes on the lectern, and without thinking, crossed himself. On a whim, he decided to pretend he meant to do that, and folded his hands and bowed his head. He couldn't think of any prayer that suited, other than *Please, Lord, don't let me mess this up,* which at least had the virtues of simplicity and sincerity.

As he stood, he took in the congregation, and immediately wished he hadn't. In front of the pulpit, ranged on either side of the nave, were the choirstall-seats for the quality. And right at the front of those seats were Heinzerling and Lennox. Which meant—

Yes, there they were. The Stone boys had reached Rome and clearly had plans in relation to Galileo that . . . Mazzare shuddered, and realized that he didn't want to think about that. *Please, let it be harmless. Let them be discouraged.*

Could he draw attention to—? No, he looked down at Heinzerling. His curate was making motions with his hands that said *go on, go on.*

Mazzare realized his knees were trembling, but his hands and face felt perfectly steady. He took a deep breath.

"Brethren in Christ, most learned fathers of the Holy Office," he began.

Chapter 49

Mazzare stepped down from the pulpit, on unsteady legs. Somewhere, behind him, he could hear a murmur. Some of the crowd must have understood some of what he'd said, but he couldn't read their reaction from the murmurs. Throughout there had been virtually no reaction from anyone, except Galileo, who had hunched in on himself more and more as Mazzare had spoken, and then toward the end sat up straighter, as if remembering where he was and trying to show—what, exactly? Had it been a response to something Mazzare had been saying?

He couldn't remember much of it. Virtually nothing, in fact. How different from an ordinary sermon! When the audience was familiar, the material well tried, the consequences only a little more of Scripture explained to a congregation who had just heard it, speaking to a crowd was easy. When the audience included princes of his Church, the material in a language not his own and the consequences—

He balked from the thought. What if the gap in his memory covered a string of incoherent babble? He looked down at the notes in his hand. He hadn't turned more than the first page, which was purely introductory material. From then on he'd been extemporizing; expounding on the spot based on nothing more, really, than an epiphany that had come to him only that very morning.

A friendly face. "Simon—how?" He couldn't get more control than that of his mouth.

"You killed 'em, Larry." Jones's voice was deadpan, but his face was grinning from ear to ear. "Couldn't follow but one word in three, but after the first couple of minutes, you really seemed to get hold of it and made 'em listen, by God!" He reached round to slap Mazzare on the back.

Mazzare felt a cold shiver run down his back. Still no idea what he'd really said. He looked across to the sanctuary. No movement there, except for cardinals leaning over to mutter things to each other and to dart glances in his direction. *What are they thinking?* Cardinal Barberini, the younger one, wasn't moving yet.

"Please, do you speak German?" Mazzare felt dizzy as he whipped his head around. It was Scheiner.

"Yes, of course, can I help you?" Mazzare mouthed the pleasantry, but he couldn't imagine what to say of any substance.

"I simply wish to say that that was very well said. My own efforts will be in the shade now, I think." The Jesuit smiled thinly, and with a little sadness as well. "Your exegesis on the subject of humility was, I think, very well taken."

"On the what?" The words didn't seem to register.

"On humility, Father Mazzare. You were aware that His Holiness was present?" The smile was still there, still a little sad; but now, Mazzare realized, with a little warmth as well.

"Ah, yes. He spoke to me while you were at the podium."

Scheiner nodded. "It always pays to use arguments that you know will go over well, yes?"

"I'm sorry, I don't follow you." Mazzare felt like his skull was stuffed with cotton, his mouth dry and leathery. "Please, forgive me, I need to sit down."

"No, I understand," Scheiner said. "His Holiness grounded much of his opposition to the Copernican hypothesis on the principle of humility, that we should not pretend to know all that God has wrought in the world and in the heavens. To turn that around to show that we must therefore not presume that we have any perfect understanding of what is in Scripture, that any word is the final word, was excellent. I suspect that will be a point of quite vital dispute for some years to come."

"Dispute which I shall be glad to hear before making my final pronouncement." Again, the pope surprised Mazzare with his presence. Distantly, Mazzare could hear Barberini addressing the congregation. "Most eloquent, Padre. I must speak with you later; my secretary"—he gestured to a youngish priest at his elbow—"will make the arrangements. We have much to discuss, little of it to do with natural philosophy. My purpose today was to hear you defend Galileo and take your measure."

Urban smiled, a bit slyly. "Galileo would approve. I made an experiment. I am pleased with the results, and there is therefore a service which you may perform for me. I shall tell you later. For now, I will address this Commission, and the congregation present."

With that, he mounted the steps to the side of the sacristy, and walked across to his nephew, the cardinal.

"Can he do that?" It was Jones.

"Do what, Simon?"

"Just order you about like that?" Jones was scowling.

"Well, he is the pope." Mazzare smiled. "And I am a Catholic priest."

"Yes, but—"

"He can," said Scheiner, in German. "And after today, I think he must."

"Thought you didn't speak English?" Jones shot back.

"Not well, and I prefer German or Latin. Herr Mazzare," he said, turning to his fellow Catholic, "I think perhaps you may find yourself advanced in the Church. Or I miss my surmise—but His Holiness is about to speak."

Heinzerling sat, stunned. He knew Mazzare could talk, had lived with him for nearly two years now. He knew that, impassioned as he so rarely was, he could speak with fire and power. *That* had been something else again. *To imagine that the truth of the Heavens as it may be seen, and the truth of Scripture as it may be understood, should contradict each other . . .* Where Mazzare had acquired the knack of such *excellent* epigrams was beyond Heinzerling. It made him regret abandoning his studies after he left the seminary.

And yet, there remained Galileo. The speech had seemed to put some spirit back into the old man, but he remained amid his inquisitors, still a prisoner, nothing yet resolved. After a short time, Barberini rose again, and began to speak further.

Inconsequential. Heinzerling ignored it. If proceedings were about to end, now would be the time for the Stone boys to do something stupid. No, he corrected himself, something even stupider.

He watched them carefully. They looked alert. They looked ready. They looked—eager. Some of them must have realized that the quality in the seats where he and Lennox had gotten themselves put would be leaving first, and so they would have a clear run. Would they realize that that would leave the two adults with the initiative to act first? Would they try and pre-empt the final *go in peace*?

There was a stir in the congregation. Heinzerling looked around.

"Who's yon laddie?" Lennox murmured.

Heinzerling recognized him only by his white soutane. Only one cleric wore that . . .

"The pope," he said.

A sharp intake of breath from Lennox. The principal fiend in the demonology of his own religion. "Aye? He's a man for a' that, is he not?"

"*Ja.*" There really was no other answer Heinzerling could give. He knew how it was with some of these Calvinists. They heard that the pope was the Antichrist from the day they were born. Most of them, naturally, would little expect ever to be in Rome, let alone in the same room as the Beast of Revelation.

Heinzerling sighed. "Please do not call him any bad names, Captain Lennox."

"Wouldnae dream o' it," said Lennox. "E'en the de'il gets his due, and I'll be polite, richt enough."

Heinzerling realized he'd been had. He didn't have to turn around. Lennox's grin over his shoulder could be felt.

The congregation fell silent as the pope raised his arms for silence.

"Who's that?" whispered Gerry.

"Dunno," said Frank.

"*Il Papa,*" breathed Marius.

Up on what Frank kept thinking of as the stage, the guy in white . . .

"Hold on. Did you say that was the pope?"

"Yes," said Marius, his eyes bright and intent.

"The actual pope? Here?" Frank couldn't believe it. He'd only ever seen one pope, and that was on TV. This was the actual pope, right here in the room with him! "Cool."

"Yes," said Marius. Something about his tone worried Frank for a reason he couldn't quite put his finger on.

But the pope—*the actual pope! right here!*—was raising his hands like he was a rock star or something, and people were going quiet.

"*Urbi et orbi,*" he said, and Frank lost him right there. Another speech in Latin. Couldn't these guys do something in one of the three languages he did know? There was a long pause.

"*Eppur se muove.*" That got a big reaction, but Frank couldn't understand why.

And then Marius drew out his pistol, shoved his way through the row of people in front of him, leveled the pistol at the pope, screamed, *"Information wants to be liberated!"* and pulled the trigger.

Heinzerling never saw how Lennox managed it, but he seemed to spring out of his seat like a child's toy and bounce out of the pew and into the aisle. The pistol that the man standing beside Frank Stone had produced was a flintlock of some sort, which meant it was manufactured in the USE. While Heinzerling's brain was still wincing from that and searching for the logic of the bizarre battle-cry, Lennox was leaping into the line of—

—nothing. The man with the pistol looked down at it, then more closely at his lock, and then colored bright red. Heinzerling noticed, in the clarity that such moments produce, that he seemed to have wet himself.

Lennox landed on his side. He'd loosened the strap of the fancy helmet earlier, once they'd taken their seats in the church. The helmet fell off, bounced oddly because of its shape, and rolled right in front of Frank. The reason it could do that was because the row of people who'd been standing in front of the Stone and Marcoli boys had frantically parted to the side.

The young idiots were now the center of attention of—

The whole world, it seemed.

Heinzerling's eyes quickly ranged about. Not counting Lennox, who was now scrambling back onto his feet, there were expressions of horror on every face he could see.

Including, thank God, the Stone and Marcoli boys themselves.

So, they couldn't have known—but would it save them?

Silence. Frank felt freezing cold all over, as the sweat started from his skin. Never had he felt so thankful for doing anything as for shaking the primer out of Marius' gun. What to say? What to do now?

Gerry supplied the lack. "You jackass!" he hollered, charging forward and drawing his own pistol. "You just fucking shot at the *POPE!*" By the time Marius looked up from his own gun, Gerry was standing in front of him and had the barrel of his pistol pressed into Marius' throat.

Everyone else in the church still seemed frozen. Frank hoped that the pause was because no one believed what they were seeing, and not because a horde of hidden marksmen were taking careful aim.

And then Frank saw two other guns, sliding forward between Ron and the two Marcoli brothers standing at his side. Looking up, he saw the faces of Ducos and his Roman Committee member.

It all came to him, then, in a flash of understanding. Not any of the details, just the essence of the matter.

He suckered us.

There was no way Frank could get his pistol out in time, he realized. "Ron! Heads up!" Frank flipped the helmet with his foot, just enough to catch it on his instep—if he tried actually kicking the damn thing he'd break his bones—and flung it at the pistols. Ron looked up just in time to duck.

The helmet missed everybody, but it came close

enough to Ducos' Roman confederate to throw off his aim. His pistol fired high, the bullet whanging somewhere above.

Ducos, alas, never even flinched. He took a step forward, thrusting Fabrizio aside, and drew a bead on the pope. With a feeling of complete dismay, Frank was sure that Ducos was a crack shot on top of everything else.

Marius grappled with Gerry. Gerry's gun went off, still stuck into Marius' throat. It looked like he'd almost been decapitated. The blood sprayed everywhere, some of it splattering into Frank's face.

Frank grabbed at his eyes. He heard a hiss of priming and another flintlock firing. Ducos, he was sure.

Someone was screaming something. Was it him?

It was him.

Again, silence. Quite clearly, he heard the pope say a word, in a church in which a pin could have dropped. *"Merda!"*

It must be okay if the pope does it, he thought.

Then something hit him on the head and he blacked out.

The gun in the hand of Ducos went off. Stunned, shocked silence. The pope said something very unpontifical, and then all hell broke loose in the church. The Swiss guards were finally reacting. One of them swatted Frank on the head with his halberd; fortunately, using the heavy shaft for the purpose and not the deadly blade. A compromise, apparently; the guard must have realized that Frank was not one of the assassins, but he still wasn't taking any chances.

But Heinzerling only caught a glimpse of that. His attention was on Lennox, who had leapt in front of the pope again and then been slammed off his feet, falling onto his backside. While a scuffle broke out in the front row of the nave, and guards rushed in from the side-aisles, Lennox was doubled up on the floor, grunting something under his breath that sounded decidedly vehement.

The pope, untouched, was staring down at him. His mouth was agape.

Ron Stone had ducked the helmet more out of reflex than anything else. The only conscious thought he'd had at the instant he heard Frank's warning shout and saw the helmet sailing toward him was: *What the hell is Frank doing messing about with soccer at a time like this?*

By the time he'd straightened up and could see what was happening, Ducos was hauling out a second pistol. A wheel-lock, this time. So was the guy from the Roman Committee. Ron still didn't understand exactly what was happening, but he understood enough to know that Ducos and his Roman companion had gone from *one of us* to *those dirty rotten bastards.*

Even if he hadn't figured it out himself, the sight of Fabrizio and Dino grappling with Ducos to keep him from shooting at the pope again would have made things clear. Clear enough, anyway. Ron didn't like Michel any more than Frank did—Gerry was the only one of the three brothers who thought the cold Frenchman was "sorta cool"—and he'd grown quite fond of Fabrizio and Dino.

He drew his pistol, to give them a hand. Then, out of the corner of his eye, saw the Roman guy aiming at the pope. Ron swiveled and pointed the gun at him.

"Drop it!" he shouted.

The Roman guy stared at him. Then, suddenly, turned his wheel-lock pistol on Ron and fired at his head. Point-blank range, not more than two feet. The bullet missed but if Ron hadn't ducked and shut his eyes at the last instant he would have been blinded by the powder blown out of the barrel. As it was, even wearing a hat—the hat went sailing—he felt like he'd been scalped.

"You son of a bitch!" Furious, he straightened and lifted his pistol. Pulled the trigger.

Nothing. It suddenly dawned on him that the Roman guy was hollering obscenities and trying to hobble away. There was blood on his leg.

Ron stared down at his flintlock. He realized that he must have pulled the trigger when he ducked and fired his shot out of reflex. He'd never even noticed. Apparently it had hit the Roman guy on the leg—or maybe ricocheted into the leg off the stone floor.

He heard another gunshot. Turning his head, he saw that Michel had accidentally fired his second gun in the course of struggling with Fabrizio and Dino. The shot went over the heads of the crowd and struck an icon of Jesus against the far wall of the church. Jesus' left arm and that part of the crucifix were shattered.

Oh, shit. We're in big trouble now.

One of the Swiss guards blew his stack at that point. He hefted his halberd and hurled it like a massive ungainly spear. Fortunately, the guy missed Ron by a country mile. He didn't even have to duck. Ron turned to see where the halberd had gone and—

Oh.

The Roman guy was flat on his belly. Slowly, the weight of the halberd pried the weapon out of his shoulder blade. It toppled to the floor, blood staining the uppermost two inches of the spike. The Roman guy groaned and lurched to his knees, clutching the shoulder. Blood was oozing through his fingers.

"Oh." Ron owed the Swiss guard an apology.

He heard another shout and turned. Ducos, with maniac strength, had finally managed to break free from Fabrizio and Dino. He clubbed Dino down with the barrel of the gun and tried to do the same to Fabrizio in the back swing. But Fabrizio caught the barrel and clutched it with both hands. Cursing, Ducos released the pistol and started racing for the exit. He had to

duck a halberd swing along the way that would have
taken his head off.

He was headed more or less in Ron's direction but
not close enough for Ron to tackle him. Ducos could
run a lot faster than Ron would have expected.

No way, asswipe! Ron threw his pistol at him. The
heavy butt struck Ducos a glancing blow to the mouth.
That split his lip badly but the Frenchman kept going,
ignoring the injury completely.

Then . . . he was gone. The Swiss guards had been
too preoccupied with ensuring the pope's safety to stop
Ducos from fleeing. The only two guards who went after
him stopped when they got to the Roman guy and got
sidetracked putting him under the Swiss Guard equivalent of arrest. Which apparently consisted of beating
him to a pulp with the butts of their halberds.

Swell. The dupes do all the work; the cops come from
Keystone; and the Mastermind makes his escape.

Bullshit. Ron raced after Ducos. As he reached the
door leading outside, he spotted some bloodstains on
the floor. That made him feel a lot better. Although
he was still really worried about that busted statue of
Jesus. God only knew what the Inquisition would do
to you for something like that.

Chapter 50

Heinzerling surprised himself with a vault over the pew rail of his own. Immediately, though, he had to jerk to a halt faced by the halberds of four of the Swiss guards. They'd leapt to protect the pope—rather later than Lennox the Protestant had done, he noted with grim amusement, not to mention the Stone brothers.

"My friend, there—my master, he is hurt." He pointed to where Lennox lay, visibly nowhere near the pope. A bit to his surprise, they let him through. No doubt the vestments helped, but he suspected the Swiss guards were just too confused themselves to be thinking clearly.

Whatever language Lennox was cursing in sounded like a good one for it. Or languages. Heinzerling recognized English and German and the Scotsman was going through at least two others.

"If you can swear so, Herr Hauptmann Lennox, it seems to me you are not so badly hurt?" Even as he spoke the mild joke he checked for bleeding, for any sign of injury.

"If I'm no wounded—ye papist swine—why the de'il dae—I hurt so much?" Lennox was getting his

breath in great whooping gasps and spending all of
them on swearing.

Blood. Heinzerling could see blood. Not much,
but . . .

He traced it to a bloody score up one ear, that was
welling up bright red and dripping onto the marble
floor. "Your ear," he said.

"No mind—ma ear—ye bampot—ma bluidy ribs,"
Lennox wheezed. "Hit on—the cuirass."

"The what?" Heinzerling tried to remember what
part of the body the cuirass was. He was conscious
of figures gathering around him.

"Here." Lennox gasped and rolled over. "Crivvens,
that hurts."

Heinzerling saw immediately. The flashy dress cuirass
armor that Lennox wore had taken the pistol ball high
on the left side, where the piece curved back toward the
shoulder-strap. It was cracked clear from collarbone to
armpit, the crack running right through a long, gouged
dent running away upward with a smear of gray lead in
it. "*Scheisse, du glücklicher Hundinsohn,*" he breathed.

"Bluidy cheap pot-metal rubbish," the Scotsman
hissed. "Nae decent proof plate'd 'ae cracked so."

"Saint Thomas should have had such as you," came
a voice. Both of them looked up. "To stand between
him and his king's knights," the pope went on, smiling broadly.

Lennox went bright pink, seemed on the verge of
either laughing or wailing protest—perhaps both—and
clutched his chest again and groaned.

"My friend is a brave man, Your Holiness," said
Heinzerling solemnly, for want of anything better to
say.

"And a true and pious son of the Church, whom
God has preserved. He has laid down his life, and
kept it!" The pope spoke these last words loudly, to a
ragged cheer from those nearby who had seen what
Lennox had done.

Heinzerling could feel the next development looming up on him like an avalanche of embarrassment. He had brought this, this—*Calvinist*—it was too much.

Too much for Lennox as well, who was gasping with pain between the sobs of laughter. "Will"—gasp, wheeze—"ye tell yon"—sob, chortle—"canna e'en call 'im a papist"—gasp, wheeze—"since 'e's the pape himself"—sob, chortle—"or will I?"

Lennox subsided in incoherent shuddering moans of agony and hilarity.

For Heinzerling, it was just the agony. "Actually, Your Holiness . . ."

The sound of gunshots brought all the Marines outside the church to sudden alert.

"Saddle up," Lieutenant Trumble commanded. "No, wait! MacNish, you come with me. We'll check the side entrance." Billy was already mounting his horse. He pointed toward the main entrance to the church. "Sergeant Southworth, take the rest of the men in there and see what's happening. On foot!"

Southworth and his three Marines ran toward the entrance, pulling out their swords and bracing themselves for a confrontation with the two confused-looking Swiss guards standing there. When they got within ten feet, all four of them as well as the Swiss guards were swept away by a swarm of screaming people charging out of the church. They might as well have been six chips of wood trying to stop a tidal wave. Fortunately, they all managed to keep their feet so none of them got trampled.

Billy Trumble stared at the sight, for a moment. Then, rolling his eyes with exasperation—doesn't *anything* go right?—he and MacNish started trotting around the side of the church.

As they came around the corner, they saw a man racing out of the side door and heading toward an alley. Maybe five seconds later, Ron Stone burst through it also. The Stone kid spotted Trumble and came to a sudden halt. He looked back at the door, as if thinking to flee back inside.

Weeks of slowly building frustration and anger at the idiot hippie kids who'd hauled one Lieutenant Trumble all over Italy till his ass felt like it would never recover came to a boil. Billy forgot all about the man who'd run down the alley.

"Halt!" Billy shouted. "Ron Stone, you are under arrest!"

Under the circumstances, it was probably a silly thing to say—just for starters, he had no jurisdiction here whatsoever—but Billy couldn't think of anything better. Given that he was being a dumbass anyway, he pulled out his sword and waved it around. "Halt, I said! In the name of the law!"

The lieutenant was now within fifteen feet of the Stone kid. Ron squinted at him. "Trumble? Is that you?"

"Who the hell do you think it is, you—oh." It suddenly occurred to Billy that wearing his dress uniform, complete with that fancy stupid-looking helmet with sidebars, Ron hadn't recognized him.

"Yeah, Stone, it's me."

Ron pointed a finger at the man who'd raced out of the church. Billy turned his head just in time to see the man disappear into the alley.

"Go after him! Get him!"

Billy turned back. "Nice try, Stone. And you're still under—"

"You jackass! That's *Ducos*. He just tried to kill the pope!"

Billy stared at him. With a look of total exasperation, Ron stood stiffly erect and raised his right hand.

"Look, I'm telling the truth. Scout's honor."

"That's the Vulcan live-long-and-prosper salute."

Ron stared at his hand. Then, started hopping up and down. *"Who the hell cares?"* Billy, goddamit—do your duty!"

Billy looked at the alley entrance. Belatedly, he realized that the guy *had* been acting kind of suspiciously. And now that he thought about it, the man did seem to match the description he'd been given of Ducos.

He came to a decision, and slid the sword back into its scabbard. "All right, Stone, but if you're lying your ass is grass. Where's the guy headed, anyway? I don't want to lose him somewhere in there. These alleys can be a maze."

"Not that one. It just leads straight through to another square. There's two coaches waiting on the other side of it. You can't miss them."

Billy headed off, MacNish following.

Ron stared after him, trying to decide whether to follow. Then five Swiss guards piled out of the church and buried him under a mass tackle.

That's what I was afraid of. They're really pissed about what happened to Jesus.

When Frank came to, the first thing he saw was Gerry. He was kneeling next to Frank, his face scrunched up.

When Gerry saw that Frank was conscious again, he wiped his sleeve over his nose.

"You okay?"

Frank nodded. Gerry burst into tears.

"I didn't mean to kill him," he sobbed.

Frank struggled to a sitting position and folded Gerry into a hug. "Yeah, I know. It just happened."

"Why did he have to be so stupid?" Gerry whispered, clutching his older brother tightly. "I mean, he wasn't really a bad guy or anything. Why did he grab me? That's why the gun went off. I didn't plan to shoot him. I just wanted to stop him from trying to kill the pope."

For a moment, Frank felt a burst of sheer hatred such as he'd never felt before in his life. "It was

Michel Ducos did it, Gerry, not you. He played us for fools—and no one worse than Marius, because the poor guy was half a fool to begin with."

Gerry pulled away from Frank far enough to wipe his nose again. "I'll get him for that."

"No, you won't. We all will. The Stone boys stick together."

Just as the Swiss guards manhandled Ron to his feet, he remembered something. He twisted his head and shouted as loudly as he could.

"Billy, watch out! There's a boobytrap waiting in—oh, damn."

The entrance to the alley was a cloud of smoke. Gerry had outdone himself.

A moment later, two horses surged back out of the alley, snorting fiercely. One of them had a rider wearing a Marine dress uniform. It was not Billy Trumble.

It took Billy a couple of minutes to recover from the fall. Then, another minute to crawl painfully out of the worst of the smoke. When he got into clear air, he realized that he'd crawled the wrong way.

"Doesn't *anything* go the way it's supposed to?" he cried out to an uncaring universe, then sprawled against the wall of the nearest building in a half-reclining, half-sitting position. His head hurt and he was still feeling dizzy.

A very good-looking girl came running up the alley toward him, her skirts flapping like flags in the wind. As she got close, Billy saw that it was Frank Stone's girlfriend, Giovanna.

When she reached him, Giovanna leaned over and screamed in his ear. "*What did you do to my husband?*"

Billy gaped at her. "When did you guys get married?"

Giovanna screeched pure fury. She reached down

with both hands and, before Billy realized what she was doing, had yanked his sword out of the scabbard. Then, held it over his head.

"If you killed my husband, I will kill you!"

He stared up at her for a moment. "Guess not," he murmured. Then, burst into laughter that was just barely this side of sheer hysteria.

"You guess not what?! Answer me or I cut your head off!"

"Nothing goes the way it's supposed to. What do you think?"

Luckily for Billy, MacNish came stumbling down the alley, groping his way through the smoke. "Are you there, sair?"

Giovanna sprang toward him, hefting the sword like a baseball bat. Pretty decent grip, lousy stance, was Billy's assessment.

"*What did you do to my husband?*" she screamed at the Scot trooper.

MacNish stared down at her. "Nothin,' ma'am. Don't even know who yer husband is."

"Liar!" She took a magnificent swing. Home-run quality, Billy thought; ground rule double for sure. If it had hit MacNish, his head would have sailed over the next building.

As it happened, the blade didn't come within two feet of the Marine. But MacNish was a Scotsman and knew a bad bargain when he saw one. He didn't draw his own sword. Just turned on his heels and ran back down the alley.

Giovanna ran after him, swinging the sword every other step.

Billy lurched to his feet and followed. Laughing softly all the way down the alley.

When he got out of the alley and back into the street in front of the church, his laughter got a lot louder. Giovanna was there, still brandishing the sword, but now surrounded by perhaps a dozen Swiss guards.

They were—in a very gingerly manner—trying to keep her at bay.

"Looks like pretty fair fight to me," he choked.

Then Frank Stone came out of the side door of the church. Giovanna dropped the sword and raced toward him. Wisely, the Swiss guards got out of her way.

"He told me you were killed! He told me you were killed!"

She flung herself into Frank's arms, sobbing. Frank held her tight. "He lied," he whispered. "That's what Michel Ducos does. He lies."

Giovanna pulled her head back, her eyes still wet but slitted. "He made his escape, then. He took the coaches and told me you were dead. Everyone was dead except him, he said. I will get him for this."

"Not on your own, you won't. Join the club."

Inside the church, Urban VIII was now surrounded by a phalanx of cardinals.

"We shall investigate this affair!" hissed one of them. "The truth will be revealed. The Holy Office—"

"Basta!" The pope raised his hand firmly. "I think I have had enough of the Holy Office, for a bit. Yes, yes, we must investigate, but . . ."

Urban's eyes moved across the crowd gathered just beyond the inner ring of cardinals, looking for a certain face. A young face in which he had come to have great deal of confidence lately.

He spotted the man and crooked a finger. When he came up—managing to do so, somehow, without *quite* elbowing any cardinal aside—the pope issued his instructions.

"Monsignor Mazarini. I wish you to undertake an investigation of this entire bizarre affair. Find out the truth, and then report to me. Alone."

"Yes, Your Holiness."

※　　　※　　　※

The pope spoke loudly enough for Mazzare and Jones to hear him, where they knelt beside Lennox. The Scot cavalryman was doing much better, now that Heinzerling had removed the cuirass. The Jesuit, who was something of jack-of-all-trades, included a certain degree of medical knowledge in his repertoire. He told Lennox he was pretty sure he'd suffered nothing worse than a couple of broken ribs.

"In short, less in the way of damage than I inflicted upon you myself, that time of our theological dispute."

"Ha!" snorted Lennox. "And I won that fight, too."

Heinzerling was on the verge of issuing a retort, when he heard the pope's informal proclamation. He twisted his head around.

"Ah. What is that handy American expression of yours?"

Mazzare and Jones considered. " 'The fix is in,' " suggested Jones.

"Yes. That one."

Chapter 51

In his private apartments, Urban VIII wore clothing that was far more comfortable than his formal robes. Considerably lighter, too, in the summertime. That was fortunate, he reflected—or he might well have broken his shoulders heaving them up under that weight of office.

"Youthful high spirits?" He managed to choke that much out before bursting into another round of laughter. The pope wondered if he might die from the strain of trying to remain reasonably pontifical when his boyish instincts were straining to slap a knee.

Possible, possible, indeed possible—seeing as God was clearly in a whimsical mood these past few years. First, the miracle of the Ring of Fire. Then, the miracle of a pope saved by a Calvinist. Third . . .

Why not? In private, Urban had studied a copy of one of the astronomy texts purloined from the Congden Library. Popes had died of apoplexy in the past. To have one die of sheer amusement in this day and age would be a fitting reminder by the God who created the improbable moons of Jupiter that men risked His irony when they mimicked His grandeur with mortal . . .

Call it pomposity, he decided. He even considered for a moment whether he should rescind his decree that cardinals be titled "Your Eminence" and be given diplomatic precedence over all but crowned monarchs.

It was not a long moment. Was there anything in the world as pompous as a secular prince? Do them good to be humbled a bit.

Urban VIII wiped the tears from his eyes. When he could look through them again, he saw that Monsignor Mazarini seemed to be enjoying this as well.

"So. 'Youthful high spirits.' Out of idle curiosity, Monsignor, I wonder what label you would apply to Alaric's sack of Rome? 'Gothic exuberance'?"

Mazarini smiled, but shook his head. "Oh, no. A most barbarous deed, that. Surely not equivalent to this." For a moment, the legate was unwontedly serious. "In truth, Your Holiness, the boys may not be precisely innocent. But I have interviewed them all at great length, these past few days, and I can assure you they are quite the innocents."

Urban did not doubt it himself, actually. With his own eyes, he had seen the youngest of them burst into tears after killing—with no intent to do so, Urban was quite certain—the simpleton who had made the first attempt on his life. And seen his older brother's attempt to comfort him. Neither, the impulse of an assassin. The pope did not think that even his dullest inquisitor would think so.

Hard to be sure, of course. There were some very dull men employed by the Holy Office.

Be that as it may, Urban had chosen another sort of man to investigate this matter. And was pleased enough at the result. "*Basta,*" he said softly. "There is sufficient wickedness in the world that we do not have to invent it."

Mazarini's nod was more in the way of a bow. "My thoughts exactly, Your Holiness."

"Ha!" This time, the pope did slap his knee, since

he felt himself under sufficient control to make it simply the gesture of a decisive man. "Monsignor, I don't doubt that was *one* of your thoughts. Among perhaps . . . a hundred?"

He moved on, not really sure he wanted to hear the answer. Mazarini was a bit frightening, in some respects. "Obviously you do not propose that explanation for the public. Please explain, then, how you *do* propose to handle the matter."

Mazarini explained. At length. To his surety, the pope counted at least thirty-eight distinct thoughts. And was just as sure he'd missed as many more.

A bit frightening, yes. On the other hand, so was the father-general of the Jesuits. Loyalty was the key. Vitelleschi's loyalties were simple, fixed by an oath; Mazarini's, more complex, and not yet fixed at all. But what mattered, in the end, was that both were men capable of great loyalties. For the moment, with Mazarini, the depth was what counted. The direction of the current could be ascertained—perhaps channeled; perhaps not—at a later time.

"Very well. We will do it as you propose. Is everyone assembled?"

"Yes, Your Holiness."

"A moment then—well, a bit more than that, I'm afraid—while I assume my robes and regalia. Await me with the others, Monsignor."

Mazarini bowed and left.

Urban spent more time than usual having himself *pontificated,* as he always privately thought of the lengthy process his servants went through to prepare him properly for public occasions. He needed that time, to be sure he had his amusement under control.

Heinzerling was having a very hard time himself, some time later, keeping that control. Mostly, because he was so vastly entertained by Mazarini's uncanny ability to utter the most preposterous statements with a perfectly straight face. Mazarini was the best card player Heinzerling had ever met.

"—clearly did not intend any misprision, whatever delusions they might have been under." Mazarini clasped his hands behind his back and rocked up on his toes. "They had no fixed plan of rescue, their preparations for flight were evidently hopeless even to the meanest wit—their means of escape left in the hands of a young girl, the betrothed of one of them and sister to two others, hardly a worthy hand in any desperate business—and they had taken almost no account of the fact that the Swiss guard was out in force and that Your Holiness disposes of sufficient cavalry to run them to ground within a day, if not mere hours."

"And the fact that I was shot at?"

"Entirely the work of a French agent, Your Holiness. A man named Michel Ducos, known to me as an agent of the comte d'Avaux. Although I hasten to add that the man was not operating within his orders. First, because I know Seigneur le Comte to be a pious man most unlikely to order Your Holiness harmed. Second, because the one confederate of his we captured—primarily due to the quick actions of Ron Stone, I might point out—has confessed that both he and Ducos were members of a secret organization of Protestant assassins. Ducos' plans were not known to any of the persons now present."

The last was said very firmly. So firmly, indeed, that not a one of the sceptical faces observing the proceedings was moved to speak. Perhaps, Heinzerling admitted, because they thought the sceptical expressions spoke well enough for themselves.

But Mazarini was unfazed, as throughout. "The proof of it was evident to any who witnessed the events." The monsignor waved in the direction of the Stone and Marcoli youngsters, standing to one side under the close watch of the Swiss guards. "I commend to Your Holiness the quick action of young Frank Stone, which undoubtedly prevented any real harm. Indeed, even before then, Signor Stone expressly drew the priming from the first weapon to fire at Your Holiness, little suspecting that he was thereby disarming an assassin. He simply wished to avoid any possible accident."

That drew a little round of choking noises—one of them coming from Heinzerling himself. Mazarini had neatly glided over the issue of why anyone had brought a pistol to the church which needed to be disarmed in the first place. But, again, no voice was raised in open opposition. None of the clerics in that room except Mazarini, Mazarre, and Heinzerling had ever seen an actual steamroller, but they understood the basic principle. They certainly understood the likely fate of anyone who thought to oppose it directly.

The pope nodded. "So it was this Ducos who was plotting against me?"

"Indeed, Your Holiness. He was last seen escaping by boat down the Tiber. I understand that fast horses have been dispatched to carry warning of him to any ship that might take him from Ostia, but I have no great hope of his capture. He is a cunning and resourceful devil, Your Holiness."

"Then there is no case to answer in their complicity in attempting to murder me?"

"None whatsoever."

"And the charge of attempting misprision of an Inquisition prisoner?" The pope had an eyebrow raised, and almost, to Heinzerling, seemed to be stifling a grin.

"I am ahead of Your Holiness," Mazarini said, with a most respectful nod. "I am given to understand that Dottor Galileo was never actually a prisoner, and furthermore today's proceedings were not, lawfully, those of the Holy Office?"

"Indeed, both matters are the case, yes." The pope's face was that of a superb card player himself.

Mazarini spread his hands wide. "Then there is no need for diplomatic upset, Your Holiness. No need at all! What we have here is a case of disrespectful behavior in church. Scandalous, it is true, but not calling for the condign punishments of a misprision or of an assassination. After all, these poor duped boys could hardly have known of the plottings of a skilled secret agent and assassin. And at considerable personal risk they aided in foiling him."

His Holiness frowned. "Doubtless there will be fines to pay?"

"Most condign fines, Your Holiness," Mazarini confirmed.

"And damages?"

"Damages. Some statuary was destroyed, and there are bullet holes, Your Holiness." Mazarini's moustaches twitched.

"Aye, an' near wan in ma ain hide," Lennox muttered from the seat he had been permitted to take on account of his injuries. He had his chest strapped up under his uniform tunic and was wearing a sling, and a bandage around his head. Rather more than his injuries merited, in Heinzerling's opinion, but it wasn't for him to speak out about how the miserable old Protestant cavalryman was hamming it up.

Heinzerling looked across at the audience for this particular play. A perfect picture: *Hope of Survival, Fear of Ruin.*

"Hmm. I think," said the pope, "in the interests of diplomatic peace and quiet we should simply leave it at that. However, the subject of damages remains open."

"If Your Holiness will indulge me," said Mazzare, speaking for the first time at this meeting, "a consular loan from the USE embassy will be available to the boys to pay the fines."

"Ah, most generous, Monsignor," said the pope. "I might have thought you would be more inclined to allow them to reap the fruits of their foolish behavior? Not, I might add, that the full story will go beyond these four walls."

There was a euphemism, thought Heinzerling. Whatever official story went out, the real version was probably already spreading as rumor, although the fanciful embroiderings would cloud the issue somewhat. Indeed, Cardinal Borja, the most ardent member of the Spanish party at Rome present at this meeting, looked like the story he was having to listen to tasted so bad that he wanted to leave and spit it out.

Mazzare heaved a sigh. "Your Holiness, I would be entirely inclined to leave them to just and deserved punishment"—here, to Heinzerling's glee, a little shudder ran through the little group of would-be commandos—"but there is the small matter that two of them are about to begin married life together. I should not like to see them begin it in debtors' jail while they await funds."

"A marriage? Splendid. Nothing better to bridle too-high spirits." The pope fairly beamed. "And that is of course a matter we can readily attend to. Cardinal Barberini?"

Three men said, "Yes, Your Holiness?"

"Ah. Young Antonio, I meant. See that the young lovers are married. We cannot have them tempted to fornication on top of all their other follies, can we?"

Cardinal Antonio Barberini the Younger frowned. "But, Your Holiness? The banns? And one of them is not Catholic."

The pope waved his hand. "We dispense with the banns. And, young lady?"

Giovanna Marcoli nodded. "Yes, Your Holiness?" Her voice was small and frightened-sounding, and Heinzerling could see a flutter in her skirts where her knees were trembling.

"Do you promise to raise any children of your union as Catholics? And never to stint in your efforts to convert this young man?"

Her eyes went big and round. She simply nodded.

"Well, then!" The pope turned to his nephew. "See to it by no later than tomorrow, Antonio."

The youngest of the cardinals Barberini nodded. "Yes, Your Holiness." And then a slight grin. "May we use the Sistine Chapel?"

"In the circumstances, I can hardly refuse." His uncle's grin was starting to creep through the card player's face.

"Can he do that?" Jones asked, clearly less *sotto voce* than he'd intended. A slight titter went around the room.

"He's the pope, Simon," Mazzare said gently. "Yes. He can do that."

"Ah."

"Your Holiness, both for myself and for the United States of Europe, I should like to thank you—oh." Mazzare had been brought to a halt by Frank crumpling to the floor in what looked like a dead faint.

Disdaining the halberds and sabers around her, Giovanna leapt to Frank's side, with a wordless cry of alarm.

"Felt the same way the night before my own nuptials, as it happens," Jones drawled. "And I wasn't facing the Sistine Chapel."

The fuss and confusion ended with Frank revived amid protestations that he was *okay, really, I'm fine*, and his being promptly shut up with a kiss from Giovanna that provoked a round of ironic cheers from the soldiers present and not a few of the priests. The Stones and Marcolis were ushered out of the room.

"Now," the pope said. "Monsignor Mazzare, I think you were about to offer protestations of a most commendable gratitude. I suggest, however, you await Our next command to you, for We have decided you are fit for a particular task We have in mind."

Heinzerling caught his breath. This would surely be it! A bishopric, at last—and rightly so. Had not the good Father Mazzare been doing the work of a bishop

these three years' past? Far better—Heinzerling had
good cause to know—than most of the—

The pope snapped his fingers and someone stepped
forward with . . .

It was Heinzerling's turn to feel faint. For what was
being brought forward, with all due ceremony, was a
broad-brimmed red hat, adorned with long tassels to
either side. Only one rank of churchman wore that
kind of hat.

Somehow, he was aware that the pope was speaking
to the man who had been his master these past two,
nearly three years. A man who was to be his master
in yet another sense from now on. He caught a few
phrases. "Common father of all Catholics," was one of
them. "Entirely separate from all secular jurisdictions,"
was another. "Recognition of the new shape of the
politics of Christendom," was still a third.

The one that truly beggared belief, however, was the
one that clearly left Mazzare staggering as well as it did
Heinzerling and Jones. As well it should. A theological
and political earthquake had just shaken Europe.

"Lawrence Mazzare, Cardinal-Protector of the United
States of Europe."

Dead silence.

"Gus, can he do *that*?" Jones again. A beat. "No,
don't tell me. He's the pope."

Urban enjoyed his little games. But, ever mindful of
the need for mercy, he waved Mazzare forward, that
he might lean over and speak to him privately.

"There *was* a trial, you see. A very real one, whose
result—unlike Galileo's—was not predetermined."

Mazzare's face was very pale, but the pope was
pleased to see that the man was still able to think
clearly when under great stress. He was not surprised,
of course. That had been part of the trial also.

"Mine."

Urban nodded. "Trial is perhaps not the right term.

'Test,' perhaps. Or . . . no, a trial, yes. May we think of it as an intellectual trial by combat?"

He spoke very softly now. "I needed to know something, Lawrence Mazzare. One thing, before all else. Had that Church of yours, in that other universe, become transformed into something I could no longer recognize at all? But, when the time came, you argued like a priest. Not a natural philosopher wearing a mask. In the end, that is all that matters. The rest is disputation. I will say I found your theological argument itself quite compelling. But—"

Here he smiled a bit slyly. "I have no doubt my horde of theologians will soon be at their disputation again."

Mazzare even managed a little chuckle. Indeed, from the hooded look in his eyes, Urban could see that he was already considering the future.

Splendid. The pope had enough cardinals who spent their time considering only the past.

"One thing, Your Holiness."

"Yes?"

"Might I request the services of Father Christopher Scheiner? The truth is, Your Holiness, we have books on astronomy in Grantville, and are creating a great university nearby at Jena—but we have no astronomers. And he is a superb one. In that other universe, quite unfairly, he would only be remembered as Galileo's accuser. I think it would be well to rectify that small injustice as well as the larger one."

Urban considered the idea, for a moment, liking it the more he thought about it. Another subtle but excellent gesture, in a world too dangerous for him to consider anything else. The pope, raising up Galileo's defender; the defender, then doing the same for his opponent.

Let the Austrian and Spanish Habsburgs choke on it; Richelieu, perhaps, learn from it. Perhaps—who can tell?—even that half-barbarous heretic Swede.

Yes, splendid.

"Scheiner is a Jesuit, Father Mazzare, so I will need to speak to the father-general. But I foresee no difficulty."

He managed to say it without so much as cracking a smile.

Chapter 52

Tom and Magda Stone arrived in Rome that evening. When they were ushered into the room in the Vatican where their sons were being held in what amounted to house arrest, Stoner gazed upon them like an pigeon might gaze upon his ostrich offspring.

"Boys," he began. Closed his mouth. Opened it. Closed it again.

"Really weird, man. First time in my life, I'm at a complete loss for words."

Magda, of course, wasn't.

But even Magda was mollified, the next day, as she observed the wedding. True, she was Lutheran and disapproved in principle of Romish idolatry and pageantry. On the other hand, like most people in Thuringia, she'd seen enough of the endless changing of official faiths as a result of the principle of *cuius regio, eius religio* to have become more than a little cynical on the subject.

Most of all, she was fiercely ambitious for her husband and her family. So she thought it eminently suitable and proper that the oldest of her three stepsons should be married under the most famous ceiling in the world. Besides, who was to say? Perhaps that divine spark of life transmitted from the Creator to Adam might be reflected downward—just a bit of it, but enough—to impart a modicum of common sense into her boys.

If God could create a Ring of Fire, surely He could create a sensible son. Perhaps even—Magda had her doubts, though she'd readily admit the girl was gorgeous—a sensible daughter-in-law.

It was an age of miracles, after all.

Two days later, Antonio Marcoli hobbled his way into Rome, assisted by his cousin Massimo.

By then, the Stone family—along with the four Marcoli boys who were now their in-laws—had moved into a luxurious palazzo not far from the Pantheon. Reluctantly, Tom Stone had yielded to Magda's insistence that he stop playing the pauper and *spend* some of those vast sums that were beginning to pour into his coffers.

Being rich was still something Stoner was coming to terms with. A settlement made all the more difficult by the fact that he was the attorney arguing the case for the other side.

He'd hoped to assuage Magda by his immediate offer to pay all the fines levied on the boys himself, thereby removing the burden from the somewhat-strained purse of the USE embassy.

"That's pocket change!" Magda snapped. "We will *not* spend our visit to Rome living in a—what did you call it?"

"Youth hostel. Hey, look, it's the way I bummed across Europe back—"

"Just what we need!" She glared at her stepsons and new daughter-in-law. It was still an impressive glare, if not the solar incandescence of the day of her arrival. "I do not need to be reminded that youth is hostile."

"Hos-tel, dear. And the youth in them are really nice

kids. Well, there's the occasional jock, but you don't run across too many of them on account of they usually can't find their way anywhere except to the mall, forget foreign travel. But—"

He shook his shaggy mane. "'Pocket change'? Is that really true? I mean, I know you keep the books, but—"

Magda sniffed. Magda had a world-class sniff. She marched over to her purse and pulled out her wallet. "Books. Who needs books for this? Will they take scudi?"

Stoner sighed. "Innocence lost. I can remember those glorious days when I'd drive for months on a suspended license 'cause I couldn't afford to pay a traffic ticket."

The three Stone boys looked at each other. "Uh, Dad," said Ron. "Is that the same traffic ticket that got you tossed in jail when you got stopped for speeding again? 'Cause, if so, I can remember those glorious days when me and Frank—even Gerry, and he was only ten—had to bust our ass in order—"

"Details, son, details. It was the freedom that mattered."

"Jail is freedom?"

"Freedom of the soul. Who cares about the prison of the body? Besides—"

He got no further. Antonio Marcoli burst through the door. Somehow he managed it while hobbling on a crutch. Massimo came right behind him.

"Tell me it is not true, faithless daughter!"

Giovanna stared at him, mouth agape. "What's not true, Papa?"

Marcoli marched over to the table where she was sitting next to Frank. Somehow he managed to march while hobbling on a crutch.

"You got married! In the church! The Sistine Chapel, I am told! It is all over the city!"

He flung himself into an empty chair. Yes, somehow managing it while hobbling on a crutch.

Then, placed his head in a despairing hand. With his other hand, he pounded the crutch on the floor. "We are ruined, ruined!"

Giovanna closed her mouth. "You *told* me to get properly married. Made us promise! And we—ah—kept the promise."

"Well, yes. But that was *before*. Now we are ruined. Our political principles hopelessly compromised!"

All the Stones and Marcolis were now gaping at him.

"Uh. Before what, Messer Marcoli?" asked Frank.

Marcoli pointed the crutch at Massimo. "Before he explained to me that our political principles do not allow us to recognize the Church's authority in such matters. How can Church and State be separated if the Church—just another set of plunderers of the poor, that's all—is allowed the right to determine such matters?"

Giovanna was almost cross-eyed. "But . . . where *else* could I get married?"

She drew away from her father, sliding a firm arm around Frank's shoulder. "And he *is* my husband. So don't think you can tell me not to get married to him. I already did!"

From the look on Frank's face, Tom Stone understood that his son was about to blow up. Would have blown up already, in fact, had he not been basking in the sudden knowledge that Giovanna's ultimate loyalties had just undergone a sea-change.

On one level, of course, Stoner approved of his son's anger. If he didn't stand up to Marcoli he'd be hopeless. He approved even more of that instinctive motion of his new daughter-in-law. Still, he was a man of peace.

"Hey, folks, ease up. Let's all ease up here. Mister Marcoli—"

He rose from the table and leaned over, extending his hand. "We've never met. I'm Tom Stone, Frank's father. We're in-laws. Please to meetcha."

Out of reflex, Marcoli shook his hand. That done, Stoner pressed on with his mission of peace.

"Look, Mr. Marcoli, this is an old problem and one I had to solve, oh, years ago now."

Both Marcoli and Massimo perked up. "There is an American solution?" demanded Massimo.

How to answer that?

"Uh, yeah. Well. One of many. You understand—ah—freedom and liberty also means what you might call variety. So to speak."

"Please. Go on!"

"Right. Well, in our old commune we, ah, had a similar sort of problem. Our own principles clashing, you know, with the uptight notions—well, never mind. The point is, we founded our own church. Except it wasn't really a church. Certainly had no connection to the state. Heh. And whenever one of our couples wanted to get away from the usual—"

Best to skip over that. Communal sex would probably not play well with a man who could burst through a door on a crutch.

"Anyway, wanted to get married, let's say, we'd have our own ceremony."

Massimo pounded his fist softly on the table. "Yes," he said, almost hissing the word. "Of course! Hurl our defiance in the face of the oppressor."

"Uh, yeah. Sorta like that. In our case, it was more like smoke our defiance—"

"Dad!"

"Hey, Frank, take it easy, I'm just—never mind. Anyway, Mister Marcoli, with your approval, we could just do it again right now. Give Frank and your daughter a *real* wedding." He waved his hand. "They just did that other, in that Sistine Chapel place, to slide one over on the enemy."

He hoped they could also just slide over the issue of consummating the wedding. Seeing as how that had already happened. Many, many, many, many times, judging from the fact that no one had seen Frank and Giovanna outside of their bedroom for more than an hour at a stretch these past couple of days.

Marcoli eyed him. "*Si?* You can do this?"

"Oh, sure. I was the ordained minister. Still got my card." He began reaching for his wallet. "Universal Church of Life in . . . can't remember the rest of it, that's odd."

"Dad!"

"Ease up, willya? You get my age, your memory starts to go a little. Oh, well. Never mind the card. Just take my word for it, Mister Marcoli. I can marry the kids right here and now and we thumb our nose at the establishment. To do it full bore, of course, we'd need a hookah and some—"

"Dad!"

"Jeez, are you anal today, or what? Okay, forget the hookah. We're not people to get fixated on the trappings, are we?"

"Certainly not," said Massimo firmly. "Superb! The contradiction resolved."

"Yes!" agreed Marcoli, lunging to his feet. Somehow he managed it even without the crutch. A one-legged lunge. "Where do we stand?"

"Uh, well. You don't. Everybody sits in a circle. Cross-legged."

That got two very cross-eyed looks.

"Hey, relax. It won't take long. Since we're passing on the hookah. Most of it is just taken up by saying *om.*"

Really cross-eyed looks.

"It's an acronym." Now he was getting cross-eyed looks from his kids. "I swear, it *is*. Stands for Omnipersonal Munificence."

"A superb slogan," proclaimed Massimo.

❋ ❋ ❋

As everyone moved around to take their places, Frank took the occasion to murmur into his father's ear. "Smooth move, Dad. Thanks."

Tom Stone basked in filial approval. "Your old man's no dummy. Besides, this is a piece of cake. I made LSD in the sixties, remember?"

Epilogue: July, 1634

Round the cape of a sudden came the sea,
And the sun looked over the mountain's rim:
And straight was a path of gold for him,
And the need of a world of men for me.

The mountain's rim

"There might be a scar, Michel, it's impossible to tell yet." Antoine Delerue finished cleaning off his hands. "Won't be a bad one, though, just a short hairline. Not enough to make your description obvious. It's the mark on your hand that'll be problem there."

Ducos scowled down at his right hand. The Buckley creature had ripped and torn it badly, leaving a large and distinctive scar. But, there was nothing to be done about that now. He rose and went to the port rail,

Delerue following. The coast of Italy was now barely visible behind them.

Another of Ducos' Huguenot confederates came to join them. Guillaume Locquifier, that was. "They'll never catch us now."

Ducos nodded.

"Too bad about the pope. Most of the project succeeded quite well."

Ducos nodded.

"He's the Antichrist, so I suppose we should not be surprised to have failed the first time." Locquifier scowled. "Curse those American bastards. Do you want—"

Ducos waved his hand impatiently. "Don't be stupid, Guillaume. Do you propose to curse every soldier who stands against us? Divert ourselves at each instant in order to punish lackeys?"

Locquifier subsided. Seeing the sour look still on his face, Delerue shook his head. "Just forget it. If we should happen to encounter them again—not likely, where we're going—we might arrange something. Even then, only if it could be done easily and without distracting us from our great purpose."

Learning that a decision had been made, Locquifier's sullen thoughts of revenge were replaced by interest. Ducos and Delerue were the two recognized leaders of their group, although their roles were quite different. Ducos the man of action, the leader at the fore; Delerue, more in the way of the organizer and the strategist.

"You have decided. May I—?"

"No reason to keep it a secret now," said Ducos. "England."

Locquifier's eyes widened. He'd been expecting Holland. With the Spanish Catholic boot now so heavy on that land, recruitment would be easy. Leaving aside the Huguenots, of whom many had taken refuge in the United Provinces in happier days, the Dutch Counter-Remonstrants should be receptive also.

"You're not thinking clearly, Guillaume," said Delerue, reading his thoughts well enough. "In Holland, we'd spend most of our time in hiding, running from one shelter to the next. In England—" He chuckled, waving a hand toward the cabin at the stern of the little ship. "With the small fortune Michel took from d'Avaux—we only spent a modicum of it on this project—we will be well set up in that land of wretched money-counters. Almost as bad as Venetians, they are."

"True." Guillaume thought about it. "Still . . . although I suppose the Puritans will be receptive."

Ducos grunted. Delerue smiled. "Not the Puritans. English to the core, they are. This is a task of the nation, not simply the faith. Scotland, Guillaume, think in terms of the Scots. France's traditional allies in the islands. We will begin in England, set up with the merchants. But our eyes will remain on the north."

Locquifier made a face. "That will mean Edinburgh and the lowlands. The highlander savages are all papists. They say Edinburgh stinks."

Ducos' face seemed more hatchetlike than ever. "So? The world stinks. Our task, to cleanse it."

A path of gold

After Servien finished his report, Richelieu was silent for a very long time. Hands clasped behind his back, standing in his rich red robes of offices, staring out over the city of Paris through a window in his palace.

That was the cardinal's way of controlling his rage, Servien knew. Simply . . . wait, until he was sure the first surge of murderous fury had passed. Richelieu was the most self-disciplined man Servien had ever encountered. That was not the least of the reasons that the cardinal could gain and hold the loyalty of men such as Servien himself. The work they did for the cardinal was often dangerous, but at least they did not have to worry—as did other men, serving other princes—that they would be punished out of sheer anger. Anger which often—as in this case—resulted from the errors and failures of others.

Eventually the moment passed. Servien could tell from subtleties in the set of the cardinal's shoulders.

Richelieu swiveled his head and gave Servien a dark-eyed stare. Seeing the waiting expression on the face of his intendant, the cardinal snorted.

"Oh, tell me. Where is the fool now? Hiding on his estate?"

Servien nodded. "So my spies place him. In the wine cellar, at last report, working his way through its contents."

Richelieu snorted again. "As if I would not find him there." He took a deep breath. Then, gave his shoulders a little shake, as if to rid himself of the last residues of fury.

"Send d'Avaux a letter. I will sign it after it is drafted. First, tell him—use plain language here, Etienne, I see no reason to pamper the comte's tender sensibilities—*that imbecile!*—that he has done more damage to France than our worst enemies could have managed. You may be precise. Blackened our name with the Venetians. Even worse—much worse—given that wretched Barberini the diplomatic shelter he needed to carry through this . . . this abomination. 'Cardinal-Protector of the United States of Europe,' no less. A nation with no religion at all. To think that the pope himself would collapse on the matter of an established church!"

Servien nodded. He would enjoy writing that part of the letter. Seigneur le Comte d'Avaux had irritated Servien often enough in the past with his haughty ways.

"Second." The cardinal paused, breathing deeply, and again giving his shoulders that little shake. "Tell him—grudgingly, Servien, make sure the tone is proper; I want that miserable toad frightened out of his wits; if he dies of the terror, he would do me the favor—that we accept his explanation that the deeds were all committed by the rogue actions of his man Ducos. *His* man, Servien—he chose him and selected him. Rub his snout in it."

"Yes, Your Eminence. That should not be difficult."

"No, I imagine not. And finally, tell him that I do not accept his offer of resignation. He may do amends for his error by serving France in other ways. Ways which are more suitable for his talents."

The cardinal eyed Servien again. "Do you perhaps have a recommendation? Don't feign the innocent, Etienne. You have that little smirk on your face."

The intendant cleared his throat. "Well, Your Eminence, as it happens, just two weeks ago we received another letter from Brest. The fishermen have fallen to quarreling again."

Richelieu nodded. "Adjudicator between quarreling Breton fishermen. Delightful. And the weather in Bretagne is miserable in the winter. Delightful."

"Don't much care for the wine of the region, either, Your Eminence. Matter of my personal taste, of course."

"Everyone's taste, I think. Certainly that of a puffed-up comte who fancies himself a connoisseur. Delightful. See that it is done."

"Yes, Your Eminence." Servien hesitated. Unusually, he was quite at a loss to anticipate how Richelieu would handle the next matter. It could be . . . anything.

"And Mazarini, Your Eminence?"

"Ah, yes. Mazarini." Richelieu shook his head. To Servien's surprise, the gesture seemed an admiring one.

"What a brilliant coup. I do not believe any man in Europe could have done better."

"Your Eminence?"

Richelieu issued a little laugh. "What, Etienne? Were you expecting me to send out assassins?"

As a matter of fact, that *had* been Servien's guess as to the cardinal's most likely reaction.

"He—ah—would seem to have betrayed us, Your Eminence. There is no doubt at all that he was instrumental in concealing the complicity of the *Americans* in the affair." Servien felt himself growing a bit angry, now. "I do not believe for a moment that ridiculous 'finding' of his, that the sons of the USE's ambassador were simply attempting to foil a plot of which they had only learned at the last minute."

Richelieu's next laugh was more cheerful. "It *is* threadbare, is it not? Still, Servien, the same report also stipulated—quite firmly—that the actions of Ducos were those of a rogue, not an agent of France. A religious fanatic—and a Protestant, at that. Which, I will remind you, is all that kept the damage to France from being far worse than it was. If young Mazarini protected the Americans, he extended as much protection to us as he could, under the circumstances."

The cardinal was intent, now, very intent. Servien understood that this was a matter to which Richelieu had spent some time applying his formidable intellect. "What else could he have done, Etienne? Think. He *had* to single out Ducos as the only villain in the piece, to cauterize the damage. You think he should have tried to place the blame on those American youngsters? The oldest of them is but nineteen, and when the actual attempt was made—all the witnesses agreed to this—he and his brothers took great personal risks to protect the pope. To be sure, Mazarini could have exposed their earlier folly and recklessness. But folly and recklessness are not malevolence—and trust Italians before all other people to understand the difference." He barked a sarcastic little laugh. "Since they have practiced both reckless folly and malevolence for centuries. It is no accident, you know, that Italian is the language that produced the term *commedia dell'arte* as well as *vendetta*."

Servien's face was set stubbornly. "Still—"

"And the suggestion of treason is simply absurd. How can a man betray something to which he has never given his allegiance in the first place?"

That startled Servien. "I thought—"

Richelieu shook his head. "No, Servien. There was not and never will be a straightforward arrangement between me and Mazarini. I thought so myself, I admit, when I spoke to him in the spring of last year. But I see now that I grossly underestimated the man. He was playing for much higher stakes than I realized." The last sentence was spoken in a tone of pure and undiluted admiration. That respect which a master gives another, when he discovers himself outplayed.

Servien was now completely out of his depth, and knew it. "Ah . . ." He cleared his throat. "I do not see . . ."

"You do not see how there could be any greater stakes in the world than becoming the leader of France? In effect, if not in name." The cardinal shook his head. "Don't be silly, Etienne. That is simply a means to an end. I have never sought power for its own sake."

That was true enough. Richelieu was almost—Servien, with silent apologies, allowed himself the thought: satanically ambitious—but the ambition was not personal. To be sure, the cardinal enjoyed the privileges and comforts of his station, but those were never paramount.

"The purpose, Etienne, is France itself. And beyond that, what *kind* of France? Or, it would be better to say, what kind of hegemony over the world."

For a moment, the cardinal seemed to be suffused with an odd melancholy. "I imagine my memory in this universe, even more than in that other one, will be dark. They will remember Richelieu's France as the France of the sword and the torch. So be it. Let another one use the power I created for him to forge a lasting hegemony. Rome was perhaps created by its armies, but it did not rule half the world for so long simply because of them. Do not ever think so, Etienne. That is the way of the Hun, or the Mongol, who terrify the world for a few decades and then vanish. Rule—rule which lasts—is a thing of peace and prosperity; a court which draws because of its splendor and glory. A court which *attracts*. I will, in the fullness of time, yield my place to another if he can create a monarchy of the sun, where I could only create one of the wind."

His face closed down. Servien, from long experience, knew that the cardinal had opened himself—a rare occasion, that—perhaps further than he'd intended. There would certainly be no more words on the subject.

Simply orders, now. "Send a letter to Mazarini—I will sign it as soon as it is drafted—giving him my warm regards. Invite him back to Paris at his earliest convenience." Seeing the little trace of doubt on Servien's face, Richelieu smiled thinly. "Oh, Etienne—of course not! He will come, be sure of it. Mazarini is far too smart to detect a trap where none exists. Not a trap lined with blades, at any rate."

For some reason, the cardinal's smile widened. "Oh, yes. And be sure to mention, at the end of the letter, that the queen has been asking about him. She much enjoyed his company, it seems, during his last visit."

Servien began to leave. As he reached the door, however, Richelieu called him back.

"One other thing, Etienne."

"Yes, Your Eminence?"

"The assassins that we dispatched to the Germanies. Have them recalled."

"Certainly, Your Eminence."

Something in Servien's face must have indicated his puzzlement.

"I make errors, Etienne. I rarely make them twice. After these three years, I believe I have finally come to take the measure of my great opponent. Who is not, you understand, the Swede."

Servien nodded. None of those assassins had been sent to kill Gustavus Adolphus.

"He is much like Mazarini, I have now come to understand. Much like me, as well. A man who seeks hegemony on his own terms, to be sure. But understands what the word truly means."

"Yes, Your Eminence."

"Ha! That faintest tremor of doubt! You are such a subtle man, Etienne. I could not ask for a better." The cardinal shook his head. "Always remember, Etienne, the possibility that you might *lose*. And then, cap in hand, have to ask for terms. That being so, make sure you did not create a Hun where none existed before."

Servien found that thought . . . too distasteful to consider.

"Easy for you," Richelieu said harshly. "Not for me. Were I not prepared to swallow that bile, did the time come—and taste it beforehand—I should be unfit in the eyes of God for the position He has chosen to give me."

The cardinal turned back to the window. "The man is not a Hun, whatever else. Of that much, I am now certain. He does not seek to destroy France, simply to bend us to his will. There are rules, Etienne. Decreed not by men but by the cold logic of the contest. Decreed by God, if you will, since He chose to allow us this freedom. One rule, in a Hun war of the knife. Another, in the far greater contest of civilized hegemony. So call off the assassins. And make clear to them—let us not have *another* Ducos—that I am no petulant English king. If they disobey or think to play the helpful knights, the penalties will be severe."

Severe, when the cardinal gave the term that tone of voice, did not mean execution. It meant something that ended in the execution of whatever was left.

"Yes, Your Eminence."

A *world of men*

"Bottom line, Francisco. Down and dirty. I've got plenty of time to chew on the fine points later. Right now I've got some quick decisions to make."

Nasi hesitated, then nodded. He preferred himself to deliberate, when faced with profound issues. But Mike Stearns was a pugilist, not an adviser. A man whose deepest instincts emphasized speed above all else.

"The French have suffered a serious blow in Venice, of course."

"Yeah, sure—but who really cares? If the wind turns, the Venetians will blow back the other way."

"Not before we can consolidate our commercial—it looks, even now, possibly industrial—ties with the city. The best of all possible holds, since Magda and Sharon had the good sense or instincts to draw in as many Venetian partners as they could. La Serenissima is a city of merchants before all else, Michael. They will blow in the political wind, to be sure, but the only winds they worship are the trade winds."

"Point. I stand corrected. The matter with the pope is still far more important."

"Yes, I agree. In essence, Urban's decision to make Mazzare the cardinal-protector of the United States of Europe is two things. First, a subtle declaration that the Roman Catholic Church is henceforth neutral in what has been so far—as fraudulent as the claim may be—usually justified as a war of faith. No longer can Ferdinand and Maximilian—or Richelieu—claim that they are pursuing any other purpose but their own political aggrandizement."

Mike nodded. "The second?"

Nasi hesitated. "I am not, you understand—"

"Yes, yes, I know. You're a Jew, not a Christian. Not an expert on the bizarre intricacies of the Christian faith. Give me your best estimate."

"The pope is launching—very subtly, you understand; he's a Barberini, after all—what amounts to . . . Well. Not the Second Vatican Council. That's too extreme. But—"

Mike nodded. "He's begun to chart the course toward it. He's decided that Larry Mazzare is right, at least in broad outlines."

"Don't expect anything quickly, Michael," Nasi cautioned.

Mike grinned. "With the Jesuits backing him up? Of course not. It won't be quick. But it will be sure."

Mike rose from his desk and went to his favorite window. Where another man might clasp hands behind his back, Stearns chose to lean his hands on the windowsill. It was the mannerism of a man who liked to have his hands free. A pugilist's mannerism.

"Okay. We can chew on all the details later. The only thing we have to decide immediately is whether to accept Larry's resignation as ambassador. And who to appoint in his place."

"How could we—"

Mike waved a hand. "Fine, fine. Obviously, we'd have to accept it, no matter what. Larry's a priest, in the end, and it's a fact that the Catholic Church is in a shambles up here. There's no way I could prevail upon him not to come back and take up his new position. But there's still a difference between that and accepting his resignation gracefully. So make sure the message we send him oozes congratulations and goodwill, okay?"

"Yes. Certainly. And the matter of his successor?"

Mike stared out the window. Something in the set of his shoulders told Francisco that he'd decided to take the gamble.

Nasi was unsure himself, but would trust Mike's instincts on the matter. It was not so much a gamble, Francisco knew, as the reflexes of an experienced fighter seeing a little opening.

"I agree," he said firmly. "We should do it."

Mike turned his head. "I didn't propose anything."

"I know you too well. You want to appoint Sharon Nichols as the new ambassador."

This time, it was Mike who played devil's advocate. "She's young—not yet twenty-five—female, and black. I'm not sure how that last part will play out in Venice in this day and age, but I know the first two are strikes against her."

Nasi shrugged. "Young, yes—but I think that issue was settled well enough on the operating table. The same for her sex."

"Medicine is not politics."

Francisco laughed. "That—coming from you! Aren't you the one who once told me that political success is ninety percent a matter of confidence?"

Mike smiled. "Ninety-five percent, if I remember that conversation correctly. Of course, I've been known to exaggerate a lot for the sake of making an argument. Truth is . . . Probably not more than seventy percent. You *do* need to be right, in the end, not just think you are. But you'll never get there if you don't have the wind in your sails. And the only wind that ever really matters is your own."

He rapped the windowsill with his fingers. "Let's do it. Nothing else, the black part, matters. Yeah, sure, it's a small and symbolic thing, but symbols are also messages. And right now, I'm trying—so is John Chandler Simpson, bless him; there are times I really like that man—to do my level best to give those greedy Dutchmen as clear a signal as I can."

Nasi understood the point. In this day and age, the still-nascent Atlantic slave trade was largely dominated by the Dutch. Not entirely, by any means. The English presence was growing and the Catholic nations of Iberia had been active in it for some decades. But Francisco knew that it was the Dutch who concerned Mike immediately. The English were an open enemy and the situation with the Catholic nations was hopefully susceptible to other measures. The Catholic Church had always been far more ambivalent about slavery and the slave trade than the Protestants. In this, as in many things, "justification by faith alone" could serve as a convenient excuse for any barbarity.

The Dutch, on the other hand, were allies at the moment. Neither Francisco nor Mike expected that to last—indeed, it was for that very reason they had urged Bedmar to return to the Netherlands and smoothed his way. But whatever eventually transpired in the Low Countries would likely leave the issue a thorny one.

Mike Stearns had an abrupt way of handling thorny problems, when he saw no other option. He expressed it again, in his next words.

"Yeah, stubborn Dutchmen. Well, the greedy pigs better start getting unstubborn. Right quick." He turned away from the window, his face set in harsh planes. "In the universe I came from, something like six hundred thousand Americans killed each other to end slavery. Some lessons do *not* need to be repeated. Do those sorry Dutch merchants think we won't kill them, in this one?"

Francisco smiled. "Perhaps they are expecting gentler treatment at the hands of the admiral?"

That was good for half a minute or so of laughter. When it was over, Mike turned to the next point.

"On the Stone boys." He picked up one of the files and scanned it quickly. "Out of idle curiosity, which pencil-pusher in the State Department—God, I miss Ed Piazza—came up with the idea of recalling them from Venice? And ask him what miracle he wants from me next? Order back the tides? We couldn't keep those kids under control in Venice—and he wants me to haul them back across the Alps when they aren't willing? Ha! How far do you think they'd get before they disappeared out of the fingers of anybody I sent down there to put them under custody?"

"Basel?"

"If that far." Snorting, Mike tossed the file back on the desk. "I leave aside the fact that Frank Stone is legally an adult—so's Ron—and now has an Italian wife. And Gerry is a minor, which means he's a ward of his father. Exactly what law I've never heard of does Mr. Pencil-Pusher think I could invoke to take a kid away from his family? Just because we've nationalized some vital industries—and damn few, at that—does he think we've got the right to nationalize children? Or does Mr. Pencil-Pusher—Gawd, what a *genyush* statesman he is—think that we ought to recall Tom Stone? Right at the point where Stoner's finally making inroads into changing sanitary and medical practices on a major scale somewhere outside our own borders. Not to mention creating the beginnings of a serious medical supplies and pharmaceutical industry in Venice and Padua. Fricking idiot."

The State Department was not Francisco's domain, but he felt a mild urge to play devil's advocate himself. "I think he's concerned that the boys might continue their involvement with those Italian revolutionaries."

Mike scowled. "They had damn well *better,* or I'll strip their hides off myself." He took a deep breath. "Pencil-pushers. Give them a suit and a title and they immediately start thinking they're respectable. Leave it to a suit to think rambunctious kids who might embarrass you are worse than an epidemic of bubonic plague. Francisco, I *am* doing my level best to lead a revolution—all across Europe, too, not just here. What the hell does the puffed-up clown think this is all about, anyway? Before I'm done—assuming I survive—I intend to see this whole stinking world of kings and nobles lying in a pile of rubble."

He took another deep breath. "Yeah, sure, I'm not stupid about it. And I don't confuse ends with means. And I don't lump everybody under one simplistic label. Gustavus Adolphus is not the same as Ferdinand II.

The pope is not the same as the Inquisition. So what? That's just *tactics*. Whether you use sugar or vinegar—or a sledgehammer, when you need to—the goal remains the same. It's called 'democracy,' and the last time I looked—"

He paused for a moment, to pick up the file and look at the name. "Christ, Mr. Pencil-Pusher is an up-timer, so he doesn't even have that excuse." He dropped the file back on the desk, wiping off his fingers. "The last time I looked, we don't have democracy anywhere in the world. Not even here in the USE, not really; just a good start at it."

It was at times like these that Don Francisco Nasi found his sense of irony stretched to the utmost. For, at bottom, he was not at all sure himself that he had much confidence in Mike Stearns' treasured *democracy*. Still, he followed the man. Did more than that, really—for Nasi was one of Stearns' closest associates.

Mike turned back to the window, once again placing his hands on the windowsill. Nasi took the opportunity to swivel his head and examine the huge painting at the rear of the large office.

It was truly laughable. Not for the first time, Nasi silently tipped his hat to the genius of the artist. He had to be genius. Only such a one could have possibly disguised a human hurricane under Roman armor and such a dimwitted little smile.

"Send a quiet message to Spartacus," Mike growled. "Tell him I want another private meeting. You understand."

Nasi nodded. Stearns was always careful to keep a certain public distance from the Committees of Correspondence. Which, in truth, was not simply a pretense. There were in fact differences—of emphasis; certainly of tactics—between him and the Committees. Still, below it all, the relationship was very close. And ultimately more trusting—on both sides—than almost any other of Mike's political alliances.

"You will send people down to Italy, then?"

"I won't," Mike grunted. "But they will. I'll let Spartacus pick 'em, of course. He knows his people, I don't—and the truth of it is that he's a better tactician than Gretchen, anyway."

"Ah. You want . . . ah, what you would call 'savvy types.'"

"Yeah. My first choice would be Red Sybolt, but he's tied up in Bohemia. Hasn't lost any of that fire in the belly, but he knows which end is up. That sort. I'm sure Spartacus knows someone similar."

When Mike swiveled his head this time, it looked purely like the movement of a predator. "Francisco, I will now tell you the ultimate rule of politics. You can teach tactics to people with heart. You cannot do the reverse. The Stone boys are okay in my book. So are those Marcolis, impractical as they might be. Just gotta be educated some, that's all."

The predator glare fell on the file. "Wouldn't trade a one of them for all the damn suits in the world."

Then, came a sly smile. "Actually . . . Yeah. Draft up a personal letter from me, will you? Address it to Frank Stone and his father-in-law and—what's the other guy's name?"

"Massimo. Massimo Marcoli."

"Yeah, him. A real friendly letter. Nothing specific. Just something to make clear Frank has my confidence and . . ."

"Something to boost their own confidence. Ah, Michael . . ."

Stearns waved his hand. "Oh, stop worrying. After the Galileo affair, even Marcoli will be thinking for a change. And now that Frank's his son-in-law, he'll have real status. Frank's a level-headed kid, all things said and done. They'll handle it well enough. With some help. But most of all—this above all—with confidence." He chuckled. "A Frenchman said it best, you know."

Nasi knew the quote himself, from the French revolutionary Danton. Mike Stearns had more or less adopted the slogan for his own. *De l'audace, encore de l'audace, et toujours de l'audace.* The words could be translated various ways into English. "Audacity, more audacity, always audacity" was perhaps the most common.

Francisco tried to imagine the best way to translate it, with the Marcolis and the Stone boys in mind.

"Eek," was all he could think of.

"Don't chicken out on me now, Francisco," Mike said sternly.

"Eek."

Of a sudden came the sea

Unlike Sharon, Ruy Sanchez was an early riser. So, when she came into his room—or her room, depending on which way you looked at it—she wasn't surprised to see that he was nowhere in sight. She glanced at the door that led into what passed for a bathroom in even the fanciest palaces in Italy. Ruy might be in there. He was able to move around now, if not very far, and the very first thing he'd insisted upon as soon as he could do so was taking care of his own toilet necessities.

Sharon hadn't objected, needless to say. Any experienced nurse could handle such things with aplomb, but it was hardly something they looked forward to.

The thought made her smile. The irony involved, not the subject matter itself. Except for sex, Sharon and Ruy had experienced a level of physical intimacy over these past weeks that very few couples ever did, even those married for half a century. Ruy made jokes about it.

Of course, Ruy Sanchez de Casador y Ortiz made jokes about everything. On his last visit before he'd left for the Netherlands, Cardinal Bedmar had warned Sharon that he would. *If Sanchez found himself replacing Brutus in the maw of Satan on Alighieri's ninth level of hell, he would claim it was because even the stupid Devil had finally realized Catalan food tastes better than Italian.*

The warning had been pointless. Sharon had figured that much out for herself some time before. It was one of the things about Sanchez she cherished.

She decided he wasn't in the toilet. She couldn't hear anything, and Ruy had a habit of singing in there. That was one of the things about the man she didn't cherish at all. Partly because he was a lousy singer; mostly, because of his selection of tunes. One of the few good things Sharon had gotten out of her relationship with that bum Leroy Hancock was an exposure to flamenco music. The real stuff, not the touristy junk. *Only good blues in the world 'cept our own,* he'd insisted, an opinion Sharon had come to share. If anything, she preferred it to American-style blues.

Alas. Flamenco as such hadn't really evolved yet, in this universe. But the Gypsy groundroots that would produce it were well in place, and well known to Ruy Sanchez. He claimed to be part Gypsy himself—a claim Sharon found a lot more plausible than the business about Casador and Ortiz—and thought he grasped the soul of the music.

Alas. *The blues* and *Ruy Sanchez* were terms that went together about as well as *the Calvinists* and *His Holiness, the Pope.* Ruy was the only man Sharon had ever known who could somehow manage to sing a song of lament as if it had been composed by John Philip Sousa.

Since Sanchez wasn't in the toilet, that left only one other possibility. Not even the Catalan would risk Sharon's displeasure to the extent of wandering away from his living quarters entirely. Yes, he was healing better than almost any other man of his age could have been expected to do from that type of injury; on the other hand—whether he liked to admit it or not, and he didn't—Ruy Sanchez was: a) human; b) no longer young; c) in fact—you always had to add this, dealing with Ruy—very far from young.

The balcony, then. Which was what she'd expected, anyway. Sharon headed for the door which led out onto it.

She paused for a moment, as she came out on the balcony, catching sight of the sea. Probing, as she did every morning when she first saw that once-hated body of water.

Hated, not because of anything about the Venetian lagoon's portion of the Adriatic Sea in particular, but simply because—names were human inventions; the sea itself was indifferent—it was the same body of water that, more than nine months before and half a thousand miles away, had swallowed Hans Richter. His body had never been found, devoured by the leviathan. Sharon had been denied even that comfort.

It . . . ached, still. A bit less than yesterday, perhaps. It was hard to tell, one day to the next day.

Not hard, though, half a year to the next. When they'd passed by Lake Constance on their winter's journey to Venice, Sharon had had to avert her eyes. Fresh water or not; frozen over or not—technically guiltless—the lake had earned her damnation. In those days, she'd barely been able to forgive creeks and streams.

She'd never used the balcony herself, after they'd arrived in Venice. Had barred the door leading to it; insisted that the drapes on the windows facing it never be opened. The servants had thought that odd, since the reason the room was considered one of the best in the palazzo was its magnificent view of the waters.

But, they'd obeyed. People usually did, when Sharon Nichols chose to be *nurse firm* about something.

Ruy Sanchez had been the one to break the command. The first day he'd been able to walk, he'd immediately gone to the door, unbarred and opened it. Sharon had begun to protest, half-angrily, but the Catalan had simply continued his work.

"I will respect your grief, woman," he'd said. That had cut Sharon's protest off in mid-sentence. *How had he known?* She'd never told anyone how she felt about the sea.

When he'd turned to look at her over his shoulder, she'd seen the understanding in his eyes. And remembered something her father had once told her: *A witty man may not be a wise one, but he'll sure as shooting be a smart one.*

"I will respect your grief," Sanchez repeated. "Even be glad for it, in the end. For you, because you need it; for me, because it tells me something I need to know as well. But I will not feed the monster."

That said, he'd finished his work, slipped through the door and vanished for an hour.

Sharon had not joined him that day. Not for a week, had she ventured onto the balcony herself. By then, she discovered, Sanchez had set himself up a table to hold his precious morning coffee—Turkish-style, of course; Ruy disdained anything weak—as well as a stool on which to prop his feet.

He'd also set two chairs. She was quite sure he'd had that done on the second day. Strange, how a man as impulsive as Sanchez could also at times be so patient. His was not a broad vein of patience, to be sure; but it ran very deep.

Perhaps that was the Andalusian side of his heritage. Sanchez was only part-Catalan, he'd finally admitted to her, although he considered himself such. But then, he'd immediately insisted, all true Catalans were only part-Catalan. *How could it be otherwise, with such a mongrel nation? Any man tells you he's a pureblood Catalan, he's a Castilian trying to give himself airs.*

His mother had come from Andalusia. That region of Spain which, if it had none of Catalonia's cosmopolitan flair and panache, had virtues of its own. Tenacity, above all. Over the centuries, the peasants of that harsh land had seen conquerors come and go—Romans, Vandals, Visigoths, Moors, Berbers—the Castilians being only the latest. Andalusia endured and outlasted them all; wailing sorrow, only in its music.

It had taken her another week before she could bring herself to use that second chair; another week, to sit it in for longer than a few minutes; yet another, to remain for the entire hour that Ruy did, enjoying her own style of coffee; and still another, before she could finally gaze upon the sea.

Gaze upon it, now, like a human being. Not stare at it, dully hating and dumbfounded and despairing, like a mouse before a snake.

She did not know, and never would, the day when she finally forgave the sea. It simply happened, as of its own volition. She did not even realize it, until one morning she understood that she had.

She did not know, and never would, the day when her grief for Hans finally closed over. Became a healing scar, not a bleeding wound. It simply happened, as of its own volition. One morning, gazing from the balcony upon the sea, she realized that Hans had become a memory instead of a haunting ghost.

Treasured memory, to be sure; and still one that often brought a pang of sorrow. But that would never change, she knew, for the rest of her life. Ruy had told her that there were still times when he would stop in his tracks, remembering that first young wife who had died so many decades ago, paralyzed for just that moment. The same, for his second and third.

He found that a comfort, he'd told her. Proof, in the end, that there was such a thing as a soul.

Sharon thought he was right, even if she didn't share Ruy's eccentric theology. Her own religious beliefs, insofar as she retained them from her mother's adherence to the African Methodist Episcopal Church, tended to run along conventional lines. Ruy, on the other hand, was the closest thing Sharon could imagine to a Sufi mystic's version of Catholicism.

She knew a fair amount about Sufism, as it happened. Leroy Hancock had claimed to adhere to that variant of Islamic faith. But if the man had had much of Ruy's wit and bravura, he'd possessed not an ounce of the Catalan's integrity. Living proof that a smart man need not be wise. Mysticism, to such as Leroy Hancock, was a way to evade all responsibility. To such as Ruy Sanchez, a guide to it.

"Sit," he said to her, smiling. "Your coffee—if I may so misuse the word—will be suitably tepid for you by now."

As she sat, Sharon smiled back. It had become a running joke between them. The fiery Catalan; the cool American. Ruy claimed to like everything hot: his climate, his food, his coffee—above all, his women. A claim which was immediately followed by sour grumbling that in his old age he'd clearly gotten senile. Abandoning a lifelong devotion to passion because he'd become besotted by an American! He was a disgrace to Catalonia.

But even Ruy Sanchez de Casador y Ortiz had a hard time maintaining the grumble. When the time came, he'd have no complaint when it came to Sharon Nichols' passion. None at all. He knew it, and . . .

So did she.

Sharon did not know, and never would, the day when she found her answer to Ruy's question. She would not speak the answer until October 8, still some months away, for she had come to believe in the power of ritual. But the decision had already been made.

Had made itself, somehow. One morning, not long before, she'd gazed from the balcony onto the sea and realized that it had become settled in her mind. In that mysterious back of the mind, which was so much more reliable in such matters than the treacherous frontal lobes.

Set and firm. As firmly set as her loving memories of Hans, which could now become a support for her life instead of a barrier to it.

"It will be a good day," Ruy predicted.

"Yes," Sharon replied.

Afterword

1634: The Galileo Affair is the fourth volume to appear in the 1632 series, following *1632* and *1633* and the anthology of stories entitled *Ring of Fire*. There are a lot more books coming down the road. David Weber and I will be writing four more novels, the next of which—*1634: The Baltic War*—will conclude many of the story elements which were left unsettled at the end of *1633*. Not all of them, though: the adventures of the diplomatic mission trapped in the Tower of London will be continued in a novel I will write called *1634: Escape from the Tower*. And some of the political issues which emerge in *The Baltic War* won't be fully resolved until a novel I'm now working on with Virginia DeMarce comes out soon thereafter. That novel will most likely be titled *1634: The Austrian Princess*, and it develops some lines of the overall story which Virginia began in her novelette "Biting Time," contained in *Ring of Fire*.

Nor will that be all the novels set in the year 1634. I'm also working on a novel which follows up the storyline I began in my short novel *The Wallenstein Gambit*, which is also contained in the *Ring of Fire* anthology. Mike Spehar, who wrote most of the flying sequences in *1633*, is my co-author on that novel. (We don't have a title for it yet. Right now, Mike and I are just calling it "1634: Bohemia.")

All that, in *one year?*

Well . . . Yes. In terms of its narrative structure—as well as the way it's written—the 1632 series could just as easily be considered a shared universe as a series in the traditional sense of that term. A shared *multi*-verse, in fact, as I'll explain in a moment.

The basic premises of the setting and the story as a whole are established in *1632* and then expanded and elaborated in *1633*. From there, the story branches in many directions. Branches—and constantly reconnects. Characters who play a major role in one novel will not necessarily appear onstage in another, although their actions will often have an indirect effect. Minor or secondary characters in one story will become major characters in their own right in another. Throughout, as the series continues, some characters will tend to remain constantly at the center of things, in one way or another—as Mike Stearns does in this book. And most of the characters, whether major or minor in any given novel or story, will tend to keep appearing and reappearing.

That initial "story explosion" will all happen more-or-less in the year 1634, which is the reason so many of the novels in the series have that date as part of the title. (Okay, one of the reasons. The other one is that it's a nifty marketing device.) Thereafter, the complexities will continue.

People have asked me many times now if I have any final end goal in mind with this series, and the answer is no. I try to let this story tell itself in the sense that I more-or-less approach each book as it comes up. I say "more-or-less" because, for obvious narrative reasons, any author has to give *some* thought to what's going to happen down the road. So, for instance, what'll happen in the book Virginia and I are working on is connected to what will happen in the books I'll be doing with Mike Spehar and Dave Weber.

But I try to keep that sort of predestination to a minimum, and I make no attempt to develop some overarching general plot outline for the series as a whole. As much as possible, I want to try to capture the often purely contingent aspect of real history—not to mention that this method (I think, anyway) tends to produce better stories because in the final analysis the key ingredient in making a decision is usually purely dramatic. I'd far rather adjust later developments to incorporate a really nice dramatic development in a novel I'm working on, than to truncate the drama for the sake of making the novel fit into a preconceived schema.

That's also the reason I like to work with so many co-authors in the series, either in the form of collaborative novels or by surrounding the novels with shorter stories in anthologies or the new online 1632 magazine I've created called the *Grantville Gazette*. (See below.) I find that keeps the series loosened up, because different writers will constantly bring in different ideas and angles than I would have thought up on my own. To give an example, except for Sharon Nichols and Lennox, none of the major characters in *1634: The Galileo Affair* are ones who played any real role in *1632*, except, to a very limited degree, Father Mazzare and Rev. Jones. Most of them, in fact, don't appear at all in that book—and few of them in *1633*, and then in cameo roles.

The characters of Stoner and his sons and Stoner's wife, Magda, were first introduced into the series by Mercedes Lackey, in her story "To Dye For" in *Ring of Fire*. True, they first appeared in print in the novel *1633*, simply because of the publication order of the books. But Dave Weber and I based the characters on Misty's portrait in her short story, which had already been written. Likewise, Billy Trumble and Conrad Ursinus were introduced into the series by Deann Allen and Mike Turner in "American Past Time," one of the many other stories in *Ring of Fire*. Mazarini and Heinzerling, by Andrew Dennis—and it was really Andrew's story "Between the Armies" which lays the basis for the important roles played by Father Mazzare and Monsignor Mazarini in this story.

Sharon Nichols is mine, so to speak. From the moment I decided to turn *1632* into a series, I planned on developing her into one of the central and major characters of the series, on a par with characters like Jeff Higgins and Gretchen Richter. But all the specific ways in which that eventually happened in this novel were shaped by the input of many other writers.

I like it that way. Partly, because I enjoy collaborative writing. But, mostly, because I think it helps keep the story lively and helps prevent the (always ever-present) danger of the series sliding into a formulaic rut. When I wrote *1632*, over four years ago now, I did not intend for it to be the first book in a series. I planned and wrote it as a purely stand-alone novel. I hesitated for some time before changing my mind, after many people urged me to turn it into a series. The main reason I hesitated was because I've seen far too many good single novels turned into tedious series which simply recycle endlessly and pointlessly the ingredients of the founding novel. Eventually, I decided I could avoid that—and a large part of the reason was because of the narrative structure I decided to adopt. The great advantage to a shared universe, as is true with human interaction in general, is that it's very different from having a conversation with a mirror.

Earlier in this afterword, I mentioned the *multi*verse aspect of the 1632 series, and I should take a little time to explain what I meant. My publisher, Jim Baen, pointed out to me some time ago that there was

no inherent reason that only *one* Assiti Shard might
have struck the Earth. From that initial observation,
he and I began thinking through some other ways to
expand the setting—both to the side and outward, so
to speak. What has come out of that concretely, so far,
are two other books which I will be writing:

One of them will be *1781*, which posits the effect
of a far larger and more complex Assiti Shard trans-
posing both George Washington and Frederick the
Great (along with their armies) into the chaotic and
turbulent period of the Roman Empire usually known
as the "third-century crisis."

You might think of that as the sideways expansion.
The "outward" expansion is a novel which I am beginning with a new co-author, Sarah Hoyt. This novel, *By
Any Other Name*, will take up the Assiti themselves
and the initial clash which the human race has with
them. Part of the novel is set in Elizabethan England,
but most of it takes place on a strange setting which
is no part of human history—indeed, exists in another
universe altogether. *By Any Other Name* will at least
begin to provide the overall framework and logic for
the Assiti Shard multi-verse, of which the 1632 series
is a subset, as well as—always the most important
thing—being an enjoyable story in its own right.

A few words on the *Grantville Gazette*. As I mentioned in my afterword to *1633*, the 1632 setting has
spawned a very large and lively discussion group in
Baen's Bar, the discussion area which is part of Baen
Books' website. (www.baen.com, then go to "Baen's
Bar" and the "1632 Tech Manual" conference.) Over
time, a lot of fanfic started being written in the setting.
Some of it is . . . awfully good. So, after discussing it
with Jim Baen and getting his go-ahead, I tried the
experiment of producing an online magazine which
would incorporate the best of the fan fiction, with me
serving as editor, as well as a number of factual articles

which bear on the series. The first issue came out in October of 2003, and sold enough copies to make the magazine financially self-sustaining. Once that became clear, we decided to turn the initial experiment into an ongoing publication. The *Grantville Gazette* will have no regular schedule, but I expect to be able to produce at least two issues a year. The second issue is already out.

"Fan fiction" usually has a negative connotation to science fiction readers—"derivative, unimaginative, poorly-written dreck" being the gist of most complaints—but there is no intrinsic reason that needs to be true. Many established science fiction authors began their career writing fanfic, after all. The main problem with fanfic is usually that the author who originated the setting either doesn't have the time or the inclination to play the needed role in overseeing the process. I have the inclination, and I can find the time. The end result is a magazine with a lot of good stories, and one which I hope will serve a lot of new writers as a place they can develop their skills. Most important of all, to me, the *Gazette* is already proving to be yet another source of stimulation for the series.

If you're wondering where the Cavriani family who figure in this novel came from, you can find out by reading Virginia DeMarce's "The Rudolstadt Colloquy" in the first issue of the *Gazette*. The adventures of the various Cavrianis will appear in later stories in the series, be sure of it. Anyone interested in looking at the *Gazette* will find a brazen advertisement for it right after the afterword.

I should also mention that a role-playing game set in the 1632 universe is coming out in July 2004, published by Battlefield Press, Inc. Those interested should look for information on BP's web site: www.battlefieldpress.com.

Finally, as always, I need to thank a lot of people for their input into this novel. First—an overdue acknowledgment, because they were also a great help to me in writing *The Wallenstein Gambit*—my thanks to Suzann Denton-Pratt and Mitch Miller for guiding me through the manifold complexities of Judaism and Jewish history and culture. I'd also like to thank Marla Ainspan, Janice Gelb and Stan Brin for their assistance as well.

My long-standing "chem group" helped a lot, as always. I'm tempted not to name names, because I like to think of them as my equivalent of the mysterious Council of Ten which the Venetian Senate used to conduct so many delicate affairs. But . . . since they don't actually break any bones—just half-baked notions, usually mine—that would probably be churlish. So, another tip of my hat to Drew Clark, Rick Boatright, Bob Gottlieb, Laura Runkle and John Leggett.

My general thanks as well, in no particular order, to Judith Lasker, Cheryl and Rog Daetwyler, Virginia DeMarce, Mike Spehar, and Pete and Elizabeth Wilcox for reading the manuscript as Andrew and I wrote it and giving us their reactions and criticisms. Special thanks to Danita Ewing and Butch Clor for their advice on medical matters, and to Enrico Toro for his advice on swordplay.

Last but not least, I need to thank my friend and longtime co-author David Drake for looking at the manuscript and advising me on some of the key details concerning guns.

—Eric Flint
December, 2003

Volumes 1, 2 and 3 are already available,
with Volume 4 on the way.

In Volume 2, stories recount the first air raid
launched by the United States of Europe against Paris, among others.
In Volume 3, among other stories, the same teenagers who appear in
the short story "The Sewing Circle" (in the paperback book, *Grantville
Gazette*) move on to conquer the financial world. These magazine
volumes also contain factual articles exploring such topics as 17th-
century swordmanship, iron, agriculture, telecommunications, and
the logic behind the adoption of the Struve-Reardon Gun as the basic
weapon of the USE's infantry.

Grantville Gazette magazine can be purchased through Baen Books'
WebScriptions service at www.baen.com (select WebScriptions.)
Volumes 1, 2 and 3 of the *Gazette* can be purchased as single copies for
$6 each, or you can purchase Volumes 2-4 as part of a $15 package.